LIGHTSPEED TO BABYLON

Booklocker.com, Inc.
2002

LIGHTSPEED TO BABYLON

J.Y. Jones

DEDICATION

To all who utilize and care for animals in any way, as domestic stock, companion animals, hunting prey, fisheries stock, working animals, wildlife observation, necessary research, performers, traditional and religious objects, and captive animals maintained for public enjoyment. May this book somehow stimulate all people to a realization that those who seek to limit human utilization of animals have a sinister and hidden agenda. Loss of animal utilization would be just as devastating to the person who enjoys a seafood dinner as to the individual who enjoys catching fish. With this dedication and this book I salute all who would resist misguided attempts to humanize animals, and to thus dehumanize mankind.

ACKNOWLEDGEMENTS

I am indebted to many people who have helped me to construct this project far better than I could have done so on my own. Michael Spence, while working on a doctorate at Dallas Theological Seminary, has been the single most helpful individual, doing three separate full reviews of different revisions of the book (all of them brutally honest with incisive commentaries). His mentor, Dr. Robert Pyne, was kind enough to assign him to this task initially. Dr. Joseph Kalt of Harvard University, chairman of the John F. Kennedy School of Government and a world-renowned expert on renewable resources, did another especially insightful commentary on an early version. Mrs. Harriett Claxton, a professor at Middle Georgia College and a close personal friend, has reviewed and commented on two separate versions. Dr. Don DeYoung of Grace College did a discerning review focusing on the book's astrophysical accuracy. Mr. Mark Lamb of Tennessee was quite effective with suggestions on science fiction and future thinking aspects of the book. My partner in medical practice, Dr. Roger D. Smith, who is now retired, also read and critiqued an embryonic version of the text and inspired me to continue. There is a very long list of people who have heard of this project, and have encouraged me to persist. My wife Linda has read the entire book several times and has been most honest and forthright in offering suggestions. Most of the time I have put into this work has been taken from her, so I am especially grateful for her help and her forbearance.

LIGHTSPEED TO BABYLON

INTRODUCTION

All my life I have been a hunter, mentored from an early age in ancient rites rooted in the outdoors. Hunting is to me not an activity as much as it is an identity. As a person is born with a predetermined nationality or skin color, I am what I am because God made me that way. I have watched in dismay as my very character has come under increasing attack, and I have been horrified that I might perhaps live to see my beloved way of life fall into abject disrepute. Ultimately, this book stems from my desire to preserve my heritage, my lifestyle, and a significant portion of my passion for living.

With opportunity to develop my immutable hunting instinct at every turn, I have always been active in this timeless activity. I also have been exposed, on many fronts, to farming and animal utilization, because both of my grandfathers spent a sizeable portion of their lives as farmers. When I was in college, I took more biology courses than almost anything else, so high was my interest in the diversity of living creatures that share our planet. I excelled in school and was blessed with a much-coveted admission to medical school. There I was exposed to animal research in its purest and most beneficial form. I have practiced medicine for over a quarter-century, and I have observed remarkable progress in this field, virtually all of it in some way riding on the strength of irreplaceable animal models for research.

I am an enthusiastic advocate of animal welfare, and an ardent conservationist. I've taken in my share of stray dogs and cats. I've got a tender streak towards animals that makes me a soft touch for anyone raising funds to "help the animals." When I leave on my early morning jogs, I often dutifully toss any stranded earthworms off my paved driveway and into adjacent grass, where they can continue to perform their vital function unhindered. This minor act of kindness would be insignificant, except that it allows me to "do justice, to love mercy, and to walk humbly with my God" (Micah 6:8).

Our mandate from the Creator of both humans and animals is that we use the creatures that share our planet in an ethical fashion, whether that is for food, clothing, simple companionship, or observation. All God's creatures deserve such amenities as a clean and undisturbed habitat, protection during certain seasons for game animals, and complete protection from humans at all times for many wild animals. Animals merit, and in fact we owe them, esteem and admiration, protection from unethical people, and rules regulating their hunting, observation, and other forms of utilization. Domestic stock deserves adequate food and shelter, protection from physical and mental abuse, and a clean and painless sacrifice as necessary to provide for our human needs, whether wool, skin, meat, eggs, or dairy products.

As a hunter, I am particularly aware of my responsibility to make a clean and painless kill when I harvest a game animal. Wounding and losing is not an option. I am obligated to my quarry to be certain of my target and to make a good and practiced shot. In the event of a rare accidental wounding, I must diligently pursue until such an animal is dispatched with as little delay as possible. I must go afield with an immutable mindset that such is the case and that any price must be paid, any effort must be expended, to be certain that ethics is highest of all on the agenda.

Hijacking of the time-honored animal welfare movement by strict preservationists is a fact of life. In the past two decades, a once miniscule fringe movement has come into its own, and it goes far beyond the concept of animal welfare and conservation of resources. This development has emerged as an offshoot of the theory of evolution, and it essentially equates humans with animals. Through a series of developments it has grown into a formidable and well-funded force. In Europe and in America, certain high-profile celebrities have led this movement opposing all animal usage. This has been made possible because we live in an age of emotion, and pragmatism has been one casualty. Pictures of cute baby seals were shown on network news programs, and public pressure was generated that entirely halted the harvest of plentiful seals of all species and age classes. Native Americans who depended on that resource were forced onto welfare in Canada. Fur usage has been drastically curtailed by using identical emotional tactics, working hardship on innumerable people who must trap in order to earn a living. Arctic foxes are not endangered and never have been, but now they die of rabies instead of providing beautiful, warm, and practical fur coats for the world.

Critical medical research is performed in laboratories where animals constitute an absolute necessity to the cause of finding treatments and cures for myriad human diseases. These have been repeatedly attacked and trashed, wrecking years of priceless experiments, all in the name of equality for animals. In this age of terrorism, the most common form of terror activity is done not for the sake political persuasion or religion, but because of a misguided and dangerous philosophy of anti-humanism that purportedly protects animals.

I tried for two years to get a magazine to publish a short story I wrote that demonstrated how radicals in this erroneous movement could easily lead to the end of our world as we know it. Taken to the logical extreme, the fondest aspirations of their more radical leaders were apocalyptic, beyond doubt. Perhaps just as bad, the world and its human population were being placed at great risk not because such ideals were lofty and impeccable, but because they *raised piles of money*!

I have published over 70 magazine articles and two full-length books, and another book is about to be published, so I'm not a newcomer to writing. I submitted that original article that led to this book to some 25 magazines that publish fiction, and it was rejected in every case. My account certainly wasn't politically correct, and maybe the story just wasn't very good in that form. Nevertheless, my frustration level began to rise because my viewpoint couldn't be aired despite my best efforts. The idea of expanding that simple short story into a full-length novel grew out of that frustration, and *Lightspeed to Babylon* is the result.

This book assumes today's current state of affairs is soundly quelled by the application of scientific thought, and that this extremist movement has been relegated to the obscure past. The book begins in 2049, in a world of exemplary animal stewardship, and follows mankind's progress to its zenith. The story covers a span of 120 years, all of it featuring a constant main character who starts the book at age five and ends it at age 42 (read the book to find out how!). The Biblical timeline of *Lightspeed to Babylon* presupposes a considerable delay from most current evangelical thinking. I am not advocating that this is the correct interpretation of Scripture, but I would submit that this delayed timeline is a possible scenario.

It has been ten years since I first began to put together the original short story, and eight years since I began the book. It has been a demanding project, but I believe all the long hours at the computer are worth the sacrifice. If some people are sensitized to the mendacity inherent in the movement to humanize animals, and if some change their minds about their sympathy towards that heresy, then *Lightspeed to Babylon* will have accomplished much of my personal ambition. On a deeper level, it is my fervent hope that someone will be inspired to connect the portrayed end times scenario in this book to their own personal spiritual needs. What every man and woman needs is a personal relationship to the omnipotent God who created man and animals, as well as the universe we inhabit. He has commissioned mankind to be stewards of His world, and by following many false doctrines we abdicate that responsibility. I hope this book demonstrates that truth.

And I hope it is enjoyable to the utmost.

CHAPTER 1

October 2049

It did not appear to be wild and savage outside. It looked wonderfully tranquil, the view down a winding country road towards low hills that were colored tan by an early killing frost. The western sky was pink with afterglow from the setting sun, an image stained only by dark wisps of cloud that banded the heavens. Venus, a gleaming gemstone in the twilight, dominated the horizon in its nearest approach to sister Earth. Such an enchanting display beckoned irresistibly.

It was time for Alice Morgan to take her usual stroll, a ritual she had begun several years before as a means of staying fit. Rugged Kansas flint hills formed a dark palisade to the west, backlit by the brilliant sunset and darkly framing the majestic scene. Stark outline of leafless trees against the panorama cast a bewitching aura, and she momentarily gazed in awe. She left her kitchen door slightly ajar and descended low steps to an irregular gravel driveway.

The cool autumn evening caressed the young woman as she strolled among mature poplars and cottonwoods that lined the quaint lane. A deep breath of invigorating air was a welcome respite, clearing for the moment persistent cobwebs that inevitably crept into her mind after a long day's toil. The stress of running a prosperous farm was taking its toll. There were never-ending management decisions, supplies to order, bills to pay, countless data entries to complete, work to be done. On top of this routine she had found that raising a precocious five-year-old son placed added demands on her schedule that were most unyielding. She needed this break. She released her long dark hair from an encumbering barrette and tossed her head a bit to feel the freedom. Her flowing locks rippled in the evening breeze like an enthusiastic banner on a sailing mast.

Jim Morgan watched from a distance as his wife left the house, and he waved a weathered hand at her from across the yard. A smile crossed his thin lips, and his sparkling blue eyes fixed on her with affection born of familiarity. He admired the ease of her gait, the sway of her pretty body, so youthful in appearance that nobody would suspect that she had ever given birth to a child. She waved back nonchalantly, leaving him to finalize preparations for night on the farm, gathering livestock into enclosures and assuring a flow of feed to the animals. Young James Lee Morgan, the couple's only progeny, was helping in his childlike way, and he too waved good-bye to his mother.

"Lee, I think there's a memory chip problem in the Epsilon unit," Morgan said to the old man at his side. "We'll have to do a scan. That should isolate the glitch."

"He's still working, though. What makes you think there's a malfunction?"

"The robot's locking onto sheep like they were an intruder. Lets them go okay. The programming checks out, so there has to be a hardware malfunction."

"Let me see, Dad," said the boy, his young mind straining to understand what his father had detected. The elder Morgan traced out the fault so his youngster could watch, and the old man nodded in agreement as a hidden defect became clear to them all.

Departure of the young wife was only a momentary distraction from the labor at hand, which consisted primarily of supervising on a giant monitor the activity of a retinue of computer-controlled robots, all of which was in process of accomplishing needed tasks. Mechanization was the watchword for farmers of the twenty-first century. Animals tagged with ubiquitous computer chips lit up the screen to reveal their location flawlessly, while wheeled all-terrain robots did extensive legwork that had been accomplished by horses, cowboys, and stock dogs in centuries past.

In thickening dusk the lovely woman walked briskly with a cool wind at her back, and fallen cottonwood leaves swirled like a miniature tempest all around her feet. The brilliant crepuscule that surrounded her spoke of coming clear weather, the atmosphere transforming silently from softer pastel tones to a deep red that was inspiring. Winter can't be far behind, she thought, gathering her modern processed leather sweatshirt around her more tightly for added warmth as an involuntary shiver coursed her spine.

A flock of geese settled into a nearby farm pond to pass the night, and numerous big birds honked loudly as they glided on locked wings toward black water, where outstretched legs groped for the surface like extended landing gear on an airplane. Alice Morgan watched as a rabbit scampered across her path and disappeared into tall grass along a fence row, as if in a hurry to make an appointment. Tilled bottomland beyond lay fallow now, but the harvest had been good and a rich supply of animal and human food was assured. It was a time of plenty, a time of gleaning, a time of blessing. The woman reflected silently as she walked, and she felt deeply grateful for all the good things that filled her life and times. As she meditated, a coyote howled in the distance, and its plaintive notes wafted on pristine air and made her hesitate momentarily, transfixed. She contemplated the sound briefly before moving on. In that cry was an indelible and sobering reminder that wildness was never far from the cultivated fields and livestock.

The wind transmitted a more aggressive sentiment now, changing subtly in its insistent and firm current past the woman. The rising flow of air caused a subtle but somehow sinister change deep in her subconscious, imparting a different and disturbing character to this particular stroll. An obscure and undefinable terror seized her, a sudden silent warning cry she couldn't visualize or verbalize. In the winding path there now seemed to be a quality that was unmistakably cold, radically unlike other walks she had taken in this place over the years. She could only vaguely, dimly perceive the difference, but her heart began racing and her short steps quickened, amplifying the noise of crunching dry leaves. Was there danger out there, or was this impression nothing more than the first icy fingers of winter extending into America's heartland, as normal and expected as each day's dawn?

She almost turned around and headed back the other way, directly back to the brightness of her kitchen, the glow of her cozy home. That would really be silly, she thought. Morgan would think she was crazy or perhaps that she was becoming afraid of the dark. She appealed to her rational mind, the normal thing to do in this age of omnipotent science, and was uneasily satisfied that her sudden visceral fear was likely to pass shortly. The frigid emotion she felt had to be an aberration, for she had never experienced such a sensation before, not in all her years of walking this path.

Just ahead, her sinuous hillside trail passed through a livestock gate and then crossed a brushy draw at a place where dwarf maples grew deeper and thicker. Alice Morgan paused, contemplating her terrifying sense that the situation was dreadfully wrong. Don't be ridiculous, she assured herself again, you've been by here hundreds, maybe thousands, of times. Just walk on by and don't think about it. Nothing's wrong, she affirmed rationally.

The woman couldn't see a pair of curious yellow eyes watching her as she walked. Crouching now a scant twenty yards away, a hungry animal observed the young woman's approach and traced every move of her lithe body. Times were tough for the old cat, a huge tom cougar well past his prime. The creature was a fourth generation lion, descended from original stock planted in Kansas early in the century. Biologists had predicted that their kind would adapt readily to life amid active farmlands, and indeed the species had thrived. Catching farm deer and an occasional stray calf or lamb had been this cat's standard fare for over a decade. Recently one of the big predator's essential molars had loosened and separated, leaving him without an important piece of survival gear. Other teeth in its mouth weren't far from suffering the same fate. Worse, agile deer could now outmaneuver the cat with unaccustomed ease. Farmers knew better than to leave precious livestock exposed at night, so meals were few and far between for the aging feline.

Humans had always been strictly off limits. They smelled bad, like death, to the cougar. They were disgusting and dangerous, creatures to be avoided, the tom knew instinctively. Still, it had been nearly two weeks since his last meal and the movement of this woman was enticing. Its eyes narrowed a bit, and the tawny furred brow almost appeared to be frowning as the animal observed this walker. Never had he come close to charging one of these upright forms before, but this one looked like a sure kill. The empty stomach gnawed hungrily inside his rib cage, triggering desperate instincts of self-preservation. The black tip of his long, serpentine tail twitched nervously, and the mountain lion hunkered unseen in the gully, every muscle quivering and every nerve end tingling. Elongated pupils were almost fully dilated due to deepening twilight, while instinct and hunger waged a soundless battle in the cat's murky mind. Demand for food was the more convincing, and a moment of opportunity pressed insistently as crunching footsteps came nearer. Without any further delay the bulky feline sprang into action!

Jim Morgan was finishing his chores at the big metallic barn when he heard a chilling scream, one terrible shriek of terror like he had not heard since his tour of duty in the war. He knew instantly that it had to be Alice. Her cry pierced the nearly dark sky with suddenness and force like a clap of thunder, conveying audibly the horror of an utterly terrified human being. He bolted toward the sound, leaving a startled old man and a deeply puzzled child to fend for themselves. He raced out the door and ran as hard as he could toward the fading commotion.

The cougar first bowled the woman over, hitting her high and sinking its long, sharp retractile claws into muscles on her back. The cat buried its long incisor teeth in the back of her neck while simultaneously slashing at her legs with rear claws. Her sweat suit was no protection at all, so soft and pliable was the leather material, and it shredded immediately at the onslaught. Blood spilled from numerous wounds as the massive head and shoulders of the predator twisted and tossed its prey almost airborne. The earsplitting wail of anguish was over almost as soon as it began, and merciful unconsciousness engulfed the woman. All was quiet except for gentle rustling from vigorous final thrusts of the animal's back legs, and then absolute stillness reigned again.

The cat crouched beside his meal, a little unsure whether it should flee or begin to feed. Warm blood covered its muzzle, and left a sweet, attractive taste in the cavernous mouth. He released the death grip slightly, noting intuitively that this creature had been much easier to dispatch than the nimble, muscular deer he had been devouring regularly in times past. There may have been a dim sensation in the cat's primitive mind that life could be good again on a diet of these hapless beings. The lion rolled his prey over and chewed tentatively on bared stomach muscles.

The cat's demeanor became more tense again as it detected the rapid approach of another of these upright creatures. He could hear noisy, rhythmic treading in the leaves, and could smell another human's foul scent wafting toward him on the unending breeze. The feline leaped over its prey and partially concealed itself from the approaching intruder. Closer came the man, and the cat's muscles contracted banjo-string tight. Yellow eyes now filled with hate at this meddler, this interloper, who would perhaps try to steal this irreplaceable kill. A telltale nervous rhythm of the tail foretold that another deadly charge was imminent, and the next victim was rapidly approaching. Defensive instincts surged, and nothing would be allowed to deprive the creature of this sweet-tasting prize.

Morgan could see the bleeding body of his wife before the cat materialized, but he knew immediately what must have happened. He rushed through the fence gate breathing hard, and in failing light he spotted an unused metal post leaning idly against the top strand of wire. He resolutely grabbed it and proceeded quickly and without caution toward the bloody scene. He was within ten yards when he spotted the cat, postured low behind the fallen woman, limbs pulled tautly into its body like an arrow ready for launch.

The man instinctively shouldered the long, heavy metal shaft, unflinching as he readied his makeshift weapon. He knew that an attack was coming, and he was certain that he would have only one chance to save himself and retrieve his fallen wife. The creature sprang like an arrow leaving a bowstring, closing the distance in a flash. Its action was unexpectedly quick, even to a farmer accustomed to dealing with animals, but his critical swing with the post was only slightly late. It caught the big cat squarely on one side of its body and sent the heavy creature sprawling out of control, a sensation the animal had felt only rarely in many years of chasing and capturing prey. Not to be dissuaded, the giant whirled, fangs bared, snarling menacingly, and slashed savagely with unsheathed scalpel-sharp claws. Morgan flailed repeatedly at the cougar, driven by the sure knowledge that if he could not drive the animal off, all was lost.

Several of Morgan's desperate blows found their mark and the old cat retreated, seeking shelter for a brief moment of nearby dense brush. Once in the thicket, it regrouped and spun once again to the attack, all in a split second. Morgan was ready and planted his post firmly in the ground with its sharp end toward the advancing animal, his crouching posture reminiscent of a Masai warrior in the ritual of taking on an African lion. The animal leaped, striking the post slightly off center, but still partially impaling itself on the dull point. Finally defeated, the animal reluctantly withdrew bleeding to safety in deeper vegetation. It fled several hundred yards up and over nearby higher terrain before seeking refuge in a familiar hillside cave.

Morgan ignored his own bleeding arm and thigh, caught incidentally by those lashing claws, and now he approached Alice with more prudence, unsure if his fierce adversary would return. He knelt tenderly by his wife's side, surveying in disbelief the abject disarray of her familiar form. He removed his shirt and tried frantically to apply enough pressure to stop active spurting of blood from a gaping neck wound.

"Oh, God! Oh, God!" He prayed repeatedly aloud, addressing his petition more in desperation than in actual hope of divine intervention. He failed to notice the approach of a light from the direction of the farmhouse until its beam fell on the awful bloodstained spectacle.

"Jim, what happened, son?" asked Lee Shealy in a shaky, labored voice. Disbelief overwhelmed the old man as he approached the gruesome setting, his stiff and aged body shuffling as fast as he could move it. A light was welcome but it only revealed more gushing arterial bleeding, so much that prospects of curbing it seemed hopeless.

"A cat. Give me your shirt, Lee. Hold pressure right here while I call for an ambulance," Morgan commanded, reaching for his wallet personal computer as Shealy took over momentarily. The device gave instant coordinates of the calamity to authorities, and Morgan gave a brief description and account of the tragic incident, his voice strained and trembling with emotion. In a mere matter of minutes, lights of a jet rescue helicopter came into view, almost silently gliding with an emphatic hiss from the Kansas sky.

Emergency personnel swarmed over the injured woman, inserting intravenous catheters into her largest veins, attaching mysterious monitoring devices, and infusing massive doses of artificial blood into her limp body. All advanced emergency technology of the twenty-first century was focused intensively on the injured woman from that instant, including dramatic live holographic hookup and monitoring by a distant trauma center.

"Lee, go check on Buck. I left him in the control room," Morgan called to the old man from inside the craft as it took off. A twinge of added worry crept into his mind as dark ground receded from view, and he could see Shealy shuffling hurriedly toward the farm operations center, his light glowing as he laboriously followed the unseen road.

The whine of the rescue chopper had long since faded by the time Shealy approached the farmyard again. Twice he had to stop briefly and rest because his chest was heaving violently and his ailing heart was fluttering from unaccustomed exertion. With relief he noted the boy's form, outlined by brilliant light emanating through the door. The old man entered and reached for the nearest chair, where he collapsed to catch his failing breath and let his wildly erratic pulse settle down.

"Where's Dad, Pa Shealy?" asked the younger Morgan as the old man entered the light. "I stayed here like Dad said. I'm watching all our robots."

"Yeah, infernal robots. 'Scuse me, Buck, I'm a little upset," Shealy wheezed, straining to get the words to come out intelligibly. "Your mom...had an accident. You...you heard the chopper?"

"Yep. She'll be okay, won't she, Pa Shealy?" asked the child, his blue eyes staring intently, inquisitively, with worry apparent in his voice.

"I hope so, son," replied the oldster tentatively. There was an unsettled and distinct hint of quandary in his gravely voice that the boy recognized immediately. He rested a gnarled hand on Buck's head and gently tousled his dark hair. Shealy hadn't driven a highway vehicle in a long time, but it seemed the only thing to do under the circumstances. "Let's drive into town."

The old man slowly rose to his feet, and then waited until the floor stopped its treacherous spinning. He began a tentative walk toward the nearby garage where a farm truck was parked, steadying himself on the boy's shoulder and whatever inanimate object he could reach. He could only hope that he could maneuver the machine safely to Adrian. He thought briefly about calling a neighbor to drive them, but decided he was feeling a bit better. Besides, he dreaded calling Alice's nearby relatives, so he and the boy would go it alone. After all, he rationalized, there was no need to alarm anyone until he was certain of the situation. The steering wheel felt familiar enough as the pair eased down the lane toward highway pavement.

"Mommy's okay?" petitioned Buck again as their vehicle motored onto the high-speed freeway. Shealy's wrinkled face grimaced a bit as the youngster spoke, and his ancient rounded cheeks almost visibly revealed pain.

"Son, some hard things happen in life. Remember when Ma Shealy died last year? Hard things."

"Is Mom dead?"

"Oh, no, son. I don't think so," Shealy answered, regretting his choice of words. "She got bit by a cougar, but let's not speculate. Let's wait until we get to the hospital, then we'll see how she is."

It seemed to take an eternity. Old Shealy was quite unaccustomed to any driving at all nowadays, much less at night. Oncoming headlights were arrayed in contrary and deceptive concentric circles of light, and he concentrated desperately on the illuminated midline to stay on course. James Lee "Buck" Morgan frowned deeply, and apprehension rolled over him interminably, a maelstrom of doubt and discord, posing fundamental questions about safety and security on their familiar farm. Finally, after an endless interval the glow of Adrian Community Hospital loomed in the distance, just off the freeway in a forest of artificial light. Soon the two were entering an emergency waiting area, where sterile surroundings projected the impersonal, the fastidious, the intimidating. Jim Morgan was nowhere in evidence as they surveyed the spacious room.

The receptionist was a pretty blonde with short, almost crewcut, hair. She looked up indifferently from her reading, glanced at them in highly detached manner, and inquired casually and with unveiled monotony, "May I help you?"

"We're looking for Morgan—Alice Morgan. Or Jim Morgan, her husband. Should have come here by rescue helicopter a short while ago."

"Oh, yeah. Mr. Morgan is in the counseling room. A preacher or somebody just went in there with him, I think."

"Counseling room?" the old man questioned quietly, his coarse voice shaking. "And where would that be, if I might ask?"

Reality dawned quickly on Shealy, and his worst fears seemed to be confirmed. He had seen the horrible wounds, and deep down he knew that the woman's chances were slim at best, even with application of all the latest high tech gadgets. Sometimes even young people are hurt too bad to live, he concluded silently and with deepening dread.

"Around that corner and then right, next to the chapel," she replied, her voice softening considerably as she called after them, "Sure sorry about the accident, mister."

A pair of doctors dressed in timeless white coats, professional medical dress for eons, met Shealy and Buck at the conclave door. Both had hurried, preoccupied expressions and neither spoke as they brushed past. Shealy caught the door before it could close and with the boy in tow he entered the dim expanse. Two men sat at a long table, one with his head cradled in his hands, elbows resting on the table, staring downward at the blank surface. It was Jim Morgan. The other man was also familiar, and they immediately recognized him to be Pastor Don Tolbert, an elderly and portly clergyman. He greeted them quietly, his somber tone telling the entire story without a word. Buck ran immediately to his father.

"Dad, I want to see Mom!"

Jim Morgan hugged him warmly, and the boy noticed that his father was crying. Buck's emotions overflowed, and before long both were sobbing loudly. Sad eyes of a grizzled old man and a corpulent pastor met somewhat awkwardly, and neither of them spoke for a long and uncomfortable moment.

"Preacher, how'd you get here so quick?"

"I was already here. Jim had me paged when he found out I was in the hospital."

"What's the story?" Shealy asked quietly. Tears welled up in the ancient farmer's eyes as the minister related a hopeless battle to save Alice's life.

"They did everything humanly possible," said the preacher, straining as his jugular veins bulged unnaturally. "Her brain was dead. That cat severed two big arteries, a major one in back of her neck and a main one in front. They think her neck was broken, too. She was neurologically dead almost immediately. They kept her body alive after the medics arrived, and her organs live on even now. They're being transferred for transplant."

Shealy nodded in understanding. Of course they would use her organs. Science being the primary basis of law, and no one was allowed to bury perfectly functional organs at the whim of relatives.

"When will we get the remains? I know Jim will want to use our old family plot, out behind the east gate," his voice trailed off a bit, remembering the funeral of his wife so very recently.

Leaving the room to do the dreaded task of calling Alice's family, Lee Shealy encountered Adrian County Sheriff Mahlon Hicks, accompanied by two deputies. All of them wore grim countenances like one would expect to see on soldiers in battle. Their concern now was the cat, and they voiced this anxiety to Shealy, whom they knew to be owner of the parcel of ground where the attack had occurred.

"No need to worry about that old cougar, Sheriff," Shealy assured him. "With one phone call I can get its carcass delivered to your door. And it won't be tomorrow."

"Really? How's that?" asked the sheriff in honest skepticism.

"I'll call Rocky Purdee. Him and his dogs will have that cat within an hour. Need to do it, too. A cat that kills a person doesn't know when enough is enough, they say."

"Why do you suppose that cat turned man—or woman, I mean— killer? Heard of it other places, but never here. Ever since they stocked those things in Kansas, we've avoided any trouble in this county. But now this," the sheriff lamented, dreading the mountain of paperwork that routinely accompanied any such incident.

"Never should have brought them here, anyhow. It seems idiotic now. Idealistic fools back then wanted to see big predators everywhere. You youngsters can't begin to remember the arguments. Some crazies were determined to put them in every state in the Union. Besides government transplant programs, there were a lot of cats released illegally by God knows who. Big bears, uh, grizzlies, in a lot of places, too. And wolves wherever they could put them, legally or not," Shealy raved. After a labored pause to catch his failing breath, he added as an afterthought, "You prob'ly don't know a lot of the varmints are here illegally, do you?"

"Mmmm, maybe so, old timer. However they got here, most of 'em are here to stay. Say, pull up that guy you mentioned and let's put this one away before someone else gets hurt—or killed."

A call to Rocky Purdee was accomplished, then Shealy notified Bill Barnes, Alice's brother. Even before the rest of her family had arrived, the houndsman called back to report the job completed. Jim Morgan had not seriously wounded the cat, and it had put up a lot of resistance when cornered. Entrenched in its deep rock cave, it had been hard to reach and to kill, but in the end an experienced veteran and his tenacious dogs had prevailed. The killer was dead.

Shealy returned to the conference room to tell Morgan, but it was empty. He went next door to the chapel and pushed open the door. In dim light he could see three figures, one small, one heavy-set, and one a trim adult. They were kneeling in prayer.

Shealy closed the door quietly and bowed his head reverently for a moment. A wayward droplet coursed down his deeply creased face, and then another. His eyes welled with more, and then he began to sob quietly.

It had truly been a night for tears.

CHAPTER 2

April 2050

Lee Shealy knew that he was dying. Each day it was harder to arise from his tilted bed in the back bedroom of the farmhouse, and each night his labored breathing kept him awake. This morning he shuffled into the kitchen and sat at the table, hacking up a night's accumulation of phlegm from his chest. It was early and neither Jim nor Buck were up yet.

Shealy surveyed his swollen stomach and leaned over as far as he could to cough and try to clear his congested lungs. During daytime his feet swelled so badly he couldn't wear his shoes, and at night he slept propped up by three pillows. The old man felt nauseated this morning as he stared at the floor and contemplated toenails like those belonging to some beast, all thickened, curved, and dark, barely visible to him over the arch of his fluid-bloated belly. It seemed that every organ in his ancient body was beginning to fail, and he knew that there was no cure for the ravages of time, even by the most advanced medicine.

"Lee, why are you up so early?" came a husky, familiar voice from a darkened hallway that led into the kitchen. "Are you okay?"

"I'm as good as I can be, Jim. That's not much good, either, anymore." He coughed deeply and expectorated some loosened material, but the clingy gunk adhered treacherously to his lips. Jim Morgan handed him a tissue and motioned for him to wipe his mouth.

"Son, I think I'm getting worse. Can't breathe at night. And not much during the day."

"You've got to go to the medical center. I'll take you. Nothing here that can't wait another day."

"Won't do any good, Jim. I've been going for months and they can't do anything. Not even with all those miracle drugs and magic gizmos they use. They don't do transplants on people my age, you know. Anyhow, you can't take time off now with all that's going on here. Alice had enough trouble finding time to take me…"

His voice trailed off and he wished he hadn't mentioned the tragedy of six months ago. Morgan had been a little better the past few weeks, drinking less, seeming to recover a bit more from that trauma.

"Look, you need to go, and everything can wait. There's nothing here so important that we have to neglect your health. Will you go?"

"Come here and sit down, Jim. I need to talk to you while I still have enough breath to do it," Shealy rasped, ignoring his question.

Morgan pulled out a chair from under the antique wooden table and sat down close to his old friend, tenderly touching Shealy's gnarled hand as it rested on a bony right knee. He loved this old man now more than anybody in the world except his own son. Shealy's breath was coming in short bursts now, and Morgan reached for a nearby oxygen mask. He slipped it over the old man's head, flipped on a valve and adjusted a computer control to optimum flow.

"Lee, we've got to take you to the doctor. I can't let you sit here and die. You're in the worst shape I've ever seen you."

"Maybe so. It gets worse than this sometimes. Especially bad when I can't sleep. I'm looking forward to a long sleep beside Mary, to tell the truth," he gasped, his labored breathing seemingly worse by the moment. "But I need to tell you something. Jim, I don't have a single living relative. I'm leaving this whole place to you. And enough cash to pay the taxes on it, I believe."

Morgan looked silently at the frail old man and squeezed his rough hand again. Shealy had indeed previously detailed to him the proposition, actually over a year before, prior to Alice's death. Time and infirmity team up to ruin the memory, he knew, as Shealy's repetitive statements had proved over and over again.

"Lee, remember when I first met you, thirty years ago? I was a kid at the orphanage heading for nothing but a life of trouble when you got involved in their big brother program. You and Mary included me in your holidays and together you two showed me how to care. You rescued me and taught me everything I know," Morgan said, groping for appropriate words. "I can't ever repay what you've already done for me."

"You're welcome. Promise me you'll make Buck the best he can be, Jim. He's smart as a whip, he is. Teach him to stay out of trouble and to work hard. He'll make a fine farmer."

"Maybe so, old friend. I'll get your clothes. We've got to get you to town, and soon."

"One thing more, Jim. You know Buck has been hurt bad by what happened to his mother," Shealy wheezed slowly. "I've noticed a change in his attitude—well, towards everything. Can't blame him, though. It's hard for anybody to understand something like happened to Alice. Why that occurred is God's secret, but someday our boy will know, too. I really believe that, Jim."

A spasm of coughing ended Shealy's labored train of thought. Morgan patted the old man's bowed shoulder, and quietly agreed to his request. Right now he had to get moving to get his elderly friend to the doctor, so he got up to make necessary arrangements. He hoped the trip would take only a few hours, but he would have to call Alice's brother, Bill Barnes, and ask him to cover the place for a while. Alice's family was so darn dependable and neighborly that he almost hated to request such a favor of them. It was always so hard to find an occasion to return their kindness. The telecom signal was answered immediately by a friendly female voice, and a pert face appeared in the monitor.

"Hello, Jim. How are things on the Shealy place?" she asked.

"Not so good, Carol. Got to take Lee to Adrian. He's sick. Can you get Bill to monitor the op center and make sure we're in the green on all units? I should be back by noon."

"No problem. I'll message him now that I'm splicing in the Shealy data stream. Is Lee going to be okay?"

"I hope so. Trouble with those lungs again. Got to run. Thanks for helping me again, and I'll be in touch."

"And Jim, don't worry about Buck. I'll pick him up right away and bring him here."

The screen went blank after parting cordialities, during which Carol made mention of praying for Shealy. Morgan contemplated Carol's peculiar final statement, spoken in childlike sincerity, while he went about the difficult task of loading his feeble friend into the vehicle.

Lee Shealy made his last trip to town that day and died before the Kansas sun had dipped below the western horizon. A blazing red sunset appeared through a big window in the spacious final care waiting room, a fiery orb sitting momentarily on the very edge of eternity as if bidding a comrade farewell. As he considered matters of significance through his sadness, Morgan sensed that somehow nature was applying an appropriate finishing touch to a life that had been dedicated to the fields, livestock, and wild things on the farm. He would miss Shealy terribly, but at least the old fellow's suffering was done.

Morgan stared at the setting sun, a streaked horizon showing myriad colors as the life-sustaining star sank out of sight. Pastor Don Tolbert had arrived only moments before Shealy passed away, and he was there to console Morgan as only he was able. The clergyman left him alone momentarily to go and make a computer net entry that would spread word of Shealy's death. Morgan held the preacher's worn Bible in his lap, and he thumbed absentmindedly through some tattered pages as if searching for something he wasn't competent to express. Was there consolation to be found here in this old book, something immediate, something that he could find now, not in some future afterlife? The preacher was more than a little vague about such specifics, but there seemed to be a measure of relief in the man's mere presence.

On funeral day, Morgan led Buck to the now-familiar burial plot on the east boundary of the farm, where they would lay the old man to rest next to his wife Mary. Weathered tombstones all around them told a saga of many generations of Shealys who had preceded these final members of their clan, and Morgan considered how those mute monuments put an indelible emphasis on the brevity and insignificance of life. Was there really any meaning to man's existence, anything of permanent value? Was the quest for worth and security one of total futility? He pondered his wife's headstone, so close by, and the stark contrast between her twenty-nine years and Shealy's ninety-three. Was there any justice in those figures? For some reason he felt ashamed of the thought.

Shealy had been a popular man in Adrian. He had established an impeccable reputation and had a penchant for extreme generosity, characteristics which assured a large and respectful crowd. A gentle spring breeze made new cottonwood leaves quake, and a slight chill caused the whole assemblage to draw a little closer together.

Morgan held Buck's small hand and made an unspoken note of how the boy was reacting to this latest loss. The words Lee Shealy had spoken to him reverberated in his mind with sudden impact, and he could almost hear the old man talking again. What was it he had said? Hurting and a changed attitude? It all came flooding back now, drowning him in a groundswell of responsibility.

"Don't worry, old man. I'll do it." Morgan mouthed softly, almost inaudibly, and then he looked around self-consciously to see if other mourners had heard him. After all, he wasn't at all certain he could live up to that promise. Nobody had apparently caught the statement, except maybe Buck, who was staring up at him with a quizzical look in his eyes. Morgan turned his attention back to the service at hand and motioned his son to look back to the front.

Pastor Don Tolbert delivered a radiant eulogy sprinkled with somber words from the Bible. John Gentry, head of the local Conservation Club chapter, spoke briefly about numerous contributions Shealy had made in the area of husbandry, referring specifically to wildlife on his farm. He recalled the restoration of bobwhite quail, particularly, and the part Shealy had played in furthering university wildlife research programs. A local couple sang two of Shealy's favorite hymns accompanied by mournful music from an ancient and rare acoustic guitar, while the melodious sound wafted on cool, crisp air.

Following the service, Shealy's polished wooden casket was lowered into the ground and workmen shoveled in dirt to fill the hole. Hollow thumping of heavy soil on top of the coffin and the smell of fresh earth brought back difficult memories. In fact, such a burial was uncommon in the times, since cremation had become the more usual way to dispose of human remains.

Morgan walked back home with the boy by his side, both of them silent. Morgan's mind returned once more to the words of his departed friend and mentor, and he tried intently to come up with something useful to say. He would think on it and spend some time talking to his son when the time seemed right.

Buck changed into his everyday clothes after they reached the farmhouse and then left via the back door, which he allowed to slam loudly as he departed. Morgan was sitting on a sofa in the living room, contemplating the old family piano, an idle upright Baldwin that stood forsaken in one corner. It had played many happy tunes when his wife had been living, but now it just sat there and gathered dust. Maybe he ought to sell it before it dry rotted and became worthless.

He got up and moved slowly to the kitchen, where he plaintively watched his young son cross the back yard and walk toward the bird dog kennels, one of the boy's favorite places. There the youngster could find solace in his love for the white English pointers that occupied the pens, feisty friends of the boy since he had been present at their birth. Those were Shealy's dogs, too, and the canines would be missing their trainer and master. Both they and Buck would be okay, he convinced himself, because the bond between boy and dogs was a strong one. There was a new litter of pups, only a few weeks old, to keep him occupied, too.

Morgan opened a high cabinet and reached inside, retrieving a bottle from the dark recess and pouring some liquid into a glass. Since Alice's death, he had begun to drink more than a little. It made him feel better and had become one of the few pleasures in his life. His liquor went down smoothly and created delightful warmth in his throat that gradually spread throughout his body. As the familiar sensation took hold of him, his worries seemed to diminish ever so slightly. Another drink and they diminished some more. Maybe Shealy's presence in the house had been a governor of sorts on his need for alcohol, but now that the old man was gone he felt strangely liberated to imbibe a bit more. So he poured himself another one. He felt pressure to communicate with the boy easing a bit too, as mellow bourbon dulled his senses perceptibly.

When the youngster returned, Morgan had begun to feel quite comfortable. Buck had never seen his father drunk, since the man reserved his heaviest drinking for late evening, after the boy was safely tucked away in bed.

"Dad, your face looks red," Buck observed, noticing a dullness that glazed those bright eyes and a limp appearance in his keen facial muscles. "Whatcha drinking?"

"A little something to lift my spirits, I guess, son," Morgan replied, trying to keep the words from slurring. He put the black cap back on his bottle and twisted it tight, shoved the liquor back into its place, and then placed his empty glass in the overloaded dishwasher.

A loud vehicle interrupted the tranquility, and he got up to see who was coming. From the kitchen window he could see Carol Barnes and another lady arriving in a farm truck, then getting out carrying a load of goods. Only now did he remember Carol mentioning at the funeral that she would see him a little later today.

Buck ran to the door, blasting it open noisily in his enthusiasm to greet them. The two women had changed into work clothes and quickly made known their intention to clean the house, in addition to providing a meal for Morgan and Buck. Housekeeping was a duty that had not been accomplished with any degree of regularity since Alice's death, and Morgan acknowledged their kindness with gratitude.

"I won't be able to thank you enough, Carol," Morgan began tentatively, his speech exuding slowly and with difficulty. He was greatly afraid that the treacherous smell of whiskey or a stumbling, mispronounced word would disclose the influence of alcohol. He made a mighty effort to be cold sober normal, but his words came out thickly and heavily, like he had a mouth filled with chewy taffy.

"No problem at all, Jim. We really feel guilty that we haven't been more diligent at this sort of thing. We'll be here for a couple of hours if you have anything you want to do. We'll mind Buck for that time," the trim lady replied, adjusting some pins in a bun that sat like an ornament on back of her head so her hair would not interfere with work.

"Thanks, Carol. I was just thinking about taking a walk over the farm to clear my mind," Morgan said in a syrup-like tone. He wondered if his perky sister-in-law had perceived that his mind indeed could use a little clearing. Maybe she had noticed, he thought, but she isn't the judgmental type, thankfully. Whatever, he welcomed the chance to get out and do a little self-examination, and he even needed a break from Buck at this particular time. Maybe it was the alcohol, in a deviant twist, sapping his confidence even as it soothed his heartache. He couldn't begin to put together a plan of action to raise and nurture his son, much less do it at the same time he managed a major farm operation. Funny, neither his son nor the farm had seemed problematic until Shealy's death.

He departed via the spacious back porch, descended weathered masonry steps, and crossed the greening lawn. He followed a path that was opposite in direction from the fatal path his wife had taken on the day of her death, and also opposite the way he had driven Shealy just a couple of days before. He chose the direction unconsciously, but for some reason it seemed the right way to go.

He crossed a little stream that bisected the property, stepping a bit unsteadily on strategically placed stones. That dependable flow of clear water was essential to prosperity on the farm, and he noted that it held plenty of water. He spotted tracks of a grizzly bear at water's edge, fresh and deep impressions in smooth, wet sand. Only a few decades ago these markings would never have been found within hundreds of miles of this spot. His mind harkened back to a conversation with the local game biologist several years ago when this same animal had first appeared, and he noted the growth in size of the footprint since then. He measured its imprint with the middle segment of his index finger: six inches wide across the front pad now, a budding giant. He had been told that this creature was a young male and that it was the only one in the immediate area, as far as anyone was aware. All such bears were strictly protected, and he made a mental note to call the biologist to report the track size and its location.

Presence of such major predators in his home area had not been particularly problematic until Alice's death. Sportsmen and farmers had opposed introducing them everywhere, and he knew that Lee Shealy had been in the forefront of resisting the restocking effort. Surprisingly, big carnivores had been low profile intruders, cougars preying on excess deer and bears eating whatever they could find. There had been no measurable impact by their presence on numbers of game animals taken by human hunters each year, a scenario that few had predicted. Mighty science had solved so many problems related to environmental degradation that now all wild animals proliferated in incredible numbers.

In springtime male white-tailed deer sport rapidly growing antlers covered with soft, nurturing velvet, giving them a fragile and elegant appearance. One such magnificent creature rose to its feet in a brushy bottom along the rambling creek as Morgan approached. Towering antlers the animal would possess by fall were rudimentary now, but in the massive developing stubs there was the promise of beauty, grace, and heart stopping potential. It struck him that his son also had that kind of budding prospects, and he paused to consider the idea. Buck's image now filled his mind as he watched the deer, its head held high and alert, staring intently at him, ready to bolt away at any movement.

It was exactly in this spot that his son had gained his nickname a few years earlier when he had uttered his first word. His strolling family had spotted one of the antlered animals and Morgan had said aloud the word for a male deer. A tentative "buck" from infant James Lee Morgan had become a repetitive litany that had followed the couple home that night. Morgan and his wife had begun to call the boy "Buck" that very day and the name had bonded indelibly. Happy memories of family time caused Morgan to smile outwardly, a momentary reflex which faded rapidly as he faced grim and unrelenting reality once more.

Ascending some low hills across the valley, he looked back on the peaceful farmhouse setting he had just left. Manmade structures were nestled into a protected nook that seemed like a picturesque dollhouse with miniature outbuildings from this distance. Lush farmland tailed off into the distance, and the crystal atmosphere allowed him to see for miles. It seemed for a time that Jim Morgan could perhaps even see infinity from his lofty vantage point. Somewhere far downstream that little creek joined a larger one and eventually flowed into the Arkansas River, then into the Mississippi, and on to the sea, although little precious water from Kansas made it that far anymore. Intensive agricultural efforts, a necessity in feeding a hungry world, used most of the liquid for irrigating innumerable productive farms.

The fertile fields he gazed upon had already been planted and green row crops were emerging, though black bottomland dirt was all that was visible from his hilltop. Cattle and sheep were congregating to be herded automatically into nighttime enclosures after a peaceful day of feeding on lush emerging grass, and he passed several contented groups of fat animals. The Epsilon robot that had been repaired six months earlier was still functioning flawlessly. It dutifully locked onto him with an identifier beam, triggering a vibrating alarm in Morgan's wallet computer that startled him at first. The machine automatically released its hold when Morgan's friendly status was routinely confirmed.

He chose a large rock near the highest point of land on the farm. And now it was his farm. Long blades of succulent grass rippled in a pleasant spring breeze, and cool air caressed him gently. He sat down and reclined against a warm boulder to watch the sun sink lower. Days were getting longer this time of year, so he still had plenty of daylight. A golden eagle, born ever to hunt, soared on graceful plumes high over the valley searching for mice and other varmints that could make a farmer's life harder.

His thoughts returned like a homing pigeon to his son. How could he help his boy through the recent series of losses that had so bludgeoned both of them? Lee Shealy's admonition to remember Buck had struck like a bomb with a delayed action fuse, with implications eluding Morgan until the old man was cold in his grave. The more he considered those words, the more convinced he became that he had indeed noticed a subtle change in Buck. He now harbored a definite reluctance, a perceptible lack of enthusiasm, about every aspect of their complex farm operation. The boy had previously relished tending animals, doing necessary chores, working the computers, whatever. No more. There had to be a connection.

Morgan thought about praying, the silence and solitude and the sweeping panorama engendering pensive pondering about eternal matters. If the preacher were here he would probably insist on it. Morgan knew that Lee Shealy had been a true believer, if there were any such thing. Shealy had been rough and gruff at times, but surely God wouldn't hold that against him.

God. Morgan pondered the thought. Was there really a God who cared, who listened, who could give assurances like Shealy had seemed to have? Or was it all an illusion generated by religious types who had to have something outside them to lean upon? Like a child Alice had believed all things the preacher taught without any discernible misgivings. And look where it got her, he brooded, such injustice seeming to argue against a caring and personal supreme being.

"God, if you're out there, please let me know," he blurted out loud, the first words he had uttered since leaving the house. "I'm Jim Morgan and I hope you've noticed I need a little help here."

Nothing happened as far as he could tell. After the longest time the sun finally set, leaving a fading red sky in its wake, and he felt an increasing chill. He rose stiffly to his feet and started back toward home, his mind now crystal clear. He hoped silently that he hadn't extended his time beyond the level of common courtesy, thoughtlessly abusing the two women who were cleaning house and looking after Buck for him.

Just before he left the hilltop, he saw it. A big cat that was all alone, moving silently through thick brush near the meandering creek, its dusky yellow color barely visible through dense cover. A cougar! He wasn't surprised that it was there because there were a lot of them around. He was somewhat astonished that he had been able to spot it, though, because under normal circumstances one seldom encountered a cougar directly. He shuddered imperceptibly as he observed its long, snakelike outline, the switching of its long tail, its powerful head and shoulders— so much like the creature that had snatched Alice away from him. The animal practically slithered through an opening, and like a ghost its tawny form was gone.

Darkness was fast approaching when Morgan crossed the little stream and slipped into his back yard. He knocked loudly so he wouldn't startle the women inside and then eased in the back door.

"Carol, I don't know how to thank you," he began, looking around in amazement at the extraordinary transformation the ladies had wrought. A wonderful meal rested on a traditional red and white-checkered tablecloth adorning the wooden kitchen table. Hunger had been most remote from his thoughts, though he had hardly eaten all day. The smell of food so permeated the kitchen atmosphere that Morgan momentarily forged a truce with his feelings.

"Don't mention it, Jim," said Carol in a sincere voice. "We're glad to do it. If you and Buck need anything, just call. You really don't call enough. But we are running a bit late. Better get on home. We'll pick up the dishes later."

Morgan walked out to the vehicle with them to bid them goodnight and express his considerable gratitude once more.

Lying awake that night, Jim Morgan contemplated. Due to human kindness, both he and his boy were safely tucked in bed in a clean house with full stomachs. Somehow, deep down in his gut, the memory of the cougar he had seen was troubling to him. It was more than being reminded of his wife's annihilation; it was something even more disturbing, if that were possible. He didn't know if he believed in signs, but he couldn't help but wonder if seeing the animal had some veiled meaning. Perhaps it had been a representation of the dark side of his own nature. Was it a portrait of something sinister inside him, something he couldn't quite identify? If that were so, could he overcome that intangible monster within and effectively parent this son of his?

Unable to drift off to sleep, Morgan slipped on his house shoes and walked out onto the front porch. Gentle animal sounds could be heard in nearby holding yards, the lowing of a cow here, a gentle sheep bleat there, all very pleasant and contented. Watchful robots winked ceaselessly from their guard positions, eternally vigilant. All seemed to be snug and satisfied.

Gazing heavenward at the expanse of stars overhead, he wondered about the meaning of it all. Life and death and cougars and stars. All were inexplicable to his finite mind, and prevailing scientific wisdom seemed grossly inadequate. As he identified the Big Dipper and North Star, he stood awestruck at the inconceivable expanse, so quiet and endless. As he looked skyward, an enormous ball of fire suddenly trekked across the heavens, illuminating the farm like broad daylight. The meteor trailed off toward the ground, burning out while traversing over two thirds of the sky, then it broke suddenly into smaller pieces before extinguishing in a long, fading trail of silent fire. Hair on the back of his neck stood up in autonomic response, and a sudden chill made him shiver.

Morgan turned and walked back into the house, his mind whirling and his soul heavily burdened. The thought surfaced that perhaps the unusual phenomenon he had just witnessed might be a preternatural answer to his plea for some unspecified sign.

He wished he had someone to talk to about his questions and doubts. Maybe the preacher?

He'd sleep on it and consider calling him tomorrow.

CHAPTER 3

June 2050

The Hat Trick Bar was the foremost of local watering holes in Adrian County. Jim Morgan seldom stopped in because quite often his boy was along. You just didn't take a youngster to the Hat Trick Bar. Today, Buck was in school as the farmer returned from a supply run, so his truck just naturally gravitated, it seemed, into the smooth parking lot.

The rustic building sat at a busy highway interchange where it easily caught the eye of any passing traveler. Its gray sides were homogeneous and freshly painted, its red tile roof was old but unfaded, and a meandering motel of matching construction stretched like a growth behind the main building. A vast expanse of darkened glass was the most prominent feature to anyone who approached the front of the bar, but internal details were hidden from outside. Constructed of concrete blocks nearly a century before, the management kept the complex in mint condition from spic-and-span polished oak floors to rugged raftered ceiling. A magnificent shoulder mount of a royal bull elk adorned the spacious main room, an impressive ornament that was outshone only by a towering rock fireplace on which it hung.

Out front on an island of green grass stood a bright, contemporary holographic display that beckoned tirelessly to all who passed by the establishment. It appeared to be a live cowboy, except that the beguiling advertisement was over twenty feet tall. The illusion was festooned in glittering multicolored rhinestones and endlessly performed impossible maneuvers with a giant Stetson. It was definitely eye catching and effective at bringing in business. The Hat Trick Bar attracted customers of all kinds, from locals who called the area home to tourist types crossing Kansas on their way to timeless sights out West.

At any given moment, Morgan could usually count on the bar being manned by several people he knew, and he always looked forward to catching up on local gossip over a cold drink. He glanced across the room and spotted two old acquaintances immediately, and he waved a tentative acknowledgement at them. Approaching the bar he greeted Leo, a veteran bartender, and a mountain of a man with massive arms, a dark beard, and sparkling brown eyes that were piercingly serious. Leo doubled as the bouncer, and nobody ever challenged him, not that Morgan could remember. The thirsty farmer ordered his favorite beverage with a simple gesture, and sat on an ancient red bar stool while his brew was being prepared.

Sam Archer sat at a table with Jesse Prestone, and he blandly returned Jim Morgan's impromptu salutation. He then stared indifferently at the farmer, a distinct measure of contempt creeping into his condescending smirk. Morgan had known Archer since boyhood and knew that the pudgy one was a little on the strange side. Still, on the surface Archer had always been lukewarm friendly, and he motioned him over to the table where he was sitting with his partner. Morgan moved toward Archer with a slight reluctance, noting with some disdain his scruffy companion. Prestone was not native to Adrian like Archer, but he seemed to be every bit as bizarre, though in an undeniably contrasting manner. Could be worse, Morgan thought diffidently as he approached their table with his usual drink in hand. Might be nobody at all here to talk to except Leo, and the big guy wasn't much of a talker.

Sam Archer leaned back and grinned a toothy smile at Morgan, revealing his trademark gold incisor tooth. The man's paunch extended well past his ample belt line, and his expansive frame was as wide as a bale of cotton. He gave every appearance of overpowering the precarious chair on which he was sitting, creating an effect that bordered on comical. His face was covered with at least three days' growth of stubby beard, and his wire-rimmed glasses sat propped slightly askew on his broad nose, where the power of strong lenses magnified the battleship gray color of his eyes. His mop of unkempt red hair was streaked with silver, but there wasn't the slightest hint of thinning.

Prestone was as skinny as Archer was overweight, and his hollow eyes stared at Morgan from deep in their sockets. His scrawny arms were sparsely populated with hair, and were propped on the table caressing a frosty beer. The lanky man wore a shirt open in front all the way to his gaunt waist, revealing a hairless chest that was as flat as a baseball field and sported more bone than muscle. His fair skin was splotched with irregular dark blemishes and scattered spots of red. Prestone's long, straight hair was pulled back tightly into a ponytail, and the frazzled end dangled limply in front of one shoulder. In one of his earlobes was a small ringlet that was apparently of gold that had been hammered into the shape of a panda, the best one could tell. It could have been some other kind of bear-like animal. Neither of the two men offered a handshake.

"Evenin', Sam. Howdy, Jesse. How's business?" Morgan knew that neither of them conducted any kind of productive work as far as he was aware. Somehow he dreaded the conversation, though he was drawn to their table like nails to a magnet.

"Same as always, Jim. You been takin' a hellish lickin' out your way lately, huh?" Archer replied, swigging his drink as he finished the question.

"You mean Lee? Yeah, that and a lot else. Sometimes seems like we get underneath a disc harrow and can't get loose."

"I know what you mean. 'Course, Lee was old as rocks, wasn't he? He was a contemporary of my old man, and he's been dead for nearly thirty years. They went to school together back in Pre-2K."

"I'm aware of that. Lee told me a lot about your dad. I know they didn't get along very well. Too bad."

Morgan took a long swallow of his drink, and the cold liquid soothed his dry throat. He needed to be careful with this subject, he knew, because there was a lingering element of feud. Lee Shealy had been a prime opponent of predator reintroduction programs years before. Clemon Archer, Sam's father, had headed a pro-predator coalition. Nobody had been a clear winner, but the battle had been protracted and bitter ugly.

"Well, I hope you can lay all that to rest now. I trust that all's well at the animal place."

"Well as can be, under the circumstances. We've some problems with Buck adjusting to recent events. He'll get over it," Morgan said with feigned confidence.

"Why don't you get that preacher fellow to fix him? A trace of religion helps some people when times get rough. Thought of that?" Archer grinned as if he had touched a nerve, and his gold tooth reflected brightly in the subdued light.

"I might just do that, Sam. No finer a man I know than Don Tolbert . I didn't know you had any religion."

"I don't. Well, in a way I do. I'm a solipsist. I'm writin' a confounded book about my faith, if you can call it that. I believe that self is the only verifiable item in existence. God is a concept dreamed up by self to sustain it. Some are strong enough to stand alone, but others need a crutch. Maybe your boy needs a crutch."

Morgan felt his anger rising as Archer talked, but he suppressed an impulse to retaliate. He could see that he needed to opt out of this discussion as soon as civility permitted. Before he could finish his drink, however, Prestone jumped into their discussion.

"Say, you know, all three of us got boys the age of yours, Jim. I got one by a little filly out west of town, 'bout six years old now. Name's Alex—Alex Prestone. She even gave him my last name. Prob'ly in school with your kid. Sam's got one all legal-like, marriage certificate and all, don't you, Sam?"

"Uh, yeah. What's that got to do with this conversation, Jesse?" asked Archer, looking more than a little irritated.

"Nothing, really. No problems with my boy. Ain't never seen him but a couple of times. Yours ain't no problem, neither, is he?"

"No, Monty is a model kid. His mother takes good care of him. I send her gobs of money. Monty's all right. He's most likely in school now, too."

Morgan hastily drained the last liquid from his glass, burning anger that had flared briefly now completely controlled. He placed his glass on the table resolutely and rose to leave, politely bidding a farewell to the two. He was back in his truck shortly and glad to be motoring toward home.

The bar mates watched him leave with unconcealed disdain, then ordered another round of drinks. Archer gloated a little about getting Morgan's goat with his religious posturing, and Prestone chimed in with gleeful agreement.

"Dumb farmers. They and their educated scientist brothers are out to pillage the planet. They make me nauseated," Archer said scornfully in a loud whisper as he hefted his new drink.

"Yeah, me too. We're gonna stick that whole bunch in the ear before they can say payday. Someday."

Morgan stewed over his perilous dialogue with Archer and Prestone as he drove along in silence. He had more to do than sit and talk idly in a bar, anyway. But it occurred to him that there was one piece of advice from Sam Archer he could accept at face value, even though it had been cast at him like a dart. Maybe he would indeed still talk to Pastor Don Tolbert about his son.

Buck had arrived home a few minutes earlier than Morgan had expected, and as he drove up to the house he could see the boy in a holding pen adjacent the sheep barn. That facility was a giant metal edifice containing the nerve center for all activities relating to sheep, from ministering health to the animals to painlessly shearing off their luxurious wool. These special creatures had been genetically engineered to fill an unused ecological niche on the dry plains, and had been a resounding success in providing a bonanza of meat, skins, and fiber that was almost free for the taking, at least from a farmer's perspective.

Buck had always loved the springtime for many reasons, not the least of which was the coming of lambs. When Morgan arrived at the pen, his youngster was sitting on the lower rail of a fence surrounded by a half dozen wobbly legged nymphs, each weighing only a few pounds. Their frolicking with the boy was as natural as could be, untainted by any sign of fear. Nervous ewes kept a respectful distance while Buck was in proximity to their offspring.

43

"Looks like we've got another good crop, huh?" Morgan queried, a bit reluctant to break the magic of the moment. Buck continued to play, stroking first one of the tiny creatures, then another, and allowing them to suckle his fingers in succession.

"They're special, Dad. Let's don't let them grow up to be sheep. I like them little and lovable."

"Everything and everybody has to grow up, son. You included. I'll head up to the house. See you there." A telltale frown creased the boy's brow, a subtle window into his heart that Morgan failed to notice.

As Morgan walked back toward home, he felt strongly disinclined to approach the boy with his concerns. This was the first time in quite some while that Buck had gone near livestock when it wasn't required by his regimen of chores. Should he just stay quiet and let time take care of any reservations the boy might have? He honestly didn't know.

That evening, Morgan pondered his dilemma repeatedly as he prepared a meal. Supper was the time when his memory of Alice seemed to be strongest, and when her absence was almost overpowering. He was particularly morose this evening for some reason, so he had little propensity toward making a firm decision or preparing a plan of action. He plopped a pan of baked protein on the table without transferring it to a plate, and began slicing it into portions. Buck sat on his knees in a chair and puzzled over his father's unusually gloomy countenance. He rested his head in his hands and propped his elbows on the table, but said nothing. The man glanced up at him as he worked, noting the probing stare.

"Son, I was certainly glad to see you enjoying the lambs today. I've been concerned about you."

"Really? Why, Dad?"

"You seem to be pretty reluctant to help me these days. What's the matter? I thought you liked farm work. I know it's been tough on us lately, but I can't have my number one helper all hobbled up."

Buck looked surprised.

"What do you mean?"

"You don't go to the control room for roundup anymore. You don't want to be there when cows or sheep deliver newborns like you used to. Seems to me you've lost your enthusiasm for feeding and tending the animals. I'm concerned."

Buck swallowed hard. His young mind raced seeking an explanation, but he was unable to formulate anything that seemed acceptable. Finally, he looked up from an uncomfortable moment of staring at the tablecloth and spoke.

"Dad, you remember when that cow died trying to have her calf?" he said slowly, shifting in his seat and showing discernible uneasiness.

"Yes. The calf was okay, even though we lost the cow. What about it?"

"That little calf didn't have a mother. Dad, do you wish Mom were here?"

"Son, you know the answer to that. Of course I do. I miss her just like you do. But remember, son, animals don't feel it like people do. That calf is being fed well and it's growing. You can't let unavoidable circumstances like that bother you. Life is full of them."

"What does unavoidable mean?"

"When something happens that we can't escape. It's on us and we have to live with it. Like what happened to Mom."

"Was that unavoidable?"

"As far as I know it was. It's painful for a person to lose a mother, Buck, I know that. But you can't compare it to an animal losing its mother. The two occurrences are of entirely different magnitude. I don't have to tell you how much I adored Mom, nor how much losing her has hurt me, too."

"We could kill all the cougars, couldn't we?"

Morgan struggled to answer that one. He stalled a little while he thought, going to the refrigerator for a glass of milk for both of them. He had actually considered doing exactly that, for a brief angry moment, in the depth of his grief just after Alice's death. It would have been quite possible with the right combination of DNA specific poison and a robot guard array with laser guns programmed to kill cats on detection. Both such approaches were strictly illegal, so he had dismissed the thought.

"You pose some tough questions, partner. Yes, I suppose that would eliminate any future possibility of such a tragedy. It still wouldn't bring your mom back, though. Do you think we ought to get rid of vehicles because people get killed in them sometimes?"

"Can't we at least kill all of them on our farm? Robots can kill instead of sending shock warnings."

The kid thinks so much like I do that it's scary, thought Morgan. He struggled to find answers, and regretted that this discussion hadn't taken place while Lee Shealy was still alive. The ancient veteran had been a whiz at explaining such particulars, and damage to Buck had obviously been done long before the old man had died. Oh, how I miss that stubborn old goat, Morgan lamented silently.

"Son, animals just do what comes natural. They don't think or consider. We can't kill off a species because one of them does something bad. There's nothing inherently wrong with big cats, nothing that says they can't live in harmony with us and other creatures. As long as we constantly harvest a few of them—like Rocky Purdee does—the older and more aggressive ones, as well as those in declining health, can be removed to prevent tragedies. I know it's hard to understand at your age, but trust me, son, we don't want to go out and kill all the cougars. Besides, it would break every game law we have." Morgan noticed his forehead was beading up with sweat, and he wiped his sleeve across it to dry it.

"Dad, I don't like cougars. Cows, I do like. And bird dogs. But not cougars."

"We're going to have to get over it together, then, I guess. Cats serve a very useful function as long as they keep their normal fear of man. It would be unethical to eliminate them, but we can control them well with proper management. I'm just worried you may make some wrong judgments—come to some wrong conclusions—with the direction your reasoning seems to be taking you."

"I can't help it, Dad. Any more than a cougar can help killing a deer. Or somebody's mother."

Morgan had no more words to return to his precocious son. He drew the boy to his breast and hugged him like he had done so many times before, and neither one of them spoke. Father and son embraced for the longest time, and shortly Morgan felt a hot tear burn down his cheek. Buck noticed the tear as he pulled away, and he hugged his father warmly once more.

Next day dawned bright and clear, and a crystal blue sky arched heavenward over the farm while a warming sun chased away morning's dew. Henry McLean from Wichita, quail hunter and outdoor writer, showed up on the front porch early with his hat in his hand. Morgan had been expecting him to come calling, since he was aware of a commitment Shealy had made to him regarding the new litter of English pointer pups.

McLean was dressed in khaki-colored leather briar britches and a matching skin shirt. His weathered face bore the marks of a man who had spent many hours afield, and little lines of white radiated from the corners of his eyes where squinting had protected some areas from the effects of excess sun. His arms were burly and still sported a thick covering of bleached, yellowish hair that contrasted markedly with underlying brown skin. The man's crowning head of hair was snowy and abundant, and the outline of his hat could be seen just above his ears, with facial skin above that line being light and untanned, and that below being quite bronzed. His broad shoulders were slightly stooped, and he was beginning to appear physically frail, though he still displayed a quiet strength.

"Welcome, Henry. Been a while," said Morgan, extending his hand as he pushed open the creaking screen door.

"Too long. Sorry I was out of state when Lee died. Pity. He was a great friend," said McLean as he reached next for Buck's hand.

"To a lot of people," said Morgan. He motioned Buck toward the kennels across the way. "Go turn the puppies out, son."

"Good looking kid, Jim," said McLean as the boy ambled out of earshot. "How's he been doing?"

"Not as well as I'd like. Say, your pup is just seven weeks old. Sure you want to take it so young, Henry?"

"Yep. I like to get them started young. Keeps them from learning wrong on their own. Or learning bad habits from somebody—not that you would allow that, of course. But not everybody is as knowledgeable as you are. My custom is to pick them up at seven weeks. Hope you don't mind."

"Not at all. You know what you're doing. I don't mean to question your timing."

"No problem. Mighty robust bunch of canines here, Jim," said McLean. The whole litter of rowdy pups was suddenly surrounding them, accompanied by Buck, and they clamored for attention, romping underfoot with boundless vigor. They climbed all over the boy and tugged insistently at everyone's pants legs, growling and tussling like miniature fighters. Both men smiled at such a swirling menagerie, and then stooped to inspect the tiny creatures more closely.

"Picked out the one you want?"

"Yep. No problem for me. I always take the runt. Makes the best dog."

McLean selected the smallest pup in the litter, a sparkling white female with a large liver-colored spot surrounding her left ear. He held the struggling puppy gently while he stroked her with measured affection.

"Lee always said so. Probably have trouble moving the rest."

"No way. People all over want a dog out of Lee's last litter of pups. There'll be a note in my column about these dogs in a few days, you can bet. You'll be out of puppies by the end of this week."

Morgan nodded in silent agreement. In fact, practically all of them were already promised. He instructed Buck to put the remaining dogs back in their kennel, which he did only a bit reluctantly. As the mob of remaining puppies drifted out of sight with the boy, Morgan couldn't resist the temptation to question McLean. He had been a close friend of Lee Shealy, and the two men had shared many long hours in the field together over the years before Morgan came along.

"Say, Henry, you're aware of all our tough breaks of late, losing Lee, and before that the cougar…got Alice. It's having a very troubling effect on my boy."

"Understandable. But how are you taking it, Jim?"

Surprised at the change in focus, Morgan stammered a bit for an answer. Caught off guard, he bowed his head and looked momentarily at the ground, searching for words.

"You're sharp, Henry. Are you thinking the problem's me and not him?"

"Could be. Kids don't usually have problems they can't work out unless somebody's compounding them. Think about it. What do you think is wrong with Buck?"

"First of all, he's really missing his mother, and I can't do anything about that, I guess. He's mad at cougars, and he wants to kill all of them now. Maybe worse, he seems to be completely turned off to farming. I can't seem to stimulate his interest in what we do here anymore. It's having an adverse effect on our ability to communicate, too. True, it's probably my fault instead of his. I'm no whiz at raising a kid, I admit. Any suggestions?"

"Jim, I lost my mother when I was young, too. I remember all the uncertainties that went through my mind. I still deal with some of them, even at my age. You never recover completely from something like that, but you do learn to cope. He'll be fine in time. The key is to stay in touch, give him every extra minute of your life, and just keep on doing what you know is right. He'll come around. You can bet on it."

"Any specific suggestions?"

"Nothing builds understanding between a father and son like a wholesome outdoor activity of some sort. Get him to help you train one of these pups. Arrange with ol' Rocky Purdee to let him kill a cougar when he's older, if you think it'll make him feel better. But make certain he does it for the right reasons, and revenge isn't a good one. Have the two of you talked this out, Jim?"

"Oh, we've talked. We probably need to talk a lot more. But how do I make him like farming? Maybe I can handle the rest."

"You don't. He may not turn out to be a farmer. And there may not be anything you can do about it. That's the straight of it, my friend. Just teach him all you can and be content to know that he'll go his own way and do fine. He's no fool, Jim. He'll be okay, I'd wager."

"Not a farmer. Never considered that, I guess," said Morgan, his voice subdued, as they watched Buck walk back from the kennels.

"Turn him loose, Jim. It's the only way. He's got to be free. There's a lot you can do to influence, but nothing you can do to control. He'll grow up to be his own man. So get used to it," McLean said as he put the puppy down and let it stroll about the spacious porch. He kept a protective eye on the precious animal as it explored.

"Would Lee say the same thing?"

"I'd bet so. He might throw in a few words that are a little more colorful, perhaps. Like you, he'd hate the thought of the boy not becoming a farmer, but he'd give him his freedom, nevertheless. Oh, you might talk to John Gentry about one of those life memberships in the Conservation Club for Buck. Isn't he still president of the chapter in Adrian? They have some great youth programs. Something to think about."

"I don't want to push so hard that I drive him away from other things that interest me, Henry," Morgan replied.

"Balance, my friend. Balance. And encouragement. It's a sad fact, but most fathers never discover that their number one task is to cheerlead for their kids. Find something else he's good at and encourage him there, too. Something perhaps very indoors. Like playing the piano. My grandson plays and I can tell you it does my old heart good to listen to him. You might suggest it and see how he responds. I'll tell you one thing—he's a step ahead of most kids just because he has a father who cares."

"You know I care, Henry. And your suggestions make sense. His mother was a whiz on the piano, and she always said she hoped he'd learn to play. I'd thought of that before, but I guess I'm a little lethargic, Henry. I never could string one note after another myself."

As the wise front porch philosopher drove away with his puppy, Morgan watched his vehicle disappear, gazing down the road with his hand on Buck's shoulder. The boy looked up at him inquisitively.

"What were you and Mr. McLean talking about, Dad?"

Morgan looked down at him without speaking, noting the boy's handsome smooth face and sparkling blue eyes. For a brief moment, it seemed that he was looking into the eyes of his departed wife, so profoundly sincere, so deeply radiant, so much like hers. He snapped out of the spell fast enough to deliver a spontaneous answer.

"I was getting advice from Lee Shealy about how to raise you, son."

"Aw, you're kidding. What do you mean?"

"They were good friends. I wanted to know an important opinion from Mr. McLean. I wanted to know what Pa Shealy would say about some of our conversations lately."

"Don't worry about me, Dad. I'm fine."

Morgan smiled down at him, and somehow he felt better for a change.

Morgan made a firm and steadfast commitment at that very moment. He would be more than a provider and father to Buck. He would do everything humanly possible to lead him into an accurate understanding of his world. He would give him freedom to develop under his guiding hand. He would have to leave the results to forces beyond himself. There didn't seem to be any reasonable alternative.

J.Y. JONES

And for reasons he couldn't fully understand, an immeasurable quality of peace permeated his decision.

CHAPTER 4

November 2052

The Morgan farm had taken the route of most twenty-first century
agricultural enterprises, specializing in only a few principal commodities.
Jim Morgan worked hard producing an unending flow of animal protein,
a desperately needed food product in a world of eleven billion people.
The United States still had a population of only 800 million, so North
America remained the least populated continent. Morgan's operation was
mainly mammalian protein, which he grew in a variety of forms,
principally sheep and cattle. His product underwent a final technological
transformation at a protein processing plant in Adrian, and was
distributed worldwide as the brand Promag, a food of astounding
nutritional content.

Other farmers specialized in growing food for farm animals or food
to be marketed directly as vegetable matter for human consumption. It
was fundamentally little different from millennia past except that
packaging was more sterile, processing was more advanced to remove
certain unwanted elements for use as fuel and other products, and raw
varieties of meat were genetically engineered for maximum nutrition and
minimum negative factors. The result was a longer lasting commodity
for shipping and storage, as well as much improved taste in a more
healthful product. Food production was more sophisticated than at any
time in history, but it was still hard, exhausting work. There were live
animals to tend and there was complex heavy equipment to operate and
repair, all of which required constant manual labor.

"Dad, when we finish this, can we take the dogs for a spin?"

"Don't see why not. Let's get this quarter panel back on, then we'll
reactivate the system. Old Omicron will be as alert as ever now."

The two had spent the better part of a Saturday morning repairing
another glitch in the electronic circuitry of a robot sentry. The
contraption had malfunctioned in lock and laser mode, tipped over, and
drilled a deep hole in one of their back fields before a sensor mechanism

had detected the fault and shut it down. Buck was amazed at the complicated design of the mechanical cowboy, and he marveled over and over at its internal structures. The dependable devices seldom failed, so he had infrequently been privileged to see beyond the impervious surface. His arms ached from reinstalling dozens of magnetic welds that held the manmade custodian together, but he was gratified to see the robot functioning again and motoring toward its assigned duty station.

"Let's go back and make sure that cow is okay, then we'll break out our gear and let the dogs out. We'll use Tip and Babe today. Sound okay?"

"You bet, Dad. I'll check on the cow. Her calf looked great for her first one, despite her difficult labor. Guess we'll have to change to a different type of semen. Maybe Texas longhorn to hold down a calf's head size when we're fertilizing young cows, huh?"

"You got it, partner," said Morgan, shaking his head at the boy's observations. "I thought we might be making a mistake. But the biologist thought our prime heifers could tolerate larger heads first time around. And they can. But not without some anxiety that we can do without. See you at the kennels."

The cow looked quite well off, and her calf was okay as well. The newborn was up and nursing without any sign of problems, so he left them and returned to the farmhouse to get ready for one of his favorite activities.

Despite a grueling schedule of school, work, and other activities, Buck and his father frequently found time to pursue their farm's abundant quail. Shortly, two gorgeous white dogs were racing in a flowing motion of pure poetry across rolling hills, covering ground rapidly in pursuit of quarry. Action wasn't long in coming.

"Come here, Buck, Tip's on point! Hurry!"

Excitement boiled to a fever level as the boy's short legs carried him quickly through dense brush to his father's side. Their aging white pointer was standing statue-still now, his tail exactly vertical and his handsome black-and-white head held high. His muscular frame fairly

54

quivered with eagerness and anticipation, but his nature and his training rendered him completely immobile at the smell of bobwhite quail. The birds hugged the ground so tightly they were invisible to human eyes, crouched just in front of the dog ready to explode airborne when anything, dog or man, moved closer. Tip's bracemate Babe, another pointer dappled with liver-colored spots, stood locked in place nearby honoring the male dog's find.

Both hunters eased up behind their dogs and stepped forward to flush the hidden birds. Buck was young for a quail hunter, but his schooling on every aspect of the sport was extraordinary. He knew that he must pick out one bird instead of blazing away randomly at the whole erupting covey. Birds which flew to his side were his, and any going straight away were fair game, but on his father's side they were strictly off limits. Safety demanded rigid attention to such details.

A dozen birds lifted off the ground like tiny brown rockets, zooming skyward, darting and twisting among intervening limbs of tangled brush. Only one broke to the left side where Buck was positioned, but he was on it in a flash. A single shot boomed from his double-barreled twenty gauge shotgun, and the bird folded cleanly and tumbled groundward as excited dogs broke to retrieve. Another bird flushed to his right, and the boy instinctively swung toward it as his father's antique shotgun thundered twice. He caught the blaze orange color of his father's hat in the corner of his eye, and immediately and intuitively lowered his gun barrel. It was over for the moment. Two birds were down safely for Morgan and one for Buck, and the soft-mouthed pointers brought all of them quickly to hand. White teeth flashed and satisfied smiles etched their faces as the dogs worked perfectly.

"Almost enough for supper already, Dad," Buck noted as he examined the handsome tan and white plumage of his bird. He counted the quills on its juvenile wing, noting that the creature was young and healthy. He smoothed a rumpled area of feathers, and then carefully slipped it into his game bag.

The youngster got his second bird off Babe's point down by the creek, and Morgan felled another from a lespedeza patch behind the feedlot, then it was time to head in. A cool breeze ruffled dry prairie grass as they walked, and the crisp, clean air carried a pungent scent of sagebrush from somewhere upwind. The two laughed as terrified cottontails, flushed accidentally by their dogs, fled in zigzag fashion before the unconcerned pointers. Both of them shouted encouragement as elated canines cavorted across prairie and scrub brush land in continuous hunting mode, perpetually seeking quail but posing no threat to the rabbits.

As they approached the picturesque farmhouse, still surrounded by Alice's flowers and shrubbery, Morgan slipped deep into thought and paused momentarily. He still grappled occasionally with his tendency to ingest too much of his favorite brew, but he was making progress. Or at least he had been until recently. He cringed as he recalled his last stop at the Hat Trick Bar, just a week before. Memory of that disaster once more washed over him, dampening his spirits palpably.

As they entered the yard, they immediately spotted a vehicle in the turnaround, a truck they remembered seeing before. Henry McLean stood leaning against his all-terrain machine, his own bevy of bird dogs housed comfortably on the back. He had without doubt been enjoying the same timeless activity, and he waved as they approached. Morgan stashed his troubling reminiscences at the sight of their old friend.

"You old bird hunter! How you been?"

"Good, Jim. Been a long time. Thought I'd come by and show you my pup. I'm real proud of her."

"Been wondering how she was coming. Let's see—she's worked about two years now, huh? Great potential?"

"You'll be amazed. Want to take her for a whirl? No guns, just us and the dog."

"Sure, love to. Buck, would you put up the dogs? I'll clean birds when I get back."

The boy nodded in agreement and headed for the kennels. Morgan shouldered his archaic shotgun instinctively, though he had no intention of using it again this day. McLean released his petite pointer from her confinement, and using hand signals he directed the animal into nearby rough terrain without so much as a word. The men walked along silently as the sleek hunting machine quartered in front of them. Shortly she was rigidly on point, the very picture of perfection. They flushed the bird and watched it fly away unmolested.

"She's a beauty, Henry. You've done a magnificent job with her. I wish I had your talent. Congratulations."

"Thanks. A dog like her is a joy to train. A natural is never a problem, unless the trainer fouls it up."

"That's true, but a steady guiding hand certainly conveys a magic touch. I can't imagine you damaging a dog."

"Speaking of naturals, how's your boy coming? I see you're taking some of my advice, at least. He seems to be responding."

"I've been meaning to call you for some time, Henry. He's doing so well I can hardly believe it. He's quite a hunter, in fact. Shot twice today and killed two birds. When it comes to fieldwork, I guess I'm a pretty good trainer. I'm trying not to foul up there, as you say."

"Two for two ain't bad. Considerably better than my average. He's got to be enjoying it to get that good."

"Buck and quail are like biscuits and syrup. He's a fast learner and he's got lightening reflexes. 'Course we spend quite a bit of time at it, too, and practice doesn't hurt. But he's really a very unusual boy, Henry. I don't say that just because he's mine. He stands out from the rest in everything he does. He's good at so many things."

"Like what? School work?"

"Oh, yeah. But so much more. He's a whiz on the computer. You ought to hear him play the piano, too. And he reads books all the time. I can't get him interested in baseball or soccer. He could play any sport, I think, but he just isn't attracted to them. It really works out better anyway, with our routine here on the farm, but it's quite strange to most people that a boy would prefer a book to a baseball. He even chooses old-fashioned paper and ink books over the three-vee," Morgan said, referring to holographic videocom that had replaced old television technology a few decades before

"How are you doing, Jim?" asked the grizzled old man. "I was a lot more worried about you last time we talked than I was about the boy. Just like in these pointers, I worry a lot more when an old dog like you develops a major fault than when a pup like Buck gets one. You can always work it out of a pup."

"I'm doing all right," sighed the farmer. Morgan looked back into the stern eyes of his friend. He knew that McLean hadn't come so far out of his way just to rave about a prize dog. Word of his recent rampage must have gotten all over Kansas. There was no use pretending.

"You must have heard about my brawl," Morgan finally allowed with obvious disgust in his voice.

"Somebody did mention you belted a guy. What in heaven's name got into you, Jim? I've never heard of you doing anything like that."

"Like I told Sheriff Hicks, Jesse Prestone had it coming. He called me a—well, he said I was illegitimate. To be honest, I don't know if I am or not, but neither does he and he's got no right to say something like that. And then he implied that Alice was illegitimate, of all things. Her dad would've rolled over in his grave if he'd heard that. And that coming from a guy like Jesse, with no telling how many kids up and down half the streets in Adrian. My blood just boiled and I lost it. I knew I never should have sat down next to him—I always come away mad. I reckon I ought to just stay out of there altogether."

"I heard you mighty near killed him. And did a good bit of damage to some fixtures, as well."

"Not as bad as you probably heard," said Morgan in a highly irritated tone of voice. "The story gets inflated with the telling. I settled up with Leo right away. And I paid the hospital to patch the weasel up, too."

Up ahead the dog was pointed again beside an irrigation ditch that coursed along a field edge. Morgan eased up behind the perfect point as if to flush harmlessly as before. An unexpected metallic clank resonated as the breech of his old shotgun slammed shut, putting the piece at ready. The quail erupted into the air with a thunderous wing beat and streaked for nearby cover. The ancient gun whipped from Morgan's shoulder in an instant, and he dropped the bird with a single shot at less than a half dozen paces distant. A spray of feathers and flesh was all that was left. The classy pointer broke to retrieve the fragments and brought the riddled carcass quickly to McLean's hand.

"Jim, too close, too close! You know better than to shoot so quickly," lamented the old man. "You must have shot with that full choke left barrel, too. Ruined a fine bird and some mighty good meat. Man, that old cannon of yours shoots a tight pattern."

McLean shook his head as he inspected crushed remnants of feathers and bloody flesh. He handed the sad specimen to Morgan, who was contrite as he held the destroyed bird tenderly.

"You can't let your temper get away like that, Jim. You know that anger is a dirt poor reason to kill anything, man or beast. You'll wind up dead or disabled, and who's going to raise the boy? Relatives? Neighbors? The state?"

Morgan swallowed hard at such sobering words. He looked again at the dead bird in his palm and felt a twinge of deep remorse for his impulsive shooting. Why did he have such a degenerate streak? He wrestled with the same old issue, a feeling of consuming desolation encroaching on his mind, a piercing perception that somehow his human frailty was wreaking subtle destruction deep within his son. External evidences indicated that Buck was progressing well, but what about internally?

"What did you tell the boy about your little indiscretion, Jim?" asked McLean, looking directly into his friend's deep blue eyes.

Morgan exhaled deeply as he slipped the mess of feathers and flesh into his game bag. He cleared his throat and spat into the irregular windrow before replying.

"I told him I was wrong. I explained what happened and how I reacted. And how I should have reacted."

"Good. I was hoping to hear that. You'll be all right, Jim. And so will he. We won't mention this one to him. But let the birds get a little farther out before you shoot."

"I usually do, Henry. Thanks for coming over. You wouldn't have shown up if you didn't care. And I want you to know I appreciate it. Stay for supper?"

"Why not? I'll toss in a couple of my birds, if you need some more. Maybe we can salvage a little meat off that one there. I'd enjoy a little time with you and the boy."

"Great! I'll get Buck to play the piano for you. You'll be impressed with his progress, I assure you, no matter what you may have heard about mine."

Delicious fresh quail fried in canola oil made a fine meal for the threesome. After supper, Buck Morgan's nimble young fingers caressed the piano keys as he deftly walked from one melody to another in a concert that lasted nearly an hour. McLean requested a few old hymns, among them the timeless *Amazing Grace*. The youngster terminated the sequence with some classical Christmas songs, and then played *Brahm's Lullaby* perfectly as his finale. It was a good practice session and a powerful favor to their old friend.

"You're right, Jim. He can play," observed McLean, his eyes misty from unexpected emotion. "Good suggestion if I ever made one."

"I'll say. Big hit at his recital two years in a row."

"Another natural. Seems like this farm produces a lot of them."

"Yeah. I'm the biggest flaw on the place, I'm afraid."

"Don't worry, my friend. You'll do all right," McLean replied, reaching over and patting Morgan on the back. "You just wait. You're going to be proud of that boy, too."

"I already am. Thanks for coming by, Henry."

After the old man left, Morgan quietly watched the boy preparing for bed while he pondered. Buck seemed to have recovered completely from the low point, just after Shealy had died, and now he was back into a routine that seemed as normal as could be most of the time. Nonetheless, it seemed to Morgan that he could always sense a measure of discontent fermenting just beneath the level of consciousness, a dissatisfaction and an ambivalence that often seemed to peculiarly mirror Morgan's own. Still, it had been a marvelous demonstration of progress the boy had demonstrated after supper.

"Mighty good show tonight, son," Morgan remarked as they cleaned the kitchen. "Mighty good, indeed. Not many farmers play like that."

Buck looked at his father thoughtfully, then turned back to the task at hand with resignation and a barely perceptible sigh. Morgan kept silent, and after a few minutes the boy spoke.

"Dad, do I have to be a farmer?"

Morgan stared at him, transfixed again by the boy's similarity to Alice.

"Of course not. You have a whole world out there. Nobody can set the agenda of your life for you. You can be anything you want to be,"

"Really? You won't mind if I don't farm?"

"Son, I've had my heart set on you taking this farm and making it your life's work. That's what I've wanted since the day you were born. But I'm not always right. I had a lesson from Henry today about trying to do things my way, about giving my own wants and desires and passions their rein. I'm wrong sometimes, and I was very wrong today. If I could line out your life for you, I probably would, but I can't. Now I'm determined that I won't protest if you don't farm or if you don't teach or if you don't drive a truck. It's your life and I'm going to do my level best to be happy watching you do anything honest and productive. I want you to go as far as your talents and abilities can take you, and I'll support you all the way. If your life doesn't include farming, I'll just have to live with it. The farm can be sold when I retire if you don't want to run it. In fact, your cousin Jerry has already expressed an interest in it, if it ever comes up for sale."

A barely perceptible smile crept across the youngster's face. In sweet relief, he hugged his father. Buck loved the farm and hated

61

J.Y. JONES

thoughts of leaving it for good. He revered the familiar fields, the dogs, the house, the quail hunting. But his heart craved adventure in faraway places he had read about, places and activities that dominated his dreams. He wanted to be a part of the images he could pull up on his computer screen from anywhere in the world. Some unknown force deep within him stirred incessantly, creating a yearning to fill in the glaring gaps in his identity with real-life experiences remote from this familiar place.

"You need to get to bed, son," said Morgan. "I've got quite a bit of paperwork to do before I can get some sleep. Got to keep the jargonauts happy, you know. And we've got to be up early tomorrow."

As Buck departed, Morgan almost regretted the words from his own mouth. They just might be decisive as far as Buck's future as a farmer was concerned. Not that he had any choice, though. And maybe it was best, after all. Farming was not the profession it had been in the past. For decades, farmers had battled an impossible flood of government regulations, the lasting residual of a time when government intruded into everyday lives of people in pervasive fashion trying to modify behavior by means of passing ever more burdensome laws. Jargonauts, as career government paper pushers had come to be called, were a continuing thorn in the side of farmers, a festering legacy of the unenlightened Oil Age when regulation was the watchword. While attitudes were officially more rational these days, nobody had told the jargonauts, and they relentlessly insisted that all mandated paperwork be duly accomplished. National government had grown ever more inert and inflexible, so compliance with regulations was still easier than rewriting odious and obsolete laws.

The boy re-entered the living room to say goodnight. Before he departed, he sat down beside his dad, and their eyes met. Buck harbored an unusually quizzical look this night.

"Dad, where is Mom now?"

"She's in heaven with Jesus, son," Morgan replied softly, remembering numerous sermons he had heard on the subject, as well as the preacher's tribute to Alice at her funeral. "That's what the Bible says, I'm told."

"My teacher doesn't believe that, Dad. I heard her say so. Do you?"

Morgan paused, trying to think how best to answer the question. It seemed so much like his own questions that it was eerie. After a deep breath, he ran his hand thoughtfully through his close-cropped dark hair. He then rubbed his square chin with a cupped hand and stared blankly at the kitchen floor.

"Son, there's an awful lot we don't know for sure. Some things you can't know beyond all doubt, I don't think. We talk about proving an idea scientifically, but sometimes science fails us at our time of greatest need. It's a question of faith, and faith can't be measured like other commodities. People of faith would say without hesitation that your mother is in heaven."

"Where is heaven, Dad? The computer doesn't know—I asked it last night. Lots of information on 'the heavens' and a definition of 'heaven,' but nothing on where it is."

"Only God knows, son, but I'm becoming convinced we will, too, when he's ready for us to know."

Buck drifted off to sleep that night with the question still poised unanswered, as far as he was concerned. He thought of myriad stars glittering like jewels in the dark sky over the farm and he wondered if heaven was out there somewhere, holding his mother captive in some ethereal state. He longed deep in his soul to go trekking across those starry skies in search of—of what? He was by no means certain. Maybe if God's heaven wasn't out there, there would be something else wonderful awaiting discovery. Someday he'd find out. Someday maybe this God people talked about would be ready for him to know. Someday, so far away, when he grew up...

CHAPTER 5

February 2059

"Hurry up, Dad, we'll be late," young Buck Morgan called as he finished packing the car and told its cargo door to close, which it did briskly at his oral command.

"Can I drive?"

"You bet," said Morgan as he flipped the car into activated mode with a pocket remote starter. Doors slid open automatically, and each of them assumed appropriate seats, noting with satisfaction the sophisticated panel arrangement. They were quickly locked in place by special sensor-driven belts, devices that appeared almost innately intelligent as they secured their living cargo. Buck punched in destination coordinates and watched a color map display light up. He knew the way to the Civic Center already, but he loved to play with the technology. Besides, the onboard computer coordinated their vehicle with traffic signals and made suggestions to avoid congested areas and other obstacles, once it grasped where you were going.

The teenager eased the silent vehicle onto the main road in front of the farm after carefully checking for high speed traffic on his scanner. In spite of such a complicated navigation system at his fingertips, he did a thorough visual crosscheck by looking carefully up and down the road before proceeding. Morgan fairly glowed with pride as he noticed the boy's methodical attention to detail, somewhat of an oddity in teenagers of any era. It was a dangerous world and he was glad to see his son doing a good job of developing survival skills.

"How's it going at school?" Morgan questioned, more by way of making small talk than to gain information. He knew Buck was studious and stayed at the head of his class. The boy was also maturing physically, and Morgan noted with a great deal of fatherly satisfaction his broadening shoulders and developing physique, the beginnings of a teenage beard, and more huskiness in his youthful voice.

"Fine, Dad. I think Mr. Russell will be at the banquet."

"I'll bet you're right. You like that guy, don't you?"

"I do. He's the best teacher I've ever had. I've learned more science this year than during all the other years put together. And the projects he comes up with are fun."

"Oh, that reminds me, Dr. Albert Hansen from the university called today. They're going to start that electrobiology deer study this summer on our farm, if they can get some funding from the Conservation Club. Mr. Russell is still going to help with fieldwork, and you'll have an extra job as assistant."

"Oh, boy, Dad! That's what I was hoping. Mr. Russell says we'll be able to eliminate animal-vehicle collisions forever if this works out."

"That's what I understand. Something about a force field Dr. Hansen has discovered surrounding all living animals. It should be interesting to see how it goes."

"It'll go great, Dad. Dr. Hansen is really smart, and so is Mr. Russell."

Morgan smiled. Such enthusiasm had to be rare in the schools today with such a high dropout rate and so many troubled youth. Buck was undoubtedly a refreshing departure from the norm for his teachers.

"What about your friend Monty? Is he still keeping up his interest in school?"

Morgan had worried a little about Monty Archer's influence on Buck, since the other boy was a member of the community's strangest family. Monty was the son of Sam Archer, and was being raised by Archer's estranged wife. Monty had seemed to gravitate towards rebellion and conflict, characteristics that were common among the day's young people. There had been some trouble with the law a couple of years before, too, but of late the young man seemed to have settled down and become an unusually good student.

"I don't hear much from Monty except at school. No, he isn't trying as hard as he did—he's seeing Mary Jane Grabow a lot. He seems to be more interested in her than he is in science or math. Or sports or anything, I think."

"Well, that's pretty normal, huh? Most guys like girls, don't they?"

"You bet they do. I have to admit they're pretty interesting all right. But it seems like girls have a way of becoming the most important thing in life to a lot of guys."

"Yes, I can tell you from experience that they can sure take over your life. By the way, does Monty ever mention his grandfather, Clemon Archer?"

"No, sir. Oh, he did tell me once how bad he felt that one of his grandfather's pets killed Mom. I guess his grandfather was a little strange. A vegetarian and all, huh?"

"I'd say so. And he hated Pa Shealy. Those two were like foxes and hounds. Pa was pretty strongly opinionated himself, though."

"Monty's father isn't into a vegetable lifestyle, is he? Aren't you and Mr. Archer on pretty good terms?"

Morgan thought for a moment before answering. What could he say that was good about Sam Archer? The man had never held any kind of job, and he had few local friends besides the insipid Jesse Prestone. Archer had kidded Morgan openly at times about being involved in the killing business, leaving little question that he found the profession unacceptable.

"We have some of the same habits, I guess you'd say. I used to have a drink with him sometimes when I went to town. He was in the Hat Trick Bar the time when I had that fight with Jesse Prestone, and he's had very little to say to me since. He doesn't eat meat, though, and we've always disagreed strongly on that point. Not many people of that particular persuasion are around these days."

"Well, whatever he eats it sticks to him well. He's as big as a silo, isn't he? And he certainly doesn't spend any time with Monty. I think I'd leave home if I never saw you, Dad. What makes a person ignore someone they're supposed to love?"

*   *   *

A man's sinister eyes, colored like cold steel and brimming with hate, watched as a retinue of vehicles arrived in the parking lot of Adrian Civic Center. He directed a vulgar epithet at emerging occupants of one sleek vehicle. Shouted from the confines of a disguising head cover, his words were lost in the prairie wind and noise of a growing crowd. Frustration mounted as he tried unsuccessfully to attract attention form the arriving horde, but few noticed his shouts, his obscenities, his gestures.

He was accustomed to being ignored. It had become an unwelcome way of life for him. Sometimes his rage was replaced by a small measure of regret, perhaps even shame, that his view of life was so much at odds with norms of contemporary society. Why did he feel so strongly? He didn't know, but grim and bitter determination ruled his thoughts. His anger seethed and he would never give up.

*   *   *

Only a few minutes after leaving home, the Morgan vehicle glided flawlessly into the Civic Center lot. Morgan and the rangy youth removed their packages from the cargo hold and turned to note a big sign on the marquee: "Welcome—Adrian Conservation Club." They paid little attention to a small group of protesters who stood in ragtag formation near the sign's base, waving and yelling slogans. Each of them was dressed up in some kind of head-to-toe animal costume. One member of the colorful band sported a grandiose maroon elephant costume, complete with massive ivory-colored tusks and a swaying mockup of a tapering trunk.

"Don't eat dead meat!" the elephant man shouted at them from his sanctuary. It became a repetitive chant that the other oddly costumed people took up immediately.

Morgan and Buck walked by, packages in arm, but the makeshift menagerie merited only a glance from them as they entered the giant hall. One concealed objector veritably shook with anger as they passed. Someday he would get even with them for their unconcerned demeanor. Murderous thoughts coursed through his mind as Morgan and the boy shrugged their shoulders, shook their heads, and smiled as they passed. What a joy it would be to one day extinguish those laughing and patronizing blue eyes. He would show them if it was the last thing he ever did.

On entering the meeting hall, Morgan and his son surveyed an endless array of donated items to be auctioned that night. There were sporting goods, guns, fishing equipment, artwork, hunting and fishing trips, and on and on ad infinitum. They delivered their packages to the kitchen and returned to do some more scouting.

"Its hard to believe how this event has grown. When I was president of the chapter, way back when your mom and I first married, we had maybe ten percent of today's membership and not much more than that in donations. But we still did a lot of conservation work—like, for instance, those quail you love so much."

"I know, Dad. Thanks," the boy replied. Buck was well aware of that great quail success, restoration of abundant quail populations despite intensive ongoing agricultural operations. In early years of the twenty-first century, quail had almost died out, but essential new research and new techniques had turned the tide.

"Hey, Dad, come here and look at this. Can we bid on it?"

"A caribou hunt in Alaska? Gee, I don't know, son." Morgan thumbed through the brochure and then looked at some awesome pictures posted by the donating outfitter. "Looks interesting, huh? Three people, all-inclusive, except travel tickets to Anchorage. Pretty attractive."

"Can we bid on it, Dad? Can we?"

Mulling it over, Morgan looked at the date and checked his pocket computer for projected pasture irrigation and animal harvest schedules. All seemed to miss the hunt dates except for one watering cycle. Maybe his brother-in-law, Bill Barnes, could help him out again by doing that one. The cost of such an adventure might be a little much—after all, he had donated a good sized portion of protein for tonight's meal and he didn't want to overextend. Still, if the price didn't go too high, it might be a possibility.

"Maybe. Let's see how it goes."

"Okay, Dad! Please, God, let us have it!"

After surveying most items to be auctioned, they entered the banquet room and began seeking their table. It was crowded and noisy but there were some familiar faces all around.

"Hi, Jim! Hi, Buck!" They were greeted with a Texas-sized grin and an outstretched right hand that exemplified courtesy. John Gentry had a farmer's tan, yet he was dressed in a business suit and tie. His teeth were like ivory, and he fixed his piercing dark eyes on whomever he was addressing in order to establish a visual grip like a bulldog's bite. The distinguished man was legendary in conservation circles for his exploits on behalf of wildlife

"Evenin', John!" came an instant reply from both Morgans. Gentry was once again president of the local Conservation Club. He was a computer dealer who specialized in agribusiness, but he always said he only ran a business to have enough money for his outdoor activities. It was also his complaint that to have enough money he never had enough time. Buck still dimly remembered the brief eulogy Gentry had delivered at Pa Shealy's funeral some ten years before.

"Buck, tell me about Rocky Mountain Ranch," Gentry requested as he shook Buck's hand vigorously. "I hope to hear someone rave."

"Well, Mr. Gentry, I sure ought to rave. What a place, and the teachers were awesome! I can't say enough." Buck said enthusiastically. He then went on to thank Gentry once more for recommending him as the local chapter's student to attend Wilderness School at the Conservation Club's Rocky Mountain Ranch the past summer.

"Well, you're a great testimony for our program. I should've put you on to speak tonight. And thanks again for the Promag, Jim. Your product is the very best anywhere, and I've eaten processed protein all over the world. By far the best."

"No problem. Glad to do it. The secret's in our grass and our feed blend," Morgan replied. He knew Gentry was right. Nobody else seemed to have the "Shealy touch," as people still referred to it. Their protein was the best of the best, and Morgan's pride in his product made him feel a satisfying sense of accomplishment. That product, and similar ones from all over the country, met much of society's need for protein. Extracted fats were excellent chemical building blocks, and most motor fuel came from such renewable sources in surprisingly adequate quantities.

"I just hope we have enough. They tell me we have a larger crowd than expected," Gentry stated, casting an analytical eye over the hall with a bit of worry in his expression.

"We solved that. Three more cases delivered to the kitchen."

"Wonderful! Thanks again, Jim. Have a great banquet!" Gentry hustled off as several other people sought his attention in the busy hall.

They found their table on the computer monitor and moved to it slowly. As they arrived, Buck instantly recognized a man sitting next to his seat. He was dressed in a comfortable casual suit, its material a brilliant burgundy color, obviously tailored from finest leather. A familiar smile emanated from behind rimless spectacles, and he had large, elephantine ears and a balding pate. The skinny man extended his right hand to Buck and they shook hands fondly.

"Mr. Russell! Are you going to be at our table?"

"That's affirmative, Buck. Seems like your dad had something to do with it. I'm the proud recipient of a prime seat next to you tonight."

"Wow! This banquet is sure starting out right!" Buck smiled broadly, revealing his uniform white teeth and his dimpled cheeks.

Across the table Buck greeted his pastor, Don Tolbert, and his wife Julie. The hefty preacher was an avid outdoorsman and sometimes even preached about the importance of caring for the world's natural resources. The preacher wasn't nearly as enamored of science as Russell, but nevertheless Buck liked Pastor Don a lot. He and his father made a special trip around the big table to shake his hand and greet his wife.

They also took out time to speak to each person along the way. There were introductions to a couple he didn't know and cordial exchanges with all others. He waved to Uncle Bill Barnes and Aunt Carol across the room, then turned his attention back to Russell.

"We might bid on the Alaska caribou hunt, Mr. Russell," Buck said, trying to suppress excitement for sake of demeanor. "And I hope we get it. It's for three people. If we buy it, can you go with us?"

"I hope you get it, Buck. It's out of the question for me, though— the club is sending me as its teacher representative to the Rocky Mountain Ranch this year. One trip at a time is all I can squeeze in."

"No kidding? Wow, I wish I could go back there and be with you. We'd learn more than ever."

"Well, I'll come back and teach you all I discover. After all, you did the same for me."

The youth smiled at the thought of actually teaching Russell something. His teacher was a living fountain of information. One thing for certain, if the teacher learned anything new at Rocky Mountain Ranch he'd undoubtedly share it.

"And I wouldn't worry, Buck. You won't have any trouble finding a third party for a trip like that."

"I hope not. But first we've got to buy it. Do you think they'll raise enough money tonight for the club to fund our deer project?"

"Maybe. If so, we'll know answers to a lot of questions about deer by the time you finish high school."

Buck looked around at the crowd, recognizing many people, among them the best of Adrian County. There was a contingent from virtually every profession, doctors and lawyers, accountants, merchants, government officials, industry executives, and college professors. There was even a stockbroker and securities dealer, Andy Rosenthal, whose industrious son Aaron was in Buck's class at school. Rosenthal was there more for business contacts than for anything else, since he was not an outdoorsman. There were many in the audience who were neither

71

wealthy nor prominent, though, with a visible blue-collar crowd and numerous other working men and women. It was a mixture of people that had to be as diverse as any gathering in rural America.

After preliminaries, including a couple of speeches and some awards for various conservation accomplishments, the fundraising auction was finally underway. The pace was brisk—wildlife sculptures, rare books, quaint paintings in gaudy frames—all sold quickly and for good prices. At long last, the auctioneer was describing that coveted caribou hunt.

"You'll fly from Anchorage to splendid Lake Clark. Then you'll go by bush plane to the caribou hills. You'll live in a splendid tent for a week, you'll see hundreds of caribou, and you'll see moose and grizzly bears. It's the trip of a lifetime for three lucky hunters."

The first bid came from across the room already near market value. Another bid at market value, and another higher. Still his father kept silent. Two more bids pushed up the price a little more, then silence from the audience. The auctioneer pleaded for more audience response, then he halved his requested raise. No takers. Buck's heart began to sink, and disappointment welled up in his soul, oppressive and heavy.

"Going once. Going twice..."

Jim Morgan's hand shot up. The spotter yelled and raised his hand. Morgan now had the top bid.

"Now back to you, sir! You can't take it with you, and your money will be put to good use!" called the auctioneer, pointing to a man who had previously held the high bid. The man's finger twitched, he scratched his nose, and looked at his wife for some unknown sign. He then shook his head negatively.

"Going once, going twice...sold to Jim Morgan!" Buck leaped from his chair and gave his dad a big hug. Then he hugged Russell. Even Pastor Don and his wife seemed to be quite happy that their parishioners had prevailed.

"Thanks, Dad. I knew we'd get it. I just knew it!" Buck bubbled like a teenager, quite out of character for the normally deliberate young man. Morgan's smile told of his deep satisfaction.

"We paid a bit too much, but like the man said, it goes for a good cause. It should be a great time for us."

Outside the hall, the earnest band in Halloween costumes had already drifted away into the night, having made their unpopular statement to a consistently uncaring crowd. The maroon elephant man took a measure of convoluted comfort in his boiling hatred for banquet participants. Someday it would be different. Someday these people would pay.

Inside the convention center, Buck was still absorbed and ecstatic. The rest of that night had an almost dream-like quality, and soon they were filing out to head back home.

Morgan let the enthusiastic youth drive the vehicle once again, and he noted with satisfaction a most happy tone of their conversation. Despite the distractions, Buck maneuvered the vehicle carefully onto the highway and accelerated to a safe speed near the limit of 120 miles per hour.

"Good job of driving, son. Say, how about that third person we need for the trip? Ever thought of asking Monty?"

"Monty? Sure, why not? Too bad Uncle Bill and you can't get away at the same time. Maybe Jerry?"

"Let's think on it. Jerry doesn't like to travel. But somebody is in for a treat."

Dark highway spread before them, and the trickle of center line lights, guiding beacons locked into the car's computer system, stretched on forever into the night. All seemed well on the road and life was good in Adrian County. In the midst of joy, disaster struck with awesome suddenness.

"Look out, Buck! Brake!" shouted his father as a brownish blur materialized from one side of the road. Too late Buck saw the figure, a supple doe deer that stopped without warning directly in front of them. There was no time to even reduce speed, and a sickening sound accompanied the crunching impact. A big protective metal shield was mounted on the front of the vehicle for just such unexpected occurrences, but it didn't help the deer at all. The poor creature burst like an oversize water balloon and showered the windshield with lumpy red liquid. Washers and wipers activated spontaneously and restored visibility immediately as rivulets of crimson streaked rearward in the slipstream of the speeding car.

"That's two for me already this year, Dad," said Buck with a definite sadness in his voice. "Gee, I hope Dr. Hansen's force field technology can do away with these collisions."

"So do I, son. What a waste. I'm glad it doesn't destroy the car, at least."

Small comfort, thought the boy soberly. The car would have to be cleaned up when they got home. There was no need to stop, but sorrow at such a useless dissipation dampened his mood considerably.

It also inspired in the boy a staunch determination. Somehow, Hansen's new method had to work. Young Buck Morgan resolved that he would do all within his power to make a theoretical concept into an effective reality.

CHAPTER 6

May 2059

For days thereafter Buck was so excited about their upcoming trip that he could hardly think of anything else. He kept up his endless studies, his farm duties, and his piano practices, but thoughts of faraway wilderness were ever on his mind. Alaska, still the last frontier! The vast state contained thousands of square miles of untamed land and places where humans had seldom set foot. It had always sounded like a fairyland place, and he could hardly wait to experience the solitude, the quiet, and the beauty he had read about and had seen portrayed on holocom documentaries.

From an on-line store they ordered all the needed items and began accumulating them in an unused room they straightway dubbed "the Alaska closet." Gear was soon piled all over the floor in a rudimentary state of order, sleeping gear in one pile, underclothes in another, socks and boots in another.

"Dad, I can't wait for this trip to get here. If I could only forget about it, maybe time would pass faster," Buck lamented.

"Good point, son. Try to get occupied in mind and body and it'll be here before you know it."

Buck usually had no such problem, staying busier than a squirrel in fall most of the time. Seeing him so excited about something they would do together made his father all the more glad he had purchased the excursion. Good work, Morgan, he congratulated himself silently.

The trip was still months away, but as days and weeks passed the grinding routine of their agricultural operation finally reestablished itself. Tractors plowed, robots churned farm roads into thick clouds of dust as they roamed on eternal guard duty, and plants and animals flourished under tender scrutiny. The eventual Alaska experience assumed a back seat to everyday life, though it was seldom more than a thought away. By summer's end all would be ready. Reservations were made and travel tickets for the boy and his father were already purchased.

It was one of those gorgeous spring evenings in Kansas, when cottonwoods are emerald green and meadowlarks sing until near twilight, and lengthening days make it hard to go inside for the night. As the sun hid itself behind distant flint hills, Buck eased through the back door to get started on his homework. He had just engaged WorldNet and was about to become engrossed in his studies when the telecom, a common audiovisual device which had replaced the telephone, flashed on unexpectedly. A face framed by big ears and a bald head appeared on the screen requesting electronic access to the Morgan residence. The boy's eyes lit up with immediate recognition, and he hurried to key in affirmative numbers.

"Hi, Mr. Russell."

"Buck? How's my math expert?"

"Fine. Is everything okay?"

"Oh, yes. Middle of the green arc here. I know you seldom watch the holographic videocom, but I think you ought to power it up. Science history was made today and you need to remember the event. Tune in WorldSpan. See you tomorrow."

After canceling the telecom access code, Buck spoke the three-vee into function mode and told it to bring up the news channel WorldSpan, which it did instantaneously. A live interview was in process, with a crisply sterile high tech laboratory as background. An aging scientist with a bald head and a thick, white beard was being questioned by famous WorldSpan anchorman Tom Druthers.

"Dr. Klas, can you tell us exactly what today's statement means?" asked Druthers, expectancy showing in his well-known voice.

"Tom, let me first emphasize that we have been forced to make this announcement prematurely," said the aging doctor. Grain-sized droplets formed on his forehead as he basked in the intense light, threatening to launch a cascade of perspiration. He spoke a bit nervously and with a viscous accent, though the voice failed to readily disclose his national origin. "An activist spy, fortunately one friendly to our work, infiltrated our laboratory and discovered over the past several months that we were researching a new technique for countering human immunodeficiency virus. We had hoped to hold our announcement until we accumulated more data, but this particular individual—well, he was going to go to the media anyway. So this announcement is made tonight without benefit of fully comprehensive and finalized research data."

"You mean you might have taken another several months or years to confirm what you're announcing tonight?"

"Hopefully not years, but now we'll never know. We've always been immaculately careful about who we employ in our lab. Security is a prime issue, you know. There were even some bombings of our research facilities way back during the Oil Age, so we've always been meticulous about getting the right people on our team."

"Doctor, please get to the heart of this matter for our viewers," insisted Druthers with a hint of impatience.

"We have finally isolated the weakest link of the virus, a link which can be attacked biochemically," said Klas. He droned on about chemical bonds, double helices, sulfur double bonds, and a lot of other complicated data before a restless Druthers interrupted him in mid-sentence.

"Doctor, please tell us what this means in everyday language."

"It means that finally, after nearly three billion deaths in the past eighty years, we can cure acquired immune deficiency syndrome caused by human immunodeficiency virus. We can eliminate this virus easily from any living system. All preliminary data indicates that our method is foolproof, although as I say, we haven't been given as much time to complete our studies as we feel we needed."

"You mean, after decades, AIDS has been defeated? Are you serious?" Druthers asked, sounding downright dubious as his inflection betrayed an undercurrent of disbelief.

"We've been close for years, Tom, but we lacked one critical bit of information. Recently Charley here provided exactly the sample we needed to fit a final, critical piece of the puzzle into place."

The doctor opened the door of a small cage, reached inside, and expertly retrieved a small monkey. The petite animal squirmed and cocked its head from side to side as the researcher gently placed it on a lab counter. The little creature stood hesitatingly on its hind legs with its long tail curled tightly around the scientist's hand. The tiny primate seemed to be smiling as it alternately pursed and pouted its fragile lips.

"Tom, let the world meet our hero. Charley was inoculated with HIV only a few months ago for our studies. A sample of his bone marrow taken only two days after infection revealed the missing clue. What we've discovered is the susceptible element of the virus replicating mechanism that I've been seeking all my life. We would never have found it if we hadn't accidentally sampled two weeks earlier than planned in our protocol. The vulnerable linkage doesn't show up later. We've repeated the test in more monkeys and it comes up the same. A simple intravenous infusion of a fairly common chemical appears to extirpate the virus from any biological system in which it occurs. Tom, Charley is already free of HIV."

Buck could hardly believe what he was hearing. This sounded too good to be true. No more AIDS? He yelled for his father to come as Druthers continued to interview Klas.

"What's going on, son?" Morgan questioned before he entered the room, kicking grime from the animal holding area off his shoes just outside the threshold.

"Dad, they've cured AIDS!"

Buck could hardly believe this impossible scourge might be defeated. All his life and all his father's life this awful holdover from the Oil Age had been a consuming blight on the human race, the one disease that defied any solution. Could this really be true? If this were so, human medicine had finally eliminated the very last of infectious diseases.

"Doctor Klas, many people labored on this project all their lives but never saw this day. To whom do you give the most credit for this incredible breakthrough?" asked Druthers.

"How about Charley here?" said Klas with a twinkle in his eye.

The interview digressed to a review of the history of AIDS since it first appeared, and the disastrous emergence of a hypervirulent Bangkok strain. That frightful mutation of the virus could pass from one person to another even through intact skin under certain circumstances. All that was necessary was for skin to briefly contact any body mucous membrane of an infected person. A single sexual contact with a person harboring the Bangkok strain was certain to produce a prolonged and painful death.

Observing the discussion, Buck calculated in his head how many people died each day from AIDS. Since the epidemic had really started rolling a decade after the change of the millennium, it had averaged nearly fifty million deaths per year. That came to almost 110,000 people a day. Why would anyone even consider holding back a cure pending absolute confirmation when it could save that many lives? He put the question and numbers to his dad.

"Why does that bother you so much, son?"

"Dad, science is supposed to serve people. Mr. Russell stresses that all the time. These scientists are guilty of pride of the worst sort, wanting to be entirely certain the thing works when all preliminary indications were so positive. Did you hear that part?"

"Some of it. What's the point?"

"Millions of lives will be saved because they were forced to announce early. Even if they find a strain that's resistant, they already know it works on most of them. I can't believe they'd let that many people die just to prove they were exactly on target with a cure."

"I see what you mean," replied his father thoughtfully, resting his chin on one hand while he stared at the ongoing holocom spectacle. "It's an imperfect world, son. Scientists have to deal with jargonauts, too, and they could be criticized if they don't do all the proper preliminaries. They may be afraid of the reaction if the thing is eventually shown not to work or to have some unpredicted side effect."

"But now public pressure will probably force them to start treating people," observed the youth.

"Yep, I think you've got it right. It's a funny thing, too. It takes public pressure sometimes. Those scientists would have proclaimed imminent doom on the basis of a fragile theory or contradictory findings, but they have a hard time embracing good news confidently, no matter how much proof they have. I've seen it happen time and again. I've heard it called the cold fusion syndrome, but I'm not certain where the phrase originated."

Buck and his father seldom watched three-vee more than a few minutes per day, just enough to get news and weather. Tonight, however, the discovery was so big and the revelry so raucous and unrelenting that they sat mesmerized for several hours, taking in coverage as absorbing as that of a war in progress. City streets around the world pulsed with excited humanity, and everywhere people danced and sang arm in arm, eager to proclaim victory with the planet's biggest ever party.

"Dad, I've got to get away from this and do my homework," said Buck in a worried tone of voice.

"Son, I think we'll probably have a holiday tomorrow," Morgan said with certitude. Shortly, he was proved exactly right when the President of the United States appeared live to declare the next day "International AIDS Victory Day" in a joint declaration with other heads of state from around the world.

While they were observing a time of unprecedented joy throughout the world, Buck could not escape a creeping sensation of uneasiness. As he watched the ongoing festivities, he recalled several past conversations dealing with just this eventuality.

"Dad, I've heard you say that if AIDS were ever cured the world would go downhill fast. Do you think that's where we're heading?"

"It's a concern. Physically the world is certainly a safer place without AIDS, but in other ways it could become much more hazardous. Pastor Don has made that observation many times. I hope he's wrong."

"I hope so, too. There's a lot I'd like to do in my life, and I want this development to mean progress. Maybe this really will make things better, after all," said the boy. After a thoughtful pause, he added, "I can't believe a little monkey was the key to providing a cure for a major disease, Dad."

True to Morgan's prediction the next few days were all a big holiday, designated by the international community as International AIDS Triumph Week, to be observed annually by all nations. Dr. Klas and his colleagues were immediate international celebrities, uncommon heroes to a grateful humanity. Buck noticed with great interest the adoration the world showered upon this small group of scientists.

Someday, he thought to himself, I'm going to do something important like that. Someday the world is going to celebrate Buck Morgan.

It seemed like an impossible dream for a farmer's son from Kansas.

CHAPTER 7

May 2059

Business was brisk early this evening at the town watering hole, and Leo the bartender was staying busier than usual. Jim Morgan gazed casually around at a horde of people as he strode into the bar, searching for a friendly place to repose. The crowd in the Hat Trick Bar was in a delicious party mood and drinks flowed freely. Most of the usual crew was there and an atmosphere of celebration and sensuality was pervasive. There were quite a few new faces that Morgan had never seen before, and more were arriving all the time. Sam Archer and Jesse Prestone sat in a dark corner by themselves, ignoring Morgan altogether, taking in the vibrant scene.

Morgan strolled to the bar and leaned against the only open spot, brushing against a brash young cowboy in the process. The strapping youth was too busy to notice him, and continued his busy advances toward the girl next to him. It was impossible not to overhear.

"Hey, baby, come on over to my place tonight. We'll play...whatever you say!"

The curvy brunette looked positively luscious in her clinging finished leather dress, the latest in revealing feminine fashion. She recognized the blonde muscle man in form-fitted sheepskin jeans, having been attracted to him previously. She knew little about him, but the usual caution flag was gone and a most welcome feeling of exultant liberation coursed through her mind. She spoke with undisguised passion, leaning up against him as she answered.

"Now whatever do you mean by that, honey?" She fluttered her long eyelashes innocently and moved her face ever closer to his.

"Like I said, come with me to my place and you'll see. There'll be some of my friends there, too. Hope you don't mind a little company."

She recalled seeing him with a rather handsome bevy of companions earlier, all of them well dressed, well proportioned, and as wild as

82

backcountry sagebrush. Her mind raced at the prospect and involuntary chill bumps covered her skin. She nodded in agreement, parting her luscious red lips in a knowing smile. He placed one hand on her trim waist and planted a passionate kiss on her open mouth.

The two scowling men at the corner table watched and listened intently, straining forward in hopes of hearing the conversation. The noisy crowd and loud music made it impossible to hear the couple's words, though their overt actions left little to the imagination. The skinny man turned to his rotund friend in obvious frustration.

"This is more than I can take, Sam. I want to join in the fun. The doctor says I'm already free of the bug, so I can get back to real business," Jesse Prestone whispered loudly to his companion. "I'm putting on weight and feeling full of pep. Before long everything will be normal."

"Oh, shut up, you lecherous fool. There's plenty of time for that later. Just be a voyeur for now. We've got some important planning to do before you start acting like an alley cat again."

Jim Morgan stood sipping his favorite concoction, one leg propped on the foot rail as he leaned against the bar, observing the pervasive stimulating atmosphere. Several younger women left with older men in tow, and he overheard another couple making plans to meet at the blonde cowboy's place. More than one unattached female cast a suggestive eye at him. Leo looked the other way while a couple partied undisturbed in a dark corner booth.

Morgan was entirely unaccustomed to such looseness, and the whole scenario somewhat unnerved him. He felt an uncomfortable stirring inside, though, a sensation he had felt only rarely since his wife's death. He found his gaze drawn irresistibly to the dark booth, and his breath quickened. He rose to his feet and made his way silently back out to his truck, reeling with powerful passions.

The defunct Oil Age had given way to the Age of Science. The world now stood on the brink of a new Age of Passion. Nothing seemed different about the roads, the houses, the fields, or the farms as Jim

Morgan motored toward home. The material world looked the same, but a profound attitude shift had occurred.

Despite changes in much of society, young Buck's world changed practically not at all. His was one of hard work, both at home and at school. He anxiously waited for school to reopen after the declared holiday. He spent his time completing a paper he had written and helping his father catch up on endless chores. The celebration period finally was over, and the boy arrived early at school, anxious to begin.

"Hi, Mr. Russell! I guess its time to go to work again, huh?"

"You bet. Great week off, though, wouldn't you say?"

The teacher had arrived exactly on time as always and began arranging his desk, bringing his computer on line and generally preparing for a day of catch up.

"I appreciate your calling and suggesting we turn on the holocom. You just don't see that magnitude of scientific progress often in a lifetime, according to Dad."

"I couldn't agree more. Solving mankind's problems has always been the prime function of research. Such breakthroughs are the triumph of applied science," Russell said, lapsing into his teaching voice. "Mankind can do it all, Buck. We just have to believe in ourselves enough and be persistent enough. I must admit, though, that I had begun to wonder if our researchers would ever solve the HIV riddle."

"Science really came through, all right," Buck acknowledged, although he couldn't shake the thought that maybe the cure hadn't resulted from pure brainpower and determination. Hadn't there been an accident that had led to the real breakthrough? But he wasn't about to bring that up to Russell.

"Someday, Buck, if you really believe in yourself and find that inner well of strength that you possess, you'll be one of the very best scientists. There's no limit to what you can accomplish. Young people like you are the hope of our world."

"I'm always dreaming about someday, Mr. Russell. It seems pretty far away. Dad tells me the years will pass faster as I grow older, but it's hard to see that from where I am. At any rate, it's a problem to mesh the thought of ever really accomplishing great things for mankind with the everyday business of learning basics. Sometimes it even gets boring."

"You've got to take it a step at a time. Yes, math and science that we study are basic but also foundational. You must have good groundwork to build upon, and the only one worth building upon is knowledge. You're making great progress, Buck."

The charisma that flowed between the two was abruptly shattered by a noisy clamor outside. Russell commanded the classroom video monitoring system into function mode as the sound grew to a tumultuous level. A whole classroom of students suddenly spilled into the room squawking like a disorderly flock of birds.

"Take your seats, take your seats," blared the classroom address system, an artificial voice booming the command so loudly that it was impossible to ignore. Two teenage boys, Buck's friend Monty Archer and industrious Aaron Rosenthal, dutifully sat down in the midst of the melee. Each of them exchanged glances of acknowledgment with Buck. Aaron was the studious type and was clearly not going to be deprived of an education by the undisciplined rabble sharing his classroom, and he showed his displeasure with a frustrated frown. By contrast, Monty sported a devilish grin, so expansive it seemed hardly confined by his ample head of flaming red hair. Another youth, Alex "Spot" Prestone, also was marginally responsive to the robotic commands. No one else paid any attention until Russell got up and walked up and down the rows of workstations, whereupon an uneasy truce settled over the room.

Russell usually held a firm grip on his class, and this iron control was one of many reasons he enthralled Buck. His threats were not idle, and more than one student was summarily ejected for disrupting class. Buck was glad he was in an advanced learning section where some semblance of order could still prevail. Lower level classes were mainly a chaotic holding action whereby teachers simply tried to survive, all teaching aside, until the clock ended that period and released the unruly mob.

"Let's get started, class. I'll take up your vertebrate comparative anatomy papers and then we'll go over a few principles. We've got lab today, and we'll be studying vestigial organs, embryonic recapitulation, and other basics of evolutionary history."

Buck handed in his paper and relished prospects of more information on the subject. The mechanisms and dynamics of evolution held a certain fascination for him, though many of his questions remained unanswered.

"In lab today we'll begin dissection of a primitive aquatic creature, the dogfish shark. Follow instructions carefully. You'll be tested thoroughly after we finish this project in two weeks," Russell lectured. "Pay attention to what you're doing, or down you go to a lower class level. That's warning enough."

Buck and Monty worked together as always. Monty was unusually talkative this particular day, his demeanor bordering on effervescent. Buck's friend had his ample crimson tresses parted immaculately down the middle, a new and impressive style for him that even Buck couldn't help but notice.

"Let's get on with this dissection. I need to get through so I can talk to someone."

"That someone happen to be named Mary Jane?"

"You bet. We've got plenty to talk about," Monty answered, pausing briefly in his dissection to comb his hair and preen a bit. "If talk's what you call it."

"Monty, that girl is nothing but trouble. You're really asking for it. Why..."

"You're such a cussed hologeek, Buck. And if she's trouble, I'll take some of it anytime. Besides, if there's anything I've learned in this class, it's that we're free to follow our natural instincts, we're just like animals..."

"Mr. Russell doesn't believe we're just like animals or else this dogfish would still be swimming free. Right?"

"We're not exactly animals, but we came from them so we have certain aspects which we must turn loose. You've got to be free to explore." Monty sliced away at the dogfish, hurrying his dissection again after giving his friend a quick sidelong glance. "You must not watch the same three-vee programs that I do, Geek. No, of course you don't."

Buck let the subject drop in favor of keeping up with Monty's furious work pace. He couldn't understand his friend's hyperactivity since class wouldn't be dismissed until the period ended, regardless of how soon they finished their dissection. Such was how a romantic relationship affected one's ability to reason, he decided. He had to admit that sensual thoughts about shapely Mary Jane came easily, and Monty's casual, graphic ravings set Buck's own mind into turmoil. But thinking intently about such matters seemed to destroy the capacity to analyze rationally, an ability he held in highest esteem.

Looking across the busy laboratory, he noticed that the Prestone kid was teamed up with Aaron Rosenthal as usual, and they were making great progress in their dissection. Why had he been saddled with a partner who was more good times than good student? He didn't trust the Prestone boy because he harbored a pernicious dishonest streak that led him to overt cheating whenever opportunity presented. Other students sometimes gleefully made fun of Spot Prestone because his closely cropped coal black hair featured a prominent round patch of pure white on the left side of the scalp, just below and behind the ear. Seldom were any taunts directed to his face, because he was more than able to fend for himself, and the wisest students left him unmolested.

That Spot Prestone was smart nobody could deny, and he was a fierce scholastic competitor. Sometimes Buck felt hamstrung beyond what he could bear being teamed with Monty all the time. Maybe he would bring up the subject to Russell, although it seemed inappropriate to ask for special consideration. Looking back at the work at hand, he noticed that Monty had almost finished today's dissection, and was moving practically at mach speed as pieces of pickled shark flew in all directions.

"Monty, are girls the most important thing to you?"

"Huh? The most important? No, I don't think so. But maybe. They fill up a big slice of my appetite. I'm just not sure they're the most important item on the menu."

No firm answers as usual, thought Buck. He really felt sorry for Monty in many ways because he had so little family support and so few friends, especially among the boys in school. Buck and Monty had endured some serious differences of opinion at times, but they had mostly come to terms and were now fairly good friends. Buck and his dad had still not found a third party for their upcoming trip to Alaska, so Buck decided that now was as good a time as any to ask Monty about it.

"If you can turn loose of Mary Jane for awhile, I've got an offer for you. Dad and I have a special trip coming up this summer. We're going to Alaska and we have a place for another person to go with us. Why don't you come along?"

"Yeah, I heard all about that. You're going to go up there and shoot some helpless animal, aren't you? My old man doesn't think much of that kind of thing. I don't think he would let me go. Even if I decided I wanted to. My mom wouldn't care a tin kilobyte wherever I go, but the old man might blow a microchip."

"It's much more than 'shooting an animal,' Monty. It's an experience that might change your whole perspective. Think about it. But we need to know within a week or two so we can get more travel reservations and so you'll have time to gather your gear."

"Don't think my old man will let me. Can I go to Alaska to kill something? Holy holograms."

"Everyone put your specimen away now and return to your seat," interrupted Russell. "Time now for discussion. We'll continue our dissections tomorrow."

"Let's talk about how dogfish and people are related, Mr. Russell," suggested Monty, piping in uncharacteristically as they returned to their seats.

"An interesting observation, Monty. How are we alike?"

"We've both got the same basic organs. We've both got survival and reproductive instincts. We should both follow our instincts to be at maximum biological potential; wouldn't you say?"

"Now we're talking about something I like," came a sarcastic voice from a kid in the back of the room. The boy was part of a local cult of some kind that practiced fertility rites. Buck had even heard they performed sex acts to worship nature. "Follow instincts, do what's natural!"

Buck lowered his head and shook it slowly in faintly concealed disgust.

"To a certain degree I'd say you might be right, Monty," answered Russell, ignoring the cynical boy's voice. "But we've evolved to a much higher level and consequently we have a higher degree of responsibility. Our number one responsibility is to make sure, in following our biological drives, that we don't hurt another person."

"So we can follow our instincts if we don't cause harm to others?" Monty questioned.

"I believe so. But it may not be as simple as you're making it sound. Do you have a specific example in mind?"

"No, sir. I was just wondering in general."

Buck knew Monty was lying. He thought about clarifying the point but he decided it best to let it drop. Spot Prestone delivered a short oratory on chemical attractants that exist between males and females of various species, and how this information related to the current discussion. It didn't appear certain that his observations applied at all.

After school Buck returned to Russell's classroom for an hour of special one-on-one tutoring in math. The young man had already made near-perfect scores on all the standardized tests but still there was more to learn, and Russell was a rare genius when it came to mathematics.

"Hi, Mr. Russell," he said as he entered the now-quiet classroom. He put his wallet personal computer on the desk and attached his terminal to the main unit in preparation for their session. When all was ready, he turned again to Russell.

"Before we start can I ask you a non-mathematical question?"

"You know that's affirmative. Out with it and let's talk about it."

"Do you know what Monty was getting at today?"

"Positively. I didn't find it necessary to pin him down on it, but he's girl crazy. The whole world is going insane like that, I'm afraid. Our world has never been in this position in my lifetime. It's marvelously liberating, I suppose."

"But isn't immoral behavior still immoral, with or without the consequence of some kind of disease?"

"It's immoral in the old-fashioned sense, I suppose, Buck. But people are people, and they're going to fool around. After all, most people have certain basic instincts they follow," said Russell. He paused and looked at his student, then added as an afterthought, "At least everybody but Buck does."

"Oh, you know I don't have anything against girls. I even had a date last year, remember? I actually like girls as much as any other guy, and I have those same impulses that Monty cultivates. But there's time for that later, and Dad says a person can't be involved physically and still function at their best mentally. At least in an illicit relationship, whether old-fashioned or not."

"What's illicit? Just remember, Buck, for many decades religious fanatics have preached AIDS as punishment by some supreme being. To see science triumph over that obstacle, and over their distorted chortling, is a wonderful thing. We must expect a period of jubilation and released inhibitions."

"I guess so," Buck conceded.

"But enough side issues. As you very well know, my young friend, Alex Prestone is right on your heels academically. His mother pushes him relentlessly, and I have a meeting with them right after your session. So we'd best get busy. Only top bird gets the juiciest worm, you know."

"Oh, yes. And I have a piano lesson in forty minutes, too."

"How's that going? You were doing very well last time I heard you."

"It's going well. I'm learning a Neoclassical Pre-2K medley of Brian Wilson songs. A piece called 'California Vibrations.' Interesting musical combination."

"Hmm. I'm not much at music. But good luck. Let's get into this math for now."

The two settled into a more mundane discussion of a set of equations designed to prove a complex mathematical theorem, and Buck relegated other issues to the back of his mind. The involved computation was much easier to unravel than such complicated social puzzles as they had been discussing.

That evening he couldn't bring himself to question his dad about events of the day. It was difficult for him to broach the subject of sexuality with his father, somehow awkward for both of them. Still, he couldn't dismiss the whole subject. He elected to ask a few general questions without bringing up specifics.

"Dad, do you really think the world will change a lot because of the cure for AIDS?"

"I'm sure it will, son, for those who carried the virus, unquestionably. Previously infected people can now look forward to a normal life."

"No, I don't mean for those who were infected. I'm thinking more of humanity as a whole."

"I suppose there will be a lot less fear about personal relationships, contacts with other people, doctor-patient interaction, and the like. Why?"

"Just wondering. I've heard we're into a behavior revolution. You think so?"

Morgan's mind shot back to events earlier in his busy day. A girl in the feed store had made a suggestive remark while they were alone together. A pretty secretary at Adrian Savings Bank had winked at him slyly. In most places the seductive changes he sensed were far more veiled than he had seen at the Hat Trick Bar. But indications of change were undeniable.

"A revolution is exactly what it is, son. Whether it will be good or bad, who can tell? Pastor Don is really concerned that morals will become nonexistent. Our society is already sadly deficient in common virtues like working for a living, being neighborly, simply respecting your fellow man. Who knows? We just have to behave morally ourselves and do the best we can. We can be thankful we live in a place like Adrian, where such qualities still are present to a large extent. We can only hope that doesn't change."

"I sure hope not, Dad. By the way, I went ahead and invited Monty to come with us to Alaska like we'd discussed. I don't know if he'll go, though. He seems to think his dad will be opposed."

"I wouldn't be surprised. Sam Archer is about as strange as they come. If Monty gets to go, maybe we can teach him a thing or two."

"You said once that Mr. Archer is always with somebody. Who would that be?"

"Prestone is the guy's name. Jesse Prestone. Why?"

"Just wondering. His son's in my class. Smart kid. Spot Prestone, we call him. Real name's Alex."

"That's Jesse's boy, all right. I've heard him say he's got a son your age. I assure you, Jesse doesn't even know him."

*　　*　　*

Again that evening in the nearby town, a voluptuous brunette cuddled up to her muscular companion and the two locked in a prolonged embrace. The triumph of science was their freedom, and they played out their roles unrestrained. Some hours later, the ravishing girl lay unconscious in the man's quiet pad, sleeping a sleep of satisfied exhaustion. Her mates left one at a time as they recovered sufficiently, a stupor of contentment hazing each depleted mind, all of their sexuality sapped. It was over again for now.

*　　*　　*

Buck Morgan finished his homework and lay in his bed contemplating his first day back at school. Where was the world going and how would he fit in? The uncertainties of his childhood had faded dramatically as he grew in stature and confidence, so he was a bit surprised at the uneasy sensation recent events had brought into his life. Still, he had a solid rock, a man he trusted wholly, to help him through. Dad could be counted on for everything he needed now, but to guide Buck's future—it was Ralph Russell, all the way.

Give me good old science over emotions any day, he thought as he drifted off to sleep. Something dependable that won't let you down. Something worthy of total allegiance. Even if the world's morals degenerated completely, he was sure research would provide answers needed by society.

It had worked many times before, and it wouldn't let society down now. He was positive about it. In fact, he might have staked his life on it.

CHAPTER 8

June 2059

The Church of the Sun and Moon was located in a fenced compound not far from the Morgan farm. Its main building was a climate-controlled temple of crystal clear glass that glistened like a prodigious jewel in bright sunlight. This day was a summer solstice celebration, and there were special preparations in progress for that exact moment the sun reached its northernmost excursion. Situated around an ornate altar were several dozen couples preparing for the most unholy of rites, timed to coincide with sacred solstice. A high level of ecstasy would mean the sun god would be pleased, and his favor would shine forth on all participants. Reminiscent of Caananite ceremonies of long ago, the proceedings honored primordial deities of nature, and would assure that goddess Earth, Mother Gaia, would be reliably warmed and nurtured.

Such activities had been greatly subdued for decades, perhaps for centuries. Quite a few new members had signed up to participate in the observance this year, strict screening rules having been suspended. A pagan priest looked out over the assembled mass of humanity with diabolical satisfaction, anxious for showtime to start. In only a few minutes he would announce the countdown and preliminaries would begin.

*　　*　　*

On the Morgan farm nearby, insects were unusually bad that sultry summer in Kansas. Walking down by the little creek, Buck spotted a garter snake entwined among the branches of a poplar sapling. In its jaws it held a grasshopper firmly in a death grip, another of the farmer's friends enjoying a meal. Usually bugs were not problematic, but perfect growing conditions had characterized this year, which had been wet and warm, so flies and ticks were especially abundant. Every trip outdoors had become a survival experience for humans, and both livestock and wildlife suffered incessant molestation by pests.

A little farther along, the boy stopped to watch a foraging family of bobwhite quail. The hatchlings were barely large enough to fly, and the tiny birds were feeding copiously on insects. The chicks seemed to prefer grasshoppers to other prey, and they followed the lead of two adult birds in attacking these pesky vermin with a vengeance, thus satisfying their considerable protein needs. Buck observed their foraging with great interest, noting that the family seemed to be strong and healthy, well nourished, with most chicks surviving so far. There should be really good quail hunting come fall.

The youth was well covered with the latest anti-hormonal insect repellent and was enjoying his own innocent brand of communing with nature when he saw a big roadster headed down the driveway. He recognized the approaching vehicle as that of their preacher. He left his diversion and made straightway for home.

Pastor Don Tolbert had remained a good friend to the Morgan family over the years. He had stuck by Morgan through those dark days that followed Alice's death and had stayed close to him. For years he had made it his routine to visit the farmer and his son virtually every month, and both of them respected and admired the affable clergyman.

"Welcome, Pastor," Morgan greeted him sincerely at the door. "I hope all is well with you."

"Couldn't be better, Jim," replied Tolbert, who was a bit out of breath from the climb up the short stairs onto the front porch. His cheeks were red from exertion and his temples pulsed visibly. "How are things on the farm?"

"Hot and buggy, I'm afraid. I feel like we're in the midst of one of those plagues that Moses called down on pharaoh," Morgan replied, remembering something about that Biblical incident from a distant sermon. "Here comes Buck now. He spotted your car."

"Ah, yes, how are you today, my good man?" greeted Tolbert as the boy strolled across the yard.

"I'm fine, Pastor Don, fine. Everything okay at church?"

"Fine as sunlight through stained glass. Attendance has held fairly well, considering. People in general don't seem to be too interested in spiritual things these days, though, I'm afraid."

"Spiritual things?" asked the boy as he shook the pastor's beefy hand, and then leaned back against the porch railing.

"Oh, everyone is too preoccupied with this life to consider eternal things, I guess. And the attitude has even deteriorated further in recent months, it seems. I'm discouraged sometimes but I know it's my duty to persist."

"I guess everybody's mindful of changes in society these days. You can't avoid discussing it, Pastor," Morgan said. "How do you think the church will weather this?"

"I'm not worried. The church has endured far worse," huffed the clergyman, looking about for a place to repose. Morgan motioned him to an ancient rocker in one corner, while he reclined on a squeaking swing and motioned his son to his side.

"Can I get you something to drink, Pastor?" asked Morgan.

The preacher nodded as he caught his breath while wiping away the sweat from his forehead. There was a ring of damp perspiration staining his collar, and in fact his entire shirt was quickly becoming soaked in the intense heat and humidity. Morgan arose and stepped into the house, and returned momentarily with a tray on which sat three frosty containers of clear liquid.

"When the millennium changed six decades ago, just about every Christian writer, philosopher, and teacher was certain Christ would return anytime," continued the preacher after a long drink from his refreshment. "They were so convinced, in fact, that it was almost promoted as a foregone conclusion. Decades have passed and we're still waiting. But he's coming in his time, not according to our schedule. Nevertheless, when it didn't happen, a lot of casual Christians drifted away. Even today the church continues to shrink worldwide while many other religions are flourishing. Christian missionaries all over the world are closing up shop and heading home."

"What do you mean, a lot of religions are flourishing? You just said there was a decline of interest in spiritual things."

"Non-Christian religions, Buck. They seem to be much more attractive now than ever before in history, at least since I can remember. For example, mystics and pagans are establishing churches all over the place and people are flocking to them."

"Are there any around here? I never knew such groups were classified as religions," Buck noted. "Oh, yeah, there is that group that meets in the glass building on the hill. There's a boy in my class who goes there, kind of a kooky kid. You've got to have a sponsoring member to get in. What's the name of that group?"

"They're Celtic Pagans. They worship trees and flowers and the sun and the moon. They're opposed to our space program because it violates their spiritual principles. They worship animals and heavenly bodies like they are some kind of god. They worship visible, created things instead of the invisible God who created those things. They hold in highest esteem Earth itself, which they refer to as Mother Gaia, the living planet. I'm glad our God isn't dead like the rocks of this planet he made. Theirs is actually an ancient religion, and its resurgence is foretold in the Bible," answered the preacher, mopping his sweat-beaded brow again with his kerchief and taking another grateful swallow of cold fluid. He then wiped his mouth before continuing.

"They have fertility rites that are hideously immoral by any standard I know. And what they do has nothing to do with fertility, anyway. It's just entertainment. Many people seem to really enjoy that kind of carrying on. I tell you, it's hard to convince people with a message of living right and being faithful when such a sensual attraction is out there to lure them away."

"I think Spot Prestone goes to that church sometimes, too," said Buck. "The kid I spoke about is chummy with him. But Spot is no fool, and I doubt if he worships flowers and animals. I don't think he worships anything except good grades."

"Do tell. Unusual if he's a good student. Not many academics in that group, in my observation. His parents must push him pretty hard, huh?"

"Just his mother. She sure pushes him, all right. I've never seen his father."

"I have," said Morgan, casting his gaze downward to the weathered porch floor.

"I think you know their mode, just don't forget our code," the preacher stated, using everyday secular slang. "We're facing false but powerful opposition. Watch yourselves lest you too be deceived."

"We'll hang in there, Pastor," Morgan reassured him, remembering with guilt his own recent sensual thoughts. "That kind of behavior doesn't interest us at all. And we need your counsel and friendship. And we'll never forget the way you've supported us all these years."

"I know you mean that, Jim, and I can't tell you how much I appreciate it. God always has his faithful few."

Morgan still wasn't sure about his being one of the really faithful ones, and he still struggled with what he really believed. But he wasn't about to take part in any fertility rites.

They talked for nearly an hour, discussing a wide variety of topics from the farm to Buck's studies to the upcoming Alaska trip. Finally he said goodnight and slipped out into the evening twilight.

"Dad, Pastor Don is a good friend, isn't he?" Buck asked and declared at the same time as noise from his departing vehicle faded away.

"Yes, he is. Why do you sound dubious?"

"He's funny in a way. He's so different here in our house from the way he is at church. You know what I mean, don't you?"

Morgan paused and rubbed his chin in his characteristic way, considering the observation.

"Yes, I do. I've always noticed, but it's just his way, I guess. He really steps into his preacher shoes when he enters that church, I suppose."

And in a big way, Morgan thought. In his visiting style he was very down to earth; at church he was untouchably pious, as if he had to act like a preacher was expected to act. The dichotomy was obvious to all except to the minister himself, perhaps. He was nevertheless quite able when dealing with parishioners who needed intensive individual attention, such as these two. The preacher really did seem to care, and the authentic person seemed to be the one who resided outside the pulpit.

"He preaches so loudly, Dad. And almost always in an angry voice. I used to get scared sometimes when he would preach. He's so condemning when he shouts like that, I feel like there's no way I can meet his expectations, whatever they are."

"Son, he's got a very difficult job in today's world. He's right that most people have dismissed the concept of a personal God from their thinking. Since the millennium changed, it's been pretty much a steady decline in general acceptance of teachings of the church. It must be hard on Pastor Don."

"I guess. But I'd still like to see him get over some of his anger and just quietly tell us what we need to know. And that's another thing, he only preaches about bad things that the Bible says are going to happen. Doesn't the Bible ever predict anything good? And does it tell us anything beneficial we could use right now?"

Buck shuddered a bit as he recalled the destructive scenario Pastor Don had covered recently in a sermon from the Book of Revelation. A horrible destroying angel had come onto the world stage, meting out destruction as part of the wrath of God on earth, the prelude to a predicted final battle between good and evil. It had been fascinating stuff, as interesting as any other classic literature. But to believe that it would actually come to pass seemed to stretch probability to the breaking point. It sounded like just so much fantasy. Science would solve all problems long before it came to that, the boy was convinced

"Dad, do you think all those terrible things Pastor Don preaches will ever happen?"

"I don't know, son. Some people say they're not real predictions but just metaphors for plagues like AIDS. I've recently come to a peace about the Christ that they talk and preach about, but I don't know what to make of some of the bizarre predictions."

"I'm really turned off by Pastor Don saying everything was created by God, Dad. If he's a good God, it seems we'd have a whole lot better world than this. And if God made everything, he must have done it differently from the way the Bible tells it. None of that squares with the science I've been taught. Pastor Don doesn't go into detail, but I get the feeling he doesn't accept much of it, either. He's a professional believer and if he doesn't believe it, how can we?"

"Maybe he does believe it but perhaps he doesn't know how to express it—defend it, if that's the word—in view of the scientific wisdom everyone acknowledges without question today. Concepts like how things got created are impossible to prove, one way or the other. What one believes in that regard ultimately distills down to a matter of faith—faith in what the Bible says or faith in the ability of science to accurately reconstruct the past. I just don't know for sure, son."

"Pastor Don reserves his strongest words for people he perceives as immoral, doesn't he, Dad? I mean, I get the feeling he looks forward to that destroying angel coming and killing left and right, like in his sermon. I thought we were supposed to love people. What he preaches sometimes seems to be a long way from love."

Morgan recalled such sermons and secretly he wished the preacher would talk a little more about the love of God. It would certainly seem a more effective tactic to temper his condemnations with forgiveness and grace, but who was he to give advice to a learned man of the cloth? On the other hand, young Buck seemed to be more than a little reluctant to consider the teachings of the church as anything more than legendary or fanciful, so perhaps another discussion with the preacher might be a good idea, perhaps a necessity. Morgan felt a great deal of trepidation at the prospect of his son rejecting foundational beliefs that the farmer had begun to embrace of late. Moreover, those same beliefs had undergirded the life of the boy's departed mother, and Alice's gentle face flashed before his eyes as he looked at his questioning boy and pondered.

"Buck, we are supposed to love. We're supposed to love other people the way I loved your mom—the way you and I love each other. It's just hard sometimes to remember that the people who do bad things aren't really bad people through and through most of the time. They're just people caught up in an activity that—to us at least—is not right. Who's to say it's not right for them, as long as they don't hurt anyone?"

With his words Morgan struggled to make some moral sense of the current social scene, and he was more than a little uncomfortable with his conclusion. Buck chimed in with his own speculation before Morgan could clarify.

"Maybe Pastor Don and my teacher aren't all that far apart in their approach to life, then, Dad—what you're saying sounds a lot like what Mr. Russell said about that same question. Could be everything's relative to your point of view."

"Maybe so, maybe so," Morgan admitted reluctantly, the quest for words overpowering him. Down deep he regretted that he lacked more satisfying answers to Buck's honest questions, and he grappled to find a way to express his reservations about such a verdict. Somehow he knew it wasn't quite right to equate the teachings of the two men, but he just couldn't articulate his own misgivings about Buck's final synopsis on the matter. Imperfect man that he was, he came away from their discussion determined to learn enough to be able to satisfy Buck's objections to the faith he professed, albeit a faith he practiced with an undeniable measure of diffidence. He needed an education, and he would give it his best shot.

* * *

At the pagan church, exhausted participants were scattered in various states of disarray all around the temple complex. Their bodies were totally exposed to the view of other worshippers, all of whom had been treated to a bizarre and infinitely stimulating visual experience. A late afternoon solstice had provided perfect timing for the entire festivity. Now all was quiet except for rhythmic chanting of the priest as he moved among piles of people, sprinkling them with oil and waving an incense urn that spewed fragrant smoke. The service had been very good, and the sun god should be highly pleased. And coffers of the church were overflowing with generous donations.

*   *   *

Buck Morgan lay on his bed contemplating recent events, wondering about conflicting ideas of truth. He dismissed the pagan rituals as simply misguided, but he had genuine questions about whether truth lay in traditional religious worldviews or in scientific cosmology. He liked parts of both and he spent several minutes marveling a bit at his hopeless attempt to splice two seemingly opposed philosophies. He gazed out his window at the expanse of familiar constellations above the farm and wondered about the vastness of the universe. Were there really absolutes of right and wrong? Was there really a God out there who created all this, or was that infinite universe a giant cosmic accident of chance? He knew his preacher would hold to the former if his life depended on it. Would man ever know?

Cruising across the sky like another small, hurrying planet, a sparkling new space station, christened Delta by the international community, came into view. Now there's something in which one could place a huge amount of faith, the youth thought. Words from his recent discussion at school sprang like spirits into his consciousness, assaulting him gently, cleverly, mercilessly. Man could accomplish whatever his mind could conceive. He watched the glistening silver dot streak across the starry sky and disappear over distant dark hills. A surpassing awe almost overwhelmed his sensibilities.

Some kind of voice inside him seemed to be whispering to him, tendering answers in near silence to his deepest questions. It gradually dawned on him once more that he had a ready source of needed knowledge. He knew where to find that truth which seemed so elusive. He'd ask Ralph Russell.

CHAPTER 9

July 2059

Bared claws, furious and determined, met the veteran researcher, giving him no opportunity to collect his thoughts or calculate a response. Dr. Albert Hansen, a man experienced with all manner of wild animals, reacted only out of stark, desperate survival instinct. He carried an electric stun device, standard equipment for field researchers, but the cat was upon him before he could activate his unit.

Unlike the cougar that had killed Alice Morgan a decade before, this one was a youngster. Perhaps it was this lack of maturity that led to an attack and, paradoxically, saved the doctor's life as well. Hansen had accidentally stumbled onto a kill site, where a half-consumed deer lay buried underneath leaves and brush so it could not be readily detected. The juvenile cat leaped at him like insanity personified, determined to protect its food cache from this uninvited meddler. A more experienced lion in good health would probably have retreated at first evidence of man, but this one attacked with violence and resolve.

"Help me! Help!" yelled the professor as he covered his head with his arms and desperately sought to ward off the assault. The creature buried its fangs in his right forearm, slashing deep into muscle with incisors as sharp as scalpels. With his left hand the beleaguered scientist flailed at the creature's face and neck, but he succeeded only in inciting more savagery.

Buck Morgan and Ralph Russell heard Hansen's frantic calls for help, easily audible from their location on the other side of a small cottonwood grove where they were positioning a force field monitoring device. This complicated instrument was an integral part of the upcoming collision avoidance project, which was scheduled to begin in earnest in early fall. They dropped several probes that would later feed data to a central computer bank at the university via satellite, and both of them hurried toward the frenzied noises.

By the time they arrived, Hansen had succeeded in beating off the attacker and had managed to recover his stun device with his uninjured hand. With it he had put the creature to instant flight. Buck and Russell arrived completely breathless after a long run uphill. Russell was almost white with fear and unaccustomed exertion, and the athletic youth arrived a half minute ahead of him. Hansen was covered with blood from head to foot and sat motionless, propped limply against a boulder with his face drained of all expression. With his remaining strength he held pressure on his right arm, trying to punctuate rapid flow from a ruptured brachial artery. Interlacing sanguine streaks cascaded down the injured arm and bright red droplets fell from his fingers in a steady stream.

"Dr. Hansen! What happened?" Buck exclaimed, aghast at all the blood and dirt.

"Cougar. Stumbled on its kill," whispered Hansen weakly. "Call for help."

The professor appeared to be near losing consciousness as a shaken Russell moved in to apply more pressure to the wound. Buck rapidly summoned assistance with his pocket personal computer, their instant link to the anywhere. Shortly surgeons at Adrian Medical Center were repairing the damage as if it were routine, using advanced tissue glues to splice severed arteries and nerves and repair lacerated muscle flawlessly.

Buck rode in the helio ambulance with his injured friend and was able to observe efficiency and current medical technology at work first hand. His mind inevitably harkened back to a similar attack with a drastically different outcome. He had only a fuzzy recollection of that episode, but an involuntary shudder coursed through him repeatedly, and images of snarling cougars, bigger than life, sprang from the dark whenever he closed his eyes.

He was deep in thought when a vibration in his wallet indicated an incoming call. He reached promptly into his leather pocket and retrieved the card-sized pee-cee, and on activating receive mode his father's image appeared in the miniature monitor.

"Son, are you okay?"

"I'm fine. But Dr. Hansen almost got killed."

"I heard. Any word on how he's doing?"

"I heard the doctor say it would be no problem. Should be as good as new in a few days."

Morgan paused and took a deep breath, wondering how this unwelcome echo from the awful past incident might affect his impressionable son. He tried with painstaking effort to keep the conversation flowing, but his hesitation was glaring. Buck seized upon his father's thoughts in an instant.

"Don't worry about me, Dad. Like I said, I'm fine. Okay?"

"Umm...okay, son. I can't get away with anything around you, can I, partner? Anyway, I know you had wanted to go on a cougar hunt sometime. Rocky Purdee is going to be here in a couple of hours. Want me to come in and get you?"

"Oh, wow, Dad! For sure!"

The houndsman was already at the farm and waiting when Buck arrived. Ralph Russell would also accompany them, along with a couple of Purdee's friends. The dogs were housed on back of an ancient ATV, and their canine sounds emanated from their confinement like the rumblings of a great machine yearning to be unleashed. Purdee went all over the country eliminating older cougars, aggressive lions, and problem cats, hardly disturbing other wildlife in the process. Despite his rough mannerisms and unpolished speech, he was highly reliable and was widely respected as a figure with nearly legendary status. Buck shook his hand vigorously, remembering tales of the man's courageous victory over the cat that had killed his mother.

Purdee was a squat fellow, lightly complexioned but with curly black hair that he wore medium long. He had on a pair of weathered leather coveralls, his standard dress, and a cowhide Stetson hat rode slightly askew on his head. Irregular teeth, clean and white, showed through a slightly parted pair of full lips. A beard, curly and dark like the rest of his hair, surrounded his beefy face. He spoke with a penetrating honesty and matter-of-fact sincerity that clearly punctuated the serious nature of his work.

"We'll have this cat in no time. Lives up in the flint rock, most likely. Prob'ly go in a cave. Doubt if it'll tree. Either way, it's dead," Purdee said with no detectable emotion as he studied the youth for any signs of reluctance. Sometimes a person was deathly frightened to deliberately go after an aggressive animal. To a discerning man such fear always showed like a neon sign. Seeing no trace of such a reaction in Buck, he continued. "Your dad says you want to come along. What do you say?"

"I'd love to, Mr. Purdee. Sounds like your dogs are anxious to go."

"They're always eager, summer or winter. They hate cats. The bigger the cat the more they hate them."

"I'm ready when you are," Buck responded. He didn't even need to change clothes, as he was still wearing tough leather work clothes he had donned for his summer job.

Shortly the group was standing at the attack site, and Purdee studied the sophisticated monitoring probe. He commented regarding copious blood on the instrument and on a lot of surrounding ground. There were large droplets scattered randomly on bare soil, and a coagulated puddle of red where Hansen had reposed. Purdee had a puzzled look on his face, but stuffed it as he stooped and examined fresh cougar prints in the soft dirt.

"Youngster. Not more than two years old. Awful shame to have to kill it. But once they taste the wrong blood, they're always a problem. Got no choice."

Buck nodded in agreement. The presence of unobtrusive lions on the farm he had learned to tolerate. A potential killer was a whole different story.

"By the way, what's this gizmo? A magic wand?" asked Purdee, looking again at the blood-smeared sensor. "Never seen anything like it, I don't think."

"A force field monitor," answered Russell. "We're setting them up all over the farm. It's a little complicated, but someday we hope to use data we get to prevent collisions between animals and vehicles. Dr. Hansen thinks it will work."

"Of all the crazy ideas. I wish him luck, though. Saw a deer blasted to microparticles as we drove over. Maybe he's onto something good," said Purdee, scratching his head as he laid the probe aside. "Wait here. I'll get the dogs."

Buck flashed a grim smile at Russell as the houndsman began unloading his charges. Of course it will work, he thought to himself. There's no reason it shouldn't.

Soon Purdee had his pack ready, which included several big spotted Walker hounds, a few burly redbones, and a couple of dainty blue ticks. The dogs began barking and whining as soon as they were out of the truck, though the houndsman and his companions restrained them with leashes until they were certain they had the scent. When they cut them loose, it was momentary pandemonium as a colorful horde thundered off across the high prairie, through cottonwood groves, and up onto the flint hills. The assorted barks and howls of running hounds was a kind of music that Buck had heard only rarely, and the hair on back of his neck stood up a little at the bewitching cacophony. He set out with the men in hot pursuit, following the old fashioned way, by the sound of running dogs.

Before long, there was a discernible change in cadence, a sudden shift from random individual dog sounds to a rhythmic baying, an assortment of voices melding into one grand and continuous symphony. Purdee paused in their furious walking to listen momentarily, cocking his head as the distant sound undulated through clear atmosphere.

"He's bayed. Prob'ly in a rock cave up in that country. This oughta be fun," said Purdee with measured glee. "We might have to go in after him. A little elbow walking after a cat is pretty excitin', boy."

As they continued up a mile long ridge, everyone's breathing was becoming ever more labored. Purdee paused at intervals to let the rest catch up, and to listen to the increasingly near sound of his frantic pack.

J.Y. JONES

Buck couldn't help but feel exhilarated as they climbed through the rough terrain. Still, thoughts of facing an agitated cat on hands and knees in a rock cave triggered a creeping dread.

Russell had some trouble keeping up the pace, his frail physique not being equal to such a level of activity. Buck dropped back to keep him company, feigning a bit of extra tiredness himself. The teacher was fine but was breathing and laboring hard on the uneven ground and steep hillside.

"This is above and beyond the research protocol, my good man," Russell wheezed as they walked. "Maybe it will all be worth it, though."

"You know it will be, Mr. Russell," said Buck, diverting his thoughts momentarily from the task at hand. "It's hard to describe to other people how this project is going to work, but we know how important this force field breakthrough might be."

"Yes, it could be," said Russell with great effort between gasps for air. "Shame we had this cat attack, though. Twice on the same farm. Hard to believe."

Buck cringed a little at the words. Russell failed utterly to gauge the depth of emotion such an experience was eliciting from his young student. He continued talking as they reached more level ground.

"Strangest thing is that cougars were put in Kansas to eliminate hunting, and we're out here in the thick of a hunt because of one. Odd twist."

"Eliminate hunting? Really?" Buck asked. "How's that?"

Russell paused again to catch his breath, but gave him no immediate answer. Both of them stood looking ahead at the whirling pack, and now they could see the cougar atop a truck-sized boulder above them. Purdee and his companions were now stopped perhaps a couple of dozen yards from the dogs, and above electrifying dog sounds they could hear the cat snarling menacingly at its tormentors.

"Eliminate hunting?" Buck asked again as they started walking once more.

108

"What a sight!" noted Russell as they closed the distance, ignoring the repeated question.

Buck wouldn't let the matter drop so easily and pressed him again to explain his comment. Reluctantly and almost ashamedly, he answered in a near whisper as they walked, practically looking over his shoulder to see if by some unlikely occurrence someone might overhear him.

"Yep, cats eat deer and humans won't need to hunt. That was their theory, but it didn't work out that way."

As they approached the chaotic scene, the absolute primeval savagery mesmerized them. Purdee and his seasoned cougar hunters awaited their arrival with a degree of appropriate smugness. Their high comfort level in such a disordered arena stemmed from hundreds of previous similar engagements. Purdee produced a stainless steel pistol, topped with a precision telescopic sight, and extended it to Buck.

"At least you don't have to make like a mole, son. Take this thing carefully right here, and be particular where you point the business end. I hear you've got a score to settle."

"No sir, Mr. Purdee. It's not a score to settle. It's only a job to do."

Buck took the firearm gingerly, and grasped it by the handle grips with both hands while he looked through the scope at a distant hill. It felt heavier than he had expected, almost as heavy as his old shotgun. He had seldom fired a handgun, so the sensation was a bit strange.

"You just pull this hammer back and put the crosshairs on the cat's chest, just like you would a deer. It's an old time mechanism, but deadly effective. When you squeeze the trigger, be steady and the gun will do the rest. Just make a good shot so that confounded critter don't kill a dog or two when it falls."

Buck nodded and swung the pistol upward toward the glowering cougar. It was close enough that he didn't need a support to shoot accurately. The hammer cocked crisply and smoothly, and the animal was easily visible through sharp optics. When his view settled on exactly the right spot, he gently applied pressure against the trigger with his index finger. The metal appendage seemed resistant and stiff at first, but it took precious little force to activate the mechanism. A deafening explosion was so loud that it startled him and seemed to shake the ground. The cougar slumped forward before careening headlong into the waiting pack. It was very dead and completely harmless when it hit the ground with a blunt thump.

As they made their way home in gathering darkness, Buck seemed to arrive at an uneasy peace about predators among them. Hansen's terrorizing experience had given him pause as he reconsidered his reluctant acquiescence to the place of such animals in proximity to human beings. There had been no other attacks nearby since his mother's death, though, so such an event had to be rare. And hadn't Hansen stumbled unaware onto a kill site, something nobody would knowingly do?

Next morning was business as usual. Hansen called early to check on the status of his attacker and was relieved that the animal had been dispatched. In the course of conversation he deemed himself fit to carry on with the project. Buck had just finished his chores when he greeted the professor as he emerged from his vehicle only a little later than usual.

"Welcome back, Dr. Hansen. I'm sure glad you're all right," Buck said cheerily. Hansen's arm was encased securely in a white sling , and there were also bandages on his forehead and neck where lesser punctures and scratches had been treated.

"Glad to be back. I couldn't let a little cat bite keep me from being here for important preparations," he said as he removed his arm from the supporting sling and flexed it for them, demonstrating near-perfect function.

"Little cat bite, you say? It sounded like a pretty big one to me. Several of them, in fact," Jim Morgan said, amazed such a degree of trauma could be nullified so quickly.

"Twenty-five centimeters, and right through the antecubital fossa of my arm. Amazing what they can do with those newer tissue glues, though. I'll be back to normal within a week. Good thing the teeth missed my motor nerves. I've got some numbness that will persist awhile, but it's quite tolerable. Buck, I understand from the sheriff that you went along and did the honors last night. Did you enjoy it?"

"I'm not sure," the youth answered thoughtfully as he began sorting through some hardware they would install that day. "That cat was a young one and I felt a little bad about removing it prematurely, to tell you the truth. There was some satisfaction in it, I guess, since we clearly had to kill it. The chase was exciting, too. I tried hard not to look on the actual kill as retribution, though. Not revenge for my mom's death or for the attack on you. Or for a quite a few lambs and calves we've lost to cougars. Overall, it was a positive experience, I'd say."

Buck started the engine of the truck for a short drive to their best deer habitat, a thicket along the creek bank, and they bounced down the hedgerow with him behind the wheel. He tried to keep the pace slow and easy for Hansen's sake, but the professor was unavoidably jostled quite a bit anyway.

They reached thick willows along the creek, and a white-tailed deer dashed from the tangle and into full view, with gorgeous velvet-covered antlers prominent in the morning sunlight. They watched in admiration as it disappeared, then descended to begin work before the temperature could climb to an uncomfortable level. Before long they reached a predetermined work area and began to position field detector devices.

"Could you hand me that activator coil, Dr. Hansen? There, that's got this one."

Buck stayed busy as they conversed, and Hansen mostly supervised and did light work. They finished setting out a necessary array in the long creek bottom, and then turned their attention to the east side of the property where the attack had occurred. There were still several unfinished sites there, and they would try and complete the task before quitting. They reached the attack location, and Hansen paused as he examined his own blood discoloring the ground. A most disturbed look of trepidation crossed his face. There was a rising stench from the partially consumed deer nearby, made worse by summer heat. Doubtless that smell added to a nauseating flashback the scientist was experiencing. They left hastily as soon as the probe was positioned and secured.

The sun was inching toward the flint hills as they finally motored slowly back toward the farmhouse. Hansen was probably tired, perhaps near exhaustion, from the dual stress of recent trauma and long hours in the sun. But almost like a hyperactive child, he seemed agitated as he talked almost nonstop, shouting at times over the noise of the truck engine.

They wheeled into the yard and Buck parked the truck in its customary location, where he shut down its rumbling engine. He thumbed once more through a printout of the research plan, a document an inch thick and peppered with technical charts and complicated mathematical formulae. With competent biologists like Hansen on the job, the presence of numerous predators should never be a generalized problem to society. Despite some tragic exceptions that had touched his life and some consequent misgivings, Buck was confident that nothing would ever impede good science. It appeared the future was secure.

Science. The word kept coming up over and over again. The more he thought about it, the more he wanted to be on the cutting edge of it. He wanted to leave this place and become a researcher or a great innovator.

"Professor, we can certainly look forward to some excellent data from this study, can't we?"

"No question about it, young man. Science will achieve what's right for mankind. It promises control of what we've already created, vehicles and the like, but so much more than that. We can control natural forces like predators, and keep them in their rightful place. And preserve our other wildlife, too."

"I agree, sir," said Buck as he assisted the professor into his vehicle and waved goodbye. He stood watching his car disappear down the road, thinking intently as it receded from view. Hansen was a man who, like Ralph Russell, held in highest suspicion those intangible human qualities such as whimsical emotions, religious inclinations, and mindless passions. Such were easily misguided and completely unreliable, it seemed.

Buck Morgan made up his mind that he would stay in the forefront of scientific knowledge and never back away from it for as long as he lived. He was setting the course for his future as surely as a finely tuned telescopic sight sets the course of a bullet.

CHAPTER 10
August 2059

Mr. Sam Archer

wwn/samafoa@econo.com

Dear Sam:

    I want to make a formal request that you let Monty accompany Buck and me to Alaska in a few weeks. We bought an excursion to hunt caribou, and I think the experience would be good for both boys. We would like your permission to take him, if he wants to go. He has expressed an interest in so doing.

    Give me a call and let me know, if you don't mind. We need to make necessary arrangements if he's allowed to go.

Sincerely,

Jim Morgan

    Nine o'clock in the morning was early for a group of late risers who emerged from an ancient brick mansion near the outskirts of Adrian. The old house sat obliquely on its lot, facing an intersection on the corner of River Street and South Main. Flowers lined the sidewalk in front, and the lawn had been freshly mowed. A hedge that surrounded the property had been trimmed recently. A long cobblestone driveway angled from curbside to the front door and back out to a corresponding point on the other street.

    A sleek panel truck parked at the house bore unusual markings, a circular emblem on which a member of every phylum of animals was included in successive fashion. In the center of the round symbol was the familiar scale of justice, depicting a human family on one side and a menagerie of animals on the other. An indicator needle on the scales registered an exact balance. Bumper stickers almost covered the back, each one exclaiming a poetic message against science, government, and conventional farming. Gathered around and loading into the vehicle were a dozen or so women of assorted sizes and ages, as well as a sprinkling of men. For the era their dress was unimaginably exorbitant, and consisted of costly plant fiber and expensive synthetics to the very socks on their feet. Each person carried a small suitcase, and they said little as they settled into the vehicle, faces set with grim determination.

Meanwhile, for Buck Morgan and his father, the long, hot summer dragged on. The brutal schedule was relentless, and they were lost in their work. Both looked forward to the upcoming trip to Alaska with ever-increasing anticipation, and as the time approached they counted off days with a digital display in the farm control station. It would be necessary to have every aspect of the farming operation in top shape for their upcoming absence. Work was harsh because of oppressive and unabated heat for weeks on end. Livestock alerts due to high temperatures were a daily fact of life. Prospects of a cool break in Alaska tantalized them through sweat-filled days of toil.

One dusty afternoon Buck came in filthy and exhausted from working the sheep medicating area. He passed the computer control room on his way to the house, and his eyes fell automatically on a flashing message light. He punched in his identifier number and the machine failed to respond. His father had a separate number, so he tried that one. They had a mutual agreement that this was permissible on incoming mail. The screen lit up with the new communication:

Jim Morgan

wwn/jmpromag@econo.com

Jim:

Monty and I don't talk much. He insists he's going and I can't stop him, since his mother has final jurisdiction. I want you to know that I'm opposed and I hold you personally responsible for his safety. You know I abhor killing in any form. I hope you don't see a living thing to destroy.

Sam Archer

By the time Buck had finished reading the terse note, it had been automatically printed out. He picked up the paper and carried it to his father, who read it with interest.

"At least he didn't veto it," said Buck. "But it sounds like he would if he could. And it looks like Monty really wants to go."

"Or else Monty's doing it for spite. In any case, I say let's take the opportunity."

The Morgans discovered later that Sam Archer and his son had engaged in a heated session of disagreement when the possibility was discussed earlier. The fireworks had galvanized Monty's determination to go. To punctuate his disdain for the whole affair, the elder Archer had steadfastly refused to provide any monetary support for the trip. For the first time in his young life, Monty had been induced to get a summer job in order to pay his travel fare.

At the farm there were plenty of good times despite the certainty of endless work. On this particular day, Buck and his father had arisen early and completed their animal care routine. Afterward they loaded a farm refrigerator truck with protein ready for the processing plant. The facility received protein from producers in the area and readied it for distribution all around the world. Buck directed a robot as it lifted each heavy box and placed it on a conveyor belt that led from the truck into the warehouse. On delivery day each week the truck stayed active moving tons of prepared beef and sheep protein from farm to purchaser. After a short drive this day, they left the highway at the protein plant, and the gate guard waved them on in to make their delivery.

Live animals had, in the distant past, been moved to intermediate facilities for fattening and eventual slaughter, but with the help of mechanization it had become much simpler, as well as more humane and less traumatic to the animals, to perform these functions at the production site. Human beings were involved but minimally in the roundup, sacrifice, and preparation of rich protein. Raw skins were preserved in a special solution and shipped to a high technology clothing manufacturer in Wichita. Every animal came wrapped in a marvelous covering which applied science had learned to miraculously transform into a broad variety of convenient and useful materials.

All waste material was used for a variety of products, principally fuel components, by being broken down, or "cracked," in a facility right there on the farm. When complex hydrocarbons were chemically digested into simpler components, they became invaluable to energy companies. In a mixture with ethanol and other alcoholic byproducts from plant farming, this renewable combination produced a highly flammable concoction known as "veganox." This solution had become standard fuel for all internal combustion engines since petroleum reserves had become depleted worldwide. It burned much cleaner than gasoline and kerosene, and the result had been a dramatic reduction in smog, even in crowded cities. The long anticipated and much dreaded end of the Oil Age had finally come as predicted, but instead of disaster it had produced a pleasant, unexpected, and welcome ecological surprise.

"Dad, here's a broken box. Shall I hold it?" Buck shouted over the hum of robotics and the noisy unloading belt.

"Hm, too bad. Yes, put it back in the truck. We can eat it or give it away. The bird dogs could use a little, too. We aren't permitted to sell it unaltered, but we might have a cookout and invite relatives and neighbors. Everybody likes a taste of the natural now and then."

"Good idea, Dad. But it'll have to be after our trip. Hey, maybe we can put a little fresh caribou on the grill with some of this!" called Buck as he placed the damaged box back into the cold interior of the vehicle.

The truck was rapidly emptied and they were ready to travel several miles back to the farm. They mounted their vehicle and approached the compound's gate, where a most unusual commotion unfolded before them.

"Dad, that guy is kicking the gate guard!"

"I see. What the heck?"

The uniformed guard was trying to get up, and each time he raised to his knees a wiry individual would knee him in the side, causing him to roll over in agony. Blood covered the guard's face, running like a river from each nostril, as well as from a deep cut over one eye. There were in fact several observers standing by, and the Morgans only now noticed their unusual garb. Like creatures from a theme park of some kind, each and every one was dressed as an animal. The assailant was wearing a mask that was a very credible representation of a snarling Rottweiler dog.

"Central security, Gate One, Gate One! Someone's attacking the guard!" Morgan barked into his communications unit. He swung open his door, ordered Buck to stay put, and dashed toward the ongoing beating. Morgan covered the distance in a flash and tackled the assailant high, knocking him to the ground and ripping away his disguise almost simultaneously. He didn't recognize the face that emerged, but he planted several quick blows between the surprised man's eyes before the individual could react. Onlooking protesters made no move to help their suddenly besieged comrade, instead shrinking back in alarm at Morgan's savage onslaught. Other plant guards shortly arrived on the scene and took over.

Adrian policemen arrived quickly and took the aggressor into custody. They found out later that the man was from New York City, and that he had a long record of previous convictions for similar assaults. Since his cohorts were breaking no laws, authorities had no choice but to leave them alone. The demonstrators carried colorful signs declaring ANIMAL PROTEIN STINKS and KILLING IS ALWAYS WRONG. As they gradually recovered from the rude disturbance, they began singing a rendition of "Old McDonald Had a Farm." The parody was a spiteful satire on the entire farming industry, delivered gleefully and meticulously, if not with any appreciable melody. Buck noticed that one dissenter was wearing the same maroon elephant costume he had noticed at the Conservation Club banquet.

Buck had seen such protests before, but never one that turned violent. There had been a small contingent of such activists at the plant on a couple of recent occasions. Once a few of them had picketed at their farm. His dad had advised that he simply ignore them, which he had found hard to do. When he had engaged them in conversation, he had been impressed at their repudiation of logical arguments and their apparent close-mindedness. Scientific facts were of little interest to them. Their inflexible mindset was entirely foreign to the studious youth, and his rational mind rebelled at what appeared to be a philosophy of self-imposed deception. Nothing he had ever learned in his eminently sensible education could provide insight into such a mentality.

After the guards had cleared the road, Morgan and Buck pulled out into the highway. Both of them were quite sobered and shaken by the incident. They drove along silently for a few miles before Buck spoke.

"Dad, I've never seen you do that before. You really hammered that guy! He had it coming, too," he said, a deep admiration evident in his voice. "What's wrong with those people?"

"You're witnessing the dying throes of a movement that dates back into the last century. I guess that attacker was pretty frustrated to take such drastic action. Most people ignore their type nowadays. They must be getting desperate."

"Is that any way to get your views accepted? He could've killed an innocent man. Or gotten himself killed, if the guards hadn't rescued him," the boy grinned. "I'll bet they never jump on anybody when you're around again."

"Don't ever be quick to do anything like that, son. It can cause a lot of trouble," Morgan said slowly, almost with regret. "But I didn't have much choice that time. My impression is that their kind doesn't feel much for people."

"What do they believe, anyway?"

"In animals, I guess. Animal worship, if you want to call it that. It peaked the first of this century, and now it's over. Those guys became a really powerful political force with millions of followers and a lot of money. There were a whole bunch of activist groups back then. In the end it was science that destroyed them. Good old solid science."

A disturbing thought crept into Morgan's mind. Why was Buck, precocious Buck, who knew every battle of the U.S. Civil War and who could name every past president of the United States, so ignorant of this particular issue?

"I wonder why they don't teach anything about this in school. Come to think of it they didn't teach me much about it, either—Lee Shealy told me about it. He knew firsthand, because he was in the thick of the battle."

As they arrived back at the protein plant on their second run, Morgan and Buck noted that the odd demonstrators had disappeared, leaving no trace of their activities except for the gate guard's bandaged forehead. He related to them that his attacker was now in jail charged with assault. Good enough for him and exactly what he deserved. They expressed sympathy to the abused guard and offered condolences for his headache.

Back home that night Morgan sat reflecting on the day's events. His shoulder ached a little from the stiff tackle he had administered so effectively, and his knuckles were abraded and slightly swollen. He stretched his fingers and made a fist to be certain all was okay. He would have his hand Q-rayed if it didn't seem to be getting better by tomorrow.

The thick leather of his recliner squeaked as he pushed back and let his tired body relax. An ultrasonic massage function in his chair activated automatically, and its soothing sensation gradually caressed his whole body. But he couldn't shake the notion that something else was wrong, something that wasn't physical at all. An unavoidable sense of concern invaded his mind as he pondered. The historical issue he and Buck had discussed was unmistakably getting little emphasis in the educational system.

An old saying kept returning to his thoughts, one that echoed from distant days of his childhood: *Those who fail to remember the lessons of history are condemned to repeat them.* The disquieting truth reverberated in his head again and again.

CHAPTER 11

August 2059

A few days later, young Buck Morgan gazed again into the night sky as he walked from central computer control, roundup finished at last. He watched with intense interest as a prominent manmade satellite moved across the heavens in its now-familiar trajectory. Space Station Delta sailed along majestically some 700 miles above Earth's surface. It moved along at five miles per second, looking like a gigantic star to the naked eye. The gleaming orb traversed Sagittarius, then flew just north of Scorpius, then it bisected Libra, as if on a tour of the constellations. His old friend Polaris, the North Star, shined brightly, a rare constant in a vista that slowly changed throughout the year. The magnificent Little Dipper pivoted endlessly around the star, taking with it the whole host of heaven. Eyes filled with wonder, the boy pondered the grand scale of the panorama he was enjoying. What could be out there far beyond that station? What kinds of discoveries awaited mankind in the far reaches of the universe? These were questions into which he longed with all of his being to delve. Someday.

Buck knew that his favorite constellation, Orion, would not appear in the night sky for several more months, and he awaited its arrival each year with anticipation. With the return of the mythological hunter came time for quail hunting. But first, he remembered without effort, there was another outdoor experience to be relished. His mind snapped back to his upcoming trip and he hurried inside to do some needed packing and other preparations.

The long-awaited date was at finally at hand. Departure time was set for a Saturday morning in August, and the boy and his dad went about last minute preparations on Friday evening. He glanced out the window as they worked and saw headlights approaching the house.

A dark sedan glided into the yard almost noiselessly and parked in front of the house. Buck recognized the couple as they materialized under the front porch light.

"Mr. Russell! What's he doing here?"

"Oh, I forgot to tell you. He called this afternoon and wanted to come over and see you tonight. He's leaving in a couple of days for Rocky Mountain Ranch Wilderness School for Teachers," Morgan replied, a little annoyed at himself for letting the conversation slip his mind.

They happily greeted the teacher and his wife, who wore broad smiles that spoke of eager anticipation. Buck had seen Russell's wife on only a half dozen occasions previously because the two seldom appeared together in public. He remembered that her name was Rhetta and that she also was a teacher, but he knew little else about her, since she taught in a different school.

Rhetta was most attractive, and she looked to be quite a bit younger than her husband. The youth couldn't tell if she was a blonde or a brunette because she always wore a somewhat gaudy wig of whatever color struck her fancy on any particular day. Her makeup was impeccable, her eyebrows pulled and penciled into a fine line that surely cost her hours to perfect and maintain. Her white dress was of the finest, most expensive leather, and it gleamed like silver in the subdued light. She always wore polished leather high heels, no matter how informal the occasion, a habit that struck Buck as a bit odd. How could a respected man of science like Russell have a wife who behaved so impractically? But he couldn't deny that the woman looked stunning. Russell wore the usual informal attire that was his trademark.

After handshakes and greetings, Russell made pointed mention of the mounds of gear packed for the trip.

"Looks like you've got everything. I'll bet you've even got a generator and lights in all that equipment."

"No, sir, we've got perpetual hand lights and a stove, though, and plenty of dry clothes and warm sleeping gear. We've been accumulating and packing ever since the banquet last winter," Buck said. "When you're way back in the wilderness, delivery service is a bit unreliable and you've a long ways to go to the store. That's what Dad says."

"You're right, son," said Morgan. "But I think we're ready. I know you're excited about your upcoming trip, too, Ralph."

"I am excited about it, all right. The experiences I've heard other teachers speak about after attending Wilderness School—usually they simply gush about how much they've learned."

"We'll be pulling out first thing in the morning, Mr. Russell. If you'll pardon me a minute, I'm taking some things to the car now, so you and Dad can just talk while I get that done."

"We'll all pitch in. We can load it into the cargo hatch while we talk."

"Rhetta, nice of you to come over. How's the summer going?" Morgan inquired cordially.

"Quiet and peaceful, so far. I wish I had an exciting trip like all you guys. Maybe next year," Rhetta answered. "I'll stay home and prepare lesson plans. To tell you the truth, this wilderness adventuring isn't my idea of fun, anyway. Give me a bed in a room with a good view."

Buck noticed her stealing a look at something in the foyer mirror, which was at an angle that made it clear it wasn't her own image she was perusing. He couldn't be positive, but he could have sworn she was looking at his dad. She glanced at the boy, and catching him staring she smiled and shrugged her shoulders innocently. Embarrassed, Buck turned his eyes away quickly.

"That's not for me," Buck stammered a bit as he struggled to regain his composure. "I've got a bed in a room with a good view. Living for a week in a place I never saw before, doing something I enjoy, now that's my idea of fun."

He struggled as he strained to lift another piece of heavy duffel, and then headed out the door.

"There are a couple of reasons I wanted to drop by tonight, Buck. I promised Rhetta I'd try to get you to play the piano for her if she'd ride out with me," said Russell as they walked. "But I have another motive, too. You know, your trip to Anchorage will be via sub-orbital shuttle plane. I wanted to tell you a few things to look for so you can get the most out of the experience. You'll actually be going out in space above the atmosphere, something only astronauts got to do just a few years ago."

"Dad's told me some about it. And I've read some. I'm looking forward to it."

After finishing loading, all four of them returned to the house and took seats in the spacious living room. Buck observed with some concern that Rhetta sat with her legs crossed revealing too much of her well-proportioned legs, but thankfully his father seemed oblivious to her display. Her repose made it difficult to concentrate on the conversation.

"Dad says transportation has really changed since his early years. People used to burn petroleum fossil fuels in cars and everything else. Pretty wasteful, huh?"

"Yep, nonrenewable petroleum, the scourge of the Oil Age," said Russell. "Dirty burning stuff, it was. Anthropologists will refer to that generation as oil people, or maybe grease monkeys, if you'll forgive the term. The trouble was that their fuel not only polluted, it ran out. We only have enough of it left for medicines and some plastics now. If civilization had been a bit more frugal we might have had plenty for a few centuries more."

"Well, our atmosphere's cleaner anyway. The cleanest it's been in some three centuries, I've heard you say."

"You're right, Buck. It's good to live in an age when things are logical. If something doesn't measure up scientifically, it's out," beamed the teacher, leaning back in an overstuffed chair and placing his hands behind his head.

"Hey, we can start our deer project when we get back, huh, Mr. Russell? The monitors are in place and the Conservation Club approved full funding."

"I know. John Gentry called last week and told me. It's going to be really exciting to be involved, even if the published work will be done by the university people. I guess they won't even put our names on the

124

research paper, but at least we can contribute positively. Dr. Hansen called today about final preparations for our gathering field data. Should be a great privilege just to participate."

"You bet," Buck agreed.

"Ralph, I know Hansen discovered the force field that surrounds animals, but what's the principle behind using that to eliminate vehicle collisions?" Morgan asked. "I've watched you guys off and on all summer and I'm still a little fuzzy about how this concept is supposed to work."

"He also found an anti-force that repels all living creatures. In the lab he can send a test animal scurrying in the opposite direction by activating it. Can you imagine what a deer or any other animal—even a person—would do if every vehicle had a device to emanate the anti-force?"

"Well, I'll be darned. Maybe soon we will have wasted our last animal."

"Actually, the savings will be a lot more than you might casually think. You know that heavy collision plate in front of your car? We'll be able to go back to an aerodynamic design if this proves out. When that plate can come off, think of the fuel savings."

"Ralph, you wanted to talk to us about sub-orbital flight," Morgan reminded. "I want Buck to hear what you've got to say. I wish Monty Archer were here, too."

"Oh, yes. I'd almost forgotten that Monty is going. He does need to be here for this little discussion. He certainly could use something to stimulate his academic interest, wouldn't you say? I hope you aren't making a mistake in selecting him for this trip."

"We'll be fine, Ralph," said Morgan. "Now, why don't you tell Buck about the shuttle?"

"I'll just let him tell me about it. You've been reading, Buck?"

"Seventeen thousand miles per hour and an altitude of over a hundred miles above the earth, a little less if you're not going very far.

You're on the edge of space," said Buck, after which he launched a very studied analysis of the shuttle, differences between the craft and conventional atmospheric flight, and a few points of historical interest.

"Very good, Buck. You've been researching, I see," replied an unsurprised Russell. He accepted a glass of lemonade Morgan offered him, took a deep drink, and looked at Buck with satisfaction.

"I pulled a lot of data up just a few nights ago. I think I raided the entire computer library on the subject. But I didn't expect to be tested on it."

"No test, no test. If there were one, you'd pass anyway. Be sure and fill Monty in on your findings. Now, any chance you could accommodate Rhetta with a little music, my good man?"

"No problem. I've got to practice one more time before we leave anyway, if you don't mind listening while I experiment a little."

They retired to the music room on the back of the farmhouse, where the old Baldwin piano stood in one corner. Buck started with a medley of practiced numbers, mainly tunes by various twentieth century authors, all of which he played without benefit of written music. He finished with a brilliant rendition from Chopin, the ancient classic filling the house with music. His finale was a piece he had performed at his spring recital, and he brought the nineteenth century music vividly to life as his nimble fingers graced the keys. After receiving congratulations for his performance and exchanging warm good-byes, Buck and his father bade the Russell couple goodnight.

The Morgans had trouble sleeping that night. Next morning they loaded their remaining gear and left to pick up Monty Archer. He was quite excited but a bit apprehensive about staying in the backcountry for a whole week, having hardly ever camped outside even for a night. They could detect no misgivings about the upcoming flight, however. Sam Archer had sent Morgan another terse web note advising that he wouldn't be there for their departure.

They drove to the Skyport, chattering all the way about the impending adventure. Buck dutifully educated his friend on the upcoming flight, but the technology portion of the trip held far less fascination for Monty than its outdoor aspect. After parking the car and checking everything in, they strolled around taking in the sights.

Finally all baggage was loaded, they had cleared security, and it was time to board. They reached their assigned seats in the cabin, and Morgan allowed Buck the seat by the porthole. The youth's excitement grew as he approached takeoff for his first taste of space flight. Maybe he'd let Monty have the porthole on the way back, but not for this leg.

Ground roll and lift off were very much like any other airplane. The landscape grew farther away and there was a short period of conventional climb. A green flashing light suddenly illuminated in the cabin, indicating the main engine was being lighted. As it ignited, they were pushed tightly back in their seats by a force several times normal gravity. They could feel most prominently their facial tissues being pulled in an unaccustomed posterior direction, so different from normal gravitational pull. The pinning force eased as the craft commander throttled back at Max Q, the point where atmospheric pressure against the climbing vehicle is highest. As they climbed past that level, G-forces again increased dramatically with throttle-up. The thunder of mighty booster engines abruptly ceased as they slipped over the speed of sound, leaving noise behind and creating a fierce sonic boom. Earth dramatically receded below them as sub-orbital velocity was rapidly achieved.

"Dad, I see the Pacific already! It looks like a big map of North America down there. And clouds and lakes and cities. And I see the curvature of the earth! Look!" Monty strained forward in his shoulder harness, trying to see past his friend to view the sight.

By now the G forces had subsided and there was a brief period of weightlessness before re-entry. Much to Buck's surprise the travel bag he had placed under the seat drifted up into the air, nudging him on back of the head as he peered through the porthole. He grabbed it, noting that it was so light he could move it with ease using only one finger. He batted the bag gently toward Monty, and his friend pushed it back as they enjoyed a playful sensation that was new and wondrous to both of them. Buck felt as free as a bird, so incredibly unhindered for the first time in

127

his life by Earth's strong gravitational field. The seat belt light was extinguished briefly, so they were free to unharness and experience the weightless sensation for a short time before re-entry.

A charming piano concerto flashed through Buck's mind and seemed to pulse in rhythm with incredible forces he was feeling, a pounding, swaying, unifying musical aria that made him feel at peace and harmony with the brief slice of space he was enjoying. The melody was a symphony he longed to play, to communicate, to live out forever in union with the natural order, whatever that was. He couldn't dismiss those exquisite notes from his mind. During their brief descent the measure began to fade, and as gravity took a firm grip on him again the song all but vanished. His memory of the astounding experience lived on, though, imposing itself insistently on his subconscious, drawing him like a lodestone.

On contact with solid ground a short hour after takeoff, the spell was almost broken. Much too soon for Buck they were deplaning in the Anchorage Skyport.

"Wow, I want to do that every day. I want to do that for a living. Can you earn enough to go on trips to Alaska sometimes?"

"I imagine so, son. Our astronauts and shuttle pilots are still a pretty select bunch, but I'd bet that you have 'the right stuff' as they used to say. They're doing missions a lot more exciting than sub-orbitals nowadays with the Mars station and all."

"Do you think I could be an astronaut, Dad? For real?"

"Son, if you continue to study hard, there's literally no telling how far you might go."

"I'm sure glad Mr. Russell came over last night. You should have been there, Monty. He made me think about this flight, and helped me get more out of it than I ever dreamed," Buck commented while they retrieved their bags. "I really do want to make this trip into the wilderness, but I'm already looking forward to the flight back."

Russell lighted a fire again, Morgan thought. He's good at that. And the stimulation had to be good for his boy.

"Dad, I'm going to go for it. I'm going to study hard, put science and math first in my life, and I'm going to be an astronaut."

Jim Morgan considered his son pensively as he helped gather the mound of bags. Kansas isn't big enough to hold this boy, he couldn't help but think to himself. How he longed to encourage him to settle down and just farm, and to be his friend and partner. He thought back to his long-ago conversation with Henry McLean, and remembered the advice to turn the boy loose.

There seemed to be a strong resolve growing in Jim Morgan. He would do exactly that, whatever the cost.

CHAPTER 12

August 2059

Big wheels on the Tundramaster airplane touched down on a barren ridge top, and rough ground pounded the struts ruthlessly as the pilot braked to a screaming stop just short of thick brush. It had been a different kind of excitement from the shuttle plane ride, much more visual and in touch with earthly details. There were hundreds of caribou along the route of flight and a grizzly bear just a couple of ridges over from their landing site. The pilot had banked just right for all three passengers to get the best views, and it had been quite a special experience indeed.

They stayed put while the bush flyer opened the door, then everybody unstrapped at his instruction. A late August chill assailed them and a brisk wind rippled the short grass and shook the big aircraft tumultuously. For a moment they wondered if the plane might be swept from the exposed hilltop. Monty had a slightly frightened look in his eyes, but it subsided somewhat as they climbed down the ladder and planted their feet on solid ground. Buck gathered his fur parka around him a bit tighter against the cold.

Plans called for spending six days and nights in the wilderness, but they could call the plane in early if they wanted to terminate before a predetermined time. All that was necessary was a call on the satellite-linked wallet personal computer each of them carried. Like most twenty-first century Americans they wouldn't be without these indispensable devices, which even let Morgan keep track of his farm business back home almost as if he were there.

"Hand me that cooler, Buck. Now the large duffel, Monty," Morgan called as they helped the pilot disgorge all their gear. Soon the plane door was shut, and the thunder of a giant engine again pierced the silence. Casting a shower of trailing debris it taxied to the other end of the makeshift runway, wheeled around, and took off, leaving the three of them alone on the ridge top.

As the plane's noise faded into sub-Arctic vastness, the man and two boys gazed in wonder at silent caribou hills all around them. These rounded elevations were devoid of trees except at the lowest elevations, while sparse brush and spongy terrain stretched alternately in all directions. Deep trails, timeless migration routes of tundra wanderers, interlaced everywhere. In the distance were mountains mantled in snow, where glacial fingers descended precipitously between green ridges. The panorama contrasted sensationally with a deep blue August sky. The only sound was of unrelenting wind, punctuated at intervals by a rock marmot whistling somewhere down the hillside.

"Dad, I can't believe we're here! We must be the luckiest people alive."

"I still can't tell if we're the luckiest or the stupidest," said Monty. He couldn't even imagine another location where he would feel so small and out of place. "Where's the bathroom?"

"Oh, for Venus' sake, Monty, don't be such a petunia," Buck said, a bit disgusted. Talking ceased as each person shouldered a pack and picked up their duffel. The three began ferrying gear down to a campsite suggested by the pilot, and the heavy work consumed most of their energy. When all supplies were in position, Morgan began directing the operation to assure they would be able to survive any eventuality.

First the tent was erected, pegs were driven deep, and ropes were pulled taut. Now in case of rain a shelter was ready. Their gear was stowed inside and all was ready for camp setup. The three pitched in eagerly, and each one accomplished his share of necessary work. Stubborn mosquitoes rapidly assaulted them once they were off the windy ridge top, and the aggressive insects shortly forced them to break out a highly effective repellent. That chemical wonder kept the blood suckers at a safe distance, but the whine of thousands of pairs of wings hovering merely inches away set the very air vibrating.

"Say, I wonder if the anti-force Dr. Hansen has identified would work on mosquitoes," Buck mused as they toiled.

"I don't see why not, if it works on deer," answered Morgan. "Give me that other duffel. If we hurry and get everything ready, we can have supper and climb that high promontory to look for a while with our binoculars. Why don't you go fill the water bucket, Buck, while Monty and I get the kitchen operational and start supper?"

"Will do," said Buck as he tossed the requested bag out of the tent. He was ready to stretch his legs and try out his new hiking boots. Their leather was so soft that he was confident the footwear would be faultlessly comfortable. Being so far from civilization was a new sensation to him but being in wild territory was not. He couldn't wait to move about some and see what was living in these parts.

He picked up the collapsible water jug and started toward a rushing stream at the foot of their hill. He had hardly left camp when he came upon a bristling porcupine, almost green from an algae coating on its sharp, spiny quills. How unusual, thought Buck—a green mammal. The creature ambled away into dense brush, making a soft hissing sound as it retreated.

A fat caribou cow with a long-legged calf stood gazing at him from the opposite hillside, mesmerized by this strange upright invader. After a while the cow snorted, stuck her short tail up into the air, and sauntered over the ridge out of sight, her head held high and her calf following closely behind. Buck watched with great admiration, and his heart overflowed with gladness.

"Wow!" he exclaimed softly as he approached the rushing stream. Its waters literally teemed with salmon, the rivulet manifesting a sizable run of the fish. They were jumping a small waterfall, each one in turn catapulting into the air and with powerful strokes of the tail ascending into more tranquil water above the rapids. In this pool there were dozens of the travelers resting for another grueling assault on the next section of fast water. Buck watched, transfixed, for several minutes before filling his container.

The crystal clear water was sweet to the taste and contained not the slightest hint of pollution. Buck savored his first sample of untreated surface water. The north country had never been subjected to heavy usage that characterized more temperate climes, and few besides outdoorsmen were aware that one could drink water from virtually any stream or lake and suffer no ill effects. Even back when defilement elsewhere had been at its zenith this fact had held amazingly true, so long as human habitation upstream was limited or nonexistent.

Buck consumed his fill of the refreshing natural liquid before embarking on an exploratory tour of the sandbar that stretched up his side of the creek. Its smooth surface was crisscrossed with caribou, moose, and small animal tracks, some of them fresh and others days old. Among them were those of a good-sized grizzly bear, apparently a female accompanied by a cub. A little farther along a pack of wolves had crossed the sandbar, leaving their prominent canine prints. The boy drank it all in, marveling at the abundance and variety of wild things here, as he moved beyond the sandy stretch into a thick area of dwarf willows.

Without warning there came a loud snarl from a brushy thicket just across the stream, and the boy was horrified! The biggest bear he had ever seen came charging toward him! Only the water separated him from the approaching bruin, and the youth's first impulse was to run. There was little time to think, but he recalled in a picosecond what he had been told—never run! He stifled his strong inclination and remained motionless, waiting breathlessly while his heart pounded violently. His rifle was still in camp, and he found himself helpless at the mercy of nature's raw power.

Deep in the recesses of his mind stirred old feelings of terror, feelings that had lain dormant or suppressed for years. Though he had not been allowed to view his mother's body until it had been prepared for burial, images of her frail form spurting blood flooded his mind, the recent incident involving Dr. Hansen perhaps providing a rejuvenated template. The memory combined without mercy with dim but powerful recollections of her pale, lifeless body in a cruel wooden coffin. Buck Morgan cringed in absolute agony, crushed by helplessness. He wondered whether his mother had been given ample time to feel this kind of terror, a sensation so intense that he could feel nausea rising in his stomach, almost to the point of retching. To die or to fear you were about to die, there was no way to know which must be worse.

The big grizzly ran vigorously into the creek's edge, galloping like a horse and sending a white spray into the chill air. The agitated animal growled menacingly at intervals and snapped its jaws with a loud clicking sound. Drenching water matted its dense hair together, causing it to drip copiously. The creature was so close at hand that individual droplets were visible on its coat. The bear retreated slightly and shook like a giant dog, sending a blinding mist into surrounding air. A horde of ever-present biting insects formed a veritable cloud around the beast, doubtless tormenting it to no end. Buck prayed inaudibly, hoping for deliverance by whatever supernatural force could hear him, begging salvation from those powerful jaws and the unbelievable claws that could rip life from a caribou—or a human being—with a single wicked swipe.

The bruin settled down ever so slightly, and stuck its nose into the air, sniffing the breeze. It seemed to be trying to determine the source of the unaccustomed foul spoor of man. The creature appeared confused, apparently having momentarily lost track of the intruder. The boy crouched motionless in heavy brush, attempting to make himself as invisible as possible.

The animal left the shallow water and paced an opposite sandy bank, still unmistakably angry. It arose several times to its hind legs for a better view, giving Buck an imposing view of its agile, muscular body wrapped in silver-tipped splendor. The wind was swirling and the bear was doubtless unable to confirm Buck's exact location. After several minutes of uncertainty and a couple more abbreviated false charges, the creature emitted a parting snort and disappeared into impenetrable alders.

The youth dared not move for several more minutes. When he finally spotted the bear crossing an open ridge a couple of hundred yards upstream, he knew that the danger had at last subsided. He took a series of deep breaths, and then quickly splashed some of the cold creek water in his face. His nausea was now passing quickly into an unpleasant memory.

Returning with his heavy load of water, Buck struggled as he ascended the steep hill. Beads of perspiration cascaded from his forehead, both from physical exertion and recent emotional trauma. He looked back down toward the stream repeatedly, but he could see no movement that might indicate the bear's return. He felt an uncontrollable and compelling sense of urgency to get back to the safety of camp lest such an eventuality should occur, so he pushed his tired legs until the muscles burned. He stuffed his cap in his back pocket so his head could cool better and finished the trip, while rivulets of sweat washed stinging insect repellent into his eyes. Voracious bloodsuckers took advantage of his exposed scalp and the diminished effectiveness of his repellent and attacked him furiously. Long before he topped out on the steep grade, he was beginning to wonder if he would ever arrive alive.

The aroma of grilling protein burgers drifted to his nostrils, announcing the nearness of camp and at the same time reminding him of his ravenous hunger. He put down the water container and tossed his sweat-soaked cap into the tent. After wiping his face with a highly absorbent chamois towel and cooling down a bit, he began to nonchalantly apply a second coating of insect repellent.

"Good work, son," Morgan congratulated him. "We'll be ready here in a minute. Looks to me like our first supper is going to be absolutely unbelievable."

"Dad, I just saw a grizzly," Buck said in as unperturbed a manner as he could muster, giving his best attempt to sound casual. "Down by the creek. In fact just across the creek from me."

He then related the events that had transpired, and his riveting account held them spellbound. Morgan ceased his cooking entirely and listened silently until his son finished his story. The man shook his head and rubbed his jaw from time to time as he relived Buck's close brush with wilderness catastrophe of the worst sort. The location and description of the animal made it very likely that this was a big male bear they had spotted while approaching in the plane.

"Why didn't you take your rifle with you? And there's a can of sure-fire bear repellent in my duffel. We can't afford such oversights," Morgan cautioned, removing his cap to wipe away a film of nervous sweat. "We won't let that happen again. You could have been killed."

J.Y. JONES

"You invite me to go to Alaska with you and then you hog all the fun," joked Monty, breaking for a moment the serious tone of their discussion. "Then you get back just in time for supper. Buck, you must be the luckiest guy alive."

"Well, lucky or not, we've got to be more careful. Could be the insects are making these bears more aggressive. Could be you just surprised it," Morgan surmised. "I would expect that a female with cubs might act like that, but with an old male, it doesn't usually happen that way. They have a natural fear of man and no cubs to protect. But one thing you can always predict about grizzlies is that they're unpredictable. In any event, no more water runs without the rifle. This isn't Kansas and bear density here is a hundred times higher than back home, so don't forget that. Now let's get ready to eat. These protein burgers are ready."

"They sure smell like they are. I've worked up an appetite, packing water, fending off grizzly bears, and all..."

"Quit bragging and let's eat," Monty interjected, clearly quite hungry himself. "See anything else interesting down there?"

"Let's begin by saying a blessing," Morgan suggested. He removed his hat and in the midst of nature's grandeur he said a halting prayer, thanking God for a safe trip and for the food they were about to enjoy. Buck noticed something different in his prayer this time, though. Back home saying grace was always a monotone, using the same words and always spoken with a sense of duty and nothing more. Here there was feeling and emotion in the simple blessing of food. What was the difference in his father? Could Monty sense this? He knew that saying grace over food was entirely foreign to his friend and he wondered how he would respond.

"That was neat, Mr. Morgan. Just like you really meant it. Say, Buck, I ask again, what else did you see down there?" Monty said with an accepting smile as they distributed burgers.

"Wolf tracks all over the sand bar. Either that or a pack of very large dogs. And hundreds of salmon are in the creek. I'm sure glad we bought fishing licenses."

"Salmon, huh? Just like the pilot said. We'll have fresh salmon steaks for supper one night. Here, try one of these burgers. You look like you could use one."

"Thanks, Dad. I'm glad I didn't become a burger for that bear." Buck heaped on a generous helping of trimmings, mustard and ketchup, lettuce and tomato, and then he savored the delicious aroma. The first bite was awesome, like food always seemed to be in the outdoors. He thought about how great it was going to be to picnic here for a whole week.

After finishing the meal and cleanup, Morgan went over the safety rules with the two youths again, covering guns and their handling in detail. Then the three shouldered their packs and set out for an adjacent higher ridge where they could command a good view of the surrounding countryside. The climb was significantly steep and footing was treacherous, and the trio found themselves laboring and perspiring. As they finally topped out, they removed their burdens at a large rock, which they would use as a table and a back rest.

"Wowee, Dad, what a view. Why didn't we camp here?" Buck uttered as he gazed in astonishment at endless, unspoiled, majestic country spreading out before him. The view made him appreciate how remote and wild was this back country, and he could almost convince himself that he was the first human to ever see that particular place. He had read about the first explorers and this was the kind of virgin land they had roamed in search of sustenance and discovery. He was gazing on sights that were unfamiliar, but in his innermost being there seemed an aspect that was as familiar as the farm back home.

"That's quite a grade to haul water up. No, I like our campsite. But this high place will be a good landmark we can see from everywhere. We can come here as a starting point each day. Of course, I've put the satellite coordinates of camp in my pee-cee, in case we do get lost."

"You mean we've got to do that every day?" moaned Monty, looking back down the steep hillside towards their campsite, where the brightly colored tent was visible in the distance as a speck of orange. "I wanna go home!"

"Dad! I see a caribou! It's a bull! About two ridges over!" Buck said, looking through his binoculars and pointing.

"Where? I want to see him!" Monty exclaimed, the strenuous climb suddenly forgotten.

"Let me find him...Oh, yes, now I see him. Nice bull. There's another to his right...and another. But one is pretty nice," Morgan surmised, reaching in his pack for a high-powered spotting scope.

The caribou were feeding along the next ridge top, grazing abundant tundra lichens. Buck watched as the fat animals moved along, and his searching eyes found several more nearby. He pointed them out to Monty, who had soon located them in his binoculars as well.

"How does he look, Dad?"

"He's mature. Let's see, his top points are a little stubby, and the bez points are a bit deficient. Great spread and a nice shovel, though, I'd say," Morgan reported as he peered through the spotting scope. He was glad he had spent some time on the Conservation Club's WorldNet site learning to evaluate various elements comprising caribou horns. "Want to look?"

Without answering Buck moved to his dad's side to take a magnified look at the animals. Monty got in position for his chance to check out the creatures in the high- powered device.

"Splendid specimens. But not what we're looking for, huh?"

"Nope. Let's not be in any hurry. There are plenty of caribou here so we'll enjoy taking our time selecting the three we want."

"Good idea," Buck agreed. He was certainly in no hurry to finish this special quest. But he did want to take home his caribou.

"Take a look, Monty," suggested Morgan. The boy stooped to place his eye to the oculars, removing his hat and letting his flaming red hair ripple in the breeze.

"Wow. I've never seen anything like that. Now I want to see a grizzly bear."

The next few days were pure heaven for three guys from Kansas, as they enjoyed one another's unhindered company while camping, exploring, hunting, and fishing in unspoiled wilderness. Morgan had almost forgotten how refreshing it was to take a break from the daily routine. Long hours of daylight gave them plenty of time for such activities. They saw no less than nine grizzlies, counting four cubs, the closest ones only a few dozen yards away, although none approached as near at hand as Buck's opening adventure. They also encountered numerous moose, hordes of caribou, and countless smaller creatures.

On the third day, Buck killed a marvelous caribou bull with a single well-placed shot from his rifle. Just like taking a deer back home, he thought to himself. The next day his father did the same. The remainder of each day was spent packing everything back to camp and hanging the meat. Now it was time for the moment of truth for Monty, who had declined his opportunity to shoot, in deference to the others, both times they had encountered a bull that was up to standards.

A high ridge separated the trio from a band of caribou they had seen crossing the creek upstream from camp. After a lung-bursting climb to get ahead of them, an ascent that consumed more than an hour, they finally topped out and spotted the herd. In it were several magnificent stags, the largest truly extraordinary.

"There he is, Monty, and I think he's bigger than either of the other two we have. Want to make a stalk?" Morgan asked.

Monty gazed at the creature through his binoculars and then lowered them slowly but said nothing. Then he watched the bull feeding for a full minute of indecision. He again lowered his binoculars and looked at Morgan.

"You know, Mr. Morgan, my dad will never understand if I shoot that animal. My grandfather might roll over in his grave, from what I've heard about him. But I'm going to do it. Let's go."

Glorious excitement and the impending shot really got Monty's blood boiling. He followed Morgan's instructions to the letter, chambering a high-powered round only when the two were within easy range. Buck watched from an adjacent ridge as Monty dispatched the creature with a perfect shot.

It was near dark when chores associated with the successful kill were completed. Finally all meat was in camp and stowed safely. Now there were no unfilled caribou licenses, so the three discussed at some length what should be their next course of action. It turned out to be an easy decision to stay the remaining time. The weather was cool enough to keep their caribou meat from spoiling, so there was really no hurry.

"Hunting is as hard as farm work, Dad. I thought we'd never get all those quarters of meat back to camp," Buck declared, glad that job was behind them. "I'm glad we're limited to one caribou each."

"Me, too. Say, these are really gorgeous antlers. The taxidermist will make some wonderful mounts for us."

"Special mounts of our caribou. They'll always remind us of this time. Dad, I can't say enough how much I appreciate this trip," Buck reflected sincerely.

"Mighty extraordinary time for me, too. Opportunity to hunt, yes, but more importantly to spend time with you and Monty unencumbered by the concerns of the world. I had almost forgotten what it feels like to be carefree. I can't tell you how glad I am that you've both had a good time."

"Who wouldn't have, Dad?" Buck wondered, looking at Monty and thinking how the experience seemed to have changed the boy's perspective. "What is it that makes this kind of trip so special?"

"Seeing the animals we love, getting close to the outdoors, just seeing wilderness and being together—all are appealing. To me, though, the best part is the opportunity to practice and to teach you a higher plane of ethics."

"Really? Ethics? Doesn't quite compute, Dad," said Monty to Morgan, his head shaking in thought. "I just killed a caribou, and that's ethics?"

"See, Monty, you're focusing on the least important part of the experience. Remember how hard the work was before and after the kill? There's just so much more to it than pulling a trigger. When I'm totally alone, just the animal and me, I decide when to take it, and when not to. Usually no one else sees but God and me. The most demanding ethic is that which only your conscience polices," replied Morgan. "The best hunters are probably the most responsible individuals in the whole world. When you're out like this, it prepares you well to make even bigger decisions down the road."

"But we have game wardens to enforce the laws, don't we, Dad?" Buck piped in. "Doesn't that give everybody strong incentive to do the right thing?"

"They only have to enforce laws when there are those who disobey them. Never forget this, son—the chance to make such critical decisions as Monty made today can take your character to the highest possible level. On the other hand, it can bring out the worst. I've even seen it destroy a person's character. That's a battle our game wardens fight, people who refuse to be ethical outdoorsmen. Fortunately we have very few lawbreakers nowadays. I sincerely hope that never changes."

"Good words, Dad."

Monty listened to the older man's answers thoughtfully, and he couldn't help wondering why these two had included him on this outing. He had benefited, to be certain, from the whole experience. And he loved what he was doing, whether his own father did or not.

*　　*　　*

Back in Adrian, Kansas, the time of year was extremely quiet, with school out and many people enjoying summer vacations. Even busy farmers could become a bit lazy, with crops growing and harvesting machines cleaned, lubricated, and ready for fall. Ralph Russell was in the middle of a two-week stint at Rocky Mountain Ranch, honing his skills at teaching his students the joys and benefits of managing natural resources in a renewable and ethical manner. He thought often of the Alaska adventurers and wondered if they were having the grand experience they had anticipated.

He had tried on a number of occasions to reach Rhetta in the evenings, but had not been able to make connections. Even her purse pee-cee seemed to be inoperative for some reason. He stewed endlessly about where his pretty wife might be, even as he hungrily drank in all the conservation information he was being fed.

Even small town Adrian had become quite tolerant of virtually any private behavior. Nearby residents paid little attention to what went on in a neighborhood back yard where prying eyes were excluded by a high fence. A buxom woman entertained a youth at her modest home on the outskirts of town, doing her own kind of natural resources management, a daily activity since her husband had been away. Cavorting around the backyard swimming pool, the mature woman taught a very young man various stimulating activities, stretching his imagination beyond anything he had previously envisioned. Spurred onward by outrageous and ebullient hormones, the youth learned quickly. As the pair rested beside the sparkling water, the woman stroked his dark hair gently, noting with interest a white patch of scalp that constituted his defining trademark. It was too bad this robust interlude couldn't last longer than a mere two weeks.

And every night she had an appointment with a friend at the Hat Trick Bar.

*　　*　　*

Sundown in Alaska found the trio of adventurers enjoying their last night in the wilderness. Tonight they consumed fresh salmon steaks, grilled to perfection. The delicious fish had done double duty, having provided great fishing fun in the rushing stream. They kept only one to eat, releasing all others quite unharmed. The plane would arrive next morning to retrieve them if good weather held.

As they settled into their warm sleeping bags, nestled snugly against the chill of night, Buck found himself strangely torn between his present and his future. He longed to stay here forever, to explore every corner of this vast land. But he sensed somehow that his destiny lay far away from this virginal location. He remembered again the shuttle plane ride and his heart leaped at thoughts of their upcoming voyage home.

"Dad, we've killed three caribou. But there are thousands more out there, aren't there?" Buck asked as they all settled in for the final night.

"Lots more will die of old age and animal predators than human beings could ever take, Buck. You know that."

"Have you ever killed a person, Dad?"

"Why do you ask?"

"Just wondering. You were in the war."

"In the thick of it. War is truly hell on earth, a life and death struggle between people who want to destroy each other. But I never killed anyone with any malice in my heart. They were just impersonal enemy."

"Does it feel different to kill a person?"

"Of course. You take the life of another soldier in battle and you feel remorse at first, though it gets to be less of a burden as time goes by. A human being has a mother and father somewhere and perhaps a wife and family, all of which love him like I love you. I could never completely disregard that. But the biggest difference is that a man has an immortal soul. The Bible says that man is infinitely more valuable than any animal, which is only a material being, as far as we know. You never quite get over killing a man, but you're free to take the life of an animal with a clear conscience."

Buck pondered the concept in the security of his sleeping bag, and Monty wondered out loud about whether animals have souls or not. Buck kept his own musing to himself, though he couldn't help but question whether even man had an eternal soul, despite the preacher's sermons and his father's beliefs. Was man a purely material being also, like his science teacher believed? And did he want to spend his life searching for answers?

"Dad, what do you want me to be?" Buck worried out loud.

"The best you can be. Nothing more, nothing less."

J.Y. JONES

"I want you to be asleep. So shut up and get to it," interjected Monty through his drowsiness. Morgan smiled in the dark at the new closeness the two boys shared.

Young Buck Morgan silently determined as he slipped into sleep that he would be exactly what his dad had suggested. The best he could be. And his dad would be proud of him someday.

CHAPTER 13

September 2059

"Dad, what were those fancy women doing at the hotel in Anchorage?" Buck asked as they pulled out of their driveway and eased onto the highway.

Alaska was now just a pleasant memory, and the warm Sunday of late summer was perfect for a drive to church. For some unknown reason the flashy women came unexpectedly into his mind as they motored along. Glittery girls had been trolling like fishermen through the ornate lobby of the Alaska King Hotel, where Morgan and the boys had lodged for a night after their backcountry vacation. Dressed in delicate leather fashions that clung in revealing manner to tender young bodies, precious little had been left to the imagination. Both teenagers had gawked at them in amazement, though Morgan had exercised fatherly discretion in pretending not to notice them. The boys had received numerous winks and warm hellos that were definite invitations.

"The ladies of the lobby? Pretty tough not to notice them, huh, partner? I guess any man would have a hard time ignoring them."

Man. Buck loved it when his dad referred to him as a man. At age sixteen undisputed manhood seemed all too far away, but his father always made it seem that he had already arrived. Jim Morgan had developed an uncanny way of bridging the generation gap and compressing their age difference into insignificance, a talent that seemed to be growing as the years passed.

"That's no kidding, Dad. They were very beautiful and dressed like I've never seen before. Monty couldn't get over them. And they were really friendly to everyone who came by, even Monty and me. Did you look at them?"

"Could anybody miss them? I'm sure those were prostitutes, son. They sell themselves to men for the night. It's a profession almost as old as mankind, they say. You know, I had never personally seen one before in my life—before Anchorage, that is. Not even during the war."

"Really? I saw a magazine that Spot Prestone brought to school that had pictures of women dressed like that, and women wearing even less. Some of them were completely naked, Dad. Monty just couldn't keep away from that magazine."

Buck had been mildly shocked, and uncharacteristically he had neglected to mention the incident to his father until now. Such pornographic literature had been a rarity until recently.

"What's he doing bringing something like that to school? Where's the world going? You and Monty would do well to avoid him, if he's into that kind of thing."

"What those women do is wrong, isn't it, Dad?"

"I believe so, and so do most people, I think. The world is beginning to change, though. And a lot of it isn't good."

"If it's wrong, I'll bet Pastor Don can preach a sermon on it. Maybe he will today," Buck hoped. So often the preacher's sermons seemed to him to be about topics of little interest.

"If he doesn't, we can ask him about it at our leisure after church. His wife is away visiting family and I've invited him to eat lunch with us."

"Okay, Dad. We'll ask him."

Buck knew better than to question the pious preacher at church about such a seamy subject, but when the man transitioned afterwards to a more earthly mode he would be much more accessible. They glided into a parking space near the church building, a modest structure steeped in twentieth century architecture, with low sloping lines and a brick facade, topped with a majestic bronze-colored metallic cross.

Morgan and his son ascended the front stairs and entered the sanctuary. Familiar surroundings emanated a churchy smell to which Buck was very accustomed. Bright sunlight filtered colorfully through ancient stained glass windows, creating a mosaic of colors that merrily lighted the main chapel. Other people were arriving as well and they were met with a chorus of greetings as they assumed their usual seats.

Buck waved to one of his teachers, youthful Judy Hancock, across the aisle. She was the only educator he knew who went to church regularly, and she always sat in the same seat with her husband Terry at her side.

There was another towering cross behind the pulpit, and numerous Bible scenes were depicted in stained glass side windows—Abraham readying Isaac for sacrifice, Moses and the Ten Commandments, Jesus at the Last Supper. The pews, mostly empty now, were of ancient wood imported across the plains at great expense back when generous offerings would sustain such indulgence. The costly seats harkened back to an earlier era when support for the institution was automatic, and money and people flowed in endlessly like the prairie wind. The congregation was much smaller than during its heyday and its numbers indeed represented a faithful few.

Pastor Don Tolbert smiled at them from his chair behind the pulpit, causing the youth to wonder again about the pastor's dual personality. Today's smile was more like his away-from-church manner, so it struck Buck as quite unusual. Probably he's looking at me that way because he's going home with us to eat, he thought. The pastor motioned to the music director and the service proceeded with a usual menu of announcements, welcoming a few visitors, a prayer, singing, and a presentation of special music by an aging woman. After the offering was collected, Pastor Don stood up and strolled to the pulpit.

"Brethren, this nation and this world are standing on the edge! We're on the edge of the abyss!"

The preacher's unexpected shout caused Buck to jump visibly. He watched as Pastor Don contorted his face like an actor and did what Buck had come to refer to as an eye roll, turning his eyes up under his lids so only the white sclera was visible. "How I long for the good old days when revival swept this land! When men and women came to the Savior by the thousands, and righteousness and justice prevailed! Brothers and sisters, when I was a young man I saw this kind of revolution come to pass, by God's grace, and how I hunger to see it again!"

Buck wondered exactly what he was talking about. A revival? Lots of people attending church? It seemed unlikely. He knew Pastor Don was

147

not happy about changes in behavior of recent times, so probably the clergyman was exaggerating.

"The years after 2000 A.D. brought about an outpouring of religious fervor that literally altered the face of the world. Expectation of Christ's imminent return caused people to search their souls for answers, and in Christ they found them. Lives changed, society was cleansed, right prevailed! Racial and social problems were improved, and then eliminated, by the love of Christ!

"Science was found to be a god that had no answers. Pollution, garbage, global warming, depletion of our ozone layer—problems that man solved through promoting individual responsibility under God— Almighty God! Now mankind is giving all credit to human achievement and not to our God who answers prayers."

His sermon went on at length to explain how profound changes in past decades had affected every segment of society and every community. The missionary effort around the world had succeeded tremendously and Christendom had been all set for the end of time. Sweat beaded on the aging minister's forehead and he wiped it repeatedly. As he overheated in his enthusiasm, he removed his leather dress coat and tossed it roughly toward a nearby chair. After three quarters of an hour of near-maniacal raving, his voice suddenly plummeted to a whisper.

"Finally, Brethren, be expecting his return. Don't be lulled into a sense of complacency, because he will return. There is great reward in being found faithful. Keep yourselves unstained by the present madness in this world. Be ready, be hopeful, be diligent. Let us pray."

Back at the farm, Morgan served the finest of caribou steaks to the pastor, and the savory aroma of unaltered meat filled the kitchen. Morgan's attraction to alcohol had been greatly moderated by his sometimes-reluctant counseling with the pastor. He wanted to demonstrate the new cooking talent he had developed, at least partially as a replacement for his drinking habit. Pastor Don had already cast off his pious nature and was as amiable as could be. Buck couldn't believe how much more comfortable he was with this side of the preacher.

"Mighty good steak, Jim. I'd say you two had a successful trip, all right," commented Pastor Don between bites. "We seldom get any unrefined meat these days. Mighty tasty."

"Thanks. We did have a good trip. And it was a great time together for Buck and me. And both of us became far better acquainted with Monty Archer, too."

"Mode and code, Dad, on both counts. You should see Alaska, Pastor Don. Have you?"

"Once I was there a very long time ago. It was attractive then, too. I preached a revival service there, in a town called...what was that name...Palmer, when I was a very young man. Good response, too. The aisles were full of people coming forward to receive the Gospel."

"We were in Anchorage one night. We stayed at the Alaska King Hotel. Of course the wilderness was the really special time, but we wanted to ask you a question about the hotel, Pastor Don."

"The hotel. What about it?"

"The ladies there, Pastor Don. Dad says they're prostitutes who sell themselves to men. Isn't that immoral?"

Pastor Don almost choked on a bite of steak and required a moment to recover his poise.

"Pardon me, Buck, but your forthright way of putting things sometimes catches me by surprise," Pastor Don hacked. "I should always expect you to come up with the unexpected. I'm just glad Julie isn't here...no, I mean...oh, well..."

"I didn't mean to upset you."

"No, no, good question actually. Did you understand my sermon today, Buck?"

"I believe so."

"I'm sure you did. Such women...and their customers...are just another sign of the world's moral slide. It's the utmost in corruption, son."

"Why have they just appeared? Dad says he's never before seen one and he's been all over. He says they've always followed armies in the field, and there were none around when he fought in Terror War III."

"Revival of spiritual values and a major disease consequence. But now they're both gone."

"But now the disease part is cured. Science is doing a pretty good job of solving most problems, isn't it?" Buck asked.

"I believe it's only a matter of time before many of our dilemmas return to haunt us, my boy. Science has installed some pretty good systems, yes, but they run on the engine of individual responsibility. And that's a mighty tired horse these days," said the preacher as he finished his last bite of caribou. He then pointed emphatically toward his plate with a pumping motion. "Understand, Buck, I know about your fascination with science particularly and with knowledge in general. And there's nothing wrong with that. Science has never been the problem. It's always been people and how they apply it."

Buck mulled the soliloquy by the pastor. How could you apply real facts wrongly? Science appeared rock solid to him. If accountability for individual actions did indeed seem to be on waning, it couldn't be the fault of science.

"When Christ didn't return as everyone predicted, people began drifting wholesale from the faith, didn't they?" Morgan asked.

"They did, and we see the effects. But you can bet the Lord will return when the world least expects it, and I look upon today's current madness as the final prelude to that imminent blessed event. We should have known back in Pre-2K that everybody wouldn't figure out the exact time of his return at once. The Church would be much healthier today if so many of its leaders hadn't been dogmatic in their interpretation of when the Second Coming would occur."

"When do you think that will happen, Pastor Don?" asked Buck in deep thought.

"We still can't say exactly, of course. The Bible says the Second Coming will occur physically at the site of the ascension of Christ, the

150

Mount of Olives in Jerusalem, Israel. There will be a period of unimaginable catastrophe and turmoil, worldwide deprivation, much loss of human life, and a terrible battle on the plain of Megiddo, popularly referred to as the Battle of Armageddon. At some point, though we're not certain exactly when, believers in Christ will be summarily removed from the earth. The Jews of Israel, God's chosen people, will be surrounded and close to defeat and annihilation when Jesus their Messiah returns to save them."

"Who's going to surround them, Pastor Don? Isn't it peaceful there now?"

"Very peaceful. But peace is always more fragile than it appears. I guess the Jews are as much at peace now as at any time since the nation Israel was established more than a century ago. The peace treaties enacted back at the first of this century have held remarkably well. Unexpectedly well, in fact."

"That's good, isn't it?"

"It is good but surprising, according to the conventional line on how the end times were supposed to transpire. As for the enemies who will entrap Israel, the Bible lists several specific nations as their oppressors. I believe that all nations will be against them. It appears to me that they will stand entirely alone in those days. All I can say with absolute confidence is that Christ will return and save them. I'm convinced of it, Buck."

"So Jews are key players in this coming event, then, Pastor Don? I have a Jewish friend, Aaron Rosenthal. He doesn't seem to care much about what I believe or what anyone else believes, for that matter."

"In due time he will, Buck, if he's around when the great day comes. Mark my word. In due time," said the big man as he leaned back in his chair and took a long swallow of tea. Changing the subject, he continued, "Oh, say, Buck, could you fill in for the pianist next Sunday? She's going to be out of town."

"No problem, Pastor Don. Glad to."

"And how about a little old time gospel music before I go?"

151

"Can do that, too."

Buck sat at the piano and opened an old church hymnal that rested on top of the instrument. He often played from the tattered book because he liked its tunes. He had developed a great respect for church music despite some profound reservations about its message, and he had an easy time deciding which songs to play. Thirty minutes later he turned around and faced the two men who were listening in silence. Both wore calm, serene expressions.

After Pastor Don left, Buck continued to think about their conversation, mulling over the remarkable degree of confidence the man had in his convictions. Nothing Pastor Don had said, indeed nothing he had ever said, was measurable. Maybe that was what faith was all about, believing in the immeasurable. It was a hard line for Buck to swallow.

"Dad, do you believe what Pastor Don was saying? About Christ returning someday? And Israel and all?"

"Of course I do, son. I'd be a hypocrite if I didn't. After all, we're Christians, and Pastor Don's explanation is what we believe. I've tried reading the Bible some for myself but a lot of it I can't follow. But what the preacher says makes sense."

Morgan readily admitted that his orphanage education had been much less than adequate, and he knew that his verbal skills had never been outstanding. Surely he could be forgiven for not ferreting out small nuances of theology. But of late he had experienced a growing confidence that the concepts he had learned at his church were accurate, at least accurate enough to hope in them. After all, Alice had staked her life on the truth of such propositions early in their marriage and had believed them with faith like a child until the day she died. If such beliefs were adequate for her, Morgan felt they were right and appropriate for him. At the same instant his mind harkened back to that dark day, just after Lee Shealy died, when he had spent time alone pondering life and its meaning. He remembered again the seemingly miraculous appearance of that blazing meteor in response to his terse, anguished prayer. Wasn't that some kind of message from God?

Buck wasn't nearly so positive about the issue. He had nagging doubts, especially about notions that didn't seem scientifically valid, nebulous concepts such as future predictions. He again wondered, too, why they didn't teach much about religious history in school and why they didn't teach...what else was it? Oh, yes, about the rise of science and how it had nullified animal worshipers. Seems like those two must have occurred at about the same time, just after the turn of the millennium.

He wondered if Ralph Russell knew much about it. Was there some inversely proportional factor working between science and these other changes in society?

It sounded like a good question for his teacher. He'd ask Russell tomorrow.

CHAPTER 14

April 2061

"Good morning, Mrs. Hancock," a handsome student greeted his English teacher. The young woman was arranging her workstation and she looked up from her computer terminal to greet the arriving pupil. She was perky and faultlessly pretty in a red and white work outfit, and she wore a bright matching bow in her auburn hair. The slightest hint of lipstick and eye makeup made her flawless complexion fairly glow, and she radiated a personality that lit up the room.

"Good morning to you, Buck Morgan. You're here awfully early today. Congratulations on your appointment to the Military Academy. Local boy makes good—sounds like a logical headline."

Buck had developed a boundless and burning affection for the young educator. Something about her made him feel...well, good but strange, a sentiment he couldn't exactly put into words. Judy Hancock was a relative newcomer to Adrian, but despite her youthfulness and her lovely face she had some unusual habits that made her stand out from the rest of the faculty. She still attended Buck's church, and this alone made her an oddity in the educational community.

Despite her youthfulness and her religious nuances, she was a determined and effective teacher who had rapidly gained the respect of a very rowdy student body. She controlled her unruly classes with the proverbial iron hand and insisted on excellence, and from young Buck Morgan she demanded an extra measure of it. He really didn't mind and worked hard to live up to her expectations.

"Thanks. I'm excited about it. I had some reservations at first, since I know several professors at Wichita State University and they wanted me to attend there. But the education at West Point is the very best. Like I told you, I want to be in the Astronaut Corps, so it's the best place to attend. Did you know that most U.S. members of the Corps are graduates of the U.S. Military Academy?"

"Vaguely. Why so?"

"You know how deeply our military is involved in the international space effort. Most top military pilots graduate from the Point. Four years from now, if all goes well, I'll graduate and start training to be a pilot, then I'll do my best to move on up to the Astronaut Corps."

It sounded quite logical. All other service academies had been closed a couple of decades previously, and their missions combined at West Point. Serious efforts to stay within a national budget had been the start of that consolidation. As well, the need for military officers had been greatly reduced by comprehensive treaties that halted virtually all armed conflict after Terror War III.

"I have no doubt that you will," she said, giving Buck her warmest smile. Somehow this teacher's confidence created a warm glow deep inside him, so intense that he felt an involuntary blush.

"I'm very glad to get the appointment, just the same," he replied, regaining his bearing quickly. "Everything is on hold unless that comes through. Dad's more excited than I am, I think."

"He's always been a big supporter, hasn't he?"

"Yes, ma'am. The best supporter I could ask for. He always puts me first and never asks for anything in return. He's a great father."

"You're giving him exactly what he wants in return. You're the best son a man—or woman—could ask for, too, I'm sure."

Buck felt his ears getting a little red again but the burn subsided shortly. He stuttered slightly as he began to express the real reason for his visit.

"Mrs. Hancock, I hope I'm not imposing, but I came in early to see if you can answer a question I have. In fact, I've been a little puzzled over this for a couple of years, and even Mr. Russell can't seem to help."

"If he can't answer it, I probably can't either. He's got a supercomputer for a brain when it comes to facts, doesn't he?"

"I thought he knew just about everything. But he's stumped by this question. Or maybe he just doesn't want to answer it."

"You've really raised my curiosity, Buck. Let's hear it."

"It's really not so important, I guess, but Mr. Russell just brushes off the subject when I bring it up. He refuses to talk about anything with any religious overtones."

"Religious overtones? Now I'm definitely intrigued."

"I've worked with Mr. Russell almost constantly for the past four years. You know, we did the fieldwork together on the deer collision project a couple of years ago. I've had a class under him every year, and he's been tutoring me extra as well. I know him pretty well."

"Oh, yes, I know you work especially hard on your academics. And I heard all about that deer project. That was truly a superb success, wasn't it?"

"Indeed it was. Dr. Hansen from the university received all kinds of awards for discovering the force field and its various applications, and we were privileged to be a little part of that project. He's one reason I thought seriously about attending college here in Kansas. But life sciences is not my main area of interest."

"Back to your question, Buck. What was it? We've got only a few minutes until the other students arrive."

"Oh, right. Uh, you're a Christian, aren't you? I mean, I see you at church every week, at least. You're different, I know that."

"Of course I'm a Christian. I decided to follow Jesus Christ several years ago. He's why I'm different," she explained. "He changed my life, and I'm glad it shows. What does that have to do with your question?"

"A couple of years ago, Pastor Don Tolbert gave a sermon indicating that there was some kind of revival about the turn of the millennium and that Christianity became the dominant force in every area of life for a short time. But Christ didn't return as expected so all the fervor died down eventually. It's not mentioned directly in our history books but he swears it's true. He's pretty old and he claims he was a part of it."

"The turn of the millennium, or farewell to Y2K, as they say. He's probably old enough to have been a very young preacher then. And we know he's truthful, don't we?"

"I'd say so, except that he acts one way at church and another when he's somewhere else. I guess that's not being untruthful."

"Is that your question, Buck? Whether there was a great sweeping revival about Y2K? Give or take a few years?"

"No, not exactly. That's only part of it. You know, today we've got the greatest wildlife program, the greatest farming operation, the greatest medical research, and the most advanced animal based clothing the world has ever seen. Pa Shealy died a dozen years ago, but he raised my dad. Well, partly raised by him—Dad was an orphan and spent a lot of years at the old orphanage. Dad says that he was taught by Pa Shealy that the world came perilously close to being taken over by a philosophy that promoted the idea that animals and people should be treated exactly the same."

"If there really were such a campaign, it didn't succeed, as you can see. We live in an age of science. Science is the god of this era, for better or for worse. Anything that isn't scientifically defensible is held in pretty low esteem, you know."

"I understand, and rightly so. But there appear to be a couple of historical events here that are mostly ignored today."

"I see a lot of loose ends here, Buck. Mind tying them up for me?" she asked, glancing at the clock.

"My question is really this: Both Christianity and that animal equality thing seem to have crashed around the same time. Are the two occurrences related in any way?"

"Well, first, Buck, for people like us Christianity hasn't crashed. The world at large doesn't accept our beliefs as bedrock truth like it once did. But real Christians have always been a small—and often a persecuted—minority, with only brief intervals of history when their beliefs were widely accepted."

"I can see a relationship that I've already thought about. Adherents to both philosophies are still around but there aren't many of either, although they still believe fervently in their doctrines."

"There are parallels, true, but there's a major difference, Buck. Christians are right and animal worshipers are wrong. One philosophy is of God, the other isn't. It's really that simple."

"But why is neither movement mentioned in history books relating to that era? Christianity is covered briefly in the centuries before that, or at least the origins of it. But animal equality is completely ignored except for references to ancient cults that held certain animals sacred, or worshipped nature in general. Why the obvious omissions?"

"Buck, they aren't mentioned for the same reason Mr. Russell doesn't want to discuss it with you. Today's scientific mind views both movements as ludicrous. They don't even want to acknowledge that such episodes have occurred. In scientific circles, both concepts represent an embarrassing time in the history of the evolving human race," the teacher sighed. "Actually, history books are probably more likely to mention pagan practices than the genuine article. Animal worship, fertility rites, and the like make good textbook material, it seems."

"Yes, ma'am, you may be right. I've read something about those from time to time. Celtic Pagans still do those things right here in Adrian, I'm told. Animal sacrifices are done sometimes, too. Seems like they wouldn't sacrifice something they worship."

"Doesn't make a lot of sense, does it? Certainly no more so than for scientists to twist history like they've done."

"Are history books written by scientists? I thought they were written by historians."

"They are written by historians, Buck, but even historians don't write with an unprejudiced mind. They reflect current wisdom, and it permeates their works, too. Like I said, science is held in such esteem by the world that it has become society's new god."

The young man thought a minute or so, hesitating between the two opinions. He really didn't want to risk hurting this gentle teacher's feelings. But his mind raced ahead, his conclusion inescapable.

"Then science killed both movements. One was based on unprovable faith and the other on emotions and distortions, but neither stood the test of scientific scrutiny. And neither merits more than a footnote in history."

"Wait, Buck. Don't relegate Christianity to the trash heap just yet. You need to think about what you're saying carefully. Christianity isn't unreasonable and distorted like the animal cult. Isn't your father a Christian?"

"Oh, yes, but he's a little uncomfortable with Christianity when it comes to scientific facts. Oh, he's a Christian. I get the feeling that he doesn't think his beliefs are unreasonable, or he'd reject the whole proposition. But he admits it isn't provable, either."

"But you're not certain, Buck?" Mrs. Hancock asked pointedly, looking at him intently with her sternest expression.

"I think I am. No, that sounds like an oxymoron. I don't know, Mrs. Hancock," Buck admitted. A rumble in the hall outside was rising in crescendo as other students began to fill the school, and already a crowd was spilling through the door.

"Buck, I'd like to talk to you some more about this. Please come by after school and we'll discuss the matter further," Mrs. Hancock spoke loudly over the rising noise level, her voice dead serious.

"I have to go to piano practice after school, but maybe for a few minutes," he replied reluctantly. He retreated to his assigned seat as other students began to enter.

After school, he dutifully dropped by the young teacher's room again and stuck his head in the door. She looked much more tattered than she had earlier, but her friendly smile was just as warm and her concern for him was just as intense. He could sense her anxiety in their discussion, but nothing she said altered his thinking in the least.

159

.   As they finished talking, she gathered up her belongings and struggled to lift a rather large box of books she was ferrying home. Buck noticed right away that she needed help. Despite their differences of opinion, he still liked her a great deal.

"Here, I'll carry that for you."

"Thanks. I was going to make an extra trip."

On the way down the concourse the pair fell under the watchful eye of Mr. Rudy McGill, the school's administrator. McGill was a masterful jargonaut, and he maintained the external appearance of a stable, progressive scholastic enterprise. The truth was much less pretty and neat, though one could never have suspected the facts from the flow of precise paperwork from the school, with reports that showed glowing academic progress and flawless achievement test results.

McGill was a big man who had a full head of hair that was cropped close all over. His scalp almost merged with his bushy eyebrows, leaving the impression he had only a rudimentary forehead. He wore reading glasses propped slightly askew on his ample nose, and his cleanly shaved beard was already showing signs of re-growth since its morning removal. His eyes were so dark that they appeared almost black, except the sclera, which had a distinct yellowish cast. His loose leather pants hung in baggy fashion, very unlike the trim cuts fashionable in that day. His chamois shirt showed signs of wear, and a colorful sheepskin tie around his neck looked poorly matched to the rest of his attire. He was leaning against a wall talking to Ralph Russell, with his substantial abdomen protruding well into the hallway. Both men spoke with a measure of sincere fondness to Buck as he passed. Neither had a word for the young teacher, but McGill watched her with a lecherous eye as she moved down the corridor. He hid the look from Russell and commented only as she moved out of earshot.

"She's a crazy one, Ralph. Good looker, but a loony from the moony. Good with kids, but I don't think she'll last long in this business. She's a holdout religious nut."

"I know. Buck told me all about her. She goes to his church. Seems likable enough to me."

"Ralph, you could get along with a rattlesnake in your bathtub, I'll bet. You never look around to see if there's anything to dislike about people, do you? Well, that's my job, and I won't tolerate her pushing any of her idiocy in the classroom. She'll be in the street before you can say 'megabyte' if she does. I wouldn't have hired her if I'd known she really believed all that ridiculous drivel. A lot of people go to church but aren't dangerous to the mental health of others like she is. Why can't she leave all that superstition when she leaves church, like most of them?"

McGill bade Russell good day and moved down the way to watch the young teacher in the parking lot, as if keeping her under surveillance. He slipped his reading glasses into a pocket and folded his arms to watch. He licked his lips hungrily as Judy Hancock bent over to put down her burden of classroom supplies, and lusted almost openly at her swaying, trim figure. While he looked, he flashed an evil grin as he considered the conversation with Russell. He wondered if the old fool had the foggiest idea where his wife Rhetta had been last night. What a great one she is, he chuckled under his breath, remembering with diabolical satisfaction the many evenings the two had spent together. And that big-eared teacher thinks he's so smart, he thought as he continued his observation of Judy Hancock. Chicken-chested old Ralph can satisfy a few teenagers in their quest for approval, but he can't even keep his wife happy at home, he smiled with convoluted glee.

The young teacher could not hear the words of her boss, and she assuredly was unaware of his licentious thoughts. As she and Buck arrived at the car, she commanded the cargo hold to open, which it did instantly. Buck placed the heavy box in the bay and she closed it. As he backed away from the hatch, he noticed an unusual emblem on the back of her vehicle, two arcs placed opposite one another, with one end overlapping to form what looked like a fish.

"What's this?" he inquired, tracing the odd emblem with his index finger.

"The sign of the fish. It identifies a true believer to another true believer."

"Interesting. I've never seen that before. Is it new?"

"It's been with us almost since the beginning. Remember it. You might want to use it someday."

"I will," he replied, his voice heavy with thinly disguised doubt.

Sure I will, he thought, even as the words rolled like sweet syrup off his lips. Sounds like it might be indispensable, he mused quietly to himself, although he took care not to let her notice his attitude. As she drove off he turned and headed toward the school building again, to attend his piano lesson in the music room.

Buck looked back once more as her car departed the school grounds, and her words reverberated in his ears. He felt a little ashamed at the condescension he perceived in himself. But the sign of the fish? What a laugh! Wait until I tell Mr. Russell about this, he thought with a faint smile.

CHAPTER 15

August 2061

JoEllen Thacker was pensive as she motored with her mother up the west bank of the Hudson River, headed for a rendezvous with her peers, the incoming Class of 2065 at the United States Military Academy. She adjusted her long, blonde locks so that her lap was virtually filled with spectacular tresses, and she somewhat nervously wrapped a thin, svelte finger with some of her hair. Her fingernails were rosy pink, needing practically no polish or other adornment. She absent-mindedly flexed her smooth index finger and noted the complicated manner in which that appendage responded. Her nose was so petite that it was almost rudimentary, and her high cheekbones and fragile mouth made for a gorgeous profile. She adjusted her firm, well-proportioned body in her seat and peered out the window at a beautiful summertime view across the broad river. As the miles slipped by and their destination neared, she wondered aloud whether she had made the right choice of schools.

"Mum, you think I'll be okay here?"

"You'll be the heartbeat of the Point. You'll blow them away, sweets. Put up with a little crap for a while, sure, but you'll come out a big winner," said her mother. She smiled at her stunning daughter as she spoke, and her mind automatically harkened back to the young girl's birth almost nineteen years before. Though the event had been an unwanted byproduct of a disastrous relationship with an abusive boyfriend, her daughter had been worth all the pain and inconvenience and expense. Valedictorian. Queen of the prom. Miss Hackensack. Miss New Jersey. Third runner-up in the big event. It had been fun.

"I don't mind a little harassment. I do hate the haircut," JoEllen responded after several moments. She twirled one of the abundant locks in her lap once more, and briefly considered a retreat to some other educational institution. Why did she need such a challenge? There were scholarship offers from all over the place, so it wasn't as if this were her only option. Still, the decision had been made. She fretted aloud again, and then both of them fell silent as an imposing fort-like assemblage of buildings materialized before them.

"Sweets, they can cut off your hair and run off your buns, but they can't take away who you are. You'd be just as beautiful with no hair at all."

JoEllen Thacker managed a fetching smile, perhaps her uncertainties making it a little weaker than usual. Nevertheless, her perfect teeth shined like gems, and her mother returned the grin. They turned into a designated parking lot at the direction of a handsome, uniformed man.

*   *   *

"Dad, thanks for coming up with me," Buck Morgan commented as the two travelers disembarked from an express bullet train and boarded a waiting taxi. "I'll be okay. Don't worry about me."

"Oh, I know. Just the same you be careful."

As the driver accelerated, Morgan glanced at his son, noting the sheer determination etched in his face. The son he had nurtured from infancy had truly become a man.

"Academically, you'll do more than fine. It's just the mental and physical stress I'm a little apprehensive about."

"After this first phase, I think everything will settle into a routine," Buck reassured his father.

"It's funny, son. You're going off to school and it's me who's worried. I guess that's the way it's always been."

"Don't be uneasy, Dad. I'll be fine. And we can go quail hunting when I'm home for Christmas."

That happy thought broke the somber tone. Morgan had a new bird dog pup that was his most promising prospect ever, and their conversation settled on that hopeful item rather than on the coming separation.

"Maybe you can get Monty to come out and hunt with you some on weekends. He's going to be closer home, at Wichita State."

"Oh, yes, good old Monty. He's done a little studying lately, huh?"

"Enough to get by, at least. He still has an ongoing craving for wild women. Maybe he'll settle down some more."

"I'll talk to Monty when I get home and let him know he can call on me anytime. He needs someone he can find if he ever needs help. I understand Sam's out of town most all the time."

Nostalgia gripped Buck as they discussed more details of old times. It would be a long time before Adrian would be once more at the center of his life—if it ever were again. His thoughts drifted back to high school and recent events that had ended his senior year at Adrian High. He would miss Ralph Russell and Monty Archer, and maybe even a few of his other classmates.

"The valedictorian race was as tight as an Angstrom unit, Dad. Two hundredths of a point between me and Spot. Close."

"I'm glad you got that honor. But it really wouldn't have mattered in the long run. Both of you achieved what you wanted. He's going to Wichita State, too, I understand."

"Full scholarship to study psychology, from what he says."

"He ought to use that kind of learning on his old man. I've never known a man quite like Jesse Prestone."

"I'd bet he'll find a way to do well there. Whatever it takes, as always. I hope the admissions committee at State knows what they're getting."

"They probably do. They say it's become nearly impossible to find academically excellent high school graduates. Son, you and the Corps of Cadets here at West Point are the best of the best."

Shortly they were deposited outside the reception area, and they stowed Buck's belongings in a designated location. Following precise directions, they headed toward the main gathering point for incoming candidates. There were people of all descriptions; most of them were trim young men and women accompanied by one or two adults. Buck's eyes were suddenly fixated on an exquisite young woman who was strolling along in front of them. Her long tresses, reaching all the way to her slim waist, swished from side to side in intriguing fashion as she walked.

For the few minutes she was visible, he wondered if perhaps the young woman had a brother who might be entering the Point. She was so beautiful that he momentarily forgot about the impending ceremonies, and walked along without speaking, practically spellbound. Seldom had he ever felt such a powerful attraction to any female, and the preoccupation was unnerving. He shook his head and looked at his father, who had to be noticing the girl, but Jim Morgan said nothing and did not return his glance. The young lady entered the huge building just ahead of them, and shortly disappeared into the crowded assemblage.

In cool, cavernous Holleder Center, an ancient edifice where generations of West Pointers had played basketball and hockey, Reception Day ceremonies proceeded as in centuries past. The drone of mighty air conditioners tempered the smell of ancient walls and ceilings, windows and grandstands with refreshing air. Summer heat outside was shortly forgotten as new sights and sounds greeted the arrivees, and both Morgan and his son were kept at rapt attention throughout the process. Buck listened carefully to an officer addressing the horde of new cadet candidates and their parents, knowing well that it was almost time for parting with his father. The officer ended his talk abruptly, and after a hug and a handshake from his dad, Buck was suddenly immersed in the traditional initiation that would qualify him for entrance into the Cadet Corps of the United States Military Academy.

All new arrivals anticipated with some apprehension the start of "beast barracks," the inaugural phase of indoctrination into military lifestyle. It lasted only six weeks but was a legendary time of severe trial and testing. This tradition was an integral part of a proud heritage stretching back for several centuries. The first indignity was a severe haircut, but that was just the beginning of trials. Many nights were entirely without sleep, and one never knew what was coming next. The period passed with amazing rapidity, and Buck weathered numerous mental and physical stresses. In rare quiet moments he would again reflect on his ultimate goals, and often the mental reminder would sustain him when going got really tough. Recognition Day, when new cadets were officially inducted into the Corps of Cadets, finally arrived.

His roommate for the fall semester was a big city cadet named Hugh Baxter, a dynamic and energetic soul who was as different from Buck Morgan as a planet from a star. Both were excellent students, however, and both had been raised by a single parent, in Baxter's case his resourceful mother. Baxter's father was unknown to him, a common fact of life in the times. He carried an impressive list of academic credits, most of them the result of his mother's constant encouragement. He was tall and muscular and planned to compete on the school's athletic teams if time and academics allowed.

"Morgan, you knucklehead, you'll never be an officer, much less an astronaut," Baxter chided as they prepared for morning inspection, his gleaming white teeth flashing in a mischievous smile as he scrutinized shiny insignia on Buck's uniform. "Look at the crap on that brass."

"Crap? It's shining like the sun! What are you talking about?"

"Well, you have to use your microscope to see it, but it's there. You'll fail inspection and be drummed out of the Corps. You'll never make it, Morgan."

"Baxter, I'll tell you who isn't going to make it—you! Look at those shoes, you tin-head. They look like you've been walking through some of our animal pens back home. Not even an ivory-mouthed dog like you could count his teeth in that shine. 'Course your expectations aren't very high so you can afford to be a little slack," Buck kidded, alluding to his roommate's more earthly military aspirations.

The whole idea of a roommate had not appealed to Buck, since he had always maintained his own room. For the most part he had also kept a distance from the other casual friends he had made over the years at home, Monty Archer being a rare exception. As a survival tactic he had kept that same kind of separation from his roommate during cadet basic training. But Baxter was refreshing to be around and the two developed a strong bond that jelled in their years at the Point. Subsequent roommates

167

never quite measured up to this first one, and the young man from Kansas established a lasting friendship with the affable cadet.

"Morgan, get your butt in here!" barked a cadet six striper, an upperclassman who was company first sergeant. Long rows of insignia on the sleeves of higher achieving seniors were intimidating, and Buck did as commanded without hesitation, laying aside his studies to comply. This time it wasn't for a drudgery detail he was being summoned into the day room, though, although the pressure to perform was no less apparent. The whole company was assembled and a piano was prominently positioned in the center of the big room.

The first sergeant began by reading a segment of Buck's resume indicating he was an accomplished pianist. As if to test the statement, Cadet Morgan was ceremoniously escorted by the student company commander to the instrument and ordered to entertain the troops. For the better part of an hour he played everything from contemporary popular music to timeless classics of previous centuries. The entire assemblage was rendered spellbound by his inspiring display of talent, and several upperclassmen made special requests, all of which young Morgan played without benefit of sheet music. Thereafter he was duly established as something of a phenomenon on the sprawling campus.

He came home for Christmas holidays as planned after his initial months of grueling academic and military indoctrination. Buck walked with his father across the familiar fields of the Kansas farm, and the young man sensed something different in the way he viewed their home place. There was no change in the layout, the fences, or the picturesque brown hills. But an unspeakable transformation had occurred nevertheless, one that seemed haunting, almost frightful. For reasons he couldn't voice adequately, it didn't really seem like home anymore.

"Strange, Dad, I've lived here all my life and now it seems so foreign, so distant. It's hard to express," he said, perplexed.

"At least the bird hunting is just as much fun, I hope," replied Morgan, watching a striking pair of swift pointers quarter efficiently in front of them.

"It's definitely a lesson in nostalgia. And yes, just as much fun."

The birds cooperated as usual, and soon both men had a day's limit of the explosive game fowl. They were almost to the south property line by now, and the walk back was considerable.

"You haven't heard about Spot Prestone, I guess?" asked Morgan as they ambled toward the scenic farmhouse.

"Heard what? Last I heard he was still at State."

"Not any more. Got caught stealing final exam codes. He should have known they'd have hacker detection modalities."

"Wow. I thought he was smarter than that. He was always willing to cheat, but it surprises me they caught him so easily."

It made Morgan glad that his son was attending an institution where old time values were respected and revered. He didn't understand why people would so readily overstep the bounds of decency in order to achieve. With a little hard work, there was a much better way. His boy was proof enough. It was too bad Spot Prestone didn't have a little more attention from his father, he thought a bit smugly. A little glimmer of devilish satisfaction flashed through his mind as he thought of his old nemesis, Jesse Prestone.

*　*　*

Buck almost ran into Cadet Thacker as he departed Washington Hall the first evening back at the Point. He found himself staring into deep blue eyes, transfixed, while a warm rush immediately engulfed him. He knew there was protocol to be followed, so he spoke only a stammering, tentative hello before hastily retreating. His heart raced uncharacteristically as he headed back toward his barracks, and he felt somewhat foolish about their chance encounter.

JoEllen Thacker had weathered beast barracks with the best of her class, and had even survived a drastic trimming of her luxurious hair. Sometimes she had second thoughts about her chosen school, but in most ways she was quite proficient and equal to the task. Buck thought of her often, but plebes at the Point had very little opportunity for social interaction with the opposite sex. It was just as well, as his studies and

169

other obligations consumed practically all his time. Still, he couldn't help but have periodic thoughts about his dazzling classmate.

Academically Buck excelled at West Point as always. He was near the head of his class by the end of the first year, and he held high hopes that he would be able to capture the prestigious top position. He had extra incentive, after all—only the top few graduates had any reasonable chance of becoming astronauts. Although this long-term objective was often pushed into the back of his mind amid a constant whirl of activity, it was always in his subconscious, pushing him to strive to attain higher levels of excellence.

When he was a third classman, as second year students were called, his superiority began to shine in certain areas as he entered the domain of such favorite subjects as physics. The biggest problem for his instructors was to find something to teach him that he didn't already know. There was plenty for him to learn in the disciplines of history, languages, and art, but in math and science there were indeed few peers to the farm boy from Kansas.

"Mr. Morgan, explain the curvature of the space-time continuum," ordered Colonel Davis, his physics professor. The clean-cut middle-aged officer was a Harvard graduate who carried on his uniform a chest full of medals from Terror War III. Subsequent to that war he had returned to graduate school and had attained the highest academic credentials imaginable. The polished eagle insignia on his shoulder flashed in intense overhead illumination as he folded his burley arms, awaiting a response.

Buck sighed as he stood briskly to his feet after an awkward pause, at first barely aware the question had been directed at him. This would be tough. Instead of his usual laser-like focus on classroom proceedings, he had been thinking placid thoughts of faraway places and unlikely companions. Sitting across the aisle from him, in the same class with him for the first time in his West Point career, was that magnificent blonde woman who intrigued him so. Nothing about the war hero-professor intimidated him, but Cadet JoEllen Thacker most assuredly did. He cleared his throat and tried to get his thoughts together. He closed his eyes and tried to shut out the stares of his classmates, and finally ordered his thinking enough to begin. With extreme concentration he was able to perform a masterful dissection of the subject that left his classmates and his professor quite impressed. As he sat down, he shot a glance at Cadet Thacker, and found her staring at him with very little expression.

Even when handicapped by such a distraction, young Morgan had a way of taking charge in a scientific or mathematical situation, where his sharp powers of reasoning always gave him an edge. He fell a bit short in military protocol and some "reasonless" subjects, as he called them, but given a scientific topic or a project that required manual skill, he was unsurpassed. He constantly amazed the instructors with his incisive mind and unerring grasp of complicated principles. Ralph Russell had taken a diamond in the rough and had produced a true jewel.

"Morgan, you nearly floored us today," reported a classmate, a big blonde cadet from Georgia named Kirk, that night at the library. "Where did you learn all that nonsense?"

"He's always doing that, man. Likes to show off," commented Buck's old friend Hugh Baxter, who had chanced upon their study session.

"Unlike you, Baxter, I had a decent teacher in high school who covered most of the subject we discussed today while I was still in tenth grade. So it's old hat, buddy." Buck replied with only a hint of joking in his voice. He turned to his study mate and observed, "Kirk, he's been jealous since the day we first met."

"Well, I had a good stable of profs, too," said Kirk. "But we didn't talk about theory in such depth. Guess that's why you're soaring and I'm struggling to stay alive. If you've got to know that kind of detail I'm glad I'm not craving the Astronaut Corps."

"Yeah, sometimes he forgets he's at the U.S. Military Academy. He thinks this is astronaut candidate school, and he's trying to get in," observed Baxter with a toothy grin. "Even his hokey name has an astronautical ring to it. Must have been named after Buck Rogers right from the start."

"I'm not just trying to get in, Baxter. I'm going to be in. There's too much going on in space now to miss it," replied Buck, deflecting his friend's good-natured plinking.

"I can tell you, there aren't enough women in space to suit me," said Baxter with a broad grin. "No more than a dozen farther out than Moon Station, hardly enough to make it interesting. And probably most of them wouldn't appeal to me, anyway. Nope, you've got to be different—like you, Buck—to want to be an astronaut. Got to have the same qualifications as a priest has, I figure."

"Holy holograms, Baxter, we've covered this before, haven't we? Like a few hundred times? Have you ever thought about how much of your mental and physical energy you expend cultivating your female friends? It's just like you to waste your time looking up how many women are at each space station, for pity's sake. I don't think you need to let the numbers concern you, though, buddy. You won't ever be out there anyway," Buck chided.

"I don't want to be out there, my good buddy. I'd rather be down here. I've got a date tomorrow with the queen of the Point. Know JoEllen Thacker?"

Buck's mouth dropped open involuntarily. He felt lightening-struck! Thacker dating Baxter? It couldn't be! But she probably dates all the time, he thought, wrestling perceptibly with the idea.

"Yes, I know her. She's in physics class with me and Kirk. How did you meet her?"

"Military science class. Nice...all over, one can't help but observe. Say, buddy, you sound interested for a change."

"She's pretty. Not like your usual fare, I must say, Baxter. Let me know how it goes."

"It always goes well, Morgan. Never miss my fun. See you later."

A sinking feeling made it hard to study for the rest of that evening, so Buck retired early. He tossed and turned uncharacteristically that night, finally slipping off to sleep long after midnight.

There was nothing different about Cadet Thacker in physics class on Monday morning, the best he could tell. He couldn't bring himself to mention her date with Baxter, though he had opportunity to engage in small talk during a break in class. Her interest in Buck seemed to be miniscule, at best, and he could find little encouragement in his shy conversation with her.

Baxter was beaming in front of Washington Hall later that day, his broad smile seeming more commanding than ever. Buck declined to question him about his date, but as usual Baxter volunteered the information.

"Great gal, that Thacker. Smart. Cold fish, though. Cold fish," he said with a rare serious look. "So delicious in appearance but with so little sugar."

"Could be she's looking for something better, Baxter."

"Nah. Couldn't be. She's just different somehow. Couldn't put my finger on it, if you know what I mean."

As the two parted company, Buck was deep in thought. Should he ask Cadet Thacker out on a date? The idea intrigued him, and at times it obsessed him, but his attempts to come up with a strategy were invariably short-circuited. Their brief conversations never led to any substantial discussions. Physics class ended without him putting the question to her, and he seldom saw her thereafter.

The years at West Point passed quickly, and young Buck Morgan had innumerable opportunities that other institutions could never have provided. For his Cadet Troop Leader Training between his third and fourth years, he went to an Astronaut Corps unit for a special time of participation. This prepared him well for his final year before graduation. His summer included an extended space experience, orbiting Earth for six days on Space Station Delta, the permanent manmade satellite. There he observed manufacture of a new interplanetary cruiser so large it had to be assembled in space.

Speed and the efficient exploration of space were ever more firmly linked in Buck's mind. Could there be anything as important to advancement of the human race as space exploration? He looked down at his blue-green home planet from 700 miles in space and wondered if there were any others like it anywhere in the universe. More importantly, were there any within the ever-expanding reach of mankind? So far modern technology had detected only giant gaseous planets outside the solar system, and not the small rocky type that could support life. But if Jupiter-like worlds were abundant, surely there were stars with planets that matched the necessary profile. He couldn't escape constant thoughts that such a place could be there, within the grasp of modern science and awaiting discovery at the right time.

Sometimes during that final year he longed to see the queen of the Point again, but their paths seldom crossed. Even when he did run into her, she showed no discernible affinity for him. Later he heard that she was engaged to an army officer who had graduated from the Point two years before.

One night there came a knock at his door and Buck bid the petitioner to enter. Through the door stepped Hugh Baxter, brimming with jovial smiles. He shucked off his cap and sailed it toward the corner bunk in a brilliant whirl of gray and gold.

"Man, I'm in, Morgan! I'm heading for Fort Benning and the Infantry School. Reliable old ground warfare, parachute training, ranger school, and all kinds of good torture. I got my acceptance today."

Buck had never seen Baxter happier.

"Well, congratulations, old buddy," Buck replied. "I'm really glad for you, but I sure hope you never get the chance to use that kind of training."

"Got to be ready, Morgan. Conflict is always decided in the trenches, you know."

Buck had seen very little of Baxter that final year of school, and in their brief encounters they never quite recaptured the fellowship and camaraderie they had enjoyed as lowly first-year students. It was beyond Buck's mathematical mind why anyone would be excited about studying infantry tactics, crawling around in the dirt and grime. He remembered well tales his dad had related, usually in grudging fashion, about his service in Terror War III. It had been fascinating to hear blood and guts anecdotes about grinding, deadly, face-to-face warfare, the essence of which had changed little regardless of how modern war technology had become. Still, someone had to be prepared to do it, and Baxter would be very good at it. There hadn't been a serious armed confrontation between nations in years, so to Buck studying infantry made about as much sense as learning to build horse-drawn carriages.

"What's all this stuff, Morgan?" inquired Baxter, examining a plethora of complicated diagrams freshly generated by the computer. The layouts had been hard copied and were now strewn about the room.

"Engines, man, engines. I've been talking with the research and development people and they've got some great ideas on speed. We can go faster, Baxter—much faster. All we've got to do is figure out how to make engines that can burn longer. Right now we're drastically limited by how much reaction mass—that's fuel to you grunts—how much of it a ship can carry," Buck said with enthusiasm. "I can't wait to get out there and try out my wings. I really envy those guys who get to test concepts put together by R&D. What you see here still hasn't even been built. These are the prototype nuclear pulse engines that will help us conquer the solar system."

"Whoa, you got wings, geek? I thought you had to earn them."

"True, but mine are coming. I can fly jet aircraft on the computer already, and I can even command and dock a shuttle. I'm ready for the real thing."

"And you're going to conquer the solar system?" asked Baxter, chuckling. "Sounds like you're using infantry terms to me. You'd better be prepared to hold onto it if you're going to conquer it, or else you're wasting your time."

"You're hopeless, Baxter. But I think you'll make a mediocre infantry officer."

"Better than that. And don't you want to go help me celebrate? How about let's call that girl you like—JoEllen what's her name—and see if she'll go out with you?"

"They tell me she's getting married, Baxter. I'm too late on that one."

"I heard that, too. Doesn't mean a thing, though. She might still go out with you. Or maybe she might go out with me again. But she's not for me, I can tell you that. Want to call her?"

"What would I say? 'Want a one-night stand?' or something like that? I can't do it, Baxter."

"Suit yourself. You're going to be an astronaut priest, I can tell already."

Buck all but ignored the final remark, and turned his attention to point out some exciting features of the embryonic engines to Baxter. Realizing his old friend was preoccupied, the fledgling infantry officer shortly slipped out into the night to celebrate with less studious comrades and a perhaps a willing woman or two. Buck waved a belated good-bye as the door closed, and then he paused a minute to reflect. He was a son of the soil, a farmer's offspring who had lived his life in contact with the earth before he came to the Point. Baxter had seldom laid eyes on bare dirt before he had arrived. The farmer's son aspired to surround himself with the latest scientific hardware, manmade to the core, and spend his life largely out of contact with the basic mud and dust of Earth. The big city kid wanted to immerse himself in the firmament, and command others to do so. It seemed an ironic twist. With a pensive shrug and another brief yearning thought of beautiful JoEllen, he returned to his analysis of the complicated printouts.

When graduation day finally arrived, Jim Morgan and Ralph Russell came to enjoy the big event. Rhetta Russell declined to attend, since she was little more to Buck than a casual acquaintance. Uncle Bill and Aunt Carol Barnes made special arrangements to be there, perhaps the only time in their lives that both Jim Morgan and Bill Barnes had been absent from Adrian County at the same time. A surprise visitor was Judy

Hancock, who unexpectedly responded to an invitation to the commencement.

As top graduate, Buck Morgan was required to give a short speech during the ceremony. He almost choked with emotion as he recalled his father's commitment to raise him after his mother's untimely death. He made mention of the lofty honor that had been bestowed on him by his being able to attend the U.S. Military Academy, and of the privilege of sharing the same podium with the main speaker, the President of the United States.

"Congratulations, son!" Jim Morgan hugged new Lieutenant James Lee Morgan warmly after the traditional toss of hats into the air. Tears brimmed in the elder Morgan's eyes, and one wet droplet trickled in irregular fashion down his sun-seasoned cheek. Ralph Russell beamed that his favorite student had lived up to all expectations.

Judy Hancock was more reserved but her congratulations were nonetheless enthusiastic. Buck had corresponded with her some during his years of college and he remembered how consistently warm and accepting she had been. She had allowed no trace of bitterness or criticism about their differences to interject itself into their communications. Ralph Russell had apparently not made known to her any indication of the mirth the two had shared over some of her peculiarities, hidden ridicule that Buck now recalled with some regret.

"My, don't you look handsome in that gorgeous uniform!" she commented sincerely, noting that all the boyish features she remembered were now gone, having given way to abundant manhood. His broad shoulders and closely shaved face were fully mature in appearance, and the lines of his body were those of a virile soldier, chiseled like a granite statue. She couldn't help but wonder what was in the heart of this striking graduate and how it might be expressed as he pursued his dreams. She was entirely unashamed as she added, "Buck, I've been praying for you to succeed here for a long time."

"I know you have. Thanks," he responded, a little embarrassed to have her say something ridiculous like that out loud. Perhaps Ralph Russell or some of his fellow graduates had heard her.

"So it's off to flight school, Buck?" she asked as the crowd began dispersing.

"Yes, Ma'am, then to astronaut school," Buck replied, his voice as confident as his body was erect.

"Here's a little something for you, Buck. I hope you'll keep it always," she spoke gently. "You might need it someday."

She handed him a package, which had to be a book wrapped in gift paper, and a nice congratulatory card.

"Thanks, Mrs. Hancock," the new officer said sincerely.

"Remember, Buck, your work may not fulfill all your dreams and expectations. Keep an open mind, okay?"

Her tone was very serious. Buck didn't quite know how to reply. He kept recalling what Ralph Russell had repeatedly stressed. This was a woman of weird and uncompromising beliefs, who for the most part ought to be ignored.

"I will, Mrs. Hancock, I will," he answered, a little ashamed of his mendacity. This was the same deceptive reply he had used in response to that solemn voice, and to her inexplicably disquieting demeanor, more than four years earlier.

But again his direction was already determined. Science had become his god and space his destiny. And he couldn't wait to get started.

He opened the package in absolute privacy that evening. Inside was a Bible with a name inscribed boldly on its fine leather cover in bright gold letters.

"James Lee 'Buck' Morgan" stood out clearly against the dark background.

CHAPTER 16

August 2065

The student pilot pulled the nose of a small aircraft up at a progressively increasing angle of attack, and the engine strained audibly in an effort to keep the machine in flight. Higher and higher it climbed as airspeed slowly bled away. Buck Morgan scanned his primary flight instruments methodically, noting as expected the drastically declining velocity as an insistent stall horn began to sound. His feet instinctively controlled the rudder pedals, keeping the tiny plane straight on course. When critical stall speed was reached the plane plummeted earthward with a shudder that shook him rudely. In the turbulent air, one wing dropped precipitously and suddenly, but the pilot's addition of exactly the right amount of rudder and aileron corrected the tendency and kept the plane out of a potentially dangerous spin. The pilot simultaneously lowered the nose and smoothly recovered, successfully completing the last in a series of power-on stalls, all of them executed with clock-like perfection. He then turned the plane toward home base and switched to tower frequency in preparation for a routine solo landing.

It had been an uneventful practice session up to this point. The first indication of trouble was a sudden drift in the aircraft's nose alignment, and an overt change in control responsiveness that initially Buck thought was a simple need for trim adjustment. A calm right hand on the trim wheel automatically rolled the device to compensate for downward drift of the nose, but only minimal modifying effect was apparent. Becoming mildly alarmed, he pulled back on the yoke to apply more elevator force, but there was absolutely no satisfying correction. The plane meanwhile was assuming a hazardous position with its nose drifting ever lower and the airspeed indicator pushing perilously close to the red zone. He pushed in the yoke and then pulled it out all the way, again with no discernible effect on the craft.

Now increasingly dismayed, he tried rolling the craft carefully, ever so slightly, with the yoke, and found the ailerons responding normally. Likewise, pressure with his feet on the rudder pedals resulted in a normal yawing of the plane's nose. He diagnosed the problem immediately from this information—an elevator failure. What on earth could have caused that? These trainers came with state-of-the-art alloy cables that could never conceivably break. Nonetheless, another series of steering manipulations confirmed the situation. In the meantime, the plane had drifted to such a crucial nose-low position that he was staring directly at the looming ground through the windshield. His airspeed had climbed far above the safety level, and extreme danger loomed. Worse, an ominous buffeting started, apparently fluttering of the limp elevator surface on the aircraft tail, and the entire airframe was beginning to vibrate violently like a flag in a stiff breeze.

His mind raced to analyze the condition, and he tried desperately to recall all he had ever read about this particular in-flight emergency. He knew the plane could be landed if he did everything right. What a time to have such a disaster, he thought briefly, with only a half dozen solo flights under his belt. No matter, the predicament was upon him, and now he would have to fly the craft or die trying.

At least the other controls worked, giving him some options. He struggled to maintain level flight in the midst of the intense and worsening flailing of the airframe, adding power to try and bring up the plane's nose. The response to more engine power was minimal but definite, so he pushed the throttle in another quarter inch, noting significant improvement in his position as the pitifully small engine roared to life. The disturbing shaking increased with higher airspeed, the result of a more rapid flow of air over the flapping elevator surface. He backed the power down slightly, and as his heart raced he coolly rotated the trim wheel to maximum up position. With this combination of maneuvers he was able to reduce the vibrations slightly while restoring to normal the angle of the aircraft nose, and airspeed began to bleed back just a bit. Beads of sweat were forming on his forehead, and he only now thought to finish his call to the tower and report his problem. By this time he was directly over the field, and the tower was already calling him before he had time to contact them.

"Six-four-niner-seven-golf, say intentions."

"Niner-seven-golf, uh, I've got an elevator failure. I'm having trouble controlling her. Can you clear traffic for me?"

"No problem, sir. Are you declaring an emergency?"

"That's affirmative. I'm having to control attitude with power and trim tab."

"Understand declaring emergency. Will clear traffic. Make downwind for zero niner. No need to report."

"Roger, zero niner. Niner seven golf." Grateful for the assistance, the young lieutenant turned his full attention to the battle at hand. He struggled to maintain control of his crippled machine, since the slightest excess power caused the nose to shoot up near stall configuration. In this disastrous position the plane could easily plummet into a deadly spiral toward the earth with little possibility of recovery in the absence of a functioning elevator surface. Too little power and he was diving, a position of equal peril. He deftly learned the necessary minute corrections, intuitively incorporating data into fine precision movements of his fingers. He also had to turn the aircraft into a position to land while cautiously lowering the nose just enough to descend, but not enough to dive cataclysmically into the ground.

By the time his heading was around to the necessary easterly reading, he was soaked with perspiration from intense concentration and extreme duress. Despite the stress, he found himself actually enjoying this tight wire experience, a paradoxical mindset that he didn't have time to analyze. He had the technique down now and was shortly descending in a smooth path toward touchdown. He could hear cheering in the background of the tower transmission as his wheels contacted pavement, and the welcome squeal of the tires was most beautiful music. He had won!

His primary instructor, Major Bill Mitchell, was waiting anxiously as he taxied the crippled craft back to the aviation school ramp. Mechanics were soon swarming over the tiny plane trying to determine what had gone wrong. Such mechanical failures were rare in current aircraft, so a detailed inquiry was mandatory. Everyone patted him on the back and told him how lucky he was to survive such an emergency.

"Morgan, I don't know what to think of you. You amaze me," said Mitchell as his protégé descended from the trainer.

"Routine, sir," returned the sweat-soaked student in a calm voice that seemed almost recovered. "I don't want to train like that every day, though."

"Talk about a fish in water, Morgan. I've had hundreds of students but not many of them could fly as soon as they got into the aircraft," Mitchell commented as they watched several mechanics begin disassembly of the tail section. "And today you've been challenged more than most pilots get in a career. You handled it well."

"I've just had a good teacher, sir."

"That's kind and I hope there's some truth in it. But you can't teach all the skills you do so well. You recruit that kind of talent. I hope the military realizes how much capability you've got."

"You're generous. I guess it's easier when you've been doing it on the computer for years," Buck replied, the pounding of his heart and the adrenaline in his veins subsiding remarkably as they talked.

"True, but not many make an easy transition from make believe to the genuine thing. And I'll bet you've never done an elevator failure on the simulator, and you handled it like it was an everyday occurrence. I'm not one to make premature predictions normally, but I'll chance it just this once. I'd bet a month's pay you'll make it to the Astronaut Corps."

"I will, or at least I'll never quit trying. I'm ready to spend more time in space."

"Yeah, I understand the attraction. It used to be tough out there, but now it's like eating cotton candy. So many improvements."

"There's a lot going on all right, a lot of changes. But I hear it's still challenging."

"While they're figuring out your trainer's problem, we'd better go on over to Flight Ops and file an incident report. We'll check back here afterwards."

After an extended debriefing by the safety officer, they returned to the shop to find out details about the mechanical problem. It turned out to be simple—a broken connector had released the cable from the elevator. Rather than a failed aircraft part, poor workmanship was to blame, because the device had been installed backwards. The mechanic commented to Buck that he was very lucky to be alive, because the undulating surface could have vibrated the entire tail assembly to pieces, even if a pilot did everything exactly right. Was it pure dumb luck, or was it something else? The important thing was that he was alive and safe, and he had done his part, and that was what mattered most.

As the two men walked back toward the officer's quarters, Buck's mind returned to the major's allusion to the Astronaut Corps. Was that space experience talking?

"Do you know much about space, sir, if I might ask?" Buck questioned.

"I spent twelve years in the Astronaut Corps. When I met this girl—she's my wife now—I just couldn't stand the thought of another six year trip to Ganymede or a long rotation to Mars Station. So I gave up a couple of promotions in order to settle down. I really like instructing, too. And I've got two boys now, so being on a regular schedule is pretty important to me."

Buck's mind harkened back to the years he had spent in blissful labor with his father on their Kansas farm. He remembered men who had been content with just the simple things in life—a woman, a bevy of kids, a steady job. Pleasant memories beckoned like an old and cherished friend, and JoEllen Thacker flashed through his thoughts, for some reason. She was probably training even now for an important position in her field, the Judge Advocate General Corps.

He shook his head to clear these doubtful notions intruding into his thoughts like a creeping Kansas dawn on a cloudy morning. He couldn't let such sentimental feelings interfere with his calling. It was unthinkable to get this far and then retreat.

"Those are valid objections for a family man, sir. It would help if we could get the speeds up some to reduce travel time to the planets."

"Yes, a little more speed would help. Our solar system doesn't offer very much hospitable real estate for planetary stations, does it? They tell me Ganymede is like living in hell, with constant ground shifts and gravity outside the station so deficient. There's perhaps some potential out at Saturn's moon Titan. But in my experience all those places except our own moon are as crude as a wooden rocket. Mars is one terrific duty station, though, I'll tell you that from first hand experience."

"They tell me the mineral wealth we're mining up there is worth a king's ransom. I've heard that there are still problems getting it back to Earth in a way that's financially feasible. It appears to me that the intangibles we're reaping, such as new data, new techniques, and new technological breakthroughs, are helping our understanding of a host of basic questions, the economic return aside. I think it will prove out in the long run that man's destiny is tied to this space program. Eventually we've got to find a way to explore beyond the solar system. Do you agree, sir?"

"No question about it. You're showing the same spirit I had when I first got into the Astronaut Corps. I guess I found something I wanted more than adventure and discovery. I'll stay right here with the wife and kids. But don't let me discourage you. Oh, congratulations on an outstanding job today. You came out of a bad mechanical problem in one piece. You're moving up to jet school next week."

"Thanks, Major. One baby step at a time for now, but I'll be docking the shuttle to Space Station Delta before you know it," Buck proclaimed confidently.

Jet training was even easier than light aircraft for the young officer. Computerized aeronautics courses he had taken over the years had heavily emphasized vintage turbine powered machines, and had practically bypassed basic propeller-driven slow flying skills necessary in the thick atmosphere near the earth's surface. Jets were young Morgan's real talent and he proved once again that his aptitude tests were on target. He was the perfect pilot, meticulous to utmost detail yet confident and smooth in flight. He lacked juvenile brashness and bravado, undesirable hallmarks of lesser pilots, finding such attitudes old-fashioned, useless, and downright dangerous.

Jet school passed uneventfully. Buck really enjoyed the incredible maneuverability of the twenty-first century fighter plane, even if his model were only a trainer. Modern engines ran flawlessly on an odorless veganox mix, like a fine timepiece. The ancient smell of Oil Age kerosene had become a thing of the past on the flight line.

During rare free time Buck brainstormed occasionally with his enthusiastic young comrades about speed, space, and beyond. Thirty young officers were in the current class, although only a couple aspired to become astronauts. Fantasy was in vogue, because in the modern age fantastic dreams regularly became reality.

"I think those nuclear pulse engines they're designing will be the ultimate," stated Lieutenant Harry Hale, another highly talented, promising young pilot. Hale was tremendously intelligent but was anything but handsome. He had a nose that was so large it had earned him the unwanted nickname of "Hose Nose" Hale.

"No way they're the ultimate, Hosey. But they're a quantum leap better than the clunkers we're burning now," Buck responded. "You know, traveling near light speed we could get to Ganymede Station in about an hour, depending on Jupiter's proximity to Earth. That's the kind of speed we need."

"Pipe dreaming, Buck. Scientists at the space lab are convinced that even nuclear pulse engines can't sustain thrust long enough to come near light speed," said Hale.

"With some design changes they can perhaps reach five hundredths of light speed or better, but they'll produce so much heat and guzzle so much fuel that they can't be burned long enough. It's obvious to me that we'll have to improve on the concept considerably to really go places. The best hope is that mass inversion mechanism they've discovered," Buck speculated optimistically. "But look, even at five hundredths velocity, we can get to Jupiter in a day. The solar system will be our oyster."

"We'll never go that fast, because space debris will clobber us," noted Buck's current roommate, Lieutenant Dexter O'Malley, another big city woman chaser from the Point who reminded him remotely of Hugh Baxter. "At today's speeds we can see and avoid larger meteors and absorb hits from minute ones, but at such high velocities, we're in a world of hurt. Even a grain-sized meteor is going to shatter your ship."

O'Malley was as darkly handsome as Hale was ugly, and their opinions often clashed as dramatically as did their appearances. Buck Morgan was perpetually uncomfortable in their combined presence because there was always an undercurrent of tension. He often found himself in the role of reluctant peacemaker.

"A plasmafyer hyperlaser could sweep constantly in front of the ship, turning smaller meteors and particles of matter into harmless plasma which would stream around the ion shield of the craft," Buck explained patiently. "If that works, though, we'll have to build spacecraft with true aerodynamic design."

His observation did little to defuse the situation. Morgan left the two young officers arguing heatedly about the effect of plasmafied space debris on the trajectory of aerodynamic machines in a vacuum, and slipped out to resume his studies. He couldn't afford any distraction at this stage. Time was short and he still had plenty to learn.

After earning his jet wings, Buck had no problem getting accepted as an Astronaut Corps Candidate. He once more prepared psychologically and physically for the toughest endurance test on the planet. In other times perhaps Marine Corps basic training, Army Ranger school, or Navy Frogman training were epitomes of stress, danger, and hardship, but in today's world nothing remotely compared to Astronaut Candidate School. Buck thought back to the depressing and wearying beast barracks at West Point and finally he was glad he had endured that learning experience.

He was constantly stressed above and beyond the other candidates, his preceptors knowing of his high goals and therefore attempting to probe daily the extent of his fortitude and stamina. Sometimes in moments of impending despair he would think back to his days on the relaxed farm, tending his chores and living a life of luxury by comparison. At times he would wonder momentarily why he harbored such a burning passion for space travel. Many long weeks of intense trial and testing finally came to an end, and not a moment too soon for him and his peers. His class graduated six new spacemen and two new spacewomen, the survivors from nearly two dozen who had started the course. He had made it!

"Ladies and gentlemen, I present to you Lieutenant Buck Morgan, Astronaut," the general smiled as he pinned the Astronaut Corps emblem on Buck's blue leather dress uniform while applause sounded. Buck's father beamed proudly in the audience as his son received well-deserved accolades from his superiors. Yep, thought Morgan, my little boy is going far. And he's well on his way.

"Well, son, where's it to now? Seems like you're moving up the ladder rapidly," said Jim Morgan as the gathering was dismissed.

"I'm going to specialty school now, Dad. It's highly individualized training designed to prepare you for a specific task. I want to eventually captain an interplanetary craft and hopefully be in position to participate in the latest innovations."

"You'll do fine. But remember, space is a dangerous place. I can't afford to lose a son. I don't have one to spare."

"Don't you worry about me. And I'll be home a lot, Dad. We'll still have time to quail hunt sometimes," Buck promised sincerely. He couldn't help but notice increasing wrinkles on his father's weathered face, as well as new streaks of gray in his thick, dark hair. It was uncanny how much older his dad had become in the last few years.

"Well I'll be there, God willing. It gets pretty lonesome there at the home place sometimes, but I've got Uncle Bill's family, as well as plenty of friends around. Nothing like having you home, though."

"Big furlough coming up the end of the year, before I get my final assignment. I should be home for two weeks, Dad."

"Great! I'll have the dogs ready and we'll just have a grand old time. Just fly the way you do everything—carefully and consistently."

"Okay. Like I said, don't worry about me, Dad."

Specialty school was designed to give personalized instruction in whatever area of expertise the newly graduated astronauts needed. Sometimes the most basic earthbound skills were taught, such as welding and metallurgy, but often their training was more academic or technical, such as mining chemistry or deep space navigation. Buck chose the most broad-based program he could get.

"Morgan, what do you want out of this program, everything?" asked an instructor, aging Captain Ben Stuart, a grizzled veteran with a scarred face resulting from a lengthy battle with recurrent skin cancer. Such an unseemly appearance was common in pioneers whose service dated from the early years in the space program. "I've never seen a guy stay down here on Saturday night pulling up data to read. All work and no play..."

"No problem, Captain. This is play for me. There's not much I'd rather do than to learn this material. I'll need it someday," said Buck, glancing up from his work into Stuart's salt-and-pepper face.

"Those newer metals are awesome, aren't they?" said Stuart. "I remember in the old days we were constantly afraid something might melt. No more. They're getting tougher and more durable every year. Better living through chemistry, as they say."

"I know what you mean. Just look at the molecular structure of this latest silicone-vanadium steel. Makes our old stuff obsolete when the first new batch is poured."

"No kidding. We're throwing things away so fast it makes everything seem disposable," said the old veteran as he rubbed his short beard while Buck manipulated some flashing equations on the monitor.

"By the way, Captain, can I have that big molybdenum alloy pot in the kitchen storage room? The cook said it was slated for disposal. Newer ones are already here, he says."

"The ten gallon job? I don't care. What are you going to do with it?"

"For my father. He's never seen one made of such advanced material. I know here it's obsolete, but in Adrian, Kansas, it'll be a hot item. Dad likes to have a group of quail hunters over to cook birds after they hunt, and he's never got a pot big enough. He's getting by with an old chromium stainless setup."

"Take it. Scrap heap stuff anyway. They're hauling back tons of the base metal from Mars every week."

"Thanks, Captain. I'm going to close out now and hit the hay."

Before retiring Buck retrieved the shiny metal vessel, complete with lid, and stowed it in his room. He couldn't wait to present it to his dad.

After completing specialty training Buck received his first space assignment, a six-month required apprenticeship aboard Space Station Delta. This initial rotation would be followed by a round trip on an interplanetary cruiser to deep space bases at Mars and Ganymede. Astronauts had once been required to wait literally years before their first space flight because missions took months or years to plan and execute, and preparatory time between missions had often been long. Space flight had become almost as routine as atmospheric flight, so the problem now was sometimes the opposite. Twenty-first century astronauts sometimes complained they didn't get back to Earth as much as they desired. Fortunately, before the lengthy upcoming voyage Buck had a well-deserved vacation at home in Adrian.

Back home at the farm the young astronaut related the details of specialty training to his father as he presented him with the sparkling kitchen hardware. Jim Morgan was delighted with the big container. After securing it in one corner of the spacious kitchen, Buck and his father took time to tour the farm and inspect the latest high tech farming gear that had been recently installed. Morgan glowed with pride as he demonstrated to Buck his new technological system.

"Pollution free fuel production, Buck. Now we'll hardly let a molecule of methane escape," Morgan explained with only a modicum of exaggeration. "The system works almost perfectly. Helps the old cash flow, too. We're doing better than ever, producing more protein and a higher grade of fuel. Everything's really jam up."

"Wow, Dad, I'll bet this setup costs as much as an interplanetary cruiser." Buck walked around looking at the amazing conglomeration of equipment, and deep inside he felt an urge to know more about how it worked. Could he have a little bit of farmer left in him?

"I doubt it cost that much. It cost plenty, though, I'll tell you that, son. But I can't help but believe it's worth it. The only concern is you really have to be careful because this arrangement cracks hydrocarbons so well they're as flammable as old time gasoline. But the computers that control everything are on top of the process so there's a lot of built-in safety."

"Just the same you be careful, Dad. You look like you're really enjoying what you're doing as much as I've ever seen."

"It is fulfilling and so darn practical. And they've even eased up on some red tape and regulations lately. Wish I had someone to pass this on to..."

Morgan's words trailed off as he thought about what he was saying. He looked at his son quickly, hoping he hadn't heard the last part. The young man had indeed heard, and he looked at his father intently with those piercing blue eyes.

"Dad, I love this farm, but you know my future isn't here."

"I know. Sorry I said that. I was just thinking out loud, I guess. I've thought about some kind of trust that would produce income for you after I'm gone. I don't know. I plan to run it myself until I can't do it anymore, but I'm getting older and the twelve hour days get longer every year."

"Hire more help, Dad. Just be a manager. Have fun, but don't let the place be a burden. With my salary and basically no expenses I won't need any more income. If you have trouble running it, lease it out. But keep the hunting rights."

"Don't worry. You'll always have the run of this place. Speaking of which let me introduce you to Hank. He's terrific. The old guy bunch from Adrian will be out tomorrow to hunt, and you should hear them rave about that dog. Say, I'll get to try out that new pot you brought me. It ought to be darn big enough."

Around at the kennels they inspected a lovely white English setter and admired its shiny, soft coat, the feather-like long hair on its legs and tail, and the intelligent head bejeweled with intense yellow eyes. The sights and smells brought back boyhood memories to Buck in a flood of nostalgic mindscapes. He was very glad to be home. He patted the gorgeous dog on the head and rubbed its strong back, ruffling the long hair as he did so.

"He's really a beauty, Dad. You say he's the best you've ever trained?"

"Without a doubt. He's almost flawless in the field. He's as much a picture of perfection at what he does as a certain son of mine is at what he does."

"Gee, Dad," Buck exclaimed, almost reverting to his teenage tone of voice. "Think we've got time to take him for a spin before supper?"

"How long will it take you to get your briar britches on, partner? Remember, these birds fly like little brown rockets!"

"I remember. But rockets I know about now, Dad," he replied, already heading back to the house to change. "Last one back to the kennel has to clean the birds!"

And so the two passed the afternoon awash in happy remembrances of many such winter evenings past, walking in contentment over cinnamon-toned hills and valleys. For a short time, outer space and its grip on the young man faded into the background as they enjoyed and loved one another and relished the dogs, quail, fields, and crisp, clear atmosphere.

"This is great!" Buck exclaimed as they made a turn toward home, exhilarated all over again by the rush of classy pointing dogs in pursuit of petite feathered projectiles. He hadn't experienced so much pure delight for quite a long time.

* * *

Neither of the two satisfied hunters could see a sinister pair of scornful eyes that watched them from afar. Hatred burned so intensely that the agitated individual could hardly hold his binoculars stationary. He followed the pair and their dogs from atop a rocky hill on the opposite side of the valley, cursing out loud and breathing murderous threats each time the hunters found success. His malevolence stirred ever more vengeful with each noisy volley fired at fleet-winged quarry. The man had restrained his hatred as long as he could tolerate it. He just might take drastic action, he concluded, his eyes narrowing as another unwelcome round of shots boomed loudly.

*   *   *

"We can do this every time you're home," Morgan said as they put the dogs back in their kennel and started for the farmhouse.

"Sounds great, Dad."

"By the way, I want to give you something, son."

Jim Morgan extended his worn Stevens Savage double-barreled shotgun toward Buck tenderly, and carefully placed it in his cradled arms. The smooth wooden stock of that old Model 311 complemented its worn metal surface, and the combination shined magnificently in the declining sunlight. Buck's mouth fell open as he ran his fingers over the antiquated firearm in awe, and swung it upward to look down the weathered barrel. A round bead sight that had been aligned with many a bird greeted his eyes as he pointed the weapon at a nearby object. The right barrel was usually fired first, since the modified choke rendered a slightly wider pattern that was better for close range. The left barrel held a bit tighter pellet group, and consequently maintained the shot together nicely for longer shots. The gun had belonged to Lee Shealy's grandfather, and originally cost only a few dollars from the Sears Roebuck Company back in Pre-2K. It was over 100 years old, but still performed like the best in modern technology.

"Dad, I can't take your shotgun. It's...it's always been yours..." He pushed the locking lever laterally and opened the smooth breech, then snapped it crisply shut once more.

"Not always. There came a time when Pa Shealy handed it over to me just like I'm giving it to you. Always think of me when you use it."

"What can I say, Dad? Thanks doesn't seem enough."

Buck admired the weathered walnut grip as he held the old gun. The original stock had succumbed long ago and had been replaced with a more superior grade of wood. This was a prize that Buck had never even considered might be his someday.

"You've said plenty already. I've got a new automatic I've been itching to use anyway. You owe yourself a well-earned quaii excursion every time you get a chance, and I want you to use this old gun. We can go again tomorrow, and maybe a few other times before you leave, so you can try it out. And we'll do it again next time you can visit."

It sounded too good to be true. He stood practically speechless, thinking about the genuine heirloom he had been presented. It should have been the happiest of moments.

But down deep, a disturbing feeling crept over him. Buck couldn't shake a pervading thought that perhaps future trips home might not measure up to this one. This visit was a special and unique time.

CHAPTER 17

May 2066

Buck Morgan reached as far as he could, grasping a power riveter and applying pressure to the trigger with a heavily gloved finger. The recoil of the instrument in the vacuum and weightlessness of space was surprisingly vigorous, and it required a bit of finesse to counter it. The result of this action was a perfect, shiny adhesion of metal to metal. He then touched the maneuver button on his belt and jetted to the next joint where he repeated the process. It was mandatory to check continually for defects in his workmanship, since lives would be dependent on the impeccable security of each bond.

In the safe confines of his space suit he was very much at ease and confident in the airless environment. The self-contained survival apparatus he wore had evolved considerably since the time of bulky, crudely encumbered relics of earlier space history. Even more wonderfully, science had discovered how to block all harmful radiation entirely. The key was practical application of antigravity physics principles that had been understood but vaguely just a few decades before.

Seven hundred miles below him he could see the world of his birth, garnished in a perpetually changing veil of clouds. The splendid planet's variable face was broken at intervals by broad areas of blue ocean and familiar brown-green land masses, all punctuated by incessant swirls and bands of white. Earth was at the same time close at hand and almost infinitely distant. Somewhere down there was the community of Adrian, a place which now seemed so alien to this new life the young astronaut was beginning, and so remote from his focus and his vision. What would his father be doing at this very minute? For some reason Buck had him on his mind as he paused and momentarily glanced in wonder at the misty orb suspended far below.

Space walks were becoming second nature to him. Every day he spent several hours suited up for sunbathing, as astronauts referred to such skywalking experiences. During this apprenticeship he had set his mind on accumulating a broad range of knowledge and experience, and he was certainly getting it. Protocol required that he spend six months in Earth orbit before being considered for deeper missions into space. Such procedures were necessary to weed out any unsuitable candidates who might have passed through the rigorous screening process with dangerous undetected physical or personality flaws. Deep space on a six-year mission was a bad time to discover defects in personnel.

"Good job, sir," complimented the sergeant who accompanied Buck.

"Well, it isn't exploring, but it's getting ready to, I guess. Someday we'll have this bird ready to fly."

Repetitive tasks in Earth orbit were a bit boring at times, but the young man knew that better things were coming. He rubbed his finger over the new weld, noting the impervious adhesion and the smoothly finished surface.

"Back to the entry lock. Time to change shifts, sir," the sergeant radioed.

The foursome jetted back toward the designated area, located on the ventral surface of the new ship. The young officer pressed another button on his belt and the door activated, allowing them to enter the outer vacuum chamber that led to the living area. When the door behind them closed, the sterile room filled automatically with refreshing air, and all four astronauts shed their outside work suits. They then stepped through the inner door into the bowels of the growing spacecraft where they lived.

Entry into the inner portion of the machine from the weightlessness outside was a startling experience when one felt the sensation for the first time. Artificial gravity onboard drew one's body toward the floor in a sudden burst of momentum that strained every muscle, and with unrelenting and unexpected force it torted and yawed one's internal organs, sometimes to the point of discomfort. Buck had quickly learned what to anticipate, and by now he gave every appearance of being highly experienced.

"They're starting to send up components for the nuclear pulse engines, Lieutenant Morgan. Today's shuttle flight will have the first shipment," commented his commander, Colonel Orson Staar, who greeted them just inside the air lock.

Staar was a veteran with many years of space experience, yet his dark complexion showed little of the awful scarring which afflicted so many older astronauts. He was completely bald except for a rim of hair that circled the back of his big head just above the level of his ears. This fine residual was kept quite shortly trimmed, such that it was hardly a factor in the colonel's appearance. He was always shaved so cleanly that one wondered if he actually possessed any facial hair. He was small in stature but was built like a bull, with massive arms and legs and a barrel chest that spoke silently of power and authority. His waist was that of a high school athlete, and his shoulders were like an Olympic weight lifter. His mind was as fit as his physique, and he had rapidly established himself as a type that young Morgan wanted to emulate.

"That's when the real excitement will begin, sir," responded the lieutenant in slightly belated fashion. There was always a bit of awe that he had to overcome whenever he spoke with Staar. "How long is it projected for assembly?"

"Four years, minimum. At least there won't be any weather delays."

"I was hoping I'd be here when you test them, sir. Do you really think they will reach projected speed?"

"Five hundredths of light speed is the target. The guys on the surface are referring to it as nickel c. I've looked over the diagrams and specs, and I think they'll do it. Say, you've got a computer for a brain, Morgan. What does that calculate in miles per hour?"

"About thirty-four million miles per hour. That's a little less than 10,000 miles per second. And these are just the first prototypes. They'll do better with the next generation, if I know anything about it."

Buck was burning to petition the colonel to let him be in on the testing, but he knew it would be a futile move. Nobody would work on that project without deep space experience. No, he would have no choice but to do his extended voyage before anybody would listen to his pleas to get involved in cutting edge research.

"Sir, how are these gizmos going to work?" inquired the sergeant, referring to the new engines.

"Controlled nuclear detonations, several per second, with all the force directed along a single vector. The opposite reaction is inconceivable thrust," Staar explained. "I've seen a lot of quantum leaps in my time, but this one should top them all. I can't wait to see this thing go. A longer burn equals more speed. And we can get it all done with far less reaction mass than anybody thought possible."

"Sir, I'd give anything to ride this baby. Need any volunteers for that first trial run?"

"We're well covered, thanks. Just be patient, Morgan. You'll get your chance to motor in one of these gadgets, I'd wager," replied Staar.

"I'm not convinced yet I'd want to, sir," said the sergeant. The enlisted man was certainly adventurous, opting for a career of space duty, but he wanted his technology to be tried and true before he staked his life on it.

"I'd love to be on board first time out. If I could get the chance," Buck said, shaking his head. "My assignment after the preliminaries here is a six year round robin trip to Mars and Ganymede, leaving from the moon. I've never even been to the moon so this will be my first big trip. I'll completely miss testing this concept."

"I'm not sure I envy you the ride, sir. I've made that journey twice. Long haul," said the sergeant, who noted a disapproving look from Staar even as he spoke.

"Sergeant, you aren't trying to discourage our young officer, are you?"

"Oh, no, sir. But I want him to have realistic expectations. Maybe I'm overstating it, but it is a long voyage."

"I know, but I'm looking forward to it," said Buck. "Even if I do end up missing the nuclear pulse testing. At least it should beat riveting."

"Yes, I'll admit, it beats this monotonous routine, but here at least the comforts of home are less than an hour away," the sergeant said as he gestured downward.

"You mean home is that close. The comforts of home we take with us," Staar reminded him.

"Oh, that's right, sir. The renewable resources gardens they put on these interplanetary cruisers make you feel like you're on Earth sometimes. The animals make the same noises, plants grow like crazy, and recycling is more serious than nature itself. They're getting increasingly innovative every year. When I was on my first trip, it was all metal and plastics and I nearly went crazy. The last trip I took was a lot better. And they keep improving the artificial gravity and the radiation shields. It's more like home all the time."

Another officer hurried down the cavernous corridor towards them and interrupted their conversation abruptly. His face was tense and showed a highly worried look that clearly conveyed distress.

"Morgan, urgent message for you. You need to come to the communications center," he ordered with an unhesitating exigency in his voice.

"Urgent?" asked Buck. "Urgent? Pardon me, please, Colonel Staar."

They walked briskly to the door marked "Telecom," and entered. There on the holocom display, to the young officer's great surprise, was his old friend Pastor Don Tolbert, appearing very elderly and gray. His complexion seemed deathly ashen in color, and his plump face was drained of his characteristic enthusiasm. His sad, tired eyes looked superlatively realistic.

"Pastor Don!" Buck exclaimed as he fought a foreboding sensation that had crept into his thoughts.

"Buck, God bless you, son. I've got some bad news, I'm afraid," the preacher began.

"Bad news? Pastor Don, is it Dad?"

"I'm afraid so, Buck. There's been an accident," Pastor Don explained wearily. "There was an explosion in the hydrocarbon extraction facility on the farm. Your dad—I don't know how to tell you gently, son—he's been killed."

"Oh, no, Pastor! He's dead? He can't be dead! Oh, my God!" The lieutenant's voice faltered badly, and his military bearing dissipated.

"You're coming home for a while, Buck. I've already spoken with the commander at mission control. You'll be leaving on the shuttle later today. We've arranged for Ralph Russell to meet you at the Cape."

"Okay," he replied weakly. He was so accustomed to a controlled environment that it felt dizzying to have command unmercifully wrested from him, like some kind of gyrating craft spinning in terminal distress. His head whirled with a mixture of profound grief and unanswered questions. He sat down and put his head in his hands, contemplating for a minute what life would be like without his father. Not since early childhood had he lost anyone close to him—indeed, no one in the world had ever really been close to him other than his father. He had been too young to remember the pain of earlier losses with such horrifying clarity. Colonel Staar slipped into the room and sat down beside him, placing a hand on one of his shoulders.

"Shuttle's already lifted off from the Cape. It docks on the construction deck in forty-five minutes, Morgan," Staar advised him gently, his own decorum momentarily set aside. "You'd better get your belongings together."

"Yes, sir," the young man replied, but his legs didn't want to move. His body seemed frozen in time, the numbing shock of the awful news still draining his energy completely. He stood up wearily and with great effort shuffled down the passageway to his quarters. He stuffed his essentials into a small duffel and returned to the docking bay.

"Can I leave my gear here? I'll be back soon, colonel."

"Will you, Morgan? You can leave your belongings here. We won't call for a replacement until we hear from you."

With his mind in a dreamlike stupor he waited, paralyzed with grief. The announcement that the shuttle was approaching came in only minutes, it seemed. Usually Buck was thoroughly enthralled when the gigantic craft ascended for rendezvous with the station. The procedure was completely familiar by now, and on most days he found himself mentally driving the big silver bird. Today was different, though, and this time he was understandably more detached than usual. Before long the connection between the craft and their sector of Space Station Delta was firmly established and all was in readiness for offloading.

He felt compelled to pitch in and help the crew unload the shuttle. Through his sorrow he was still able to find a bit of excitement in some complicated components of the nuclear pulse engines he knew so well from schematics. How he wished he didn't have to deal with the catastrophe at home. What could have happened? His dad was so careful and so unerringly competent.

Prior to disconnect, a huge plate of Martian platinum was loaded aboard the shuttle and secured firmly. It was a regular ritual that taxed the craft's re-entry carrying capacity to the maximum. Descent back to the Cape was uneventful, and a rear seat held a passenger wishing, even with his overpowering sadness, that he could be up front guiding the vehicle back home. As they touched down and coasted to a stop, he continued to mull over a plethora of questions with no obvious answers. At the entry gate, he immediately spotted Ralph Russell, waiting in the company of an Astronaut Corps representative. Russell looked tired and haggard, even more so than Pastor Don had seemed earlier on the holo.

It was at first good to see Russell, but the joy of camaraderie and adventure they had shared in the classroom, in the field, and in the laboratory was sadly muted. Something seemed terribly awry in his old mentor, something oppressive and burdensome. Or possibly it was simply the dreadful circumstance in which they found themselves. Whatever the cause, there was no spontaneity or authenticity to their strained conversation, and the young astronaut found himself simply enduring the time. There was a dark pretension in Russell that he had never noticed before.

A scant seven hours after receiving the devastating news the astronaut arrived back home. His uncle, Bill Barnes, greeted him warmly with a sincere handshake. Bill had naturally made sure that the Morgan livestock had been well attended since the accident. Bill was a kind-hearted soul whose fragile outward appearance and strikingly fair complexion seemed somewhat out of place in a farmer. His hair was almost white, another oddity on a man who looked otherwise much younger than his years.

"Wow, Buck! From space to middle America in an instant, almost," noted Barnes, placing his arm around Buck and looking him over with affection. "And you look more like your mom every time I see you."

"Half an hour from the space station to the Cape, four hours by levitation express train to the Metro terminal. It's fast, all right," he replied. "And if I look like my mom, I probably look like you, too. Dad always said you really favored her."

"How fast does that thing go, anyway?" Barnes asked, postponing all painful questions for the moment. "Maybe I'll go for a ride sometime."

"The train? Around 400 miles per hour. Suspended above the track by a superconducting magnetic field. Quite a deal. They're even using the same levitation principle to slingshot the shuttle into space now. Saves fuel for maneuvering in orbit."

"I'm glad I'm just a farmer. My work incorporates enough of that high tech stuff for me," Barnes commented, sensing that the inevitable discussion of the accident was fast upon them.

"Tell me what happened, Bill," young Morgan requested, feeling the same urgency that the time had come to cut the small talk. "Mr. Russell told me some on the train, but he was terribly vague. He's hard to talk to, for some reason. Anyway, I want to hear it from you."

"It just blew up, Buck. I don't understand how. If I knew what happened, I'd tell you. I've got the same system over on my side of the fencerow. There's a fail-safe mechanism that just didn't fail safely. The sheriff has searched for clues that someone might have tampered with it, but so far they haven't found anything. We just don't know."

"Was there any reason for anyone to alter the thing? Dad didn't have any enemies that I know about."

"The possibilities are being investigated. Your dad had a verbal altercation with a guy demonstrating at the protein plant a couple of weeks ago. The guy laid down in the road and wouldn't let him pass. Your dad got out and tried to reason with him to no avail. The security camera got it all on holo."

"Those guys! They can be mean sometimes. I've seen them in action. They need to check all of them out, because Dad has had confrontations with them in the past. But I hope they're not capable of murder."

"So far it's impossible to say, according to the sheriff. A simple intentionally misconnected line could have done it. There was so much damage the evidence is going to be hard to read."

"He didn't suffer any, did he, Bill?"

"No, that's the only good thing. It was instant death. Just look at that building. We had to put down several badly wounded sheep, and lost about forty in the adjacent pen."

The two walked the length of a cluster of buildings that constituted the main farm facility and inspected tangles of steel girders and twisted sheets of metal that had been the fuel processing plant. The blast had created a hole in the ground more than fifty feet across and thirty feet deep at the main storage area.

"What about the remains, Uncle Bill?"

"Pastor Don is going to talk to you about that. I'd rather leave that to him. Here he comes now," Barnes answered, pointing to an arriving vehicle.

Pastor Don got out, accompanied by his wife Julie, as well as the astronaut's former teacher Judy Hancock. There were hugs and handshakes and tears flowed freely, though the young officer tried to fight back his emotions, however unsuccessfully.

"We're waiting for you to finalize funeral arrangements, Buck. We've tentatively scheduled it tomorrow afternoon. The U.S. Army is sending down an honor guard to conduct a full military funeral."

"Where is his body, Pastor Don?"

"At Adrian Funeral Home. It's so damaged I wouldn't want to look at it if I were you. I know that's painful, son, but it's the truth," the old preacher explained gently.

The young man winced perceptibly. Recovering quickly, he answered in as masculine a fashion as he could muster.

"All right, Pastor Don. Full military honors is fine. We'll bury the remains next to Mom in the east cemetery. That would please Dad, I think."

"I know it would, Buck. He loved your mom dearly and hardly looked at another woman from the day she died, as far as I know. And he really gave his whole life to this place, so it's more than appropriate that he rest here. People around here will fondly remember Jim Morgan for a very long time, I can tell you."

Somehow the kind words brought a measure of comfort, a solace that had been lacking up to this point. It was a balm that an anguished young soul sorely needed.

"He was the greatest father a boy could ask for, Pastor Don. I'm really going to miss him," Morgan said quietly as a faint quivering crept into his deep voice.

"You'll see him again someday, Buck," interjected Mrs. Hancock. "I know for certain that he was a Christian and that he will rise again at the Lord's call."

Young Morgan considered the statement silently and gazed out into the distance over the picturesque pastoral landscape, the blue sky, and the fluffy white clouds. How could she know something like that? Where was the evidence? It almost made him angry and he felt the blood rising hotly to his head. He was able to calm himself without revealing his thoughts, and he settled down momentarily. She was just trying to comfort him, but this type of fantasy just could not be. Dead is dead and gone is gone. And if that's indeed the truth of the matter, perhaps that was why it hurt with such an agonizing pain. Oh, Dad, why did this have to happen? The healthy man should have lived fifty more years, but he was suddenly lost to mysterious circumstance. Could a divine providence be so cruel?

There was a flurry of necessary activity in preparation for the funeral, and by evening Buck was totally exhausted from twenty-four hours without sleep. He felt so numb that he gave only brief, sad thought to the fact that he was alone in the farmhouse for the first time in his life. Next morning he slept late, and was awakened by an insistent knock on the front door.

Fighting off his sleepiness, he made his way to the front room, drawing on a housecoat and rubbing the stubble of emerging beard as he walked. He pulled aside the colorful curtain, and there was an army sedan sitting in the driveway. He could see a distinct row of military buttons close to the door, plainly part of a dress uniform. He turned the knob and tugged, and the door creaked open. He found himself face to face with a smartly dressed female officer, accompanied by a somber sergeant.

"Lieutenant Morgan? I'm Lieutenant JoEllen Thacker. Remember me?"

Sleepiness fled completely as Buck tried to gather his composure. He felt himself stammering as never before in his life, trying to fathom this turn of events. His first thought was that he had to look simply awful, just up from bed after crashing for many hours. Finally, he uttered through faltering lips, "The queen of...of the Point. Or should I say that?"

"I've heard that nickname. I never felt like a queen, frankly. I'm commander of the funeral party. It's part of my job. I'm sorry about your father."

"Yeah, thanks, Lieutenant," he said with little emotion, throwing out his hands in a gesture of resignation. The young woman's eyes were as sparkling and alive as ever, and the fit of her uniform was immaculate. Just like he remembered. "Want to come in? I'm a little in disarray, I'm afraid."

"We need to talk some about the physical details of my detachment's duties, Lieutenant Morgan. I spoke with the minister yesterday. I just need to confirm a couple of items."

"No problem. And you're welcome to call me Buck, if you like," he said as he backed from the room, shooting a glance at the sergeant. "After all, no need to be so formal when we're old classmates. If you'll give me a few minutes, Lieutenant Thacker, I'll get dressed. Might take more than a few minutes, matter of fact."

"Not necessary. And you can call me JoEllen. We've plenty of time. I'll wait."

As he showered, shaved, and dressed, Buck's heart was racing, and he had that same old feeling—is it helplessness? He wasn't sure. When he was spic and span, he returned to the living room.

"I still can't believe this. A classmate from the Point on my front porch. And the prettiest one in my class, I must say."

"Don't be a chauvinist. And I'm here because your father was a hero of the first order. We don't do two Silver Star funerals a year. He must have been special."

"Indeed he was. I've never hurt over anything so much in my life. The old home place here will never be the same. By the way, didn't you get married after graduation?"

The lady's demeanor changed only slightly, and pain was only distantly visible. She looked at Buck with her face devoid of expression.

"It fell through. Turned out the guy I was going to marry was already married—to somebody else. I'd already sent invitations. I thought I knew him, but I didn't. I learned a lesson, but it was kind of embarrassing."

"I'm sorry, JoEllen. And I regret that you had to come here for another sad occasion."

205

"Life is full of them. Now, about the funeral..."

*   *   *

An adoring segment of the community attended the funeral the next day, most of them to pay homage to a departed solid citizen. Some came for a look at a local hero, a youthful West Pointer turned astronaut. The church overflowed with people in uncommon fashion. Pastor Don delivered an uncomfortable sermon on the brevity and uncertainty of life and the need to walk with God while we're here. He made the point that Jim Morgan's soul rested with God because of the life he had lived and because of important eternal decisions he had made. Buck Morgan was buoyed beyond reason by such confident statements, though his circumspect mindset still rejected the idea as absolutely implausible.

He felt a little guilty about the dichotomy he was experiencing, profound grief over the loss of his father combined with a teenager's giddiness at seeing Lieutenant Thacker again. She smartly directed the six enlisted men throughout the proceedings, and their contribution to the proceedings was flawless.

Amid the crush of mourners, the young woman loomed like a giant. Soil was landing in the new grave with resounding thumps on the coffin, burying a huge part of Buck Morgan's past. Her duties finished and the squad dismissed, she walked over to Buck and stuck out her hand.

"Once more, my deepest regrets."

"And mine for your recent tragedy," he said with feeling. He swallowed hard before continuing, as her hand lingered ever so briefly in his. "JoEllen, could I see you again sometime?"

"Aren't you off on a big trip in space?"

"Not for a while. Where are you based?"

"Fort Leonard Wood, Missouri. Here's my card. You can call me if you get a chance."

"Thanks. I will. And I appreciate your coming."

She turned and walked away, while his eyes followed her almost to the point of becoming conspicuous. He felt an almost visible tremble as he turned to shake hands with another person offering condolences.

Ralph Russell walked with him over the farm the next day reminiscing about old times, quail hunts, deer research, and the like, while they visited all Jim Morgan's special places. There were distinct, fresh tracks of another grizzly bear in the creek bed, this time a female accompanied by a half-grown cub. Neither of them was surprised at the finding because the magnificent giants were becoming ever more common in farm country.

The weather initially was pleasant as they walked to the top of Jim Morgan's favorite hill and surveyed the broad valley where the life-giving stream disappeared into the distance. They talked extensively of life and science and the relationship between the two. As had been the case on the train ride from the Cape, the words of his former teacher were of little comfort to the hurting young man. There was a notable deficiency of soothing consolation in Russell's comments, and nothing at all to really help the ache in his heart, except for the succor of the company of a man he had long respected. Young Morgan surmised that the death of a loved one was an area where science was glaringly deficient. Who could understand it?

As they tarried enjoying the view, storm clouds were gathering, at first in the distance and then looming closer and more threatening. They hurried back toward the safety of the sturdy farmhouse, and arrived just in time to avoid a thorough drenching from a subsequent downpour, though thumb-sized droplets did chase them the final distance across the farmyard. Included in the sudden violent rage was a hailstorm of such intensity that neither of them could recall a similar tempest.

When the furious weather had subsided almost as abruptly as it had appeared, a gorgeous rainbow appeared to the west of the farm, as if summoned by the gods. It created a complete semicircle of prismatic colors that formed an overarching frame for the pastoral setting. Young Morgan was no less than completely speechless at the occurrence, and he and Russell watched in silence until the phenomenon faded spontaneously.

Selling the farm would be left with the Morgan attorney. Buck's first cousin Jerry Barnes, Uncle Bill's son, had already offered a very fair price. Accepting the proposal was easy, because Buck couldn't think of another person in the world he would rather own the farm than a member of the Barnes family, his only living relatives.

Back at the venerable farmhouse, it was a painstaking task to go through the many personal effects his father had left behind. He picked up the old shotgun his father had presented him, so plain yet so priceless, so worn and so old. He admired the well-preserved firearm at some length while he almost choked with unfamiliar emotions. More than anything else he could imagine, the cherished fowling piece evoked profound memories of happy days with Jim Morgan. He put a coat of synthetic preservative on the smooth external surfaces before setting it aside.

He packed his father's personal items, pictures of Buck's mother, several medals from the war, and the like. He would arrange storage of these in a bank vault, and he would also put that precious old shotgun there for safekeeping. He rummaged through the house putting everything in order, and noted the now-blackened quail cooking pot in one corner of the kitchen. He took special pains to scrub it up and then placed it prominently on the aging stove. The young man almost got a tear in his eye as he remembered how impressed his father had been when he had demonstrated the amazing properties of the high-technology vessel to him. Unquestionably it had been used repeatedly.

While cleaning out one closet he saw a book he hadn't seen before. It was his father's Bible, hardly worn at all but quite fragile and old. The date of his parents' wedding was prominently inscribed in his mother's handwriting inside the front cover.

He picked it up, and it fell open to a place with a passage underlined. Buck read it thoughtfully:

Thus says the Lord,

Cursed is the man who trusts in mankind
And who makes flesh his strength,
And whose heart turns away from the Lord.
For he will be like a bush in the desert
And will not see when prosperity comes
But will live in stony wastes in the wilderness,
A land of salt without inhabitant.
Blessed is the man who trusts in the Lord
And whose trust is the Lord.

Buck Morgan was by no means convinced, but he did remember for the first time since graduation day that he had a Bible of his own, the one given him by Judy Hancock. He had left it among his belongings in his old room, and he went straightway there and located it. He placed the heirloom Bible among the items to be placed in the bank vault.

But he put his own unused and forgotten Bible with the gold lettering into his duffel. And he underlined that same passage before he tucked the book in securely.

CHAPTER 18

September 2068

Ralph Russell sat in a darkened room thinking, simply thinking. He had spent a lifetime doing just that, and by Mother Earth, he had accomplished a few meaningful victories over the years. He leaned back and reflected on some of the prize students he had turned out, and naturally his thoughts gravitated to Buck Morgan, perhaps his most outstanding contribution to the world. The astronaut was away on a deep space mission that would perhaps launch him into even greater endeavors in the future. Yes, there was some degree of satisfaction in such successes as Morgan.

Russell stared blankly at the opposite wall, and with undisguised gloom he wondered where his wife Rhetta was at that very moment. He hadn't seen her today, though she was usually in and out of their home regularly. Russell's declining ability to be intimate with his spouse had driven a wedge between them that gnawed like a cancer at the aging teacher. Worse, her attraction to other men had become epidemic, and she seldom even pretended to be his wife any more. In the prevailing loose moral climate, a one-night stand was available at any bar, so he shared her with whomever she chose. Share, he thought darkly. The infrequency of the couple's nights together could hardly even qualify as sharing.

Perhaps the most painful aspect, though, was the man she selected as her most frequent partner. Everyone in the school business, and half the community besides, knew that Rhetta was engaged in a torrid, long-running affair with Rudy McGill, who had now been promoted to chief administrator of the entire system. McGill smirked openly at Russell every time he saw him, and did no small amount of boasting to colleagues behind Russell's back about his adventures with Rhetta. Shame was returned to poor Russell in myriad ways, often in the form of veiled taunts from other teachers or overt snickers from groups of rowdy students he passed in the corridors. Russell fumed now at the thought, and his anger and hurt boiled into a raging hatred for his overbearing boss. Someday the insensitive and uncaring jargonaut would be held accountable, he resolved grimly. Somehow. And he just might get his wife back, too.

Groping in the darkness, he grasped a knob on the bottom drawer of a chest next to his chair. Rummaging among the potpourri that littered the space, he located what he was seeking. It was heavy, metallic, and ominous as he retrieved it from the dim recess. The shape of such instruments had changed little over the last couple of centuries. The pistol was an old Smith & Wesson .357 Magnum, passed down from a grandfather who had died years ago. Russell practiced with the weapon only rarely, but now he fingered the pitted metal and the wooden grips pensively. He wondered if there was power to right wrongs in the sinister device. He had always disdained, and even railed against, such actions as he now idly contemplated in his profound depression. No, he decided adamantly, to do something like that was unthinkable to a rational mind.

His finger traced over the stern outlines of the gun, and he gripped the handle like a frontier lawman or outlaw of old. He lifted the weighty piece and pointed it here and there in mock action. He then placed the muzzle to his temple, wondering what sensations a blast from that fearsome orifice might deliver to the recipient. No, he certainly wasn't likely to activate such destructive impulses, no matter how depressed and lonely he became. He lowered the pistol. That approach would be too easy and too convenient. There had to be a better and more efficacious way. He needed more time to think.

He placed the weapon back in the drawer, covered it with papers and journals, and closed it emphatically. Indeed, he would find a solution and a way to vindicate himself. Somehow.

* * *

Far behind the speeding *Delta Dare* lay Mars, the Moon, Earth, and the vastness of interplanetary space. Ahead of the ship stretched a void of unimaginable infinity. The ship had slipped easily out of the iron grip of Earth's gravity almost two years before, and now the sun continued to shrink with the passing of weeks. The home planet initially had begun to look like a magnificent dark moon backlit by the majestic life-giving luminary orb, but now even the sun was gradually fading in glory. Earth was so remote as to be almost impossible to locate with the naked eye. When the sun had become the only significant body in the sky in terms of brightness, the study of the universe had begun in earnest. Conditions for scientific observation couldn't be better, and Buck Morgan was in best form.

On his return to his assignment on Space Station Delta, young Morgan had found solace in his work, a measure of consolation that was unavailable in Adrian, Kansas. His relatives Bill and Carol Barnes, as well as his cousin Jerry, had done all they could to make the loss easier, but there seemed to be little real comfort to be found. The young man's enthusiasm for the dangerous work of space had been temporarily dampened by the savage death of his father. He had briefly considered a more extended stay on the planet's surface to regroup and re-establish his identity and priorities. He finally had rejected such thoughts and had opted for what seemed the logical and reasonable course. His father was irretrievably dead so it had made no sense to prolong and magnify that unpleasant period of grief. His best choice had been to get back to work in his chosen vocation.

He had taken an eventful trip to Fort Leonard Wood. His chances with beautiful JoEllen Thacker had seemed remote, but he had finally spent enough time with her to know that she was more than something special. Their date at the Officer's Club had been intimate in terms of conversation, and she had seemed to really like young Morgan. Instead of another trip back to Adrian to see relatives, he had returned there to Missouri on furlough once more before his ship had departed. JoEllen had seemed eminently glad to see him, and they had laughed together over some of the cadet escapades that occurred during their years at the Point. He had developed a deep feeling for her, but he wasn't at all certain it was reciprocal. After all, he was going to be away for an awfully long time. They stayed in touch via holo-mail, but the conversations seemed distressingly superficial and devoid of real meaning. Nevertheless, her fascinating image never failed to make his heart sing with inexpressible joy.

By now the months were stretching into years. The young astronaut still chafed at the research work he was missing back in Earth orbit, where scientists should by now be putting the finishing touches on the new nuclear pulse cruiser, the *Chuck Yeager*.

Sometimes it could get a bit boring aboard the *Delta Dare* during its six year run to Mars and Jupiter's moon Ganymede. Stops had already been accomplished at Moon Base and Mars. At Moon Base the interplanetary cruiser had picked up supplies for the long voyage, and Morgan had walked on his first alien world. At Mars Station, they had offloaded supplies for the mining and exploration effort there and had taken on many tons of platinum and titanium blocks. At Mars they had also picked up the *Delta Dare*'s new first mate, Lieutenant Jeremiah Smith, with whom Morgan had rapidly established a growing friendship. There was a crew of twenty-four souls on the cruiser, most of whom were non-commissioned personnel. Three women were among the enlisted crew, but fraternizing with them by officers was strictly prohibited by Astronaut Corps regulations.

Smith was proud of his western heritage, being the descendant of pioneers who had settled in southern Montana. He had finished a couple of years ahead of Buck Morgan at West Point. The two hadn't known each other there, but they had so much in common that they never lacked for interesting conversation. Smith was also a dedicated outdoorsman and a member of Morgan's old conservation club. The two swapped hunting stories with regularity and occasionally joked about renaming their organization the Interplanetary Conservation Club. Smith was of about the same medium build as Morgan, somewhat more slender but strong and vigorous just the same. His ample sandy hair had a way of looking very wild, defying his attempts to control it, even with the latest in twenty-first century hair management technology.

"Don't look so serious, Bucko. What do you see out there?" asked Smith as he entered the observatory section.

"I've been studying the Proxima Centauri group for the past few watches, Smitty. They say there are no planets around any of the stars, but I'm not so sure. Look at this tracing of Alpha Centauri A," Morgan commented, laying out a computerized graphic to demonstrate his point. "See this blip and that one—couldn't those be planetary?"

"I doubt it, Bucko. Those aren't new discoveries, you know. I think those are just the effects of two nearby stars in the complex. For decades everyone has been convinced that our nearest neighbor couldn't have a solar system. I wish it did, but it's unlikely," Smith responded. "Anyway, even when the new nuclear pulse engines come on line, we'll still be over eighty years away from Centauri, so it's only academic at this stage."

Young Morgan looked up at the mention of the nuclear pulse engines, a distinct look of yearning crossing his face.

"Not out of the question, though, Smitty. There'll be another generation, or two or three, of those engines and they'll get faster. And I think we're on the verge of a basic breakthrough on that new engine type."

"Ah, yes, antimatter conversion. I've heard a lot of excitement brewing over those babies lately. We didn't even have schematics when I left Earth."

"I spent a good deal of time with Dr. Gerald Schultz at the Cape during training. He's the lead scientist researching antimatter conversion. He seems to think we'll be well on our way to actually building a prototype of such an engine within a very few years. Perhaps by the time we return. With antimatter conversion, they can apparently invert the mass of matter, actually helping to propel the craft, at least theoretically, instead of mass becoming an increasing drag as light speed is approached."

"Bucko, they could just run out and pick us up before we get to Ganymede, couldn't they? Nah, it'll take years of research and development. That kind of project always takes more time than the eggheads forecast. We won't even have the first nuclear pulse engines up and running when we get back unless everything goes remarkably smooth with testing."

Both the men respectfully acknowledged entry of Colonel Maxwell Scott, commander of the *Delta Dare*, into the observatory. Scott was a slightly balding veteran who was trim and fit, and whose face was marred by the near-universal facial scarring that afflicted older space explorers. He had a scraggly mustache, which he wore neatly trimmed, and like many career astronauts he kept his scalp trimmed almost to the skin. In his gruff voice he spoke in his typical British accent on overhearing their conversation.

"Those n-p engines will allow them to shrink planetary trips to the level of global travel in terms of time," he said to them. "No more of this conventional rocket travel. I'm glad you men got in on some of it, though. It's a long trip, but you'd be like sailors who never used sails if you hadn't been able to experience it."

"Good point, sir. By the time we get back, they'll be decommissioning and recycling these old cruisers as they arrive back in orbit. Barring a stunning failure of the n-p tests, this could be the last voyage of the *Delta Dare*," Smith prognosticated.

"Could be," said Scott. He gave an almost imperceptible sigh and just a hint of nostalgia crept into his voice. Maybe the colonel did feel like an old salt making his last wind-powered ocean trip before switching to a steamer. It was possible to imagine a strong mariner voice calling out commands to batten down the hatches or to furl the canvas.

"Activating gamma thruster group! All hands and cargo must be secured! Ready for firing when ordered," called a metallic artificial voice.

Morgan stowed the instrument he was using to scan the remote skies, quickly locking it into position. He already knew what was coming. He briskly made his way back to the ship command post and assumed his seat.

Asteroid watch could be boring, but it was a necessary drill. There on the screen was indication of a car-sized boulder closing with the ship. They had passed hundreds of them, some close enough to actually see when they passed, but others detectable only electronically. Several times since entering the asteroid belt they had taken evasive maneuvers, and grains of matter impacted the craft from time to time, most of them striking the frontal plate that was designed to absorb such impacts. Rarely a melon-sized chunk would ricochet off the shield with thunderous effect, but anything larger they meticulously avoided.

Five more inauspicious blips were now showing on the screen adjacent the largest onrushing body. They were spread out in virtually a star-shaped array, and the ship's profile on the screen electronically overlay the flight of asteroids. Morgan lifted and turned the image of the *Delta Dare* to try and fit it between them graphically, a task that was now routine to him. One had to be sure the big guy would miss. The others were of various sizes, up to about six feet in diameter. They needed sorely to miss all of them, but if the big one should hit, it would be absolute disaster. An intense shower of smaller asteroids pelted the ship as he twisted and rotated the craft's profile.

It wouldn't fit! Collision with one or more of the streaking boulders seemed inevitable. Alarmed, Morgan summoned help from the computer, and ignited a thruster that would move them out of a collision course with the big one.

"Colonel, trouble! We're getting red indicators all over the flight envelope we're entering. The computer's searching for an avoidance possibility."

"What? Collision with a big one?" asked Scott, leaning over Morgan's shoulder and examining the screen as more insistent small impacts reverberated through the craft. "My God, it looks like the whole asteroid belt is shooting at us!"

"Two minutes to impact as we now fly, sir," said Morgan as he worked, a bit of anguish finding its way into his voice. "Got to find a position to fit us through here."

Several more of the orbiting meteors were now on the screen, all of them bearing down on them at many times the speed of sound. The computer had all the trajectories plotted, but that only confirmed that they had a colossal problem. Morgan furiously examined and rejected every suggestion made by the computer, and noted that the ship had already edged away from the trajectory of the largest body. Small comfort, he thought, if two or three of the others hit us.

How to get this ship past these flying rocks, Morgan pondered. Nobody online in the control room had found a solution so far, and time was running out fast. He looked up momentarily and noted nervous perspiration staining Smith's face, and frantic activity all over the room. In desperation, Morgan rotated the screen image of the *Delta Dare* to a radically nose-up position, a possible attitude but one that would expose the soft underbelly to damage from any undetected debris. The big one was just off the screen in the new cyberenvelope, a safe but perilously close passing distance away.

There appeared to be a sufficient space for asteroid number two to fit in the gap between the meteor shield and the ship's main control room in this position, but it would be crowded. There were indentations in the profile of the *Delta Dare* that would allow numbers three, four, and five to pass literally through the ship's structure without touching it. Only number six would clip the right half of the front control room. Man, you only read about this kind of thing, thought Morgan as he worked feverishly. There were just seconds left to make the move and find somewhere to tuck number six.

"Sir, pull up this flight profile," he exclaimed to Scott. "I've got all but the last one trimmed in tight!"

"That's the best we can do, Morgan!" returned Scott "Thrusters ignited!"

The massive ship trembled as the small side rockets came to life and spit streaks of fire into the dark void. The rotation was maddeningly slow, and all hands frantically sought to find a space in which the last rock could pass without damaging the craft. They had precious little room to maneuver the ship lest they shift position so that they were imperiled by one of the other asteroids. Morgan tried every conceivable perspective, and finally hit on a remote possibility. Turning the nose of the ship ever so slightly on his computer screen, the last rock could be made to strike a glancing blow to the collision shield and still leave just enough room for the others to pass. With just a little bit of luck.

"Colonel, I've got it!"

"Bully good show, my good man," said Scott when he saw the profile. "Attitude thrusters firing!"

The ship moved imperceptibly as the small rockets fired as ordered, and then reversed themselves to stop the motion. Suspended like a giant spider on a bulls eye, they waited while several hundred tons of rock avalanched toward them with unstoppable momentum.

They could only hope the calculations were exact within inches. They could hardly see the asteroids as they swooped by the ship. The big one passed first, hidden below them out of sight. The one between the control room and the collision shield zipped through in a hardly perceptible dusky blur and was gone. The three that passed more rearward were seen only on the computer, and as they passed without contact the men breathed a sigh of relief. The blast of the last rock careening off the collision shield shook the perceivable universe and sent mighty reverberations throughout the *Delta Dare*, sending earth, plants, and animals flying as shock scrambled the renewables section badly.

"Wow," said Morgan, only now noticing his sweating palms and face. "Was that ever close!"

"Fun, huh, Bucko?" asked Smith of no one in particular.

"Same thing happened to the cruiser *Ernest Warren* a few years back. Third trip to the planets for that great ship. Only it didn't make it," said Scott. "Lost a bunch of good people on that one."

"Pretty awful fate for a ship named for the guy who explored Mars," observed Smith. "Ironic, too. He died on his third voyage there, didn't he?"

"Sure did. Yes, there's an element of irony there. You guys visited the Warren Memorial on Mars, didn't you?"

"Yes, sir. Incredible," responded Smith. Morgan looked up at him as he recalled the dead man on display there. An eerie play of lights danced on the perpetually frozen face of Ernest Warren, who had died in a "red-out," or Martian dust storm. A little quiver tickled his spine as the thought of death and its inevitability surfaced in his mind. They had just come so very close to such oblivion.

"Colonel, have you heard of the solution they've designed? I mean to eliminate these collisions?" Morgan asked the commander.

"Eliminate them? Oh, yes, something about a laser. How does it work?"

"It's called the plasmafyer hyperlaser. Dr. Gerald Schultz has a design they're going to use on nuclear pulse cruisers. It'll dissolve the panic in such a situation as this one," said Morgan.

All soon returned to business as usual after they adjusted the ship's position and configuration back to normal. All in a day's work, thought Morgan as he helped put the finishing touches on the maneuver and rechecked coordinates for Jupiter.

Inside, the *Delta Dare* was comfortable and spacious, with generously outfitted living space and crew quarters. It had an ongoing bioresearch facility that housed numerous species of plants and animals in a nearly natural setting. These were not only experiments in progress but also provided an important renewable food source for deep space journeys. The artificial gravity wasn't as good as the latest technology, but it was quite passable, and the radiation shield had been upgraded to the very latest design.

After his watch was over, Morgan settled into his quarters with a mind toward doing a little reading and researching. He sent off his monthly inquiry to the Adrian County Sheriff's Office requesting a status report on his father's case, though the replies lately had become more terse and Morgan sensed the case was hopeless. With some sense of despair he contemplated the situation, and while he pondered, Jeremiah Smith entered his quarters after a tentative knock on the metal door facing.

"Why so glum, Bucko?"

He looked at his wild-haired first mate and forced a smile. He hadn't realized his feelings were so transparent, and he was a little surprised that his friend was becoming so perceptive about his moods.

"You might not understand, Smitty," he replied, trying to sound upbeat. "My father was killed three years ago, and nobody's doing anything to find out why. I told you he died in a farm mishap, but I've never been convinced that it was accidental."

"How so, if I might ask? Wasn't it an explosion in a fuel facility? Happens every day."

"Not to people like my father. He was a stickler for keeping all the rules. Anyway, the law enforcement people back home are losing interest."

Smith rested a hand on Morgan's shoulder and gave him a resounding and masculine pat. A human being's touch always felt strange to Morgan, unnatural. Smith was the only person on board who ever touched him purposefully, or with the slightest degree of understanding. The hand felt as comforting as a warm cup of milk, yet it was applied as casually as a mother might touch a son.

"Come on down to renewables after your rest. We're planting broccoli and turnips. Time to go low tech," said Smith as he slipped out the door.

"I might see you shortly," he called after him.

During the long trip, the renewable resources garden was a spot Morgan loved to frequent. Everything on the ship was recycled, even the human waste, and the garden grew like nothing he had ever seen. Protein-producing animals fattened and reproduced at an astounding pace, their forage was so rich and nutritious. Maybe he had a little streak of farmer left in him after all, and he took great joy in pitching in to help with the work involved. He found himself quite often at the finish of his watch with dirt under his fingernails from working the fertile loam. How unlikely that such simple non-technical pursuits could bring unending satisfaction. His dad would have been proud of him for carrying on so naturally in his established family tradition. It wasn't mining like they were doing on Mars, but it was still playing in the dirt.

Ah, yes, he thought as he lay in the subdued light. The mines. Would they ever supply enough metal to make the space program pay for itself? With improved speed from the new edition engines, the cruisers could hopefully make the mining effort far more worthwhile. The *Delta Dare* was hauling back several hundred tons of pure metal, which had been shuttled up to the orbiting cruiser as the planetary landers made their repetitive runs. The solid bricks had been amazingly easy to transport up to the cruiser because of the relatively low Martian gravity, only thirty-eight percent as strong as Earth's. When cross loading pure metal ingots from lander to cruiser, the gigantic blocks had been remarkably easy to handle in the weightlessness of space.

One of the enlisted women was assisting with the farm work, and Morgan couldn't help but notice her as she stooped to dig in the productive soil. Thoughts of graceful JoEllen Thacker were seldom far from his mind, and naturally her image clouded his mind at this prompting. There had been trouble on some interplanetary flights because of women, and rules regarding them were now rigorously enforced, so officers on this trip faced no real temptation in this regard. Morgan wasn't so sure about what went on in the noncommissioned quarters of the ship.

Morgan often relieved his own monotony, and contributed to the mental health of his co-voyagers, by playing music on the piano. Such an instrument was a central part of the entertainment complex for all interplanetary craft, but not every voyage had such a talented player. During off hours, many happy moments were spent by the crew listening and relaxing to magnificent music, played to perfection by the young astronaut in tune with the mood and events of the day. Sometimes, when duties allowed, enlisted men and women danced as he played, the ladies passing among the males as if to distribute their feminine charms as widely as possible. It seemed to be good for all of them.

The giant sphere of the planet Jupiter grew ever closer. A dozen moons of all sizes were visible now, and Ganymede was one of the more prominent. The big moon had been selected for a base because of its size and the fact that the gravity there was nearly as strong as that of Mars. The cruiser slipped into orbit around the planet-sized satellite after a powerful reverse thrust burn, mimicking exactly the procedure used to achieve orbit around Mars.

"Ganymede Station, prepare to receive landers," the radio operator barked.

"Roger, *Delta Dare*. Welcome back," came the voice. "We're glad to see you."

"What's for dinner?" inquired Lieutenant Smith, making small talk as the crew finished loading the landers. It was his job to monitor the radios constantly and maintain contact.

"Home grown potatoes, beans, and protein. Straight from renewables. Nothing canned for our guests."

"Sounds great. See you shortly," returned Smith. He smiled wryly as he turned to Morgan, "Truth is, I'm the guy who has to stay with the ship, Bucko. Maybe I'll get down there before we leave, though."

"Sure you will. If the Colonel will let me take over for you, you make a trip down."

"Thanks, old buddy. He will. How am I going to repay such favors?"

For now it was Morgan's turn. He and the other lander pilots ferried the goods in record time. There was then plenty of time for food, good times, and exploring.

Ganymede Station was much newer than Mars Station and had a shiny, glistening appearance throughout. The base there had been designed in painstaking detail to function on the frozen surface, the most hostile environment into which human beings had thus far ventured to establish a permanent presence. The renewables garden wasn't yet complete, and towering girders for a massive canopy were just taking shape. A temporary bubble inflated with an imported atmosphere served as a fresh food source for now, but later a permanent facility would be much larger and more substantial. One marveled repeatedly at the rising and setting of the magnificent planet nearby, its size dominating the entire sky. It seemed to be looking at them with its stormy red eye, a prominent feature that was so large it could swallow hundreds of bodies the size of Earth. There was much to see and do here, and everyone was anxious to complete the ferrying runs.

*   *   *

Back in Adrian, Kansas, Rhetta Russell slipped out the door of the modest home without so much as a goodbye to her husband. He knew where she was going, and he was pitifully powerless to stop her. How he longed to be held by her, to just be close to her. He would give anything to feel that tender touch just one more time. He had grown far more despondent in recent weeks, and he wasn't sure how much longer he could take the loneliness and depression. Abuse from hecklers at school had increased as his retirement date neared, and it was now unending, tenacious, and vicious.

Gone were challenging projects like he had done so many years ago with students like Buck Morgan. Gone was the esteem of a grateful community. Gone, woefully, was the love he had shared with a beautiful young wife, a love that was giddy and fun, whether it had been genuine or not. More than any other time in his long life, he doubted the wisdom of the course he had chosen for himself. Where were the elusive answers to the real questions of life? Did anything at all really matter? Was there any purpose to this existence? These were questions he pondered incessantly in his isolation and his despair.

Yes, Ralph Russell was bitter, too. He hated the school system that now mocked and scorned him. He hated his wife's lovers, accumulated with such ease and abandon. He hated—yes, he hated Rudy McGill more than anything else. He hated him with a malevolence that was more than hate, it was absolute disgust, profound and putrid. Rhetta would be with Rudy tonight, almost certainly. Tonight was their regular night. He was almost certain he knew where they would be from a taunt he had heard recently, a caustic jeer directed at him from a group of students that mentioned the Hat Trick Motel, famed for just such illicit trysts.

Russell again opened the drawer of his chairside chest and fumbled once more for the pistol he had not summoned the courage to use. Could he somehow overcome his own doubts and purge the tormentors from his life? He didn't know. He stood up and held the weapon at arm's length, sighting down the ominous barrel. He opened the magazine and counted the deadly shells that the device contained. Nine. He extracted one and examined it, his scientific mind dissecting the mechanism that propelled these blunt and elementary lead projectiles in such deadly fashion. It was really a very simplistic system, indeed. He dropped the tiny monster back into its launching pad and crisply snapped the cylinder shut. He then jammed the pistol behind his belt and covered its protruding handle with his shirttail.

Maybe he would just take a drive with the steel companion at his side. He could not imagine actually taking any drastic action, but somehow the feel of cold metal against his belly was comforting, tightening his waist and tenting his leather trousers in a very masculine way. He felt an irresistible attraction to his vehicle, and shortly he was motoring toward the celebrated intersection where the holographic cowboy stood guard.

As he drove, visions of his lovely wife in the arms of Rudy McGill haunted his anguished mind, bringing anger of intensity such as he had not experienced before. Frustration, irritation, even mild raving was nothing new. But now the emotion blossomed into a deepening rage that was soon brimming over, clouding his judgment.

In a short time the bright undulation of the Hat Trick sign loomed just ahead. As he pulled into the motel yard, he immediately saw his wife's vehicle parked near the main door. By now a sinister plan had formed in his mind, a course of action that was most irrational, but seemed to be a legitimate alternative to an infuriated man.

Nobody was stationed at the desk this time of night. That was all the better, anyway. It was easy to find out which room she had entered. He engaged his wallet pee-cee to the desk terminal and quickly identified the password. His tiny computer then handily bypassed the motel security code, and soon he was scrolling the guest list unhindered. Rudy McGill. Room 215.

Approaching the door with that number, he could hear inside undisguised sounds of passion. It was clear what was going on, and a seething jealousy magnified many fold in the Russell's heart. He put his shoulder to the door and heaved with all his might as a rush of adrenaline energized his small frame with almost supernatural strength. The structure gave way and burst open, revealing a horrified couple in the most intimate of embraces. Shots rang out repeatedly, a total of eight times. There was brief silence, and then one more explosion sounded. Ominous silence then prevailed in room 215 of the Hat Trick Motel.

*   *   *

Time at Ganymede Station seemed even more attenuated than their stop at Mars Station. Considering time to relieve Smith for an extra couple of days, Buck Morgan's visit seemed much shorter than he desired. Soon they were saying good-byes once again and preparing for departure.

"All systems are go, Smitty," Morgan relayed from his station.

"Ignition, Colonel Scott," chorused Smith.

The *Delta Dare* groaned as all four massive engines awakened and rumbled to life once again. The hungry beasts had been revitalized again with hydrogen and oxygen distilled from the lunar base. Gargantuan tongues of flame spit a half-mile of pyrotechnic magic into the dark vacuum over Ganymede as 200 million horsepower drove the monstrous ship forward, pinning the inhabitants with multiple G's for the duration of a white-hot rocket burn. Computer trajectory for Earth was locked into the navigation system and the exact number of seconds of thrust to achieve that objective had been calculated. Forward motion was smooth but incredibly energetic, virtually the same as departure from other stops.

"Coordinates for Earth captured and secured," said Smith.

The burn to escape Jupiter's gravity used up a huge quantity of precious fuel, leaving just enough for braking to enter Earth orbit three years down the road.

"Smitty, this old ship's a paddle wheeler compared to the *Chuck Yeager*. Should have been named *Delta Queen*. Really neat they're naming the first nuclear pulse ship after the man who broke the sound barrier, don't you think?"

"Appropriate in a way. They say those engines are apt to let us break the 10,000 miles per second barrier. If this works out as expected, we'll be able to legitimately measure our speed as a fraction of c for the first time in history," Smith replied, referring to the c for light speed in Einstein's relativity formula. "Nickel c, for five percent of light speed, is what they're calling it. I really believe we're going to come up with a method of achieving within an eyelash of c itself."

"I think so too, Smitty. We'll shrink the solar system to a day's travel if we do."

"Interesting, isn't it? Those nuclear pulse engines won't do it, though, they say."

"No way, Smitty" said Morgan. "They produce sufficient thrust, but it can't be sustained long enough to push anywhere close to light speed. Two problems are the heat generated and the fact we can't carry enough nuclear fuel to burn the power plants continuously. It appears to me that our best bet is antimatter conversion. There's power there that makes nuclear look like a peashooter. The people in Research and Development really know what they're doing, and recent findings are colossal. When you power up antimatter conversion, there's a mass inversion effect that comes into play..."

"Sure will help cut down travel times, huh?"

"You said it. I guess the trip home is always longer, eh?" Morgan asked, feeling a deepening anxiety to get there, thoughts of nuclear pulse engines beckoning silently.

"Not only in time but in millions of miles, Bucko," said Smith. "I understand preliminary runs of the *Chuck Yeager* were only marginally successful."

"Some problems with the nuclear reactors and some unpredictable vibrations. They're working on them, though."

"Man, with speed like that, a married man could be an astronaut and be home for supper once in a while. Say, is that girl still sending you messages sometimes?"

"None of your business," said Morgan testily. "Nah, she doesn't communicate anymore. Six years is a long time, Smitty."

"How well I know. We'll both have to upgrade of our address books some, Bucko."

Word of the death of Ralph Russell and his wife came to Morgan on the return leg, though the astronaut would not learn all the heinous details until after returning to Earth. He was deeply saddened at the revelation, relayed through mission control by Morgan's cousin Jerry Barnes, who skillfully neglected to fill in all the particulars. Morgan couldn't imagine what could have killed both of them at once, but he assumed it was a traffic accident. Looking out over the vastness of interplanetary space, he said a melancholy goodbye to his old friend and mentor, and a quiet word of thanks for all the diligent and competent tutoring. He knew he wouldn't be where he was today apart from his old teacher's leading. And he was confident he had been taught the best way to fulfillment. Ralph Russell could always be trusted to lead you in the right direction.

Arrival at Space Station Delta finally came almost exactly six Earth years after departure of the *Delta Dare*. All available personnel assisted in disgorging a fantastic amount of deep space metal, and Morgan noted with some dismay a growing stockpile of monstrous rectangular plates moored in temporary bays all around the space station. A load of it went down on every shuttle flight but still it accumulated in massive quantities. How would they ever be able to get that valuable commodity down to the surface with limited weight requirements for re-entry into the atmosphere? Oh, well, he sighed. Project scientists would figure it out eventually.

He put all such thoughts out of his mind for the time being. There were more important matters to consider. With any luck at all he might be able to land a position on the team that was testing nuclear pulse engines. And now he had the experience to request that job.

And there was a lady officer he planned to contact as well.

CHAPTER 19

November 2072

Beauty and infinity spread before the travelers, stretching beyond the Kansas prairie's distant broad horizon. It was so dramatically different from the austere artificial environment to which they had become accustomed for so many years. Hills around the farm conveyed a soft, pleasing brown tone that spoke mutely of early winter. Flint-crested ridges appeared vaguely reminiscent of rugged but sterile escarpments they had visited in the Martian highlands five years before.

Buck Morgan was filled with a nostalgic gladness evoked by this view of the land that had nurtured him as a youth. This was a planet so rich and diverse, so amazingly productive and alive, and so different from other bodies in the solar system. The places he had visited had been so awful, so dead, and so unpromising by comparison. He couldn't help but wonder if there were another place in the entire universe that was comparable to this vibrant sphere of rock and water and friendly atmosphere. This was home.

"Dad's been dead now for six and a half years, Smitty," Morgan said with more than a hint of sadness. He was speaking to Major Jeremiah Smith as they motored toward the old home place, where his cousin still conducted an ongoing high tech protein operation. Both astronauts had earned another well-deserved promotion on returning to Earth, in addition to one received while in deep space.

Cleanly harvested fields and manicured pastures greeted them as they drove down the familiar lane, while animals grazed in contentment and watchful sentry robots noted the movement of their vehicle. A white-tailed deer bounded across the road in front of them, a big buck bent on finding a female. It was quite evident that the farm had been very well managed since Morgan's departure.

"Looks like whoever is minding the farm is doing a good job, Bucko. It appears mighty productive to me," said Smith, admiring the symmetrical fields, cropped close and ready for the plow. In one place a covey of quail lofted skyward from the road edge, zooming like tiny fighter jets toward velvety tan meadows where prairie grasses grew tall and wildlife teemed.

"Jerry Barnes is really some producer. His dad is my uncle Bill, who's always owned the adjacent place. They're good at what they do."

"And you're sure they'll let us hunt?"

"No doubt about it. Jerry tells me Dad's old bird dog Hank is still alive and well with six more seasons of experience. I gave that dog to Jerry when he purchased all the other livestock. I can't wait to see him work again."

In his mind Morgan could see the immaculate white setter running free as the wind, searching for a whiff of the birds he lived to seek. The thought put Morgan into an ambivalent mindset that recalled both pain and pleasure. Despite intensive efforts to put the past aside for a while, he just couldn't relegate that last hunt with his father to his subconscious. He unintentionally revealed a tender side to his friend Smith, shedding a tear or two as they visited the east cemetery where his father and mother were buried.

Jerry's payments for the farm had gone into an escrow fund, and the proceeds had grown to an astronomical amount. Morgan didn't need money, his own salary having accumulated rather dramatically in a similar account during his absence. To his amazement, he was practically rich when he added up the totals. He considered briefly donating the whole amount to some charity, but decided against it. The universe was an uncertain place, and one couldn't be too careful, after all. He did make a generous donation to the local chapter of the Conservation Club, and another one to his old church for upkeep of the ancient building.

Pastor Don had died the year before and the church had come on hard times. Morgan's timely donation was sorely needed just to maintain the physical facilities. Finding a man to pastor a church had become next to impossible, according to Judy Hancock, who was still teaching at the local high school. Morgan had a joyful reunion with her, and from her he learned the seamy details about the death of Ralph Russell and his wife. He was surprised to discover that Rudy McGill had also died in the same incident. He couldn't understand why a man of science like Russell would commit both murder and suicide, although he somehow felt that Rhetta and the pernicious McGill had deserved what they got.

Judy Hancock seemed to understand the unspoken hurt her former student felt as she related the tale. At one point she stopped and wiped away a tear, a drop of liquid regret that was shed for a man and an adulterous situation that she had known about only remotely. Perhaps it was something else that touched her, though Morgan just couldn't tell. She tried ardently to engage him in meaningful conversation about Russell and the tragedy, but communication faltered as she spoke of spiritual matters and human inadequacy. Morgan really loved this aging woman, but he snapped his mind shut to such improbable and immeasurable concepts. He chose to change the subject abruptly.

"What about old Spot Prestone, Mrs. Hancock? Ever hear from him?"

"No. I hear about him, but not from him. Once in a while I do see him around town on his jet cycle, but I don't know what he does. He's always got a girl or two with him."

"I guess he never went back to school, huh?"

"Not that I'm aware. But like I say, I never hear directly."

Morgan and Smith stayed a whole week with Jerry Barnes. Remembrances were tough on Morgan, and he wandered the familiar house in a virtual trance at times. The old molybdenum steel pot was still being used in the kitchen, though it was much too large for most cooking purposes. It was being used as a repository for other smaller household vessels, and it was crammed to capacity. Seeing the aging canister brought back poignant memories of his father once more.

He went to the bank one day and got out all the old mementos from the storage vault. His father's war medals were a bit tarnished, and the pictures were getting an aged look, but each article brought another tide of memories. His father's old shotgun looked none the worse for the passage of years, and he fondled the three main disassembled pieces affectionately. He snapped the stock piece back together with the foregrip and long double barrels, and the firearm assumed the familiar appearance he remembered so well. He raised the gun to his shoulder and noted the smooth, whip-like action he had seen his father utilize so many times in the past. His eyes once more clouded with tears as he restored everything except the gun to the deposit box. He reverently tucked the old shotgun under one arm as he left the bank. He had plans for the gun on this trip.

His father was always in the background, but most powerfully when he immersed himself in the joy of pursuing quail. It was great fun as always, and watching the dogs work was a superb treat. But without Dad something wonderful was now missing. For the first time in his life Morgan had developed a profound sense of the value of roots, a connection to other human beings beyond mere friendship. It was a bittersweet kind of discovery and he tried to suppress it. Such an intimate association seemed impossible for him, anyway, so why wallow in such baneful thoughts? He resolved to shed no more tears for anything at all, if he could help it.

Attempts to contact JoEllen Thacker had perhaps contributed to his melancholy mindset. She was out of the army, still single, and was working as a consultant for a firm in Manhattan so she could be near her mother. Morgan had perceived evasiveness in her voice and in the expression on her holographic image. While she had asked polite questions about his voyage, she had seemed distinctly disinterested in him personally. He had been deeply disappointed, but had made no determined attempt to see her. He might call her again.

As a life member of the Conservation Club, Morgan had continued to receive the organization's publication *World Conservationist*, even while he had been off in space. As he reviewed six years' worth of magazines, he found one containing a moving obituary to his father. Despite his determination, his eyes clouded and another tear spilled from his eyes as he read the short article.

His visit home passed with extreme rapidity, and shortly it was time to plan their return trip to the space station. Morgan broke the old shotgun down into its three main components once more and placed it in a box designed for this purpose. He returned to his bank and stored the cherished firearm in their massive steel vault. The huge steel door closed behind him with a resolute slam as he departed.

*   *   *

As a tested and seasoned veteran of a deep space mission, Morgan now commanded considerable respect among his colleagues. He approached age twenty-nine filled with optimism about the future and his role in the international space effort. Now nobody could question his credentials.

Back at the Cape after furlough Morgan made it a point to approach Dr. Gerald Schultz, project engineer for the nuclear pulse engines. Schultz was a balding and bespectacled veteran of many intricate projects, and was easily recognizable around the research complex. He looked so much like a cartoonist's caricature of a scientist, sporting a crisp white coat, grandfather half glasses, and a flourishing forehead that gave abundant meaning to the term highbrow. His hooked snout almost touched his chin because of the near-absence of maxillary bone under his nose, giving him a most peculiar profile. He had a residual ring of white hair, left to grow as it willed, that had a fly-away look reminiscent of Albert Einstein or Mark Twain.

"Major Morgan, in answer to your question," gummed Schultz, "I think we've worked out most of the bugs. We're on the verge of a tremendous breakthrough. We will have conquered the solar system if this works."

"Any chance I might get in on the project, sir?" Morgan inquired, feeling he had nothing to lose by asking.

"We've got astronauts from all over wanting in. I got a holocom inquiry from Agryre Basin on Mars just last night. I don't do the hiring and firing, for Gaia's sake."

The downcast look on Morgan's face made Schultz have second thoughts about such harsh words. Despite his overt negativism, he knew that this officer was exactly the kind of man who would get the most out of his invention. Unfortunately, it was also true that several more senior astronauts were in line ahead of him. But he had seen enough of Morgan to have a good visceral feeling about him.

"Tell you what, Major, let me talk to the project commander. He's the one who ultimately makes all personnel decisions."

"Who is that?"

"General Orson Staar."

"Really?" Morgan exclaimed. His old commanding officer! He hadn't realized he was now in charge of the nuclear pulse project. "Please do speak to him, doctor. I can pilot that ship. I'll make it work if anyone can."

Schultz looked the strapping young astronaut over thoughtfully. The old engineer had been disappointed and highly displeased at the somewhat bumbling efforts of the second officer in early trials. It wasn't so much that the last man had been unable to make the machine run smoothly, because there had been some technical problems beyond immediate solution. But he had disintegrated under fire and had caused a public relations disaster, one that had blossomed into a nightmare and delayed the program. Schultz needed a truly cool hand in the seat next to his test pilot, and Morgan appeared to be a perfect fit. He'd mention the promising young man to Staar at first opportunity.

Morgan couldn't wait for Schultz to run into Staar. He went calling on the general himself. Sometimes you need to be aggressive, he reasoned. He made his way down a manicured walkway toward the headquarters building, a low structure with bright, cheerful flowers lining the approaches from every direction. Old Glory whipped in a brisk afternoon breeze alongside the resplendent ringed planet flag of the Astronaut Corps, with bright moons on a field of black representing each participating nation. Pride welled as he drank in the inspiring sight showcased against a crystal blue sky.

Inside the building smelled strongly of cleaning solution, adding to the spic-and-span appearance. Everything was artistic but tasteful, a bit formal but certainly not elegant. Following the computerized directions, he easily found the commander's spacious office.

233

"May I speak with the general?" Morgan requested of his secretary, a dazzling dark-skinned girl who was the picture of efficiency, her ivory teeth flashing as she smiled. The pretty young woman recognized him as a member of the Astronaut Corps from his distinctive uniform, but she couldn't recall ever having seen him before.

"May I tell him who you are?" she questioned, looking Morgan over admiringly as he stood straight as a rifle barrel, his broad shoulders and handsome profile the picture of virile manhood.

"Morgan. Buck Morgan. Major Buck Morgan," he replied, a little embarrassed by the look over he was getting, though he had become accustomed to it since his return to Earth. He resisted a strong temptation to return the look, even though some powerful force tugged at him as never before. He was more than a little uncomfortable with the new morality, an extreme sensuality that seemed to pervade every relationship. And he certainly didn't want to get his hopes up that something more satisfying and permanent might develop. He smiled back at the beauty, trying to look both friendly and disinterested at the same time, a tightrope walk he had mastered sufficiently to stifle most advances. Disappointment at his unintended rebuff showed visibly as the secretary stood up curtly.

"Wait here. I'll see."

Within a few minutes Morgan was standing face to face with the general, shaking his hand and receiving congratulations on his successful maiden voyage.

"Somehow I've been expecting you, Buck," the general began, extending his burley arm toward him for a handshake. Staar had changed little in appearance, with his closely cropped ring of silver hair still almost imperceptible, and his face so smooth that it looked as if he had just finished shaving. Morgan couldn't miss that the general's first-name salutation as he waved him toward an empty chair. "I've heard you really had a productive six years in space."

There was really no need to engage in small talk with Staar. Mission Control followed the progress of every craft in space daily with virtual word-by-word accounts, transmitted continuously to all headquarters personnel who had a need to be informed. He knew every detail already, and it was not necessary to fill him in on the recently completed trip.

"General, I'm not here exploring for compliments, but I do appreciate your kind words. I'm here to ask for a job. Do you need a pilot for the *Chuck Yeager*?"

"Matter of fact, we might. Our current copilot got cold feet when those cussed vibrations almost shook the ship apart on the first run. We never got her up anywhere close to a thousand miles a second. Good thing you took so much care with those rivets."

"What caused the vibrations, sir?"

"Non-sequential thermonuclear detonations in one engine. It sounds simple sitting here discussing it, but it took nearly three years to iron out the defective hardware. And unfortunately it shook public confidence and we've had to scramble to keep our pet funded. But now our problems are fixed, both from the standpoint of hardware and public relations. We'll be ready to try again in a couple of months."

"Can you get me transferred from interplanetary cruiser to R&D?"

"Probably. There will be a few senior astronauts who will want my head for it, but I've thought before about putting you on this project. Let me work on it."

Morgan left the general, his hopes buoyed. He knew there were plenty of reasons he could be cut out, not the least of which was his relatively short tenure on deep space duty. Oh, well, it can't hurt to try. If it didn't work out, he would probably ship out on another *Delta Dare* mission within a few weeks. This time he dreaded even more acutely the prospect of being left out of ongoing development work.

The next day a video phone rang early in Morgan's quarters. It was General Staar. He had talked personally with both Dr. Schultz and with *Delta Dare* commander Colonel Maxwell Scott. Both men had unequivocally recommended Morgan. The transfer was in progress. After thanking the general, Morgan turned off his phone and whooped for joy!

Before long Morgan was back at Space Station Delta, where he had docked initially after his space voyage. The *Chuck Yeager* was still moored to the station, by all appearances completely ready to fly. On the other side of the station the *Delta Dare* was being outfitted for yet another voyage, this time a short hop to Mars and back. It couldn't be decommissioned as planned until new technology was on line to replace it. Morgan was glad that the aging cruiser would leave without him this time. As he approached the *Chuck Yeager*, he encountered an older astronaut wearing a most serious expression.

"Major Morgan, I presume," said Colonel Joe Hemingway, first pilot of the *Yeager*. "I hope I'm glad to meet you. I understand you want to fly this beast and that somehow you've secured the blessings of the powers that be."

He seemed to have more than a trace of disdain in his voice. Hemingway knew that Morgan was competent and had a superb reputation, but he didn't understand how he had succeeded in leapfrogging over more senior candidates.

"Somehow I have, I guess. I'm just glad to be on the project. Can you show me around?"

"Glad to. Let's start on the flight deck."

Hemingway was extremely big for an astronaut, perhaps tall enough to be a professional basketball player. He had a full head of salt-and-pepper hair that was combed impeccably. He was perhaps twenty years senior to Morgan and had the characteristic facial scars of a long-time astronaut.

Scars fit well with Hemingway's demeanor and his cast iron expression that seldom wavered. He had a practiced nonchalance that gave one the impression that he truly cared not if he lived or died. Not that he was less than meticulous or thorough—he wasn't—but taking chances was second nature to him. Morgan couldn't help but wonder if this man couldn't face a guillotine unperturbed if he had the remotest chance of escaping unharmed.

The tour was thorough, and afterward Hemingway presented Morgan with microchips for his computer, key information that detailed the ship's innermost secrets. Morgan had worked on it before, so only the more immediate developments were new to him. Even the latest work had been relayed to the *Delta Dare* while he was in space and he had already spent long hours perusing the data. He felt ready.

Morgan studied the latest plans exhaustively. Before he could be a capable second officer he had to know everything he could about the *Yeager*. The principle that one shouldn't fly what one doesn't understand went all the way back to early days of flying, when accidents were epidemic among people who bought expensive airplanes but didn't take enough time to study and learn them. He scrutinized the plans exhaustively and was especially glad to note an expanded section on sequencing detonations in the firing chambers. He concluded that the original problem had likely been eliminated.

"Preparations for the next test are well under way, Morgan," Hemingway stated as he returned to the workroom. "You're still sure you want to be second pilot?"

"Are you kidding, sir? I wouldn't miss it for the whole solar system! What kind of time frame are we looking at?"

"In two weeks we'll actually fly. We'll light the engines several times before then just for checkouts. If all goes well we'll make a thousand miles per second in a just a few hours of burn on the first run. We don't have as much of the old problem of insufficient reaction mass in this buggy, but it generates so much heat we can't burn the engines continuously. If we could, we might be able to push it pretty close to light speed. But then the increasing mass phenomenon would become highly significant, I'm afraid."

"I know the physics. Too bad about all that heat. I'd love to bump light speed."

"The guy you're replacing was scared off the project by some little vibrations we experienced. Can't say I really blame him. I'll tell you, Morgan, I've been in some tight spots but I thought we'd earned an obituary notice on WorldNet."

Morgan was amazed that anyone would voluntarily opt out of such an opportunity, even under awful duress. This was the chance of a lifetime. He hadn't experienced those earthquake shakes, but the ship had held together and everyone was still alive. He'd never let anything spook him off the project. Not now, not ever. He'd go maximum speed or bust, and he would never quit.

Increasingly it seemed to Morgan that delay was an inevitable part of the human experience, and this project was no exception. After another spate of postponements, it was finally time to get down to the very serious business of testing. Engine light ups went smoothly, and the atomic thrusters glowed cherry red with intense heat. Everything appeared to be ready.

"Now we ride, Colonel," Morgan beamed as the pair took their stations on test day. At this initial stage they would be the only occupants of the sleek machine.

After successful ignition, the *Chuck Yeager* shuddered slightly as thrust was gradually increased. Delta Station quickly faded out of sight behind them and the blackness of space loomed ahead. The speed indicator was climbing—slowly at first, then more rapidly as the minutes ticked past. The first milestone was 200 miles per second, the maximum speed attained by the initial testing phase before the vibration problem had occurred. Soon they were pushing 400, then like a streaking lightening bolt they were groping for 1,000 miles per second. There were none of the infamous vibrations as the impressive engines ran smoothly. Morgan counted off miles per second while the Colonel pushed in more and more power. He stopped at ten percent throttle, the predetermined maximum for this run, and the speed indicator edged toward 1,000 miles per second. Wow, Morgan thought, we could be back at Mars at half power in a few hours! Impressive thrust built slowly, and with it came increasing potential for reaching the magic number of 10,000 miles per second. Only a few hours of gradual acceleration would achieve that figure easily, and project engineers were certain that nuclear pulse engines could sustain acceleration for that long without danger of meltdown.

They docked back at Delta Station to the cheers of the assembled technicians. They were already the fastest men of all time, and in subsequent runs they would see what this new space machine could do. It would take several days of debriefing and re-tuning the engines before they could make another run. All data seemed to indicate that every parameter was in order to push for more speed.

It actually took over two weeks before they were able to settle into their harnesses for another lightup of the *Chuck Yeager*. At last everything was in readiness, and they checked and rechecked their instruments. This time they would try to double their previous accomplishment and move up to 2,000 miles per second. Both pilots were confident in their machine, and had anyone authorized it they would have gladly gone for maximum speed. There were protocols to follow, though, and sticking to them was mandatory.

A thousand miles per second came as easily as before, and shortly they were setting new speed records every instant. Everything was progressing smoothly as they progressed past 1,200 miles per second, and then began approaching 1,400 miles per second.

Without warning there began a series of shudders, initially a low rumbling that was barely perceptible. Morgan scanned all the instruments while his commander radioed for a readout from the remote sensors being monitored by the research team at Space Station Delta. There was absolutely no other indication of trouble at first, the groaning of the hurtling machine subtle in its protest, so subdued that detection was more in the realm of instinct than hard data. There was practically no measurable indication of any malfunction, just a distinct feeling that the whole ship was in a high-pitched vibration mode. Unobtrusively, however, the navigation indications began to drift slightly askew, and craft attitude drifted minimally out of trim. If the trend continued unabated, the ship eventually would begin a disastrous rolling action that would rip it apart. Bright red lights shortly began to flash, ominous beacons warning of exceeded tolerances all across the panel, and the two test pilots fought frantically to bring the shuddering craft back into a sustainable flight envelope and find the answer to this unforeseen hazard.

"Morgan, our flight profile is completely out of synchronization. We've got less than two minutes before we go into a disintegration spiral. Don't think I can hold her! Shut down the main group!"

Hemingway shouted the obvious, his steely voice tainted by unaccustomed dismay. He was attempting valiantly to pull the attitude back into appropriate profile using small hydrox rockets designed for just such duty, and he simultaneously directed Morgan to pull breakers on the massive nuclear engines. Of course, thrust from their awesome burn could not be reversed without those same engines running smoothly, and there was no telling where they might end up in the universe because nobody could conceivably be in a position to rescue them. Traveling at this velocity an emergency intercept was impossible, a docking unthinkable. They simply had to find the problem and bring their main engine group back on line to decelerate. If they couldn't, they were destined to become a disorganized swirl of radioactive debris.

After deactivating the nuclear burners, Morgan scrolled frantically through his systems analysis menu, and finally located what appeared to be a malfunction in one of the microcomputers that controlled nuclear detonation sequencing. Bad news. The damage might be already irreparable, and reversal could prove impossible. Without a word to his first officer he pushed a disconnect control button, releasing himself from the confines of his seat, leaving Hemingway to wrestle the streaking ship into proper flight profile if he could.

Morgan hurriedly dropped to his knees and opened an access door to the main computer housing. He crawled along the firewall, groping in black darkness for the emergency lighting switch, the autolight having apparently malfunctioned in this sector. He searched frantically in the dark recess, and finally laid a tense finger on an auxiliary switch. A gloomy light flickered on, casting haunting shadows into every obscure corner. It was no easy job to orient oneself amid the confusing maze of circuitry and electronic hardware, all of which looked the same. There was no time to test each unit individually, so he would have to guess where to start. If only he had time he felt he could isolate the culprit and repair the problem, but even then there was no assurance the ship could be brought back into a non-lethal flight envelope.

Working from learned intuition, he jerked off a side panel that potentially contained the incapacitated unit. As he did so, a thought hit him like a hurtling meteor, a lesson he had learned in advanced gravitational physics at the Point. There was indeed a scenario that would get the ship back under control. There was only one possible way, and those impotent hydrox rockets wouldn't do it alone—they were more for docking maneuvers than for flight profile adjustment, anyway, and were barely adequate for either. But if he couldn't solve the basic problem it was simply all over, anyway.

As he opened another accessory panel, this time an internal automatic light dutifully came on, and he immediately found a loose microcomputer connection in the sequencing control mechanism. Pitifully poor workmanship, he grumbled aloud in the tight confines, cursing mildly under his breath at the quality of aerospace technicians being produced these days. Using a repair kit designed for just such a purpose, he reunited the faulty connection and began a reset sequence that would check out the system before re-tuning it. If all proved out, they would be able to re-ignite the engines, for whatever good that would do them. It just might already be too late to prevent a catastrophic disaster in space, an eventuality that would inevitably set back the program for perhaps decades. Not that it would matter to Morgan and his first officer—they would shortly be quite dead if they couldn't reinstate control immediately.

The young test pilot extracted himself from the tight space, sweat beads rolling off his brow, and crawled back into his seat next to Hemingway. The first officer was losing the battle, despite lines of grim determination that creased his scarred forehead. Red lights flashed hopelessly, and their crippled ship apparently was doomed to become a mach 6,000 garbage heap, possibly ejecting itself entirely from the galaxy in time.

"Colonel, we've got to re-ignite the engines," Morgan said as he took his seat. "Our only chance is to stretch out the envelope and use the auxiliary thrusters to realign the profile. We can do it only at a higher speed."

"Do it, Morgan. We're dead anyway if we don't come up with something. She's drifting further askew every second. Delta, we're re-igniting n-p engines," he radioed the space station, where nobody, it seemed, had any better ideas.

The surge of mighty power plants was now smooth and secure. Both men knew that engine re-ignition possibly would accomplish nothing more than to add velocity to their demise, unless the flight profile could be brought under control. As the miles per second indicator climbed once more, the first officer strained to get every ounce of thrust from the appropriate attitude control, and the long tunnel display on the computer lengthened out to indicate the new conformation of their flight path. Nothing discernible happened, and the ominous deviation continued to grow, apparently indicating their fate was sealed. Then, as if by some miracle, it stabilized, holding steady but still perched at the very edge of cataclysm. The miles per second indicator climbed steadily as minutes crawled by, and they were now well above the 2,000 miles per second goal of this mission.

Ever so slowly then, with judicious application of appropriate lateral thrust, the ship inched back to the very edge of the envelope. Morgan dutifully called out the latest readings to his captain. Over the next few minutes, several ominous red lights winked out, indicating that stress on the ship's structure was lessening. Morgan glanced at the speed indicator and noted that it read an astounding 2,500 miles per second. Another record, if they could only regain control and live to savor the victory.

Hemingway prodded their swaying ship ever so slowly back toward center on the yawning cyber envelope, finally realigning it like a bullet in the exact center of a target. Morgan then asked for and received permission to shut down the n-p engines for a 180-degree rotation required to use reverse thrust to decelerate. Rotation with hydrox rockets was easy, and the ship stayed well within stress tolerances. By now all the red lights were extinguished. Engine re-ignition was shortly accomplished, and the craft began decelerating smoothly and steadily, the speed gauge showing a rapid decline in miles per second. Soon they were stopped dead still in the vastness of space, many millions of miles from Earth but safe nevertheless. The two men looked at each other and Morgan chortled a hearty laugh.

"I'd say we overshot the mark a little, partner," Hemingway said with characteristic absence of emotion.

"Only a few million miles, sir," replied Morgan, suppressing his tense mirth and trying to emulate some of the insouciant manner of his superior. "Close enough for the second time out."

"It'll have to be. It's good enough just to still be alive, in fact."

"If I may say so, sir, I wonder if you aren't tempting fate in this ship? Didn't something just this bad happen before?"

"Not this bad. Scared my copilot out of his flight suit, though, like I said. You ready to quit, too?"

"Not on your life, sir, if you'll excuse that phraseology. I'm going to go over every connection and every wire with the engineers when we get back, though. This whole episode was caused by poor quality installation of a connection. We get some real dimwits these days, even in the space program."

They powered up the engines again as they chatted, requesting and receiving permission from mission control aboard Delta Station. They would go back at a turtle's pace by comparison to the ride out, but nobody was in any mood to take any chances until more checking was done, not even the unflappable Hemingway. Hours crawled by and the two men had plenty of time to talk.

"Say, exactly what was the problem under there, Morgan? The deficient labor you mentioned?"

"Simple loose connection, like the kind that has crashed many a vehicle and many an airplane. If it had disconnected anytime before power up, we'd have detected it. My readouts showed where the problem might be, and sure enough, there it was. A couple of wrong guesses and I would have missed it."

"Thanks, Morgan," Hemingway said, again without emotion. "Welcome aboard any flight I'm on."

The remainder of the trip was uneventful and their return to Delta was triumphant, despite the scare.

"Quite a smashing success, I'd say, small problems aside. Good job, gentlemen," General Staar commented as he entered the *Yeager*'s flight deck after its docking. A few hours before the pilots had been within an Angstrom unit of oblivion, and now the general talked as if little out of the ordinary had occurred. Indeed, the engines and other systems had performed flawlessly. "Once we iron out some small details, men, we may be on the verge of interstellar flight."

"We've possibly shrunk the solar system to manageable size, sir, if more testing goes well," Morgan responded. "But we need one more revolutionary development to reach the stars. We need antimatter conversion so we can bump light speed. Reaction mass in a tea cup."

"Could be coming down the pike, Buck. I hope I live to see it," replied Staar.

"Right now I want to get in line to pilot one of these n-p ships. What a quantum leap! We've just moved the equivalent of foot travel up to jet planes, all in one step. Somebody ought to nominate Schultz for the Nobel Prize."

"He's already got one. But I'm sure he'd take another."

Further testing pushed V max, top speed, to the projected 10,000 miles per second, making Morgan and his first officer the only men to achieve "nickel c," or five hundredths of light speed. Hemingway was repeatedly glad he had lucked into having a second officer who knew the ship so well, because several times more aggravating minor problems came up which were easily repairable with minimal work, and Morgan demonstrated his mettle again and again. After more exhaustive tests and several short trial voyages, the *Yeager* was ready to be outfitted for its primary mission of supplying deep space bases. Hemingway wanted to pilot the ship for a few runs; then he would recommend Morgan as first pilot. The older astronaut wanted to stay closer to home now and assist in testing each newly constructed n-p ship. And he wanted to chew the butt off any incompetent technician, like the one that had almost killed them on that second run. Buck Morgan was not interested in such assembly line work, and he was more than happy when General Staar named him as next commander of the *Yeager*.

*   *   *

Adrian, Kansas, like the rest of the world, had been utterly transformed in recent years. There were prostitutes on some street corners and the rustic Hat Trick Bar was overrun with sensual shoppers. Spot Prestone was a frequent visitor to the old watering hole, and he had established a reputation as a counterculture leader. He arrived each afternoon on a jet cycle, a travel sensation of the late twenty-first century. The whining machine looked like a Harley Davidson without wheels cruising along on a cushion of air, fueled by potent and omnipresent veganox. Prestone always arrived with his plentiful, long black hair flowing in the breeze, his trademark white lock rippling prominently.

A lady's man would have been his defining label in centuries past. In the bustling sensuality of the times nobody made any special note his flamboyance, nor of two buxom girls, clad in expensive synthetics, riding behind Prestone.

"Go, Spot!" shouted a red-haired beauty closest to him as they cruised into the parking lot and flashed underneath the holographic cowboy's whirling lariat. An ample expanse of pale skin was briefly exposed by the whipping wind, causing a rowdy crowd of onlookers to fairly leer in admiration.

"Hang on, honeys," he called to his girls as he put on a show in an open field adjacent the Hat Trick Bar. Gunning his machine, he raced all the way to an opposite tree line, pivoted 180 degrees, turned the craft up on its side so the trio of riders was practically horizontal, and then streaked like lightening back to his mooring, delighting the throng of spectators.

Ever since Spot Prestone's ouster from Wichita State, he had been a rebellious perpetual teenager. He made plenty of money in the illicit drug and sex trade, wealth he spent lavishly on himself and his legion of friends, most of whom were shapely young women. For the majority of his girls, direct contact with their employer was no more than a one-night stand, but inevitably one or two became repeat fascinations for the willful and dangerous young man.

Entering the Hat Trick Bar, he ordered a round of drinks for all the women present, and looked defiantly at a room full of glowering men to see if any would make the mistake of retaliating. He smiled a diabolical smile as none rose to challenge him. His drink was already sitting on the bar as he turned his attention away from the crowd, and he picked it up and took a long swig. Turning back to the horde of merrymakers, he lifted his glass high and bellowed a toast to all the ladies. Few of the men joined him, but the women saluted him mutinously with their free refreshment.

The young blonde who had entered with him was less than enthusiastic about the proceedings, but Prestone failed to notice. Betty's gloomy countenance spoiled the radiant beauty of her fair face, but her man seldom looked her in the eye anyway. She looked around at the raucous mob, and felt an overwhelming revulsion knot her stomach. All the people looked so—so ugly. Despicable. Dirty. She felt a wave of nausea wash over her, an extreme loathing of mankind that made her recoil from the leering throng.

She desperately needed to talk to Prestone, if she could get his attention in the right situation. She momentarily blocked out the disgusting mob of people and concentrated on the need at hand. It was with a trembling hand and a deep sense of fright that she touched his shoulder and pulled him toward her when she felt the mood was right.

"Spot, I'm pregnant. Got a few bucks so I can get an abortion?" asked Betty. Prestone had consumed a few drinks, and she hoped he was in a merry mood. It was Betty's job to prevent such inconveniences, and she knew he would be quite irritated, to say the least. Still, she had no money for the needed procedure and he had to be told. The old saying that abstinence was the only sure prevention rang in her mind as she made the dreaded confession to the volatile young man. She had done everything twenty-first century medicine dictated to prevent a conception, but still it had occurred. A pregnancy test had proven her worst fears to be true.

Prestone snarled at her like a mad dog, swinging his fist at her with all his might. She recoiled in fright, and he missed her fragile face by inches, but he compensated by coming back and smacking her soundly with his backhand. Blood spurted from her burst upper lip and the right side of her petite nose, causing less hardened patrons to gasp at such an obscene abuse of pure beauty. She staggered backward and collapsed into the arms of a stranger, an older man with a skinny frame, who took the opportunity to fondle her freely as he lowered her to the floor.

Spot Prestone was on the man in an instant, lashing and slashing with bared blade, his laser knife finding its mark in the man's vital zone, collapsing him like a limp dishcloth. The rest of the crowd retreated, not wanting to foolishly challenge the man who was reputed to wield the fastest and most indiscriminate laser blade in the whole state of Kansas. The remainder of the glowering mob was content to lust after the unconscious woman from a safe distance, while the unlucky groper wallowed his last breath away in a pool of his own stinking guts and gore.

Prestone moved to the young woman's side as blood from the dying man gushed and created an encroaching red tide that washed relentlessly toward her. Lifting her from the floor, he looked menacingly at the assembled crowd, his laser knife pointed at them perilously, and backed out of the room. Such incidents were common in the unwholesome drinking establishments of the time, and the authorities seldom bothered to investigate unless the victim was prominent or wealthy.

Prestone carried the unconscious young woman to a room he maintained, where he flung her limp body on the bed. By this time she was rousing somewhat, and he finished awakening her by pouring her face full of water, an inappropriate and callous move reminiscent of old Western movies. She moaned and moved heavily, her eyes dull and her face swollen and crusted with fresh blood, before finally gasping and becoming fully awake.

"Oh, Spot, you hit me. Why?"

"Bitch. You can just have that baby now for being so careless."

"No. I won't. I don't want a baby."

247

"Don't give me that garbage. It's your fault. You let your genes get loose, and you bear the consequences."

"I'll get an abortion anyway. You can't stop me."

Producing the laser knife, he flicked it on and traced the white-hot tip along the woman's bare abdomen. The heat licked at her exposed skin with malice, singeing the fine, soft hairs around her navel and curling them away. Prestone's eyes were cold and indifferent, so threatening that the girl shuddered in fear and suppressed an impulse to scream. There was nobody in the world that would care a whit if there were no tomorrow for her.

"I'll kill you if you do. A Prestone died tonight on account of you, and you're going to replace him."

She hadn't been conscious when Spot Prestone killed his father, but she had seen him kill enough men—and a few women, as well—to know that it was no idle threat. She shrunk back at prospects of her body lacerated and disemboweled, lying in an alley for dogs to devour. It happened frequently in the unmerciful and deviant world in which they lived. She buried her bloody face in her hands and wept loudly.

"Why, Spot? Why? You don't want a baby," she pleaded. Her cries went unheeded, and a complete absence of compassion showed in the sinister man's demeanor.

"I don't have a baby, honey. You do. And you'd better shut up and get used to it."

*   *   *

The next few years saw Buck Morgan make multiple trips back to visit all his acquaintances at the deep space bases. The veteran astronaut requested and received with no significant objections his choice of first mates from all the available astronauts—his old friend Jeremiah Smith. With his favorite sidekick on board, he could enjoy the conquest of the solar system even more. The two buddies rejoiced at being reunited and being in command of the fleet's most modern ship.

The *Yeager* was so fast it could have made several trips to the bases each month were it not for the laborious task of onloading and offloading, demanding work which still necessarily employed conventional planetary landers. Even so it was now possible to make a round trip every month instead of every six years. The plasmafyer hyperlaser, meshed in tandem with an ionizing shield, worked to perfection whenever they crossed the asteroid belt, and this, plus the ship's sleek aerodynamic design, eliminated almost all possibility of collisions. Morgan and Smith were back and forth many times before the last of the older generation planetary cruisers docked at Space Station Delta, where they were decommissioned and recycled as they returned. The last one in was the *Delta Dare*, Morgan's old ship. It seemed a shame to recycle the only remaining conventional cruiser.

"Sir, we need to see if we can keep the *Delta Dare* intact as a museum. I sure hate to see her destroyed," Morgan pleaded with Colonel Hemingway, who was now commander of Space Station Delta.

"I respectfully agree, sir," added Smith, a wistful look in his eye. "Isn't there anything we can do to preserve her?"

"Guys, she's obsolete. I understand your feelings, but the High Command won't hear of it. We need some of the components for the next nuclear pulse ship, too. Hauling new hardware into orbit is too expensive, so we have to make the most of what we already have up here."

"We understand. But we still hate to see her go. After all, we spent six years in the old girl."

Much more interesting to Morgan than cargo ferrying was the frequent side trips on scientific assignment. With the speed of the *Yeager*, it was possible to visit Pluto and return in just a couple of months. When the new cruisers came on line, such missions were given regularly to Morgan and his men, since they were by far the most experienced crew. Morgan reluctantly gave up his old friend, Smith, so he could become commander of one of the newest cruisers.

Morgan and his crew, often accompanied by Smith's ship, the *New Ranger*, made numerous runs to all of the planets and moons. The involved astronauts became the first humans to set foot on many of the small, rocky worlds. Mercury was found to have a fairly temperate polar region, as suspected, and in the deep vertical cracks and protected crevices there were vast deposits of water ice in unlimited quantities. Because of very favorable findings and a wealth of usable natural resources, a polar base on Mercury was shortly on the drawing boards.

The only possible drawback to the speedy nuclear pulse ships was that each carried a boundless burden of enriched plutonium. In the weightlessness of space large amounts of material were of no practical disadvantage, so each new ship carried ever-increasing quantities of the hazardous fuel. In their wake these cruisers left a trail of radioactive ions scattered across the enormity of interplanetary space. Hardly anybody gave a second thought to such emissions nor to the enormous load of high-grade fuel. After all, what harm could come from polluting infinite space?

"Colonel Morgan, head home," crackled a voice on the radio as the *Yeager* probed ever deeper into an unknown portion of the solar system. The transmission went on to explain that Dr. Schultz at the Cape wanted Morgan home for important discussions of his latest project. He was about to announce another quantum leap in space travel. They were so far out that the transmission had taken many hours to reach them.

But with its fantastic speed, Morgan's ship would be back on Earth in only a few weeks.

Buck Morgan didn't radio any questions en route. He already knew about the project. He was ready for the speed of light. As close to it as matter could travel, at least.

CHAPTER 20

March 2076

A meeting was taking place at the Planetary Propulsion Lab, where a team of scientists was gathered with aerospace experts who would test some promising new technology. Several distinguished men wearing sparkling white lab coats sat on one side of a gleaming electronic conference table. On the other side were a half dozen trim, athletic men of varying ages and nationalities, all wearing crisp, distinctive leather uniforms with the ringed planet emblem featured prominently on their sleeves. From every seat graphic information was presented to each participant in exactly the same perspective via the magic table.

After his opening remarks Dr. Gerald Schultz looked sternly at the astronauts. He spoke in his most fatherly voice, trying to sound soothing and confident, but an irritating rasp in his elderly voice betrayed a most distinct element of doubt.

"You're talking about real danger here, men," he said with a conspicuous smacking sound, as his chin closely approached his upper lip while he lectured. He reached up and adjusted his wire-rimmed spectacles, quaint pieces of glass that regularly dislocated from his pointed nose due to the anatomy of his face and constant trauma from his rattling speech. "Any way you cut it, it will be hazardous. I can give you advice but you will be the ones whose lives are on the line. Understand?"

"We're accustomed to danger. We've been there, sir," Buck Morgan said thoughtfully. "In a situation such as we're discussing the only thing to do is realize the danger is there, then forget about it. You can't live in fear that one of these inventions might turn on you."

"Anyway, you've been warned. Has everyone finished reviewing the data? What do you think about it?"

"Doctor, I think you've got it," said General Orson Staar, senior astronaut at the table. "The indescribable amount of energy available from the matter-antimatter equation is no surprise, since we've known for some time its limitless possibilities. But your latest studies seem to confirm a most useful mass inversion effect you've theorized. Do you really think we can achieve pragmatic c?"

"Begging the general's pardon," Schultz commented, wrinkling his brow as he ran his finger over one pertinent section of the equation. "Prag c appears to be within our reach. And the low temperatures emitted will allow us to burn the engines virtually continuously, if need be. Gentlemen, I think we're set to really explore a little, with just a bit more testing."

"Prag c. A dream I never thought I'd live to see. Since we now know we'll never achieve full light speed, this is the best we can do, men. Let's go for it," said Staar, shaking his head as he tried to comprehend the significance of the awesome information before him. "This is truly a giant leap for mankind, to quote Armstrong. We can finally start reaching for the stars!"

"I think this breakthrough will allow us to scrap the n-p engine before we ever construct any newer prototypes," replied Schultz, talking as he shut down the giant tabletop screen. His pointed nose practically buried itself in the white beard on his chin as he sucked in a breath of air and made an odd slurping sound, further collapsing what little tissue normally separated these two parts of his anatomy. "They're infernal blowtorches, anyway, more heat than thrust. And as you know, their best speed potential is no more than about two tenths of c, no matter how much we tweak the design. To reach prag c, we have to have a whole new concept. This is it, I believe. Questions?"

"We know the mass inversion factor is there, doctor. But will it adequately neutralize increasing mass as such a craft approaches light speed?" asked Morgan.

"Adequate to achieve light speed? You know better than that. But to significantly counter increasing mass, yes. You pilots are the ones who need to be most convinced, though," replied the aerospace genius. "If it doesn't, you'll be able to back off some power and the mass should decrease accordingly. I don't think it will be a problem, according to these calculations, but we're dealing with a lot of unknowns when we put this into action. I want all of you to understand this thoroughly before you pilot this monster anywhere close to light speed. Then you'll be in the best position to deal with whatever happens."

"We'll be jam up, doctor," said Morgan. "Thanks for bringing all of us in at this stage. You just design us some of these fancy engines and we'll learn as much as we can about them. I think I can speak for all of us when I say we want to stay abreast of the engineers as they try to come up with ship specifications. If this works, we'll be putting together a real starship. And soon."

"We'll have to build an experimental ship this time to test the concept after we have working engines. If we can achieve prag c, we can start constructing a starship, all right," the scientist mulled as he reached into his shirt pocket for his computer and casually scrolled through several personnel files. "Of course, with the experience represented here, you'll all be of great help to engineering in producing any proposed starship, so I know the project engineers will be glad to get your input on that phase as well. Morgan, most of your experience has been in nuclear pulse ships, not in the larger cruisers designed with a wealth of renewables. You're a little deficient there. You did have the one long voyage on a conventional cruiser, though."

"Doctor, I've worked my entire life in renewables. I was a farm kid in Kansas growing up. My life back then was all about renewable resources and what it takes to maintain them. I've flown the faster sport version for a while, it's true, but I've never forgotten my time on the *Delta Dare*. I want my name in the hat to ride that starship, when we get that far."

"Maybe so, Morgan. Let's see how it goes," said Schultz thoughtfully. "It's premature to make such a commitment now. But in due time we'll choose our crew."

It quickly became an obsession for Morgan. He became so engrossed in the project that he reluctantly relinquished command of the speedy *Yeager* to devote all his energy to the task. The Research and Development Lab was a beehive of simultaneous activity, with men and women working night and day to complete various phases. Some were researching the test craft, but for the most part that aspect had been completed and awaited final assembly and mandatory test flights. Confidence was high and most current action was based on the assumption that upcoming prag c trials would be successful. Experts were already at work on the design and specifications of a functioning starship.

Morgan had some opportunity to give input into this aspect, although his main job was in proposing cockpit layout and human resources schemes, since he was a pilot and not a laboratory researcher. Nevertheless, he had quite a bit of time to spend with systems engineers. Since the craft would be capable of such exhilarating speed, its design had to be modeled after the *Yeager*. It would have a laminar flow exterior and a sharp aerodynamic nose so hyperlasered space debris could easily flow by the ship's ion shield in plasmafyed form with little risk of damage to the hull.

"Dr. Schultz, how are the engines coming?" Morgan inquired as he encountered the scientist hurrying to a meeting with an armload of intricate models fresh out of the three dimensional printer. The scientist's twin shafts of towering white hair rose from either side of his balding head, looking more disarrayed than usual this day.

"Great. Lab tests are all in and we're on track. Just a few glitches to work out before we incorporate all our newest data into the prototype," he replied, furrowing his high brow and pushing up his glasses as they talked. "Morgan, I know you're way ahead of me in contemplating the final product. Sometimes you forget that thinking can be done a lot faster than assembling hardware. I'm not sure where you are, to be frank, but let me suggest something. You need to have a proposal ready on a possible mission for this ship. The High Command is going to have to be very interested in the possibilities before they issue funding for actual starship construction. You know how expensive it will be."

"I have indeed been thinking, doctor," Morgan replied confidently, producing a tiny chip he had stowed in a compartment in his vest pocket. "Our theoretical think tank here at the Planetary Propulsion Lab actually did the mathematics in this presentation. Slip this chip into your computer and you'll get a complete game plan."

"We've still got a lot of testing to do on our end. But I'm glad someone else is putting some brain power to it, too."

"Don't worry. We've had some time to gestate the idea lately and we're just preparing in advance. Actually I'm looking forward to the testing phase. Got to hurry to a meeting of my own, doctor. See you at the briefing."

As Morgan turned and walked away, the elderly scientist swept back his wild ruff of receding white hair with one hand and regarded the young, enthusiastic astronaut. He had the man's life history at his fingertips and he knew virtually everything about him, including triumphs and tragedies. He noted that Morgan still looked even more youthful than his thirty-one years, and that he was truly a handsome specimen. He knew that he had few living family members and no lasting attachment to any member of the opposite sex. Shame, somehow, he thought. But this man—James Lee Morgan, he read the astronaut's real name on the mini-holo monitor that barely filled his palm—could be the logical pilot of Schultz' life work: a genuine, functioning starship. Some day, people would probably refer to the kind of starship he was going to build as a "Schultz class cruiser," or something like that. It would indeed be a miracle machine.

Nuclear pulse ships had been a dramatic breakthrough that had captured the imagination of the public for a long while and had already made Schultz famous. But this latest project had potential to turn those clunkers into instant nickel c dinosaurs.

Conventional wisdom would have dictated that a maiden voyage be made to Proxima Centauri, the nearest star, a distance of 4.3 light years from Earth. Even at the nickel c speed of the *Yeager*, such a round trip voyage would take over 160 years in Earth time. At prag c the time shrunk to a mere eight and a half years, not much more than Morgan's first long space voyage. It was tempting to suggest a trip to this group of stars, since the data would be available so soon, and the crew's time in space would be so short.

There were, however, compelling reasons to bypass the nearest star group, and even the next nearest, as well as almost all stars nearer than forty light years away. The most indispensable criterion was the probability of inhabitable planets in orbit around a star. In order for this guideline to be met scrupulously, it was essential that the selected star have a temperature and radiation emission spectrum compatible with planetary life. Most stars closer than forty light years away had already been extensively studied by conventional means and those with systems of giant gaseous planets like Jupiter were duly charted. There might well be small rocky worlds orbiting them that still couldn't be detected by current technology, but almost certainly none would be able to support life. Such stellar systems were places of searing, deadly radiation levels, confounding companion stars, or inhospitable gravitational tides for one reason or another. All such destinations had been eliminated because reasonable chances of finding an inhabitable planet had been judged absent.

As well, the speeding ship could gather data on other stars from a far different perspective than could be achieved within the confines of the home solar system. Signals from such a starship would return to Earth continuously in a stream of information that would be in some ways as much a boon to scientists as the actual return of the mission, even though that data would necessarily carry a significant time lag. Mankind's destiny could well be tied to the discovery of another planet like Earth to colonize. That lofty goal simply could not be compromised for mere convenience of the starship crew or any selfish desire on the part of mission designers to see a final result. Neither could the nuances of government and funding be allowed to jeopardize this imperative, it was deemed of such importance.

The scientific team at the Planetary Propulsion Lab recommended that the first voyage be to the distant star 47 Ursae Majoris, the closest sun-like star at about forty-four light years away. It was a part of the Ursa Major constellation, situated "in the paw of the bear," the English name of the star arrangement being Great Bear. A giant gaseous planet orbited the star at a distance about twice as far as Earth was situated from the sun. Its positioning left adequate room for other smaller planets closer in to the friendly star, and ample freedom from the giant's fierce gravitational pull.

"How do you like the lab's proposal?" the astronaut inquired of Schultz during a chance cafeteria encounter.

"I think it's feasible. Their analysis of possible useful data from such a trip is most impressive," replied Dr. Schultz. "The downside is that we wouldn't get the whole body of information in the lifetime of anybody living today, so it could be rejected on that basis. A trip to a nearer star would return here in less than ten years of real time. General Staar is presenting the plan to the High Command next week. Morgan, you know such a voyage is going to give the crew a very long lifetime, don't you?"

"Yes, sir, I know," Morgan answered. "Simple math says the ship will be gone from Earth about ninety years, perhaps a bit more since it won't be moving quite at light speed. The formula is simple to plug in for .995 of c, prag c as they say, and it comes out to one-tenth of the time for the crew. All theoretical, of course, but the mathematics should be accurate. It'll be almost like riding a one-way time machine into the future."

"This has always been the theoretical wisdom ever since Einstein proposed the relativity principle back in Pre-2K. We should be able to calculate our time differential exactly with test runs here in the solar system after we build a working prototype ship. But I'll bet the formulae are as certain as a sunny day on the moon."

Construction of a test ship was well along by the time the news media adopted the project as important daily news fare. Reporters constantly hounded Morgan and Schultz whenever they left their confines. Morgan was already a well-known celebrity for his exploits as a nuclear pulse ship jockey. Shultz had indeed received a second Nobel Prize, and appeared well positioned for a third.

Morgan's growing influence eventually assured his position as test pilot of the experimental craft. There was no argument about that, and from early in the project everyone referred to the emerging test ship as Buck's Baby. The name stuck as tight as the astronaut's own nickname.

All vehicle assembly, including refining and most manufacturing involving metals, was done with material already in orbit. Extensive

J.Y. JONES

preliminary testing had been done on the earth's surface using gigantic vacuum chambers to simulate outer space. No full lightups of antimatter conversion engines could be done until the miraculous devices had been assembled in space. To unleash such power in any situation except a vacuum was unthinkable, since disastrous consequences were certain in Earth's atmosphere. This would be the very first time a ship had reached a stage of complete function before anyone knew for certain that the most key component, the engines, would work as projected.

"You never go home, do you, Bucko?" inquired a voice from behind him as he pored over his work. He turned to face the speaker.

"Smitty! Where have you been?" Morgan exclaimed, glad to see his old interplanetary companion. The two shook hands and embraced briefly, and as they did so Morgan couldn't help but remember his father for some reason. Was it that he had practically never touched another human being since his dad died, other than the occasional handshake? It felt strange to get so close to another person. His dad had embraced him like that the last time they were together.

"Cruisin', man. Just got back from Saturn last week," Smith explained, talking as he perused the partially assembled test module. "We're exploring to try and find a suitable base site there, maybe on Titan—stomping around wearing a survival suit in a cloud of frozen methane isn't much fun, you know. We were just polishing up some of the work you and I did earlier, before you got distracted. And I guess you heard they're proceeding with the Mercury base, right on the north pole of the planet. I'm heading there when I leave here."

"I envy you, old buddy. I'm stuck here in a testing phase until I can get this buggy functional. Then we've got more work to do before I get a chance for a real ride."

"Looks like you're onto something big, my friend," he continued. "The whole Corps—in fact, the whole world—can't talk about anything but prag c. And you're going to be the first man to achieve it, I'd wager. You'll be more famous than Yeager or Armstrong or Warren. You'll be in an entirely different class from the first man on Mars and the like."

"Maybe so, maybe not. I think we're on track to capture the mark, but we won't know beyond doubt until our engineers get it assembled," Morgan explained. "We can't even fire her up for a test run until we're functional in space. But Schultz is razor sharp and I have no doubt we'll make prag c."

"Nobody does. Is the old man positive that increasing mass can be negated?"

"Looks like it to me. I think the doctor has all the right answers."

"Where you going in this thing, Bucko?"

"Just around the solar system in this little module. It's much too small to hold adequate renewables for interstellar flight. A tremendously expanded starship is on the drawing board, with an awesome renewables section. But man, oh, man, can you imagine to Ganymede and back in an hour? Pretty impressive. Ultimately the starship we're hoping to construct will go to 47 Ursae Majoris as the initial goal, more than likely."

"Forty-seven Ursae Majoris? That's forty-four light years away!" Smith whistled as he spoke. "Bucko, you realize you'll never see anyone you know again after you blast off? You'll have to hold a funeral for the entire planet while you're enroute."

"Oh, don't be so morbid. We'll all live to normal lifespans. Mine will just be suspended—or drawn out—over a longer period of Earth time. But it won't seem any longer to me. And I'm convinced it's the best star to visit. Possibly the paw of the Great Bear has a planet we can colonize someday."

"Well, we'll miss you. And who knows if there'll even be a world here when you get back. Ninety years! Can you even imagine the changes?"

"You know me well enough to know that I've got to do it, Smitty. I predict the High Command will approve the long trip instead of a shorter one. Of course I'll miss everybody if they decide to go with the 47 Ursae Majoris voyage. Nobody can predict what the world will be like the way things are going. Scientifically we're progressing by leaps and bounds in our little research enclaves. But out in the world, it just looks to me like society is degenerating. People have become so—there's no other way to put it—so immoral. Have you taken a look around lately, old friend?"

"Hey, people are just people. I've heard you say that quite a few times."

"Yes, but I wish people would act differently. It's a depraved world and I wouldn't be too sorry to leave it behind, if only for a while."

"Could be a lot worse instead of a lot better when you get back, old buddy."

"Might be, but I believe we'll find a way to alter human behavior. We've got to re-establish a work ethic and do something about getting people to stop being so selfish. People won't even raise kids anymore. Very few people have a family of any kind these days, you know. Such concepts have become oddities instead of the norm, Smitty."

"I was supposed to be heading back up to Delta on the afternoon shuttle, but I've got to stay around a few days, on orders from old flyaway hair Schultz. He's doing an electronic profile on me, to include personality, ideals, and even all my eccentricities. He hasn't told me what for, but I'm in for some pretty intensive scrutiny, Bucko."

"I don't envy you, Smitty. They're always coming up with something new. Good luck and I hope you're back on the *New Ranger* before they give the ship to your second in command."

"No chance. This is a voluntary deal, Schultz tells me. Anyway, I ran into a very interesting lady last night, and we've got a date tonight. I'll see you around for a short while, anyway."

The pilots returned to a discussion of the prag c quest at hand, and in the process they got around to planning another trip to the Barnes farm to hunt quail over the holidays. In what was otherwise a dismal and dangerous world there was still joy to be found in small town America, and they looked forward with gusto to some time together in the outdoors. They parted when it became time for Smith's appointment with Schultz.

*　　*　　*

The quail population in Kansas that fall was truly exceptional. Morgan and Smith toured extensive field edges with cousin Jerry as their guide, enjoying the companionship and hard-working dogs. Barnes filled them in on many challenging changes in society in recent years, a society from which the two astronauts were increasingly isolated. Science ruled the land officially, but chaos was an increasingly potent reality. There were unsolved murders and assaults on every hand that were never even investigated. Most crimes were accepted as normal by society and by authorities.

"You probably heard about Jesse Prestone, huh, Buck?" asked Barnes.

"Not a word, Jerry. I get all my news off WorldNet. Did it make the net?"

"Nope. Nothing. Not much on the net about murders, you know. They're too common."

"Was he murdered? I'm not surprised. It's funny, though, that so little negative news makes the net. You'd think from monitoring it that we're a most civil society. When was it?"

"It was several years back, right after your last trip home. His own son killed him. Bar fight at the Hat Trick."

"Spot killed his dad?"

"He did. One of my farm workers was there. Killed him in cold blood."

"Spot always was a bad actor. That's hard to believe, though. Is he in jail?"

"No way. They don't prosecute such crimes anymore. The law stays away from local activities like fights and domestic disturbances, unless they're forced to intervene by somebody. There's not much justice anymore, except the street kind."

"That's a bad kind of justice, Jerry. Where's justice for Jesse?"

261

"He got it in a distorted way. Jesse had just killed old Sam Archer not a month before. Same scenario, too. They had some kind of disagreement. Nobody really knows what it was about. And everybody thought at first that old Jesse had gotten away with it clean."

"I guess there is an ultimate justice, after all, huh? I don't understand why there's so little attention to such social problems," Morgan said, shaking his head.

"It makes a lot of things hard to explain to our kids."

"Kids always take a beating, don't they? I guess I was one of the truly fortunate."

"Your father was one of the best, Buck."

"How well I know. How's your dad?"

"Failing health in some ways, but still active. We'll stop by and see him before you have to leave. We'll probably lose that farm of his to taxes when he dies."

"Your boy Billy not interested in purchasing it?"

"I'm afraid not. Billy shows every sign of abandoning farming for good. He's the original good time boy. I'm lucky to get any help at all from him."

"Don't be too hard on him, Jerry. He might turn out all right yet. I know you and Cindy have been the best parents you could be. Kids are hard to figure."

"Sometimes. Say, did I mention about Spot having a boy?"

"No kidding? Spot Prestone? A child?"

"Yep. By one of his girlfriends, like most kids nowadays. But he's a cute little devil, I must say. I saw him in town one day with his mom. She's a girl named Betty Hoyle whose mother once worked for Cindy here on the farm. And I looked at the boy carefully when I talked to her. He doesn't have a white spot on his scalp like his father, but he still looks a lot like him. She told me Spot was the father, but she apparently hasn't even seen him since the baby was born."

"What about ol' Monty? Is he doing okay?"

"Far as I know. He married Marge McCoy, but Marge acts like she's single all the time, from what I hear. I don't think Monty had much feeling when his father was killed."

"I'd like to see him sometime, I think. Where does he hang out?"

"Hat Trick, I think. You might go by there sometime."

Morgan never did get by the place. It had never appealed to him, and for some reason he had an aversion to entering the building. Monty Archer would have to wait until the next trip to Adrian.

The renowned astronaut had always felt a special admiration for his relatives and hosts, the Barnes family, but this trip home the difference between them and the rabble on the streets was even more apparent than before. He knew that they represented a stronghold of integrity in a ruthless and uncaring society. Jerry had three children and with his wife Cindy they faced a daunting task as they attempted to keep them on the right track. Public schools were mandatory for all students and the values taught reflected those of an increasingly corrupt and impersonal government. Raising children had to be an impossible chore, given the atmosphere that prevailed. Morgan remembered the disorder that had predominated in his own high school over fifteen years before, and he imagined that it could be logarithmically worse today.

It was too bad about Jesse Prestone. And in a strange way, it was even worse about his son Spot. Such promising intelligence, totally misguided and out of control. He couldn't help but think back to the careening experimental nuclear pulse cruiser he had almost ridden into oblivion. Power, potential, and purpose all out of synchronization, the envelope decaying so badly that it was heading for inevitable demise. That kind of chaos had to be the hallmark of Spot Prestone.

* * *

A few months later Morgan was back at the space station, attending the nearly complete test ship, which had been officially given the apt name *Velocidad de Luz* in recognition of the international nature of the space effort. It really didn't matter what official name the vehicle carried, because to the public it was indelibly nicknamed Buck's Baby. Even Schultz was at Space Station Delta with his pet project, donning outside clothes and working on the ship in hands-on fashion. Finishing touches on the engines were in final stages, as most of the assembly work had been completed by this time.

"Buck, we're almost ready to ride. Aren't you a little nervous about this? I mean, nobody has ever approached the speed of light," said Schultz, staring intently into Morgan's face to try and discern any hidden reluctance.

Morgan hesitated only slightly at the sobering thought. He couldn't back down now, no matter what. An implacable determination galvanized in his mind. He would ride, whatever the outcome.

"Doc, I'm ready when the bird is ready. I wonder how Yeager felt back in 1947," Morgan observed, running a hand over the smooth alloy that constituted the surface of the new craft. "You know, nobody had the slightest idea if the speed of sound would be fatal or not. And before that, back in the nineteenth century, they used to debate whether the human body could withstand speeds of forty or fifty miles per hour. It's all a stepwise process. I'd be a fool to claim I'm not in the least afraid. But really this is no different from our testing of the nuclear pulse engine design. I don't plan to die, but even if I do, I'm certain in my heart that I'm involved in something of great significance."

"I appreciate your frankness, son. I just personally wouldn't want to be the first to push it so close to c. You already know it's different from the lower speeds. There are unique things that happen. I'm certain our calculations are correct and that the ship will hold together and perform as expected. But you—you're betting your life on it, and you've got to be certain it's worth it to you."

"So did Yeager. Don't think I haven't considered that—all of it. But I can't imagine voluntarily moving over to let anyone—and I mean anyone—take my place. That would be like Christopher Columbus, after being convinced the world was round, finding another seaman to make the trip. No, I'll hang in there, doctor," Morgan replied emphatically.

"At least you have a bit of extra incentive now. You must be pleased that the High Command approved Project Ursa. We're stepping up to the stars."

"Couldn't be more pleased. And it is extra incentive. For a dream to come true sometimes you have to ride out a few nightmares. Not that this project is a nightmare, unless everything goes space garbage on us."

"The time is approaching fast. First full lightup of our antimatter conversion engines is next week. Once we're sure they work it's only a short step to the first test run."

There had been intensive discussion about doing an unmanned run before risking the life of an astronaut, but in the final analysis, the possibility had been rejected. Someone had to be in the craft to adequately monitor all systems and to do any necessary repairs. Besides, space flight had become so common that nobody gave much more thought to testing a new concept than had been given flying a new airplane in earlier times. No, the human element couldn't be dispensed. A living pilot would have to be on board.

The space station pulsed with intensive activity. The deceptively simple engines fired perfectly except for some necessary tuning, and shortly Morgan was in the driver's seat for the first flight of a ship powered by antimatter conversion. His mind raced as he inspected the familiar but complicated panel, with dozens of extra digital gauges and monitoring devices making the layout a virtual Christmas tree of color. He was intimately familiar with every one of the instruments and how each was connected to thousands of other parts of the dazzling machine. Now the only question was whether the device would function as planned. He looked at the holo display of the technician in Space Station Delta and nodded to him that he was ready.

"Ignition!" He radioed from his position in the single pilot's seat. Morgan's heart pounded with excitement as the ship shuddered and vibrated like the business end of an ultrasound probe. His palms cooled with sweat as powerful engines sprang to life for the first time, and vigorous energy surged through the entire airframe. The complex instrument panel required all his attention, even with assistance from onboard artificial intelligence and an array of supercomputers that were the most modern ever assembled. Because of the unbelievable power of the engines, it was necessary to cast off from the space station as soon as they ignited. The whole sky behind Morgan lit up as if a gigantic lightning storm were bearing down on him. He eased the craft into a predetermined arc around the station, avoiding pointing the ship's tail anywhere near the manufactured moon. He waved to the pilot of his old ship, the *Yeager*, as he eased by, and felt some comfort that the speedy old craft had been assigned standby duty.

Easing away from the station, he monitored his instruments carefully for an hour, measuring every aspect of the machine's performance. On signal from control through the holographic technician, he throttled up just above idle, and slowly but surely felt a frightening outpouring of pure energy. This flight would be only to circumnavigate the earth and rendezvous once more with Space Station Delta, effectively "lapping" the manmade satellite in the process. Within mere minutes, it seemed, he had caught up with his origination point and was docking back in the test bay.

"I don't know what to say! It's hard to believe so much light and thrust is produced without any appreciable wasted heat. I can't wait to push in that throttle," he told Schultz at the debriefing, his face beaming with measured enthusiasm.

"Only with antimatter conversion, my boy. You haven't seen anything yet."

The first few flights were carried out just above engine idle. Several uneventful partial power flights were then conducted in preparation for the big event. The level of excitement onboard Space Station Delta hadn't been so high since nuclear pulse testing several years before. At long last all preliminaries were complete and the go-ahead was given for a run at prag c.

"Morgan, I want you to chop the power at the slightest hint of trouble, understand? We can't be certain how this will go so don't take any chances, okay?" Schultz insisted as the final orientation was completed and the room began emptying.

"Don't worry, Dr. Schultz. I know this ship and I'll be careful. I value my hide."

Engine ignition and disconnect went as usual. Morgan took a deep breath, put the ship through the prescribed arc, and set the navigation system on coordinates for Mars. If he achieved prag c, he would be there in a matter of hours, counting acceleration and deceleration times. There was a nuclear pulse ship orbiting Mars, Jeremiah Smith's cruiser *New Ranger*, standing ready in case it was needed. Morgan took a measure of comfort knowing his old friend would be there in no time to pick up the pieces if anything went wrong. If it went wrong at a low enough speed, perchance, that the *New Ranger* could intercept the debris.

"Power forward quarter throttle."

"Go, Buck's Baby!" came the reply from Delta. The hologram of the Delta technician on the monitor flashed him a resounding thumbs up sign.

The light behind him literally illuminated the sky as he quickly achieved better than 0.2 c, producing an intense Doppler effect on his radio signals that the artificial intelligence automatically calibrated. Every added increment of power was a new speed record for mankind, and he had barely begun the process. He was almost on his own, into an unavoidable period of delayed radio contact due to increasing velocity. He pushed the power lever forward to half, then three quarters, slowly increasing thrust over a period of minutes. The awesome force kept him pushed back firmly in his seat as speed built to levels never before achieved by mankind.

"Three quarters throttle, 0.8 c," he radioed calmly. Special processing of his message would be required to make it intelligible to the station. "Should be power enough for prag c."

Feeling intensifying heaviness in his body, Morgan reached over and manually engaged the mass inversion augmentation control, since increasing mass would soon start to apply a force of unknown consequence to him and the craft. Immediately he felt the weight lifted and he confidently eased the power almost to full throttle. The bright stars ahead of him took on a definite bluish tint, a most striking and peculiar phenomenon. The prag c mark on the speed indicator was still a fraction away, but he seemed to have plenty of available power. As the indicator nudged to the desired velocity, his mass inverter indication began to waver, plunging from well into the green to the top of the red arc in his monitor. There was no more mass inversion compensation available if he pushed beyond his current power setting, and his whole ship might be converted into photons, or some other unanticipated effect might occur. He knew better than to push his luck. He was out of options, but the speed readout was pegged and the mass was equilibrated at 0.995 of the speed of light. Prag c!

All systems were humming, but he knew he would have to rotate the ship and reverse the process with equally effective deceleration if he was to keep from shooting by Mars and the *New Ranger* like a sunbeam. Morgan tried the controls to see how they functioned at prag c, and found the craft as maneuverable as the mathematics had predicted. Soon Mars was looming ever closer in his computer flight profile envelope and he knew he would have to immediately begin deceleration. When power was chopped for the rotation, the craft quickly slowed just below prag c, proving that some degree of intermittent energy input would be necessary to maintain such high velocities, not an unexpected finding. Once reverse thrust was applied, the ship slowed quickly over time to a minute fraction of its top speed. As the planet loomed, he had the ship positioned to enter orbit at the side of the *New Ranger*. He established radio contact and could hear the crew of the ship cheering.

"*New Ranger! New Ranger!* We've got prag c! We've got prag c!"

"You're telling me, you old shotgun toter," came the familiar deadpan voice of his friend Smith. "Dock beside us for tea. Then you can zip out to Ganymede and have a spot of brew with them, too."

"Maybe next time. I'm due back at Delta in a few hours. Can you believe it, Smitty?"

Jubilance reigned and protocol was put on hold for a few minutes while he celebrated on the radio with his old buddy. The artificial intelligence display and the holo-technician appeared genuinely triumphant as well. He did a couple of orbits of the planet just to check out essential systems while the *New Ranger* did a thorough visual examination of the ship's exterior. Finding all in order, none the worse for wear, the artificial intelligence set coordinates for Earth. Orders were to return to Delta at half power so engineers could thoroughly check the ship for damage before doing any more high speed work.

The welcome back to Earth orbit was nothing short of spectacular. Even the celebration of the cure for AIDS was nothing like this revelry. Morgan had a call waiting and had to speak with the President of the United States immediately. Then he tuned in the holographic videocom and viewed news reports of people literally dancing in the streets heralding his achievement. Morgan and Schultz were darlings of the whole world.

Morgan was hungry for more work, but the High Command determined that public relations demanded a pause for the world's fastest man to accommodate his adoring fans. Morgan endured it out of duty but all the while he chafed at being deprived temporarily of his ship. His backup pilot became the second man to achieve prag c, and succeeded in working out many of the fine mathematical details and most of the time dilation calculations while Morgan was unavoidably detained by a worshipful public. There was a lot of fine adjustment to be accomplished, a lot of theoretical design work to be tested, and a lot of conceptual honing to be done before they could build a functional starship.

A starship! Mankind was at long last ready to grasp for the stars.

CHAPTER 21

February 2078

Project Ursa was more than off the ground; it was the talk of the entire world. Humanity was preparing to break the bonds of the solar system and reach out, finally, to probe the far reaches of the galaxy. Interplanetary flight had become boring to most people because every heavenly body in the solar system had been visited, explored, mapped, and mined multiple times. Masses of people caught a tantalizing vision of the unknown beyond nearby planets and moons, and there was no stopping its momentum. Buck Morgan had become a central figure and was the obvious choice to insert flesh and blood into the machine that would bear mankind's first mission to the stars.

"Bucko, you'll go crazy spending nine years alone in space. What will you do to occupy the time?" asked Jeremiah Smith. "You know how boring long hauls can be. Sometimes I almost got suicidal myself spending months between planets. I must admit the disease didn't seem to affect you as much, but it still has to exact a price."

"If you're so concerned, why don't you go with me?"

"No, thank you. I've got other plans. And I understand they've ruled out sending along a second crewmember, anyway. I wonder if even you and I could get along as the only fishermen in the same boat for nine years. And we're best friends."

"You know how complete they make the entertainment center on these big ships. For conversation, the artificial intelligence is the next best thing to a real person. This complex is so real they've named it 'Calvin.' They've even personalized it to fit my disposition and needs. I haven't seen the final result, but they tell me that some of the improvements make the holo display seem alive. I'll miss flesh and blood people, but I'll get by fine. I hope."

"I've heard some talk about the artificial intelligence they're building for your ship. You know, there had been some question about sinking so much money into a project that won't show full results for ninety years, but public pressure has won out. Besides, we've got to do some far-sighted planning if the human race is to succeed in exploring space."

"Yeah, that's one big problem with society nowadays," said Morgan. "Everything has to be instant gratification. It's refreshing to see the public behind a quality venture like this. The motivation may be wrong—sensationalism—but the result is the same. Mankind gets a chance to do something worthwhile. I'd rather see the effort pushed because its noble and right, but I'll take it any way I can get it."

Additions to Space Station Delta had made it truly a satellite of Earth, almost a new moon. It was tremendous in size and had become the third brightest object in the sky, after the sun and the moon. It was so big, in fact, that it could easily be seen in the daytime, the only manmade object ever to be clearly visible above the atmosphere. Incoming nuclear pulse ships continued to add to its mass almost daily, attaching massive rectangles of purified high grade plutonium, platinum, gold, silver, and other less valuable metals mined from the various bases on the moon and beyond. There was still an unsolved problem in getting the final product back to the planetary surface, however, because of Earth's thick atmosphere and strict load limitations for landing shuttles. Every piece of mined material had to await a ride in a shuttle in order to enter the marketplace on Earth. Naturally, only the most valuable metals were landed with priority, meaning several square miles of lower value metal such as iron and copper were destined to wait indefinitely for a ride to the ground, and more accumulated all the time. Despite such distractions, the new starship, the *Ursa C*, was nearly complete at the main construction bay, its antimatter conversion engines already installed. Morgan offered to give Smith a grand tour.

"Smitty, you remember how we begged them to keep the *Delta Dare* intact as a museum? Nobody was very sympathetic to that idea, but they did hold up recycling it. Now they've removed key components to construct this new starship. I think you'll recognize the cockpit and navigation modules. They're the same except for the instrumentation," Morgan explained as they approached the construction area. "And we're keeping one planetary lander aboard, just in case I want to go down to the surface and check out some place in person."

"Wow! They're really going maximum G's on this project. How long did it take to build the old interplanetary cruisers? Four years? Five years? But this machine will be complete in less than a year, you say?" Smith queried. "What's the diff, Bucko?"

"Well, for one thing, the old components we're recycling, like I just showed you. Most of the basic ship was already assembled, although we've had to do some major reconfiguration of the exterior to make it aerodynamic so hyperlasered plasma will stream past smoothly, just like it does on our nuclear pulse ships. And we've had to do a lot of interior remodeling—like for example renewables. We've removed most of the old crew quarters for an expanded garden. Since there'll be only one crewmember, we don't need all that excess sleeping space. But for interstellar voyages we've got to have immense renewables."

"How are you expanding renewables? What are you adding?"

"Eight more animal species and twenty-two more plants. We've even included both a mammalian and an avian predator, just in case a starship commander ever wanted to colonize a planet that would support life. It's the most thoroughly studied, all-encompassing renewables garden ever conceived, it's safe to say. Plenty adequate for several people, it appears to me. There's no question I'll be trashing perfectly good food that ought to be eaten before it's recycled."

The pair inspected the forward section, noting once more its streamlined aerodynamic design, and commenting on the similarity in appearance to much smaller nuclear pulse cruisers.

"The big difference is these engines," Morgan continued, demonstrating the peculiars to his friend. "Schultz is truly a rare genius, not only in developing the antimatter conversion formula but in instantly recognizing its practical application. The bottom line is absolutely unbelievable power, Smitty. This starship should reach prag c as easily as the *Velocidad de Luz* did. The engines are so much larger that acceleration should be little different."

"Ah, yes. Buck's Baby. Everyone's forgotten the real name, you know," Smith corrected. "Even the Smithsonian is planning to label it with the nickname. By the way, I like what they've chosen to name this vessel—*Ursa C*. Ursa for the constellation you'll visit, and c for the speed you'll use. At least, as close to that speed as we can get. The public loves it."

"I like the destination, too. Forty-seven Ursae Majoris is mighty promising for finding a livable world. I might make the greatest discovery of all time—hopefully, Earth's twin planet. Another intriguing fact about this particular star is that it's in the paw of the bear. The Great Bear Constellation, that is. I hope I can escape unscathed."

"You sound like you might be a little scared of the bear," teased Smith. "I didn't know you had any fears about anything."

"Of course there are some old fears, maybe a little apprehension. But what really matters is discovery, and I hope there'll be plenty of that."

"Doesn't sound like Bucko is really frightened. Maybe you're a little remorseful about leaving us all here to die of old age while you streak across the heavens? There's a lot of turmoil on the surface now, you know. That's why I stay up here as much as I can. You never know what kind of changes might occur," Smith worried out loud. "I sometimes ponder the ancient Mayas in Central America. Their civilization collapsed because only an elite few were allowed to learn the immense volume of knowledge their kings and priests accumulated. Their common people were kept uneducated, and eventually that whole society came crashing down. I hope we don't wake up one day and discover that none of the illiterate clods on Earth gives an Angstrom unit about our science."

"Oh, for the love of Venus, Smitty, you sound like I do sometimes," said Morgan. "You've said it before, I think—people will always be people. They'll be hungry for my return, I'll bet. The quest for knowledge never gets old to any generation. I believe science will solve some basic human problems while I'm gone. If not, I'll just have to pick another star."

"Any last requests, Mr. Bear Paw?" asked Smith as the tour concluded. "We have to plan quickly because your time to depart is approaching fast. I hear the High Command wants to blast you off before year's end."

"Only one request. Let's take a two-week furlough in September and go to Alaska one more time. I've always wanted to hunt Dall sheep and I can't think of a better companion than you, Smitty. This will be our final time together so we need to make it the best it can be. Can you make it?"

"Can I? You betcha. I'll make it a point!" Smith replied enthusiastically. "In fact, I'll make some telecom calls and get it arranged for us. Great!"

The construction phase drew rapidly to a close and then live testing of the interstellar ship began in earnest. The engines worked marvelously and it was no problem achieving 0.5 c and better. The mass inversion factor required some re-calibration to compensate for greater size of the enormous starship, but that job was soon accomplished. Achieving prag c was actually easy, and the massive proportions of the starship made no real difference in performance. Morgan first went to Mars and back and later he did more work at sustained prag c out to Pluto and back. He gave a distinguished bevy of high-ranking officials, including the brilliant Schultz, their first taste of deep space in the sparkling new craft, including close-up tours of the lunar arrays of both Jupiter and Saturn. The newest version of the plasmafyer hyperlaser worked even better than the old model, essentially eliminating collisions with particles and small asteroids when used in conjunction with the ion shield. Every aspect of the *Ursa C* was as smooth as bird leather.

Docking back with the space station after final testing, Morgan entered data from the trip into a central computer system for analysis, and then returned to his quarters for a well deserved rest. He had not left the space station in some nine months and he now looked forward to a furlough on Earth's surface.

*   *   *

Monty Archer had always struggled in his relationships with women. He was at first determined to make his hurried marriage to Marge McCoy a success. No one expected it to last more than a few months, since seldom did such unions last very long anymore, except among religious nuts. To be sure, the girl didn't care if it was permanent or not. Her raucous nights at the Hat Trick Bar hardly ceased during their brief period of romance. But Monty tried to make it endure, as much so as he knew how.

Marge's terminal indiscretion was when she failed to return home late one night, and Monty went looking for her. He had reluctantly placed a tracking device in her watch, an easily available espionage unit one could purchase at any discount store, smaller than a period at the end of a sentence. When she failed to arrive home by 3:00 A.M., the young man went searching. He found her in the willing arms of two men in room 221 of the Hat Trick Motel.

In that brief moment, Monty's mind gravitated to an indelible image of his murdered father. The bar and motel had become places of death, rotten to the very foundations. Sam Archer had died at the hands of Jesse Prestone very close by where he was standing. Not that it made any difference, because Sam Archer hadn't cared a proton for his son. But something spoke to the young man as he stood, transfixed at the live image of his wife naked in bed with these men, and he was miraculously able to control his anger. Despite his disgust, he wanted their child to live. He couldn't explain why he cared, but neither could he avoid noticing that she was already showing with their child, her pregnant abdomen mirroring the bulging beer bellies of her lovers. Monty knew her tumescence was his own doing, because somehow he had kept her away from other men for the first couple of months they had been married. It had to be his child.

Before anyone could cover up, he laughed at the trio, a mirthless chuckle that hung heavy with contempt. He had all the information on his adulterous wife he would ever need. His angry impulse turned quickly into an intense loathing of Marge, but he concluded at once that he would rather die than risk interrupting her pregnancy.

"Have a good time, babe," he said with total disdain.

"Don't worry. I will," she returned as he slammed the door.

Sometimes a cuckold husband could be deadly. All three lovers breathed a sigh of relief as he spun on his heels and retreated.

Monty seldom ever spoke another word to Marge. They shared a child when she delivered early the following year, a girl who was named Hilda by her mother. Monty had little input into the upbringing of the child, though he contributed money to an account for her as his means allowed, and he sneaked in a visit with her when opportunity presented. That the youngster shared his genes he could not doubt, as her flaming red mop of exuberant hair and her fair, freckled complexion bore undeniable witness.

*   *   *

Morgan and Jeremiah Smith enjoyed a great wilderness experience in Alaska. The white sheep were still the pride of Alaska, a superbly managed renewable resource that was carefully harvested under intensive scientific scrutiny for sustained yield. There were more of the magnificent creatures than at any time in history and each astronaut took a heavy-horned ancient ram after a truly grueling two weeks of backpacking. Each was required to climb a mountain of several thousand feet to complete his final stalk. Both trophy sheep were old and were likely in their last year of life, had nature been allowed to take its course.

Two astronauts lay out under the stars, viewing with awe the universe stretched out before them. Enjoyment of such a primitive outing seemed to run inexplicably in their blood. There was nothing in the world so inspiring as a starry night on a high mountaintop, where the Milky Way galaxy created a luminous arch of light across the heavens that was a mere hazy streak when seen from lower elevations. The Big Dipper, ever visible in these northerly latitudes, hung like a celestial drinking gourd before them, constantly reminding Morgan of his upcoming travel to 47 Ursae Majoris, a part of that same constellation. He pointed out his destination to himself and his companion repeatedly.

The glistening orb that was Space Station Delta, where both men had spent so much of their professional life, traversed the crystal clear sky. Morgan watched the station track by and disappear slowly over the far horizon on its endless trek. It was as familiar to most human beings as the moon itself, and it stayed aloft just as mysteriously.

"You know, old buddy, there are billions of points of light up there," said Morgan. "It really sticks in my craw that we can visit only a handful of them. Makes me feel a little guilty that with so much work to do, I'm here having the time of my life. Sometimes when I feel a little crazy, I wonder why I'm not a big game guide instead of an astronaut."

"You'll never be a guide, my friend," replied Smith, removing his cap and smoothing his wild mop of hair with his fingers. "Maybe a guide across the heavens to some distant star, but not for any kind of game, I'm afraid. You're completely committed to scientific endeavors. But you're right, Bucko. A trip like this seems to rekindle a passion that I had almost forgotten."

"Smitty, why are all my heroes outdoorsmen of some kind? My Dad is right at the top of the list. But there's also John James Audubon, Teddy Roosevelt, Chuck Yeager, Norman Schwarzkopf, Ernest Warren. Have you read Warren's biography? When the guy landed on Mars, his first words were 'Looks like there'll be mighty poor hunting here!' Can you imagine? It was a totally impromptu comment, they say."

"Beats me. I guess they share a tendency towards open boldness. Maybe you're attracted to some honest spontaneity. Maybe there's just plain old selfless sincerity in them. There's also something especially adventurous about those guys. My favorite quote is from Roosevelt. He said, 'The chase is among the best of all national pastimes. It cultivates that vigorous manliness for the lack of which the possession of no other qualities can possibly atone.' Profound, huh? I wonder if we'd have any astronauts if we didn't have people like that."

"Interesting question. And what Roosevelt said is certainly profound. And time has proved him correct. The words hunter and conservationist are absolutely synonymous in this last half of the twenty-first century, I'm happy to say."

"You're right. And now you blast off on the ultimate adventure, continuing the outdoorsman's contribution to scientific and technological progress. Some privilege, huh, Bucko?"

"Indeed. Smitty, I do hope you have a happy life. Are you ever going to settle down, get a family, anything like that?"

"Why should I? Nobody else does."

"I don't know, I somehow hoped you'd do it differently, I guess. The happiest people I know come from a family background."

"Well, with that comment, I guess now is as good a time to tell you as any. Bucko, there's something I've been reluctant to admit. I'm marrying an old classmate of yours. I've been seeing her for a long time now, and we're going to do it."

"Really? That's great news, Smitty. Who would that be?"

"JoEllen Thacker. I'm going to give up space duty in a couple of years and go back to ground-based work. For her sake, I'm moving back to Montana for now."

The words struck Morgan like a fist in the face, and mentally he staggered a little before righting himself. He looked incredulously at his friend, at first not knowing whether to believe him or not. Smith's expression was sincere and decidedly resolute.

"Seriously? Where did you meet her?"

"At the Cape. She was there on her job, and I ran into her one day. It's been interesting. You know, she's never been married, and she's getting on up in years, like me. But wow, what a woman! I could immediately see why you had an interest in her. Sorry it had to go this way, old buddy."

Morgan stared into the campfire for the longest time before speaking again. An old heartache seemed to burn in his chest like the glowing coals. But if she couldn't be his, he couldn't think of anyone else he'd rather have JoEllen Thacker than his friend. After all, his own relationship to her had never been anything more than possibility. He had to wish them nothing but the best.

"Smitty, that's a mouthful for me to swallow. But it never could be for me, anyway. I wish both of you well."

"Thanks, old friend. I'll pass on that sentiment to JoEllen."

Before he headed back to Space Station Delta, Morgan made one more trip to Adrian. He said an emotional goodbye to the Barnes family, and was almost tearful during his final meeting with Judy Hancock, who was now a relatively young widow with an adolescent son to raise. He assumed that he would never see these people again, and it was harder to take than he had imagined up to that point.

From the Adrian Bank vault he retrieved some special items, including the antique shotgun that had belonged to his father. There would be no shortage of room aboard the starship, so it was no problem to carry along a few keepsakes. These precious belongings of his father were his choice, naturally. Meaningful bits of the past would hurtle into the future with him. Morgan got a tear in his eye as he examined the memorabilia, which included pictures of his mother and father, his father's medals from Terror War III, and a very personal old-fashioned letter his father had written to him during his U.S. Military Academy years. This precious merchandise would all travel with him to the Paw of the Bear.

As an afterthought, he went by the hardware store and purchased a single box of high brass number eight shotgun shells, his favorite quail load. He needed the obsolete style with two and three quarters inches of length, since the ancient shotgun could handle nothing any longer. He noted by the print on the box that each one of the twenty-five shells had an ounce and a half of lead shot, and three and three-quarters drams of powder. Some things never changed. The *Ursa C* was plenty large enough for him to do a little target practice, if he so desired, though he had no real intention of doing so.

*   *   *

The final months of preparation passed smoothly and Morgan was engulfed by last minute details. Stocking the renewables section brought back meaningful memories of his father's farm, and he took great pleasure in the work. It seemed highly improbable for a light speed astronaut to be handling plants, animals, and soil, but it was not only necessary for his interstellar survival, it was immensely enjoyable.

"Morgan, come into the control room with me," ordered Dr. Gerald Schultz on encountering the young astronaut in a long corridor between Space Station Delta and the *Ursa C*. Schultz had a happy twinkle in his eyes, and his collapsed mouth smiled as he spoke. "I've got a surprise for you."

A surprise? Morgan couldn't imagine anything on the ship that would surprise him. He followed with hardly a comment, so puzzled was he by the statement and by the gruff old scientist's obvious glee. They entered the starship control room, and all looked quite familiar, with all buttons and panels unchanged. Without a word, Schultz activated a master switch designated "Artificial Intelligence," and a ghostly image appeared in the co-pilot seat. It took several seconds to completely form, but as it did so the visage caused Morgan's jaw to drop.

"Smitty!" he exclaimed out loud.

"Calvin is the name," said the artificial being. "They've basically cloned all the characteristics of your friend Jeremiah Smith into me. He sat for hours while we extracted all necessary information. Kind of like sitting for a portrait, you might say. I hope you don't mind me going along, Bucko."

Morgan walked all around the apparition, amazed at the similarity to his old friend. Now this was an unexpected and most welcome surprise. Most artificial intelligence holograms were rather generic and looked more or less like a well-groomed holocom newsman, but this one was truly wonderful. A broad grin creased Morgan's face as he contemplated, and with just a few questions to Calvin he became astonished at how comprehensive was the illusion. Unless they could make the hologram look like JoEllen Thacker, he couldn't think of a more fitting companion.

Adding to his delight, Japan's foremost piano manufacturer donated a magnificent instrument for the centerpiece of his entertainment complex. The High Command was well aware of the unheralded talent of their man in this respect, and promptly ordered the piano lofted into orbit for inclusion in the nearly complete starship. Morgan happily installed and tuned it personally. The *Ursa C* would resonate across vast interstellar space to the sound of Earth's finest melodies. The onboard memory system that was a part of Calvin's complex brain easily held the music and words to every piece ever composed.

Just before the scheduled departure, Morgan was best man in Jeremiah Smith's wedding. JoEllen Thacker was resplendent in a pure white gown, as ancient marriage rites were conducted in an archaic church near the Cape. Morgan actually felt great joy that the two were committing to each other in marriage, and he finally got to hug the beautiful blonde after the ceremonies were over.

For the departure, General Staar and the High Command arranged a sendoff never before seen by the Astronaut Corps. Morgan was required to return to the surface briefly for the festivities, where he was given an official farewell by the President of the United States and members of Congress, as well as by many world leaders from other nations. Everyone who knew the handsome celebrity was there. Some surprise visitors included Judy Hancock with her son Bob, and the entire Barnes family. He had to do the final farewell one more time for these special people, and it was even harder the second time around. His old teacher was in the waning stages of youthfulness, that time in life when the face and figure are beginning to show the effects of time, but she was still pretty. She was immensely proud of Morgan and the role she had played in his life, though she couldn't escape the disturbing feeling that somehow she had failed him. With much fanfare the shuttle finally departed carrying the astronaut back to Space Station Delta.

Last minute details were eventually complete and the big day arrived. Morgan and his technical crew had long since programmed the starship's complicated navigation system with data necessary to reach 47 Ursae Majoris. He and Calvin rechecked every detail as all systems except the engines were activated. Pushing back from Delta, Morgan had no reservations about his role or his destiny. He would certainly return to a changed planet in ninety years, only nine years older but probably infinitely wiser and literally light years more experienced. How the world would change was a matter of impossible conjecture, but he harbored no discernible uneasiness in that regard. For now unfathomable adventure

J.Y. JONES

lay before him and consumed most of his thoughts. What would he find at his destination? What important scientific discoveries would he make? Only the trip itself would answer the questions.

The radio crackled a bit, or was it the crewman's voice cracking? "*Ursa C*, bon voyage, sir. We'll be praying for you."

Praying for me? That's an odd good-bye, he thought.

"Please do, Delta. I'll be out of contact in a minute. Say good-bye to everyone."

A true good-bye, Morgan thought. The parting with the real Jeremiah Smith earlier in the day had been painful. It had been similar to the burning, inconsolable pain that he had felt at the untimely death of his father many years ago. Grief had flooded back in a cascade of memories that had threatened to overwhelm his staunch dedication to the task at hand. He hoped nobody had noticed the tears that had clouded his eyes during their farewell embrace.

The crewman on the radio sounded a lot like his friend, but he didn't have the heart to ask him if it were or not. Both of them had suffered enough anguish over it already. Rats, he thought, I didn't mean to get so close to the guy. But when you work so closely like the two of them had, friendships develop. And the hunting adventures they shared had created immutable bonds Morgan would never forget.

"Ignition. Putting her in arc. Throttle forward. Sound speed. Climbing for prag c," he radioed in sequence. The words became stretched and elongated by Doppler effect as the craft accelerated dramatically. The whole earth celebrated the fireworks display that announced the greatest adventure mankind had ever undertaken.

And then he was gone at almost the speed of light.

CHAPTER 22

August 2097

In a dirty ditch near the Colorado-Kansas border, a reptilian hiss of devastating automatic weapons fire echoed through black darkness. Efficient low noise electric firearms burped lead fragments with deadly effectiveness, and the main body of Kansas soldiers sprayed a forward observation post manned by the Sixth Colorado Range Volunteers. In the confusion that followed, a detachment of specially trained troops from the Jayhawk Home Defense Regiment managed to avoid detection as they crouched low in shadowy prairie grass, concealed by the night. Gradually the commandos inched their way toward the base of a huge earthen dam, belly crawling the last fifty yards as high intensity flares began to light up the landscape with an eerie luminescence.

"High explosive depth charges over the top! Prestone, dig in the tunneling rockets!" commanded Colonel Hugh Baxter, a graying infantry officer who was leading the Kansas militia on this crucial mission. The toothy, boyish grin that had helped make him a favorite at his West Point alma mater had faded with age and circumstances over three decades of his military career. Ground warfare was his chosen way of life, and he was a master of the craft. Gone was the broad smile, but his command voice was still clear and intimidating as he barked orders to his troops. "And make it fast. There'll be cowboy reinforcements coming before you can say Gettysburg."

Scrambling men set about performing the assigned tasks, all efficient and calm in their sinister skill with weapons. Baxter coolly surveyed the situation, noting with satisfaction that his snipers were keeping the Colorado cowboys, as enemy soldiers were called with gleeful disparagement, pinned down with murderous accuracy. The West Pointer had been demoted quite a bit from his former glory days when he was a lieutenant colonel in the shrinking United States Army. When he had been "rifted" in another never-ending round of personnel cuts, he had reluctantly taken an unsavory job with the rowdy Kansas Militia, a miscellaneous assortment of volunteers that had been recently augmented by a large number of involuntary conscripts. He wasn't part of a grand army, but at least he was employed doing something he was trained to do. It wasn't much better in the Astronaut Corps these days, he thought wryly as lead fragments whistled deadly notes on all sides.

Alex Prestone Jr. was Baxter's greatest fear. The young man knew firearms and ordinance, all right. Explosions held a fascination for him that was doubtless pathological. As a youth Prestone had been a suspect in a series of bombings that plagued southern Kansas for years, though nothing had ever been proved. Because of his well-known proficiency, struggling Kansas had pressed him into service in desperation. Baxter didn't trust him and hated this forced dependence on him, but he was the only competent munitions expert available. Prestone could easily arm and deploy their astounding burrowing rockets, and destroy for the foreseeable future an odious barrier to the flow of lifeblood to southern Kansas.

And to Kansans, that was exactly what the Arkansas River represented. With headwaters in Colorado's Rocky Mountains, for all the history of the United States of America it had been protected from over utilization, and an equitable amount had been allocated to all parties along its entire course. The ballooning megalopolis of Denver covered the east side of the Rockies almost from border to border in Colorado, and thirsty masses of people craved every drop of available water. The burgeoning crisis had forced the state to take the hard step of claiming all waters that originated within Colorado's boundaries. Colorado's leaders knew that this drastic step would be regarded as an act of war by downstream states, but it was considered necessary. Survival Dam at Holly, Colorado, had been constructed under the watch of a virtual army of security personnel, but nevertheless blood was spilled by deadly Kansas raids on the project early in construction. When the floodgates were finally closed, strangled Kansas had no choice but to declare war.

The plan was for modern subterranean explosive devices to be activated with delayed detonation mechanisms that would allow the raiders time to escape. Even Prestone, for all his snake-eyed instability, seemed efficient tonight. Baxter radioed his second wave of infantrymen into position to cover their retreat, creating an intense barrage of electric small arms noise, the sound of which reverberated like a million rattlesnakes. The cacophony was entirely different from the shocking sequential explosions of past wars, and far more lethal. Indeed, Baxter thought to himself with a measure of satisfaction, warfare has come a long way. There were Colorado infantrymen lying dead all around the dam by the time his explosive charges were activated.

Suddenly, without warning, the Kansas warriors came under precise artillery fire, originating from somewhere far to the northwest but zeroed exactly on their position. Disaster! How could this be? Intelligence had indicated no heavy artillery within striking distance of the dam, but this deadly barrage had no doubt been programmed precisely to hit this strategic location. In a sudden change of events Baxter was caught up in a confusing maze of high-intensity explosions, flying body parts, and bloody dirt. He watched in horror as his commandos disintegrated into sanguine soil, and melted into a mixture of burned flesh and sticky mud, scorched and stinking like a bowel freshly opened. His helmet and his left ear were instantly missing, and what remained of him was thrown some unknown distance by another mighty blast.

Despite the shock, his training made him force himself into a degree of composure, though in the blackness he could see nothing except the incessant flash of small arms and a dazzling burst from more incoming artillery rounds. He fumbled on the trembling ground for his own weapon, which had been ripped away and flung from him by the terrible concussion. He groped blindly in the mud and filth, and finally laid a torn hand on an electric rifle. To his amazement he was unable to use the device because his left arm was also gone. He tried valiantly to fire the weapon but it was almost impossible. He felt himself spinning dizzily and he struggled to maintain consciousness as warm liquid spurted inexorably from his severed limb.

Looking around, he spotted in the confusing melee a dark figure approaching, and noticed the man was also injured, though he was still functional. It was Prestone.

"Prestone, make a stand! We'll have reinforcements shortly! Stand with me!" he ordered the soldier as he worked feverishly to get his weapon in position to operate with his remaining hand, all the while bleeding profusely. "And I need a tourniquet, fast!"

"Do it yourself, colonel. I'm getting out of here!" yelled the departing soldier as he broke into a run. The wounded officer was near collapse, but he shouted an expletive at the fleeing man, cursing him for desertion and cowardice.

Poor Baxter never knew the unspeakable irony of the situation. He died in that grimy ditch before the planted charges exploded and erased Survival Dam and all clues about the disastrous but effective raid. Baxter fell nobly like a warrior from West Point ought to, true to his calling to the end, taking with him in the process a number of brave charging Colorado soldiers. The irony was deepened by the fact that the State of Kansas never suspected his heroism in the daring mission that restored the flow of precious water. No one would ever know that the real hero died for the cause, and the state mistakenly heaped inappropriate and unending praise and adulation on the sole survivor of the explosives detachment: Alex Prestone Jr.

* * *

Hilda Archer's parenting was average for the times, with a mother who was partying and a father who was missing. Education was seldom emphasized, and challenges to achieve were nonexistent, except simply to survive. Such was the state of contemporary society, and the distorted process was perceived as perfectly normal by virtually the whole world.

Her father Monty Archer had been repeatedly rebuffed in attempts to influence the child's development. Marge McCoy seldom even let him see the girl, and he almost never was allowed to spend any time with her, except on the sly. Marge did tolerate one small favor Hilda's father did for the girl, one that Monty hoped might be helpful. He gave her copies of every book her ancestor, Clemon Archer, had written. Monty had inherited the volumes, and he passed them on to give his daughter a sense of family history. Of course, he totally disagreed with much of what was written in the books, but it didn't occur to him that Hilda would actually read them anyway. Maybe the girl would get some stimulation from simply knowing that her ancestor had been a learned man.

"Hilda, see me after class," commanded Judy Hancock sternly. "Class dismissed."

The whole motley herd disappeared raucously through the door, glad to be free of her evenhanded discipline. Few of the day's young people had experience with such a controlled atmosphere and she had become something of a dreaded legend among the students. The government pension she had been promised had vanished in a wave of uncontrollable inflation that had finally resulted in the collapse of the American dollar, and it looked like she'd have to work indefinitely, probably long beyond usual retirement age. Her husband Terry had perished two decades before in a vehicle accident, leaving her little security, no money, and a young son to raise.

"You wanted to talk to me, ma'am?" inquired Hilda, puzzled that the older woman would make such a request of her.

"I did. Don't look so worried. I just want to discuss something with you. Hilda, how old are you?"

"Eighteen. Almost nineteen. My mom didn't let me start school until I was seven."

"Hilda, this is your last year of high school, and you've some major decisions coming up. What in the world is important to you?" she began seriously.

"Clothes. And a man I know. Why?" And what business is it of yours, she thought to herself. Nosy teacher.

Hilda's most unorthodox dress had been apparent for a long time, and consisted of rare plant fiber and synthetic cloth. She wore hardly a trace of common animal skin attire that was worn by virtually all her classmates. And she says clothes are important? The teacher stared at this chirpy girl with flaming red hair, so bright and intelligent that she bordered on brilliant. She remembered having the girl's father, Monty Archer, as a student many years ago. Monty had been through a couple of divorces but seemed to have settled down into a mostly routine small town life. With just a little encouragement, his daughter had tremendous potential, if only someone could direct it.

The teacher wasn't sure how much input Monty had given toward his daughter's well being—she hadn't seen her old student for years. Monty had lived a life that was more stable than most and had kept a steady job, but consistency in his relationships with women remained a glaring weak point.

"Hilda, don't you have any inclination toward trying to do something significant with your life? You're so smart and you have so much aptitude and ability that it shines through, even when you're not interested in what I'm saying. I know your friends might be shocked if you excelled in class, but wouldn't it be worth it? Can't you see down the road a little ways beyond the immediate?"

The look on Hilda's face was highly dubious. The teacher considered again the unquestionable fact that the girl showed flashes of promise—a keen intellect that she couldn't always hide, even under threat of ostracism by her peers; an ability to grasp concepts that regularly escaped other students; even a brightness of eye that reminded her of youngsters of an earlier time. Why couldn't she reach any of them anymore?

"Hilda, why can't you see what I'm trying to tell you? Did you know your father was a good friend of Buck Morgan, the famous astronaut? They took a trip to Alaska together when they were boys. And look what a contribution Buck Morgan has made to society. Don't you want to do something great like that?"

"I don't see much of my real father. My mother has a man in the house to provide guidance for me, though. She changes boyfriends periodically so I get a well-rounded view of the world. I've got my own steady boyfriend, too. And I don't know very much about this Morgan fellow."

She had heard about the hero-girl relationship that was going on between Hilda and Alex Prestone, Jr. Alex, of all people, a self-sacrificing hero. She had taught him for a brief period and knew him to be anything but heroic. He had seemed to despise people, and had been very irresponsible in his studies. She couldn't escape the feeling that there was something wrong with the gallant image he was projecting.

"So you aren't interested in your father, Hilda?"

"Oh, sure, Mrs. Hancock, he's tried to be nice to me. But I find my grandfather more interesting. And my great-grandfather is the most interesting. His name was Clemon Archer and he wrote books. I've been reading them."

"I've heard about him. At least you're reading." And at least you know something about your family history, which is a lot more than most kids know, she thought before adding, "What did you find out about him?"

"He was a perfect conservationist. He loved animals more than anybody else in history, maybe. He did a lot of really great things, including putting lots of wild animals where there hadn't been any."

"I've heard about his exploits. You enjoy his books, then, Hilda?"

"More than that. I'm going to try and finish what he started. Things like eliminating abuse of animals. They have as much right to die of old age as we do."

"You're swimming upstream, Hilda. Science makes such determinations now, unlike in your great-grandfather's day. He lived during a time when emotions were a major part of the decision-making process and many people were strongly influenced by how they felt. Today the facts are the supreme authority. You may find your task a bit of a struggle."

"I don't care," the girl retorted. "Please don't mention my biological father to me again. He means well, but something must have happened that ruined him. Have you read any of my great-grandfather's books?"

"Yes, I have, Hilda. Pretty impressive. I can't say I agree with all he wrote."

"What you or anybody else thinks isn't important. I'm going to make sure his dreams for the world come true. You'll see."

The older woman pushed her long hair aside and adjusted the quaint spectacles on her nose. My stars, she thought, Clemon Archer lives! For better or for worse, the girl was at least ambitious about something, even though her cause was more than a bit odd. The girl's great-grandfather had been a gifted author, whatever else one could say about him, and his books were classics. But his passion had been one of those impossible fantasies that had been roughly thrust aside by the god of science.

"I'm told the world is changing, Mrs. Hancock. And I've got help. We've got to start treating animals with due consideration. This mindless obedience to heartless science has got to stop," Hilda declared, edging toward the open door. "But I've got to go now. My friends are waiting outside. They're probably wondering what we're talking about. We've got plans this evening. Excuse me?"

There was steely determination in the girl's voice that surprised the widowed teacher, a metallic hardness of opinion. The chill she felt was enough to ignite a deep sense of apprehension in the woman, and she sensed an uncanny presence—some kind of force she couldn't identify. What was it about this girl?

"Okay. But just remember, if you're ever interested in talking, come and see me," she concluded. "See you tomorrow."

She walked to the window and followed Hilda with her gaze as the young woman ambled across the school grounds, her flaming red hair bouncing energetically. On a grassy islet she met and embraced a mature man and planted a passionate kiss on his lips in full sight of the whomever might be watching. The fellow had the profile of her old student, Spot Prestone, but it couldn't be him. Spot had been dead for several years now, killed in a gruesome jet cycle crash. That has to be his hero son, Alex Prestone, Jr., though the distance was too great for her to be certain.

With a deep sigh she gathered her books and headed for the door. It had been another hard, frustrating day trying to do the impossible. The age of science, she muttered under her breath with unconcealed contempt.

* * *

290

Tonight was midweek church service at Buck Morgan's old church, where Judy Hancock had been attending now for many years. The church had been without a pastor for several decades and relied on one member or another to do whatever preaching took place. Still, here was the only place she could find any confidence for the future, any semblance of an ordered and disciplined lifestyle. Among the handful of believers there remained an attitude of optimism and hope, a distinct divergence from the prevailing disposition of society.

"Evening, Jerry and Cindy. Things okay at the Barnes farm?" the gray-haired teacher inquired of an aging farmer and his wife. The couple still lived on the farm where Buck Morgan had grown up, and she knew them to be rare solid citizens and excellent stewards of the land.

"As well as they can be under the circumstances, Judy. How does Bob like his new job?"

"Fine, I believe. He's quite capable, I think," she replied with some pride showing through. Her son, Bob, had become one of the most respected young men in the area, with rare and unwavering integrity. The local protein plant had hired him as the new operations supervisor.

"Gets tougher every year to stay in the black in our end of the business," said Barnes. "Seems like the shorter the food supply gets the harder the jargonauts work to impede our production. It's worse than ever now."

"What's changed, Jerry?" she asked, sensing the couple was more than a little down, their usual smiling optimism replaced by despairing frowns of frustration.

"Besides jargonauts, you mean? Well, now I've got a lawsuit against me charging cruelty to my stock. On top of everything else I've got to defend against that. I'll tell you, since Dad died the whole world has gone absolutely crazy."

"Cruelty? On what basis? You've must have the most modern, humane farm operation in the world. And you produce the best protein imaginable. Cruelty?"

"The very fact we utilize animals in any way is unacceptable to some people," he replied, his voice showing an unusual impatience. "I guess they want all us protein farmers to start growing yeast. Since yeast are microscopic animals, I guess they aren't cute enough to qualify for special protection. Yeah, they were out demonstrating again last week. Mostly strangers, but I recognized a couple of people from Adrian, too."

"You know, I had an interesting conversation with a student today. We discussed exactly what you're talking about. That movement really died out many years ago—almost died, at least. I thought we'd never hear from that kind of thinking again, but I guess they're back."

"Unquestionably. Trouble is that nobody's much interested in facts anymore, either," Cindy said with resignation. "It's all following your emotions, doing what seems good, and there's no respect for anything past, present, or future. We have the hardest time with our kids. No disrespect to you, Judy, but the schools are full of indecency and rebellion. Times are ripe for slipping back into the dark ages, if you ask me."

"You're not telling me anything new. I had a couple of kids trying to have sex in class last week. Other students crowded around my desk to shield them so they could do it. Kind of like a dare thing. Not a single child in my class had the integrity to say no to it, or else maybe they just don't even know it's wrong. I wouldn't have blamed you a bit if you had just kept your kids home, if you could. But the courts and the jargonauts eliminated that option years ago, didn't they?"

"Too late now. Billy and Charlotte are both grown and immersed in popular culture. We're still hopeful they'll see the light, and we pray for them constantly," added Barnes.

"I think there will always be a faithful few, and our kids may come around. They know right from wrong, even if they aren't acting like it now," said Cindy. "If we could just get them away from some of the ungodly influences they're exposed to all the time."

"I know Billy has a good head on his shoulders, and so does Charlotte. I think they'll see the light. It's not too late," Mrs. Hancock assured him. "Just keep praying. We all will, in fact. And we'll pray about this lawsuit, too. God has a plan for all this, and we'll just have to keep trusting that everything will work out."

"I haven't given up. But in the meantime I've got my work cut out for me," Barnes railed on. "Those people are even trying to make everyone go back to plant fiber clothing. Where are we going to get enough land and water to grow that stuff? It takes every acre and every high tech trick imaginable to produce sufficient food on what we have now. Where do they think our food and fuel come from?"

"Empty lives are easily filled with foolishness," said Mrs. Hancock. "And most lives are empty these days."

"They're showing all kinds of gory graphic details about our farming operations on three-vee. The presentations are really slick and they use various baby animals extensively to get the viewer's sympathy," Barnes lamented. "Lots of celebrities are signing on to assist."

"Is that right? I don't ever watch the holo anymore so I wasn't aware of that," marveled the teacher. "I'd wager Buck Morgan wouldn't believe what's happening in the world today. He was a real fanatic about sustained utilization of all our resources. He'd be completely repulsed by ideas these people are pushing. You know, he should be over halfway to that star by now, assuming he's still alive and well."

"I know my old cousin trusted in nothing that couldn't be measured and calculated," Barnes noted. "Every discussion I ever had with him we always seemed to dwell on scientific matters. But you know, deterioration of society has stopped scientific progress cold. I don't see how anyone could possibly become a trained scientist when excellence is so out of style. The space program seems to be winding down, too. I haven't heard much about it lately."

"If you've noted how much excellence is out of style, you ought to try teaching," sighed Mrs. Hancock.

"What you hear on the news is invariably about wars," Cindy said. "We didn't have a major war for nearly fifty years and now there must be two dozen going on around the world. Country against country, and internal civil wars, too. I've heard that Kansas is mobilizing the militia again to invade Colorado because they're back at it, building that illegal dam up the Arkansas River, same as before. Oh, Lord, please don't let us wind up with a major conflict right here in our back yard. Heaven help us if we do."

The three sat silently for several moments contemplating the drastic changes that their generation had experienced. The Federal Government was so bankrupt it couldn't pay for much of an army any more, so the various states had reverted to volunteer militia with paid officers recruited from the semi-defunct U.S. Army. A war between states would run its awful course without interference from outside authority, more than likely. Hardly an eyebrow had been raised in Washington about the earlier dam-destroying raid that had killed several hundred soldiers.

"Come to think of it, I haven't heard much about Buck Morgan's mission lately, either," observed Mrs. Hancock. "We used to get a progress report on the holo every now and then, but they've tapered off and stopped. The news media seems to have relegated his departure to obscurity. I still teach about it, but I'm the only one who does, as far as I know. And even after I cover science and historical material, the students don't know much more than when I started. Today, for example, the smartest girl in the class hardly remembered Buck Morgan. And that child is Hilda, none other than the daughter of his old friend Monty Archer, of all people."

"Hilda Archer? She's one of the Adrian people who were out demonstrating, along with that Prestone guy," Barnes observed thoughtfully. "Old Monty's a real story, isn't he? A genuine aberration in that family. He never had any sexual morals, but he has a certain kind of integrity. He loves the outdoors and he even helps me train bird dogs sometimes. I understand his father was a committed vegetarian and never gave up his convictions."

"If you think Monty's father was strange, you should have known his grandfather," confided Mrs. Hancock. "I was a little girl when he died, but I still remember him. He was renowned around Adrian. I wonder how Bob would've handled it that time when Clemon Archer assaulted the protein plant with a bulldozer. Another time he crashed a

Passover meal at Andy Rosenthal's home. He called him some dirty names right to his face."

"Nasty names? Why?" asked Cindy.

"The Passover meal has consisted of roasted meat for nearly 4,000 years, ever since its inception. Clemon was also a dedicated vegetarian."

"Oh, I see," said Cindy. "I guess I knew that."

"So what do you think Buck would say about these protests and such?" asked Barnes.

"Well, I think he'd be appalled at what's happening here today. But I think he knew society was on the brink of some drastic changes before he left," Mrs. Hancock said thoughtfully. "I think it would be terribly ironic if his science god had tottered and fallen over while he was gone."

The ancient door of the building creaked and opened, allowing a half dozen newcomers to enter the darkened sanctuary. The group looked up from their somber discussion and welcomed the arrivees. One of them was handsome young Bob Hancock, a blonde giant with curly hair and a smile that captivated. He warmly embraced his mother before greeting the Barneses and taking his seat. Another small group filed in within seconds and joined the gathering.

"Here come the others," said Mrs. Hancock. "Let's share with them this lawsuit problem you have, Jerry. Then we'll pray about it. Only God can solve society's problems, but we individuals have to take it one obstacle at a time."

*   *   *

Buck Morgan awoke with a start, sweat pouring from his furrowed brow, as the seeming reality of a horrifying dream slammed into him. It had appeared so real, so frightening, so imminent. He swung his feet off his bed and felt the pull of artificial gravity sucking them toward the metallic undergirding of his sleeping quarters. He blinked sleepily and looked around, half expecting to see a grizzled old man or his father somewhere in the immediate area. Both were long dead, though, and that certainty dawned upon him slowly. He rubbed his head and ran his fingers thoughtfully through his ruffled dark hair.

It had seemed so tangible and convincing, the nightmare that had just left him. He could almost feel cold claws ripping at his own flesh, and the dead woman's appearance was so awful. Blood was everywhere and chaos had littered the darkened, ethereal landscape. It had been so grotesque and so frightening.

How could something that happened so long ago rush upon him like an armed man? Somehow, it had seemed so immediate. Was there more to this time warpage phenomenon than scientists could calculate?

His body seemed to weigh twice as much as normally. He pulled himself erect on shaky legs and struggled to steady himself. Pictures on the wall and pleasant music emanating from the artificial intelligence console somehow belied his present loneliness and desolation. The *Ursa C* was designed to be eminently livable and human friendly, but for the moment it didn't seem to be so. It looked rigidly artificial, devoid of life, empty of love such as he had felt from his mother so many eons ago in those nearly-forgotten times.

Mother and home were two concepts he had long since relegated to utopia status. Indeed he had lost his beautiful, warm, and affectionate mother those many years ago, long before details could be stamped indelibly into his memory. Many subsequent conversations, both spoken to him and overheard by him, had cemented numerous aspects of the tragedy into his consciousness. Some minute parts of that ordeal he couldn't confirm, but most stood out like truth carved into granite. He knew what had happened, even though his exact recollections were foggy at best.

With some effort he shook off the commanding presence of the dream and forced himself to rationality once more. He had always prevailed by implementation of this virtue, and this time would be no different. There were measurements to be taken, calculations to confirm, and a scientific journey beyond description unfolding before him.

He glanced at a calendar clock on the wall, noting rapid movement of its digits as Earth time flowed by at an astounding rate. He had left orbit around his home planet less than two years ago, and yet the timepiece was already registering nearly two decades. Warpage of the space-time continuum was already exacting its toll on the world he had left behind, while he was experiencing the expected slowdown.

He slowly moved into the adjacent control room, the brains of his machine that could hardly be labeled a cockpit. It measured ten meters by ten meters, exactly symmetrical dimensions reflecting a zeal for uniformity and balance which were hallmarks of the scientific community. He moved toward the comfortable captain's chair, but before he could reach his command seat a pleasant and reassuring voice greeted him.

"Good morning, Commander Bucko. You rested well."

"I guess I did, Calvin. I wish I had your endurance," Morgan related to the person in the holographic display chair. The image looked so much like Jeremiah Smith, and was so extraordinarily lifelike, that Buck Morgan was rapidly coming to look upon the apparition as a real person.

"Endurance has its drawbacks. You creatures of flesh and blood hold many advantages over laser diffraction patterns and aggregations of microprocessors such as myself."

"True. But we've several downsides. Ever dream, Calvin?"

"Dream?" came the question in a tone of voice that Morgan had come to recognize as a query delay. It never took more than a few microseconds for the artificial intelligence to research even the most complicated issue, and usually such a pause came only when there was an abstract concept involved. Dreaming was beyond the normal reach of even Calvin.

"Yeah, dream. I had a dream," reiterated Morgan as he scanned his mechanical helper for any sign of consternation or feeling. A tremendous amount was programmed into the artificial intelligence, but he found himself hoping continually for some burst of spontaneity like the real Smitty would display.

"Dream. An instance or series of images, ideas, or emotions that afflict carbon-based beings during periodic physiologic states of rest. No,

I do not dream, although Jeremiah Smith dreamed extensively," stated Calvin. The holograph's handsome features flashed with satisfaction as it solved the puzzle, and its wild hair radiated in even more random fashion.

Morgan checked the navigational readings, finding all to be as expected. Systems were humming like a Swiss clock, never missing a beat. The immense engines had performed miraculously. They were currently in shutdown, but unlimited fuel and completely automatic speed-sensitive ignition made them fire up periodically in order to automatically maintain 0.995% of light speed. They had run continuously for several days on leaving Earth orbit, but now they were needed only to occasionally boost the craft back to the desired velocity as the sun's fading gravity and occasional contact with interstellar molecules slowed the machine ever so minimally.

The key star to which they were traveling, 47 Ursae Majoris, lay some twenty-eight light years ahead from them. At their current speed, they would reach their destination just a fraction over four years and eight months from takeoff. Could they find a planet there like Earth, with water and oxygen, and with a size that would allow normal physiologic processes for human beings? It was a long shot at best, but it should nevertheless be some adventure.

Morgan was satisfied that all was well on the *Ursa C*. He advised Calvin that he was going to visually check the rest of the ship, a task that would consume several hours, and he strolled from the control room. Everything from the dairy to the animal lab required his personal attention, although Calvin's electronic tentacles extended throughout the ship as well. There was nothing better than a human eye to actually look at their charges, though.

His tasks finally at end, Morgan retired to his quarters, leaving Calvin to perpetually supervise the complex craft. He took a hot shower, donned his soft leather robe, and then sat down at the gorgeous Japanese piano. He fingered the keys thoughtfully before settling into a concert of Mozart's *Jupiter*. The haunting strains reverberated throughout the starship, and the effect was satisfying. Afterward, Morgan retired to his plush cabin and reclined thoughtfully on his bed. He stared at the ceiling in disconnected fashion, his arms limp at his side and his legs crossed. He closed his eyes momentarily, but was not successful in shutting out images conjured up in the disturbing flashback to his earlier life.

He would be all right. He had a job to do, and he would do it like always. He would do it well. Anything for science and anything for human progress. Morgan had already paid some awful prices, and this latest foray was nothing really new. Just longer and more adventurous, but not really new.

Still, there remained something disquieting in his dream, something he couldn't put away. He hoped the whole memory would dissolve, but it clung to him like dirt. For the longest hours, he tossed and turned and sought a comfortable position. Finally, in exhaustion, he slipped off into deep sleep.

CHAPTER 23

January 2119

"I have an appointment with Mr. Henderson," the man told the receptionist crisply. "Please tell him Waymon Prestone is here."

"He's expecting you. Come with me, please," replied a pretty lady behind the desk as she looked Prestone over with admiration. His thin frame was clothed smartly in the latest in fashion suits, made of expensive and rare synthetic material. His red hair was swept back from a stylish middle part, and his long locks almost covered his small ears completely. His petite nose adorned a face that could have easily been that of a choirboy, angelic and serene. The only discernible flaw was his snake-like eyes, so reptilian that one almost expected to see vertical pupils. Small distraction, she thought to herself, considering all the positives. "I'm Terri. I'll see you in. Welcome to the Continental Humane Society."

He followed the well-endowed woman's swaying hips as she led him into the organization's swank executive office. Prestone noted with palpable envy the paneled walls, deep carpet, and polished antique furnishings. After a courteous knock, they stepped through a monstrous oak door bearing a brass nameplate that announced the suite's occupant. A portly man sat at an oversized desk, surrounded by a plethora of congratulatory plaques and other tokens of appreciation. He arose as they entered and extended a manicured hand in mock welcome.

Prestone knew instinctively how to take control of almost any situation. The young man had grown up under Hilda Archer's driving iron hand, and she had successfully instilled an uncommon desire to excel, and a fierce aspiration to change the very fabric of society. Hilda suffered a deep loathing for everybody within her sphere of contacts if their philosophy or behavior in any way conflicted with her own views, and had successfully passed along that attitude to her son.

Waymon Prestone had grown up in a home where discord and parental fighting, punctuated by frequent breakups and makeups, were the norm. Hilda had finally put a stop to their incessant bickering by killing the boy's father, Alex Prestone Jr., before the explosive and unpredictable man had found an opportunity to do the same to her. As was usual in the times, there had been no visible penalty and she had continued to live a libertine lifestyle as she moved from man to man almost monthly. Through it all young Waymon received thorough indoctrination into her philosophy, including the unspoken message that good times and frequent sex were a top priority in life.

Waymon fled home after high school to get away from his testy and capricious mother, and he fell under the influence of a cult of vegetarian nature worshipers. Prestone had never been fed a bite of meat in his entire life, except for yeast extract. Association with the pagan cult seemed like a perfect fit. Besides, women at their compound were free for the taking and continuously available.

But the youth was a born power broker, and his tenure there was short lived. He began jockeying early for a position of authority, feigning a strong desire to further the sect's aims. Unfortunately, he had great difficulty working under supervision, and in less than a year his clashes with the authoritarian leadership had led to his unceremonious ouster from the glitzy compound.

Prestone flourished despite this setback. He began a journey that had taken him to the doorsteps of power all over North America. Never content, he had left his Kansas home and set out on a highly visible protest tour that covered the continent. Wherever there was any form of creature utilization, Prestone would show up, bringing with him his growing cadre of volunteers. By the time he walked into the lavish offices of the Continental Humane Society, he had become a youthful force for species equality that could not be ignored. At age twenty-one he was already an expert at incessant and convincing argument, a powerful wizard with words who skillfully clouded scientific facts, and a masterful guru of high visibility, high confrontation protests. His determination, his nerve, and his bold tactics had gained him widespread notoriety. In his wake followed an increasingly sympathetic and adoring news media with holocom cameras ever at ready.

"Mr. Henderson, I want to join your organization," began Prestone, his unblinking eyes fixed like an attacking cobra on the pudgy man behind the desk.

"Well, you're certainly welcome. Our membership is open to all people with an interest in animal welfare," replied Henderson as he squirmed perceptibly and shifted around some nondescript papers on his desk. "The secretary out front can sign you up if you like."

I'd like to sign up with her all right, thought Prestone. But that can wait.

"I've got a proposal that I believe will interest you. I want to increase your membership and your visibility dramatically and advance the war for species equality by uniting my organization with yours," Prestone explained, his serpentine eyes still riveted on Henderson.

Henderson knew that Prestone's group, the Species Freedom Foundation, was deeply despised by most animal utilization groups. He shifted uncomfortably in his chair under Prestone's unrelenting gaze.

"Mr. Prestone, you may be talking about trying to mix oil and water. You see, the Continental Humane Society has been on the scene for over 200 years. We think we have a creditable record on behalf of humane treatment of animals. I don't know about merging our groups. Your approach is different, you know."

Henderson could feel the intensity and the burn of Preston's unmerciful scrutiny. He again changed positions conspicuously and drummed his fingers nervously on the mirror-like finish of his desk.

"At the Species Freedom Foundation we're probably more aggressive than you are in promoting the welfare of disadvantaged species. That's to your shame and to our credit. Our organization fervently believes that our fellow organisms should be treated exactly like people. After all, it's common knowledge that we humans descended from animals and that we are in fact ourselves nothing more than a highly evolved life form. Why should humans be allowed to take advantage of other creatures just because they are handicapped by the impersonal whims of evolution?"

"Mr. Prestone, you realize that we work with dozens of diverse groups who utilize animals. I'm saying utilize, you understand. Sometimes that means killing animals and using their bodies for food, clothing, fuel, and the like. Other organizations and individuals that use living animals are voluntarily policed as well—pet owners, zoos, aquariums, rodeos, circuses, and so on. But the ultimate utilization group is where I certainly don't think we could fit together. Exactly how do you propose we join forces?"

"I don't believe you're truly serious about helping disadvantaged species, sir. I've researched the Continental Humane Society and I find among your members a groundswell of interest in a fundamental change to your approach. These people you say that you police only tolerate you, you know. They don't necessarily support you, and who cares what they think, anyway—we're in this for the abused, aren't we? Unite with us and we'll have total commitment to these issues. We'll get equality for all species and the inalienable rights they really deserve."

Prestone paused to assess Henderson's response and astutely perceived that he was wavering, undecided what to do. He assumed his most convincing voice as he continued.

"We need to merge our two entities for increased clout. We'll have more politicians joining if we're big enough and vocal enough."

Henderson was silent for a moment, studying this focused young man before him. He then released a deep sigh of resignation.

"I'll study your proposal and discuss it with our board. I can't promise you anything, mind you. I can see some merit, as well as some risk, in what you're suggesting. I can't help but think we'll be hurt badly if we take this approach. Think of the backlash from farmers, dermal clothiers..."

And that's not all of them, thought Prestone, but he didn't say so. He was appalled at how small this man thought. All he really wanted today was for him to agree to put it before the board.

"Don't worry, Mr. Henderson. We'll prevail over all of them. I guarantee it. I'll wait to hear from you."

But he did nothing of the sort. Prestone and his aggressive henchmen fanned out and confronted personally every member of the society's board of directors. Surprisingly they found a lot of support for their radical position. It turned out that most board members were city dwellers who had little idea about various groups of utilizers policed by the Continental Humane Society. Their measure of sympathy for them was amazingly low. Becoming more vocal and more confrontational in advocating for the rights of non-humans had a distinct appeal. There were precious few holdouts, but Prestone's men made sure that nobody with a negative view of the proposed merger made it to the board meeting. The offer sailed through virtually without a question being raised. It had really been remarkably easy.

Waymon Prestone in an earlier time might have been a banker or a Wall Street broker. He was intelligent, resourceful, and well educated. He kept himself immaculately groomed and unblemished. He was strikingly handsome in appearance, as the good-looking receptionist had noted. He kept his ample head of crimson hair combed perfectly, his trademark central part in place, and his smooth face shaved cleanly. Makeup dutifully applied each day kept him perpetually holocom ready for frequent impromptu interviews, although his fair, flawless complexion really didn't need much assistance.

His speech was his most arresting quality. He was articulate to a degree that was astonishing to both admirers and adversaries. In debate he was scalpel sharp, and he always kept any unlucky opposition hopelessly outmaneuvered. His ability to capture an audience and to convince it of the correctness of his position was almost supernatural.

And capture and convince he did. He quickly displaced Henderson as head of the suddenly expanding Continental Humane Society, and sent his shortsighted predecessor to an early and unplanned retirement. Prestone's job, as he saw it, was to grip the nation and beyond with his message. He was so dedicated and so amazingly intense that one had to believe in his sincerity if nothing else he espoused.

Despite being raised in small town America, Prestone had never had any contact with animals in his entire life, except for the processed type he loathed. He had never even owned a pet of any kind. He was interested in nature in only the most detached sense, and had obtained virtually all his education on the outdoors and its creatures by strolling in the city park or watching an occasional three-vee documentary. He had devoured all of his great-great-grandfather's books repeatedly. What had originally been required reading assigned by his overbearing mother he now knew word for word.

He had been raised a strict vegetarian, and rebellion had entered his mind only rarely. Once he had tried concentrated protein, but he had recoiled from the morsel at mere thoughts of eating animal flesh. While attending high school he had been exposed to a protein packing facility as part of an economics assignment. The smells and sights had turned his stomach, and he had left physically nauseated, not unlike a medical student might respond to his first session in the anatomy laboratory or operating room. Thereafter he fully accepted the ideas of his ancestor Clemon Archer, as well as his mother's teachings. He had sworn off meat to become a dedicated vegetarian to the core, except for the unavoidable yeast extract.

Like his mother, he really strongly disliked people, a trait he was most adept at hiding. While he regularly attended fundraising and publicity banquets featuring the upper crust of humanity, he was disgusted by all of them. He absolutely refused to mix with any of the teeming masses, which he viewed as a form of pox upon the earth. Non-humans were to him far more noble and more worthy than despicable mankind.

In line with his convictions, he disdained processed leather garb and became a peculiar sight in his highly unusual all-cotton-and-fiber clothes. In an earlier time man-made clothing would have been an obvious option, but scarcity of petroleum made synthetics entirely unavailable except to the very rich.

Prestone had the ability to attract disciples in a remarkable way, and shortly other strangely dressed followers began to appear all over North America as he spread his gospel. This cadre of hardened activists viewed the charismatic Prestone as a rising messiah of species equality. His soon became a movement that spilled over onto the national news scene and was rapidly nationwide in scope.

He steadily built his empire on the foundation of rampant ignorance among the great mass of common people. Scientific facts were his worst enemy, he discovered early in the business. Anything he could do to discredit or negate them was positive for the cause. Often the best and most effective attacks he could devise were presented in deceptively objective format, citing pseudoscientific supporting studies by supposed authorities who actually worked for the Continental Humane Society. The general population was entirely unable to sort out the true facts, or else they simply didn't care. Whichever way, the effect was the same.

Fundraising was one of Prestone's most important functions. His life was one of continual movement as he hopscotched about the country and the world promoting his goals. Smooth speech and a polished appearance made him a favorite everywhere he went.

"Nice crowd tonight, Mrs. Johnson. I do hope everyone is primed to be generous toward our essential cause," Prestone said in a soothing voice, riveting his small eyes on the woman as he casually groomed his flamboyant head of hair. "Of course, your chapter is always so hardworking and dedicated. I know your efforts will pay dividends, my dear."

"Thank you, Mr. Prestone. We all do our best," gushed a matronly woman who was head of the local chapter. She adjusted her tight, stylish processed leather skirt and continued, "I'd do anything for my two dogs—the darlings! I'm going to give the Continental Humane Society a big piece of my will in their name."

"Why, that's marvelous, Mrs. Johnson. How generous! I can promise you that we'll use it for the highest purposes," enthused Prestone. "Isn't that wonderful, Terri?"

The young man wore a charming smile on his face and his striking girlfriend clung to his arm with a cold drink in her hand. As was his policy when attending such functions, he ignored offensive leather clothing worn by many unthinking participants, assuming a patient attitude toward their lack of education and discretion.

"Oh, yes, dearest. People are just so generous," replied the shapely brunette, drawing a little closer to Prestone and pressing her body against him. "There's no end to what we can accomplish when people give unselfishly. Thank you, Mrs. Johnson."

After the event, at which Prestone delivered a resounding attack on the evils of current farm practices, the two motored to a luxury hotel in the next city in their European sports vehicle, talking quietly as they rolled along. As protection against ever increasing rural gang violence, an armed escort vehicle bristling with firepower led the way, intimidating any would-be attackers.

"Sugar, I love this business!" Terri marveled. "And I must say, you do a great job when you speak. You avoided offending all those pet owners and doctors. And they really gave to fight against farmers. And in that farm community last night we raised just as much defending research animals and neglected pets. You're a genius."

"We're doing well. I'm booked completely the rest of this year and we've got a two-month stint in Europe next summer. All we have to do is show up in the evening, do a little talking, shake a lot of hands, and walk out with a significant contribution," said Prestone. He rolled his eyes toward her and enjoyed a view of her exposed upper leg. He couldn't hide a sly grin as he stroked her soft skin. "I enjoy it, too, because we're helping the disadvantaged."

"What ever gave you the idea to do this, honey? I mean the species equality thing?"

"It's in my blood. And we're having fun doing it."

Takeover of the Continental Humane Society by Prestone represented a major triumph and for the first time gave the movement access to a network of legitimate chapters nationwide and beyond. These chapters were important grassroots groups within each community that ultimately carried out the directions of their charismatic leader. In an odd twist, many members of these local chapters were themselves active animal utilizers of some type. Prestone brilliantly managed to keep them working to eliminate other categories of use without most of them realizing the broader implications.

"Does any of this money really benefit our fellow species, sugar?" Terri crooned from a luxury suite hot tub later that evening. "I know your speeches help them and the legal actions we initiate and all, but are we really doing any good?"

"Of course we help. I dropped a big percentage check in the mail this morning to that chapter where we were last night. It came to nearly $2,000. So don't worry—we're helping them. That's seed money for next year's fundraiser. It's a good system. Anyway, why do you worry about it, beautiful?" he asked, slipping into the hot tub beside her. "Something bothering you?"

"Well, that awful man who stood up last week and called you names. He sounded mean and I'm afraid a person like that might hurt you. I wouldn't want to see you get hurt, honey!"

She leaned close and planted a passionate kiss on Prestone's lips, and for the longest moment they lingered in the embrace with eyes closed. Prestone then shoved her away in mock roughness.

"Oh, for Gaia's sake, Terri—that ignorant sodbuster was harmless. He reminded me of those idiots I used to have to deal with back in Kansas when I was a kid. Besides, if a guy like that ever tried anything, he wouldn't get anywhere near me. We've got the audience salted with our people. And listen, it would be great if one of them would attack me. Can you imagine 'Animal Defender Attacked' in the headlines? Our contributions would double. So I'll just keep on telling it like it is and see if one of them won't oblige us."

Prestone always enjoyed such a confrontation, anyway, as long as he could be confident the audience was on his side. Under such circumstances he had no fear, and he was intellectually equipped to outmaneuver practically anyone who verbally opposed him. He had demolished the poor farmer with his polished words and had received a hearty applause.

By the end of his first year at the helm of the Continental Humane Society, Prestone was an internationally known personality who was hated by his hapless victims but was increasingly adored by most urbanites. Times were very good for the slick young man with flaming red hair.

*　　*　　*

Bob Hancock trudged through the Kansas snow, trying to make it to an ancient farmhouse up ahead. His old vehicle had skidded off the road into a ditch, and was now lodged in a deep drift. He would have to see if Billy Barnes could bring a tractor and pull him out. He had promised his wife he would be home by dark, but he wasn't going to make it. His wallet nav-com had ceased to operate, and getting a replacement had become a slow, expensive, and uncertain process. He would try and contact her from Barnes' house.

It was cold in Kansas, and the fields were covered with drifted snow. Some of the high technology robot sentries still functioned, but many were now parked uselessly along the lane, mute reminders of the glory days of farming in this part of the world. He stopped briefly to examine one of the rusting sentinels, and noted with dismay that someone had ripped out the insides of the machine. Maybe Barnes had been scavenging to fix up others. Maybe it was simple thievery. The back panel of the machine was open and swayed forlornly in the icy wind, and bare wires protruded while snow accumulated inside the cavity.

The protein plant needed a load of raw material as always, but that wasn't the reason for the visit. He hoped to get some herbal medicine for his sick wife. Billy Barnes' spouse Robin was an expert at the ancient art, and conventional medicine had become highly unreliable and distressingly unavailable. Hancock's young wife Gayle had fallen ill, and her cough was getting worse by the day. The middle-aged Hancock had married late in life, but he had truly grown to love Gayle. He hoped Robin could help. He didn't know what he would do if she couldn't.

The white tempest blew snow sideways, stinging his face and infiltrating down his collar, stiffening the leather and making it scratch his neck uncharacteristically. Still, he was warm and he was grateful for the fine skin clothing he was wearing as protection against the cold and wind. As he plodded along, Hancock had increasing problems staying on the windswept road. If it hadn't been for the fence alongside it, in near whiteout conditions he might have lost his way in several locations. There hadn't been a snowplow in these parts for years, so the cleanly plowed rural roads of yesteryear were but a distant memory.

In the deep snow up ahead, something had left a wide track that came from the bottomland field and disappeared over a hill to the east. Perhaps a big deer had passed, furrowing the new-fallen snow. As he approached closer, it became obvious that such was not the case. The track was not that of one animal, but a score or more that left dog-like paw prints. A wolf pack, and there were at least three or four of the creatures which had left impressions fully five inches across. He had heard about such a pack in the area, but this was as close to them as he had been. He felt for his old .44 Magnum pistol, an armament he always kept in his car, and found it where he had stowed it, snug behind the belt of his trousers. He had never heard of a wolf attacking a human being, but one couldn't be too careful.

The lane passed a plaintive cemetery, where white headstones jutted skyward from their eternal vigil, protruding from a knoll like irregular teeth on some snaggled monster. Hancock hurried past the place, not from fear of the dead but from dread of contemplating it. His wife's condition really worried him. And his beloved and influential mother, Judy Hancock, had passed away only a few years before, leaving a huge void in his life. Hancock had been deeply devoted to the old woman, and had postponed marriage until after her death, by which time he was over forty years old.

The farmhouse loomed in front of him, low and white and well kept, but with no sign of life except a dim light in one room. There was also a speck of illumination in one outbuilding, marked by a winking window across the way. The smaller structure was where elderly Jerry Barnes lived with his wife, Cindy, leaving the larger structure to his son and family. Hancock ascended the low steps, taking care not to slip on the accumulated snow. The ancient boards creaked as he approached the door, where he eased open the screen and knocked firmly.

He drew his collar around his neck for more warmth and waited. He could hear a scramble inside, and very shortly the door creaked open.

"Jamie! Is your dad home?" asked Hancock as he recognized the child.

"Yes. Come on in," replied the boy, who appeared somewhat irritated at the intrusion. He disappeared and within seconds Billy Barnes appeared in the door. He greeted Hancock and fumbled to light a candle against the impending darkness.

"Too bad we don't get dependable electricity out here any more. Come on in and have a seat, Bob," said Barnes, motioning toward a dilapidated sofa along one wall. "It's sure getting harder to make farming produce anything, I'll tell you that."

"And protein processing, too. At least the snow drives the protesters in for awhile," replied Hancock. He removed his outer coat, shook out the snow, and stepped into the cool room. The sputtering candle soon emanated enough light that the two men could see one another. Both of them were well into middle age, with Hancock the older and larger by quite a bit. Hancock still had a full head of blonde hair, though it was thinning some on top. Barnes had the weathered appearance of a farmer, with skin that was deeply tanned. His gray eyes looked tired and somewhat hollow, an effect magnified by the subdued light.

"What brings you out on such a rough night, my friend," asked Barnes. "Can't you pick a better time to make a business call?"

"This is purely personal. By the way, my car's in a drift down the road. Can you pull me out?"

"No problem. We'll get out the tractor, if I can get it started. Tractor parts have become hard to get. I'm thinking about getting some horses, in fact, just to have a backup system. Now tell me, what else do you need?"

"It's Gayle. She's got a terrible cough. I tried to get a doctor today, but I couldn't find one. I even took her to Adrian Hospital, and they had nobody on duty. There was a nurse, but they had no medicine. Billy, she's going to die if something isn't done."

311

"Robin! Come in here!" called Barnes into the darkness toward the kitchen. A muffled answer came, and within seconds the form of a woman materialized through the open door.

"Yes, Billy?"

"Robin, got any of your cough remedy? Bob's wife is real sick, he says. Got a fever, does she, Bob?"

"Real bad. I'm afraid we'll...we'll lose her if we don't hurry."

"Back in a minute," said Robin, spinning on her heels and disappearing back into the darkness.

"Let me go and get the tractor ready. Just filled 'er up with veganox today, so I hope it'll go. If it does, we'll have you on your way in no time," said Barnes. He got up and retrieved his leather overcoat from the recesses of the hall closet, then immediately rushed out into the heavy snowfall. He had no sooner left when his wife returned to the room.

"You have her drink one packet of this in hot tea," Robin said, thrusting a small box toward Hancock. "And another tomorrow morning. Dissolve another in this turpentol and apply it to her chest overnight on a cloth. It needs to be spread over her entire chest and taped in place. Smells terrible but it works."

"Thanks, Robin," said Hancock. "By the way, how's Jamie doing? He seemed preoccupied. And the baby?"

"Jamie's no good right now, Bob. He's upset with us. We've been trying to do the parenting thing, but he refuses to listen. It's been tense around here for several days. Baby Faye is fine, but it'll be tough raising her, too. Someday you'll find out what it's like with your baby Daryl, if I know kids."

"They'll be okay, Robin. Just pray for them and give them a good example. Jamie's just doing the rebellion routine. You probably don't remember, but your man Billy was the same way when he was that age, and look at him now. Daryl will do some of that, I'm sure, when he reaches that stage."

"Well, I'll be glad when Jamie grows up some. This is more than I can take."

"He'll make you proud someday. Just keep up the good work. It seems like they aren't listening to anything you say, but they are. I assure you. Oh, I hear the tractor. It started this time."

They were drowned out as the roar of an engine intruded on the silence. The machine's lights cast bizarre shadows all around the room as it approached.

"I don't know how to repay you, Robin. I've got to hurry now, but I won't forget this. You can be sure."

"Think nothing of it. Just get home fast. We'll be praying."

It took Hancock two hours longer than usual, but finally he was back in Adrian. There had been some occasional places where the snow plows still worked, and he made better time after he reached the city limits. He wheeled into the driveway of his small house and parked, then rushed in through the garage side door.

It was musty inside. That was unusual. Gayle had been an energetic addition to Hancock's life, and usually kept an immaculate house. For the past two weeks, though, she had been unable to clean or do any other work. It was cold in the house, too, and Hancock resolved to fire up a veganox heater he had purchased for just such a time. Their infant son needed a warmer place.

It was as quiet as a tomb in the house. He called his wife's name softly, but there was no response. There came a soft whimper from the nursery room, an infant fussing quietly.

Hancock entered their small bedroom and sat down tentatively on the edge of the bed, clasping the precious medicine in one hand. With the other he reached out fearfully and touched his wife's smooth cheek with great tenderness and love. Then he collapsed beside her on the bed and cried.

*   *   *

Aboard the *Ursa C*, mighty engines surged to life intermittently to maintain the dazzling machine at light speed threshold. Buck Morgan and his amiable synthetic companion made masterful and amazing measurements of the galaxies in the Andromeda Cluster. They used unprecedented parallax effect to ascertain unimaginable distances exactly, a task they repeated on many important segments of the universe. The stream of data they were sending back homeward would not reach its destination until years of Earth time had passed, but the complex material would assuredly enlighten and astonish even the brightest and most introspective of scientists.

Every piece of the *Ursa C* continued to function perfectly, and absolute peace and order reigned on the ship. Despite ongoing scientific triumphs, Morgan's greatest joy had become the renewable resources garden, a vast onboard Eden that teemed with life. Some of the animals were regularly sacrificed as food for the astronaut, after which their flesh was routinely transformed into healthful pure protein in the ship's processor. An automatic skin converter turned out new clothes that fit the explorer exactly. Morgan avoided looking upon the essential creatures as pets but inevitably a few became his favorites. As he had in his days of youth, he particularly relished frolicking with newborn lambs and calves in a wide-open pasture sector.

Enroute they were able to take extraordinary holographs of an immense pair of eclipsing binary stars, deep red in color and previously undetected. Both were relatively cool red giants, with so little luminosity that they could not be observed from Earth. Their elegant presence so near his trajectory was totally unexpected, and finding them added immensely to the magnificence of the journey. Myriad comets surrounded the complex, absolutely awesome in panorama yet equally invisible from Earth. The bodies closely resembled the Kuipper and Oort belts of comets around the home solar system, except that the clusters were much more extensive and were situated nearer the stars. Morgan theorized that the proximity of two stars orbiting one another and the pull of their gravity somehow produced an extraordinary comet array. Calvin's analysis could add little except some complex gravitational and mass calculations. Whatever the origin of the comets, the view was astounding and perhaps unparalleled in the history of space exploration.

An enormous gaseous planet in that convoluted stellar system was an equally stupendous surprise. Alternating pull of the nearby stars, first one exercising maximum influence and then the other, resulted in wild oscillation of the planet, an effect akin to a water balloon tossed spinning into the air. Unfortunately, there were no moons or other solid worlds anywhere in the system that were large enough to support a landing to gather valuable samples. The *Ursa C* dutifully recorded position, size, and radiation spectra of the gargantuan stars and their companion planet after slowing only momentarily below pragmatic c speed.

After reviewing and confirming this exceptional series of precision calculations, Morgan relieved the strain on his mind by retiring to the euphonious Japanese piano he had come to love, where he played with emotional inspiration. It took some instinctive adjusting, but he was able to perform on his instrument Haydn's thrilling chorale, *The Creation*. His nimble fingers caressed the keys like a mother gently grooming the hair of a baby. The melody stuck in his head for many watches after his encounter with the star complex, so enthralled was he with the wonder of discovery.

Buck Morgan went about his duties with boundless satisfaction, knowing that humanity awaited the data stream and his ultimate return with great anticipation. He reflected on the triumphs of mankind in his lifetime, and he frequently spent time remembering the days of his youth. He was confident that he would return to a better world, one of ever improving scientific principles. Diligent research would have doubtless solved the profusion of nagging physical and social problems in the long interim.

His learned artificial friend, Calvin, researched the subject and agreed vigorously with this assessment. Even the advanced reasoning programmed into the intricate machine couldn't foresee anything other than multiplied progress back on Earth.

Buck Morgan seemed to be in control of his situation, but he still had recurring dreams that sprang from childhood memories. Thankfully, his vivid cougar dream was now far less frequent in occurrence. Unfortunately, another sleep apparition had replaced it, a dream equally threatening and terrifying, and one that featured an unreal beast that he could not identify. His unseen antagonist growled and snarled in the darkest part of his mind, but it would not emerge into the light. During these disquieting episodes he always longed to see the creature, but afterwards he was always glad that he had not.

Dreams were minor distractions, and they never interfered with his work. They couldn't be understood, anyway, so he ignored them as much as humanly possible.

CHAPTER 24

December 2125

Leroy and Jeremy, two of Jerry Barnes' farm hands, were making a routine run to the protein plant to make an essential delivery, a task they accomplished several times per week. Jeremy fingered an automatic weapon on his lap, lifting its sinister black metal barrel so it would be easily visible to any observer through the truck's window. He also played absent-mindedly with a control panel that governed an array of electric mini-guns that were mounted like stingers in strategic locations about the exterior of the vehicle.

There were marauding bands of thieves that preyed on truckers along all highways, and some fairly effective countermeasures had been permitted by the authorities in an effort to prevent such attacks. Such destructive armament had been contraband for many decades, but these days authorities looked the other way and let the populace defend itself any way it could. Bandits were usually armed in like manner, so it was simply fighting fire with fire.

With precision moves like those of a fine watch, a band of sinister men moved their vehicles into position just out of sight down the highway from the protein processing facility. That they were heavily armed was not easily detectable, since the only external evidence of their deadly purpose was their grim, determined expressions. One man watched from a high hill, keeping the others appraised as to the location of their objective, a protein-laden farm truck that was moving rapidly toward them.

In centuries past, such a transport would not have been a likely target for major crime unless it carried gold, money, or some other precious commodity. In the twenty-second century economy, protein was becoming so valuable that it was guarded like legal tender. There was a lucrative and growing black market for it in any big city.

Disabling and stopping the truck by means of force would not have been easy, and these criminals were remarkably experienced and far too smart to make that mistake. This particular band of outlaws was a cut above average, and had devised ingenious techniques to succeed consistently. They knew that there was every possibility the truck's guard would start shooting wildly at the slightest hint of trouble. Newer protein trucks were outfitted with as much firepower as an old time attack helicopter.

Rather than a direct shootout, there was a much more effective and infinitely safer way to get the job accomplished. The trick was to kill both occupants, yet leave the vehicle functional and intact for a quick getaway. There was only one way to carry out the task, a ploy that had worked repeatedly for the gang. It seemed that these dirt farmers never learned.

Getting the truck stopped involved setting up a license check roadblock, where two fake police vehicles were used to make the scene appear realistic. Dressed in uniforms of state patrolmen, four bandits looked every bit the part, down to nearly shaved heads and radiant black leather shoes on their feet. Three more gang members were posing as halted motorists, with their vehicles pulled over on the roadside. Their key man was the hilltop spotter, who also was their main gunner. He kept his laser scoped rifle, a heavy yet compact shooting machine, sitting at ready as the truck moved ever closer.

The two rough-talking men in the farm truck were not particularly concerned about the possibility of a heist. They were longtime partying buddies and both of them had a hot date at the Hat Trick Bar that night. They continued describing to each other the unrestrained particulars of their performances the night before, and never gave more than a passing thought to the possibility they might be in danger. This was a routine run they had made dozens, perhaps hundreds, of times.

"Stupid police," said Leroy as they encountered the tangle of vehicles and flashing lights up ahead. "We'll never get this load off fast enough to make quitting time. They'll want to check every permit we've got. And probably do a computer check on our love life to boot. Curse the luck."

"No sweat. Your girl will still be there if you're lucky. And the drinks will be as cold as ever," said Jeremy.

A counterfeit patrolman motioned both men to step down from the high seat, so LeRoy secured the truck and left its engine running. Jeremy dug in the storage compartment for necessary papers, then both men climbed down. Their deadly automatic rifle, technically illegal, was left forgotten on the seat as they dutifully assembled as indicated by the uniformed man.

The advanced multiple objective sniper rifle held by the unseen gunman fired twin bullets traveling at over 4,000 feet per second, each projectile laser guided, and each entered the frontal bone of a victim almost exactly at the slight depression that lies between the eyebrows. These high velocity missiles completely penetrated though bone and brain, and both men simultaneously collapsed into lifeless piles beside the truck. Blood and scrambled nervous tissue spewed from the exit wounds and splattered for several yards beyond them. The shooter was a terrific executioner, and he had never hit any of his teammates or any important vehicles during the course of these highly profitable enterprises. Such talent could earn one a lot of money, and his cut of the profits would be considerable, as usual.

The team immediately shed their deception and jumped into unconstrained and highly practiced activity. Two imposing patrolmen quickly dragged both dead workers into a ditch, and hurriedly draped their bodies with camouflage leather netting. Another team member leaped into the truck cab and roared away to a predetermined rendezvous point on an out-of-way back road. Within minutes, the two phony patrol cars and other vehicles arrived in a cloud of dust. A swarm of thieves utterly transformed the truck with a new paint job and a new logo, complete with a fresh set of false papers. The designated driver and his appointed guard then set out for Denver, where a hefty profit would be made selling raw protein to unscrupulous grocery dealers. The job would be complete before anybody in locally was even aware a crime had been committed. The rest of the band meanwhile set up nearby for another quick series of hit-or-miss robberies of passing motorists.

*　　*　　*

Elderly Jerry Barnes arrived for midweek church service that evening more pessimistic than he had ever been in his life. He had learned of the tragedy that befell his workers, and the loss of his vehicle, only moments before he was to leave home. His snow-capped head was still spinning, trying to adjust to the shock of such a devastating loss. The shrinking number of Christian believers left him very few solid friends in whom he could confide, but his desperation begged expression. He was glad for the small congregation that still attended his church.

"Evening, Roger, how're things on your farm?" he asked a younger man on entering the darkened sanctuary. The only light emanated from two dim candles burning at the altar, since the church could no longer afford to pay an electric bill. Roger Walker had purchased the fertile farm that once belonged to Jerry's father Bill after the old man had died a few years before.

"As good as can be expected under the circumstances, Jerry," responded Roger, intense concern creasing his round, tanned face. An ample abdomen tented his leather coveralls, but despite his workingman's dress he was clean, neat, and closely shaved. "To tell you the truth, I'm worried to death about Leon. He comes home from school with such crazy notions."

"Crazy notions? What do you mean?" asked Barnes. "Sounds like what I used to say about my own kids all the time."

"Probably. I just hope I can get his head back on straight. He's been to that pagan church, or whatever it is, a couple of times lately. It just drives me insane," said Walker with undisguised resignation. He sighed deeply before looking directly at Barnes. "How's it going at your place?"

"Terrible. Cindy's sick and my latest shipment to the storage warehouse was hijacked today. Stolen. They even took my truck," lamented the aging farmer. "I can't afford another. We'll just have to make do with the old one. It's all I've got left. I left Billy in the garage trying to get it operational."

320

"That's pretty awful, but I can't say I'm surprised. It happens all the time now. I'll tell you, if we didn't ride armed nothing would ever get through."

"I haven't told you the worst part. They killed our driver and guard."

"Oh, no, Jerry! Things are going from bad to worse. What are we going to do?" asked Walker. "Were they family men?"

"No, solo drifters like most of them, but they had an honest streak that's rare. I sure hated to lose them. Stable workers are hard to find anymore, you know. It's a darn shame. No, it's worse than that."

"Did they catch the culprits?"

"Of course not. If they did, they'd be out for lack of evidence in a day. Nobody—and I mean nobody—will testify against anybody else. I tell you, it's every man for himself," Barnes responded, patting the automatic pistol on his hip. "Having to tote a gun to church, of all things."

Bob Hancock was also on his way to that same weathered brick church building, and his silent vehicle hummed along with well-oiled efficiency. His sky blue eyes squinted as flashing lights materialized out of deep darkness up ahead. High intensity strobes cast an uncanny ricochet effect in the evening's gathering fog, blinding and eerie as dancing light reflected off innumerable droplets of moisture in the saturated atmosphere. Hancock rode entirely alone, and his instincts urged extreme caution as he approached the reverberating beacons blocking his way. He still had not heard about the piracy of the farm truck earlier, but he was nevertheless aware of manifold danger that awaited the unwary.

A man in an officer's uniform motioned him to pull off the road, pointing to a space between two patrol cars. He complied reluctantly but promptly, not wishing to incur wrath from the authorities. They could and would make life at the protein plant unbearable if he was identified as a troublemaker. Extreme caution was in order in all one's dealings with the police, or anyone else in a position of power.

As he glided into the space between vehicles, he could not escape an acute sensation that something was amiss. There was another vehicle pulled over up ahead, but he could see no occupants, either in the vehicle, in the patrol cars, or outside. He squinted through the misty darkness, hoping to see the vehicle's driver. Abruptly he noticed that the police vehicle in front of him had a private license plate, rather than the distinctive Kansas seal that adorned tags on legitimate patrol cars. With little question, something was not right about this roadblock.

He let his right hand drop to a .44 Magnum pistol at his side, a constant companion that was situated permanently in a gap beside the seat in a most inconspicuous position. The hammer rested safely on an empty chamber, but he applied a crisp cocking motion to the mechanism and the cylinder rotated to put a deadly cartridge in launch position. One of the patrolmen approached in nonchalant fashion as if on routine assignment, holding in one hand a computer that flashed signals suggesting constant activity. Everything looked pretty standard except for absence of people in the other car that was stopped, and the disturbing private tag on the patrol car. Maybe I'm being too cautious, he thought. Maybe so, maybe not, his sharp mind warned, and his vigilance rocketed off the scale once more. The officer's uniform looked quite regulation, crisp and wrinkle-free, and his badge appeared authentic. Hancock relaxed slightly, but he scanned the surrounding area for anything else that might offer a clue to the legitimacy of this delay. He manually turned off the car's interior lights in order to gain an extra thin margin of safety, a move that he hoped would be perceived as unpretentious.

The patrolman passed through the headlight beam, and Hancock hit the bright switch, illuminating much more surrounding terrain. The ephemeral scene he could see was unnerving, though his view was far from clear. There was a flash of color in some tall prairie grass along the road, just beyond where another officer stood impeding his view. Was that a prone figure he could see? He couldn't be certain. The glimpse was enough to keep his suspicions at a high level, especially when the officer he could see acted inordinately irritated by the bright lights. His deceased mother, Judy Hancock, flashed through his consciousness for some reason. She had admonished him from her deathbed that he must stay vigilant for danger, both physical and spiritual. This could be either or both.

The officer now stood at his window, holding what appeared to be a glowing supercomputer linkup, and motioned for him to disembark. Hancock had seen enough that he closed his hand around his pistol and deftly took it with him as he commanded the door to open. He emerged without arousing any obvious doubts that he was anything but completely compliant.

"Your car scans in violation of the tax code. I'll have to see your registration," barked the uniformed man. "Mind getting it for me?"

"No problem, officer. Must be a mistake. Computer glitch or something."

"Maybe so. We'll see. Just get your papers for me."

Hancock now knew beyond doubt that this was a trap. His vehicle had been checked in full daylight only a few days before by legitimate authorities and had passed without the slightest hint of problems. He warily edged back into his car, never taking his eyes off the impostor. He knew trouble was coming, and that the unlucky driver of the other car had already paid an awful price. The only question was whether he could ward off the same fate. He took advantage of the darkness to feign groping in the recesses of the vehicle for papers, all the while watching for any false move by the man. In the dark interior he moved his weapon into the ready position, just in case. He had to be absolutely certain he wasn't overreacting, not wanting to be fooled into taking action if it wasn't warranted. There was no turning back if he made a mistake.

One of the uniformed man's hands was in clear view, handling the computer linkup deftly. It had to be that other hand which would reveal his intentions, and Hancock concentrated on that extremity with all his being. Suddenly, there it was, an electric auto weapon rising, as if in slow motion, from the man's side. It never made it to lethal position, though, because Hancock's .44 Magnum exploded with ghastly effect, striking the man in the mouth and practically decapitating the outlaw. He commanded his vehicle to maximum acceleration and thundered away in a spray of lead particles from the other bandits, several of which had remained hidden until his desperate and effective gunshot. None of their bullets did anything more than pit the surface of his car as he sped away unscathed. He called the sheriff within seconds to report the incident, but by the time the authorities arrived there was nothing they could do except notify the next of kin of the murdered citizen Hancock had spotted.

As he slipped in the door of the little church, he was still trembling badly. If he had been only a micron less wary, he would have surely have died. Then what would his young son do? It was a dangerous world and the child needed him in order to have any chance of surviving. As he approached this gathering of a few faithful, he couldn't help but notice the particularly somber mood he encountered. Well, he thought gloomily, I'm going to have a hard time brightening things up any tonight.

"Evening, Bob. How's everything with you?" asked Roger Walker, a dusky tone hanging unmistakably in his words.

"Not too good, Roger," said Hancock in a shaky voice. "Had to kill a man about thirty minutes ago."

"What? You killed somebody?" asked Jerry Barnes as his mouth dropped open.

"Fake officers stopped me. They'd already murdered another motorist. Fortunately, I spotted the body—and a couple of other inconsistencies. I took quite a few hits on my car as I left, but nothing serious."

"Did you hear about my guys getting blown away today?"

"Your protein truck? No! I knew it didn't come in like we expected."

"Killed our men, stole our truck and all the goods. Got away clean. I just found out about it when they didn't come back from the run."

"Oh, no! Was it Jeremy and Leroy?" asked Hancock, his speech calming considerably. "Pretty good pair, in some ways. Sorry, Jerry. Could be this same bunch I ran into. At least there's one less of them now."

"Yep, I hated to lose Jeremy and LeRoy. If it was the same bunch, I'm glad you got one of them. But you know that won't stop them, unfortunately. What's going to happen, Bob?"

"I wish I knew. Mom always said that we would eventually see disintegration of society. Lots of reasons for it, and she could see it coming."

"I wish your mom were still alive so she could talk to Leon. I don't know what I'm going to do with that boy," said Walker.

"My kids were the same way, Roger, and look what a solid citizen Billy is now," said Barnes. "But I think our grandson, Jamie, is worse than Billy was. He's just gotten into his teenage years, but he's already a pill. I guess it runs in the family, unfortunately. At least we never lack for things to pray about. Is everyone ready to get started? And let's pray for my old cousin Buck Morgan tonight. And if you don't mind, pray for my grandson. Jamie's out with friends tonight doing who knows what."

"I'm ready," answered Hancock. "Yeah, Buck's been gone, let's see, over forty-five years now. Someday he might return to Earth and be absolutely astounded at the changes. If he's survived the trip, that is. You know, my mom said to never forget him, but I think the rest of the world already has. I never hear any mention of the space program anymore."

*   *   *

At the time the meeting in the tiny church was in progress another meeting was taking place some forty-four light years distant. Buck Morgan was within a few hundred million miles of his destination, and he was filled with inestimable marvel. The alien sun was so much like his home star that it triggered a deep sense of nostalgia. Forty-seven Ursae Majoris had a distinctive corona that was exceptionally prominent, a brilliant crown that gave the star a kingly appearance that nobody had suspected. Buck Morgan concluded a bit smugly that his was the most magnificent of obsessions. His racing scientific mind devoured the latest measurements he was taking and hurried on to another series of mandatory tasks. He would set the scientific world on its collective ear with this astounding information.

Morgan had initiated a smooth deceleration of the craft a billion miles out in interstellar space so he could easily orbit his objective, a transition that super-intelligent Calvin supervised expertly. He positioned the *Ursa C* some 100 million miles from the star for a good view, then set a complete array of scientific experiments into motion. Telescopes remotely reminiscent of the defunct Hubbell orbiting device scanned nearby space efficiently, and quickly pinpointed virtually every sizable hunk of matter within hundreds of millions of miles. Radiotelescopes, spectroscopes, and intricate radiation analyzers hummed as he quickly and effectively became intimately familiar with a new system of planets, moons, and other orbiting bodies. All sizes, orbits, and trajectories were calculated perfectly within a matter of hours.

"Reminds me of the time when you and Jeremiah Smith explored Mercury, Commander Bucko," stated Calvin. "Same thrill, same feeling of exploration—and perhaps the same sense of danger, I suppose. Do you remember, sir?"

"I do, Calvin. What continues to surprise me is the way you delve into my friend's past and make it your own. I appreciate you, but every time you come up with something like that it makes me homesick, I've got to tell you."

"Shall I delete the Smitty function, sir?"

"No, no, really it helps to keep me sane, I suppose. A little homesickness is probably good. Carry on as before, Calvin. Just remember that old remembrances are a bit tough on me sometimes. I know you don't understand fully the concept of emotions, but it's a weakness I can't avoid."

"I'll do my best to be conscious of the effect, sir," replied Calvin. "All continues to perform well in all sectors of the ship. We're ready for an influx of new facts, with all memory banks cleared of unnecessary data. Shall I begin planning a surface foray?"

"Do it, Smitty—I mean Calvin—and check out all systems on the planetary lander while you're at it. The fuel cells especially."

The ship was four years, eight months, and four days into his voyage, slightly more time than anticipated. Slowing to see and examine the eclipsing binary star, and a bit more interstellar matter than anticipated, accounted for extra time consumed. The Earth calendar/clock showed that about forty-seven years had elapsed back home, shoving his home planet forward in time even as Buck Morgan enjoyed a suspended animation of sorts.

Sometimes the interstellar man longed for human companionship and wished he had insisted on another crewman. But finding another person willing to make this voyage had been only one insurmountable obstacle. There had been no other volunteers. Too, the renewables section had been conservatively calculated to be borderline for two people, though he had found that there was plenty of production to support several more.

A smaller person, such as a woman, would have satisfied the scientists when it came to resources, but no female astronaut had shown the slightest interest in the trip. Morgan missed people, and in weaker moments he sometimes wished such a situation had developed. Every time he thought about the idea, beautiful JoEllen Thacker in an astronaut's uniform flashed through his mind, making it very hard to concentrate on whatever task was at hand. He kept quite busy with his scientific observations as well as necessary work in the renewables garden, and he found the solo situation tolerable though depressingly inadequate. Calvin was not quite real, certainly in terms of humanity, but he was so cleverly designed that sometimes even the holocom display seemed not to grasp this fact.

The 47 Ursae Majoris stellar system was phenomenal in every way. There were twelve discernible planets around the star, and one of them was a giant that dwarfed his old friend Jupiter, being some three and a half times as large. It was dusky orange in color with a plethora of gargantuan elliptical storms, like Jupiter's famed red spot, that looked at him from his position like multiple eyes on some unknown goddess. There was an astounding array of several dozen moons about the world, but none of them was as large as Ganymede, and none had any detectable atmosphere. Two of them orbited in tandem, and the amount of rocky debris that surrounded that pair of conflicting moons indicated that they sometimes collided with thunderous consequence. The rest were fairly distinctive but not extraordinarily different from moons in the home solar system.

There were ringed planets, too. This system of planets had not one prominent ringed member, but three. All were more distant from 47 Ursae Majoris than the giant planet, which Morgan tentatively named Oculi because of all its eyes. There were multiple moons around each ringed planet, too, but again none with any promise of inhabitability. The nearest ringed planet was 260 million miles from the star, much too distant for life-giving warmth to be possible. Morgan determined to explore each planet in detail before leaving for Earth, but the outer bodies were no more promising than those in the home solar system, by all appearances.

There were only two planets, plus myriad asteroids that were massive but sub-planetary in size, orbiting nearer than 180 million miles from the star. Both planets had atmospheres, but the inner one had the same suffocating problem as familiar Venus. There was a thick, impenetrable cloud cover and surface temperatures near 1000 degrees. The planet orbited a scant fifty million miles from the hot star, close enough that Morgan marveled at why the atmosphere had not been blown away by intense stellar wind, as had been the apparent fate of the sun's planet Mercury. The astronaut concentrated his exploration efforts initially on the more interesting of the two inner planets, one he unofficially dubbed Schultzi, a fitting honor to the creator of the technology that had propelled him to this unimaginably remote location.

That emerald green planet appeared from space to be superficially similar to Earth, but it lacked the characteristic blueness of home. It orbited 100 million miles from the star in an elliptical orbit. Both poles of this new world were capped with an Earth-like white, and in the southern zone this mantle extended almost a third of the way to the planet's equator. There were obvious swirling clouds of white that mimicked storms and frontal systems of home. It was a brutal disappointment when spectroscopic analysis revealed that the churning weather systems were not made primarily of water vapor, a necessary ingredient for carbon-based life forms.

One hundred million miles from the stellar heater of 47 Ursae Majoris was within the envelope for life sustaining temperatures and radiation levels, so the planet was still a possibility. Two gorgeous moons about half the size of Earth's satellite traveled at about 200,000 miles from the planet in nearly circular orbits. Analysis of the new world's atmosphere revealed more carbon dioxide than on Earth, but also more oxygen. Equatorial diameter of the planet was greater than Earth's by about twenty percent, so a person walking on the surface would have to adjust for increased gravity. There appeared to be no oceans, but surface temperature was a balmy sixty degrees Fahrenheit at the equator. There were a number of large blue spots which analysis revealed to be that most rare extraterrestrial commodity, liquid water.

There was plenty of time for a run to the surface in the planetary lander, so he checked out the craft in detail before setting out. Calvin already had a program in his software for such a mission, but Morgan nevertheless briefed him extensively before embarking. His instructions to his inorganic friend included how to complete the mission back to Earth without Morgan if something drastic should go wrong. Morgan was confident as he unpacked his long-dormant outside suit for the foray, and found that it was extremely well preserved and no worse for the passage of years.

Descent to the surface was no problem, little different from returning to Earth aboard a shuttle. The atmosphere was a bit thicker and the heat of deceleration caused him some concern, as the planetary lander was better suited to landing on sparsely aired planets or moons. There were some fairly stiff winds blowing on the surface, and he knew that a mistake could be costly indeed. He relied heavily on a computer feed from Calvin to help him correct for drift, and set the machine down next to a greenish-blue lake on a stretch of rock that was almost as smooth as a polished mirror.

Despite having the unequaled protection of his miracle suit for work on this hostile surface, Morgan repeated measurements of all parameters before disembarking. On reaching ground level, he sank mooring cables into the hard surface to prevent the brisk wind from upsetting his ride back to the *Ursa C.*

There was a strong hint of sulfur in the atmosphere, and indications that the toxicity level of the planet's atmosphere would be outside tolerances for life forms from Earth. He rapidly confirmed his spectroscope's indication that the greenish color was from oxidized copper, an element that apparently comprised a major portion of the new world's surface metal. As suspected from his orbiting analysis, there was no hint of life. He found that oxidized metal heavily tainted the lake water.

He chanced a short breath of ambient air, and then withdrew choking to the safety of his artificial environment. This world would never meet his purposes, but it would be a wonderful and comfortable location for a truly deep space station, one that would be exceedingly rich in natural resources. He dutifully collected samples of surface ore and some small containers of atmosphere and water, which he stowed in a special compartment of the lander.

He briefly considered siphoning a load of water to replenish his supply, but decided against it. It might be dangerous to introduce metal-tainted water into his system, since he was unsure what effect it might have on the living ecosystems there. Additionally, he needed to save weight for his ascent, since it would require a heavier fuel burn than for most such missions, due to Schultzi's stronger gravity.

Despite the fact that this world would not be easily inhabitable, the data were extraordinary and Morgan was already anticipating the day when he could share it in person with excited twenty-second century scientists back on Earth. His transmission to Earth was progressing well, but he knew that most of the material would be terribly delayed in arriving. He could imagine the maddening, slow trickle of information toward home, and considerable frustration of breathless scientists who analyzed it.

The planetary lander docked back at the orbiting starship unscathed by its excursion into the rotten egg atmosphere of Schultzi. A potential problem was that now he would be unable to use the lander again without robbing hydrogen and oxygen from his renewable resources garden, critically depriving it of precious water. As he stowed the craft, he fretted briefly about not siphoning a partial load of water onboard anyway, just in case another landing were needed. Oh, well, that shouldn't be necessary, he was confident. He would doubtless be given a royal ride in an updated space shuttle once he got back to Space Station Delta some four and a half years future.

As he rejoiced and rested after his successful exploration, music by his ancient hero Chopin filled his head with song. After completing necessary tasks and filing his debriefing in the computer log, he retired to the piano to soothe his tired and harried demeanor. The music in his mind spoke well to the happy situation he now faced, that of carrying good news back to planet Earth. He deftly glided his fingers over precision keys, making wonderful sounds in the process. The real ivory felt solid and undeniably good. The flexible rubato tempo of Chopin's "F Minor Fantasy" permeated the *Ursa C* like an application of healing oil. He retired to bed where he slept soundly and without dreaming.

*　　*　　*

Back on Earth, the deterioration of the space program was nothing short of appalling. Exploration incentives were soon exhausted by flights of the efficient nuclear pulse cruisers, and reports of new journeys assumed a boring sameness to a fickle public. Mining, once held out as the great salvation of the space effort, ultimately proved to be expensive and economically unprofitable. Moreover, minerals found on distant planets and moons differed little from Earth's basic composition, and few rich deposits of extremely rare metals were discovered elsewhere in the solar system. Worse, the problem of ferrying many square miles of metal blocks down to the surface was never solved. Only cessation of regular cruiser runs to the mines halted the foreboding accumulation alongside Space Station Delta.

As Morgan orbited 47 Ursae Majoris unaware, an order was issued to abandon all deep space bases. The proud Astronaut Corps, that indomitable legion of the elite, was reduced to a fraction of its former

331

membership in very short order by additional decrees. Moon Base lasted a few more years and then it, too, was deactivated and deserted as too expensive and useless for continued operation.

The most devastating destruction of the space program, perhaps, came when Space Station Delta was vacated. Shuttles could easily keep any needed satellites in orbit, and servicing of deactivated deep space stations was no longer necessary. Complex nuclear pulse cruisers were soon docked idly at all bays, and its former masters soon abandoned the massive man-made moon.

Aerospace experts insisted in vain that a certain amount of maintenance was necessary to counter orbital decay. Regular firings of booster rockets were more essential than ever to keep the artificial moon aloft because of its unbelievable weight. These firings had been accomplished in regular and automatic fashion for decades, and subsequent to its abandonment the station was visited on a fixed schedule by shuttles as they maintained various communications satellites. The danger always existed that the unstable and bankrupt governments on the surface would fail to live up to their commitment to maintain the unused station.

Buck Morgan had no way of knowing any of this. His data stream from Earth was over forty years old as he explored the planetary system of his objective star. Experimental runs in the solar system before his departure had confirmed the impossibility of communication while approaching a radio source at pragmatic c, so he would be effectively out of contact on the return leg until he slowed enough for ordinary processing of incoming signals.

Buck Morgan was now in the hands of destiny, and only time would tell his fate.

CHAPTER 25

February 2129

AN ACT

FOR THE NATIONAL PRESERVATION OF WILDLIFE

WASHINGTON, DC

Be it enacted into law that this day that the killing, taking, or harassment of any wildlife on any land, air, or water on or within the national boundaries of the United States of America shall be prohibited. No individual shall use any weapon, snare, trap, or any other means to kill, intimidate, or otherwise harass the wild creatures of this nation. By this Act the Congress of the United States incorporates this mandate into the law of the land.

It is furthermore enacted that any citizen of the United States of America who conducts activity involving the killing or harassment of any wildlife by any means anywhere in the world shall be guilty of a felony and punishable to the full extent of the laws of this country, regardless of whether such taking of wildlife is legal in the country in which it occurs.

* * *

On the sagebrush plains of Eastern Colorado, a battered jet cargo hauler eased along a remote range road, far from the teeming city to the west. There was money to be made now in jackrabbits, and the bearded, unkempt men in the vehicle were armed with an aging shotgun so as to kill as many of the tough, stringy hares as possible. Sale of the leathery flesh in Denver would net big bucks for the unscrupulous poachers.

Most big game animals had already disappeared from the state, even though the Colorado government had banned legal hunting several years before. Poachers rapidly decimated elk herds to feed a hungry population. Even formerly common deer meat was becoming a rare commodity on the black market. The last thing these two poachers expected to find was a bonanza in the form of a pair of pronghorn antelope, an animal that had numbered in the millions less than two decades ago.

"Karl, there are two speed goats over here," whispered one of the men to his companion. "I thought we had them all. Let's get these two! We'll be rich!"

The driver accelerated the hauler alongside the two fleeing creatures while the other broke open the gun and changed to buckshot, a load he seldom used anymore. With just two accurate blasts he dropped both of the pronghorns. The driver slammed on the reverse thrust and banked around to retrieve their prizes. The doe and her fawn flopped limply in the vehicle's rusty bed, with lifeless tongues protruded between dead lips, and blood staining their gorgeous beige and white coats. Their ordeal of survival was over, and their unlikely luck at being missed by the raging carnage of poaching had finally come to an end.

There was only one item remotely positive about this episode. The two men would never kill another pronghorn antelope in Colorado. These two residual animals were the very last ones in the entire state.

Meanwhile, in neighboring Kansas, Scott Gentry was a worried man. As chapter head of the local Conservation Club and a fourth generation leader in that organization, he felt a high obligation to continue the legacy left by his forebears, a legacy of excellence in conservation. Unfortunately, he felt himself fighting a losing battle on behalf of his hunting and fishing heritage and on behalf of outdoorsmen and women who pursued these time-honored activities.

Like his father and grandfather before him, Gentry was an avid sportsman. He had assumed leadership of the local chapter of the Conservation Club the year before, following in their footsteps. His goal was to revitalize the group, instill some lost enthusiasm, and raise funds to oppose the juggernaut that was threatening to outlaw his beloved avocation.

The Conservation Club had fallen on hard times. Hunting especially had always been an activity that required extensive personal tutoring, so a dynamic and effective father-child relationship was vital to its propagation. Few traditional families survived, so hunters who were well schooled in outdoor ethics and who harbored a profound need to hunt were correspondingly fewer in number. Many of those who did go afield seeking game approached the activity without benefit of instruction, so their moral and ethical base was deficient or nonexistent. Instead of being devoted stewards of wildlife as in past times, vulgar outdoorsmen sought animals with the undisciplined attitude of ruthless killers. The hunter was held in ever-lower esteem by society as each year passed.

The Continental Humane Society and similar groups targeted elimination of all hunting as "the first real progress in equality for disadvantaged species." They had the media in their pocket, numerous powerful legislators on their side, endorsements from high profile celebrities, and an uneducated public that was incapable of intelligently evaluating the issues. As an emotion-based society, the population never considered any long-term consequences of eliminating legal human utilization of excess wildlife. Many laughed openly at the concept of a person needing such contact with nature for fulfillment, and labeled this a throwback to Neanderthal times. Gentry, as a hunter, had every reason to be worried. Hunters were outmaneuvered and outgunned on every front. He was on his way to attend a meeting of his small board of directors to formulate strategy.

"Evening, Tom, evening George. Good to see you," he mouthed as he entered Tom Ailey's office and sat down across the table from his friends. Ailey was a fit and trim accountant and George Worthington was a handsome physician. Both were avid hunters and anglers.

"Evening, Scott. We're in big trouble, man," replied Ailey without hesitation, his voice heavy, regretful. "Have you seen the news this evening?"

Ailey strived for excellence in every area of his life and stayed immaculately in shape so he could continue to do harder types of high mountain hunting. As a consequence his body showed little to reveal his late middle age.

"No. What's happening?"

"The bill to ban hunting on private land passed the House today. Looks like it'll sail through the Senate. It could be the end," reported Worthington. "We may be a defunct organization."

Gentry flinched. Hunting had been banned completely on all government lands for several years despite the fact that the impotent Federal government lacked enforcement resources. Initially the ban had affected only wildlife refuges, but subsequently was expanded without much dissent. Several urban states had already outlawed the practice. Now the bold step of taking away the privilege altogether from law-abiding people nationwide seemed to be practically assured.

"The idiots! Why don't they learn? They strangle our state game departments by cutting off funding and then eliminate legitimate sportsmen from the field. That leaves nothing between the animals and greedy poachers. No more hunting, lots of poaching, no more seasons or limits. Men, we're going to lose our wildlife! And we can't stop it!"

"Is there anything we can do, Scott?" inquired Worthington, hopeful his resourceful friend could manufacture a miracle.

"We can become fishermen—until they get around to banning that, too," Gentry replied, a disgusted expression creasing his face and a deep despondency in his voice. "I notice that the act's wording doesn't distinguish between land animals and fish, so fishing may already be on the brink of illegality, come to think of it."

"How did it come to this? Where did we go wrong?" asked Worthington.

"I don't think it was us who went wrong," Ailey responded, shaking his head slowly in disbelief. "America has changed. People don't understand the concept of sustained utilization anymore. The population is so uneducated I doubt if they have a hazy notion where their processed food comes from, much less grasping something as complicated as wildlife management. Men with guns kill, that's all they know. And politicians respond to such arguments if enough people feel strongly about it."

"I really hurt for our wildlife," Gentry said sadly. "Now we can watch it all dwindle away."

As Worthington had predicted, the bill to ban all hunting, even on private land, passed both houses of Congress without serious opposition. In a paradoxical twist, the legislation was dubbed "The Wildlife Preservation Act of 2129." With quite a bit of fanfare, the measure was signed into law by the president, who gave a short speech indicating how the wild species of America deserved utmost protection and that this bill would accomplish that. There was glowing commentary from media analysts. Totally ignored were a few frustrated sportsmen who expressed opposition.

It was truly a sad day for the small but dedicated hunting community. Aftershocks continued for months after the bill's passage, as state after state announced closure of its game department or consolidation of all personnel and equipment under its fishing division. Conservation programs funded by American sportsmen in many other countries gave up altogether, leaving animals there in the unenviable position of having no economic value except as food or as items of illicit trade. Fishing continued to be allowed under the bill, which had language added at the last moment defining wildlife as birds and mammals.

*   *   *

Waymon Prestone was strangely quiet as he sat at the bar in a plush Washington hotel, sipping on a martini from time to time. Traci, his striking new escort, sat beside him and observed his somber frame of mind. She took a sip of her tall, frosty red drink, and then stroked his leg under the bar. She couldn't quite understand why her famous boyfriend wasn't in a party mood. Prestone had been actively working the Congress for months, and a holocom newscaster had just related proudly the eradication of wildlife consumption as a legitimate activity. The program had featured an impressive interview with Prestone, and the celebrated species equality guru had come across in grand and convincing fashion.

"Honey, you're so quiet. Why don't we celebrate?" she whispered in his ear, nipping playfully at his earlobe and blowing softly on his neck.

"I don't feel like it, babe," he replied with more than a small degree
of irritation. He stroked her graceful thigh and admired her delicately
beautiful face, yet he was strangely distracted and disinterested.

"This is a big win, of course," he said as his voice trailed off
uncharacteristically and he let his probing hand drop limply from its
impulsive petting.

"What's the matter, sugar? You sound depressed. You never act like
this," the girl observed, pouting her luscious lips a little to protest his
somber mood. "What's wrong?"

"This is good for our movement, all right. But it has a subtle
downside, too. Hunting has been a real money maker over the years.
People have given generously to stop it. I hope our contributions don't
drop off now that the law has been changed."

"Don't worry. You'll keep everybody fired up, sugar. I know you.
You don't need any single issue to keep people interested. Besides,
there's still fishing and all those other inhumane practices that you talk
about," encouraged Traci as she ran her slender fingers through
Prestone's thick red hair, which was now beginning to show an
occasional streak of appealing gray. "So don't worry. We won!"

"I know. I'm glad. But I don't know how many times we can win
before contributions start hurting. But we'll be okay for now. I think
you're right," he conceded, putting one arm around her waist while
placing a soft kiss on her lips.

*　*　*

The wholesale shutdown of state game departments had little
immediate effect. Western states had mostly eliminated these useless
divisions years before. Huge chunks of their land were owned by the
federal government and hence already closed to most human access and
to all legal wildlife utilization. Most animals in the Western national
forests were already gone, lost to poachers long before the total hunting
ban was passed.

With legitimate hunters gone and with no enforcement personnel,
poaching heated up with a vengeance. The few remaining game officials

were hopelessly inadequate and felt compelled to simply stay out of the way lest they be ruthlessly gunned down. Spurred on by chronic protein shortages and astronomical meat prices, poachers rapidly devoured more than two centuries of wildlife stewardship.

The hunting ban on private land took a little longer to decimate the wild species found there. For one thing, such lands by definition had interested owners, many of whom kept their wildlife as protected as possible, even though they couldn't legally harvest any of them. It became increasingly risky business to protect one's resident creatures, however, as the best wildlife lands were the most tempting targets for ubiquitous poachers. Many a landowner was murdered trying to defend his property and its animals. The mean, unconstrained mood of society hastened the demise of wildlife because poachers never hesitated to meet force with force. Murder had devolved to the level of a minor offense in most cases, and was seldom addressed by authorities.

Soon, wildlife was reduced to historically low levels. Deer were particularly hard hit because they were an excellent food source and because of their susceptibility to nighttime poaching. Other animals suffered in like manner and entire populations wound up as priceless contraband meat shipments. Before long even traditionally non-game species were shot on sight to maintain the flow of illicit flesh to hungry metropolitan areas.

In spite of this inestimable destruction, doggedly stubborn Scott Gentry never gave up. He shifted the focus of his chapter to fishing conservation and continued to be a voice for sensible wildlife utilization. By hard work and discipline the local club was able to preserve a small segment of undisturbed wildlife for a time. They did so by forming a volunteer wildlife patrol and keeping poachers away by force of arms. It was dangerous business and resulted in many sleepless nights and occasional fire fights with poachers. It was worth it to maintain a tangible memory of the wildlife legacy of his forebears. Political emphasis of the club shifted to maintaining the privilege to fish, an activity increasingly under attack by insatiable species equality groups.

The decline in wild animal populations certainly did not go unnoticed by government, news media, or the public. Annihilation of wild creatures was obviously caused by people with guns, and there arose a strong sentiment that all firearms should be taken out of the hands of private individuals.

Momentum built until a constitutional amendment accomplished the long-sought complete ban on private firearms ownership. While this was not a direct project of Prestone's Continental Humane Society and like groups, they heartily applauded the move as good for animals. They assumed there would be no more guns in the hands of men with which they could kill helpless animals.

Scott Gentry wept quietly as he tossed his grandfather's worn hunting rifle onto a pile of obscure guns at the confiscation station. The old man had passed the weapon down tenderly to his grandson before he died, along with stories of his hunts with the rifle in many parts of the world. It was truly a sad day for Gentry and for the dying remnant of sportsmen all over the country.

Loss of weapons by landowners and conservationists removed their ability to effectively patrol their shrinking wildlife reserves on a voluntary basis. Despite heroic attempts they were left with little choice except to stand by while the remaining animals were illegally consumed. The day finally came when they were forced to cease the unarmed patrols altogether. To the nearly defunct Conservation Club chapter in Adrian, Kansas, it eventually became crystal clear that the time had come to cease resisting. Scott Gentry, unarmed and totally dedicated to the end, was killed by poachers on his organization's last wildlife salvation patrol.

* * *

Buck Morgan stared absent-mindedly at the Earth calendar/time gauge that was clicking off days in rapid-fire fashion. Calvin noticed his fixation and commented.

"Got home on the mind, Commander Bucko?"

Morgan glanced at his holographic companion, ever amazed that an artificial intelligence could be so astute. The seated form looked so real that the astronaut had to continually remind himself that it was an electronic illusion. Sometimes he forgot to do so for many watches, and Calvin seemed even more genuine to him. Calvin had turned out to be very nearly a perfect companion, and his recollection of so much of the life of Jeremiah Smith provided endless conversations.

"Sometimes I do, Calvin. Fifty-one years of Earth time since we left, but we've been gone only a little more than five years here on the *Ursa C*. Amazing, huh?"

"Why are you so contemplative, if I might ask?"

"Just wondering how it's going back home, I guess. We—I mean Smitty and me—we had a great time on that Dall sheep hunt before I left. Scenery and sights beyond belief back there in the wilds of Alaska. I look forward to doing something like that again someday."

"Ah, yes. That experience was most prominent in the memory of your friend. No doubt he felt the same way."

"Say, Calvin, you never mention Smitty's wife JoEllen. Any recollection of her?"

"Wife? No, Commander Bucko, I don't remember him being married. Why?"

"He was married just before we left. To a girl named JoEllen. No doubt after his computer portrait was struck."

At times Morgan retired to the entertainment complex, leaving Calvin on his eternal station. Whenever the gleaming Japanese piano beckoned, the astronaut was drawn inexorably, and shortly he was caressing to life one of Beethoven's piano sonatas. There was no one to hear except himself and Calvin, and to the artificial intelligence music was not comprehensible as a pleasurable sensation. To Morgan, though, it was indispensable therapy.

For some reason this music reminded the astronaut of his deceased father, and he reflected on the many lessons he had learned from him during their years together. He wondered how the quail and other wildlife he loved so much were faring back on the productive Kansas farm.

At times he wondered if the Barnes family might be propagating a descendant of his favorite bird dog for him to enjoy someday. Surely so, since they were doubtless awaiting their relative's return with confident anticipation. He hoped his tremendous mounted Dall ram trophy from Alaska, and his father-son caribou mounts, would survive the century. These mementos were displayed in the Barnes home, and he hoped to once again visualize them and relish those memories all over. His old friend Smitty would certainly be dead by the time he got back home, but their experiences would live on in Morgan's mind.

It ought to be a wonderful world to which he would return, and he looked forward to it with great anticipation. Calvin agreed unemotionally with Morgan's musings, and confirmed that such projections were highly probable. They would find out for certain in just a little more than three short years of onboard time.

Buck Morgan was an adventurous man returning to a happy planet. At least, by all indications, that was the case.

CHAPTER 26

July 2131

Familiar cries of a woman in childbirth filled a tiny apartment, and the cramped space reverberated with intermittent groans. An old woman pushed back her white hair with a gloved hand, and then unceremoniously greeted the newborn as it emerged from the womb. This was a ritual she had performed thousands of times during her long career. The panting and perspiring new mother was a stunning dark-haired woman named Carla. She had almond eyes and a perfect petite face. Her figure was temporarily distorted by the rigors of pregnancy, but even so she had remained strikingly beautiful. She had been widely regarded as one of the most gorgeous women in Rome, Italy, since her early teens.

"What did you want, Carla, a boy or a girl?" asked the midwife, slapping the child into its first breath and noting with satisfaction its loud, lusty first cries.

"Who cares? I'm still not sure I wasn't wrong. I've aborted five. I can't explain why I decided to let this one be born," she gasped, her labor pains subsiding now as she collapsed backward, exhausted, with her long black locks piled in deep and tangled disarray around her head. The midwife clamped the cord and cut it with a bloody spurt of red, then handed Carla the slick, crying infant.

"You've got a boy. And he's a healthy one, by all appearances. He's got good lungs. So this is your sixth pregnancy, huh?"

"It's dirty and ugly. Put it somewhere for me," she directed the old woman coldly, ignoring the question.

"Hold onto him until I'm done. Got a couple more steps."

The midwife shrugged as she finished her work, delivering the placenta in a flood of bloody fluid, then nonchalantly cleaning up. It was not unusual these days for a woman to have had many pregnancies but few children. Twenty-second century midwifery had become high on abortions and low on live deliveries. The old woman had grown to hate killing fetuses, though she had extinguished more of the tiny creatures in recent years than she cared to remember. Unsettling memories and tiny, microscopic screams kept growing relentlessly in her mind as the years crawled by, haunting and vivid and never completely still at night. Nonetheless, she was sure that way was best, Europe being so incredibly crowded. She reflected on the situation as she finished her task, and wondered why interruption of pregnancy had become so common. In the old days, it had been so easy not to get pregnant in the first place. Sign of the times, such lack of forethought, she sighed.

"You going to care for this little fellow?" she asked the mother, half expecting a negative answer.

"Huh? Oh, sure. Can you clean him up some? I'll be working a lot, but there are plenty of people around to help. Neighbors and all," replied Carla. "Come to think of it, they'll have to help me or both of us will starve."

Lack of parental attention usually leads to slowed intellectual development, a major worldwide problem of the day. This child likewise was destined for little regard from his wayward mother. At first glance he was a child not unlike millions, indeed billions, of others. Remarkably, to counter maternal neglect, he had a large number of surrogate fathers in the apartment complex. The baby's mother was so promiscuous that almost any one of them could have been his actual father. In an unusual and anomalous way they all offered some kind of developmental guidance to the inquisitive child, a set of factors that helped him to grow and mature far beyond the norm.

"Little guy, you're always here, always ready to speak Russian with me," noted an ancient immigrant with a stubby white beard and a missing left ear from a long ago injury.

"Like he speaks German with me," came a thick German accent from an onlooker. "He isn't afraid of anybody or anything, is he, Boris?"

The old man with a Rhineland accent tousled the boy's hair in mock affection, but received in return only a hard stare that chilled his soul.

Looking away, he continued his observations without making another direct eye contact.

"You're a most unusual boy, aren't you?" questioned the German in his native tongue this time. The boy nodded coldly and responded with near perfect German, inserting appropriate expletives like an earthy native of *der Vaterland.*

Through his persistence and constant presence the boy learned, all right. The community housed a good sampling of people who spoke various European languages, and the boy sought out a new language bearer frequently, whether consciously or by accident nobody knew. By the time he reached school age, he was perfectly fluent in six widely diverse languages. He rapidly became legendary around the complex for his quick aptitude and his insatiable quest for knowledge.

"Good boy! Good boy!" encouraged Mario, the parish priest, praising the boy for his latest linguistic accomplishment. The elderly priest had one of the strongest relationships with the boy because there seemed to be a special affinity between them. Their closeness was not openly apparent, though, because never was there allowed any visible suggestion of affection or fondness.

Mario was unusual for an Italian, since his homeland was in the far north of the country where a lighter complexion is prevalent. His bald head bore traces of white hair in circular fashion about a well-centered hairless expanse on top and behind. His eyes were the color of an algae-covered pool, and his skin was almost white, except where exposure to sunlight had created blotchy patches of brown. He was medium in physical size but well above average in intensity and intellect.

"You're going to be a priest someday, boy. I just know it," added Mario with a hint of coldness like polished steel in his monotone voice.

In other times, such a relationship would have been considered healthy. But times had changed. Parish priests of the twenty-second century simply maintained a phony pious presence in the community and generally didn't expect anyone to actually believe any church doctrines. The priest himself didn't believe there was any relevance to official religious teachings, and he sent to all an unmistakable signal to that

345

effect. He confirmed his disbelief by a hedonistic lifestyle, which consisted of drinking, partying, and womanizing that in no way distinguished him as a man of the cloth.

Physically, the boy developed dark Italian features like those of his mother, but he had eyes that were as blue as the sky and almost as deep. Gazing directly into those mysterious orbs inevitably ignited an inexplicable terror in a person, a fear that seemed utterly misplaced. After all, this was a mere youngster, however unusual he might be. Nevertheless it was real, albeit unnatural, and the child seemed to be indwelt by a force which one dared not challenge for reasons inexpressible. In a vague way he resembled all his potential fathers, and nobody could point to any particular feature that indicated who was responsible for the impregnation of his mother. Laboratory testing to determine such matters was still available, but nobody seemed interested in knowing the truth. The idea was never considered.

"Mario, are you my father?" the boy once asked, the question arising naturally as the priest emerged from Carla's bedroom after one of their frequent trysts.

"Who knows, boy? Your mom gets around," was all the old man would answer.

Carla herself could not begin to answer the question of paternity. She did indeed get around. She vaguely remembered a dark sexual encounter at about the time the pregnancy began, though, when she had wrestled with an unknown partner for much of one night. The mysterious man had accosted her seductively as she was walking home from work, and had never identified himself. He had emanated a sweet aroma when she met him, and she had been highly attracted to him at first.

During the act of intercourse she had developed a terror that she had never felt, and she had struggled mightily to escape his lusty grip. Unable to prevail, she had accommodated him joylessly and with somber resignation. During that episode the sweet scent of her lover had changed slowly and subtly to a most offensive odor, a stench like something dead that clung to her for days. She couldn't explain any of this and had indeed actively suppressed the memory, refusing to acknowledge even to herself that such a rendezvous had occurred.

Her attempts to deny that ordeal were only partially successful, and eventually Carla began to slip into a state of chronic depression. Over the years her demeanor gradually changed from carefree and vivacious toward a deepening despair, a despondency that eventually resulted in a form of madness, raging and unabated. In the final stages she began to rant from dwelling to dwelling day and night, pounding on doors and demanding to be let in. If any unlucky occupant complied, she would tear through the home in a destructive frenzy, furiously destroying everything breakable and doing bodily harm to anyone who was incapable of restraining her. More than once she was beaten unconscious by stronger people she chanced to attack, and several times she almost killed people she was able to surprise or overcome physically. After her insanity became widely known, she was mostly left to walk the streets alone, shouting obscenities and cursing her way from one locked door to the next. Everyone who had ever associated with promiscuous Carla now avoided her.

Increasingly the boy was totally neglected by his mother, and was abandoned to the care of the community and most particularly to the man who represented the church. The old priest was inescapably compelled to show some interest, because the boy demanded spellbound attention from all who knew him except his demented mother.

Carla's ranting finally ceased when she suddenly disappeared. It was almost as if she had never existed, except for the tangible reminder of her son. Rumors abounded that Carla was the crazed woman who committed suicide by torching her fuel-soaked clothes in St. Peter's Square while loudly and vehemently cursing the pontiff and the church. The body was burned beyond recognition and no one could say with certainty if it were her, nor did anyone really care.

Even before Carla's disappearance, Mario had become the child's prime mentor, and hypocrisy was the old priest's hallmark. His protégé was unusually perceptive and from a very early age he rejected all things represented by the tarnished residual church. All that he saw and heard confirmed that the church was either irrelevant or an implacable adversary. He even found religious ceremonies and sacraments hilarious, and often he would interrupt the most somber of services with loud and uncontrollable laughter, much to the consternation of image-conscious Mario.

Despite his peculiarities, the boy developed an extraordinary and unconventional spirituality which defied description, and which often served him well. From time to time, physical hunger gnawed at the boy's insides, causing his stomach to growl like a wild animal. The world was becoming a desperate, negligent place, and children often literally starved to death. When such a lack of concern manifested itself in a threatening way, a miraculous compensation often intervened on behalf of the boy.

"Mario, did you see that?" marveled Boris in his thick Russian accent as they observed the child one rainy afternoon.

"I did, Boris. I can't explain it, though," the priest admitted, a look of bewilderment crossing his wrinkled face He had meant to feed the boy, but other thoughts had sidetracked him.

The boy had struggled briefly to reach a food jar that was well beyond his reach. With no hint of frustration he extended his hand, closed his eyes, and with obvious concentration he "wished" the container into his grasp. It moved visibly and resolutely, as if on command. The boy then wolfed down the contents until his hunger was completely satisfied.

On another occasion he was able to locate Mario in a massive, milling crowd of people after they had become separated. He seemingly homed in on his mentor's location unerringly as if he knew instinctively where to find the old priest. Examples of the boy's unusual abilities abounded and were frequent topics of conversation among his community of acquaintances. This clairvoyance became the basis of both fear and no small degree of reverence toward him.

People called this unusual set of traits the boy's sixth sense. It was by no means an abstract, impotent concept, but a living and active spiritual dimension. The talent was much more than an ability to perform inexplicable physical acts, but it also allowed him to know concepts he had never been taught, and to perceive information he couldn't possibly know of his own accord. It would have been easy to attribute such capabilities to the outworking of an inscrutable mind, or an accident of nature that produced astounding mental capacity. Conventional wisdom was that he was simply unusual, because few believed in the supernatural. More perceptive souls who knew the growing boy weren't so certain.

While most children aspired to involve themselves in common juvenile pursuits such as games and holocoms, this youngster viewed such diversions with deep condescension. He gravitated almost exclusively to adults, whom he constantly amazed and baffled with his astounding wisdom and precocious knowledge. Most phenomenal, however, was his unnatural control over other people and even inanimate objects. In primitive times he might have been thought demon possessed, but not in the enlightened twenty-second century, where naturalistic explanations held absolute sway.

"The boy won't eat animal protein," complained old Boris to the priest. "He has no idea where any food comes from except by his sixth sense, which he says won't let him eat certain food. What he won't eat is animal protein. Almost everything else is acceptable."

"Lots of vegetarians around, Boris. Put him on yeast extract so he won't get stunted and let him eat vegetables."

"He won't like that, either, but maybe he'll take it like medicine."

The boy had seldom seen any kind of animal, since even pigeons, sparrows, and starlings were fast disappearing. But preparations of commercial protein were still available for a price, and the mere presence of these substances put the youth into a furious state of mind characterized by strong and uncontrollable emotion.

"I'll kill you if you eat that," he surprised an innocent boy at midday as they prepared to dine at school. No one could hear the threat except the one to whom it was addressed, but the terrified recipient easily recognized a genuine quality in the cold words. Being new, he had been unaware of the intimidation that was part of being in the same classroom as this one with the evil eyes. A fearsome chill rocked the new boy as he looked into those awful blue globes that threatened from across the dining table. Laying aside his protein morsel, he turned and fled from the room, only to be retrieved by an irate teacher who meted out abundant punishment. But he had learned his lesson. Everyone was a vegetarian in any setting attended by the ominous son of Carla.

Fits of rage were common occurrences in the unconventional boy's life and were yet another distinction that set him apart from his less eminent peers. He was especially inflamed when anyone admitted consuming some animal product, even at home. No one could guess where this peculiar passion originated, but it seemed more a curse than a gift.

The boy had never had an animal friend, since pets were uncommon and farms were remote from the crowded city. There were practically no wild animals about, and zoos were in abject disrepute worldwide. Ubiquitous cockroaches swarmed in his apartment complex, and they became his companions. He frequently let them crawl all over him while he squealed with delight. He would stroke their chitinous backs and tenderly touch their long antennae, while the ugly bugs most unnaturally cavorted and buzzed their wings excitedly as if preparing for a nasty takeoff. The boy inevitably became soiled with their excrement, but nobody dared make an issue of it. Roaches and other dubious creeping things would leave their hiding places and swarm to him. Why these creatures behaved so unnaturally toward him was beyond comprehension.

As the boy grew, it was ever more apparent that he was meant for distinction. The son of a loose woman, a product of a random conception, and fathered by anybody's guess, he did not seem to be a candidate for greatness. Somehow, though, genetics had come together in this one human being to produce unusual abilities, strong passions, fervent desires, and a powerful sense of destiny.

Early in life the youth had a craving for authority. His curious power over other people seemed to grow logarithmically as he matured. While he was still at a tender age, he was clearly in charge in his neighborhood, his school, and his circle of adult friends. How could one so young command such fear and respect?

"Mario, you and Boris are going with me tonight. There's a man from America speaking at the Roman Conference Center. His name is Waymon Prestone, and he's supposed to be a great protector of animals."

"Is that so? Of course, my young friend. What is he going to be talking about?"

"Protecting animals, you old fool. What else would the head of the Continental Humane Society talk about?"

"Of course. I should have known," replied the tottering old priest, completely oblivious to the disrespect. He had become hardened by repeated verbal abuse, and he knew better than to protest.

The boy came away from the speech by Prestone in an unusually thoughtful mood. The crowd had been adoring and appreciative of the graying activist and had contributed generously to his organization. But there was something that the youth sensed that was not apparent to less discerning people.

"This man is raising funds, and I'm not interested in money," the boy said.

"What do you mean? He told it straight, I thought," replied Mario, trying hard not to sound challenging or disrespectful.

"Old man, something has got to change. If this Prestone is America's best, we've got to do better."

Later, the youth sat silently in Mario's room, pondering his future while the exhausted old clergyman slept soundly. A firm and immutable destiny crystallized in his mind, and he stayed up until near dawn planning. He would make a difference. An unquestionable and powerful difference.

There could be no mistaking it. He had a purpose on planet Earth, and now he would make his vision and his future glory a reality.

* * *

Twenty-second century England was the world model of stability, a bastion of social graces and culture, a remnant domain of those qualities that had always signified authentic civilization. True, the crown was bankrupt, as was the people's arm of government, but the population was generally well fed and mostly contented and lethargic. There were occasional brawls, and there were sometimes riots over some insignificant point of disagreement. But conditions in the island nation were far superior to those in the world at large.

Six months before Carla gave birth to an illegitimate son in Italy amid filth and deprivation, another delivery occurred in a plush hospital outside Oxford. A well-to-do widow delivered a baby by Cesarean section, a common procedure that had become quite routine for live births among the very wealthy. Unlike the birth in Italy, this infant was the product of a precisely planned pregnancy, using a selected sample of sperm from a vast listing of available genetic material. It would be only the very best hybridized sperm that would unite with the wealthy woman's ovum to create her dream child. Cutting edge medicine still existed in the world, and a person of sufficient means could purchase it with ease.

Oh, how the woman did hope in this baby! It was a boy by design, and it would be her constant companion and her joy in old age. She had always wanted a son to develop, a son she could cherish and nurture. This child would be a champion of the planet, a defender of right, and an engineer of human destiny. More than that, he would show the world how superior was the House of Ersatzson, a dying line of dukes and dutchesses, knights and nobles.

The widow's deceased husband had been unable to live up to the expectations she had treasured since she was a little girl, the revival of the glory days of her ancestry and recognition of her boundless worth by upper crust English society. The man had appeared to be a picture of strength and vitality when she had met him. Her husband had been a kind of misdirected environmental warrior on a quest to save the planet from "the blight of humanity," as he had called it. She shared his passion and vision, so she had married him with grand aspirations.

But she had felt bitterly disappointed when he cracked quickly under constant pressure to perform, sexually and otherwise. Worse, their name was regularly left out of important WorldNet gossip columns, and they were almost never included on the most coveted guest lists. Her husband had many innovative ideas about ways to restore the balance of nature and reform the world, but none of his grandiose schemes would ignite. To his exacting wife, the social ladder looked higher and more inaccessible with passage of each depressing year. The woman chafed and fretted for quite some time as she tolerated the nobody she had married, and his conspicuous weaknesses became ever more obvious. Her burning contempt for him amplified daily.

The useless husband mysteriously disappeared as the couple took a moonlight cruise on the River Thames. She now wore black all the time, ostensibly in his memory, and she became well known about the city for her show of deep sorrow. She reverted to her own family name and lived without companionship, save occasional visits by distant relatives. Her search for a perfect sperm donor began in earnest shortly after her husband's unexplained death.

The child looked exactly like his mother in practically every way. This was most satisfying to her, since Lady Ersatzson had used all available technology to pinpoint genetic characteristics that fit her own family line. Using standard gene splicing methods, she was actually able to pick and choose desired characteristics from various donors. She effectively selected her own family traits, so her son truly typified Ersatzson family attributes in a most phenomenal way.

He was a handsome child, and in keeping with tradition she named him Christian, a name held by nearly a dozen of his forebears. She believed in nothing religious, not even a little, and it infuriated her when anyone pointed out the literal meaning of her son's name. Her anger caused her to redouble her intensive efforts to shape and mold the youngster to her exact specifications.

"Look at this, Bruce," said young Christian to a playmate. "I can make this disappear."

"You're crazy, Christian. You can't make things disappear. It's a trick."

"Is that so? Watch this." The boy then put a deck of cards in his left hand, covered them with his right hand, then turned his hand position upside down. Opening his hands, indeed there were no cards there. His short-sleeved shirt allowed little room for deceptive sleight of hand, so his poor companion was left in awe. On firmly clapping his hands, the cards reappeared as if by magic.

Christian Ersatzson was a most likable and personable youngster right from the start. He didn't particularly like people, but they most assuredly liked him. He was a tremendously unusual young man in many ways. He was educated in the very best private schools and lived a life of luxury on his mother's family wealth. His interest in magic was no passing fancy, and he early developed a penchant for the occult and mysterious. He kept an unending stream of acquaintances mesmerized with his odd repertoire of talent, which demonstrated a mystifying mastery over material objects. As he matured the "tricks" became increasingly complicated and ever more impossible to explain.

"I can even make an animal appear," he told one classmate, whereupon he produced a wing-flapping pigeon with precision. The boy jumped back in shock, amazed but not surprised. Nothing magical Christian did was unexpected.

"Can we eat it, Christian? My mom cooks them sometimes."

"You barbarian! No, we can't eat it. Aren't you a vegetarian like normal people? But let me show you one more thing. I can kill it and bring it back to life."

"Now that I won't believe until I see it."

Grasping the bird by its head, he spun it around several times, by all appearances snapping the creature's neck. It looked very dead. With his fingers he opened the pigeon's beak and blew gently, and immediately the bird began struggling and beating its wings violently, very much alive. The surprised companion praised him loudly as the bird flew away, leaving him completely baffled by such an astounding feat.

Maturation of Christian Ersatzson was rapid and complete. By the time he entered his teenage years, he had completely mastered the black arts and had even become an expert at communicating with assistance from "helpful spirits." He passed so quickly from childhood to adulthood in his thinking and his speech that even his mother became bewildered. His growing spiritual dimension troubled her quite a bit, since she was totally materialistic in her own thinking. But the young man's drift toward outright clairvoyance was undeniable. She accepted the development as odd but permissible, and she even found his extrasensory abilities a convenient tool for getting her name on the right guest lists. His divination often provided delicious disasters for her social rivals, a talent he displayed readily and repeatedly to her great delight.

As they drove to a grand social engagement, one of the year's top events, the young man pointed to crowded ghettos lining the streets they were traveling. Southern England was practically wall to wall with endless homes, and humanity was everywhere apparent.

"Is there any solution to overpopulation, Mum?"

"Kill off a lot of the pitiful wretches, I suppose. Perhaps a plague of some kind."

"Hmm. Too bad we can't turn them into pigeons or rabbits."

"Keep working on it, Christian. What a marvelous thought!"

They entered a grand ballroom in an ornate mansion, and noted the gay decorations and finely dressed men and women standing about. There was a vast sea of tables, all set with finest china and silver. The head table was embellished with colorful decorations, and behind it was a stage prepared for a performance. Over the stage was a giant circular emblem of complicated design that proclaimed to all "The Continental Humane Society."

An usher took the boy and his mother directly to the head table, where they were introduced to all dignitaries present. One of them was a very mature man escorted by a very young and beautiful woman. The man was an American who would be the featured speaker tonight. Efficient waiters then presented the guests rich and delectable foods, but the boy instinctively pushed his portion of animal protein to the back of his plate with an upturned nose. He picked at his vegetables but ate very little. He noticed that the man who would speak did likewise. Thankfully, the meal was soon over and waiters competently removed all plates and utensils.

"Ladies and gentlemen, presenting our night's entertainment, the eminent and infinitely talented Christian Ersatzson!" said the announcer as the fair-haired young man stepped into the spotlight. It was a distinct privilege to appear before so many important people at the momentous Continental Humane Society fundraiser, one of Oxford's premier events. Young Ersatzson stupefied the crowd with impossible feats of utter supernatural dimensions, and applause was thunderous after his astounding finale.

Introduction of the speaker was next, and handsome, mellow Waymon Prestone strode confidently to the podium. His immaculate red hair, now charmingly muted with copious gray, displayed his characteristic central part as always. He congratulated Ersatzson on his performance and thanked everyone for their part in staging the event. He then went quickly and efficiently into his polished routine.

Prestone's theme for the night involved the evils of fishing, terrible pain felt by a fish when it was hooked, and the inherent brutality of such an uncivilized practice. He was able to hold the attention of his audience as always, but the diversion created by the guest entertainer strangely blunted his usual oratory perfection. Despite this slight embarrassment, coffers of the Continental Humane Society swelled considerably that night.

Prestone's charisma and speech were not his best, but he was still very, very good, and almost nobody noticed that he was below his standard performance. Prestone's speech was truly unimpressive to only one person: young Christian Ersatzson. The youth watched the presentation with skepticism from the start, and somehow he knew deep within himself that the entire affair was nothing but a sham. There could be no doubt that Prestone was against fishing, to be sure, and so was

Ersatzson. But a visceral stirring deep in his spirit told him all he needed to know about the polished impostor.

He knew he wouldn't be able to stomach this Prestone fellow, not for long, not if he could help it. His very essence retched at the prospect. He couldn't wait to escape the glittering ballroom after such a nauseating experience.

CHAPTER 27

July 2156

A rotting dock stood almost abandoned, its heavy lumber stained with fading seagull droppings that were barely visible now under the relentless assault of sun, wind, and rain. There were very few of the familiar and graceful birds left, because traps and snares had practically annihilated them. Staunch timbers under girding the pier still stood at attention, but slumping boardwalks were not maintained, and there were no bobbing boats moored at dockside. Decaying hulks of a few rusty trawlers could be seen scattered up and down the way, situated forlornly just out of the grasp of high tide. None appeared to be even remotely seaworthy. Ancient lobster pots were stacked here and there in lofty, disorderly piles, with decomposed netting slowly but surely falling away in useless and pathetic strands. The tide washed up on shore in its ceaseless rhythm, but there was little human presence to appreciate the timeless phenomenon. The smell of salty air had changed little, but the town of Bar Harbor was just a shadow of its former glory days.

Roscoe Wiggins sat in a shabby tavern looking out over the rocky shores of the cove as dim late evening light cast shadows into the surging surf. He was sipping a cold beer, the last one he would likely be able to afford for a while. He looked out at his old boat, the *Laughing Gull*, and spit in disgust toward the sawdust floor. Wiggins followed the arching blob of spittle with interest, and noted that it hit exactly in the center of his target, a rusty bucket that sat generally in the direction of one corner.

As was the case with all the craft, the hopeless state of his *Laughing Gull* was obvious to all. It might just as well be submerged somewhere offshore for all the good it was doing him. Now completely ruined, its rusty bottom seemed to be taunting him. A yellow government condemnation paper was plastered to its side, and the document tortured him even more and added to his misery.

For four decades a well-maintained version of the *Laughing Gull* had propelled him daily into the North Atlantic, and he had made it pretty well on the ocean's fertile bounty. His father and grandfathers before him, for no telling how many generations, had been able to extract a living from the restless, heaving waters. They had not done this easily or without considerable peril, but rather by means of ceaseless toil and a high tolerance for very real danger. The vintage boat had indeed been his father's last craft before the old fisherman had died. Now it would never take to the sea again, Wiggins was more certain every day. There was no way he could afford to bring her up to increasingly rigorous government standards. It had been hard enough just to keep the boat seaworthy in the past. Now he had relinquished her to merciless salt spray and the pitiless onslaught of unopposed decay.

"What we really need is a jargonaut excluder," quipped Wiggins to another unemployed fisherman, the only other patron in the establishment.

"Maybe we ought to join the pirates. They're making money hand over fist, seining and dredging day and night and selling just about everything they pull up," said his companion. "That black market's mighty profitable and tempting."

People still wanted succulent flesh from all kinds of sea creatures, and certainly the public paid well for it. Armed renegade launches outgunned government regulators with the latest contraband armaments, so there were no authorities with the means to effectively stop illegal operators. Anyone with a legitimate outfit was caught in a maze of government paperwork and regulations, and was required to fish unarmed to boot. Their only hope of gainful employment was to get an unregistered boat, or simply sign on with one of the buccaneers on the sly.

Wiggins knew that he had to do something. He had several women he slept with from time to time, and the children he had by them were in need of food. There would be no peace until he could provide some support. He swigged the last swallow of his brew and plunked the bottle back down with a resolute thump. His mind was made up. Without another word Wiggins slipped out the door and headed down the sagging boardwalk.

More than half a continent away, handsome Charles Smith kissed his wife and hugged his pretty teenaged daughter. His thick blonde hair came down almost to his eyebrows, and had a wild, flyaway look no matter what he did to get control of it. He sported a rugged yet clean-cut full beard and mustache that gave him a most masculine look. He slipped his fishing vest on over his broad shoulders and climbed into his vehicle for the drive from Livingston, Montana, to his favorite catch-and-release trout stream. Smith was the last living member of the formerly influential Conservation Club in all of Montana, but he still took his avocation seriously.

"You be careful, Daddy," called young Eva Smith as her father departed with a broad smile and a wave of his hand.

Today he would use an antique Battenkill bamboo fly rod, a prize piece of equipment handed down from his grandfather, Jeremiah Smith, the well-known astronaut. A passion for fishing had been quite naturally passed from father to son to grandson, and the vintage tool was a valued heirloom that was inherited in similar fashion. It was guarded closely, greatly valued, and deeply personal to Smith. To use it to land a trophy fish was a rare treat, and he had high hopes this gorgeous summer day. The angler had gone several trips without so much as a strike, as most fish, even in protected catch-and-release waters, had been trapped and eaten by hungry residents.

It took an hour or so to reach his destination, a place where majestic mountains towered heavenward to the south, and snowy glaciers reached like tentacles toward broad lowlands. It was from these stretching tongues of white that the headwaters of the Stillwater River arose, and the icy flow tumbled in an ever-magnificent cascade toward lower ground. Trout were rare, but fishing was officially legal if one followed the rule to release unharmed anything caught. Smith was a stickler for doing everything exactly right, and he carefully filed away every residual of damaging barb from his fly hook as he watched the swirling current for a telltale ripple that would indicate a rising trout.

The crystal water beckoned like a magnet, drawing the veteran fisherman inexorably to his supreme passion. A sound of rushing water filled his ears and launched his mind into a state of incomparable expectation. Smith passed a fine tapered monofilament line through the eye of his hook, the shaft of which was finely wrapped by hand to strongly resemble the body of a caddis fly nymph. The wings and legs were artfully formed as well, and the craftsmanship in his creation pleased him greatly as he threaded the leader into place. He passed the tippet back through the notch in the thread between the eye and the curve of the hook, and then drew it through the resulting loop. On pulling it up tightly, he had forged the ultimate fisherman's knot, a perfect succession of circular monofilament segments that welded the fly to the line. He bit off the short excess segment and inspected his composition with pride. It was beautiful and should be effective.

Along the plunging Stillwater, the dedicated fisherman cast a long line into sparkling, cascading waters. Ingenious arching of line from the antique rod followed a series of staccato strippings by hand from the reel. Motion of the tip created a series of symmetrical circles of twine that eventually straightened perfectly at the end as if by magic. The simulated caddis fly deposited gently into a swirl of calmer water just below a protruding boulder. Many yeoman casts later there had been no response to his repeated offerings.

He moved on downstream, working each likely spot in succession, taking care that his backcast stayed clear of confounding vegetation along the bank. There was a very good spot just ahead, and he wanted to be certain all was perfect for his next cast. He heaved the tip of his rod high into blue sky, and waited expertly until the line straightened out behind him. His forward cast placed the fly perfectly in a quiet pool below an overhanging rock face.

This time he felt the strong slam of a colorful rainbow trout rising to engulf the tiny lure. He set the hook and began to play the fish tenderly, almost lovingly, enjoying immensely the surge of this powerful multicolored creature. It leaped from the water several times before it finally acquiesced to his efforts. In short order he was cautiously removing the barbless hook, after which he reverently and gently

361

released his catch back into the crystal stream. With a grateful sigh and a tip of his fishing hat he bid the fish a fond farewell.

"Die, you filthy torturer!" came an unwelcome greeting from a brushy hillside next to the stream. Almost simultaneously Smith's whole world became one of sudden loud noise and searing pain in his chest. A load of buckshot slammed into him, ripping through his ancient craftsman's vest in a scatter of crimson holes. He slumped forward head first into the waters, and his prize bamboo rod and dislodged hat both floated forlornly beside his drifting body. Long streaks of blood stained the clear water and rushed downstream away from his still form. A malignant laugh echoed through the valley, a mirthless chuckle of triumph and pernicious achievement.

"Hunt the hunters, trap the trappers, butcher the butchers. And now we float the fishermen!"

Riotous laughter broke out once more as the corpse hung up on rocks just below the pool he had been fishing. A victorious assassin emerged from nearby bushes. A second explosion echoed in the canyon as another blast of hot lead shattered Smith's lifeless skull.

*   *   *

Waymon Prestone cleared his throat and stepped to yet another podium to begin his address. He had carefully sized up his audience ahead of time, noting the mix of people before deciding on which of his poised performances to deliver. Tonight's group was heavily urban and mostly professional people, so he knew many would have pets and some would be doctors.

"Ladies and gentlemen, we stand on the brink of significance as a movement. We must press ahead to true excellence! We must never retreat from the course destiny has chosen for our world!" his clear voice resonated throughout the banquet hall.

Prestone commanded respect and he had a significant following of adoring fans from his frequent three-vee appearances. An entire table in back of the hall was filled with his books, all of which fetched a handsome price. Turnout this night was superb, and many people came just for a look at the international celebrity.

"We must never forget that all creatures can feel pain. All creatures deserve our utmost consideration. There are those barbarians who cast deadly pieces of bent metal into our lakes and streams to extract our scaly friends against their will. And they do it just for fiendish fun. Even those who release these creatures immediately are guilty of gravest savagery. Who among us would submit to being so treated?

"We must push on to equality for our disadvantaged brethren—disadvantaged by the impersonal but omnipotent forces of evolution," he railed as the audience sat and listened in bewitched fascination. "And it's not just our wild fish who are being mistreated. There are many others who are suffering even worse persecution. I can see them in my mind's eye all over our nation and in far corners of the world, living in cramped pens, eating a bare subsistence of food and starving to swim free and drink in life-giving sunshine. We've got to end this suffering once and for all!"

He stepped around the podium to better confront his hearers and his voice rose in crescendo, booming his message, "And you, ladies and gentlemen, must commit to changing yourselves if we are to eliminate such misery. You must swear off animal protein altogether, and you must insist on plant-based clothing. And you must give generously so we can press this battle on—to victory!"

The hall broke spontaneously into thunderous applause as he concluded his talk. Prestone knew he had been inspiring, and he walked back to his chair in triumph before the noise abated. He gave a sly wink to Tina, his newest girlfriend, as he took a seat beside her at the head table. He had done well, and this was confirmed as the Continental Humane Society piled up a hefty amount in donations that night.

Then it was on to the next fundraiser. His engagements just seemed to have no end.

* * *

363

Billy Barnes was deep in thought as he drove toward the main road, gazing over familiar fields and fence rows. He had lost his father, Jerry Barnes, over a decade before, and the weight of the business operation was heavily on his mind. The elder Barnes had died quietly in his sleep at nearly 100 years of age, and they had buried him in the ancient cemetery plot east of the farmhouse. Barnes still missed the old man's companionship terribly.

Cattle grazed in the distance and crops were growing well. But disquieting thoughts kept surfacing, bits of negative information he couldn't completely suppress. In recent years changes in society had increasingly instilled a deep dread in him. Just this week poor Barnes had received notification that there were pending new regulations that would make his production costs much higher.

He stopped beside his brightly colored mailbox, expecting perhaps his first shipment of the latest government commodity forms. Instead there was a single gaudy envelope inside. He reached in and retrieved it, then opened it with a quick slice of his pocketknife. The card inside was engraved like a wedding invitation.

PROTECT MOTHER GAIA

All over the world mankind is seeking ways to defend and nurture our heavenly Mother, our goddess Earth. One way you can help is by eschewing the temptation to consume any kind of animal product. Animals are our blood brothers, no matter how small or fragile, and we must protect them at all costs. With a simple ingestion of spirulina daily, you don't need anything else to eat except a normal vegetable diet. It's only a small step, but it is an essential step. If everyone did it, we would live in a healthier, happier, and more contented world. For more information call the Church of the Sun and Moon, or come to our Friday evening fertility service. You'll be smarter and a more progressive component of Mother Earth for doing your part.

Most mail arrived nowadays electronically, but sometimes flyers and other junk pieces still came the old fashioned way. Barnes snickered a little at the incongruity. Spirulina was yeast extract, and yeast was considered an animal. The hypocrites are getting away with it, he thought condescendingly. He stuffed the card in his pocket and motored on down the road to the deteriorating brick church his family had attended for generations. His old friend Roger Walker was already there, and the other farmer spoke before Barnes could say anything.

"Billy, if things get much worse, I don't think I'm going to keep farming. Did you see those protesters out there again today? What do they want us to do?" asked elderly Walker.

Billy Barnes' family had always been protein farmers, and his ancestors had arrived in Kansas almost three centuries ago. He had grown up proud of his heritage. He had inherited the Kansas farm operation known as the Morgan Place, and he was well schooled in animal husbandry and protein production in the most modern sense. Roger Walker still farmed down the road on the property that had once belonged to Barnes' grandfather.

"Well, Roger, I guess we can always switch to soybeans. That's their ultimate aim, anyway. To get us all completely out of the animal business."

"I'm thinking of putting in a yeast operation, actually," mused Walker, running his fingers through his white hair and leaning back against the church pew as if very tired. "There's already a useable building on the place, all laid out to do the job. I'm convinced there's no profit in it because people still want real protein. Most of them don't know how to survive on a purely vegetable and micro-meat diet. But it's strange how silent the majority seems to be."

"Yeah, Dad tried the yeast business," Barnes recalled. "He built that old building while Grandpa Bill was still alive, but the whole idea bombed out in a hurry. Pretty dismal financial failure, in fact. Maybe the time is right now for another attempt. Look at this card I found in my mailbox, wanting everybody to switch to micro-meat. Free advertising, you might say, if you decide to get into the yeast business. I don't know what they think we'd mix for fuel, though."

"Yeah, I know," he responded, looking over the card as he spoke. "I got one, too. Those idiot demonstrators motor all the way out here on our veganox to protest our using animals to make it. Devil of a note."

"Maybe we could do with less fuel in this country, but food and clothing, I doubt it. We're on a thin edge now and there are sporadic shortages of both in the cities. Like last year when those riots broke out..."

"That was bad. 'Course it'll happen again, too," continued Walker. "Frustrated and confused city people. They nearly burned out every big city in America. It's amazing how Bob Hancock predicted that, too. He's convinced we're heading into the end times, the way society is deteriorating."

"Right. That old man's really got a grip on what's happening in the world, doesn't he, Roger?" observed Barnes, remembering a conversation with Hancock many years ago. Their quiet private discussion had changed the entire direction of Billy Barnes' life.

"Always has, Billy. 'Course, he had a good teacher. I knew his mother Judy, one of the finest teachers who ever lived. He learned an awful lot from her. But I don't think he quite knows what to make of this species equality steamroller. It seems to be unstoppable."

"Say, Roger, how is Leon coming along? Hasn't Bob been a big help with him, too?"

"You can say that again. Leon even married that girl he's been living with. 'Course not before they had a couple of kids."

"Are they back here to stay?"

"I think so. He's had enough of Denver. He wants to help me on the farm and raise those boys out here like he was raised. That's answered prayer."

"Sounds like Leon may be coming around. Dad had the same worries about me, and I can tell you he was on target. Some of the things I used to do make me shudder now."

"Didn't you have problems with Jamie when he was a kid? Wasn't he visiting that pagan church, too?" asked Walker.

"And worse. But he's becoming a terrific farmer now with a good work ethic. He makes me proud, if I do say so myself. His sister Faye even gave us cause for concern at one point, but she's as solid as a rock now. The problem now in our little family is Jody. He's the worst egg in the basket so far, best I can tell," said Barnes as a frown creased his face on thinking of his adolescent grandson. "Jamie's tried everything, I think, but Jody's unreachable. Even Jamie doesn't even think he's salvageable, the way the boy's acting. Jody and I get along just fine, and sometimes I think he listens to me. We had a great time last week just roaming over the old farm. But his mom and dad are totally exasperated with him."

"Just pray, Billy. I cling to prayer, and I'm convinced it's effective. I've got a couple of grandsons of my own to be concerned about," said Walker. "Cute little devils, but mighty mean, too."

"I can identify with what you're saying. And I've seen Leon's boys, and you're right. They are good looking kids. You know, life is funny. You want to do right, but it's so hard when you're young. Sometimes it isn't easy when you get older, either. I just wish I'd gotten my life moving more in the right direction before Dad died. He wouldn't believe I've changed so much. Too bad farming isn't the same, though."

"You know, Billy, these same bullies that we deal with every week here at the farm, carrying their signs and making obscene gestures at us—I've heard we aren't the only ones they're after. Now researchers are doing experiments on people because such a stink is raised over using animals. Sounds like the Third Reich again to me."

"The Third what?"

"Reich. It was supposed to be a dynasty back in the middle of the Oil Age, a kingdom that would last a thousand years. Started by some crazy guy named Hitler. I read a book last year that told how dedicated he was to what we call species equality. He wouldn't allow any animal research, for one thing. He apparently used the charge of 'vivisection' against numerous medical doctors, accusing them of doing animal research and then killing them, whether they were guilty or not. Of course he was strictly vegetarian, like our friends carrying the signs."

"No kidding? That's peculiar. A vegetarian leader way back then? I never heard of that. Sounds like an interesting book," said Barnes, genuinely uninformed of the vague nuances of the Pre-2K dictator.

"He wasn't even a smart vegetarian. He apparently suffered from chronic flatulence and vitamin B12 deficiency because of his vegetarianism. He evidently had no qualms about killing millions of people, but he endured poor health in order to keep from eating animals for food."

"That's interesting. Did the book say whether he had any problem with pets, horse racing, and so on?" asked Barnes. "They're really after all uses of animals now."

"Nothing mentioned about those. Hmm...maybe that means these people today are crazier than Hitler. They're determined to eliminate 'animal slaves' of all categories. No, I don't think he was as vocal about those kinds of things. He was pretty kooky for his day, though."

"You know, Roger, not too many decades ago it wasn't this way. I read a book myself recently entitled *Recollections of Excellence*. Have you heard of it?"

"Of course. That's the book about Buck Morgan written by his old sidekick, Jeremiah Smith. We used to have a copy of it at home. The two of them met on their first interplanetary voyage, soon after Buck's dad was killed in that accident on your farm. As you know, your father bought the place from the Morgan estate after that. I haven't heard anybody mention that book in years, though. You and Buck are kinfolks, aren't you?"

"Yep, second cousins. I found that book in Dad's library after he died. Really interesting reading. Those guys traveled all over the solar system together. And when they were together back here on Earth, they participated together in that old time activity called hunting for wild animals. And in the book their reasons for doing it seem pretty darned sound to me. Can you imagine that? Dad took me hunting pretty often back when I was a kid."

"Lots of people hunted when we were young. Long time ago. I remember those days—listening to bobwhites calling in summer, watching deer feeding along the field edges at night, hearing an old turkey gobbling in springtime. None of that goes on now. Darn shame."

                         *   *   *

If Buck Morgan hadn't been nearly a dozen light years away, streaking back toward Earth with his computers crammed to the brim, his ears might have been sizzling. The mention of his name occurred only rarely now, even in his old hometown farming community. The world had virtually eliminated all reference to the interstellar traveler, almost as if he had never existed. The spaceman passed his idle moments playing Bach on the piano and considering his latest dreams. He had been on another fantasy quail hunt, this one evanescent and charming, a tour of misty prairies amid fleeting dogs and transitory quail. It had been brief, but pleasant thoughts had filled his mind. The sensation was a welcome respite from more disturbing nightmares he had experienced so often. Still, the old home place was different from before, and an abiding peace about his dream was elusive.

He had a hard time conceiving of what it would be like to get acquainted with an unknown relative, if there were living a descendant of the Barnes family he had known and loved. Would they have anything at all in common? Would he seem backward to people on Earth after all his years isolated from human progress?

He couldn't help but wonder again if perhaps an offspring of that pure white English setter might be there to greet him as well. He had respected and appreciated his father's dog so much, and that part of his dream was something he could certainly hope would come true. Surely leaders of the modern space effort would spare a couple of weeks for him to enjoy a supreme Kansas vacation for old times' sake.

"We're going to be home within a year and three months, Calvin," Morgan noted as he looked at the Earth clock on the instrument panel. They had just passed the complex of binary red giant stars a few weeks before, and more holos and measurements had added to their vast storehouse of onboard data.

"A year, three months, four days, five hours, and twenty-seven minutes, give or take a few, Commander Bucko," replied the precise holographic co-pilot. "Orbital rendezvous with Space Station Delta will be on April 5, 2169. Earth time."

"You're a genius, partner," conceded Morgan as he noted Calvin's satisfied grin. His electronic hair seemed even wilder than usual on this particular watch. "Think you're darn good, don't you?"

"Just well programmed, Commander Bucko. Just well programmed. Our trajectory looks good all the way home."

*   *   *

As Waymon Prestone motored toward yet another in his endless series of fundraisers, he became aware of pattering insects against the windshield of his car, hapless creatures splattering themselves into oblivion. My Gaia, he thought, I'm killing animals! Horrified, he slowed a bit to lessen the repetitive cacophony of deadly impacts.

"What's wrong?" asked a comely blonde in a plush seat next to him as she adjusted her short skirt over her sensuous legs. Her perfect face contorted slightly and her seductive red lips pursed as she posed the question.

"Nothing, Tara. Just bugs. Making a mess on my windshield. Curse it, the only animals we ever see anymore are these stupid insects."

"We're running late, honey," cooed the scantily attired girl. "If you keep going so slow we'll miss this next fundraiser. And there'll be some important representatives there from that Italian organization. You remember, that young Hammer guy's group."

After a brief hesitation Prestone ran his speed back to its original level. There were big plans afoot involving Europe, and a troublesome young man named Antonio Malleus had called Prestone personally about receiving his delegation. The staccato splashing of insects increased to its previous level, incessant and deadly.

I don't care, he thought angrily. They're just detestable bugs. You've got to draw the line somewhere. What do these Europeans want me to do, anyway?

Even veteran Waymon Prestone wasn't ready for total commitment to species equality. But he wasn't about to reverse his position, not when it was so profitable. Not when they were winning.

Or were they? Of course they were. And as far as he was concerned, the splashing of insects against his car had nothing to do with his degree of commitment to the cause.

CHAPTER 28

April 2159

As do most healthy boys in due time, a youngster had grown to manhood in Italy and another in England. Their youthful enthusiasm was directed toward a common consuming passion, and their unusual and extraordinary talents invigorated them to levels far in excess of their peers. The youth in Italy was somewhat ugly in appearance, small in stature, medium in build, and darkly complexioned. He was set apart from other men by a piercing pair of frightful eyes, his only really distinctive physical characteristic. The English youth was his opposite in many ways, larger than average, with broad shoulders and over six feet of height. He was a handsome and imposing specimen with thick blonde hair.

In order to better his name recognition and broaden his personal appeal, the Italian youth was forced to take certain highly practical steps. He had a clear vision of his destiny as a leader of mankind, and he changed his original cumbersome name to one easier to pronounce, to remember, and to use. Out of a deliberate search he arrived at the name Antonio Malleus.

As a youth Malleus founded the Progress League to address a broad range of social problems. Most members were enthusiastic young people who made it their business to police the populace in vigilante fashion. A special emphasis was placed on pushing various animal welfare ordinances, which were often enforced with laxity by fund-starved governmental agencies. Malleus and his cohorts also demonstrated and argued vehemently for passage of additional and more restrictive laws. By their activities the League caused much suffering among the various animal user groups, but particularly among Europe's beleaguered farmers. While it was not their exclusive emphasis, the Progress League recognized no rightful place for animal utilization of any kind, and their legacy became one of brutal hostility.

The Progress League was constantly seeking a scapegoat to blame for the many maladies that plagued society. Jews around the world, and particularly in Israel, were aghast at rekindling of anti-Semitic passions that had mostly been suppressed or dormant until that time. The youthful leader of the League always publicly disavowed any involvement of his organization in persecution, and nobody could ever prove otherwise. Besides, society's have-nots held a deep envy and dislike of relatively prosperous and educated Jews, so there was no determined effort to catch the tormenters.

Unlike the generally illiterate population, the budding young leader abhorred any deficiency of knowledge and he voraciously consumed information on many current topics. He completed every advanced course available in his native country by the time he reached age 27. Soon he began looking at other, more challenging places to learn. He decided to attend a prestigious university in Switzerland, a place to which he had good connections through old Mario. He noted that the institution appeared to ascribe no credence to the defunct beliefs of its founding religious sect. This seemed most logical and appealing to young Malleus.

*   *   *

Alexander Dubrov was an energetic young Russian Jew with a growing family to support. His family had started out from their homeland to immigrate to the Middle East a generation before. Economic circumstances and a friendship with another local Jewish family had led them to change their original plans and remain in Rome. Society there had seemed friendly to them, and prosperity had appeared achievable for anybody who would work hard. They established a family import business, and the Dubrovs had done quite well indeed.

It was an incomparable springtime in Italy, when brilliant flowers begin emerging all over the countryside, olive trees turn emerald green with new growth, and the cycle of seasons starts all over again. Everything seemed to continue unimpeded as from the beginning of time.

It was the day of preparation among the devout members of the Jewish community in Rome, a serious ritual that was as ageless as their ancient faith. In timeless commemoration of miraculous delivery of the Jewish people from national slavery millennia ago, each family prepared to slay a traditional Passover lamb. It would be eaten in a traditional *Pesah* feast and celebration that most powerfully symbolized what it meant to be a Jew. The European Jewish population had rebounded remarkably from near annihilation during recurrent bouts of barbarous ethnic cleansing in previous centuries, and in Italy alone there would be thousands who participated.

Each family group was required to secure its own lamb if possible. This innocent sacrifice would be killed and cooked in accordance with ancient traditions and explicit written instructions in the *Torah*. Much of the Jewish community of Rome had rejected modern revisions of these practices and had returned to literal adherence to the letter of their religious law. According to mandates of the *Torah*, the animal was to be served with a specific set of accompaniments, and was to be consumed completely in a very ritualistic and reverent manner. This meant that numbers of people were purchasing and transporting live lambs in and around the city of Rome.

Young Dubrov was a splendid specimen of a man, with dark Semitic hair, wonderfully thick and perfectly straight, and a typical prominent but elegant nose. His skin was slightly olive, and he was built as solidly as a block of concrete. He was deeply enamored of his heritage and the ancient traditions of his people, and he loved being a leader in his family and his community.

Dubrov's household was happy, filled with maturing children, vibrant and dynamic beyond description. His family was the center of his world, and he was passionately devoted to his wife and their three adorable children. Unlike many of his more secular peers, he never allowed work to interfere with his responsibilities at home. His elderly parents would share this Passover meal with them, as would his sister and her family. At the proper time, all was in readiness for the family *Seder*. Passover was a blissful time of abundance, a time of holy holiday, and a time of family reunion, joy, and festivity.

At sundown an ancient chant began in earnest, a haunting and rhythmic melody that was expertly led by Dubrov's white-haired father, Levi Dubrov. The lamb had already been sacrificed, prepared, and made ready for consumption. The family joined their voices in Hebrew tradition, and strains of the solemn mantra filled the small apartment. As they sang, they failed to notice a steady thumping of heavy footwear coming down the hallway. The obtrusive noise gradually increased in intensity until it was impossible for the family to miss it.

Alexander Dubrov stopped singing and looked at his elderly father with considerable alarm. There had always been an occasional idle threat this time of year, but nobody ever got hurt. Nevertheless, it was lamentable for any unwanted intrusion to spoil or detract from this special occasion. The elder Dubrov broke away from the others and tottered to the door.

Without warning, the door came free from its jambs with a resounding thump, and crashed on top of the old man, its weight and force rendering him unconscious. Into the room stormed several big men wearing black head covers. They shouted obscenities at the screaming family and simultaneously unloaded on them point blank with automatic weapons fire. High velocity bullets spit in a merciless stream from the wicked muzzles, raining a deadly hail on the helpless group. Walls and floor were instantly spackled with blood and bits of bone and flesh. One intruder swept the entire prepared meal onto the floor into a completely disordered pile, and then roughly heaved the large center table upside down.

"Filthy murderers! Now it's your turn to die!" shouted one of the executioners as the deafening sizzle of firearms reverberated. Pieces of furniture and plaster ricocheted like exploding popcorn in all directions. The firing continued until the family showed no evidence of life, then silence reigned as the gunfire ceased. The dark figures then hastily dashed from the apartment into a waiting vehicle, and quickly disappeared into the evening rush hour as nighttime fell.

*　　*　　*

"Christian, I want you to attend school where you can get the very best education," said Lady Ersatzson to her mature son, who already held a doctorate from Oxford. "There's a famous school in Switzerland—it's a cheap and churchy kind of place, but that doesn't hinder their ability to dispense knowledge. Now that you've completed all academic work to be had in England, I want us to check it out. One can never have too much education."

"I'm aware of your selection, Mother. I fully agree. Perhaps we should visit the campus and see it for ourselves. I feel a call deep within me to attend there. That school does indeed have something special to offer."

Progressive and supremely academic, the ancient institute was a bastion of higher education that was renowned around the world. For centuries this university had produced priests and scientists, futurists and historians, virtual legions of influential people. Their thinking and writing had shaped and molded much of academia and the values of human society. The decision to attend there to complete Ersatzson's education was brilliant and appropriate.

To the finite human mind it was inexplicable why young Antonio Malleus would gravitate toward that same Swiss institution of higher learning. The boy was absolutely without economic means, but provision was made for him everywhere he turned. Old Mario had somehow, by some unknown mechanism, mysteriously accumulated enough money to educate the budding genius. In fact, Mario's will named the man with the awful eyes as recipient of his entire estate. Few people noticed the old priest's death, and only a handful attended his funeral. His last rites were a most bland and secular liturgy, and there was no visible sorrow associated with the proceeding.

Antonio Malleus' spiritual development seemed to take off to even greater heights when Mario was gone. He had become known as an unusual phenomenon all around Rome and its environs. Many people were drawn to his magnetic personality. Wherever he went, crowds gathered and peculiar incidents were commonplace. He delayed finishing his formal university education until his late twenties because of ambitious projects and organizational duties in Rome.

As a student he distinguished himself in all respects wherever he studied. Academics were easy for Malleus, and his superior mind rapidly assimilated so much information that attending classes was quite optional. He built upon his original Progress League successes by establishing the European Union for Human Salvation to further his basic message, which crystallized in his keen mind more clearly with each passing day. He entered training for the priesthood well known for his exploits in various arenas of activism, and he appeared poised for a life of determined advocacy for his chosen position.

Who could forget the day he met Christian Ersatzson? Now as good-looking in body and face as a Norse sailor of old, Ersatzson sported a full beard and an outrageous head of curly blonde hair. The youth was the epitome of northern European manhood, muscular in arm and leg, narrow in waist, and with massive upper body dimensions. When his eyes first met those of the more diminutive Malleus, there was a surging sensation of recognition and camaraderie between them, even a strange form of gladness neither had ever known before.

Ersatzson felt none of the numbing fear that struck others when they gazed into those frightening spheres. The young Englishman recognized Malleus as a brother, and the two shared many characteristics in common. There existed a depth of understanding and identification between them that was extraordinary. The Hammer, as Malleus gradually came to be called, was the unquestioned leader and Ersatzson instinctively played the role of dedicated follower *par excellence*. Their years at the Swiss university annealed their relationship and melded them into a single unit that was inseparable. By graduation they were well known throughout Europe as leaders who would doubtless make a true impact on the world. For a number of years they settled in Geneva and solidified their position of leadership and their growing reputation. It was soon apparent that a move was needed in order to keep pace with the unending demands of their public.

"Ersatzson, I feel a strong call back to Rome. I've got bigger plans than this city can accommodate. We need a recognized international base of operations that is easily accessible to the rest of the world. Work it out!" said Malleus. The nefarious voice was not truly speaking a command to his partner, despite directive wording, but rather it conveyed a decree that both men understood and agreed upon perfectly.

"I'm halfway there already. Your plan is going to be accomplished by next month. We're preparing letters to call together all our fellow workers from around the continent for a conference in Rome, as soon as we are established there. Per your suggestion we will call it the European Human Advancement Congress."

Even Malleus should have been amazed, though he emphatically was not. It was the first time either had verbally mentioned Rome, and they had never discussed such a meeting. But the rapport between the two was such that verbal communication was most often a mere formality.

Ersatzson's role gradually evolved into one of advocate and promoter of Malleus, whose message the blonde giant constantly edified and expounded. In their unique relationship, the two young men were the major reason European movements for human progress and species equalization far outstripped gains on any other continent. Europe was the vanguard, the Hammer was Europe's leader, and Ersatzson was his mouthpiece. The charisma, the commanding presence, the intellect and oratory, and the mysterious ability to effect incomprehensible acts at will—all these attributes contributed to their growing reputation and to their domination of the European continent. Any who might oppose them were slowly and gradually strangled, almost without detectable resistance. They consolidated their entire movement under the European Union for Human Salvation.

Planning for a major meeting of Europe's power brokers proceeded at a feverish pace. Nothing could be left to chance because the future seemed to hang tantalizingly in the balance. News personnel gathered in unprecedented numbers to observe the landmark convention that would presumably launch a new age of progress, and a movement which could hold great promise for the planet. Hopes were buoyed that this conference would finally set the stage for formation of a cohesive European government.

"We are gathering to address the problems of mankind," reported Ersatzson to the world press in one of many public information forums leading up to the continent-wide conference. "Since the dawn of history, humanity has lived with a legacy of failure, frustration, wars, competition, and violation of basic rights. We will finally solve these difficulties. The human race is on the threshold of great progress, and the inevitable outcome will be establishment of worldwide peace and safety."

"How do you propose to accomplish this?" came a question from a bright, fresh-faced reporter. "Can you give us any specifics?"

"Are you tired of unsolved crimes, recurrent wars, schools which do not educate, numbing poverty, inefficient national governments, and troublesome uncertainty?" the charismatic and eloquent Ersatzson asked. "We have answers. Our plan will accomplish victory in all these areas and more. We will put forth a complete strategy for consideration at the appropriate time. Final solutions are easily within our grasp once we are irrevocably unified."

"Who will make decisions on what precise steps need to be taken?" asked the youthful holocom journalist again, this time drawing an irritated stare from Ersatzson.

"Perhaps you will," answered Ersatzson icily as he gazed angrily at the correspondent. "Trouble yourself no more, ladies and gentlemen. The best answers are already strongly determined and well established in our leader's mind. You can report to your audiences with all confidence that Father Malleus will share all details at the proper time."

The young journalist was not satisfied with Ersatzson's response, and he left the press briefing grumbling audibly. He was disturbed only briefly, however, since he suffered a regrettable fiery, fatal accident before he reached News Channel offices in downtown Rome. Reports distributed via the network regarding the impending conference were uniformly supportive and positive.

* * *

"Son, you be careful out there. Those demonstrators have been nastier than ever. And more aggressive," said Bob Hancock as he left the protein plant. Accompanying him was his twelve-year-old granddaughter, Molly. They were about to take a short drive back to Adrian, where the three of them lived. Molly's mother had deserted her husband, young Daryl Hancock, shortly after their daughter was born.

"Don't you worry, Dad. They're all talk and no action. We'll keep right on refining protein, and I can take care of myself," replied the blonde man who was approaching middle age. His smile was infectious, and his profile was virtually a carbon copy of his father's sturdy frame. He had not remarried after his wife left him, choosing instead to concentrate his attentions on raising his daughter and doing his demanding job as manager of Adrian Protein Works. His growing daughter was a bit lanky and self-conscious, and she carried herself in the awkward, gangly manner of most girls her age. Despite this she was showing inescapable signs of maturing into a most attractive young lady.

"Watch yourself, anyway. Molly and I are going by to see Billy and Robin Barnes before we head in. Got to pick up some medicine."

"Try and get home early, Dad. I worry about you driving at your age."

"I'm only ninety-one. And I can drive better than you can," replied the elder Hancock as he closed the door, waving a fond goodbye to his son.

By the time Daryl Hancock was ready to shut down his office for the day, it was dusky, that time when visibility is waning but darkness has not yet fallen. Days were long this time of year, and today he had worked unusually late. Before opening his vehicle, he looked around and noticed that there was no guard on duty at the nearby front entrance. That's strange, he thought to himself, and he immediately purposed to go and find out why the man was not on station.

"Lord, what's happened," he asked out loud as he approached the gate. There was a cascade of red liquid running down the inclined roadway, and he could see the guard sprawled with one hand draped limply over the curb while the rest of his body was slouched in the street. His clothing was saturated with blood from his waist up. Hancock hurried to the man's side, but there was no sign of life. The watchman had obviously died trying to reach an alarm signal just out of his reach in the security post. Hancock hurried to sound the alarm himself.

He never made it that far. A bullet struck him in the neck before his hand touched the distress signal device. No one could hear the muffled explosion of a laser-guided cartridge a hundred yards away, though the sharp supersonic crack of a projectile colliding with air molecules at 4,000 feet per second could not be concealed. Hancock had no time to hear the sound of a slug's crisp sonic boom, so there was no opportunity to react before the horrifying impact. He collapsed on the pavement next to his employee, his head almost disconnected from his body by the force and velocity of the round.

*   *   *

Meanwhile, a tiny dot of a spacecraft in the awful void of interstellar space was approaching the sun's solar system like a blinding flash, though in terms of miles it was still an overwhelming distance away. Buck Morgan was preparing a meal of venison steak, along with a bountiful portion of garden fresh vegetables and tantalizing warm bread. The robust aroma of roasting meat filled the ship's galley as he extracted it from the oven.

He would soon be back on Earth. In a way he could foresee missing this solitude and his unencumbered lifestyle, because once he docked and finished debriefing he would unquestionably begin a mandatory and laborious public relations tour. He dreaded the prospect, but he knew it was doubtless inevitable. Despite this unpleasant necessity, at the moment he was looking forward to being home with more fervor than on any other voyage.

Loneliness was often apparent, even though he could converse with marvelous Calvin for hours and hardly realize he wasn't talking to a real human being. Calvin was programmed with abilities to display human-like emotions and to empathize with Morgan's every mood, and his extreme similarity to Jeremiah Smith made their relationship all the more enjoyable. Though he never did so, Calvin could have easily changed himself into another appearance by manipulating his internal holographic display module. Sometimes Morgan toyed with the idea of having the artificial being transform into a woman, or even simply into a different person with a novel personality. He always resisted the temptation, fearing it might somehow upset the stability of his relationship to Calvin, or might contribute to surfacing of some unexpected deep-seated anxiety.

He had considered before the voyage whether he might long for human companionship, and had decided back then that he could survive without it. Now he had become much less secure in that knowledge. Calvin had mostly filled that need quite well, but frequently, indeed constantly, Morgan could feel a longing for an actual person in his life.

Morgan was happy and satisfied with the important work they had accomplished. Humanity's knowledge had taken a quantum leap forward by his sacrifice on this voyage. But his personal needs were slowly, almost undetectably, changing. Sometimes he would find himself idly contemplating his long-ago infatuation with the blonde woman from New Jersey; the romance that never developed. He wondered how that relationship had ultimately turned out for his old friend Smitty.

At times he would even play on the piano a series of old Nashville Pre-2K numbers that reflected his plaintive sentiments better than any of the classics. Lonesome songs, he called them, though Calvin could see little to distinguish the mood of the various kinds of music Morgan played. The astronaut had learned these somber tunes as a child in Adrian, Kansas, and the melodies so often seemed to fit his state of profound yearning, a deep desire for something that he couldn't quantify.

He knew there would be many changes on his home planet since he had left. With Calvin's competent assistance, he many times constructed probability models to try to predict what Earth had become. Most scenarios gravitated toward inescapable progress as the human species reached upward, outward, and onward. There should be great social advancement, and stability should be the watchword. Perhaps there would even be true permanent human colonization of the solar system, and even a major city on a planet or moon where once only a desolate outpost had stood at the edge of endless frontier. Morgan often wondered if the High Command had launched additional starships in other directions, and what the results of those missions might be.

There were a few worrisome possibilities devised by Calvin as well. All were quite low on the probability scale, fortunately. Morgan worried only a little that perhaps democracy might not have survived amid growing chaos when he left. If that had indeed become the case, some of his computer scenarios were disturbing. He reflected on those unlikely projections as he finished his sumptuous meal, but he automatically discounted them. Science would surely have found a way to make up for lack of ambition.

Morgan rested unusually well in the interval before his next watch.

CHAPTER 29

January 2164

"...and a crown was given to him; and he went out conquering, and to conquer." Revelation 6:2

It was a gathering of unprecedented scope for progressive societies of the world, a meeting that had been in planning for several years. The European Human Advancement Congress had been a resounding success, and now the Roman contingent was reaching out to the rest of the world. This meeting would be so big and so energetic that it would be beyond all comparison. The confluence of great thinkers was to be held in the Imperial City, where Antonio Malleus was easily the most powerful player on the European circuit.

Waymon Prestone's group had been invited to attend, and it was with some nervousness that the aging activist paced the floor of the grand meeting hall. There was a hurried commotion all about him, but somehow he experienced a strange sensation of being alone. He felt very much out of his element as he walked down lavish curving hallways decorated with ornate original oil paintings. There were columns in the great corridors that extended in all directions as far as the eye could see, and between each pair of marble monoliths was a flamboyant baroque statue of some god or goddess. Possibly each piece of artwork represented some religious hero of ages past, though Prestone couldn't be certain. His very footsteps echoed as he walked, and his expensive synthetic shoes made a most hollow and conspicuous sound. It almost startled him when he heard someone call his name.

"Mr. Prestone, congratulations on your humanitarian progress in North America. Welcome to the World Human Advancement Congress," said the approaching young man, who was speaking in fluent Spanish.

Prestone was mildly surprised that the person knew his name and his association with North America. *Oh, well, we Americans always stand out,* he thought with a degree of tentative pride. *Maybe he could get through this conference in good standing and arrive home in time for* his next scheduled fundraiser. He ran his fingers through his reddish gray hair, brushed it back from the midline part with his fingers, and sighed deeply. He couldn't help but wish that he didn't have to be here.

"*Gracias*," replied the mature American to the younger man. Prestone had become fluent in the language in order to effectively solicit the large and influential Latino population in the United States. It immediately dawned on Prestone that the short man in front of him was most unimpressive in appearance, being in fact quite ugly. His facial features were anything but handsome, and his squat body, blocky and shapeless, was mostly hidden by priestly garb. Prestone knew immediately that this was Antonio Malleus, because both the face and the clothing were the man's manifest trademarks.

"Looks to me like we're going to change the course of history here, Mr. Malleus."

"You can be certain of it," replied Malleus, switching smoothly to flawless English. "By the way, all the sessions will be in English, in case some of your contingent is concerned about language differences. There will be headphones for simultaneous translation into more than thirty languages."

"Clever and convenient," replied Prestone, going against his instincts and avoiding eye contact with the lowly appearing man before him. English was still used quite often for international conferences, a holdover from the days when the United States had been important in international affairs. Prestone could hardly hide a twinge of contempt as he spoke to Malleus. "I understand we have many heads of state here— including our own president."

"Quite a change from a very few years ago. We've traveled a long road to get here, but now nothing can stop us," the Hammer asserted confidently. The steel in his youthful voice was surprising, and it sobered Prestone and made him cringe a bit. "We're within an eyelash of achieving our goals. There will be equality for all. No more abuse, no more slavery, no more exploitation anywhere. And it's about time. As it now stands, *Homo sapiens* is destroying the planet."

"I agree. What happens when we achieve this equality as universal law?" asked Prestone, an unusual authenticity accompanying his words.

"Oh, you think too small, Mr. Prestone. We'll be in charge. We'll settle all questions and make all decisions. We'll bring this planet and all its despicable masses into compliance and eliminate all problems," glowered Malleus, catching Prestone's direct gaze for the first time. With deep malice Malleus looked intently into the older man's reptilian eyes, and he could see terror residing there, fear like a common snake must feel when it is caught in the iron grasp of a bird of prey. Prestone winced in pain as the accusation rang in his ears, because it was a smear he had frequently used to ridicule others.

This man before him really did have immense plans, not just the whimsical quest for recognition and affluence. His aims were far bigger than wealth and prestige. He craved power—absolute power. Prestone had always thought that kind of authority would be nice, but attaining it—just a pipe dream. But not so for Malleus. And those awful blue eyes, far more piercing and uncanny in appearance and effect than his own serpentine pair—drilled a devastating hole right through him, making a mockery of Prestone's pretentions. Even for Prestone, a famous man by any standard, the chilling contact with Malleus was threatening—even deadly.

"What can we expect at this conference, sir?" asked Prestone as his confidence fled. The awe he was experiencing infiltrated heavily into his tone of voice in a most peculiar way. This overwhelming person before him radiated a strength that Prestone could not fathom, and he found himself writhing internally under scrutiny of that dreadful personality. He swallowed hard and his voice almost squeaked, "How far can we advance here in attaining that mandate?"

"All the way, Mr. Prestone. Just stay alert and ready and you can play a big part. Your job is to showcase North American progress and unity and fit it into the world scheme. These national leaders must go home with a mindset that compliance with our agenda is the wisest course, indeed their only choice, and that to resist is folly. You must communicate that message with authority to your government, such a government as you have. Do your part and don't fail. Understand?"

The man's voice felt like ice water cascading down on Prestone, leaving him with a helpless sensation he had never felt before. He felt a creeping, insidious dread spreading like a malignancy through his uncertain mind.

"Don't worry, sir, I'll do everything in my power," he replied weakly and with great effort to the squat young leader. There was a shaking in Prestone's voice that revealed a torrent of outright panic.

"In your power?" Malleus shot back impatiently. "Try some of mine. Use my name as much as you wish in dealing with your people. To do so is real strength. But don't come up short."

The man turned and walked away, leaving Prestone standing with a slackened lower jaw and a disturbing sense of helplessness. He swallowed hard and reached into a pocket for a kerchief to wipe his sweat-beaded brow. His makeup smeared and stained the white cloth a fleshy pink. Quickly regaining a measure of composure, he headed toward the restroom to freshen it up a bit lest someone important should detect an unsavory blemish in his appearance.

The Hammer took charge from the opening ceremonies and orchestrated a stunning series of victories. It was a predetermined conclusion that his basic agenda would reign preeminent, but who would be in control and how all national governments could be brought into line certainly were unanswered questions. It appeared to be miraculous, the hold Malleus had on the delegates, both representatives from transnational non-government organizations and those from various governments. It was almost as if he had cast some kind of medieval spell on the participants.

One particular instance defined the meeting for all. There appeared to be dissent over the issue of horses in the military, a practice increasingly being utilized as an alternative to mechanized transport with its dependence on animal-based fuels. Constraints on protein farming had made most fuels expensive to produce and periodically unavailable, so mechanized cavalry was reverting to true horse cavalry once again. In fact, Waymon Prestone had earned a fine contribution to his organization at a recent fundraiser where his speech was highly critical of forcing horses into such servitude. A sharp disagreement arose regarding the ethics of horse utilization, with a sizable segment of delegates favoring horse cavalry over the alternative, and other delegates viewing this as another despicable form of animal slavery. It appeared the issue had potential to tear the conference apart along pro- and anti-horse cavalry lines.

It was the Hammer's finest hour so far. Malleus' chief deputy, Christian Ersatzson stepped briskly to the podium as debate boiled hot and heavy, and red-faced delegates shouted and shook their fists at one another in raging anger. His announcement was loud and authoritative.

"Friends, be quiet. Our wise leader, Father Antonio Malleus, is coming to the podium."

An eerie and stunning silence fell most unnaturally over the vast audience. As thousands of delegates watched, Malleus strolled confidently to the podium, his entire countenance glowing inexplicably. A panoply of gyrating light and shadow accompanied him, as if shepherding him into the limelight, and numerous hideous, undulating forms were just barely visible to the audience. The effect grew in intensity until the entire meeting hall was filled with reverberating radiance. A loud rushing noise and a sound like thousands of wings seemed to fill the air, but not quite audibly enough that a human ear could be certain the sensation was real. Not a word was spoken, and the unbreakable hush seemed to be enforced by some unseen power that all could feel but none could challenge or explain.

Malleus stood before the assembly like a powerful dark angel, small in stature but with intense majesty and overpowering charisma, casting a gaze so dreadful that nobody dared look directly at his face. The delegates stared at the floor in subdued fascination with heads bowed reverently in a worshipful posture. The unearthly light engulfed Malleus' dusky figure and a deep sense of unaccountable fright suffused the mute audience.

"Esteemed delegates, the reason we have this disagreement regarding the status of horses is quite simple to explain. For untold millennia our own species has been pursuing a doctrine that is hideously unfair and devastating in its effect. Our treatment of horses—and all other creatures—is so immoral and so perverse that it has infected our very languages. You all know well the awful prejudice to which I refer. I am speaking, of course, of that degrading label we have attached to those precious beings that share our planet with us—*animal!*

"My friends, if you search your hearts deeply, if you consider long and hard the marvelous and inestimable contributions these souls have made to our way of life and to the history and prosperity of our world, you cannot but realize that this insensitive label is the worst form of abasement. Referring to any of myriad fellow citizens by means of such a crude term makes one no better than the Nazis of history, who long ago called their fellow Germans *animals* as an excuse to incarcerate and destroy them in dreadful concentration camps. To even speak the word makes us akin to owners of human slaves long ago who considered their fleshly property *animals* and used this term as justification to maintain their charges in abject misery.

"For time untold governments, churches, social organizations, and dedicated individuals have fought against discrimination according to race, according to sex, according to national origin; yet we have been inexcusably blind to a more fundamental discrimination taking place before our very eyes. I fully realize that in times past we have been unintentionally guilty in many cases, but now we are at a point of historic *satori*. We must recognize our grave mistakes with deep repentance, and follow the shining path of light and truth. Friends, it is now time to call our living companions in this world, regardless of their form, their covering, their circumstances of birth, or their level of intelligence, by their true name—*HUMAN!*"

There was a brief silence as the implication dawned on the delegates, then there was then a smattering of hand clapping scattered about. As more and more people realized the brilliance of Malleus' declaration, the hall erupted with applause, and delegates shouted and poured out a show of enthusiasm such as had never before been seen in the movement. The energizing was so powerful that it rapidly built in crescendo, and the panoply of lights and shadows whirled and engulfed the delirious audience.

What a stroke of genius! Of course the revelation had to be true! A spontaneous outpouring of spiritual intensity inundated the entire hall and overflowed into the surrounding corridors. Something truly extraordinary was occurring here. The glowing figure up front gazed with unquenchable fire in his eyes at the raucous scene, enjoying his moment of divine triumph to the fullest. His lieutenant stood smiling in the shadows, the taste of approaching victory making him drunk with anticipation. Could anything stop this team? The Hammer raised his hands high over the podium, and an immediate whispering quiet returned to the cavernous meeting hall.

"In truth, our friends are as human as you or I. However they may differ genetically from us and from one another, they are, as we, equal in the sight of Mother Earth, and they are full participants in the great dance we call life. Let us purge our languages of demeaning speech and cleanse our minds of elitist attitudes. We can thus throw off the shackles that have kept these fellow human beings in servitude and suffering. My friends, this is a historic day. You and I shall bring forth a declaration of full and final emancipation of humanity, when all human beings on this planet—whatever number of legs they might possess or whatever their form or the mechanism of their metabolism and locomotion—all human beings may look at one another and say to themselves, in the words of that American prophet of long ago, 'Free at last! Free at last! Thank God I'm free at last!' "

An explosion of spontaneous enthusiasm again filled the vast arena, the noise and supernatural gyrations of light and shadow gleefully animating every participant. The answer to their petty dilemma was now obvious to all. Of course horses could serve in the armed forces, the same as humans. They *were*, in fact, human. They carried the same obligation to world peace as the rest of humankind.

The uncanny light and shadows faded with passage of the moment, but the effect was permanent. Ersatzson strode confidently to the podium as his leader sat down, a knowing smugness adorning his Viking-like face. He eloquently glorified Malleus for a half hour, and held the delegates virtually spellbound again as they drank in his invigorating words. His conclusion was almost as dramatic and emphatic as had been Malleus' original pronouncement.

"And finally, friends, I believe that this historic occasion deserves much more than a passing endorsement from the world. We must go a step further at this Congress. We must agree to the observations of our wise Father Malleus, and initiate steps that will not only proclaim the truth of his word, but we must by it transform our world. Much work needs to be done, and it is up to you. I have faith that you will accomplish the needed resolutions in your home nations."

There was nobody present who would challenge even a word the two had uttered. The council meetings and policy sessions that followed were unparalleled shows of unity and purpose. As excited representatives reconvened for the afternoon session, an air of expectancy prevailed that made the entire World Congress brim with enthusiasm. From the floor came an immediate move to develop and implement a comprehensive Concord for the Development of Humanity, a code of enlightened rules for living that would incorporate the central idea of the humanity of all flesh. The idea passed with no opposition, and Malleus was immediately chosen by acclamation to head the movement. Forces of the European Union for Human Salvation could now drop the name as obsolete, and unfurl their unified banner under the sweeping new Concord.

From that moment, Malleus enjoyed worldwide recognition. He was courted by heads of state and sought relentlessly by power brokers all over the world. His authority went absolutely unchallenged in most places in the Western world.

The final days of the astounding conference resulted in a tremendous singularity of purpose for the first time in history. Seminars detailed how activists could augment their growing influence back home and set forth a credible plan to accomplish the entire agenda. News media coverage of the conference was exhaustive, and carried their usual positive and progressive bent regarding the movement.

Politicians in attendance were particularly mesmerized by the World Human Advancement Congress, and most returned home with a steadfast determination to complete the prescribed agenda. In country after country, national leaders actively identified themselves with the movement and proceeded to establish a legislative agenda to accomplish forthwith all provisions. Legislators fell in line without significant resistance, endorsing and actively pushing all recommended positions.

The one proclaiming and promoting the program loudest and most often was Christian Ersatzson, the main worldwide mouthpiece for Malleus. The young Englishman was daily featured prominently in media all over the world, praising his master Malleus and giving him credit for all manner of accomplishments. In every way he called on the world to accept this man as anointed ruler and to pledge their unwavering loyalty. Malleus was sure to lead the world out of the present darkness into a golden age of unity, light, and truth. His would be a reign of fairness to all creatures, great and small. The desired effect was achieved most remarkably, and the worshipful adoration Ersatzson lavished on Malleus was far more effective in establishing the leader's credentials than had Malleus been directly promoting himself.

The World Human Advancement Congress had been an enormous success, but the real breakthrough was the emerging Concord for the Development of Humanity. The dynamic document that came forth declared truth from Malleus, and his every word was recorded and expounded by a bevy of ever-present scribes. His daily dissertations gradually gave shape to a new world order that would have the same name, though it was soon shortened to simply "the Concord." Several more important steps remained, however, before the total agenda could be implemented in full.

"Father, the groundwork is laid for your new project. Parties from all nations are in agreement. Well, almost all, and I think the holdout will come around," Ersatzson reported to Malleus. He had begun calling him Father at the recent World Congress, for obvious effect, and had simply continued doing so. Most of the world referred to him as such, and "Father Hammer" was translated into hundreds of languages.

"Then we are approaching our objective. Who is the problem?" asked Malleus, irritation showing in his voice. "As if I didn't know."

"Israel, naturally. They're a stubborn group. Jews have always been a thorn in the the world."

"No matter. They'll have to go along to survive. They can't stand alone against us. And how it will delight me if they try."

"The Pope called this morning. He wanted you to come to the Vatican for talks. I told him to come instead to your office, that you're too busy to go there. He'll be here this afternoon," reported Ersatzson. "I knew it would meet with your approval."

"Ah, yes, my old employer. He needs us a lot more than we need him. Still, his endorsement will carry influence with some," Malleus concluded smugly. "Our network is assembling nicely."

Indeed. The Concord was in control and grassroots work was being concluded in every nation in Europe, Africa, and the Western Hemisphere as they spoke. By acclamation the old meaningless dating system was shortly abandoned, and the date of signing the Concord became the new *Anno Humanitatis*, the start of the year A.H. 1 and a completely new epoch.

While Malleus' authority was not yet absolute, it was rapidly approaching that stage. For his part, he was determined that nothing would impede his agenda. He would, by any and all means, become the ultimate authority in the world. Most who heard about him quickly came to reverence and fear omnipotent Father Hammer.

* * *

Waymon Prestone came away from the meeting in Rome a dramatically changed man. The challenging encounter with Malleus and subsequent events at the conference had shaken him badly. He was accustomed to raising funds and promoting his program ad infinitum, and with that role he was comfortable. But this idea of practically worshipping a man—and a man who, by all appearances, possibly deserved it—was highly demoralizing. The playboy head of the Continental Humane Society was as nearly irreligious as any man had ever been—totally materialistic, in fact. There was a disquieting spiritual quality to Malleus that completely unnerved the veteran activist.

On returning to the United States, he was disastrously ineffective at communicating Malleus' agenda. As the most prominent of the North American contingent, he had been personally commissioned by Malleus to provide needed leadership. An especially hard assignment, and one which he dreaded, was promoting Malleus' decree to liberate all pets, which were now referred to as animal slaves. Pet owners constituted a major segment of his contributors.

His failure to carry out the agenda stood out like the proverbial sore thumb. Leaders of other groups quickly usurped what should have been his rightful position, and more potent organizations soon overshadowed the fading Continental Humane Society. Prestone was still active, cruising with his incessant stream of cars and girls, but with neither the fervor nor the success of previous times.

Most tragic of all was his delinquent oversight, his disastrous blindness to the high cost of ineptitude. In the rising new world order, failure was not to be tolerated.

His expensive imported vehicle, sleek and sophisticated, was parked at the back corner of the civic center lot under the watchful eye of a paid guard, as was Prestone's custom. It never occurred to Prestone that any unusual precautions might be in order. The whole event was a deliberate and deceitful sham, a deadly diversion designed to lure him to this spot on orders from Rome.

While the seasoned campaigner delivered his last oratory, a shadowy figure joined the guard. The two skillfully attached a modern explosive device to the car's undercarriage, a mechanism so tiny and unobtrusive that detection was impossible even by highly refined sensing devices built into the futuristic vehicle. When Prestone reclaimed his vehicle, vibrations from the engine activated the timing device, giving him and his ever-present female escort exactly enough time to reach the open road. Within minutes of their departure from the parking lot, a terrible, jarring explosion ripped the vehicle and its occupants into oblivion.

Prestone's fate would stand as a lasting reminder to any who might serve the cause with less than utter blind devotion.

CHAPTER 30

March 2164

"...and it was granted to take peace from the earth, and that men should slay one another..." Revelation 6:4

As with many conflicts by which the Concord consolidated power, the war in Kansas was brief but bloody and exceedingly violent. Ragtag state militia mobilized, and on a broad plain near Overland Park men and machines rumbled into action against the oppressive Concord army. The Concord had assimilated remnants of the U.S. Army into its loyalist military, and augmented it with several European units. The battle cost the lives of tens of thousands of brave, determined militiamen, but in the end the Concord's greater firepower, air superiority, and overwhelming numbers prevailed against Kansas. Like most of the formerly united states in America, the Sunflower State was soon completely assimilated into the Father's growing world empire.

There were other holdouts that were more resistant, but victory by the invincible Concord seemed certain. Few states or nations had the means to effectively threaten the new world order. But there was one group that remained problematic and defiant.

"They wouldn't dare oppose us. We'll annihilate them!" snarled Malleus. "Its suicide! Stupid Jews!"

As it turned out, an armed confrontation between Malleus' forces and the Israelis was averted at the last moment. Rather than risk a disastrous and decisive battle, the Israelis agreed to join the world government under certain conditions. A preliminary peace treaty was signed, and negotiations were shortly under way to effect a permanent solution. These meetings were destined to be more difficult and more protracted than Concord operatives had expected, however.

The Concord agenda was well along with implementation worldwide. Politicians were falling all over themselves to align with the European juggernaut, with few exceptions in the Western world. It appeared that there were no major obstacles to a complete takeover by the Concord.

The world had been altered drastically under the auspices of the Concord. By reason of recently ratified international agreements, entered into voluntarily and with uniform enthusiasm by every European, African, and Western Hemisphere government, the Concord rapidly assumed the position of supreme authority, with all jurisdiction vested in one man, all-powerful Father Hammer. Some Asian nations were still resisting, but all of them had given indication that they approved of the Concord, at least in principle.

In reality, Asian reluctance mattered little for the moment, despite the region's economic clout and productivity. The Concord had numerous near-term objectives to keep it occupied for the present, and they could deal with any recalcitrants later. Father Hammer had a certain amount of military and economic leverage with the holdouts, and in a crisis he would not hesitate to use it. For now he had a more important agenda, consolidation of recent gains and a tightening of Rome's iron grip on the rest of the planet.

* * *

Back in Adrian, Kansas, a few people still attended the red brick church down the road from where Buck Morgan grew up, although believers were increasingly a rare phenomenon, even there. The metal cross still towered high, but instead of a bronze color it was now dirty brown, and a long, rusty stain trailed from it onto the sagging roof.

Bob Hancock was an old man, but he came this Sunday despite increasing infirmity to worship like his ancestors had done before him. He brought with him his only descendant, Molly Hancock, his deceased son's child. She had just turned sixteen years old, and she wore tiny earrings the shape of a pansy in each pierced earlobe. Her soft auburn hair was clipped almost as short as a boy's, but her face and her figure left no room for error as to her gender.

Memories of the murder of Molly's father Daryl outside the protein plant several years before still haunted the girl and had left her with a distinctly melancholy disposition. The granddaughter was a great help to old Bob Hancock, a supreme comfort in many ways, despite a determined and understandable rebellious streak that surfaced in her with regularity.

"Evening, Bob. Evening Molly. Good to see you both. You're here early," noted Jamie Barnes. "Dad always said eager prayer is effective prayer. You guys must be eager."

"We're eager to pray, all right, Jamie," replied Hancock tiredly. "The world is coming apart, and nearly everybody thinks it's coming together. It looks like this Concord machine won't be stopped."

"Sh-h, don't say that out loud. Not even here, Bob. You know they listen to everything."

"I really don't care, Jamie. So what if they kill somebody ninety-five years old?"

"Christians shouldn't talk like that, Bob. What about Molly? What's she going to do if something happens to you?"

"Aren't you a cat of a different color, son," said Hancock to Barnes. "I remember when you wouldn't come near this church building, and gave your daddy fits with your behavior. Now you're offering me tips on raising my granddaughter?"

"Things change, Bob. Like me. I just wish I'd changed before Dad got died. Too bad I was over thirty before I saw the light."

The old man stopped and looked at Jamie, then turned to Molly. He thoughtfully considered the pretty teenager who followed him, then pulled her to him and gave the girl a bear-like hug.

"You're right about my mouth, though, Jamie. I'll tone it down. But I'm disgusted with the way things are going," he whispered. "Where will it all end? I really feel for you younger people. It's hard to believe that only a few years ago we had it so good and didn't even know it. Now look at the way things have changed. We don't even have our own country anymore."

"I still can't believe Congress voted overwhelmingly—almost unanimously—to enter the consolidation agreement with the Concord," fretted Jamie Barnes. "I'm not much of a history student, but this can't be good. Land of the free, my eye. You know, our congressman was one of the few to vote against it, and I heard they can't find him now."

"Really? Oh, no," mumbled old Hancock quietly. "He was a good man."

"Now really tough edicts are coming from Rome. And these Concord police we've got now—I've never seen such zeal at enforcing regulations. The old protesters at least stayed outside the gates. Now they're armed and they can legally walk right into your house. What are we going to do?"

"The best we can, son," the elderly man replied, "Just like always. Sure wish your dad was still with us to help us devise ways to cope. Billy just got old and worn out like me, didn't he? But I miss him."

"We all miss him, Bob. Especially Jody."

"How is Jody, by the way?"

Hancock knew the youth had completely abrogated all family involvement of late, refusing to socialize or take part in any of his parents' activities. Losing his grandfather had devastated him, because they had shared an irreplaceable rapport. He lived on the farm still, sharing a small dwelling with his common law wife, a practicing pagan named Sarah, but participated only in activities that were required of him. Jody was Jamie Barnes' only child, and the youth's rebellion and withdrawal had been a source of unending pain for Barnes and his wife Martha. The old farm seemed to be their only common bond.

"Same as always. Seldom talks while we're working. I think his eyes are completely blind to what is going on in the world," said Jamie sadly. "I don't know where we went wrong. I just don't understand why he doesn't feel free and open enough to talk through his doubts and hostility. He always got the best Martha and I know how to give. I still think he's just angry at God, but he won't talk about it. Even Mom can't get through to him. She can't communicate with him like Dad could."

"He reminds me a lot of Leon Walker," said Hancock. "You know, he was even worse than Jody when it came to disobedience and a bad attitude. His dad Roger—God rest his soul—prayed for that boy every day right up to his last breath. But when Roger died, the boy made a complete turnaround, and now he's one of the best farmers anywhere. He's a fine Christian man, too, and so is his wife. They still live on that place they call the old Barnes farm. Your great grandfather used to own that spread, way back there."

"I've noticed the similarity between Jody and Leon before, Bob. Who knows if I'll live to see Jody turn around like that? But I'll keep praying he will. Say, haven't both of Leon's boys left home? I understand one went to Denver and the other somewhere else. Maybe Wyoming?"

"Yes, Leon told me all about it. You're exactly right. Those two boys are as just rebellious as Leon ever was. And every bit as bad as Jody is now, or worse. Both of them are absolutely adamant they'll never be farmers. Jeff, the one who went to Denver, has his heart set on being an artist. Luke loves the outdoors and wants to be a cowboy, of all things. He can't do that anywhere but Wyoming nowadays. I understand he's working at an uncle's ranch near Cheyenne. Those two boys are as opposite in nature as any two brothers I've ever known."

Molly Hancock sat quietly, listening to the whispering men with wide-eyed fascination. She was a most unusual child in her world—well into her teenage years and still a virgin. She had been taught old, defunct Biblical values by her late father and her grandfather. She wasn't perfect, and a recalcitrant streak in her had caused her grandfather quite a bit of distress of late. The old man seemed so prudish and backward, and her personal freedoms so restricted.

Molly had witnessed plenty of the world and she was frankly very attracted to much of what she saw. She often wondered if there were really a God out there who cared anything about people, since there occurred such tragedies as her father's murder. Molly still came to church with her grandfather, but much of the time she seemed to be in a chronic state of depression.

"The protein business has certainly fallen on tough times," said Hancock in classic understatement. "Never thought I'd see the day.

Officially vegetarians, or else we're cannibals. How's your yeast operation doing?"

"Okay, I guess. I'm producing quite a few of the little critters, but nobody much wants them," Barnes sighed quietly. "You'd think the people would be starving for vitamin B12."

"The population won't go vegetarian even under penalty of death until there's no choice. They're still eating illegal meat," said Hancock. "You know, they did what I never believed possible when they figured out how to do satellite surveillance for gunshots. No more guns. Got some old guys left over from the space agency to reprogram the satellites somehow. Guess we can't actually go up into space and work on them anymore, but they did it. But even with no guns out there, animals are still disappearing. I don't even see any birds anymore—not even starlings."

"It's wire. Best snare material ever designed. When the animals are gone, somebody is going to be caught short. I don't think we can produce enough yeast for everybody," said Barnes.

"Too bad we don't have the means to oppose them anymore here in Kansas," said Hancock in a voice that was many decibels too loud. "I understand Wyoming is resisting like Kansas tried, but we know who will win, don't we? I'd sure give my worthless old hide to try and stop them."

"We're certainly under their thumb, but you're doing some dangerous broadcasting again, Bob. You know the penalty for rebellion, and they listen everywhere they can, maybe right here in our church," whispered Barnes. "But you're right. It's only a matter of time until the only animals we ever see are bad dogs, big cats, and bigger bears. And I heard a wolf howling the other night, too."

"Good thing all of them are scared of people, even kids if they hear or smell them. Peculiar, huh? But it's just like the Bible says, God put a terror of mankind on all of them, thankfully. And as for birds, at least we still have buzzards," Hancock noted. "If it weren't for the stinking vultures, I think all birds would be extinct."

"You know, I had a poacher tell me that you couldn't trap some animals with wire. The big guys are too smart. It's uncanny how they avoid snares. And buzzards are practically impossible to catch, too," noted Barnes. "More predators and less prey. Something's got to give at some point."

"Don't worry. There's enough bugs that a major predator can survive on them, I think," said Hancock. "People could, too, if push came to shove. Long as nobody sees them. I got a feeling some of them are doing it now."

Eating of insects by mankind was strictly forbidden, but privately everybody who couldn't get yeast had to do so, unless they lucked into a rare mouse or some other small creature. With no ready source of vitamin B12 and a chronic calorie deficit, it was consume bugs or die. But if you were caught, justice from Concord police was swift, deadly, and hopelessly decisive.

The love affair with technology that the modern world had enjoyed for centuries had completely ended at the death of the United States of America. Airplanes were banned early in the Concord takeover in order to avoid impact with "flying humans," and vehicular speed was likewise limited severely by law. Veganox fuel, the old standby, had been replaced by ethanol, but such small quantities were produced that foot transportation had again become the primary means of travel.

All medical research involving animals was quickly outlawed in a world where methodical study had essentially eliminated man's diseases. Clothing was purely plant fiber by law, but increasingly people mainly wore shredded rags. Gradually even these gave way to the dress of Eden, leaves sewn together as a covering. Because fish were killed in hydroelectric operations and moving large amounts of fuel to power plants placed animals at risk, most electricity had been terminated. Pervading darkness, both physical and spiritual, covered the planet.

In the gloom, a small group of believers knelt, dressed in remnants of clothing, to come before their acknowledged Maker in prayer. They were an enigma, a tiny fraction of the original contingent of believers, torn and ragged and insufficient like their clothes. In faith they petitioned their God on behalf of their world, their circumstances, their families, their neighbors, and their destiny. In that hour of despair it seemed that nobody was listening.

*   *   *

Drawing ever nearer to the solar system, the stupendous *Ursa C* continued its swift journey back home. The ship was a small and oblivious island of plenty and health in a universe of need and despair. Buck Morgan increasingly anticipated his arrival home as time slowly crawled by. He reflected often on what kind of world he would find on his return to Earth, seldom imagining anything less than astounding scientific progress since his departure, over eighty-five years before in Earth time. Surely the timeless foundations of the United States of America, the Declaration of Independence and the Constitution, would still be standing firm. He wondered if West Point had changed very much and he longed to visit the campus to find out. Perhaps they would ask him to speak to the Corps of Cadets on his public relations tour.

Morgan got out his father's ancient Stevens Savage shotgun while working a particularly introspective watch, and looked over the well-preserved firearm with tenderness and care. The wooden stock was interestingly patterned in walnut grain, and he traced his fingers along it in awe. The way wood grew was remarkable, and the shotgun contained one of the rare pieces of the material onboard the starship.

The gun broke down easily into three pieces, and assembly was equally effortless. He fit the metal double barrel into the slot that attached it to the stock and snapped it together, then positioned the foregrip so that finger pressure fastened it perfectly in place with a click. Morgan applied force to the release handle just in front of the top-mounted safety, and the breech opened smoothly. He noted that the shell ejectors jumped outward crisply, and then he held the piece up to the light and looked down the barrels. Both bores were squeaky clean and shined like new stainless steel. He slammed the gun shut satisfied. It was still in perfect condition.

The old firearm strongly reminded him of his father as always, and once more in his mind's eye he could see Jim Morgan staunchly swinging the barrels in the direction of a winging bobwhite quail, and the bird folding in a fragile arc at the report. Those halcyon days of long ago seemed to have been the very best of times, in retrospect. Perhaps he could find a hunting partner when he got back to Earth, and some small portion of those memories could be relived.

Morgan's age had crept past forty years, and he hoped he would have no more upcoming birthdays in the loneliness of space. He couldn't wait to download his bulging computers to the delight of wide-eyed twenty-second century scientists, sharing grand discoveries with them that none could remotely imagine. They would have received a good deal of his initial data, but the best could arrive no sooner than he would, and beyond doubt the quality of his onboard information would far outshine that of transmitted material.

The seasoned interstellar traveler had been given lately to deep reflection, unlike on his voyage out to 47 Ursae Majoris. He remembered some of the peculiar beliefs that his father had held, and he thought often of his old teacher, Judy Hancock. She would be dead now, beyond any reasonable question. He thought rarely of Ralph Russell, his old science teacher, dwelling instead on those bits of wisdom that the others had dispensed—those timeless concepts he had always viewed in highly skeptical fashion. Perhaps it was that he simply had filled up with measuring things. Perhaps it was something else. But he thought more than ever before on matters that were utterly unscientific, subjects that were infinitely profound and defiant of objective analysis.

Even mighty Calvin's mind seemed preoccupied with analysis of factors that transcended logic. The artificial being was programmed to identify and react to Morgan's moods in a way in which even the real Jeremiah Smith could not have attained. Calvin's spontaneous interpretations of any theological question raised by Morgan, however, were usually grossly inadequate, but this was doubtless to be expected of an inorganic being.

Morgan had plenty of time to study that most immeasurable of documents, the Bible. Since his father's death, he had never gone into space without the one he had been given by Judy Hancock. He had read it through several times on this trip and he remarked to Calvin more than once that it seemed to be getting to him. In a rare burst of spiritual wisdom, Calvin had countered that the human psyche seemed to need such support for optimum health.

Often when entertaining himself at the piano he would find himself almost idly gravitating toward old sacred songs he had known since childhood, those written lovingly and pensively by Wesley and Crosby and their like, and he sometimes scrolled the archives to find the needed music. Christian melodies had to be the most beautiful in the world. Deeply religious men had composed most timeless classics from past centuries, and their creations were often solidly constructed on spiritual themes.

Still, simple and unsophisticated people had written those songs, and their fantastic beliefs couldn't be literally true. He had to allow himself some diversion, though, some new thoughts and some rethinking of old ones. Those razor sharp scientists with whom he would spend endless hours in debriefing would purge that kind of foolishness from him, anyway.

Buck Morgan was streaking toward a most shocking homecoming.

CHAPTER 31

November 2165

"And authority was given them over a fourth of the earth, to kill with sword..." Revelation 6:8

It looked like a great day to have a war. Dawn broke clear and cold, and a promise of winter hung expectantly in the air. A heavy frost glazed the ground as sunlight's first fingers caressed the prairie, and the brilliant sparkle of myriad ice crystals created an appearance like a bejeweled fairyland. The sky in the east glowed brilliant crimson streaked with ebony until the sun rose and drove the color away.

A young soldier from Casper, Wyoming, was enjoying the grand vista spread before him. He found himself daydreaming of quieter times before this conflict. It was easy to for the young warrior to fantasize of fun days and happy occasions, letting the harsh circumstances he faced this morning fade into the background for a moment. Yes, it would be wonderful to go home one day soon. He removed his helmet and tucked it under one arm, then took a deep breath of cool morning air, noting with contentment the pungent sage-like smell.

He stood erect on a hilltop, his close cropped hair and trim appearance imparting to him a battle-hardened profile that contrasted with his innocent, boyish face. He scanned the southern horizon with his holocom binoculars, feeding through them live information to his headquarters. He had been well briefed, and he kept watching dutifully for inevitable columns of billowing dust that would herald the long-anticipated enemy approach.

The youth could at first see nothing of interest among the glistening brown grass and ubiquitous sagebrush, and everything seemed quiet and still. He lowered his binoculars tentatively and gazed momentarily with his naked eyes, a disquieting uncertainty suddenly clouding his mind. Was that something moving out there?

He was dead from the second an impact struck his exposed forehead, as a speeding bullet shattered his frontal bone, then skated downward as it penetrated the skull cavity. The shock wave made jelly of the frontal lobe of his brain, exploded both ventricles, and destroyed the brain stem before exiting low on the back of his head. The handsome soldier was mercifully oblivious to the disaster that had befallen him, and he dropped his optical instrument abruptly as he slumped lifeless onto harsh, cold ground.

Invasion plans had been kept secret, but people in Wyoming knew beyond question what was coming. In compliance with dictates from the Concord, Colorado had declared war on Wyoming several weeks before. There had already been some firefights, fierce and bloody, but the free people of Wyoming had so far prevailed every time. Their young soldier was the first casualty of this latest engagement, killed by a sniper in a forward Colorado patrol. The infiltrator's unit had crawled into position undetected during the night to provide covering fire for the main body of invading troops that would follow. The sniper's orders had been to wait until the main unit was in sight, but the uncovered soldier with the field glasses had presented such a tempting target that he couldn't hold his fire.

Discipline among soldiers was difficult to instill, given the quality of conscripts in the Concord army, so the Colorado platoon leader was not surprised that the fatal shot had prematurely broken the morning stillness. He dutifully noted the identity of his impatient commando, writing it in his logbook and penciling in beside it the telling words "firing squad." That is, if the impetuous fighter survives the coming battle, he thought grimly to himself. Then the officer radioed the commander of the main force that the element of surprise had been lost. It didn't really matter. They had troops to spare.

Jeff Walker, recently pressed into service in the attacking army, was initially an unwilling participant. The fragile young man looked somewhat outlandish in his ill-fitting camouflage battle dress, mottled pants gathered at the waist by an encircling belt and sleeves rolled up so he could use his hands. Military service had been the farthest thing from his mind when a street sweep by Concord police had netted him for this unsavory duty. The hasty training he had received consisted mainly of mass movement tactics and proficiency drills with an electric auto weapon that spit out dozens of tiny lead fragments per second. On orders from his commanding officer he crawled forward with his comrades to clear the way for the main invading force, his mind obedient to the utmost.

The unlikely soldier had demonstrated above average aptitude in training, a circumstance that had qualified him to serve in an elite forward unit. His instruction in military discipline had been marginal, at best, but he was no fool. Jeff Walker knew better than to do something so stupid as to go against orders. He knew the penalties were severe and irreversible, and he cringed to think of what would be coming for his impatient compatriot.

There was another reason besides simple natural capability that had placed him here in this regiment of crack Colorado troops. He hated the Wyomingites they would be attacking because they reminded him of the crude, unsophisticated clods he had known while he was growing up in Adrian, Kansas. There just might be some satisfaction in this endeavor, after all, however involuntary it might be. Maybe he could get this war behind him and get back to his art studio in Denver before long.

The Colorado Army had submitted without protest to becoming a sub-unit of the Concord army. Their objective was to assault and capture the affluent town of Cheyenne, Wyoming, a rare bastion of prosperity and plenty. The official reason for the attack was to punish the renegade state for continuing a policy of livestock utilization that had persisted far longer than anywhere else in the entire world. Unofficially, urbanites from the south were jealous of the lifestyle, riches, and independent arrogance of the people of Wyoming.

Wyoming had parlayed its revolutionary status into incredible wealth. The rebel state had significant residual oil, innumerable cattle, and potent agriculture. They had early followed the lead of these very Coloradans they were facing by claiming and holding all waters originating in their state. With that immense supply of water, Wyoming had utilized vast reservoirs as irrigation sources for cultivating much previously non-arable land. Most wildlife had already disappeared to cowardly poachers, but consumptive use of cattle and other livestock was still sanctioned by the state. As a result, people in Wyoming had all they needed in the way of protein and clothing and they were able to use their excess for illegal but lucrative interstate barter.

Outlaw states had long operated with impunity whenever they defied the bankrupt central government of the United States. Such precedents would be allowed to continue no longer. All state militias were assimilated into the Concord army and made to serve the purposes of the ruler. Rome cared not a particle how many people died in the resulting conflagrations so long as the end result was absolute submission.

Wyoming was practically the only holdout left in North America, except for parts of Pennsylvania, and the southern Appalachian Mountains, where a few isolated enclaves of resistance still existed. Wyoming's army was well supplied, well trained, dedicated, and determined. Nevertheless, the armies of envious puppet states on all sides hopelessly outnumbered the state's rebel troops. Odds against Wyoming were long indeed, but one had to admire the courage and conviction that motivated men to defend their beloved home state.

Sonny Hester was a tenth generation Wyoming rancher, and it was his piece of ground that the Colorado Army was using to attack entrenched rebel soldiers. An onrushing swarm of Coloradans was utilizing a broad, open prairie in an attempt to outflank the Wyoming soldiers. Hester mustered his outnumbered irregulars in an effort to counter them. His small private army was strictly forbidden by the state, the Concord notwithstanding, but nobody in Wyoming was complaining about this breach of state law in light of the current crisis.

Luke Walker loved his uncle Sonny like a father, and served with distinction in his security force. Here in Wyoming, Walker had been able to learn about horses, cattle, and riding the open range like free men had done for centuries. It was an experience unavailable anywhere else in the world now, and he would fight and die to preserve the privilege, if necessary. He nervously fingered his automatic weapon and waited for approaching Colorado soldiers to come within range. He could see telltale blue and white arm patches identifying the urbanites as servants of the Father, and he determined to do everything in his power to stop them. He nestled a little deeper into his position and checked to make certain his extra munitions were ready, along with a spare weapon. He glanced toward a nearby bunker where Uncle Sonny was on a field radio, and could hear his ongoing conversation.

"I can see them coming from the southwest, like a cattle stampede! They're flanking you! Move your butts over here!"

"Colonel Hester, can you stop them?"

The radio crackled loudly and the soldier who had made the query dropped the device, dead on his feet. A well-placed bullet exploded through his chest before he could hear any answer, rupturing his aorta and shattering his spine. The force literally picked him up and tossed him backward several yards, another casualty of vicious Colorado snipers. Sonny Hester didn't know for sure why he suddenly lost radio contact, but he couldn't miss that the moment of testing was fast upon them.

"Bet your buns we can stop them!" he shouted defiantly into the useless radio. Unable to make a verbal connection, he flung the worthless apparatus aside in disgust and set about preparing his charges. It was futile to hope for help against the approaching wave of troops. They would live or die by their own defenses this day.

The Wyoming army's trenches had been constructed along a low ridgeline that ran east to west and consisted of a series of fortifications. These imposing bulwarks were well-planned killing zones that covered the approach up a long valley from the border. The location was on one side of Hester's spread, and an adjacent highway was the main route to Cheyenne. Colorado had precious few military vehicles that still functioned, and any such entrenchments were bound to be only marginally effective against masses of highly mobile foot soldiers. The brief word from Hester had revealed the enemy's intentions. The only practical defense was a moving one, and the main body of Wyoming troops quickly pulled out to set up another battle line farther north.

The entire column of invading troops was in constant fluid motion, now with weapons blazing, and the pitter-patter of deadly lead pellets kicked up prairie dust on all sides of Luke Walker. He pinned his weapon

410

on the charging column of men and noted with diabolical satisfaction its weed-eater effect on the moving mass of humanity. But there were now thousands of aggressors approaching, far too many to be stopped by a paltry few hundred men. No matter how rapidly he and his compatriots fired, the column approached ever closer, and growing piles of dead soldiers failed to stem the implacable advance. A bullet creased Walker's skull as he reloaded, and he slumped motionless to the ground. Several stumbling and dying Colorado soldiers fell all around him, and bright red blood from the carnage stained virtually every square inch of ground for hundreds of yards around the main ranch house.

Living Coloradans used the dead for cover and returned murderous fire to the remaining militiamen, eventually climbing over gory piles of corpses as resistance subsided. The lifeless body of attacker Jeff Walker was near the bottom of one of the nameless heaps, completely riddled with bullets from Hester's militia. He never even knew he was attacking his own uncle's ranch, nor that his estranged brother's bullets had been directed toward his unit.

There is a disquieting quality to a war involving brothers, something idyllic, even perhaps poetic. Inherent in such conflicts is a disturbing dichotomy that adds an extra measure of fervency and lends a touch of nobility. This was obvious in all the wars between various states. Passions burned with each infantry charge, and exceptional valor was common. These emotions actually worked to the advantage of the brutal regime in Rome, because it brought necessary results quickly. Both submission and progress in the Concord's agenda were inevitable outcomes, whether by attrition or by outright victory.

Sonny Hester and his men fought a valiant holding action, but in the process every man was apparently killed, along with Hester's whole family. Fat cattle that Hester had been able to protect from poacher raids were soon dead in a wicked crossfire. The shrewd commander of the Colorado troops carefully documented that Hester's men and not his own soldiers had fired the bullets that killed each cow. There would be an awful price to pay if anyone in the Father's army were negligent enough to accidentally shoot one of these rare members of the human family. Swarming troops left the burning ranch house and myriad bodies strewn all around, advancing toward the fortifications they knew must surely be waiting just to the northwest.

The gallantry of Hester's militiamen almost paid off. The outflanked soldiers of Wyoming rallied to an unfortified hill in the brief delay and rapidly reorganized. From this high ground they succeeded in completely halting the onrushing Colorado troops. The dry wash literally ran with blood from the slaughter, so numerous were the dead and wounded. But human waves kept on coming, delivering lethal fire of their own, gradually clipping off more outnumbered infantrymen from the hill. Just when it seemed the brave rebels would be overwhelmed, a loud, deep-throated yell filled the air to the east. General Tecumseh Early, one of the last Wyomingites to have graduated from West Point before its shutdown, did his own brilliant flanking movement on the Colorado troops with his battle hardened reserves, taking them by total surprise. Yelling like wild men, fanatical warriors of Early's Wyoming Corps started rolling up the east flank of the Coloradans, destroying them wholesale as the urban soldiers fled in panic from the maniacal charge.

With perfect coordination, General Joe Jackson's Wyoming Cavalry, a mounted unit of merely 500 men, came screaming in from the rear of the trapped Coloradans. The development was another total surprise to the Colorado army. The battle raged, hand to hand at times, bright sabers of the horse soldiers flashing in the morning sunlight. Wyoming troops on the hill stood up and joined in the throaty bellowing, sure that victory was within their grasp. The abject terror of the Colorado infantry as they were systematically cut down was a horrifying yet bewitching sight.

It just wasn't to be, despite all the heroics of that fateful day. The sound of rotors in the distance was replaced within seconds by sightings of deadly flying machines. Suddenly the air was full of hissing, fire-breathing helicopters, all bearing familiar blue and white markings of the Concord. Some of them belched awful streams of high velocity lead particles while others sprayed Wyoming troops with solutions designed to snuff out life instantly, employing chemical warfare in total violation of outdated international rules of war. The Wyoming soldiers resisted valiantly and stubbornly against impossible odds, even shooting down quite a number of the awful choppers, but in the end their effort proved futile.

Intelligence had indicated that all the Father's helicopters were in the east, helping New York and New Jersey to overpower spotty resistance in Pennsylvania, but here they were, no matter what the spies had said. Having flown all night to this rendezvous, they were the decisive force.

*   *   *

Sunlight washed over Sonny Hester's obliterated and deserted ranch, illuminating a scene of horror never before seen in that part of the world. All became deathly still as the victorious army moved away, and the tumult of battle faded into the distance. There was no noise on the ranch now except the rustle of the prairie wind and a subdued, distant roar like thunder as the battle raged in another place.

In the afternoon warmth, a slightly detectable stirring occurred in one of the piles of lifeless human bodies. The movement increased dramatically as a young man slowly lifted a stiff, mangled leg and pushed it away from his shoulder. With great effort he then heaved a bullet-riddled corpse off his chest. The young soldier looked into the dead man's eyes, which stared dryly and blankly from deep, sunken sockets. He recoiled a little at the disgusting symbol on the corpse's arm, a shoulder patch of blue and white strained with clotted crimson.

Luke Walker slowly raised up, feeling his head and noting a deep bullet track along the right side of his skull just above the ear. His clothing was soaked with blood, whether his own or that of adjacent dead men he couldn't tell. His whole body ached, and behind his eyes he felt an extreme sensation of pressure that made his whole head pulsate. He stared vacantly at the awful piles of human carcasses that stretched as far as he could see, and cautiously peered around for signs of life somewhere. There was none.

For another hour or more he sat without moving, gripped by an impulsive fear that perhaps someone out there was still alive and might yet try to eliminate him. He had to think, but the effort was excruciating and his mind revolted. He felt compelled to systematically study all surrounding piles of bodies for any possible danger, and he did so without so much as another minuscule movement. He noticed that there were no weapons anywhere visible, the deadly armaments that each soldier had carried having apparently been collected by someone.

A sudden rising noise, eerie and filled with agony, startled him. Someone far out in front of him was moaning, someone in terrible pain, although the anguished words were unintelligible. There was doubtless another survivor of the slaughter, but the person had to be a Concord soldier. None of Walker's fellow defenders had been anywhere near that position. Over a period of hours the intermittent noise became less frequent, and finally it ceased altogether.

He waited out the afternoon in the warm sun, his wound caked with dried blood and his discomfort persisting tenaciously. For short periods he slept, or else lost consciousness, he didn't know which. The day was becoming later and the sun sank behind him while a creeping darkness slowly chilled the land. He would have to move out or else perhaps freeze to death. He slowly staggered upward, using every ounce of his energy. His knee struck something hard and metallic as he rose, and he felt in the darkness for the object. His electric auto rifle! He shouldered it, and then stooped back down to feel around for some ammunition. He could find none, but there were a few rounds left in the gun. Whoever had collected the weapons in the sweep after the battle had miraculously missed at least one of them.

Walker sensed that there was nothing but futility in searching for other survivors. The place seemed to be populated exclusively by the dead. He made his way toward the burned-out ranch house, where smoldering embers offered warmth if nothing else. He passed the night pretending to be one of the corpses, but he occasionally chanced to move enough to stoke and feed a small fire that persisted in one corner of the edifice. He felt no hunger, but his thirst burned relentlessly and his throat felt like it were filled with sand. In the cold and dark he knew it would be fruitless to waste energy looking for relief. He slept fitfully from time to time, always awaking with a start, incessantly shivering and hurting.

A welcome pastel dawn finally came, but it illuminated again the horrible sight of hundreds, perhaps thousands, of dead human beings, some of their carcasses bloating grotesquely already. He again searched the battlefield carefully for any sign of life and found everything still. It wasn't long before a dark vulture began cruising the sky overhead, and shortly there were many more, the only living beings he could see. The ominous black birds soon began settling to the ground in various locations, practicing their ageless vocation with abandon. Naked, ugly heads bobbed as they pecked and pulled at any loose flesh, often spearing first the eyes of their unmoving and uncaring victims.

He could see that the women and children that had sought refuge in the house had not been spared. Their charred remains were visible as hideously contorted figures, their limb positions and body postures suggesting that they had been burned alive. He was revulsed at the sight, and nausea overwhelmed him and drove him to unmanageable retching. Suddenly a pervasive desire to get away seized him, an uncontrollable urge to run. He had to force himself to stop and think. What could he do?

He decided the least he could do was arm himself and see if he could find something to drink. The elevated well tank was shot full of holes, but on ascending it he found that there was still a few inches of useable water. He drank his fill and then thoroughly washed his wicked wound. He then rummaged boldly among the corpses, stirring up clouds of raucous protesting vultures. He finally located another rifle and several canisters of bullets. There were plentiful field rations on the bodies of the dead, and despite the sickening stench of death he was able to fill his stomach and a knapsack with valuable food.

It would be execution on the spot if Concord forces spotted Walker. He would have to travel only at night and be very careful. He briefly considered moving in a southeasterly direction, back toward his hometown. But he knew that his home state was under absolute domination of the Concord, and that his arrival there would be noticed. He needed to move westward to the Rocky Mountains, where there was still impenetrable country in which a man could hide. He would spend the day concealed in a nearby brushy draw he knew, and move out when it was dark. He spent the afternoon recuperating, basking and sleeping in balmy sunshine.

As the sun set, he plotted a northwesterly course and prepared to embark. He stayed in the bottom of abundant sandy arroyos, and walked as quietly as possible. Regrettably, it was a moonless night and he had no artificial light, so he repeatedly stumbled in the rough terrain. At one point he noted a significant improvement in visibility, and he looked up to see enormous Space Station Delta cruising by, so near and so bright that for some reason the silver sphere reminded him of a realistic holocom game. He journeyed quickly along for the few minutes that it dominated the night sky, but soon he was once more immersed in faint starlight.

It was breaking day as he desperately sought shelter in a place where he could rest unnoticed. He had consumed half his water already, and his mind was preoccupied by that concern as well. He ascended a rocky ridge where he could see in all directions, hoping he could find a place to hide. He walked until it was almost broad daylight, perhaps pushing his luck to its limit.

"Hold it right there, mister! Drop those guns! *Now* or you're dead!"

Startled and certain it was all over, he quickly complied. The metallic clank of his two rifles hitting the stony ground made him jump once more, so loud was the noise after endless hours of near silence.

"Now turn around slowly! Move!" came an authoritative voice behind him. "And get those hands high! Do it!"

The youth complied, and was soon face to face with an intense pair of emerald eyes. The fiery orbs stared from the center of a ring of dark hair that completely encircled them, disheveled locks mingling wildly with a bushy beard and a complete mustache. The man wore a torn and bloodstained tan leather camouflage outfit, the army uniform of the State of Wyoming!

"And who in blazes might you be?" the man asked, looking his prisoner up and down as he spoke.

"Luke Walker. Hester's militia."

"Wiped out, weren't you?"

"Completely. How 'bout your outfit." The man lowered his gun as Walker answered.

"Same. Glad you saved some guns and ammo. We'll take a few more of the scoundrels with us if we can."

"Pitiful lot of good it'll do us. But I'm for it. They burned our ranch house down on forty of the finest women and children I've ever known."

"And they're doing as bad as that all over Wyoming right now. I spent last night this side of Cheyenne, hiding in a basement. They're shooting every Wyoming soldier they find. Even shot all the wounded. They're raping and killing and burning and stealing—Wyoming will never recover."

"What's your name, if I might ask? Uh, can I pick up my guns now?"

"Hester's militia, huh? Yeah, you're all right. I'm Jacob Thompson, Early's Wyoming Corps. A fine unit. Of dead men."

"I was making my way toward the Rockies," said Luke Walker as he gathered his weapons, checking them to be sure they were undamaged. "Got to be somewhere to hide out there."

"I was heading that way, too. Wonder how many survived this thing. I figure we can find some others like us, and then we'll hole up and do our part against this Father guy, whoever he is. We might not lick him, but we can give him a run for it, I'll bet," declared Thompson with passion, his voice dripping vengeance and determination.

The bearded man had a full canteen of water, and he shared it with Walker over a Spartan meal of confiscated rations. They then settled into a deep crevice in the rocks to pass the day and plan their next move. Maybe there was some hope after all, Walker thought as they finished their discussion. On that notion, he drifted into deep and exhausted sleep.

* * *

The final outcome was the same all over the Western world. Wherever the authority of Father Hammer's Concord was challenged there were death, destruction, and defeat for the antagonist. All of civilization's fading technology and its best weaponry were at the Hammer's disposal, so no opposing force could stand indefinitely.

The deciding factor in many localized wars was the incomparable helicopters. No one had any idea how many of them the world government had at its disposal, but there had to be thousands. They wouldn't always be available, though, because few in the Concord forces knew anything about repairing or servicing them. Every populace that came under attack longed desperately for the day when those terrible machines would fly no more, though practically all means to resist had been eliminated long before that time could arrive.

The situation was only a little better near Adrian, Kansas, where the Barnes family was now watching apprehensively as the last of their farm animals were confiscated. The only livestock they had left were two sturdy draft horses they had managed to keep from poachers by practically living with them. A unit of the Concord Army, consisting of men who had formerly been part of the Kansas Militia, arrived unexpectedly to conscript the creatures. Shortly they had boarded the animals into a trailer with a few other residual local horses for transport to the coast, where they would be placed aboard an ocean vessel destined for wherever the Father dictated. Jamie Barnes knew it was futile and perilous to resist the seizure edict, so he helped the soldiers with apparent willingness. In his last contact with the horses he made certain the sleek animals were safely and securely on board for a long ride.

The family had somehow avoided being directly involved in the earlier slaughter that had accompanied overthrow of the Kansas government. They knew a woman down the road who had lost three sons, and there were numerous people who had lost a relative in fierce battles between the Kansas Guard and Concord loyalists. Most major battles had occurred in the eastern part of the state, but there had been considerable local fighting as well. Shells had fallen in their fields as they all had huddled terrified in the basement of the main house, but graciously none had impacted anywhere close to them. As a noncombatant, Jamie Barnes was accorded a small measure of protection from the occupying troops, but he was nonetheless fearful for the safety of his family. For the most part he just kept on farming, doing what he knew best and trying to produce enough to be useful to the residual society that existed.

Leon Walker was left to wonder about the fate of his two sons. He never heard from either of them again. Jeff was left unburied where he fell, and his rotting body became food for clouds of buzzards that descended on the battleground. The omnipresent carrion birds moved about with changing battle locations, and seemed to gather instinctively at the sound of gunfire. There was no priority or respect given to the dead, and bodies of fallen soldiers were routinely left to this ignoble fate.

There had been a move to conscript the only Barnes son, Jody, into a local militia unit, but so far he had been spared. This was partly because he was also a farmer and necessary for food production, but mostly because Jamie Barnes had paid handsomely to Darwin Archer to spare him such duty. Archer was a former friend and schoolmate who was now the local Concord military commander. While the boy and his father had their differences, Jamie loved his son dearly and was glad the deadly conflicts seemed to be dying down, so hopefully the need for more soldiers would not again threaten to take his son from him.

* * *

Buck Morgan, Jamie Barnes' third cousin, could know nothing about the seething conflicts that were inundating his home planet. During one of his periods of deep reflection, he thought again of his deceased father, and he remembered that he had been a hero in Terror War III. He wondered sometimes what it would be like to be involved in that most insane of human activities, and he was glad that prospects of war seemed remote. In the world he remembered, there had been little or no international hostilities for a long time simply because such mindless destruction was scientifically indefensible. Science demanded cooperation and unity to achieve progress, and great strides had been made in the decades before Morgan's departure. He couldn't imagine a scenario that would change such a logical approach to international problems.

In one time of relaxed reflection, Morgan retrieved his father's war medals from their secure niche and examined them. There was a Silver Star and a Purple Heart, among others, still nestled in their original cases. He carried the articles thoughtfully to the control room, where eternal Calvin sat monitoring all ship functions. The holocom man had never seen the pieces, so he stared at them somewhat like an inquisitive child.

"You've never shown me these, Commander Bucko. What are they?"

"Your flesh and blood twin, Smitty, knew all about them. But I'm afraid you wouldn't understand, Calvin," Morgan replied as he spread the open cases on the utility console. The bright star still had a pristine shine like a mint condition coin, and all the ribbon colors were perfectly preserved.

"You must be right, Commander Bucko. Why don't you explain it to me anyway?"

"Terror War III, Calvin. These are medals my father won for heroism in that war," said Morgan as he began to carefully, tenderly close the small boxes one at a time.

"Terror War III. I do know all about that, sir," said Calvin, pausing briefly for another query delay as he scanned his archives. "Indeed your father did serve then and was highly decorated. Jim Morgan served with the Third Infantry Brigade, and he saw intensive action for eleven months in Macedonia and Kosovo. He finished the war as a sergeant. Want to know about any other soldier in any other war?"

"Not now, Calvin. Maybe we'll do that later. I must say you astound me sometimes."

"I don't know everything, though, Commander Bucko. War, for example. Why do humans fight and destroy one another? Almost any other answer to a problem is better than war."

"You're right again, my holographic friend. Thankfully, wars are virtually a phenomenon of historical interest only. Mankind finally came to the same conclusion your electronic brain has derived so logically."

"I'm glad for that. No medal is valuable enough to kill and destroy as the price for obtaining it."

"Don't misunderstand, Calvin. My father wasn't a hero in order to gain medals. He was simply a hero who did his duty, and the government recognized that by giving him these tokens of appreciation. He regarded war as insanity."

"Then he also agreed with my conclusion, no doubt. Your father was a wise man."

Morgan nodded as he stood up to leave the control room. He stowed the medals back in his private desk, and went to the entertainment complex to practice a few melodies.

It was significant that he had purged from his musical memory virtually all the old martial songs he had learned and played for his cohorts at the U.S. Military Academy. He had been well known as a solid piano practitioner while he had been there, and had been called upon regularly to perform for his peers in informal settings, and occasionally to play at prestigious official functions. But the tunes he had played so often back then now seemed strangely inappropriate, an affront to an advanced world of harmony and order, a world without war, current twenty-second century Earth to which he would soon return.

From time to time, Morgan couldn't help but think about his old friend Hugh Baxter, and wonder why he had chosen such an unfulfilling career as an infantry officer. He had felt a little sorry for him then and he still felt that way now. What a study in folly, pure and simple. It was glorified in history books, but Calvin's learned analysis was perfectly accurate. It was still indefensible foolishness, beyond all question. He knew Baxter had to be dead now, probably dying from boredom, he assumed.

He was thankful that Baxter's occupation was one the world no longer needed.

CHAPTER 32

May 2166

"...and with famine..." Revelation 6:8

"Sweet sixteen and never been kissed," gasped Bob Hancock, his voice barely audible over his labored breathing. Dim light illuminated a quiet room where his big frame rested limply on a rumpled bed. His tired, bulging eyes had lost most of their familiar sparkle, and his stately hair was a commotion of disordered white locks. He was weary in countenance and he could feel his life slowly ebbing away.

"I'm almost eighteen, Grandpa, and who says I've never been kissed?" asked his granddaughter as she sat beside him. Pretty Molly Hancock used a damp cloth to mop the old man's wrinkled brow.

"I do," he rasped. "Not by somebody outside the family and serious, anyway."

"Oh, Grandpa, you're silly. But I love you anyway."

"Just be careful who you kiss. I love you, too," said Hancock, with his last few words highly labored and trailing away to a whisper.

Hancock coughed deeply and the girl got up to get some refreshing water for him. He had eaten little lately, and just keeping him from getting dehydrated was the best she could do. Grandfather Bob was ninety-seven years old, and he had been her provider and friend all her life, especially since her father's death. She returned to the bedroom with a glass, and immediately a deathly silence conveyed that she was now suddenly alone.

Bob Hancock lay stone still with a faint smile gracing the corners of his mouth, and his eyes were closed. She could tell that he had stopped breathing. His battle was finally over.

Molly sat down next to him and bit her lower lip while a tear trickled down her tender face. She took his big, frail hand in hers and pulled it to her cheek, caressing it gently. Her quiet sobs were the only sound in the room.

*　　*　　*

In the town of Adrian, a nameless baby with a tumescent belly cried weakly as a woman tried to breast feed it. She handled the limp infant tenderly as she adjusted a filthy loin cloth that hung loosely about her waist. A look of desperation welled in her dark eyes, and exasperation showed as she worked.

"Come on, little one, eat," she coaxed, putting her breast nipple in the tiny mouth repeatedly, only to have it slip out of the baby's feeble suckling grip before it yielded any milk.

"Ma, he's weaker every day. I don't think he's going to make it. What can I do?" pleaded the frightened mother. "There's no doctor anywhere. Nobody to help. What can we do?"

"You're doing the best you can. Just keep trying. I don't know what to tell you," replied the girl's unkempt grandmother, the nearest thing to a mother the she had ever had. "You haven't eaten in days yourself. How can you hope to feed him?"

The old woman shook her dirty head sadly, noting a lack of color in the child and its loose skin. The bloated baby was in that latest stages of terminal dehydration. Next day the infant's stomach was more swollen than before and he had entirely ceased any attempt to take nourishment. Its skin had now lost all tone and was as wrinkled as that of an old man. That night, the baby expired without a whimper.

For the first time in history North America was experiencing the horror of African-style famine, featuring dying infants, piles of inflated corpses, and flies—everywhere, swarming on everything, making life utterly miserable for the living, whom the harassing insects hardly distinguished from the dead. This famine was different from those experienced in the distant past in other parts of the world in one major respect. There was no possibility of emergency response by other nations to help ease suffering.

*　　*　　*

"Molly, eat some of this, hon," advised farmer Jamie Barnes to his young friend. He had just taken Molly Hancock into his home after the death of her grandfather. The resourceful old man had managed to keep her healthy somehow, even when there was rampant starvation in cities all around them. With his death the girl had begun to slip slowly into malnutrition. Barnes' wife Martha had checked on her and found her without food and despondent, and she had insisted that the young woman join their family.

A female living alone had little chance of surviving. There was great competition for meagerly available food, and there was a constant threat of rape and robbery by wandering homeless men. Additionally, Concord police frequently used their power over life and death to force any available woman to accommodate them in whatever perverse manner they devised. On the Barnes farm there was some relic of protection, however tenuous.

"Thanks, Jamie," replied Molly gratefully as she chewed the offered morsel of food. "Hey, this tastes like...animal protein!" She dropped her voice to a whisper on the last two words.

"It is. It's from a cache I have down by the old barn."

"I can't believe this. Thanks, Jamie."

"We're stretching the supply as far as we can. There's no replacing it."

The efficient farmer had begun growing vegetable matter with a vengeance after the Humanity Proclamation and he was a major supplier now. Concord police, who patrolled his farm and others nearby, gave good producers special protection from marauding bands of thieves. Almost nightly, automatic weapons fire resonated through the night like a giant coiled rattlesnake as police shot trespassers.

A most nauseating spectacle was daily rumbling of big trucks as they eased by the farm at the prescribed twenty mile per hour speed limit. The trucks were inevitably loaded with fresh corpses being taken from the city to a rural landfill, which was really nothing more than a vast feedlot for swarms of circling vultures. By the thousands came the dead, presumably victims of starvation, though prominent bullet wounds on many bodies proved the danger of trying to get food illegally.

Along with the slow parade of trucks came a veritable cloud of flies, so numerous that they formed a haze all about the high piles of human bodies. This living vapor streamed toward the rear of each vehicle as the insects hovered in an attempt to gain a foothold on fresh flesh. Yellowish spots showed on all the bodies where new caches of vigorous eggs had already grown into writhing masses of ravenous maggots.

"Poor souls," Jamie Barnes muttered quietly as he stood in the open door one morning. He shook his head as yet another truckload eased past. Atop this awful pile of carcasses were those of several emaciated young men whose naked bodies were completely riddled with bullet holes. "When you're starving, I guess its better to die quickly trying to get something to eat. You've not much to lose."

"I can't believe how quickly society collapsed," noted Martha. "I know things have been bad, but why this sudden starvation?"

"Well, like I've said before, I think their food just doesn't contain sufficient calories. Animal protein was always excellent in that respect. So to start with everybody is suddenly calorie deficient. Add to that the absence of some amino acids. Then the crowning blow is lack of vitamin B12 from not eating meat."

"Grandpa said it would be this way," said Molly as she finished her food.

"Your grandpa was no fool, Molly," said Grandma Robin in her best motherly voice. The white-haired old woman was Jamie Barnes' mother, and the widow of deceased Billy Barnes. "He harbored an uncommon amount of wisdom about practically everything, and he was a keen observer and student. You remember everything he tried to teach you."

Molly looked at the floor as the widow spoke, uncomfortable to hear a sermon from her on the subject. The girl held a half-buried obstinacy that had been fashioned by the times. She missed Grandfather Bob, but she didn't need a lecture about him. There was depression enough without having to listen to this.

She sulked toward a nearby window and kicked nonchalantly at a large, aging alloy cooking pot. The grand vessel was used mainly for holding raw grain, and it was sitting underneath the sill. Its well-fitted top jostled and made an irritating metallic sound that partially obscured the old woman's nagging voice. Grandma Robin continued to irritate with more words of praise for her deceased grandfather.

"He wasn't a farmer, Molly, but he knew a lot about it just from living around here. He talked every day with protein farmers when he managed the plant," said Barnes, entering the subtle mental duel between the girl and Grandma Robin. "When the powers decree that you can't kill insects while you're farming, productivity can't help but plummet. Grasshopper excluders on the combine, for goodness sake. We leave tons of grain and soybeans on the ground because of those excluders."

"Not to mention that you can't use insecticides. We're to share with the bugs, which was a command that Grandpa just couldn't get over," Molly remembered, halting her insouciant noisemaking and directing her comments obviously at Barnes. "If there were still any birds, they'd eat well on wasted grain and insects, wouldn't they?"

"No doubt. Not many of our feathered friends around nowadays, other than buzzards. I did see a couple of mourning doves last month. Three guys were trying to sneak up on them. I told them to leave or the Concord police would get them. Fortunately those birds flew away and the people left. But they wouldn't leave until the birds did."

"Would you really have told those Concord brutes, Jamie?" asked Martha quietly.

"Of course not, dear. But a threat was the only defense I could offer to perhaps save those birds. And those guys were already in grave danger of being shot. They were out on the grain field without authorization, so all it would have taken was for a Concord patrol to happen by."

"Another factor in starvation for so many is their ignorance," Molly said blandly. "In my case, I just couldn't find any food. But even when people have food, most of them are illiterate and nobody tells them which plants they have to eat to get the proper amino acids. And I don't believe anybody has told the general public how necessary it is to eat micro-meat for vitamin B12. I listen to Concord radio and I haven't heard any nutritional information. What they're pushing now is those chip implants the Father requires."

The girl's knowledge of the facts demonstrated that she had not been completely deaf to her grandfather's teaching. There was a level of knowledge there that showed a great deal of promise. Grandma Robin ceased her attempt to lecture and wisely decided to stop pushing. She nodded silently at Molly's words, and a faint smile showed.

"The man who came to church last week—he was saying there are still lots of animals in Israel," said Martha, keeping her voice low in case anybody was listening. "The Jews continue to raise and protect all kinds of them. They signed a peace treaty with the Concord some time ago, you know. He said because of that Father Hammer gave them some degree of autonomy. But back to the point—there are no other large concentrations of animals in the entire world, according to what he was saying, except for vultures and big predators."

The man to whom she referred had a forbidden clandestine radio, and he received news regularly from other parts of the world. He distributed information to select people he was sure could be trusted. Such a radio was strictly contraband and would subject him to immediate and final retribution if authorities discovered it. Come to think of it, thought Martha, they'd kill us, too, if they knew we had knowledge of it.

"Well, folks, I've got to retrieve Jody and get to work. We've got to produce in order to stay alive," Barnes called as he slipped out the door heading for his son's small house across the yard. "Stay out of sight as much as possible. We'll be on the front field."

It was planting season and Barnes was putting in a crop of soybeans, a commodity needed desperately by everybody. He left Jody driving the tractor and headed for the harvest collection point in his heavily laden old farm truck, carrying the last of his spring wheat for delivery. Concord police were everywhere as he eased the big truck toward the delivery area. It was very simple—all he had to do was back up, dump, and drive away. The Father had socialized the whole world, promising unhindered goods and services to all people, so Barnes received nothing for his labor except what he could eat. It was functionally a moneyless society. Barnes and his family had so far been able to continue to operate without the mandatory computer chip implant, and with the onset of severe famine that requirement seemed to be forgotten for the moment. Nobody inquired about the chip and he left the collection point unhindered and with no questions asked.

Weeks of hunger and death dragged on and there appeared to be no end in sight. Barnes continued to dole out his precious vacuum packed protein, retrieving enough from his stockpile every few days only for immediate consumption. He began to be concerned that the obvious excellent health of his little clan might arouse suspicions so he had first one, then another, feign illness in plain view of ever-present Concord police. They never questioned him about the state of his family.

*   *   *

Along a stretch of highway in the Rocky Mountains, a caravan of food trucks moved slowly along at the prescribed pace, heading toward a major Concord army base. There were vehicles in front and behind that bristled with armaments to protect the precious commodities from scattered bands of rebels that still persisted in these parts. Every vehicle in the column bore the Concord emblem, a familiar circle of blue with a design and inscription in white. Smug Concord soldiers drove escort cars and manned the weaponry, while others were at the controls of the transports.

"Get down! Here they come!" whispered a bearded figure to a group of men that crouched on either side of the road. "Wait until the front vehicle is just past us, then watch for the signal! Remember our plan!"

An immense boulder had been rolled off a high bank alongside the road, completely blocking the narrow passage. Several Concord soldiers dismounted, wary and uncertain whether this was a simple case of an unexpected landslide. One trooper manned a frightful electric machine gun that could pivot 360 degrees and fire thousands of lead particles per minute. It was an awesome weapon that dreadfully intimidated any potential adversary. Soldiers on the trailing armored car also dismounted for a look at the obstruction.

Jacob Thompson's guerrillas knew exactly when to strike. Their first victim was the one capable of inflicting the most damage, the soldier manning that saturation gun atop the lead vehicle. A high explosive charge cast at him by one of the raiders detonated virtually in his lap, completely obliterating him in a bloody spray of body fluid, macerated flesh, and pulverized bone. Simultaneously, hidden warriors blazed away with their ancient weapons, cutting down every one of the Concord troops. The job wasn't completed for several seconds, though, and the faster and better weapons carried by the Father's forces hummed out deadly bullets, some of which found their mark. In the rapid exchange, several guerrillas were also killed, valuable men Thompson could ill afford to lose.

Luke Walker was wounded for a second time by the gunfire. He crawled quickly to another injured rebel nearby, a friend who was writhing in the dirt in his own puddling blood. A huge loop of bowel protruded from one side of his abdomen, and out of an extensive exit wound there was a spurt of liquid crimson as big as a garden hose. Walker tried to comfort his compatriot as the man expired in his arms. He gently laid the man's head on the ground with a grief-stricken moan. He then rose wearily to his feet clutching his own bleeding arm, while scarlet droplets cascaded from his fingertips. He walked to the mangled body of a dead Concord soldier and cursed as he kicked it repeatedly.

They would all miss Walker's friend, who had been a fierce and effective warrior. He had joined up with Walker and Thompson even before they had reached their mountain sanctuary. In fact, all the fighters were formerly members of some force that had been vanquished by the Concord. In the rugged high country they had established a unit that was one of the last opposing the world government in North America.

"Luke, you okay?" asked Thompson as he finished his own part in the attack and began to take stock of his dead and wounded. It had been costly. It always was, it seemed.

"Yeah, just another crease. But we've lost a good one here."

"Those auto weapons they use are lightening," said Thompson, tossing in expletives liberally. "We had them dead to rights. Looks like we've got four dead and two serious injuries. Plus your arm. We kicked their high and mighty butts, but we lose again."

He picked up one of the enemy's formidable guns and examined it, hoping to discover something encouraging. The weapons were absolutely useless without the combination of a chip implant and the warm print of that individual soldier's palm. The technology pre-dated the world government, but the Father had successfully implemented it to keep lethal arms from falling into opposition hands.

"Let's get the heck out of here. Load up the dead and wounded and let's go get these trucks disposed. And hurry up! Helicopters will be swarming here in no time!"

They were no more than an insignificant and remote nuisance to the Father, these Rocky Mountain guerrillas. With each attack their unit became weaker in terms of ammunition, arms, and men. Their old auto weapons used ammunition that the Concord forces disdained as antique, so they couldn't really re-arm effectively, even though they used ingenious but time consuming reloading techniques to refurbish captured enemy bullets.

"At least we won't starve to death for awhile," Walker commented as Thompson wrapped a dirty bandage around his injured arm. "Man, look at all the groceries."

"But we've got to get moving. We've got less than thirty minutes before arrival of the flies," he responded, referring to helicopters that monitored all movements of Concord forces. They would come, all right. But not before the group had scavenged what they needed and fled back into majestic and rocky high terrain.

*   *   *

Around the dinner table that night, the little group on the Barnes farm thanked God for preserving and protecting them. Jamie Barnes opened his Bible and read a few passages. After he finished, he closed the worn volume and looked straight at Molly.

"You know what, young lady? There's an awful lot in this old book I don't understand, but I believe every word of it is true. Your grandfather was a master at explaining the hard parts and something tells me his interpretation was right on the money. I hope you won't forget anything he taught you. And I hope Jody comes to a realization of the truth, as well."

She looked at him with a hint of surprise, by her eyes anticipating and dreading yet another sermon. A serious look then crossed her face as she seemed to reconsider what she was going to say.

"I can tell you one thing," she answered back slowly and with more than a hint of sadness. "I really miss Grandpa, Jamie."

"We all miss him. But at least we're not starving—not yet, anyway. We'll trust the Lord that we won't. But when the protein is gone, we're going to have a harder time of it. How I wish this Concord thing had never happened. Tell me one good thing they've done."

"They kept the horses from being eaten, Jamie," replied Martha after a brief hesitation. "They're in the army now and they're protected. Darwin Archer says that each one is assigned to a cavalryman, and if the horse is stolen or lost for any reason the soldier faces an immediate firing squad."

"Say, I wonder whether the horse is executed if the cavalryman comes up missing," observed Barnes with a sly grin. The others laughed out loud, a rare sound of mirth in a mostly humorless world.

Finally the prolific flow of human corpses from the city began to slow. Whether food supplies were arriving more efficiently, or the population was learning how to better cope with vegetarianism, or remaining people were genetically stronger, no one had any idea. But eventually the flood slowed to a trickle and then finally halted. Maybe everything will be okay now, thought Jamie Barnes as he noted the lack of ominous traffic out front.

Easing of the immediate crisis brought about intensification in enforcement of rules by Concord police. There was still a small band of Christian believers in the Adrian area, but they came under increasing scrutiny and lived in knowledge that their lives could end on the slightest whim. For reasons nobody could fathom, the police had so far neglected to check any of them for the mandatory microchip implant.

The church building had been taken over by a band of irascible vagrants, refugees from the city. They were mean and confrontational, and refused entry to the small group that had formerly owned it. There was the option of appealing to Concord police to evict the intruders, but they chose instead to avoid attracting undue attention by meeting in individual homes.

The Father had not yet specifically forbidden such meetings. The Hammer had made it clear that he took no pleasure in the idea of a personal supreme being with more authority than himself, and his own spiritual beliefs were solidly grounded in Mother Earth. Christian Ersatzson regularly declared that the primary expected spiritual emphasis was to worship that savior of nature, the incomparable Father Hammer. In an extraordinarily uncertain atmosphere, believers in Adrian gathered despite knowing that they could easily commit a capital transgression and endure the wrath of Concord police. Miraculously they were left untouched and continued their weekly home meetings.

* * *

Aboard the *Ursa C*, Buck Morgan observed his progress with great satisfaction. If all continued unhindered, he would be back in orbit with Delta Station within a very few months. When it came to food, he almost regretted the imminent termination of his voyage and more Spartan meals at the orbiting station, ingredients for which had to be lifted by shuttle at great expense. Maybe they've built their own renewables garden at the station by now, he speculated.

"Calvin, do you have any concept of what it means to eat?" asked Morgan of his electronic companion as he entered the control room with a heaping tray. "You know, ingesting food to fuel metabolism?"

"I know all the definitions, Commander Bucko. It must be much like an information feed—like you sent up to me from the surface of planet Schultzi. Is it like that?"

"Maybe a little," replied Morgan as he chewed his first bite. "But you're missing the idea of pleasure. Know what that is?"

"Of course, but I must admit it is highly abstract. Just enjoy your food and I'll observe and monitor your vital readings as usual. From this I get some explanation of the sensation of which you speak. I think it comes through adequately."

"Not quite, my friend. But it probably gives you some idea, at least," said Morgan as he forked up another mouthful of dainty morsels.

Later, Morgan retired to the venerable piano and ran through whatever selection came to mind, a few melancholy tunes offset by some highly animated and happy refrains. His time at the piano was a time to think deeply, and he reflected with gratitude on the extreme adequacy of his ship's renewables section. Each sumptuous meal was a dining experience *par excellence*, and he knew that only the bounty of Earth itself could provide any better for his needs. Calculations showed clearly that the renewables garden could sustain more people than it was originally designed to support, up to five at a minimum, and possibly even six. Like combination biologists and botanists Morgan and Calvin surveyed the health of all animals and plants and found them to be disease free and in excellent condition.

*   *   *

Back on Earth, the radio man came to the Barnes home once more bearing astounding news of numerous disturbances around the world. Not only had the famine been worldwide, but also there had been unimaginable loss of life everywhere. There had been numerous natural disasters such as earthquakes and tidal waves, as well as huge unforeseen storms of inconceivable magnitude, lashing a reeling human population with blow after blow. Unless one considered the Biblical flood, nothing close to this extent had ever befallen the world previously in human experience.

A few days later they learned bad news from Concord officers when they came to the farm asking questions.

They had found a man talking on an unauthorized radio. They wanted to find out if he had been sharing his information, and they brusquely interrogated the little group for some time before they were apparently satisfied.

The man and their source of information would be missed. Their minds were filled with gruesome questions about their friend, questions that they dared not ask. They knew he was dead.

CHAPTER 33

August 2166

"...and with pestilence..." Revelation 6:8

A small band of shaggy animals was slowly moving toward three hidden men, feeding on low sedges and arctic willow as they ambled lazily along. Half a dozen sleek muskoxen, their coats just recovering from their annual summer molt, were unaware of unseen danger just ahead. The lead cow looked briefly at a benign expanse of rock-strewn tundra in front of her, then lowered her head once more to clip off another bite with her sharp incisors. A large pair of ivory-colored horns on the herd bull practically touched the midline of his forehead, and curved shafts angled outward to end with sharp upshot tips. These horns were formidable weapons that could skewer and kill any adversary.

Tense, desperate men crouched low in a boulder field to avoid detection by their prey. They were dressed in contraband caribou skins, and the hairy exterior of their clothing blended well with the gray-white terrain. Each man carried a lance tipped with razor-sharp metal, hammered and stone ground to keenest edge. They had positioned themselves with the wind blowing directly into their faces, and the muskoxen were thus unable to detect telling human scent.

One of the cows again stopped and looked at the still parcel of rocky ground, and for a breathless moment Iqaqsaq Padlug thought their quest was ruined. After the cow stared for a full minute, she again dropped her head and resumed feeding. She gradually moved to within ten yards of the crouching men, so it was now or never. On a predetermined signal, all three launched their deadly missiles as hard as a man's arm could cast them. Even with the sharpest of tools, it took a lot of force to penetrate six inches of coarse wool, thick hide, muscle, and bone so that the vitals were reached.

One of the spears sailed high and clattered uselessly on hard, stark ground, spooking all of the animals into a vigorous run. Another lance entered the cow's belly just behind her diaphragm and sank in only slightly before rebounding and falling away. The third scored a perfect hit just behind the shoulder, entering the chest cavity with enough strength that its tip passed completely through and protruded behind the opposite shoulder. The animal ran only a short distance with the others before collapsing. A trio of successful hunters ran up jubilantly and congratulated one another before beginning the rigorous butchering chores.

A rising gale driving intense rain assaulted them before they finished the bloody and difficult task. Despite the warmth of their clothing, dampness could spell big trouble if they allowed themselves to become soaked. They stashed the quarters of meat and sought cover.

"Let's get in here. We'll freeze in this rain," called Padlug. The elderly Eskimo yelled loudly so he could be heard over the howling wind. The trio scrambled through the opening in the rocks and entered a small underground chamber in the hillside.

It had been a relatively warm summer on Ellesmere Island, considering the location some 800 miles north of the Arctic Circle. In this remote location, men still pursued remnant herds of muskoxen and even occasionally encountered a residual caribou. Compliance with frequent mandates issued by the Father was not easily enforced here, as such orders tended to be swallowed up by great distances and determined appetites. Still, in the interest of hiding their prohibited activities from authorities, the natives had reverted to hunting with spears and snares instead of guns.

"Much better in here," admitted David Kalluk, the old man's nephew, drawing his caribou skin parka around him for comfort. "Now we can warm up."

Bitter summer wind outside had begun spitting snow, a condition that was more familiar and less threatening to them than liquid precipitation. Rain could be deadly with so many miles to go back to camp. Kalluk retrieved a seal oil lamp from his pack, and lit it for heat and light in the manner of his ancestors from the nearly forgotten past.

"Good place to hide from helicopters," observed Adam Angohiatok in his native Inuktitut tongue, the halting but beautiful language that Inuit people had spoken for millennia. He had been on a hunting party some time before when their gunshots had been picked up by satellites, a fact which was not known to them until it was too late. Attack helicopters of the Concord had swooped in unannounced on the alleged cannibals, and had virtually wiped out his party. Angohiatok had been severely wounded but had escaped barely alive by playing dead. Their experience was repeated all over the Arctic, and thus the Inuit had rapidly learned that guns could no longer be trusted. They reverted with surprising ease to more clever ways of their ancestors, plying remote Arctic wastes on foot or with forbidden dog teams. They now hunted only with primitive weapons that were impossible to detect by treacherous technology.

The Father had targeted the Inuit, or Eskimos, as white men still called them, for elimination if they would not conform. Little provocation was needed to bring his wrath down upon them with intense brutality. They had always been a problematic people, even for species equality extremists of unenlightened times before *Anno Humanitatis*, because animal utilization was the essence of their heritage. They were meat eaters and had never switched to processed animal protein even when it was the principal amino acid source for the world, preferring natural meat instead. Furthermore, living at such high latitudes, they were unable to grow significant amounts of food from plants. Even their dress, constructed mainly of animal skins, was an affront to Father Hammer. They were considered by the inflexible authorities in Rome to be intractable and unruly cannibals who deserved to be extirpated from the face of Mother Earth.

Even the very real threat of annihilation had not been sufficient to force them to forsake their heritage and their ancestral practices. Token shiploads of vegetable matter sent to them went unconsumed as the Inuit returned to their old nomadic way of life, avoiding the white man and living off abundant Arctic wildlife in defiance of official decrees. Here, where the population was small and the remote location made poaching by outsiders more difficult, there was still terrestrial game as well as the bounty of an icy sea. In bitter cold, helicopters couldn't fly efficiently except during the brief summer, and even then vast distances made their reach less effective. The long winter's darkness provided resourceful northern natives with additional tenuous security.

The Father viewed the small Inuit population as a special project and sent in the best-equipped units of his army to bring them into compliance or else exterminate them. There were some larger villages that, to the superficial observer, appeared to have conformed and switched to vegetarianism. But even in those settlements contraband meat was still consumed on the sly by everyone.

When the weather broke Padlug and his friends would begin the slow and dangerous process of ferrying their illicit prize back to waiting families. In the meantime, they would wait and warm up in the sheltered niche.

"What's this?" asked Padlug, groping in the dark frozen recesses of the ice cave. It felt like a filamentary form of moss, long and stringy, protruding from eternal permafrost.

"What's what?" asked Angohiatok, reaching into the same place. He held up the flickering oil lamp and gasped as illumination filled the recess. A human body! No, two bodies!

Closer inspection revealed that both corpses had apparently been locked in permafrost for a very long time. Clothing on the bodies was like nothing the men had ever seen before, drab wool trousers and jackets with corroded brass buttons. Both bodies were longhaired white men, and remarkably well preserved.

It was possible to dig one body out completely, because apparently a recent partial melting of superficial ice had occurred in the unusually warm weather. This they did, hoping to find something useful. Both preserved corpses wore knives, and except for some superficial rust they were still serviceable.

They tried to remove the clothing, but it literally came apart in their hands. The partially thawed body was oozing some liquid, and Kalluk got the slimy substance all over his hands before he was aware of it.

"Nothing but a big mess. Must be Englishmen. There were several expeditions that lost men here a long time ago, and one large group of men disappeared completely. In the old days, this would be a big find," said Padlug. "I think I'll report it to Concord police when we get back to Grise Fiord. Maybe it will distract them for a while."

"I got some dirty material all over me," complained Kalluk. "I'll wash it off in the river when we start to leave."

Hours later the three emerged and completed the final steps of butchering their muskox. After several treks to and from the village, ferrying was complete and the essential meat was hidden in strategic locations, preserved indefinitely in permanently frozen ground.

Padlug never got around to telling the Concord policemen about the two bodies, although he had every intention of doing so. After postponing the unpleasant task of approaching Concord headquarters several times, he forgot about the incident.

Two weeks after the muskox kill, Kalluk awoke in the middle of the night with a hard chill. Shaking uncontrollably, he sought more blankets and skins in which to wrap himself. He lit another lamp, then two, but he simply couldn't get warm.

"You've got flu, I think," diagnosed an elderly native woman who came to check him, reading the symptoms in an ancient first aid book. She examined him quizzically, having rarely seen an acute febrile illness in her entire life. "I don't know where you got it, but the chills and high fever are typical. Stay in bed and stay warm."

"Yeah, sure," he replied through chattering teeth. He could hardly believe how debilitated he felt, and he began to have waves of severe nausea. His stomach was emptied repeatedly, and he was unable to eat or drink anything. His head felt like it might explode from pressure.

By the fourth day he was increasingly weaker, and his friends were becoming more concerned as they visited in a futile effort to comfort and help him. Late that day he felt a little better and was able to sit up and drink a small portion of liquid for the first time. It was then that he noticed a red rash appearing on his face, gradually spreading to involve his whole body. At the same time he developed a mouth full of sores.

The next day the skin condition was much worse and poor Kalluk was covered with clear blisters, so numerous that the lesions ran together. Clarity of the initial lesions gradually gave way to a cloudy appearance and then they became colored like pus, yellow and ominous. Like Biblical Job, Kalluk was wrapped with agonizing sores from head to foot. His level of consciousness began to fluctuate, and soon he slipped into a hopeless coma. On the ninth day of his illness, merciful death ended his suffering.

Communicable diseases had been extinct for over a century, so not many people were aware of any of their signs and symptoms. Concord policemen came calling a few days into Kalluk's illness, and they were completely baffled. Having no one with any medical expertise in the village, they had simply shrugged it off as some weird Eskimo disease. They had noted contraband animal skins on the young man's bed, and marked him for ultimate punishment if he survived his infirmity.

A week after Kalluk died, the whole village started getting sick, one by one. The Concord policemen surveyed the situation now with a new urgency. They reviewed the course of the dead Eskimo's disease, and decided that the prudent course of action would be to evacuate to a safer location.

"Northern Sector Base! Northern Sector Base! Send a chopper immediately! Request permission to abandon Grise Fiord for now," the policeman radioed urgently. After he explained the situation to his superiors, his unit was shortly retrieved from the outpost. There would be a temporary postponement of northern pacification while sick Inuit fended for themselves.

Even at the main base in Montreal, medical care was rudimentary at best. No one considered isolating the evacuated policemen, and they were not examined or questioned by medical personnel despite their story of sick Eskimos.

The men evacuated from Grise Fiord reveled in the freedom of a larger base and kept late hours partying and making merry with their peers. Several days after their arrival, however, they each gradually developed the same high fever, the same headache, and all other symptoms that had afflicted citizens of the Arctic village. Before anyone considered the implications, everyone on the base had been exposed to the disease in the crowded barracks.

Men and women in Concord forces were constantly coming and going to all parts of the world from the base, and swarms of jet helicopters disseminated them efficiently. It would not have been too late to halt the disease completely at this point with simple quarantine measures, but weeks passed with no one contemplating such a move. Only after bodies began to accumulate did the base commander send out a call for help, and by then it was too late. Smallpox, an old nemesis believed long abolished, had been resurrected from the banks of that remote Arctic river to mete out destruction on mankind once again.

It would have been much better a hundred years earlier. In the squalor of the twenty-second century regime of Father Hammer, hardly anyone had even a basic education. Filth and ignorance prevailed, making transmission easier and quicker than it had been in the Dark Ages. A torrent of virus swept first across North America, leaving a staggering percentage of the remaining population dead. By the time the outbreak reached other continents, it was fully appreciated by the remnant medical community that this unknown disease was clinically identical to smallpox of old.

"Can we confirm that this is really smallpox, Dr. Reason?" asked Dr. Andrew Swift. Both were physicians in the Concord army stationed in England.

"In the old days we could have done viral cultures," replied Reason. "But I'm afraid we've lost that capability, doctor. From clinical signs it has to be *variola major*, and a brutally virulent strain at that."

The aging physician peered into an ancient laboratory microscope at a sample of blood while his bald head reflected overhead light like it was polished. "The blood count is consistent, too."

"And there are no vaccines," noted Swift, running his fingers through his hair.

"Even if we could do the research, Swift, where do you think we would get billions of doses before this disease runs its course?" asked Reason, folding his arms and looking out a window, a look of resignation crossing his face. He rubbed his right hand and felt a small bump where his implanted chip was located.

"Then our only tool is quarantine. We must advise the Father of this necessary course of action," answered Swift.

"Of course," replied the older doctor with resignation and a touch of sadness in his voice. "I'll call our commander and request permission to transmit to Rome."

The Father received news about the epidemic with no hint of surprise. He knew all there was to know, and never admitted any deficiency of knowledge. Still, it would be necessary to take steps to protect his loyal troops.

"Ersatzson, you have your instructions regarding protection of our forces. Nothing is to interfere with implementation," he ordered. "There are other diseases lurking undetected as well. The people have little strength to resist. It is an opportune time."

"Yes, Father. I have already instituted appropriate steps. You have another matter that you will express as well?"

"You never fail to perceive my true intentions, comrade. Announce to our world that we will experience an invasion from a force that is unstoppable. I am in contact with the leader of this principality, and it is useless to resist at this time. The energy of this invader will come upon us against our wishes, but it will remove many troublesome people from our midst. It will then withdraw and leave us unhindered. Tell them that I have an agreement with an alien power that is approaching. Tell people that it is not of this world and will trouble us only momentarily as we move on to triumph."

"As you say, Father. I will be proceeding as you have directed. Glory to the Father."

Ersatzson ordered only a limited quarantine. Restrictions applied only to Concord forces, who were to identify and isolate all cases and exposures within their ranks. They were to totally withdraw from the civilian population until the disease burned itself out.

No instructions, no assistance, no hope was offered to suffering masses of people. The plague proceeded like a red tide across all continents, leaving billions dead in its wake. Corpses piled high in the cities, and governing authorities were nowhere in evidence to effect their removal. Clouds of vultures and flies converged on the stinking bodies, adding immeasurably to a climate of hopelessness and dread among the living. The dreadful sores always left those people who managed to survive the disease horribly scarred.

*   *   *

Jacob Thompson was getting sick of war. He lost five more men during their latest raid on a Concord warehouse, many more than he could spare. His band was now down to little more than a dozen, including hardened and deadly Luke Walker, his lieutenant. Supplies were ever harder to come by, and Concord tactics seemed increasingly difficult to counter. Thompson himself had almost been killed some time ago by a round that skimmed his chest cavity, necessitating a lengthy period of recuperation.

As they made their way back into hiding under cover of darkness, he pondered what the future might hold. Death, he concluded grimly. Death for him and all who followed him. They had killed perhaps hundreds of Concord soldiers, but was it worth it? He honestly couldn't answer the question, and had indeed never before considered it seriously. They had enough from this latest raid that they could hang on for a while longer. Long enough to do some serious thinking, and maybe long enough to let his men rest and ponder some, as well. In their isolation they had at least avoided the epidemic that stalked the world, and they lived as rare free men. Their ability to resist became more feeble with each hazardous attack, though, and he felt more and more convinced that his quest was futile.

They had been able to rewire a captured radio, and by trying different frequency bands every night they had found a few isolated groups and individuals who were resisting, but they were all far away. It was depressing to communicate sometimes, because none of the fighters seemed to have any good news of any kind.

The only hope was of the spiritual variety. There was more religion plying contraband airways than he ever thought existed. Sometimes he would sit and listen, intrigued at the fervency of some radio operators. It all sounded very interesting, this promise of rest and peace they seemed to be offering.

*   *   *

The little group on the Morgan farm fared much better than the general population. They established their own quarantine system as soon as they heard about the disease, laid in a supply of food and water, and essentially sealed themselves off from the rest of the population in a kind of reverse isolation not unlike Concord forces were practicing. Their farming operation was shut down completely during the epidemic, so it was actually a time of respite for the beleaguered little group.

"Uncle Jamie," asked Molly as she scooped a ration of dried soybeans, their main diet item, out of the ancient metal pot that sat in one corner of the kitchen, "How long do we have to keep this up?"

She had developed a great deal of affection and respect for Jamie Barnes, and had taken to calling him "Uncle" after several months as a new member of the family. She set about preparing a meager meal for the others as she awaited his answer.

"As long as Concord police are gone, we'd better stay in. They left because of the epidemic and they won't be back until it's over. We come out when they come back."

Eventually Concord police did return, and Barnes cautiously questioned them about what had happened. He learned from Captain Darwin Archer that many billions of people, perhaps a third of the world's population, had died. Even the hardened policeman seemed a little less condescending as he related the appalling statistics.

And this was only the beginning of the havoc of disease. Many other viruses and bacteria inexplicably resurrected, and a weakened population suffered substantial additional sickness and death.

*   *   *

As he worked fertile soil in a remote section of his renewables garden, Buck Morgan encountered resistance to his effort to spade through a dense root system. He pushed harder, and the loam still failed to yield. He applied a ferocious shove on the handle of his implement, and resistance broke free suddenly, smashing his hand against a metal retaining wall. Blood spurted from the gash, and he dropped his tool and placed his other hand over the raw wound. He headed back via a long walkway to the control room, where he knew that competent help was readily available.

"Calvin, I've cut myself. Might have broken a bone, too," said Morgan as a deep pain in his hand started to throb. As he wiped the area with a moistened towelette, he continued, "Formula for repair, please."

"No problem, Commander Bucko. You creatures of flesh and blood are so fragile," replied Calvin in a voice so carefree that Morgan would have sworn it was the real Jeremiah Smith speaking. Morgan inserted his injured hand into a diagnostics module and awaited the result.

"No tendon or nerve injury is apparent, but there is a small crack in the third metacarpal. Apply stem cell tissue glue externally and overlay with a living cast. You'll be fine tomorrow."

"Thanks, Doc Calvin," said Morgan. A soothing balm oozed in layers from the module onto all appropriate places, and his pulsating pain subsided almost instantaneously.

There was cutting edge twenty-first century medical care on board the *Ursa C*. Buck Morgan had no way of knowing his home planet was now deprived of such advances. Morgan didn't have to worry about disease himself—he had come from the golden age of human achievement, and had been given a universal anti-infection vaccine as a youth. His excellent health throughout life was adequate testimony to the effectiveness of science at combating human disease.

Two watches later, his hand was well enough that he easily played "*2001: A Space Odyssey*" on his now-worn Japanese piano, while he contemplated his utter confidence in science. He sometimes doubted his

445

sanity for taking this long journey, but the progress of mankind and advancement of science had to be worth the sacrifice. A defining attribute of Buck Morgan was this conviction, a hallmark he wore with considerable pride. After all, he had never even suffered from a cold in his entire life. And mighty science was the reason.

But Pandora's box had been opened on the earth once more, and centuries of scientific progress had been canceled in the process. Fiery chariots with rotary wings had carried disease in their wake to all parts of the world, and it would never be the same again.

CHAPTER 34

September 2167

Molly Hancock awoke with a start, as if some unseen hand had grasped her long, velvety brown hair. Her dark eyes widened in horror as she looked out the window into a still night sky. There were streams of light, like she had heard the Northern Lights described, but flowing like a vast river of white, seeming to ascend from the ground all around the horizon, as far as she could see.

In addition to magnificent rivulets of light, there was an indescribable rushing sound, a resonance like nothing she had never encountered. It reminded her vaguely of wind in the trees, but there was no wind at all. There was also something in the sound that conveyed a clear impression of distant screaming—no, shouting was more like it! Yes, like a crowd shouting and celebrating, but far away and indistinct.

She groped in the dark for a lamp, and finding none within grasp she moved toward the door of her bedroom. Her way was unexpectedly lighted by an inexplicable glow emanating through the window. The hair on back of her neck stood up and she felt a body-shaking chill as goose bumps appeared all over her. What on earth is happening? She stifled an impulse to scream and made her way through the opening into the dark hallway.

Halfway down the corridor she stopped, transfixed, at the sight of a luminescence coming from the Barnes' room. An unearthly light glowed brightly underneath their closed door, like a thousand high intensity bulbs. Heaven help me, she cried deep in her soul, what is going on? Across the hall from their room, that same supernatural glow emanated from Grandma Robin's room, like a mirror image of the Barnes' door. Just as she was about to open her mouth, the intensity of the phenomenon began to subside, and then suddenly all was completely dark. The rushing noise outside began to gradually fade as well, and just as quickly, it was gone.

All became as quiet as death. No movement. No sound. No light at all. She moved cautiously toward the room she knew Jamie and Martha Barnes occupied. Feeling her way along in absolute blackness, she bumped into a small hallway table, upsetting it and causing it to come crashing to the floor. She shrieked involuntarily, but stifled the noise with her hand as the sudden commotion dissipated.

After an eternity of groping carefully along the narrow passage, she at last reached their door. She tried to call the names of her friends and benefactors, but she was unable to make a sound, for reasons that escaped her. She tapped tentatively on the door, and her feeble knocks created a hollow ringing tone that was illogically terrifying to her. She forced herself to knock harder, and unknowingly she began to hit the door harder and harder, each blow making a noise that seemed thunderous. Finally she stopped, her hands bleeding from the pounding, and tried again to say their names. Why wouldn't they come to the door? Why wouldn't words come out of her mouth?

"Jamie? Martha?" she finally squeaked, the most difficult words she had ever spoken. The ice broken, she repeated with her voice what she had previously done with her fists, resulting in a veritable screaming of their names. The effect was made even more pronounced by an utter absence of response. Feeling her terror rising again, she grasped the doorknob and tried to turn it.

Everything seemed to be resisting her. Even the doorknob wouldn't turn. She was soon holding the inanimate obstruction firmly in a grip like a vise, her own bloody hand lubricating the knob and making it slippery and unresponsive. She kept turning and pushing, struggling with all her might to enter the bedroom. With a sudden burst of strength she managed to rotate the contrary device, and she crashed suddenly, unexpectedly, through the dark opening. The force of her entry sent her sprawling in total disorder on the floor, her nightclothes in disarray around her.

She lay still for a short interval, letting her senses catch up with her emotions. Where are the Barneses? Where are you people? Questions kept flooding in with no obvious answers. She sat up in total darkness and looked with unseeing eyes in the direction of the bed where the couple slept each night. Again she tried to use her voice.

"Jamie? Martha?"

No answer. She determined with resolve that this time she would be more methodical and less emotional, so she deliberately raised her voice and repeated the names with more force. Still no answer. Where are they?

She rolled over on her hands and knees and crawled to the side of the bed, running into it with some force. She put her hands up on the side and felt her way along to the top. She then pushed cautiously toward the center of the bed, encountering no resistance this time except for rumpled covers. With more confidence she explored deeper, but she never discovered anything more than sheets and a blanket, all peeled back as if the two had arisen deliberately.

But where could they have gone? Is this related to the eerie lights and the rushing noise? Could they have gone into the yard to see what was happening? Not likely, she concluded, or they would have returned immediately when they heard me making this racket.

Finally she located an old perpetual hand light in Jamie's bedside table, and tentatively switched it on. Everything in the room was in place, it seemed. Worn clothes the two had removed at bedtime were neatly hung on a closet door, and their tattered shoes were still beside the bed. To her amazement, remnant garments the couple had worn to bed were also there, jumbled now among threadbare bed linens.

After searching thoroughly, she dashed across the dark hall to Grandma Robin's bedroom, where she shoved the door open harshly and assaulted that bed like one deranged. The old woman was gone, too. The world had gone completely crazy.

Frantic now, she began to move about the house to see if she had somehow missed them somewhere. In the dark kitchen she stumbled over the heavy metal storage pot, dislodging its heavy alloy lid, which clattered across the room. Loud noise and clamor once more startled her brutally.

She recovered shakily and completed another scouring of the place. There was no trace of them and no evidence they had vacated of their own volition. Nothing was missing except the three people, as far as she could see. She finally eased back to her own room, noticing that the light of dawn was beginning to infiltrate the eastern sky. She had no idea how long she had been awake, but she felt a weariness creeping over her that was oppressive and heavy, like a necklace of cast iron. Puzzlement filled her mind anew as she gazed blankly out the window. Yes, it was now definitely getting daylight outside.

She moved with stone-like inertia toward a window to gaze at the quickening light. A smaller house across the way, where rebellious Jody Barnes lived, looked exactly the same as it had the night before. It appeared that nothing had changed in the farmyard, where all out buildings were in place and undisturbed. Is this some kind of weird dream? She purposed to look again in the bedroom down the hall, and having done so she found it exactly as it had been earlier in the dark. Returning to the old woman's bedroom on a thought, she rummaged among her worn bed coverings, and sure enough, it was there. Grandma Robin's shabby nightgown, just like the couple's clothes, remained undisturbed on her disheveled bed.

Returning to her room once more, she removed her scruffy gown and placed it carefully in a drawer for safekeeping. She put on her own remnant clothing, little more than rags, and her worn-out shoes. She would go to Jody Barnes' house and see if he knew anything about this mystery.

The old screen door squeaked noisily as she exited. The creaking sound awakened thousands of insects that were resting on and around the front porch. Myriad whirring wings created a familiar dark cloud all around her as she walked. Oh, come winter, she thought to herself, and end this merciless bug assault.

Halfway to the low, white house across the way she stopped short and cupped her hand over one ear. An awful noise in the distance made her blood run cold. Someone far across the valley was screaming. Now who could that be, and why are they so terrified? The plaintive noise became a short series of shouts, and then all was quiet again. Strange, she thought. There shouldn't even be anybody on that part of the farm. But she wasn't surprised that there were trespassers out there, since it was almost impossible to keep marauding bands of desperate outlaws away from a food source like the farm. Maybe Concord police had caught and punished someone. No, she concluded, she hadn't heard any telling hiss of gunfire.

She now hastened her steps toward the smaller house, and amid a dark cloud of droning flies and mosquitoes she ascended some low steps and approached the rickety door. A dread seized her at this point, a burning apprehension that she might somehow be completely alone. Composure fled from her and she banged loudly, pleadingly, on the wood, wincing a bit at the renewed pain in her bruised and bloody hand.

"Yeah?" came a welcome salutation from inside, sleepiness heavy in the voice.

"Jody? Thank God you're here!" she exclaimed, relief rushing over her like a flood.

"Where did you think I'd be? What do you want, Molly? Dad want me for something?" the youth inquired in a distinctly annoyed voice, his usual impatience showing. "I wish he'd let me rest just one day. The only time I get off is church day. Sarah isn't feeling too well. I need to stay home today."

"I can't find your parents. They just disappeared last night. There was this weird light and a strange noise when I woke up. When everything got back to normal, both of them were gone. Got any ideas where they went?"

"Gone? Can't be. The only way we have to travel is the big truck or the tractor. Or walk."

"I see the truck and tractor over where they always are, beside the barn," said Molly fretfully. "Let me in before these bugs make me disappear, too."

She waited as patiently as possible, warding off troublesome insects as best she could but carefully avoiding slapping or damaging any of them. Finally, after some bedeviled and impatient minutes, an unkempt Jody Barnes opened the door and let her enter.

"You say they're gone?" His sleepiness had dissipated, and he was fully alert.

"Gone. I have no idea where. What a crazy night."

"Did they take anything with them?"

"No. Not even their clothes. Nor shoes. Nothing, as far as I can see. Jody, I got scared out of my wits last night."

"Wait, Molly. Back up and tell me the whole thing from the start."

"What's going on, you two?" asked Sarah, her pretty face appearing in the doorway in the subdued light.

Sarah was very likable, and had assimilated fairly well into the Barnes family. There had remained tension between Jody and his parents over her, even though the boy had reluctantly agreed to treating the relationship as if she were a real wife. Jody and Sarah, still unmarried in a formal fashion, were expecting their first child within days. Jamie and Martha Barnes had hoped that arrival of the baby would be an occasion for improving the smoldering feud between them and their son.

"Sarah, Molly says Mom and Dad are gone. Just like that, they've disappeared. She was trying to tell me about how weird last night seemed. Go ahead, Molly."

"Well, something woke me up. I looked out the window and there were these streams of light in the sky, so bright it was almost daylight outside. And there was a strange noise, too, kind of like a big crowd of people shouting far off. I went down the hall to get your parents to look, but there was a brilliant light coming from underneath their door, and it scared me. Then everything settled back to normal, except they were gone. I don't know any more than that. Oh, Grandma Robin is gone, too."

"What? Grandma Robin, too! This is getting crazier by the minute. I know Dad wouldn't leave us like that, no way. He's behind in his work. We discussed the schedule last night and we have plenty to do. He wasn't planning to leave. He is so truthful it makes me sick sometimes, but I'm sure he wouldn't do anything drastic without telling me," the unkempt young man raved as he pulled a bedraggled shirt over his head. "Let's go have a look around. There's something strange going on here."

"Hurry back, Jody. These pains are getting more persistent by the minute," Sarah called after them. She grimaced as she held her bulging abdomen, and sat down to let the sensation pass.

Molly and Jody waded through hordes of insects back to the main house, leaving Sarah in relative safety in the smaller dwelling. As they reached the steps, Jody grabbed Molly's arm and hurried her along, practically dragging her swiftly across the porch. He then roughly pushed her through the door and slammed it briskly behind them.

"What are you doing, Jody? Are you crazy?"

"Whew, that was close! Did you see them, Molly?"

"See what? I didn't see anything. Except that you nearly dislocated my arm."

"Dogs. They were crossing the barnyard toward us in a dead run. They must have smelled where you crossed this morning. They've been a little aggressive lately, but they've been keeping their distance. That's the first time I've seen them when I thought they might actually attack. But I could see blood in their eyes this time."

"Everything's going haywire, Jody. As you can see, no sign of your parents or your grandmother here."

They toured the house, and Jody concluded in deep puzzlement that Molly was entirely right. As they entered scanty light in the kitchen, Jody noticed the floor was literally covered with dried beans.

"Holy smokes, what happened here?" asked Jody as the two of them sat down at the kitchen table.

"An accident in the dark. I'll clean it up," replied Molly in a monotone.

Jody sat quietly in thought for a while before he spoke again.

"We've got to find out if they're the only ones. If there are major numbers of people gone, especially one category of people, this could be—I hate to even think this could be the case, because I've always laughed when he mentioned it—but this could be what Dad has been predicting for years. This just might be a true act of God."

"Jody! I thought you didn't believe any of that. Wait…Father Hammer did say the other night—according to that Ersatzson guy who talks on the radio all the time—that some people were going to be removed by some kind of force. He said it was an extraterrestrial power, like some kind of space creatures. But God? The prediction by Ersatzson seems more plausible to me."

"We'll see. I don't see how space creatures could be involved in what I'm thinking about," he said as he pulled up an ancient window shade and looked outside. "Meanwhile, those dogs out there are a problem. I need to somehow move Sarah over here, where we have a pretty good supply of food, and then I'll take the tractor and see what I can find out. If the police ask, I'll try to convince them I'm on official farming business."

Jody decided to wait until the dogs were sleeping or out of view, then he would make a frantic dash for the big tractor. Inside the cab he was safe from both insects and dogs. Thankfully, he had seen his dad filling its fuel tank the evening before, so there should be sufficient quantity to take him on a lengthy scouting trip. If he could just get aboard the machine.

As soon as it seemed the coast was clear, he opened the rickety screen door as quietly as possible and looked around carefully. Seeing no animals, he leaped from the end of the porch and ran like a greyhound, hoping against hope that his father had not locked the tractor cab. Out of one corner of his eye, he caught sight of a fluid movement to his left, but he dared not slow down to look. Grasping the door handle, he twisted it gingerly, and the handle moved gratifyingly. Opening the cab, he jumped in and slammed the door shut, just in time to hear a large, hurtling object smash into the clear window with a tremendous thud. A dazed canine lay on the ground, a giant brute that looked to weigh well over 100 pounds. It recovered quickly and was soon erect and alert again.

Whew, he thought gratefully. That was close! He looked down at the snarling creature, saliva dripping from its gruesome mouth, and shuddered at the prospect of those sharp teeth ripping at his flesh. The dog was soon joined by several others, all of them looking hungrily at him through the protecting glass. The pack backed off to a respectful distance as the tractor engine began churning loudly.

His immediate aim was to get the women together, so he drove the machine to the kitchen window and motioned Molly to open it. When she did, he shouted over the motor's din.

"I'm going to get Sarah and bring her over here right now. Be prepared to help her in when I come back. We don't have room for any mistakes."

Molly nodded in agreement, indicating she understood. She had watched his close call and knew now the danger those canines presented. Off the young man roared, the overpowering motion and noise temporarily putting the pack to flight. He used the respite to load Sarah and then drove the short distance back to the main house with his precious cargo. Molly opened the front door, and finding the area appearing safe, she ran down the steps to help Sarah. They breathed a sigh of relief as the door slammed behind them, and listened as the tractor's noise faded in the distance.

"This is pretty darned unusual, huh?" Sarah stated, overlooking the obvious affirmative. "I wonder where they went?"

"We may know when Jody gets back. Jody has some ideas. Say, Jamie has a legal radio, you know, the kind permanently fixed to the Concord band, in his room. Let's turn it on. I should have thought of that earlier."

Molly hastily retrieved the instrument, which she hadn't seen in some months. Jamie Barnes had seldom listened to it because it broadcast only programming designed to promote the Father and his grandiose plan for planet Earth. Maybe there would be something about the strange phenomena if it were widespread.

Molly pressed the activate button, and it crackled to life, indicating its battery was still functional. The familiar and authoritative voice was exhilarating, stimulating, even electrifying. Christian Ersatzson extolled jubilantly and incessantly about the joys and benefits of the Concord for the Development of Humanity, astounding progress toward multiple goals, and diverse plans and dreams for humankind. Finally a newsbreak was announced, and the two waited patiently to see what they might learn.

"Do not be dismayed, brothers and sisters, at the disappearance of some of the most troublesome among you. The Father has decreed that such individuals be removed to another location in the heavens, and in his infinite wisdom he summoned followers from one of his advanced planets to retrieve humanity's worst for re-indoctrination elsewhere. Objects seen in the sky some hours ago were not unidentified, because the Father knows all things, and he knows the purpose thereof. Do not be troubled or afraid. All is well and the Father bids you light and persistence in our quest."

"Space creatures? That's exactly what he's claiming happened!" Molly exclaimed, her mouth a wide oval.

"Sh-h! Listen!" Sarah whispered loudly, putting her finger to her lips. "How many disappeared?"

The question was directed at an unhearing radio but Ersatzson answered as if he were in the room.

"A few million zealots, all restless and rebellious, are gone. Our Earth will profit infinitely by their absence. Calm and peace and rejoicing in heart are orders from the Father. All will comply."

The program switched back to a propaganda-style format, praising endless benefits of the new world order. Molly switched off the radio and placed it firmly on the table.

"So, aliens got Jody's parents because they were troublemakers. Well, that part sure doesn't make sense. The Father and his strange visitors knew a lot more than the Concord police, because they didn't look upon Jamie as a troublemaker. They gave him special protection, in fact. He was one of only a few farmers who still produced a lot."

"Maybe the guy does have supernatural abilities and knew who needed to be taken out. Maybe we should believe in him, Molly. Our priest says to listen to him."

Sarah exhaled deeply and patted her bulging stomach as she said the words. Molly looked at the expectant young woman with pity, knowing that she had the ordeal of birth to accomplish shortly, but without benefit of any medical help. The Adrian hospital was now a barracks for Concord police and soldiers, so the people were left to their own devices in all situations.

"I think I know another possible explanation, Sarah," she said quietly. "We'll have to wait for Jody to return before we get too involved in details, though. What he discovers will tell us for certain. Let's wait until then to talk about it."

"I believe I'm going to be too busy to talk, anyway. I'm having hard contractions," she groaned. "Know how to deliver a baby, Molly?"

"What? No, I don't! Oh, I wish Jody would come back. I wish Martha were here. Oh, God, help us!"

"You don't have to do anything. Just let it happen. Just boil some water and sterilize a string to tie off the cord. And we'll need a sterile knife to cut it with."

"Oh, really? You've done it before, I guess?"

"Oh, not me personally. But I've been there when my sister had two or three. It isn't that hard for the standby person. But it hurts like blazes for the one going through it," she groaned as more labor pains seized her.

Molly took her tenderly by the hand and carefully led her into the spare bedroom. There she placed a torn sheet on the bare mattress, the extra bed covers already having been used to make clothing. Returning to the kitchen, Molly used a small amount of precious ethanol to heat some water, and then she placed a length of string and a paring knife in it. She left them in the boiling water for several minutes while she hurriedly scooped handfuls of spilled beans back into the steel pot, then she went back and shut off the fuel. If that were all there is to it, she could handle it. She wished she had chosen to undergo midwife training when offered the opportunity many months ago by a lady at church.

The quiet was broken shortly by the loud noise of the tractor as Jody returned. Molly ran to a window and watched as he entered the farmyard. All the dogs seemed to be completely out of sight, so it should be safe for now, she thought to herself.

Riding in the tractor cab with Jody was a tall, gaunt man wearing clothes that were the best preserved any of them had seen in years. Molly had known Abraham Rosenthal all her life. He was an impassioned Jew whose family had lived in Adrian forever, it seemed. Jody parked jam up to the front stoop and dashed quickly through the door after checking carefully for danger, but Rosenthal seemed unconcerned as he sauntered deliberately into the house. Jody entered the erstwhile labor suite with a deep look of bewilderment.

"They're all gone. I went to Aunt Faye's first, and the whole family is missing. And so are all the others I suspected might be."

"What? Faye and her family too? Jody, what is going on?"

"The whole church is gone. Need I say more?"

Rosenthal had a full day's growth of beard shadowing his face, and his dark hair was in such tumult that it imparted an angry look. Despite his appearance, his bright eyes glowed with a deep and genuine concern. He knew that he could do little to help physically, but he was determined to offer what he could. And what he could give them was the facts as he saw them.

"Kids, don't believe any false explanations. You're going to hear plenty."

"From whom, Mr. Rosenthal?" asked Molly as she adjusted a dilapidated pillow under Sarah's head.

"The Father, sweet girl. His version of this great disappearance of people is nothing but an absolute lie. Don't believe a word he says."

Sarah groaned as another labor contraction wracked her. Molly squeezed her hand and looked up wistfully at Rosenthal. She said nothing, but her sadness was obvious, glaringly transparent.

"Believe me. Get on your knees and get to know Jesus the Messiah before it's too late. Ask him into your life, no matter what it costs you. Don't give in to any demands of the Concord, even on penalty of death. It's the only way. And may God bless you all."

He pointed a bony finger at them as he spoke in order to make his point, and his voice was as serious as a graveyard. It was obvious that they were listening intently, but they had their hands full with this progressing labor. He turned on his heels and walked briskly outside and down the road without another word.

"Jody, stop him! The dogs will get him," Molly said in alarm, running to the door.

"I don't think so, I don't think so. He's completely safe, he says. I picked him up within a hundred yards of a pack and they were avoiding him like he was the dogcatcher. They seem to be afraid of him, for some reason."

"Really? That's strange. Uh, I hear Sarah groaning. I think she needs us."

*　　*　　*

Aboard the starship *Ursa C*, inscrutable Calvin was routinely scanning a cluster of deep space monitoring instruments, twenty-first century technology that was able to detect and analyze all known spectra of radiation. He trained the group's main antenna on the oncoming solar system around the Sun, where a colossal burst of energy appeared to be emanating from that direction. He adjusted all monitors to finest focus, and pinpointed a source of activity so intense it appeared to be more powerful than an immense pulsar. Like a black hole swallowing the home planet, the source seemed to be voracious, so profound it appeared to be capable of devouring matter at an astounding rate. What could that be? He queried all his archives, but found no ready explanation.

"Commander Bucko, take a look at this before I blow a circuit. You're going to have to input some new data if this phenomenon is to be analyzed accurately," said Calvin to Buck Morgan, who had just entered the control room. Bewilderment permeated the artificial man's voice in highly uncommon fashion.

"Let me see," said Morgan in a concerned manner as he took his seat. Not much confounded his artificial partner when it came to analysis of incoming data.

Calvin's holographic finger traced the energy measurements, and the extraordinary implications quickly dawned on Morgan. He had never seen anything like it.

"I'm considering the possibility of a colossal alien spacecraft, almost planetary in size, to create such an energy vacuum. That's a very unlikely scenario, to be sure, but one of the few phenomena that might explain such a bizarre occurrence where no such disturbance ought to exist," said Calvin, his speech coming through as if he were afflicted with genuine worry.

Despite searching all the chronicles thoroughly, Calvin could find no logical explanation. The huge eruption of energy was of astounding proportions and was traveling at—they couldn't believe the reading—infinity! Intensity, speed, and frequency were all completely off the usual scales. How could this be?

The burst lasted only a few minutes, and then subsided leaving no trace. Perplexed, Morgan asked Calvin to repeat his data bank search of all possible conclusions. None seemed to make any sense. The search for extraterrestrial life had been abandoned after more than a hundred years of intensive searching, so an alien spacecraft seemed far-fetched. The only explanation offered was—again, Morgan couldn't believe the readout—*theological* in nature.

* * *

Evening came to the farm back on Earth, and stars sparkled normally overhead. Even the moon, in a full phase, shone pleasantly through the window. Hours were whiled away amid talk about penetrating, eternal thoughts, and nearly forgotten bits of obscure information. Much of what they discussed pertained to ideas left by the departed couple that had influenced their lives profoundly. There were some moments of sorrow as they reflected on the convictions and faith of the missing people they loved. Why hadn't the three young people had better vision before this happened?

"Jody, what do you think really happened to your mom and dad?" asked Sarah, her bright eyes seeking real answers for the first time in her life. She had known many men intimately in her time as a priestess in her family's pagan temple, but she now treasured this one man more than all of them, and she knew that she could trust his judgment.

"I'm afraid to tell you, hon. I don't know if you'll believe it."

"I know what you're going to say, Jody," said Molly in a low and melancholy tone of voice. "I can't believe what fools we've all been."

Jody nodded in agreement, and Molly thought she saw him wipe away a tear. He regained his composure and looked directly at them.

"There's a principle at work here that I've never before recognized. We're blind unless God himself opens our eyes. I think Mom and Dad are with God, Sarah. They were the wisest of people, believing as they did and making no apologies for it. I regret that I was such an idiot. We could all be with them instead of being here under the heel of this fanatical regime."

"Is it really too late for us?"

"Too late to go with them, yes. I remember what they taught me, even if I didn't believe a word of it. How did it go, Molly? You had even more instruction than I did. Or at least you were more willing to listen."

"Believers removed. Great tribulation. We're doubtless in that ordeal, unless the Father is telling the truth and space aliens got all the people who are missing."

461

"But is it too late for us?" pleaded Sarah, an extreme anxiety intruding into her pain between frequent contractions. It appeared that she might be on the edge of delirium.

"No, dear Sarah, it's not really too late for us," counseled Molly gently. "What we have to do is accept God's offer of free grace and salvation in Jesus Christ—the Messiah who died on a cruel Roman cross nearly 2,200 years ago to pay for our sins. It's all about that gift of God's son that Abraham Rosenthal is preaching now. Abe didn't believe it either until these last few days. Now he's convinced it's true. And it's clear to me now, too, but it's impossible to see until the blinders are removed."

Jody nodded in agreement, and cradled his head sorrowfully in his hands as he looked at the floor. He broke into spontaneous, halting prayer a few minutes later, the first time in his life he had been so bold and sincere in any such matter. Sarah cried.

While the labor progressed naturally and normally, all three people came to some mystifying conclusions, and made some deep commitments. They innocently dedicated their newfound faith to the memory of Jamie and Martha Barnes, not knowing if it was right or wrong to do so. Somehow, they all found a profound degree of peace in their simple act. Jamie and Martha, wherever they were, had to know they would be okay.

And just after midnight, a new Barnes entered the world, a healthy baby boy. He was as beautiful and flawless as any baby ever born, with eyes as dark as ebony and a head full of curly hair. The three rejoiced richly in the newness of life, and reveled in the timeless wonder of new birth.

They named him Abraham.

CHAPTER 35

September 2167

"...and by the wild beasts of the earth." Revelation 6:8

A scrawny man swung hard at an attacking mongrel, striking the creature on its jaw and lacerating his hand. His pitiful wife screamed loudly and desperately as she was pulled to the ground, mingling her blood with dust that billowed from swirling chaos on a narrow field road. The force of Chip Hansen's blow sent the dog momentarily sprawling into the wheeling pack that surrounded his struggling, terrified wife. One big canine grabbed the petite woman by her throat and a massive spurt of blood told Hansen instantly that all was lost. He turned and gave his second daughter a hard push up a cottonwood tree, where she joined her sister in relative safety among some lower branches. He made a final desperate glance toward his dead wife, and felt a sickening in his stomach as her fragile frame was pulled apart. He spun around and jumped as high as possible to try and join his girls.

"Climb, girls, climb! Higher!" he screamed at his sobbing, filthy children. He hugged the tree and made several frantic pushes with his legs toward refuge. He had one hand on the lowest branch when a big, growling animal lunged at him again. Before he could get enough elevation, his left foot was fastened viselike in the grip of a mouth like that of a pit bull. Blood and saliva mixed together ran down the animal's flanks, quickly tinting its light hair along the length of its muscular body. The man struggled valiantly, pain from his crushed foot causing him to grimace in agony as he tried to wrestle free. The dog shook its entire body fiercely, using its body weight to try and dislodge the man.

Another dog in the mob spied Hansen's flailing right leg, kicking fiendishly at the cur clamped like a steel trap on his other foot. The second creature left the bloody carcass to the rest of the surging, ripping, voracious swarm. It whirled like lightening and launched itself into the air on the second bound. It seized the free foot and quickly broke it in jaws like iron. The man cried out and looked pleadingly at his girls as his hands began to slip, and his fingernails tore away like paper. Over two hundred pounds of crushing teeth and agile shaking bodies clinched to his pulverized feet were too much for him, and he fell between the terrible beasts. Both animals immediately released the disabled feet and surged simultaneously for the man's throat. He made a feeble effort to fend them off, but it was hopeless. His last sounds were a gurgling scream as he drowned in his own blood, and mercifully lost consciousness as his carotid arteries were severed.

*   *   *

Jody Barnes wiped his brow with a worn and soiled shirtsleeve and put his grimy hat back on. Dirty sweat burned his eyes as he worked a soybean field under the watchful eye of nearby Concord police. A blue and white cruiser eased along a farm road at the prescribed twenty miles per hour, its slow pace prolonging the uncomfortable and unwelcome scrutiny. Finally, the threatening vehicle moved out of sight down the long road that led to Adrian.

It had been several days since the family discovered that so many of their clan were missing. They had said nothing to the police, who seemed to have scarcely noticed the absent people. So many people were disappearing for various reasons now that it was a common occurrence. Thrust suddenly into the role of chief farmer, Jody rose to the challenge and determined to do everything in his power to help his little band survive.

As he drove in the tractor, he felt quite safe from the unnaturally emboldened predatory beasts that abounded around the farm. That morning there had been a giant grizzly in the end of the south field, crossing nonchalantly as if it owned the place. It had showed only marginal concern at the approaching noisy machine, and had risen up on massive hind legs for a closer look. Jody remembered shuddering as the beast bared white fangs and mouthed an inaudible roar before disappearing into dense bottomland brush.

The maturing young man had shored up the walls of the big house, using lumber scavenged from the barn and the unoccupied smaller house. He had boarded up each window as well. Inside the group should be safe from wild dogs and mountain lions, but he wasn't so sure about grizzly bears. He hoped none would come calling, since he was pretty certain a big bear could tear through almost anything he could construct.

As he neared the field edge, his cultivators smoothly pitched plowed earth toward the stems of the growing beans. He looked back at his work and was quite pleased at the progress. Yes, his dad had taught him well, even if he had been a very unwilling and recalcitrant learner. Thoughts of his father stirred some deep regret that made him feel sad as he worked the field.

There was something that wasn't quite right about the tree line along a lane that led up a hill away from the main road. He couldn't be certain, but it looked like there was something different, maybe a touch of unnatural color in the trees. His cultivating finished, he locked the left brake and pivoted his tractor around for a closer look.

He motored through an open gate and wheeled up the lane. Before he got there he could see a mongrel pack slinking away slowly, retreating ever so reluctantly. He was obviously disturbing a kill site. There was a large spot of oily stain sprinkled with red at the base of a big cottonwood, and another farther over. There was no carcass, nor any visible bones, so he could only imagine grimly what the dogs might have eaten.

As he reached the bottom of the tree, he was surprised to see two tiny figures cowering about halfway up. The small girls huddled in the crotch of a massive limb, covering themselves with green leaves and trying to make themselves as invisible as possible. Jody eased his big machine up beside the massive trunk and shut down the growling engine. He popped open a side window and leaned out.

"Hi, girls," he began a bit awkwardly. "What happened?"

They said nothing but tried all the more to hide, retreating like squirrels to the opposite side of the cottonwood.

"Aw, come on, I'm not going to hurt you. I might even help you, if you'll let me. Come on down and I'll ride you to my house."

Neither girl moved a muscle or said a word, presenting a growing dilemma for Jody. He knew he couldn't stay here indefinitely, because the police would deal with him severely for wasting fuel, should they return right away. Yet something drew him to persist, despite the danger.

"Now girls, I've got to go back to the farm. If you've got a better plan than coming with me, fine. If not, you'd better start down right now. You're going to get awfully hungry and thirsty up there, and if you come down, the dogs will do the same thing to you they did to your, uh..."

Now the reaction was immediate. The smaller girl burst into tears, and the other shook uncontrollably and began to shout.

"Please, mister, don't let the dogs get us. Please!" She made some tentative movement as if she were going to climb down, then retreated with a pitiful whimper.

"For heaven's sake, come on down. I'll take you where you will be safe. And we'll have plenty to eat there."

Jody tried to be as soothing as possible now, feeling a little guilty as he realized the immense trauma these little ones must have endured. Were the dead people the family of these waifs?

Slowly, both girls unfurled their skinny arms and began to descend. When they finally reached Jody's tractor cab, he reached out and took each in turn and placed one on either side of him. He then started the motor again and backed down the narrow lane before wheeling the tractor toward home. During the short trip he was able to elicit only limited conversation with the two panicky adolescents.

As had become a necessary standard for him, he parked his machine virtually in the door, keeping to a minimum the dangerous distance to be traversed. He deliberately tucked a girl under each arm, and then dashed inside. Molly met him at the door and opened it, and then she slammed it resolutely behind them.

"Whom in the world do we have here?" she inquired, inspecting the half-starved girls. "Looks like they needed a little helping hand, huh?"

"Couldn't have been any more desperate. These are the Hansen girls. Dogs got their parents. They were trapped up a cottonwood tree and scared to death when I found them."

"Oh, no! I've never heard of anything so gruesome. Don't tell Sarah that, Jody. She's being stressed enough just having to nurse the baby."

"She'll have to know it in time, anyway. For now, let's just take care of these two little ones."

Both girls were excellent talkers, and they loosened up considerably on realizing that they were no longer in danger. They were sisters from Wichita, and both of them were twelve years old, one just barely so and the other approaching her thirteenth birthday. They could actually read and write, an uncommon talent in the world. Also, they conversed with a far higher degree of intelligence than the average vagrant. They were quite a bit smaller than typical children their age, due to chronic malnutrition and the effect of confluent insect bites. The older girl had a face badly scarred from smallpox. They related a disastrous tale of desperate flight from hopeless circumstances in the city to the east, traveling unmarked backcountry roads and seeking a refuge. There had been insufficient food, no clean water, hordes of biting insects, and misery all around them. Their father had been a biology professor at Wichita State University before recent monumental changes had cost him his employment. He had moved to get away from there and try to find a better life elsewhere.

"He was going to get us to a safer place, and then get us chipped there. He knew we couldn't move once we got the implants or the authorities would know we belonged elsewhere. They demand that you stay put, you know," said Rhonda Hansen, the larger and older girl.

"They're becoming more insistent about that chipping, too," observed Jody.

"When we got out of the city, there were lots of other people wandering around in the fields. None of us had any food. We drank water from streams, but it was impossible to find something to eat. We wound up eating bugs. I know the Father says that's wrong, but we were dying of hunger. Dad was a biologist and he said eating insects wouldn't hurt us. But we were careful that no one saw us doing it."

"Poor babies! You can just stay with us," Molly said as she stroked the matted hair of the smaller girl, whose name turned out to be Wanda. "I hope the Father gets what he deserves for all the suffering he's caused."

"I agree, but say that softly or not at all, Molly. You know how numerous their listening devices are," cautioned Jody in a whisper. "We can't afford to be glib in our conversation."

"You're right, but it makes me so angry," she replied, lowering her voice considerably. "There's nothing we can do anyway, I suppose, except try to care for urchins like these. I've been alone like they are now, so I know a little about how they must feel. Come into the kitchen, children, and we'll get you a good meal."

Beans retrieved from the big metal canister were shortly boiling on the stove. Over a nutritious soybean dinner the girls related how things had initially gone fairly well despite lack of decent food. Then suddenly the animals out there "went crazy," as their departed father had put it, and lost their instinctive fear of human beings. An enormous grizzly bear attacked another group of people in a creek bottom, killing all of them before they could escape. The Hansen family had watched in horror from a nearby hill, and had been frozen with terror. They faced the unavoidable prospect of coming down to drink water, despite the danger. Later, a large mountain lion had killed a big man near them as they slept, precipitating a harrowing midnight move to another location. Then it was packs of hungry feral dogs, the meanest and most ugly of all. Some mongrels were former pets that still wore collars, but in their newly liberated state the animals had mercilessly slashed into several groups of humans camping nearby. The Hansens had been miraculously spared from harm until that very morning, when luck had run out.

"Say, Rhonda, when did the animals 'go crazy,' as your dad put it?" asked Jody. "Was it four nights ago?"

"About, I think. It was that night the sky had all those funny lights and the wind made a weird rushing noise. All that commotion woke us

468

up. Everybody said it was creatures from outer space removing misfits from the earth. They said the Father had predicted something like that was going to happen."

"And next day you began seeing all the big predators—including wild dogs—aggressively eating people, didn't you?"

"That's right, now that you mention it. Dad kept saying he needed one of Grandpa Hansen's force field repulsers to keep animals away from us, but nobody knows exactly how he made them anymore. He was famous for inventing them."

"Really? What was that again, Rhonda?" asked Jody.

"Grandpa Hansen, Dad's grandfather. He invented some kind of thing to repel animals. Dad said nobody remembered how to make it now. He called it 'technology regression,' or something like that. He said he wanted to try and discover it again."

"I remember hearing about that device. Seems like it was used to prevent collisions between animals and vehicles back last century. There's one on the front of our old truck, but it doesn't work anymore, and I remember asking Dad what it was. Nobody knows how to fix it, though. I think my Dad mentioned your ancestor—your great-grandfather, I guess he was, Rhonda."

"All I know is we weren't able to do anything to protect anybody. Poor Mom and Dad," she sobbed as tears flowed once more.

"You'll be safe here," Jody assured her. She tried her best to stifle her crying as he hugged her, but she was only partially successful. "Did you see anything else unusual?"

"The strangest thing we saw was a person who appeared to be immune to animal attacks," she said with some difficulty. "He seemed to be able to walk safely anywhere he wanted. He came through our camp preaching against the Concord and against being chipped and about somebody named—what was that name, Wanda? I can't remember. The Concord police came by looking for him, but I don't think they caught him. He just walked right past all the predators and kept on going."

"Abraham Rosenthal, I'll bet. He was by here the first day of this madness. Did your mom and dad listen to him?" asked Molly. "Were they still going to get the microchip injection?"

"They listened to him, all right. No, they changed their minds about getting chipped after that. Dad was dead set against it. So was Mom."

"Kids, there may be some hope after all. Let me tell you a story." Molly told them the whole series of circumstances that had led them to that moment in time, including the deep spiritual experience the three adults had shared a few nights before. Shortly, both girls understood what she was explaining, and they accepted it without question. A brief prayer later and both kids embraced the woman in emotional release, sobbing uncontrollably in hope of someday seeing their parents again.

"That's the expectation we all hold dearly now, girls, and we can cry and cling to it from now on without shame or fear. Never forget it as long as you live," said Molly as she returned the hugs.

"Well, you're quite a little preacher, Molly. I'm impressed," said Jody after the two girls were tucked safely in bed. "Where did you learn that?"

"From my grandfather, I guess. He had a way of going over that story, or one like it, with almost everybody he met. He even told it to me more times than I can remember. I can't believe it went right over my head. I guess I thought the world had something better to offer."

"You know, we are still in a world of hurt here. Everything out there wants to eat us. I turned on Concord radio before I went out this morning and I heard that the Father has noticed this tendency for wild beasts to lose their fear of humans and become man killers. He promised that if one goes ahead and gets the chip injected it would impart protection. That pledge ought to skyrocket the chipping rate and put nearly everyone directly in his grasp."

"But it's probably a lie. After one is chipped, there's no turning back. They track all your movements and can even monitor every word you say for life. Can you imagine how many jargonauts it takes to process and screen all that information?"

"Well, I can tell you we're going to avoid it for the duration. We're..."

His words trailed off as he realized that something was walking outside. Light but substantial footfalls in fallen leaves made an ominous crunching sound, and whatever was out there was circling the house. Jody rushed to the nearest window.

It was twilight and there was just enough remaining light to see dimly. Through a wide crack between the boards, he could see an enormous grizzly bear, its nose sniffing the air as it shuffled from side to side in characteristic gait. It was in no hurry but had apparently locked onto the smell of a potential meal. Terror hit Jody immediately, and he dashed swiftly to bolt the door.

"Quick, Molly, get Sarah and the baby into the center hallway. The girls, too! We may not have much time."

He dashed to the back window, and to his horror he noted that the beast was coming up the back steps and was straightway on the dusky porch. What could he do to stop such a monstrous bear? He had no weapons other than—that's it, a knife! He rummaged in a drawer and found a formidable butcher knife, mostly useless these days and almost forgotten, in the bottom. He grasped the weapon by its wooden handle and lifted it from its repository.

The bear was now pawing at the door, and he had to act quickly. He lighted the ethanol burner and with it ignited a worn straw broom. The flame from the dry implement licked high almost immediately in a frightful blaze. He would attempt to ward the beast off with fire, and if that desperate act failed he would do his best to destroy it with the knife. He gave little thought at this point about how he would explain it to the authorities if he killed the bear, a capital offense regardless of circumstances. He would have to handle that eventuality only if he survived, anyway. He shoved the knife into his waistband, then grabbed the nearly empty alloy cooking pot from the corner and moved toward the vicious scratching noise.

Jody jerked the door open and flung the pot in the air, startling the giant bear completely. He shoved the leaping blaze at its muzzle, curling

471

some hair around its mouth by the flame's heat. The sensation was so new and so shocking, and the clattering metallic noise so unexpected, that the beast retreated in a flash, bounded off the porch, and disappeared.

Jody overturned a large and ancient oak table and jammed it up against the door, hopefully to thwart or delay any subsequent attempt. He knew the fire trick would probably work only once, and he laid his smoldering broom on the masonry steps as he descended to the ground. He extracted the knife from his waist and settled his hand securely around its wooden handle.

The bruin had gone left, so Jody ran right around the house, keeping his ruefully impotent knife at ready in case he was charged. He emerged in front of the house where warily edged past the tractor, noting that the baby was crying loudly. He could hear the wailing of the girls, as well, and maybe one or both women. He had heard that cries of young animals had always been attractive to predators, so he surmised grimly that such noises might encourage the bear's instinctive quest for food. Jody's heart pounded in his ears as he eased forward on shaky legs.

To his disappointment the great bear had not left after all, but had raised itself on its massive hindquarters and was now pawing at a boarded window, flinging wood and glass in all directions. Jody's first impulse was to run up and stab it, even though it would be a suicidal move even if he succeeded in killing it. The police would doubtless kill everyone in the house if they found a dead bear. Not an enviable position, but he had to do something.

A thought hit him like a thunderbolt. The tractor! Of course! Use the tractor to chase it away! Why hadn't he thought of that? He retreated to the enormous machine and climbed briskly aboard. He saw the bear look his way as the engine roared to life. The animal then went back to ripping away flimsy paneling that separating it from a promising meal. Jody spun the tractor toward the animal just as it finished tearing away an entry opening of sufficient size. The beast had just crouched to jump through a sizable breach in the side of the house when the big implement's front tire smashed into it, sending it sprawling.

The giant animal was up and after the tractor with a primeval roar, but Jody was ready. As the creature charged, Jody gunned the engine and met the beast head on. The resulting collision left the tractor no worse off, but the bear was reeling, enraged, and confused. It attempted one more charge at its tormentor, then retreated toward the brushy creek in a dead run, apparently now bent on finding a meal elsewhere.

The women in the house had heard the engine start over the din of weeping, and Molly had chanced to look and see what was happening. The others joined her, and when Jody parked the tractor back at the front steps and descended, he was greeted with an entirely unexpected cheer. He smiled from ear to ear and relished his unanticipated triumph. He had won! And they were safe, at least for the moment.

*　　*　　*

Buck Morgan was approaching ever more rapidly, drawing his protracted mission toward an inevitable termination. He had entered the paw of the bear, the star 47 Ursae Majoris, and had come away unscathed. He reflected on his remarkable journey with pride.

For some reason he was reflective this moment, playing out his fears and repressed anxiety as he brilliantly keyed Beethoven's wistful *Appassionata* sonata. He couldn't shake ominous thoughts about the death of his own mother many, many Earth years before. He remembered the terrible descriptions of her injuries, information his father had given him only reluctantly, and then only after he had achieved adulthood. It had been disquieting to him then, and such thoughts disturbed him even now.

He reminisced at the same moment about the close encounter he had experienced with an angry grizzly bear on his first hunt in Alaska, that time with his Dad and Monty Archer so many years ago. And he recalled those awful bleeding gashes on Dr. Albert Hansen from the cougar attack while they were preparing for the deer project back when he had been in high school. An indelible image of spurting blood and slashed, hemorrhaging muscle tissue haunted his psyche like the recurring dream of a shell-shocked soldier. For some reason he had an uncomfortable and persistent chilly sensation, and he couldn't seem to shake the foreboding feeling. He strolled thoughtfully back to the control room for an update on their progress.

"Commander Bucko, your heart rate and blood pressure are up some. More than usual, I mean. They always peak somewhat when you assemble musical notes," said Calvin as Morgan entered.

"I've got some old ghosts in my closet, Calvin. Understand that phrase?"

"Of course. Troubling incidents earlier in life. Why are yours bothering you at this late date? Erase them from your memory, at least to the extent a biological unit such as yourself can do that."

"It's not that easy, my holo amigo, and you know it. But I'll be fine. I don't expect I'll ever encounter anything remotely similar to those episodes again," said Morgan.

"Odds are exceedingly small, but it could happen if you wander into the wrong place when you get back on Earth. But we know that all animals have a natural, evolutionary fear of human beings, so another of your unprecedented close contacts is highly unlikely to occur," calculated Calvin.

Morgan's eminently rational mind dutifully sorted out the facts, and he felt additional easing of his misplaced apprehension. After all, Calvin was exactly right. Human beings had always held unquestioned authority over such creatures, and science had controlled their numbers through logical management programs for a long time. There was no place for troubling thoughts about aberrational occurrences, he concluded. He slept fitfully that night, though he was unaware of any reason why he should be distressed as he streaked toward a fateful rendezvous.

CHAPTER 36

September 2167

"...and something like a great mountain burning with fire was thrown into the sea...and a great star fell from heaven, burning like a torch..."
Revelation 8:8,10

"Jody, look! What is that?" Molly cried, pointing skyward as she gazed between two boards covering a window. "I saw something burning!"

The young man ran out on the front porch, cast about warily for ever-present dogs, and then looked upward. He watched in amazement as a colossal irregular ball of fire descended from heaven, spawning numerous smaller crimson and white orbs as it partially disintegrated. The object and most of the debris fell far to their south, perhaps near the Arkansas River.

Jody gulped in amazement, such a terrifying scene fascinating him nevertheless. What could this mean? Is the sky falling, like the storybook says?

"Stay in, Molly. I don't see any dogs, but stay put just the same. Something just fell. And here comes another one! A daytime meteor shower!"

This one was much closer and to his astonishment there were actually several objects visible at once. Smoke could be seen rising from where the first one had landed, and the nearer one had also started a grass fire just out of sight over some low hills. A slight tremor could be felt underfoot as well, the whole house shaking to its foundation from the impact of larger fragments.

Jody retreated inside when particles of debris began landing in the yard, smoking and unbelievably hot. Fortunately, none of the incendiary missiles struck the house, or it most certainly would have burned down. The rickety barn wasn't so lucky, and in no time at all it was entirely engulfed in flames.

"Oh, Lord, what's happening? Are we going to die?" pleaded Sarah, clutching her suckling baby closely. Molly tried to comfort her, while the two orphan girls clung to her and cried.

The next phase was far worse. Chunks that followed the initial barrage were incredibly large, though there weren't nearly so many of them. Immense fiery objects hurtled toward the ground and gave off sparks in all directions. When they struck, the whole surface of the earth rippled and bucked. The cataclysm hurled mountains of whirling dust and debris high into the air, obscuring the sun like a monstrous thundercloud. It appeared that the house would surely crumple as soil heaved underneath it, but amazingly it stayed intact, though all of its occupants were tossed airborne. The girls wailed desperately, and the two women had eyes glazed with renewed terror.

"God help us!" Jody prayed out loud over and over.

There was no forewarning of any kind. When the plunging, burning masses of white-hot metal began their catastrophic descent, gravity ruled supreme and there was no stopping them. Downward they hurtled, with nowhere to go but to the planet's surface.

Poised in the heavens like a giant pinata, Space Station Delta had cruised by on its seemingly endless journey, 700 miles high, for more decades than anybody on the earth could remember. For many years nobody had given much thought to the orbiting manmade satellite, taking for granted that it was securely positioned for all time. Only a handful of people knew that it would inevitably come crashing down if it weren't maintained properly. Unfortunately, the voices of science had long been stifled. The rare man of science wisely kept his knowledge to himself.

In the twenty-second century, all thought of space travel had been abandoned in favor of more earthly ideals. Worldwide communication still depended on a few permanent, functioning satellites, and the world government still utilized these. The ruling powers had demanded at one point that the satellite system be used to track down lawbreaking men with guns. Such pragmatic uses of high technology could be tolerated, if only barely.

Space shuttle flights had been out of the question for quite a few years due to mankind's loss of necessary complex technology. Regular maintenance flights to Delta had become impossible with loss of shuttle capability. Some brave scientists had tried initially to sound the alarm and had sought desperately to have funding restored, but their protests had gone unheeded. The most vocal members of the remnant scientific community had simply disappeared, warning enough for any who might try to resurrect the issue.

Space Station Delta had reached a diameter of several miles in its heyday, including two dozen parked nuclear pulse cruisers and an immeasurable quantity of purified metal hauled in over the course of nearly a hundred years of deep space mining. Transfer of those metal plates to the surface had once taken place by shuttle, but even later heavy payload shuttles had been unable to bring back more than a fraction of the materials the efficient cruisers delivered. As a result, the station and its attached components were absolutely of gargantuan proportions.

Keeping everything aloft had always been the responsibility of the Astronaut Corps and its highly trained technical and scientific supporting team. When all deep space stations had been required to close, scientists had redirected their priorities, with major emphasis on regular service flights to keep Delta safely aloft. Even when Moon Station had been abandoned, regular flights to Delta had continued for years. Booster rockets built into the complex were used to thrust the whole mass of materials a few miles higher as needed to compensate for inevitable orbital decay.

Most people who remembered the technical details were long gone by the time there was an imminent problem. There were none to sound a warning and nobody who would listen, had one been given. Calamitous fall of millions of tons of metallic debris was as certain as sunrise, though the world waited entirely unaware of impending catastrophe.

The highest layers of atmosphere licked first at the outer ring of the station, creating an accelerating cartwheel, much like a beach ball on a rolling ocean surface. Centrifugal force generated by this motion quickly snapped flimsy mooring cables and hurled innumerable plates toward the

JONESJ.Y. JONES

earth at fantastic speeds as metallic meteors of absolute purity. The rectangular pieces behaved like a flat stone hurled into a stream, skipping back and forth, and heated to a molten state quickly in a precipitous plunge at terminal velocity. The consequent rain was like an airborne volcano, spewing superheated liquid metal all over the globe, hotter than the very bowels of the earth. Ensuing fires and panic led to wholesale loss of life everywhere and flushed many hysterical people from relative safety into jaws of patient predators.

What happened next was even more disastrous. Nuclear pulse cruisers were much more firmly attached to Delta, so their disconnection awaited attainment of additional centrifugal force. The cruisers were extraordinarily big machines, though they were not as large as older interplanetary cruisers. The actual weight of one was equivalent to hundreds of the tethered metal slabs. However, the most dangerous problem the cruisers presented was not mass, but payload.

Nuclear pulse cruisers were heavily laden with plentiful reactive mass in the form of radioactive enriched plutonium, fruit from nuclear breeder reactors of a century before. The dizzying plunge to the surface heated their mainframe metal to molten state and scattered it all over the world. Massive quantities of accompanying fuel poisoned many waters and killed much residual plant and animal life in the sea. Had the plutonium fallen freely and been completely oxidized it might have been better, but in its white hot metal cocoon most of it survived to mete out unimaginable devastation. Destruction was so widespread that it could not be calculated, with buildings burning, people dying of radiation poisoning, and even ships at sea aflame from sizzling fallout.

There was a delay before the main body of Delta fell, but shortly the entire massive station descended to an orbit brushing the upper atmosphere, heating the rolling complex to a reddish white appearance.

Fall of the station was a spectacle never before witnessed in human history, the crash of an object the size of a medium class asteroid, and it had absolutely pillaging effect. The final plummet began on the other side of the world and had been only partially accomplished when the melting station passed high over Kansas. It would impact many miles to the east, but its effect would mete out destruction worldwide.

Jody Barnes was driving his tractor, plowing a firebreak to protect what was left of their soybean crop, when he felt an awesome sonic boom and saw the shocking sight. He hurriedly headed back in, desperate to warn the women before the concussion arrived, but he was too late. The ground fairly shook as an outrageous ripple in the earth's crust passed by him at the speed of sound, tossing the heavy tractor into the air like a child's toy. Fortunately, the machine landed upright and still was miraculously intact. The house likewise surged skyward at the impact, and landed somewhat askew on the ancient foundation. It was still whole, thanks mainly to a forgotten craftsman named Lee Shealy, who as a young man had constructed it so solidly.

Jody hurriedly parked the machine and tied a rag around his bleeding forehead, which had sustained quite a gash. He then descended to the porch and rushed inside filled with dread at what he might find. To his amazement everyone was okay, although Molly had also banged her head badly. The baby crib was crumpled when it was thrown against the ceiling and then to the floor. Baby Abraham was crying loudly and had a few bruises, but plainly had suffered no permanent damage. The kitchen was once more littered with valuable soybeans, as the ancient metal storage pot had been hurled recklessly into the ceiling with the shock wave. The antique vessel lay several feet from its lid, and was completely empty now.

As soon as he had caught his breath, Jody described the scene to the women, who had heard the sonic boom but didn't know what had caused it. The station had been such a familiar fixture that most people would have been no more surprised had the moon fallen.

"Now we'll have a giant dust cloud, most likely. The first chunks of the station threw a lot of particles into the air. This piece may blot out the sun," Jody said with alarm. "We might be able to see it now."

They rushed outside and shielded their faces from a fire-tainted wind and searing smoke. With irritated eyes they searched for the impact billow Jody had predicted. Far to the east through a reddish haze they could see a tremendous mushroom cloud of dust and other debris extending from below the horizon into upper levels of the atmosphere. The top of it was already being sheared off by stratospheric winds, and it was tailing away from the farm in the shape of a high altitude celestial anvil.

"Well, at least it'll have to go all the way around the world to get back around to us," Sarah said, trying to look on the bright side as they watched spreading of the dreadful nebula.

"Do you think there's radioactivity in this dust that's falling, Jody," asked Molly. "There's no way to tell, I don't suppose."

"Fat chance. I've heard about something called a Geiger counter, but I wouldn't know one if it bit me," Jody replied. "We'll just treat all of the new dust as dangerous, since I don't know any way we can be certain. I'm really more concerned about our crop than anything else right now. Without those soybeans, we'll starve. They've got to have sunlight or they just can't grow. I hope we keep enough warmth and light to let them mature. Just another couple of weeks and they'll be edible."

The sky was light red the next day and a premature chill in the air felt ominous. The group prayed specifically about the beans, and it seemed that temperatures held at a respectable level for the next ten days despite reduced sunlight. A killing early frost then browned the entire soybean field. To the young farmer's great joy he found the bean pods were adequately developed. Now if he could just keep someone from plundering them before they had dried enough for harvest, they might just make it and have enough production to survive and to keep Concord police off their case, as well.

Deep crimson skies heralded the onset of a type of aberrant winter, similar to what might have been caused by nuclear war. The phenomenon lasted for more than a month north of the Gulf of Mexico, and then it gradually subsided as dust particles settled back to earth. They could anticipate a very cold winter to follow, but on the bright side there was temporary relief from incessant insects.

Another unexpected benefit was that marauding predators suddenly became somewhat less apparent. Hot debris from the station destroyed some of them outright, or poisoned them with radioactive fallout. Stronger predators had by now killed off weaker animals when a human meal had been unavailable. Those awful dogs in the Adrian area had been consumed by a marauding pack of ferocious wolves. The wolves seemed uncommonly susceptible to the effects of radioactivity, and a number of rotting wolf carcasses could be seen scattered about the farm. For the first time in many weeks, the small group felt marginally safe when they ventured outside.

* * *

Aboard the *Ursa C*, Buck Morgan had finally concluded that the earlier unexplained powerful burst of radiation must be evidence of some new, unknown branch of knowledge that he would learn about when he arrived home. It should be some homecoming, he anticipated. He contemplated a possible need for some kind of special course to catch up on the newest and most complex technological advances. For Calvin, updating would not mean classes, but simply a brief information download, more than likely.

As his thoughts turned ever more toward Earth and home, he often reverberated the cavernous spacecraft with strains of popular music from his own lifetime, everything from songs of his childhood to hits of his adult years. He had never been particularly a fan of current musical rages, preferring the ancient classics. But sometimes the modern was appropriate and entertaining.

He thought about Space Station Delta from time to time, and he often wondered how they had finally solved the problem of getting those massive metal plates transferred to the earth's surface. He also speculated about what changes might have been made at the station, such as automatically firing booster rockets that required no human input to function, a system he had heard project engineers discuss in months before his departure. Perhaps the energy burst he had observed had something to do with the solution of one of these chronic questions. Yet so, the burst had not recurred, so its explanation was still highly elusive and annoyingly mysterious.

He was secure in the knowledge that Space Station Delta was as stable as an ocean liner, and practically impossible to sink. He couldn't have known all the intervening details of its demise. Had he known, he might have suggested changing its name.

He might have preferred to call it Space Station Titanic.

CHAPTER 37

May 2168

"...and their torment was like the torment of a scorpion when it stings a man. And in those days men will seek death and will not find it..."
Revelation 9:5,6

Anyone would have thought that Darwin Archer had gradually lost every vestige of compassion and decency in his unending quest for approval by his superiors. He had been known to kill at the most minuscule inducement. He had even once executed a member of his own family when faced with a choice of doing so or defying the new world order. He was well aware of the role his great-great grandfather, Clemon Archer, had played in bringing in the present age. His ancestor was a revered prophet, one who helped clear the way for the great scheme of progress now in motion. Darwin Archer was determined to do his part to fulfill the Father's plans. His family connections were well known to the Concord hierarchy, so he received a modicum of deferential treatment not generally available to members of the Father's forces who bore a less distinguished heritage.

Archer was thinking soberly this day, and his mind wandered down the long road toward the Barnes farm. That peaceful rural homestead was a place where he had spent some happy, halcyon days during his boyhood. He had grown up with Jamie Barnes, and they had been best friends at one point during their teenage years. They had parted company when the Barnes boy decided to return to the family business and involve himself in more than pursuit of good times. Archer had himself been tempted to settle down at one point, because for several years he had been deeply enamored with Jamie's younger sister Faye, a striking brunette with a classic, petite face and the tempting body of a movie star. The young lady had spurned his attempts to instigate an intimate relationship, and Archer had for a long time been obsessed with her to a degree that bordered on pathological.

Faye had ultimately married a young man from her own church, and Archer had been absolutely dejected about her matrimony. As a result he had for years nursed a brooding ambivalence towards the entire Barnes family. Still, he held a fond remembrance of his old friendship with Jamie, and for these reasons he couldn't quite escape having an unusual respect for him. Barnes had always been generous and handed out whatever he had to Archer, and the policeman in turn had used his unseen influence to keep his Concord unit from pushing the family any harder than was entirely necessary. But he knew deep down that he wouldn't be able to do so forever.

Being a native of the area, a descendant of Monty Archer through an illegitimate son, he had an uncanny knack for monitoring local people, even down to attitudes and demeanor. Archer was expected by his superiors to find and destroy any unchipped rebels, using his knowledge of the local populace as his prime asset. Archer had been warned not to let any personal feelings interfere with his duties. His own commander had already raised questions concerning people who failed to conform.

Archer knew that the little church had been virtually emptied by that alien spacecraft, and his old friend Jamie Barnes had disappeared, leaving the farm with his son. It seemed odd to him that aliens would zero in on that particular group, but bizarre occurrences had become the rule rather than the exception. In any case, he wondered how many of the old Barnes family might still be around. He specifically wondered whether Faye was gone, too, an old unquenched passion surfacing once more. He had to check it out.

"Sergeant, get the vehicle ready. I want to cruise up toward the Barnes place today. Might be something funny going on up there," commanded Archer.

"Yes, sir," returned the sergeant crisply, firing back a brisk salute. He then opened the tap and began to pour some precious liquid into the car's tank. Fuel was becoming so hard to get that Archer wondered sometimes if they would be able to continue policing their district if a better source couldn't be found. But there was certainly enough left to get to the Barnes place, and there he ought to be able to appropriate some freshly distilled ethanol.

Shortly Archer returned, his blue and white linen uniform resplendent, the Concord emblem prominently displayed on his cap and on one shirtsleeve. The unusually severe winter was finally subsiding, and there was only a sprinkling of frost today. Maybe things would return to normal now, or as normal as possible, considering recent catastrophes. The patrolmen stowed their sinister automatic weapons in ready position, then they got back into the battered vehicle. The sergeant started the engine, and shortly they were easing at crawling speed along the road that led north.

As they drove, Archer thought at length about the Barnes place they would be visiting. Jody Barnes was the only person he knew who assuredly had not been chipped. He had seen him drive up repeatedly to the harvest collection point and dump farm produce, yet his old feelings for the youth's father had so far kept him from fingering the boy. He knew he wasn't getting soft, because he had no trouble executing average rebels like the most dedicated Concord police. The worst part was that should he be caught letting Barnes slip through undetected, he would himself be summarily executed. The legacy of his renowned forefather carried only so much clout.

Since the alleged great space alien invasion had taken Jamie Barnes from the scene, Archer's ambivalence towards that family might be nearing an end. His conscience now felt oddly clear to proceed with an investigation of any remaining family members. A pleasant thought was the remote possibility that he might still have Faye, if she happened to have been spared by the aliens and if she had been chipped as required. The only way to know for sure was to check. He knew there were probably others in the family who also had skipped the mandatory microchip injection, and he would make some points today by finding out who could be implicated.

The two men noticed with satisfaction that the grass was returning to its customary green color, even in the vast burned areas. Spring had finally arrived with the warm weather of late, and throughout the whole area tender sprouts were emerging all over. There were a few groups of people out pulling tender green shoots, stuffing them in their mouths raw and munching like cattle. The officers scrutinized each person carefully to determine whether any might be disobeying some rule that would require that they use their weapons, but all seemed to be in order. Some residual wolves had a kill far up the broad valley, and the animals swirled about an unidentified carcass in a feeding frenzy. The sun was almost back to its usual brightness, the dusty haze improving almost daily.

Suddenly, unexpectedly, their vehicle veered off the road and plowed through thick brush for a dozen yards. The sergeant clutched his calf and writhed in uncontrollable agony. Archer yelled an obscenity at him, cursing his inept driving and threatening to have him before a firing squad immediately. The vehicle emerged from the rough area and lurched to a stop against a large elm tree in front of a dilapidated house, crumpling the front fender a bit but doing little other damage in the low velocity impact.

"Curse you, sergeant, I'll have you....Arggg! Mother Gaia, what's got me? Owww!" moaned Archer as he twisted and rolled in anguish, and a knife-like pain seared through his back. He had never felt anything like it, and the depth of torment was such that his whole body hurt. Before they had time to think, both men were seized with additional pains in other parts of their bodies, and suffering consumed them.

The two men hurt intractably for the longest time and entirely forgot about their mission. All they could think about was somehow returning to the Concord station and seeking relief. Despite their misery, they found that they could still function, and shortly they had the car turned around and headed back toward Adrian. Along the way, they noticed that the diffident feeding on new grass had ceased, and that person after person was now curled up and writhing in pain. Most afflicted people they could see were on the ground along the roadway, but often there were screams of agony emanating from ramshackle houses that stood here and there. There were also some peculiar large flying insects the men had never noticed before darting to and fro.

New pains were breaking out on them almost constantly, and the sergeant had trouble keeping the vehicle on the road, repeatedly veering right or left. At one point a nearly naked man, his hollow face gnarled with anguish, flung himself in front of them as if trying to be run down. Uncharacteristically, the sergeant swerved and missed him.

"If I have to live with this, he has to live with it," he said out loud in a callous, stone cold voice.

Strangely, there were a few people in evidence who apparently were unaffected. The two Concord men felt hatred rising in their hearts for those walking about as if nothing were wrong, or who were attempting to comfort those in pain. Despite their own contorted agony, they stopped the car and accosted one of the untouched people. The man was scarcely intimidated, and on a hunch they retrieved the chip detector device from the car. There was a negative reading. The man was doubtless another detestable rebel who had refused to be chipped. The man's lack of fear seemed peculiar, but the two hardly noticed through their own torment. A burp of automatic weapons fire ended the man's life, and his riddled body was left lying by the road in a sickening, disordered pile.

"Sergeant, it's a devil of a way to find out, but we can now easily distinguish those who aren't chipped," groaned Archer. "Whatever this is doesn't seem to affect them. I wonder if the chip is disintegrating or something. Nah, couldn't be. They're made of something called silicone. It's harmless, they say. Couldn't cause something like this."

He pulled up his pants leg and inspected his latest point of pain. There was a disturbing welt there about two inches wide with a small black spot in the center. The swollen area was quite crimson and was elevated above the surrounding skin by more than a half inch. It looked like a very bad spider bite, but it couldn't be. He had never heard of an epidemic of poisonous spiders bites.

By the time they finally reached the station, nausea had overtaken them, and they were heaving and vomiting violently. They had to stop the car several times to empty their stomachs along the roadway. Their arrival was scarcely noted by other Concord police, all of whom were lying about in various states of prostration. One man was sitting up in a corner, his mouth twisted in a horrible grimace. He was quite cognizant, and he motioned heavily to the captain to come, which normally was an offense considered insubordination. Such a transgression was punishable by death, but Archer ignored the indiscretion and complied.

"Sir," the man gasped, "I found the animal—uh, human—that's doing this!"

"What is it? A spider?"

"No, sir, I don't know what it is! Oww...!"

Through clenched teeth, the captain demanded to see this creature. The tormented underling produced a quart jar, and inside was the strangest insect anyone had ever seen.

"Look, sir. It bites but at first it doesn't hurt. It must secrete some kind of anesthetic that allows it to suck blood. I saw this one on Corporal Harrell's neck, and he didn't even know it was there. Now look at him."

The corporal was now piled on the floor with several others, moaning in deep distress and clutching his neck. Archer now noticed that there were dozens of those horrible insects flying about looking for a place to land. They were definitely bloodsuckers and were attracted to human skin like flies to a corpse. Only with great effort could they prevent the organisms from burying their siphons once alighted. Intervening clothing deterred the unearthly creatures not at all; they simply burrowed right through to obtain a meal. The air was virtually filled now with a sinister whir of wingbeats, a reverberating din that drowned out normal conversational tones.

"Get on the radio, sergeant. Find out if these devils are anywhere else. Must be some kind of mutant insect from radioactive fallout."

The radioactive mutation theory soon became the official line. The radio confirmed that everywhere the peculiar arthropods were meting out pain such as mankind had never before endured. The Father was himself beset by the creatures, and assigned a large detail of men to watch and protect him full time. Despite colossal effort, the insects still were able to penetrate the defense and get to him with regularity. When this occurred, he pronounced the death penalty on those who had failed him, but none seemed to be able get enough control of their faculties to carry out such orders. The agony-stricken ruler increasingly found himself surrounded by condemned men who couldn't be executed because of horrible pain being endured by their designated executioners. Pain, frustration, and anger caused the Hammer to rant and rave like a madman, cursing everything and everybody in wild fits of blasphemy and rage.

A few relic scientists were rounded up and convened to study the creatures. They worked under the burden of their own excruciating anguish, and were unable to supply a satisfactory antidote or repellent. The best they could do was to describe the creatures and offer mainly untenable ideas for avoiding them. Their best suggestion was to team up with two others, and let two watch while one slept. This tactic was adopted, and it completely immobilized Concord forces for some five months. The only hope for relief in most places was the faraway killing cold of deep winter.

These insects appeared to be a kind of large grasshopper, almost three inches in length, but they flew and hovered like mosquitoes on flimsy wings that supported their feathery bodies with ease. The head was most peculiar, being gold colored on top and pinkish underneath. If one looked carefully, an outline strikingly similar to a human face could be seen in the head's pink lower portion, an effect created by a pattern of pigment that penetrated the rose-colored shell. The thorax was covered with hard chitin that could be crushed only with massive force. The abdomen had no such hard covering, but from it grew a wealth of most unusual long, hair-like filaments, similar to those found on many caterpillars, and some of this same material grew from the head as well. The filaments varied in consistency, color, and configuration, and individual insects were distinguishable from others by the length and amount of curl in the filaments. The mouth had a group of round teeth above and below. Two teeth above and two below were longer than the rest. These canine-like teeth were designed to penetrate skin so the internalized siphon could be inserted into a capillary for drawing blood.

Their most terrifying feature was a long tail, scorpion-like, which was not even apparent until one looked closely. It was kept curled under plentiful abdominal hair until needed, when it was unfurled to apply the horrible sting. When the creature alighted on a victim, it immediately swept the tip of the tail forward to wherever a bite was to occur, and injected a powerful toxin that initially acted as an anesthetic. It then fed at its leisure in a numb area several inches in diameter. Shortly afterward the dreadful bloodsucker departed, and enormous torture began for the unfortunate victim.

For the first time since the Humanity Proclamation, the Father made an exception through an official declaration of war. Humankind was given the right to kill these insects on sight. When this unusual word went out, a wild frenzy of killing broke out all over the globe. *Homo sapiens* stomped, swatted, and pulverized the flying fiends with ceaseless zeal, but their numbers never seemed to abate in the least.

A most bizarre feature that nobody could explain was that the creatures attacked only people who had undergone injection with the identifier microchip. The Father's advisors speculated the insects were a product of radioactive mutation and that perhaps something in the high tech chips attracted them only to those people. The Barnes household was given a merciful respite for a time, while most of the world battled an awful plague, a scourge that was the worst mankind had ever experienced.

*   *   *

Buck Morgan was streaking back toward his home solar system, and the distant sun grew more visible daily. He was still much too far out to contact anyone, but at least he was back in his own corner of the universe, and it felt good to be nearing home. He and Calvin had already practiced rotating the ship in order to test all systems for the prolonged process of deceleration. It would surely be good to be able to contact Earth and get some welcome news from home. He wanted to enjoy this homecoming to the utmost, so he didn't want to be forced to end it in a rush. He had his holographic co-pilot check and recheck all components of the starship, which continued to function perfectly.

The commander of the approaching *Ursa C* had no insect pests of any kind on board, so his comfort and the productivity of his plants and animals was ever at highest level. All parasites and diseases had been eliminated systematically before each of the varieties had been placed in his extensive renewables garden. Nothing could change that unless contamination were somehow introduced.

Morgan sat in the control room next to Calvin and did some reading before turning in for sleep this watch. For no particular reason he read a passage in his Bible: "They have as king over them the angel of the abyss...in the Greek he has the name *Apollyon*."

"Calvin, check the Greek language. What does *Apollyon* mean?" he asked.

"Query delay, Commander Bucko," said the holographic man. "It means destruction, sir. In Hebrew the word is *Abaddon*. The information is most accessible in the Bible lexicon program. Does that help?"

"Have you been reading this book, Calvin?"

"It's in my files, Commander Bucko, like all other human literature. Every passage and every possible interpretation are there. Do you need to know more?"

"The Book of Revelation, Calvin. It predicts worldwide destruction. Crazy fairy tale, huh?"

"That's one interpretation, sir. There are many others, most of them highly improbable, even to the point of being fanciful. Want a complete printout?"

"No, that's okay. Destruction, huh?"

Hmm. It didn't seem to make a lot of sense. These unbelievable things he had been reading lately couldn't be anything more than fantasy.

Morgan retired to his quarters, and briefly considered the implications before drifting off into fitful sleep. He was sure he'd forget all about that kind of foolishness when he got back to Earth.

CHAPTER 38

April 2169

Buck Morgan awoke after his restless sleep with the planet Jupiter just ahead. He had already determined that he would try to contact Ganymede Station at this point, since the base on Saturn's moon Titan had failed to answer earlier. Perhaps that experimental project had been abandoned in favor of a polar station on Mercury. One never knew how feasible a space enterprise might be until the mining operation was up and running.

It was time to deactivate the antimatter conversion process in his main engine group to allow for rotation of the ship. This accomplished, their speed was soon plummeting rapidly as he manually ignited his engines once more for deceleration. He smiled with satisfaction as he watched the speed gauge click to lower and lower numbers. The reverse thrust was measured and smooth, but it tugged at his body in a most peculiar way as the powerful slowing imparted an unfamiliar feel. The array of heavenly bodies around Jupiter would be impossible to visualize at close range while traveling at the fantastic maximum speed of the *Ursa C*, so a lower speed was welcome.

The giant planet loomed with ever-increasing clarity as the lower speed stabilized, and Morgan once more halted the antimatter conversion process. Jupiter's familiar lunar arrangement was dazzling against the orange-red glow of the alien world. Ganymede beckoned with distinctness and familiarity.

Calvin was using the electronics system to scan exhaustively for active frequencies, but he wasn't having much luck. Morgan knew the usual wavelength without looking it up, so he deactivated automode and manually dialed in Ganymede Station, hopeful for some long-delayed word from fellow human beings. Calvin was unaccustomed to being overridden, and his facial features seemed to reflect an almost human-like perplexity.

"Ganymede Station, *Ursa C*, over," Morgan radioed. The system crackled a little, but still there was no response. He waited a short time, then repeated, "Ganymede Station, *Ursa C*, over." Again, dead silence greeted him.

"Some welcome home. They must be excited I'm here," Morgan muttered, scrutinizing the frequency bands to see if he could find the base in an unexpected place. There was detectable radio activity, but not a word coming from Ganymede. Hmm, he wondered, is anybody home? He switched radio scan activity back to Calvin and directed his companion to keep searching.

He considered briefly orbiting the Jovian moon and checking things out with the planetary lander, but he rejected the idea. He had used up his fuel supply at Schultzi, and it would take a couple of days to charge the lander for such a mission. Robbing his renewables garden for fuel components would put a strain on its water supply, a stress that he had been certain would not be necessary when he was this near such a plentiful water source as Earth. Maybe they had abandoned the base, he rightly concluded, and it would be silly for him to delay, or even jeopardize, his mission without at least checking with the Cape. A radio signal to Earth could now be sent and received in less than an hour.

The orbit of Mars had placed it on the opposite side of the solar system, far away from the *Ursa C*'s trajectory, so Morgan decided to reactivate his main engines to half of light speed. He could still talk to Earth without interference at that velocity, but travel time would be reduced to less than an hour. For the first time in quite a while, the plasmafyer hyperlaser surged to life as the asteroid belt approached, protecting them from approaching matter. Run-up accomplished, he turned his attention back to Calvin and the perplexing radio complex.

"No luck, holo amigo?"

"There are several active signal bands emanating from Earth, Commander Bucko, but none apparently directed at deep space and none evidently capable of receiving long distance transmission. It does not compute why no regular frequencies at the Cape are active, not even their emergency frequency," replied Calvin with highly unusual distress in his voice.

"Select another band that has activity, and see if you can contact them," Morgan directed. Calvin tried repeatedly and without success to communicate. Attempts to reach Space Station Delta resulted in responses of dead silence.

"I'll be darned," Morgan whispered aloud, his brow creased with a deepening frown. "They must not be expecting us, Calvin."

"Quite apparent, Commander Bucko. Most bizarre."

Since he couldn't talk to Earth, Morgan elected to increase sensitivity on his receiver to maximum to try to at least get some news from home. To his surprise, every frequency in use was loaded with military talk, the kind one would expect to hear in a combat theater. Still, it sounded good to be in contact with live human voices after so many years.

"Strange. We can't raise the Cape. We can't raise Delta. Let's try Moon Station," said Morgan, becoming ever more concerned.

"I did. No response, Commander Bucko," reported Calvin. "No logical explanation is available in my files."

Eavesdropping on the military talk, Morgan soon surmised that a major military operation was in progress. None of the talk was about people or places that made a great deal of sense to him. Much radio chatter was in various European languages, so he had to get Calvin to activate his autotranslate mode in order to understand the conversations. The Concord, Israel, troop movement, the Father, ship rendezvous points, horses, supplies. The mumbo-jumbo didn't figure at times, even for Calvin's sophisticated mainframe, and he repeatedly dealt with flashing red lights that required adjustment of language bands. As an off-the-wall experiment, Morgan told Calvin to switch the century code for the computer's lexicon back a couple of hundred years to a nineteenth century setting. To his surprise, Calvin's language barrier decreased markedly. Now that's really weird, thought Morgan. Even though the translation was smoother afterwards, it still made no more sense than before.

494

Well out from Earth, they again deactivated their primary engines, accomplished the necessary rotation, and began slowing once more. Earth was looming ever larger, ever more radiant and familiar with its single gorgeous moon. The only visible change he could detect from space was a strange, reddish brown haze that made Earth's atmosphere look more like that of Mars. It was good to be home nevertheless, the confusing radio situation notwithstanding.

The worst news yet was that the *Ursa C* couldn't get a lock on Space Station Delta. An exhaustive scan indicated no activity of Delta's magnitude in any sector around Earth. The only action originated from a few low intensity communications satellites, and precious few of them, compared to when he had departed. Something was dreadfully wrong, or else some unimaginable new technology had replaced all these missing pieces. Unanswered questions kept piling up.

It would be necessary only to lock into Earth orbit, since no orbital harmonization with Delta would be necessary. He elected to orbit for a few turns and see if he could figure this out. His heart slowly sank as he gradually realized that the breathless welcome he had envisioned for so long would not be forthcoming. With the data we're carrying, scientists ought to be scanning the heavens constantly in anticipation of the *Ursa C*'s return, he fretted repeatedly. The data stream he had dutifully sent back was old by the time it arrived, but even it had to be revolutionary in content. And as for non-transmittable data, those rocks from Schultzi should alone be coveted material for a Smithsonian Institute display.

Electrical activity from Earth showed a much lower level of than before he had left, another totally unexpected finding. In fact, readings were so low he briefly wondered if he hadn't, through some obscure quirk of relativity, gone backward in time a century or more, rather than forward as forecast by quantum physics. That would square with Calvin's ease of translation being greatly enhanced in a language mode of several centuries ago. He had Calvin run a quick probability calculation and found that such an idea was scientifically preposterous. Calvin actually chuckled at the suggestion.

Morgan continued to monitor worldwide military conversations, and eventually he began to get some idea of the operation in progress. Some government was massing troops and supplies in the Middle East for action against Israel. Hmm, he thought, I wonder what the Israelis have done? They always were a defiant and feisty bunch. At least that bit of data confirmed in his mind that Calvin was correct, and that he was indeed returning to Earth later than he left, since he knew that modern Israel had been founded as a nation in the middle of the twentieth century.

One item he repeatedly heard was most puzzling. There were innumerable references to horses. Why was a military operation so closely linked to horses? One transmission announced "all horses in the European and African theater will mass at Haifa before moving inland." There were convoys of ships, apparently, converging there bringing men, supplies, and horses. A quick geographical search by Calvin confirmed that Haifa was a port city in northern Israel.

Perhaps most surprising was that nobody seemed to notice the *Ursa C.* Even a rudimentary scan of the heavens should have led to a great stir that a major spacecraft had entered Earth orbit, but there was not a peep about it. Military chatter continued unabated with no reference whatsoever to Morgan's ship. How could any military be so unconcerned about strategic positioning of such an overwhelming craft above them? Morgan was extensively schooled in military tactics, and this smacked of a nineteenth century mentality. Could it be they didn't detect him? Could it be they didn't care? Could it be that nobody was looking up anymore, even electronically?

Morgan orbited for hours, checking over the planetary lander before pressing it into service. He fretted repeatedly that a heroic docking at Space Station Delta, an event that he had anticipated and rehearsed in his mind for so long, would not take place.

"I'm going to have to leave the ship with you in orbit and descend unaided for a look," he commented to Calvin.

"As you say, Commander Bucko. It is the only viable course. Perhaps you will have to go down and remind them we are home," said Calvin.

Morgan nodded a response, but said nothing. Maybe they had their dates mixed up. Maybe they had simply forgotten, he worried.

The planetary lander had been added to the starship almost as an afterthought. It had been placed on board in case a need arose to explore the surface of some distant, promising planet, exactly the use Morgan had already made of it. It had no heat shield, since one was not needed for descent through thin or absent atmospheres prevalent on most heavenly bodies that would support such a landing. But its metal alloys were extremely heat resistant, and he had in fact encountered no problem in the thick atmosphere at Schultzi.

The lander's hydrogen/oxygen fuel tanks were completely depleted by the trip to the alien planet more than four years previously. Morgan fretted repeatedly about not having hauled up a load of water from Schultzi, because he had seriously considered doing so. If he had, he could have saved himself stress and worry over a water shortage in his renewables garden. It was too late now.

"Calvin, how much water will be required to fuel the lander?"

"Approximately 21,552 gallons, to the nearest gallon, Commander Bucko."

"And how long can our renewables section survive with that much water extracted?"

"Sixty days, sir. All growth will be attenuated until replenishment. There will be no lasting harm up to that point."

"How long to convert the water to fuel?"

"Forty-five hours, twenty-seven minutes, and thirteen seconds at maximum distillation rate, Commander Bucko," answered Calvin.

It seemed achievable. There was no way it could take sixty days to get back. He carefully began to re-prime the lander tanks, efficiently manufacturing both necessary elements from his reluctant robbery of the precious onboard supply. Monitoring the process consumed most of his time for the required interval. It was alarming to watch the renewables water supply plummet to a dangerously low level. When all was completed, a brief test firing of lander engines was superbly successful.

Morgan got a few hours of erratic sleep before attempting the descent. This is a fine kettle of fish, he kept dreaming—almost nine years in space, and ninety years of Earth time—and nobody cares, apparently. This horrible thought kept reappearing in his restless dreams.

Morgan awoke with his head full of grim resolve. He knew from their radio monitoring that he faced an uncertain situation on the surface, but his options were few. It was obvious there was a war going on, or at least that a conflict was imminent. There were only two weapons on the ship. One was the old Stevens shotgun his father had owned, and the other was a tiny electric stun gun that was part of an emergency kit. He had only bird shot for the shotgun, so it would be of minimal value in any hostile confrontation. He was going into a war zone practically unarmed.

He put the stun pistol in a bulging pocket of his flight suit, and retrieved his father's ancient firearm from his quarters. The box of shotgun shells was now nine years old and each had a fine film of corrosion on the casing, though they appeared intact otherwise. Perhaps the powder had lost some of its potency. He took one cartridges out and rolled it in his hand, then he held it close to one ear and shook it. Rattling of the tiny shot inside sounded terribly impotent.

Then a promising thought struck him. Buckshot was terrifically effective as a weapon against almost anything, even when fired from an antique shotgun. He took the whole box of shells with him into a gravity-free laboratory.

He would save a couple unaltered. The rest he carefully pried open at the crimped end, and then emptied the grain-sized shot into a covered beaker. Soon he had the vessel half full of the tiny balls of lead floating in weightlessness. In the lab's superheater, the metal was quickly dissolved to form a blistering hot liquid.

His next step was to re-form the material into larger balls. This was easily accomplished in weightless conditions using a special ball-bearing manufacturing device. He set ball size at 0.33 inches on the meter and placed the beaker in load position. On activating it, buckshot of desired size began forming at the nozzle. In the cool of the lab the liquid condensed rapidly, making perfect lead spheres. Morgan captured each one as it floated from the port. He lost some volume of lead in the process, but he had plenty to refill a dozen of the opened shell casings, with some to spare. Nine balls went into each cartridge, and to secure the cartridge ends he applied a wax sealer designed for use on plants. He held one up and inspected it, quite content with his inventiveness.

He felt better about having some buckshot along, but this was still a mighty small amount of firepower. If this were a planet at war, he wouldn't be able to help either side very much. As he returned to the control room to give Calvin a final briefing, he passed by the plasmafyer hyperlaser module. Too bad I can't take this baby, he stewed as he thoughtfully patted the panel.

He assembled the shotgun and stowed it in the lander, secured carefully to avoid damage on descent. Beside it he fixed firmly his newly re-crafted shells so they could be easily reached if needed.

Deployment of the lander was smooth and uneventful, and Morgan watched in awe as the starship, so much a part of him for nine years, was left behind. The inconceivable size of the craft from the exterior view impressed him once more, and he marveled at the sight all over again. A reverse burn quickly slowed the lander, while Calvin masterfully supervised the whole disconnection and descent profile. His craft plunged toward the earth, leaving the *Ursa C* parked in high orbit. It quickly faded to a pinpoint in the bright daylight sky, but he maintained radio contact with Calvin as he descended.

It again became quite warm in the lander as the hull glowed from atmospheric friction, but as Morgan had predicted, advanced metallurgical concepts in the hull were up to the task. As he dropped into the atmosphere on a trajectory for the Cape, he was amazed all over again at the beauty of his home planet, so different and so dynamic in appearance as compared to dead Schultzi. He noticed a lot of unusual dust in the upper atmosphere, but perhaps there had simply been a major volcanic eruption lately.

As the Cape came into view, he did a reconnaissance run around the site. To his dismay, the place was overgrown with vegetation and appeared altogether unoccupied. This was getting monotonous. Was anything going to be like he expected?

Landing on the expansive runway by means of wheels would be impossible. A couple more passes were needed to find a place to set down his craft because the asphalt was so damaged. This runway had been the pride of the solar system, home of the famed Astronaut Corps, a place where presidents and other heads of state often landed. Why had it been so totally neglected?

The condition of the runway left him no choice but to use a vertical landing mode, exact reverse of a rocket departure, and the same mode he had used landing on Schultzi. The lander was equipped to manage such a feat without difficulty, but it was a little trickier than a wheeled landing, especially in a thick atmosphere. While it had gone very well at Schultzi, Morgan still couldn't believe he would be forced to do another landing at all and he felt terribly rusty after long years in space. Oh, well, here goes, and only my life depends on doing it perfectly again, he thought wryly. He made certain Calvin was involved in essential electronic input, and initiated the landing sequence.

Vertical landing required coordinating several factors at once, plus adding minute corrections for drift in any direction. Calvin's advice helped, but sudden manual override was necessary repeatedly. There was a stiff westerly breeze, he could tell from waves on the bay, so he compensated and made a slight adjustment in thrust to correct. A sudden puff of wind almost caused the nose to tilt eastward again, but he got the craft realigned quickly. Final touchdown was soft and secure on the battered strip.

"Big welcome home, Calvin. Man, you should see all the bug strikes on the cowling!"

"Glad you're safe on the ground, Commander Bucko. Be careful," returned the holographic man in a voice that sounded sincerely concerned.

He shut down the engines and waited patiently for the high-pitched whine of cooling fans to subside. During the interval he switched off the electronics and secured the cockpit. As he did so, waves of mind-boggling questions continued to besiege him. Because of overwhelming uncertainty, he went ahead and prepared the craft for takeoff once more, minimizing the time it would take for him to get airborne should a rapid departure become necessary. A most unexpected precaution, he thought as he finished the priming sequence.

He decided to leave the obtrusive shotgun in the lander, not wishing to appear belligerent to whomever he might encounter. He patted the stun pistol in his pocket, and found it reassuringly in place.

Here goes. He put out his hand, turned the handle, and opened the canopy. It popped free effortlessly, and genuine Earth air rushed in to engulf him.

Now he would find out some answers.

CHAPTER 39

April 2169

The Father in Rome was in a stomping, huffing rage. He sent three lieutenants to their deaths via firing squad that morning alone. He was highly annoyed and deeply agitated, and he let it be known as he bellowed commands to his cringing underlings. White-haired Lawrence Foxx, an aging Irishman who had risen through the ranks to become Commanding General of Concord forces worldwide, had thus far been able to deflect criticism to other men of lower station. Now he tried desperately but in vain to pacify the raving dictator. Foxx had earned the Father's partiality for rooting out and destroying strong European resistance forces early in the effort, and he had been a favorite follower ever since. Now he was under direct scrutiny for the current situation, and he trembled imperceptibly as he tried to maintain his military bearing.

"Incompetent slobs! Insolent scum! Find out the missing information, and bring me the truth! Now!" demanded Father Hammer.

For the first time ever the Father pointed an accusing finger directly at Foxx and shook it in his face, terrifyingly close. His speech churned with expletives as he repeatedly screamed at the cowering cadre around him. He asked again with an acid voice whether anyone among his servants was capable of doing anything right anymore, cryptic words implicating Foxx as never before. He called for Christian Ersatzson, and his terrified underlings scrambled madly to find him. Maybe Ersatzson could restore some sanity and reason to the ranting strongman.

The Father's mental state was an outgrowth of a peculiar occurrence he didn't understand, quite an uncharacteristic state for the clairvoyant Father. There was a sudden embarrassing presence on the scene that he had not predicted. The perfect Father was not going to admit any deficiency of wisdom, certainly not before his hapless subordinates.

It had not been long since that horrifying invasion of hairy flying insects had ended as mysteriously as it had begun. Now this new crisis had arisen to take its place. The Hammer would find out the meaning and intentions of this unwelcome intruder if he had to execute every one of the unfit rabble that surrounded him. Nothing would be tolerated which might threaten his well-crafted plans.

A watchman, an alert Concord policeman in France, had noticed something unusual in the nighttime heavens, even though a smog-like haze obscured much of the sky. The Father had been sent word of this peculiar finding and had confirmed with his own eyes that indeed there was something out of the ordinary floating high above the earth, something that looked like a prominent moving star but which glistened like silver and appeared to be manmade. Even while the Father fumed and cursed, elderly technicians who knew something about the defunct space program were being sought desperately all around the world. The few who were found were rushed to Rome for consultation. Within two days, everyone with any space knowledge or expertise was in Rome working feverishly to meet the Father's demands.

Foxx breathed a deep sigh of relief as Christian Ersatzson, his flowing priestly robes rippling, appeared majestically at the grand entrance of Concord Hall. Uniformed escorts quickly ushered the imposing wizard into the world leader's presence. Now all should be well.

"My Lord, Father, Exalted One, we bring conclusive word on our unannounced visitor," said Ersatzson triumphantly.

A noxious smile spanned the darker, smaller figure's face. Everyone in attendance seemed to relax at the announcement, and welcome relief flowed almost audibly. Foxx pulled a kerchief from his pocket and wiped beads of nervous sweat from his brow.

"I had no doubt you would. Let's hear it," said the Father, his mood cooled considerably by Ersatzson, who always seemed to have a calming effect on the malignant ruler. Ersatzson respectfully motioned him to sit down on his gold and ivory throne. He then ordered all the others, including Foxx, out of the room. Familiar but frightful eyes met in glorious union, and charisma flowed abundantly. It was Ersatzson who broke the moment's magic with serious words.

"About ninety years ago, the powers that existed in those unenlightened times launched a spacecraft at very near the speed of light toward the heavens. That voyage was directed at a star in the Ursa Major constellation. We have discovered forgotten records of that mission in the archives. The pilot went entirely alone and unarmed. His name is James Lee Morgan, and his voyage was for purposes of scientific discovery. He should pose no threat to your progressive empire, Father. Invasion of the Holy City can proceed unhindered."

"Tell me everything about him. The world laughs at our lack of insight. Why did we only now discover his existence?"

"An oversight, my Excellency. Science is folly, as you know. Even the memory of such unsavory projects has been purged from most records and from people's recollection. Nobody except us knows anything about this man. I have placed the team which researched the annals on indefinite quarantine," Ersatzson reported with a sly smirk. "Exalted One, do not worry yourself about the perception of the masses. They are entirely unaware."

"Anything else?"

"Yes. Something of extreme importance. Morgan is carrying a cargo of limitless value. Records show that he has onboard a 'renewables garden' containing some one hundred species made of flesh and an even higher number of plant species. Some are beings formerly known as domestic in type, but also numerous varieties which once existed in a wild and free state. Most of these are now extinct on our Mother Earth."

"Superb," said the Father thoughtfully, stroking his chin with smooth fingers that were tipped with sharp fingernails. It was good news that few people were aware of this debacle. And with those creatures, he could feign actual creation of life. The world would never question his right to rule if he accomplished that. And more significantly, lands cleansed of human vermin could be repopulated with more majestic and deserving creatures. Would not such a desirable eventuality give all the world reason to praise the Father's power and majesty?

"We must make arrangements to capture this man and transport his garden creatures to Rome unharmed. We must have them, Ersatzson. We can give all humanity a living vision of my glory through that cargo. Send Foxx back in."

"I understand, Father. An alert has already been communicated to our forces, and plans are well under way, as you suggested."

*　　*　　*

Unaware that he had been discovered, James Lee "Buck" Morgan descended at the Cape from his planetary lander. He stood on unbelievably battered tarmac, savoring his first breaths of real Earth atmosphere in more than nine years, testing his legs in authentic gravity and enjoying the sensation of a firm breeze in his face.

He sucked in a big chest full of unfiltered air and gazed about him in amazement at the changes that had transpired. There was a different smell, he was certain of that, and the air was undeniably dirty. There were trees and other vegetation all around the runway, but they had a strange dead appearance. Stark, blackened limbs clawed upward into a reddish-colored sky. There was a resurgent greening underneath the dead canopy, but something had killed a lot of larger plants. This eerie scene could have resulted from a nuclear holocaust or something equally devastating, and his instruments did show an increased amount of radioactivity, though not to lethal levels. Anyway, he couldn't believe mankind would allow such a calamity as atomic war to occur, since nuclear disarmament had been completed well before he had even been born

"Ow!" he uttered out loud. Reflexively, his hand swung to his neck and nailed a big mosquito that was sinking its siphon through his skin. The healthy insect splattered and he brushed it, whereupon it windmilled inertly downward. Others were soon buzzing around him, and he nailed them in swift succession.

"Hey, man, you're in big trouble," came a squeaky voice from behind him. The voice startled him visibly, and he jumped involuntarily. He wheeled to face two gaunt boys, apparently of adolescent age, staring at him with big, dark eyes from the runway edge. Both were completely naked except for a large leaf strategically placed fore and aft, and their exposed skin was tanned as gingerbread.

"Big trouble? That's no way to welcome a guy home. What do you mean, trouble?"

"Concord policemen will kill you for that. It's against the law to harm insects. They're as human as you are, and they have as much right to live," said the other boy, staring first at Morgan and then at the lander, then back at Morgan. He spoke in a dialect that seemed to be a mixture of Spanish and English. Using his considerable knowledge of Spanish, Morgan followed his speech with minimal effort.

Looking over the pair, Morgan could tell they were having a hard life. The larger boy had horrible scars all over his body. Both had slight pot bellies, skinny arms and legs, and deep-set hollow eyes. They moved like beasts of prey, as nervous as squirrels, seemingly on the very edge of bolting away at any moment. The pitiful sight reminded him of haunting pictures of Oil Age famines, when people had actually died of starvation in Africa and elsewhere. That kind of catastrophe had been nonexistent anywhere in the world when he had departed. How did these boys get into this terrible condition?

"Boys, I never heard of letting bugs suck your blood instead of swatting them."

"We don't mind these bugs. They only hurt a little. Flying scorpions were a lot worse. And the Father did let us kill them."

"Flying scorpions? That really sounds bad. And what did you say—the Father and some kind of policemen? Why would they care about me protecting myself from insects?"

"It's murder, mister. Insects are humans, too. They have a right to live. Don't you know anything?" asked the smaller boy in a dead serious high-pitched voice.

"Who says?" Morgan said, trying to sound as friendly as possible.

"Our Father, the Hammer, says so, and he's master and ruler. You have to do what he says," asserted the older boy with a bit more confidence.

"What? You say some guy named Hammer?" Morgan exclaimed. "Listen, can you boys take me to a grownup?"

"A what?"

"A grownup. You know, an adult." He noted blank expressions. "A big person."

"Oh. I don't know about that. You're a murderer. Our Memaw tells us to stay away from trouble. You're trouble, I think," said the older boy, staring again at the planetary lander. He pointed a finger at it and momentarily forgot the serious charges he had leveled.

"What's that thing, mister? An airplane? Memaw saw airplanes once, but they're not allowed anymore because they go too fast and kill our fellow creatures. The Concord army has helicopters that fly."

"That's my lander, kind of like an airplane. I came down from my starship in it. Now, can you take me to your, uh, Memaw, you said?"

"You're a murderer. We can't."

"Look, boys, I didn't know about that rule. When I left Earth it was okay to swat bugs. Let's go see her. Don't you have parents?"

"My mom's dead and my dad's in the Concord army somewhere. And I don't think Memaw wants to talk to a murderer," replied the smaller boy firmly, confident enough now that he was looking Morgan sternly in the eye.

Morgan put his best logic to work and finally convinced the boys that he had left before the law was changed. He had to promise that he would kill no more insects before they agreed to lead him down a winding trail to meet Memaw. Morgan waved his hand gently back and forth across his face to ward off ever-present bloodsuckers, following the technique used by the boys. Their walk was unusual in that the jungle consisted mostly of dead brush, and the only sound was a constant whirring of insect wings and an occasional chirp of a cricket. Notably absent were calls of birds, and he heard not one during the entire walk. He could see a several vultures circling high overhead, so perhaps there was more life here than was readily apparent.

They arrived at a row of tumbledown buildings he recognized as what had been the base command center—the place that should have communicated with him in space. There were unrecognizable hunks of rusty metal sitting around in various locations, and one could surmise that these were decaying remains of vehicles left to rot away.

The old woman lived in one of the sagging government buildings, a dilapidated structure that was now just a shack with a leaky roof and broken windows. The boys called to her before entering and requested permission to bring in a visitor.

"Come on in," came a voice from inside, a raspy sound that was actually a little more robust than that of the boys. "Who is the visitor?"

"I'm Buck Morgan, ma'am," the astronaut answered for the boys. He was somewhat taken aback when he saw the slight woman with the strong voice, because her appearance was much less impressive than her speech. She sat on a bamboo mat in one corner, dressed in a tunic of large leaves sewn together with coarse string.

"Glad to meet you, Mr. Morgan. I'm Mary Troy—or I used to be. Now I'm Memaw, as the boys call me. I'm actually their great-grandmother. What do you need?"

She adjusted her garb to be sure she was completely covered. Her sunken eyes looked him up and down as she studied Morgan's highly unusual clothing.

"Information, Memaw. Call me Buck. I need to know a lot, and fast," he explained. He then went into detail about his identity, the mission he had just completed, and the time dilation phenomenon that had placed him here.

"Buck Morgan, you said? Say, I do remember that name! Now you're starting to make some sense. I used to teach about you in school—over sixty, maybe sixty-five years ago. That was a long time ago," she recollected, a sudden look of recognition brightening her eyes. "It took years for your name to die down after you left. They said you'd be back someday. And here you are! Never thought I'd ever meet you, though. Haven't heard anyone mention you in years, come to think of it."

"Can you explain? I really need to know what's going on."

"What's happened? A new world order. A shift in focus. A brave experiment. Call it what you like," she replied, a look of disgust creeping across her wrinkled face and tainting her voice, something she tried to hide from the boys almost as an afterthought.

"How old are you, Memaw?"

"Pretty old. I'll be ninety in a few months. Not many live that long nowadays. I've seen a lot of change in my time."

"And you say you were once a teacher? Of what?"

"History and government."

"Would you mind sharing some of what you've seen with me? And what is this Concord bunch your boys have mentioned? And who is this man, Father the Hammer or whoever, that supposedly rules the world?"

"Supposedly is the wrong word," explained the old woman, an unmistakable undercurrent of disrespect invading in her voice. "He does rule the whole world. He's supreme master of the Concord for the Development of Humanity. He's got power beyond imagination, more than any other man in history. And I know a lot about history, or at least I used to. He's set himself up as more than a man. He's even being worshipped by many of his loyal subjects. It won't be long before he's demanding it, I'd wager. And everyone will do it, too."

"Worship? Worship a man? Whatever for?"

"He's worshipped because some people really believe in him. Some people worship him because he's so powerful. But most people worship him because they're afraid of him," she continued, lowering her voice on the last phrase to a whisper. "It's a very long story how it all came about."

"And he's in absolute power? What about democracy and elected government? And the United States?"

"No more. None of them. There's only one government now and one man heads it. What he says is law," replied the ancient woman with resignation.

She explained how the takeover had occurred, from the first victories of the species equality movement to formation of the Concord for the Development of Humanity and final consolidation of power under the Father. Morgan listened in total fixation as the wrinkled old woman related details of the new dating system. His mouth dropped open in amazement as she revealed telling details about the new arrangement.

"Why didn't people resist? Where were the medical people? How about sportsmen's groups? Where were farming organizations and ranchers? Pet lovers? Animal welfare groups? How could this have happened?"

"Complacent. Urbanized and disconnected. Disunited. Too tolerant and deceived or perhaps just too compromising. Who knows? When it became obvious it was too late, they disappeared," she replied sadly, again her words a mere whisper, as if she feared telling a secret. "While all those groups were fading away, the winners were pushing hard for equal treatment of humans and animals at every level. Once they all got together under the Concord, nothing could stop them."

"I can't believe this," Morgan said in bewilderment. He then gestured toward the heavens with a slightly uplifted hand and asked, "What the heck happened to the space program?"

"No need for it," she explained softly, barely audibly. "When the emphasis switched to equal treatment of animals and humans, science became the enemy. Progress on that front stopped cold. As you can see, the world has regressed to an amazing degree since I was a little girl. We used to have miracle medicines but they didn't seem important because we so seldom needed them. There was a smallpox epidemic a couple of years ago that killed my daughter and my granddaughter and almost got one of her boys. We old people did fine since we received universal anti-infection vaccine when we were children."

"Space Station Delta! You've got to know what happened to it, living here at the Cape like you do. What did they do with it?"

"Oh, that. It fell. Almost burned up the world. Dust blocked out the sun for a long time. See those dead trees? Caused by that fire and a big freeze that followed."

"So you can't eat meat…"

"No such thing anyway. Most animals have disappeared. We have to make do with a vegetable diet. Oh, we eat yeast sometimes, but it's the only animal product we're allowed. It's hard to get, though."

"No meat? This is absolutely inconceivable. How could this happen?"

Morgan sat in stunned silence, and put his head down, resting his forehead on his hands. For a full minute nobody said anything as awful reality settled in. It was Memaw who finally broke the silence.

"We're lucky that we ourselves haven't been eaten, as a matter of fact. Predators are a big problem, eating people everywhere, I understand. Here they never got the foothold they did most places. Worst thing we've had to deal with is wild dogs. And once in a while a panther."

"Eating people? What? Why don't they shoot them?"

"You've got a lot to learn, Buck Morgan. You can't do that anymore."

"Oh, yes, I forgot. No guns. Is there still commerce? Can you go somewhere and buy things you need?"

"We go to Central Supply for Concord bread and other things we can't grow ourselves. All you have to do is wave your hand over the sensor and get whatever they have that you need. Problem is that they don't have much. And I hear there'll be no more bread after this year," the old woman explained, lifting her right hand and showing him a small bump even as she again lowered her voice to a barely audible level. "We all have implanted microchips to identify us as eligible to receive supplies. And through the chip they are able to monitor every conversation we have, if they want to. They usually don't, though. And if they do I don't care anyway."

"Why no more bread?"

"They're going to stop large scale harvesting. Too many insects die. Everyone will have to harvest by hand so we can share with the bugs without harming them. It's the latest decree from the Father."

The veteran space traveler was silent again for a moment. He looked around once more, noting the deplorable conditions and awful deterioration. For some reason visions of ancient Mayan ruins, grand cities completely covered with rubble and vegetation, came stalking into his tormented mind.

"You say you were a teacher, Memaw? What did you say you taught?"

"History. And government. I once knew a great deal about the subjects. I've forgotten a lot. I've kept a lot of books but there's not much left up here," she stated wearily, pointing to her head.

"Books? Where, Memaw? Can I look at them?"

"In there. A whole shelf of them. Pretty worthless, all of them. I'm going to burn them, I guess."

Morgan went into a dark adjacent room, where indeed there were dozens of books on various subjects, some written since his departure. He longed to spend hours going through them. One bright green one, which looked newer than the others, caught his eye, and he pulled it from the shelf. On the cover it proclaimed the title: *Heroes of the Cause* by Hilda Archer Prestone. It had been published fifty years after his departure. Intrigued, he pondered its title thoughtfully. The author's name struck a familiar chord, but he couldn't remember why. He returned to the dim main living area with the book in hand.

"Can I have this one?"

"I've no need for it. Take it."

He slipped it into the thigh pocket of his white leather coveralls and thanked the old woman.

"The boys say their dad is away, serving in the—the Concord, is it? In the Concord army? Why do they need an army if this outfit rules the whole world?"

"Oh, my grandson was in the Middle East, last time we heard from him. He's a cavalryman in a great army that's assembling there. Did I tell you that?"

"But who are they fighting, Memaw?"

"They fight anyone who opposes the Father."

"But who's opposing him in the Middle East?"

"Jews. They've been a real problem for the world government. First they wouldn't join, then they relented and did join. But they've continued to be disobedient. They still have lots of sheep and cattle, and they officially allow meat to be consumed in defiance of the Father.

"So," Morgan mulled aloud, "they eat meat and the Father is willing to wage war on them because of it? Now I understand all the radio talk about Israel."

"Worse than just eating meat. We all keep up with the latest word on our Concord radio and the news is shocking, even to an old woman like me. They refuse to pay homage to the Father. He made peace with them sometime back, but it's been an unsteady truce. He let them rebuild their worship place under certain conditions, I understand. Now they've started doing the unthinkable there."

"What do you mean by unthinkable?" Morgan queried, something vaguely familiar crystallizing down deep in his consciousness. "What's happening over there?"

"They've really got the Father angry. They've started performing sacrifices in their holy place. Sacrificing living creatures to some kind of god. The Father has vowed to stop it at any cost. The army is gathering to carry out his orders. He's promised to solve the Jewish problem once and for all, and then we'll always have peace. That's what the Father says."

Something Morgan had recently read came cascading back into his mind. He felt his knees becoming shaky and his head was practically spinning. A lot of things just wouldn't compute, and at the moment there didn't seem to be much hope for anything better tomorrow.

CHAPTER 40

April 2169

The planetary lander did not go unnoticed as it broke the sound barrier in its precipitous descent to the Cape. Concord Forces all over the world had already been alerted to be watching for just such an occurrence. Buck Morgan had not noticed any sign that he had been detected in his monitoring of Concord frequencies. He would check with Calvin as soon as he got back to the lander. There had been little reason for concern prior to his conversation with the old woman and two boys. Now he understood something of the fanaticism that ruled, and he knew that his very life could be in danger if he fell into the hands of authorities. His practical mind stuffed the awful depression that assaulted him, and simple survival became the driving force.

* * *

"So he landed in Florida. That makes sense, with the defunct space facility there. He would naturally return to home port," surmised the sullen Father, who was personally supervising capture of the spaceman. "Are our forces there complying with orders?"

"Beyond all question, Father. We will assuredly have him in hand shortly. There is already a guard at his craft and a team is approaching the old base, where he was seen walking with two natives. He won't elude us for long," reported Foxx confidently. "We shall not do him bodily harm, shall we, Father?"

"No, he isn't to be harmed—at least not yet. We must entice him to retrieve his precious cargo. As worthless scum is purged from an area, we can restock the land with more deserving creatures. But we must be very careful that Morgan stays functional until a complete repatriation is accomplished."

"Yes, Father, I understand. All will be concluded as you wish, my Lord."

Even as the ruler and his underling were speaking, Morgan was walking back toward the idle lander, unsure what to do next. He was abruptly shaken from his sober thoughts by the unwelcome sight of several blue and white uniforms coming toward them from up ahead. The boys who had been accompanying him suddenly disappeared without a word and melted into gray underbrush. He could see several more policemen farther along, as well as a battered car that bore a strange blue and white circular emblem. For a brief moment he felt an overpowering urge to flee, and he had to fight the impulse with determination to prevent it from taking over his mind. But where could he go anyway?

Ultimately, he decided rationally that he had no choice but to continue and confront the police. Surely they could find no real reason to detain him, his innocence, indeed his complete ignorance, regarding the current world situation was so clear. Just the same he fingered his stun pistol and concealed it where it would be completely unobtrusive yet readily available if needed.

"Halt! You're under arrest!" shouted the first policeman to spot him. He used an amalgamated dialect similar to that used by the boys, a bit difficult at first but not at all unintelligible. The patrol had been well versed and knew that their quarry was not to be harmed. Morgan was in no imminent danger, but he had no way of knowing this. There were two policemen approaching him with automatic weapons drawn, a type of gun he recognized immediately as being quite the latest technology when he had left. Would he be an instant victim of the Concord police?

Morgan raised his hands in mock surrender and approached the two men, while the other four now left their station by the lander and headed toward them. It seemed highly prudent to use an innocent and unaware approach, and to that end he greeted the scowling men in uniform with a broad smile.

"You boys are mighty nervous, aren't you? I parked in a no parking zone, I guess?"

"Shut up, smart boy. You just killed about a thousand of our fellow humans with that speeding vehicle. Their precious parts are smeared all over it. You're in a deep pile of trouble, I can tell you that," snarled the lieutenant who was leader of the detachment. "Get those hands higher!"

"Can I shoot him, sir?" asked the patrol's lowest ranking member. "He's not just a killer, sir. His leather clothes demand the death penalty, too."

"You shut up, too, you idiot. We have orders direct from Rome that this one is not to be harmed under any circumstances. Get on to that car now, Mister Universe, and be quick about it."

The voice was as cold and unemotional as any Morgan had ever encountered, and its icy sound erected fine hair on the back of his neck. These guys were conditioned and hardened. He would have to be careful.

"So you already know about me. I don't suppose you would answer any questions for me about how I got to be so wanted and all? And you must understand, I know nothing about your new laws. Everything was quite different in the world when I left. Do you have any idea how long I've been gone?"

"There are no excuses, so don't ask irrelevant questions. You can expect to be dealt with finally by the Father. He wants you flown immediately to Rome by special helicopter courier. There is no way of knowing what he has planned for you, but he demands that your cargo be unloaded immediately. You have earthly creatures, right?"

The officer knew he was perhaps overstepping his bounds in telling Morgan this bit of information, but he couldn't resist showing how much he knew. It was bound to impress his subordinates.

"If I cooperate fully, will the Father overlook my ignorance of his law?"

"How would I know that? He's the supreme authority and our omnipotent spiritual guide. No mere man can presume to anticipate his thoughts. But I can tell you he never accepts excuses from anyone."

"Then I'll have to negotiate with him about that. If he wants those animals, he'd be wise to overlook transgressions that I didn't know were against the rules."

The policeman's hand shot out and slapped Morgan hard, bursting his upper lip and almost knocking him off his feet, catching him by complete surprise. Morgan shook his head dizzily, incredulous that such force was applied so casually.

"Insolent one! Never imply that the Father could be anything but right. And never refer to your fellow creatures in such derogatory terms. Animals, indeed! You are the animal! Your attitude shows disrespect that would have you swimming in your own blood even now, if you weren't protected by the Father's direct orders. From now on, keep your mouth shut. Imbecile!"

Morgan did just that. He pulled a kerchief from his pocket and wiped the oozing corner of his mouth; he was grateful he apparently still had his teeth intact. The lip swelled considerably as they walked back to the lander. Morgan came to a resolute conclusion while they moved along in silence, as dry ground crunched underneath each step. Never could he or would he willingly submit to the authority of such fanatics. But was there any way to escape these heavily armed men?

The Concord lieutenant escorted Morgan dutifully around the lander, cursing repeatedly as he demonstrated a plethora of incriminating bug strikes on the nose and cowling. The officer repeatedly fingered his automatic weapon, exercising unfamiliar and grudging restraint to keep from killing Morgan on the spot.

In the distance they could now hear a mechanical rhythm, the sound of helicopter rotor blades beating in heavy atmosphere. It had to be Morgan's ride to Rome, perhaps via a series of ship platforms across the Atlantic where they could refuel, he speculated. He marveled that airplanes were now banned because of their high speed impact on bugs, a voluntary abrogation of technology that had to be unprecedented in human history. He silently wondered if they somehow prevented such impact with helicopters, not being aware of speed limits imposed on regime pilots when flying less than 5,000 feet above ground level.

Morgan began to watch and wait for exactly the right moment as a plan formed in his mind. He knew he would have only one opportunity, so he had to be absolutely certain that all was perfect. He pretended to be very concerned and contrite about the insects he had killed and tried to feign a deep regret, to which his captor simply growled all the more menacingly.

The helicopter was coming closer so he had to do something soon. Morgan used his minimal amount of freedom to maneuver to a spot near the lander stairs and watched carefully for all the Concord police to move into a relatively small area in front of the lander. He needed all of them within approximately the same thirty degrees of arc in front of him. Only one man was outside that zone now and he kept moving away. Meanwhile, the ominous rotor noise was coming ever closer. He decided to take desperate action, so he simply started walking away, heading purposefully back in the direction of the old woman's home. He hoped the group would remember their orders that he was to be taken alive and would not simply gun him down. If he had perceived correctly, they themselves would be in mortal danger if they failed to hold him alive.

"Hey, dummy! Come back here! Where you going? Stop, you fool!"

Morgan just kept walking until he heard the hiss of an automatic weapon. There was no impact so the policeman was obviously firing into the air. Nevertheless, the threatening sound caused him to stop, and he suppressed a powerful recurring urge to flee uncontrollably. He raised his hands and slowly turned around. The whole group was now moving toward him, tightly bunched up. He let his hands drop as they approached and slipped his hand into the pocket where the stun pistol was located. The patrol failed to notice as they scrambled in his direction, and he suddenly hoisted it to fire position and let fly an electronic blast.

All six policemen piled up on the ground, and their weapons clattered away in all directions. He grabbed one of the guns, but discovered quickly that the mechanism was tightly locked and inoperative. Maybe something to do with that chip thing, he puzzled. He hurriedly dragged two of the men a little farther from the lander lest they be incinerated by his takeoff, and then he speedily ascended the steps as the helicopter appeared at one end of the runway.

He was thankful he had already prepared for takeoff. He didn't have time for a thorough check of all systems as mandated by his training and experience. This was war and he had to get moving or die. He pushed the lightup switch as soon as the canopy closed and with a sudden and mighty roar he was instantly airborne. The helicopter fired a volley at him as he ascended, but pitiful pieces of lead did no damage whatever to the impenetrable hull of the lander. He had made it!

Now where to? Why not the farm in Kansas? There might even still be relatives living there!

"Coordinates for Adrian, Kansas, my old home place! All navigation aids are inoperative, so lock it in, Calvin," he yelled into the mike. "Man, do you have some catching up to do, holo amigo!"

"I'm getting educated pretty well, Commander Bucko. Their radio transmissions are extremely telling. Sorry I couldn't warn you about that patrol. Coordinates for the Morgan place are plotted and locked in. You're going to be getting low on fuel by the time you land there," returned the artificial man with no query delay.

Perhaps Calvin had already been thinking about Morgan's next move. There wasn't enough fuel left to rendezvous with the *Ursa C*, so the old home place was the most logical next stop, in view of the situation. The efficient machine instantly adjusted course to take him there direct.

As he accelerated, inevitable questions dogged him. Would things be any better where he was going? Would not there be pursuit in place shortly? Did the crafty and insightful Father already have people waiting at the farm this very moment? If not, did these primitive chasers still possess the technology to track his craft? They certainly had functioning computers of some type, as evidenced by the microchip implants and the worldwide surveillance system. But were all these focused only on the surface?

There was no way to know but to try. The answers would come momentarily.

It was too late to change his mind now. And he honestly couldn't think of anywhere else to go, anyway.

CHAPTER 41

April 2169

Dust swirled in the cool, dry air, stinging the eyes and soiling everything it touched. Blackened limbs of dead elm trees clawed skyward, starkly framing a dilapidated metal building. A train of shabby farm trucks churned brown dirt into miniature tornadoes as each one backed up in turn and deposited its precious produce into a collection bin. Tattered and tired, Jody Barnes was at the wheel of one of the rigs, and he eyed an overseeing Concord policeman warily as the man perused an instrument he was holding. To Barnes' great disappointment, the man helpd up his hand requiring him to halt.

"Mister, I get a no read indication on the scanner," sneered the policeman. "You know that's serious, don't you? You're in rebellion against Concord authority."

Barnes swallowed hard and said a brief, inaudible prayer. He knew that he had been approaching the end of his ability to resist, and probably this was it. The chip question again, posed unavoidably by an unblinking officer.

"Sir, I work hard. I bring in more loads than anyone else. Making deliveries while doing this year's planting requires double duty. I haven't even had time to leave my fields and get last year's crop transferred," lied Barnes necessarily, searching the cold eyes for some vestige of compassion. The man kept his automatic weapon at ready, and Barnes had seen him execute more than one hapless victim on the spot for less significant infractions. The local police commander, Captain Darwin Archer, walked up at just that moment, and recognized Jody Barnes. He motioned his underling away to supervise another arriving truck.

"I'll handle this one. Move to the next one," he commanded. The policeman lowered his weapon and complied.

Archer looked the dingy, ragged young man up and down, trying to muster some indifference, but he couldn't miss the unmistakable similarity between the youth and his missing father, Jamie Barnes. That long ago childhood friendship the officer had shared with the departed farmer cascaded back into his mind, and he felt a rare twinge of compassion. He shook his head, dubious about this unfamiliar sensation. It would be risky, since his underling had discovered Barnes' noncompliance, but he would try to get away with it just once.

"You do produce, dirt man. Tell you what, kid, I'm going to make a note of your name and farm. If you aren't chipped next visit, you're dead," the officer said in his iciest voice. Both men sensed that it was a delicate situation. Barnes breathed a silent prayer of thanks as he pulled out for home.

"Jody, what's the big deal about the chip injection?" asked his cousin Harold Atkins after Barnes related the incident to the family. Atkins had joined the family as a refugee from Wichita a few weeks earlier. He had been a welcome addition for Barnes, who needed all the help he could get. "I know lots of people who've been chipped. They all tell me it doesn't hurt. They use an air puff injector, and you need only wave your right hand as you pick up supplies or drop off produce or anything. Sounds like a good system. People with a missing right hand get it in their forehead, I've heard."

"I'm glad you asked that. You hadn't arrived when we reviewed that the other night," answered Barnes. "There's impelling reason to reject such a mark. The Concord identifier chip is identical to an astounding prediction we read about."

He went on to explain the whole issue to Atkins thoroughly, pointing out to him beyond question why none of them could accept the procedure under any circumstances. In relating this steadfast conclusion, young Barnes was astounded at his passion even as he spoke the words. It was an unlikely development that he could believe anything so fervently, certainly absolutely implausible that he would be willing to die for anything. My, how your attitudes change, he reflected silently. He wished secretly that his father could be there to see how he had been transformed.

A new hired man made the next few deliveries to the collection point. He was a starving drifter they had taken in despite the fact that he had been chipped. Barnes compensated him well with extra food, but he knew down deep that the makeshift arrangement would not last long. Archer and his henchmen were bound to make note of the change in drivers. Even if they didn't, someone else would soon be around because Barnes' name and address had been recorded as being in noncompliance. Even if neither of these happened, Barnes was sure the hired man would betray them, anyway, as soon as he figured out why the farmer had stopped making deliveries personally. There were attractive rewards for legal subjects who reported infractions.

"Tonight we pray fervently," Barnes advised them all. "In fact, let's pray constantly all day, too. I hate to think about the next time we're checked. God help us."

Barnes was working diligently in his field a few days later, trying to get some hybrid soybeans planted. This was the best variety, and their excellent protein content was playing a critical role in keeping the family healthy. Their high quality animal protein stockpile had long since been consumed, even before his parents had disappeared. Plant alternatives were now essential, unless they were prepared to risk capital punishment for eating insects.

Barnes had schooled himself well in the amino acid content of various plant-based foods, digging in his dad's small library for the information. Sarah and Molly had become efficient at preparing vegetarian meals, too. All of them topped off their meals with micro-meat, or yeast extract, each day for essential vitamin B12. Overall, they were faring much better than the poor, ignorant masses, who subsisted on far less knowledge and a considerably smaller amount food. Sarah and Molly had recently tried to hold a class in nutrition for needy people in the area, but few people had attended, and those who came had great difficulty understanding the concepts. A pervading absence of basic educational background had been a distinct hindrance.

The latest decree from Geneva, bearing the official Concord seal, would signal the end of large scale farming anyway. It had been forecast by Concord radio that the declaration was coming, but no one had been required to make the change pending official notification. The Father had determined that large machinery contributed hideously to the deaths of innumerable innocent, tiny humans, and he had set a firm date for termination of all machine-assisted farming. There could be little doubt that many in the cities would starve as a direct result, but if the little family could survive it would make their job somewhat easier, since planting would be reduced to a fraction of their current acreage. Hopefully pervasive Concord oversight of their activities would even diminish. Barnes went about his current project with full realization that this would likely be his last large planting.

The young man pondered this latest requirement as he worked, but suddenly he had all thoughts of farming chased from his mind. A blue and white Concord police vehicle turned off the main road through the gate leading to the farmhouse, and began easing slowly down the lane. Trouble, he knew instantly!

He spun the tractor around immediately, grinding one wheel into the dirt as he locked a brake and pivoted 180 degrees. He set his sights directly on the house and shoved the big machine into high gear. Irregular ground of the field pounded him badly as he drove homeward, and his front wheels intermittently left the ground from such unaccustomed speed. His heart raced as he swung into the yard, slid to a skidding stop, and jumped to the ground before the engine was completely dead.

There were six policemen in the vehicle, and four of them were on the porch by the time breathless Barnes arrived. They had already checked the hired helper for chipping and had ordered him out of the yard.

"Officer, here I am! What do you want?" he called as he approached. He looked around desperately for Darwin Archer, but his father's old friend was absent. He gulped hard and blurted out hoarsely, "I'm Jody Barnes. Where's Captain Archer?"

"Shut up, scum. We'll ask the questions. Your buddy Archer's a fool and he got what fools deserve."

Barnes tried to make his dry throat swallow as crushing disappointment swept through him like a life-draining infection. He had held a dim hope that the officer would question him alone, but it was clearly not to be. The brusque man was exceptionally irritable and demanding as he barked commands.

"Get everyone out here now or we're going in after them. We know there are three children, you and your woman, and another man and woman living here. Get them out here! And do it *now*!"

Barnes groaned perceptibly as all prospects of anyone hiding in the house suddenly dissolved. Sarah was already at the door, her crying toddler and the two orphan girls with her. A policeman roughly dragged her through the door and shoved her and the children down on the floor. Another uniformed man entered the house and returned in a few minutes with Molly. One of them retrieved Harold Atkins from a garden plot behind the ramshackle barn. Barnes wondered why Atkins had not hidden or fled at the first sign of trouble.

"Just a little scanning procedure, folks," the leader of the patrol announced, his voice heavy with unconcealed malice. He produced a digital scanner as he spoke. "I'm in charge, and nobody gets any breaks. Each of you, extend your right hand!"

He went from person to person in turn, the instrument giving no indication on Barnes, Sarah, the children, or Molly. When he reached Atkins, however, the indicator sprang to life, displaying a prominent green number.

"Harold, you got chipped!" Barnes blurted out in genuine bewilderment. Before he had finished speaking, the brusque officer's backhand caught him directly in the face, sending him sprawling with blood gushing from his ruptured nose.

"Shut up, rebel! You, get out of here!" He motioned Atkins off the porch with the menacing point of his weapon and made him keep moving on out of the yard.

"The rest of you line up against the wall!" the man snapped harshly. Barnes was still woozy from the stiff blow he had suffered, but he forced himself to his feet and complied. He used the ragged sleeve of his shirt to wipe his nose as crimson cascaded over his upper lip and dripped from his chin. He tried to hold pressure against his injury with the other arm, though the effort was only partially effective. Sarah and Molly had tears streaming down their cheeks, and both of them tried to assist Barnes while acceding to the man's ultimatum. The porch was a madhouse as two little girls sobbed uncontrollably and a small child cried loudly.

Two policemen readied their automatic weapons for firing. Barnes regained a bit of composure and courage, enough to urge his frightened family gently but with an understandably subdued and stuffy voice, "Let's pray the Lord's Prayer, girls."

The snake-eyed men raised their weapons and the group of condemned prisoners began to pray quietly.

Suddenly, a blinding flash from above interrupted the desperate situation. Heat and light increased rapidly in intensity, emanating from high over the farm. These effects were accompanied by a rising swell of deafening noise. The whole group, executioners as well as intended victims, watched in absolute astonishment as a strange craft descended slowly from the sky. It touched down gently in the front yard, scorching away grass down to bare soil in the process. Intense wind blasted debris in all directions, soiled the whole group and speckled the crisp police uniforms with copious black dirt and bits of dry plant material.

"What the blazes!" exclaimed the head policeman, shielding his eyes and shouting expletives over the thunderous roar, while he clung to the porch railing for support. "You people, back against that wall! Nobody moves!"

As the object ceased to resonate loudly and its hot blast subsided, the group waited nervously while the whine of high tech machine parts gradually wound to a stop. The canopy popped open and out stepped a most unusual looking man, dressed in sparkling processed leather coveralls.

"Who in Hades are you?" called the officer. "And get your butt over here now!"

"I'm coming, sir. You'll doubtless tell me my clothes are in violation of Concord law and that you're going to mete out justice, right?"

"You're cussing right we'll mete out justice, you stupid idiot," replied the Concord officer. "You're about to see how swift it is, too!"

"Lieutenant, this has got to be that Morgan fellow the Father wants alive. You remember the bulletin this morning?"

"It's captain now, jerk. You think I didn't hear the bulletin? Trying to make a little rank, are you?" he scowled with obvious contempt. His dark eyes narrowed with menace as he stared frostily at his underling. Turning back to Morgan, he raised the threatening intonation in his voice a couple of notches and questioned him maliciously, "Your name Morgan, mister? Answer quick or you're an instant carcass."

"I might be him. Who's asking?"

"Blast you, I've got a good mind to...you've got about two seconds to answer me!" bellowed the officer, forcing a spray of droplets from his mouth.

"Yeah, I'm Morgan," came the cool reply. "And you'd best know that there's a penalty you don't want to pay if you damage me. Orders from the Father."

The effect was instant as the officer exploded in a string of expletives, uncontrollably infuriated.

"Get your stupid butt over there. We've got some business to take care of before we get to you. You've got yours coming whether I have the distinct privilege of triggering you or not," he fumed.

Morgan was ushered to the other side of the spacious porch at gunpoint, well away from the trembling family. He waited until the entire patrol was separated from the family before he acted. When the two executioners lifted their weapons, he could hear the click of their safety locks being released. The position of the men was not ideal, so he could only hope he could envelope all of them, and that the charge in his stun gun was still sufficient. His hand flew upward before any of them could react, and he activated the device. To his great relief, all six officers suddenly toppled into a pile, their limbs in paralyzed disarray. Their weapons bounced noisily but harmlessly away on the ancient wooden floor.

"What the...? Who are you? You saved us! At least for now..." Barnes stammered, the rapid sequence of events leaving him dizzy and weak. He stared up from the family huddle with a solid sheet of drying blood adhered to his nose and mouth, and the front of his dirty clothes a dark scarlet. He could hardly force himself to release his arms from the terrified women and children and struggle to his feet.

"I'm Buck Morgan. And you're Jody Barnes, I presume," said their deliverer as he extended his hand to assist him.

"How...how did you know that?" Sarah asked in awe. Her voice was quaking and she was still trembling all over, as she remained prostrate on the porch deck, trying to comfort the children.

"Easy. These guys don't have any radio security whatsoever. My partner Calvin in the *Ursa C*, my ship up there, knows all about them already," said Morgan, pointing a finger skyward. "He picked up that patrol's orders as soon as they did and relayed them to me. I was afraid I'd get here too late, though. This little stun pistol does a good job, doesn't it?"

"Buck Morgan! Oh, my, you did come back! We've always called our farm 'The Morgan Place'! I just now recognized the name!" exclaimed Barnes, recovering significantly. He took a kerchief offered him by Morgan and began to clean his face and chin. "What a time to return! You saved our lives! You're an answer to prayer, Buck Morgan."

"I guess I am, at that. I hope you know that we're relatives, Jody. I've hunted quail with several generations of your ancestors. I don't know how close we're kin, but you've got to be a cousin of some kind."

"Your cousin? You know, you're right. Grandpa Billy told me once before he died that I'm your fourth cousin, I think. I haven't been one to dwell on family history, though. My dad was Jamie Barnes. He and Mom disappeared some time back."

"I never knew your father. Billy was just a kid last time I was here, and I only saw him a couple of times. Jerry Barnes must have been your great grandfather. Jerry was a young man when I took off on my mission, and still had no children. He was my first cousin."

"Then our son, Abraham, would be your fifth cousin, Buck. This is my wife Sarah, and our friend Molly Hancock. These girls are the Hansen sisters, Rhonda and Wanda, from Wichita. Welcome home, such as it is."

"Thanks. But we're all going to need a lot more prayers answered if we don't figure out something quick. They've put out a bulletin to shoot me on sight since I eluded them at the Cape. Fortunately, it wasn't issued until these guys left their vehicle or we might all be dead."

"Shoot you on sight? Why? For your clothes or what?" asked Molly, able to speak for the first time since the rescue. She looked admiringly up and down the smartly cut coveralls Morgan was wearing, the only decent clothes she had seen in years except for plant fiber linens worn by Concord police. "They usually at least interrogate people."

"I had to stun a patrol of them at the Cape like I did these guys. I dragged a couple of them away from the ship, but Calvin heard them say that the blast burned them pretty good anyway when I took off. I don't think it killed any of them, but their commander is really livid, I guess. Their radio transmissions are quite venomous right now when they refer to me," Morgan replied, his gentle, confident voice somehow inspiring the group to a revitalized hope. Molly couldn't keep her eyes off this apparition from the past, and she kept reviewing in her mind all the legend-like tales about him that had been passed down for decades in their little community.

"Who is this Calvin you keep mentioning?" she asked, her composure recovering more by the minute.

"My artificial intelligence complex, up on the starship. The holographic display is in the form of a man I once knew, and Calvin is his name. He's pretty darn real to me, though, after living with him for nine years."

"I've never even heard of anything like that. An artificial man? Weird."

"Weird, maybe, but he's more than smart. He's super intelligent. And he'll help us all he can."

"Are they trying to kill you just because you toasted a couple of guys somewhere?"

"Not exactly for that, I don't think. They apparently told the Father I used some kind of special weapon to escape. He doesn't want me around causing trouble. He gave them permission to kill me just before I initiated my landing sequence. I just took the chance that this patrol might be acting on the old orders to capture me but not harm me. Fortunately, I was right."

Only now did Morgan notice how beautiful was the young lady to whom he was talking. She was soiled and wore nothing but rags, but her raw loveliness was impossible to hide with such superficialities. Or was it just that he hadn't seen a female in nine years? He looked Molly up and down inquisitively.

"Did Jody say your name is Molly Hancock?"

"He did," she replied. "Does my name sound familiar? I'm your old teacher's descendant. In fact, I'm her great-granddaughter. I know all about you, Buck."

"Well, I'll be darned! You even favor her," Morgan marveled, looking her over again and again as he reached out his hands and took her shoulders in a firm grip. Her petite nose and perfect mouth drew him like a lodestone, and somehow he felt a powerful urge to kiss her, a tantalizing feeling which was totally irrational, and which he fought off with some difficulty. He almost felt like a fool, having to resist such a preposterous impulse. Still, her perfectly aligned white teeth and stunning eyes mesmerized him for a long moment. It was a distinct instant of soaring joy in an otherwise devastating homecoming. The two Hansen girls were still clinging to Molly, and Morgan had little choice but to break away his gaze and acknowledge them.

"Did somebody say Hansen, from Wichita?"

"Yes," said Molly, "These girls lost their parents to predators sometime back, and they've been with us since. Their father was a professor at Wichita State until recently."

"Really? I once knew a professor named Hansen from that same university. An electrobiologist, Dr. Albert Hansen. Recognize the name, girls?"

"Dad's grandfather, sir. We never knew him," said Rhonda. "But we sure do miss Mom and Dad."

"Predators, you say? Shame. Some of Dr. Hansen's force field medicine could have prevented that. But I'm not surprised the technology is lost, considering what I've seen so far."

It was Barnes who snapped their attention back to the menacing situation at hand. Pointing to the unconscious patrol, he verbalized its gravity.

"Buck, how long will they be out? We can hide their weapons, but at best we won't have more than an hour before someone comes to check on them," Barnes lamented. "And then there's Harold and that hired guy—they're out on the road watching us right now. We can't even trust Harold not to flag down another patrol, now that he's chipped. The hired guy is most likely hoping somebody will come by so he can put them on us and collect a reward. They'd both be executed if they didn't."

"They'll be out an hour or so," Morgan estimated. "But somebody probably already knows something is amiss here. They're probably monitoring our conversation even now through these guys' chips. If nothing else, they had to see me landing, so we've got to hurry. I can't believe how serious they are about this chipping thing."

"Oh, yeah, another of the Father's decrees," Barnes explained. "Only new Christians are refusing, and the penalty is instant death when authorities find you in noncompliance. It's happening everywhere, I'm told. We just can't submit to it because of our beliefs, and we were on the verge of being administered their brand of justice when you arrived and saved our lives. There aren't a lot of us who hold to our beliefs, I guess, but because of our convictions we have no choice but to refuse the chip."

531

"Resisting to the point of death? Pretty severe. And this Harold you mentioned? Who's he?"

"He's my cousin—actually, my cousin's husband," Barnes clarified. "She died in the smallpox epidemic. But Harold had seemed to fit in well with us—until now."

"Smallpox? You'll have to explain that one. Seems like I've heard of it. And did you say *new* Christians, Jody? What do you mean by new?"

"All the old ones disappeared some time back, including my parents. The only Christians on Earth now are those who have become convinced since the great disappearance. I'm ashamed to say none of us here believed in what seemed to be nonsense until someone we loved disappeared. The Father blamed that incident on aliens from outer space, and claims he even predicted it ahead of time, so he says no one should be surprised they're gone. But we're convinced that something else happened to them."

"I see. I've read or heard somewhere before about a phenomenon like you describe. What about this smallpox thing? Isn't that a disease?"

"Oh, you bet. A killer disease. Swept the world and killed billions. You wouldn't believe how awful it was."

"I think I'd believe almost anything now."

Morgan looked over the beleaguered group, noting how much better nourished—and dressed—they were compared with the pitiful creatures he had encountered at the Cape. Their cotton garments were rough and ragged, to be sure, but they were relatively intact and functional. What havoc this Concord bunch has wrought on this world, he thought woefully. If only he had the means to fight them and perhaps set up a resistance organization. But the world he had left was one of peace, at least on an international level. Being prepared for this kind of catastrophe had never entered the minds of his mission planners.

Morgan checked the weapons of the immobilized policemen to see if they were the same as those he had inspected at the Cape. The integrated firing mechanism was likewise programmed so that operation could take place only when the appropriate fingerprint was holding the rifle, and the wielding hand had to be implanted with the correct microchip of one specific policeman. The devices were even temperature sensitive so that severing a hand and using the correct detached member to activate them would not work. They were completely worthless to any other individual except the one for which they were programmed, making an armed rebellion all but impossible. Without weapons, no opposing army could stand. It appeared completely hopeless. He took Jody aside, well away from the sleeping soldiers, and whispered to him.

"Say, Jody, you tell me it seems that Christians are the only group resisting the Concord's authority? Are you aware of any enclaves, any safe havens, anywhere? I could take you there, if there are. I have fuel enough for only one more short flight, but I'll try to get you to a secure location, if there is one. I can't return to my ship without refueling and taking on a new supply of water, anyway."

"No, I don't think so. Wait—my Dad said one time that there was a group in the Rocky Mountains, come to think of it. A friend who had a secret radio used to talk to them. Unfortunately, Concord police killed him, so we haven't heard any news from that group since," Barnes remembered sadly. "They possibly were discovered and destroyed, too."

"It doesn't take much figuring to see that we've got to go somewhere besides here," Morgan said, his eyes wistfully probing the familiar hills again, his gaze finally fixing on the east cemetery knoll where his father and mother had been buried so long ago. "Oh, how I'd love to spend some time here on our old farm. I've anticipated returning here for a long, long time. I recall so many pleasant memories as I look around. So many quail hunts and other happy times. Bobwhite quail, my favorites."

"Well, the quail are gone, anyway, Buck. They've been extinct for years now. So you aren't having to leave your favorite animals behind, at least."

"It's a disaster, but I don't even have time to visit my parents' graves, just over that hill there," Morgan said softly, pointing. There was a thoughtful pause, and then he broke suddenly from his nostalgic trance.

"Get your essentials and anything else you might need. This old ship is a cargo lander, so bring out everything you can carry. It'll haul a bunch."

For safety, Morgan bound the policemen and threw their weapons into the deep well while the others gathered their belongings. He couldn't help but watch Molly, beautiful in face and body despite her hard life and recent abuse. He wondered how this pretty girl had become a part of the beleaguered Barnes family, and he was almost embarrassed by the way his eyes were drawn to her over and over.

The astronaut helped the family finish moving the assembled materials to the craft, and each of them made multiple trips into and out of the house. Molly brought out a huge, stainless metal pot, which she was struggling to carry because of its weight. Morgan recognized the vessel immediately as he relieved her of the load and carried it to the lander. It was the very cooking utensil of space age alloy that he had brought home to his father so many years before. He was almost overwhelmed by deep, bothersome emotions as he stowed the pot and secured its lid tightly. For sure he didn't want soybeans floating all over the lander during their flight.

After all the items had been gathered and stowed in the cargo hold, Morgan strapped five new spacepersons and one new space child into available seating. As he prepared to lift off, Molly requested to sit up front with him, and he was more than glad to oblige her. He helped her get the seat adjusted and the compulsory safety devices in place before returning to his cockpit instrument panel to do a bit less hurried and more thorough preflight check this time. After all, he had picked up some pretty precious cargo and much more was at stake on this flight than on his earlier hop.

"Jody, this has got to be a quick flight. We're almost down to red line on fuel already. I'm going to take off on a west-northwest heading, and get Calvin to help me do a scan of North America. If we can pick up that Rocky Mountain group, I'll try to get a read on their position. It'll have to be a quick find or we're landing blind," he called as he did his preflight check. "By the way, Jody, quail aren't really extinct like you thought."

"No joke? Where are any?"

"On the *Ursa C*, my ship. A whole healthy colony of them."

Morgan radioed Calvin after completing his normal preparatory steps and initiating takeoff sequence.

"Look for a low intensity beacon—a regular old-time radio— somewhere in the Rocky Mountains," he transmitted sharply to his parent ship.

"I've got it already, Commander Bucko. Initial heading three-two-two from your present position. For security I'm loading final heading and distance into your onboard computer under security file. Pull up code four-four-six-Romeo for final instructions."

"Roger, good work, Calvin. We're off," returned Morgan. "You're a darn good warrior, holo amigo."

The policemen were just arousing from their enforced sleep when the lander blasted off. Through blurred eyes and dull hearing, they perceived dimly, like a dream, its departure for parts unknown.

Morgan didn't know if he could find a safe haven. One thing he did know—the old home place was certain death, so they'd have to take their chances almost anywhere else. The acceleration pushed him back into his seat as force generated by the powerful engines roared onward. The mighty blasts surged their craft skyward atop a fountain of fire while exhaust gases licked the scorched ground a second time. For the moment, they were safe.

Finding a secure landing place might be impossible, but they had some idea where to go. Or at least Calvin did. God help us, they all prayed silently. Whether it would turn out to be a safe haven was out of their hands. Buck Morgan had never felt such a need for divine intervention in all his life.

CHAPTER 42

April 2169

Even while initial G forces made his arms feel deadweight heavy, Morgan was able to function with effort. He pulled up the code Calvin had indicated, which opened a secure file of his computer. In that digital repository were explicit heading and coordinate data, and within seconds Morgan had adjusted the lander's trajectory toward the central Rocky Mountains, and hopefully a place of safety. He locked the autopilot on his destination so that only manual adjustment would be needed for final approach. In a bittersweet flashback, he couldn't help but think of a previous joyful trip to the Rockies as a teenager in happier times long ago.

"Molly, I'm trying to raise the group on the radio. They've got to be there. Calvin is seldom wrong, but I'm getting nothing yet," he told his untrained copilot as they flew. His impeccable expertise on the complicated instrument panel fascinated Molly. "Wait, here's a non-directional low frequency beacon, just where Calvin said it would be, and remote from usual Concord frequencies!"

"What are they saying? Who are they?"

"Don't know yet. They're talking about...let's see...families and...friends. Let me break in and...No, you talk to them, Molly. You speak their language. Your microphone's operative."

"I don't know how! I've never talked on a radio..."

"Who's that who doesn't know how?" crackled a response to her transmission. "This is Double Arc Overlap, over."

"Double Arc Overlap? Double Arc Overlap! This is Molly Hancock! We're coming to you. We're friendly. Buck, it's them!"

"The transmission is cut now," Morgan interjected. "They don't want to give away their position, but Calvin's put a lock on it already. Boy, if those Concord guys were into technology they could pinpoint this group—and any like it—in just about a minute." He paused, and then asked as an afterthought. "Say, how do you know they're the group we're looking for, Molly?"

"Easy. Double Arc Overlap. Maybe it isn't very sophisticated, but that's got to be the sign of the fish in radio talk. Grandpa Bob told me all about it. Christians once drew it in the dust to identify each other during times of persecution."

Morgan was silent for a moment as he observed the trajectory of his craft on the computer screen, while his mind simultaneously scanned his memory. There was something vaguely familiar in the young woman's description. Something he had almost forgotten, a revelation from long ago. The faint connection slowly emerged from a most remote corner of his mind.

"Oh, yes, now I remember something about that," he said thoughtfully. After a short pause, he continued, "You probably don't know it, but your great-grandmother had that exact sign on her car, for goodness sakes, over a hundred years ago. Strange. I'm ashamed of it, but I laughed when she said I might need it sometime."

They were still fifteen minutes out, and Morgan filled Molly in on the bare essentials of his mission to 47 Ursae Majoris, his planetary exploration, and other facts. She was most curious about the orbiting starship, and she was highly intrigued by the unreal holographic man who was tending it. For her part, Molly gave Morgan an abbreviated account of how she had come to be a part of the Barnes family.

Morgan felt deep compassion for her as she related the sad loss of her father and grandfather, and he couldn't help but notice her crying softly. He felt a most unfamiliar urge stirring inside, a burning sensation in a barely functioning part of his heart, a desire to comfort her and wipe away her tears. The very thought made him uncomfortable, but he ached to do it nevertheless. This particular situation was certainly new to him, but still there was something vaguely familiar about this strange emotional deliberation he was experiencing.

They could now see details of numerous jagged peaks below, a vast panorama of perpendicular faces that stretched endlessly in all directions. It would be absolutely necessary to land the ship vertically, and the precise location of the now-silent beacon looked peculiarly unapproachable. Morgan decided to try and put his craft right on top of the indicated coordinates, no matter how impossible the terrain appeared. He would have to trust Calvin's expertise completely, though from his perspective the place appeared highly unlikely for any habitation. He expertly rotated the plunging vehicle and began slowing it for landing. Imposing cliffs soon towered all around them, ever closer and more threatening. This could be a disaster if there were any mistakes at all.

"Fuel's down to absolute minimum reaction mass. We aren't coming back up, no matter what. Got just enough to set her down. I hope," mulled Morgan with a grim look, a sharp vertical frown creasing his forehead and his mouth a thin line as he concentrated with all his might.

"Heaven help us!" cried Molly as a jutting lip of rock came to within only a few feet of contacting the lander's glass canopy. They continued downward below the overhanging granite, and finally broke precipitously into a slightly wider valley. The course of the ship never varied from the selected coordinates as it sank into an abyss, but now the concave base of the mountain receded, and Morgan breathed a sigh of relief.

Touchdown was frightening despite the central open expanse. Sheer stone walls of utterly terrorizing proportions guarded the sanctuary on three sides, and only a narrow chute allowed the craft entry. Morgan maneuvered the ship to a small flat area near the radio beacon he had pinpointed, perilously close to one perpendicular cliff. No other landing site was possible, however, and mercifully the wind was still, so they settled to earth with hardly a bump. An insistent flashing red light confirmed that the tanks were completely depleted.

Doubtful residents of the enclave were all hiding from this unexpected trespasser. Morgan and his passengers disembarked and stood beside the lander, with Sarah holding the struggling toddler, expecting something to happen. Morgan unfurled a rectangular white kerchief to let any inhabitants know that this noisy entry was peaceful.

After several long and uneasy minutes, a lone man appeared high in the rocks and made his way slowly down to them. He was unarmed and cautious, but alert for any hint of danger. At least the craft didn't carry Concord markings, the man noted as he moved closer. He sported a full curly beard that was as black as coal, except for a prominent streaking of gray.

"Hi! I'm Buck Morgan," called the pilot as the man neared them. "We're friends."

"At least you don't look like Concord goons," the man surmised as he stood before them with his intense green eyes blazing. "Which of you girls is Molly Hancock?"

"I am. I was elected to talk to you on the radio. First time, too."

"Good job. You Christians?"

"Yes. Well, I think. I mean, most of us, at least," Molly stumbled a bit.

"You make more sense on the radio," the man interrupted. "I'm Jacob Thompson, leader of our band. Whoever you people are, welcome to our humble shelter."

The new arrivals followed Thompson up over the rocks, from the top of which they descended into a narrower valley. They could now see neat rows of crops, recently planted and growing luxuriously, and there were even some sheep grazing on emerging grass along a steep hillside. A young man appeared from one of the rocky side passages and approached them a bit nervously.

"Luke, meet our new arrivals. This is Buck...what did you say, Morgan?"

"Right. Meet Molly Hancock."

Morgan introduced all his charges in order, ending with a somewhat agitated and fussy Baby Abraham, who squirmed and whimpered repeatedly.

"I'm Luke Walker," said the young man. "Hester's militia, as I used to tell everybody. Where'd you people come from in that big rush of racket?"

"Adrian, Kansas. Home for these folks, and it once was for me, too. Not very safe in Adrian these days, I'm afraid."

"What? Adrian? My home town!" exclaimed the young man with considerable excitement. "Molly Hancock? Jody Barnes? I know you people, for goodness sake! Do you remember my father, Leon Walker?"

"Leon Walker?" exclaimed Molly "Of course I remember him! He...he disappeared, Luke. Now that I think about it, I remember you, too, even though you were a few years older than me. How in the world did you wind up here?"

"Dad and Mom vanished from the face of the earth together, I'll bet. I'm not surprised. I've learned to make sense of a lot of things since Jacob and I came here. I shouldn't have been such a fool."

"You said Hester's militia? What is that?" asked Morgan.

"The best fighting unit ever assembled. Actually, it was my uncle's ranch security force. The whole unit was wiped out by the Concord during the Wyoming War. Except for me, that is."

"How did you wind up here?" asked Molly.

"It's a very long story. Jacob and I met up after the final battle of the war, and we set up a resistance movement. We settled here and conducted guerrilla raids on Concord troops. Most of our men were eventually killed, a few at a time. Then a man brought an older woman and a girl up here, but some Concord troops were in hot pursuit. We ambushed the Concord patrol and saved their lives. And what was the guy's name that brought them here, Jacob? He was from Kansas, too."

"Rosenthal. Abe Rosenthal."

"Yeah, that's him. We thought we were pretty hotshot fighters and we were going to save the world, but he convinced us that we had been wrong about a lot of things, including our revenge campaign. Then old

Abe just drifted on out of the compound and we haven't seen or heard from him since."

"Abe Rosenthal! We named Baby Abraham after him! Jody, did you hear that?"

"Sure did, Molly. Astounding. And I remember you, too, Luke. We were several years apart in school, but your antics were legendary at Adrian High. Unfortunately, I tried to emulate most of them."

"Sorry I wasn't such a good role model, Jody. I've changed, though. I'm married now, too, and loving it. Thanks to Abe Rosenthal, I've been given a remarkably new perspective in a lot of ways. My wife is that girl he brought here. Her mother died not long after that, unfortunately."

"I'm sorry to hear that. Didn't you have a brother? What was his name?" asked Barnes.

"Jeff. Haven't heard from him since he moved to Denver."

"Bad news, Luke. He didn't come back from the Wyoming War. I heard Dad say that before he...uh...disappeared. Everybody thought you were dead, too."

Walker looked at the floor for an uncomfortable moment, seeming to ponder the news about his brother with deep sadness. He noticed the others were watching him, and he hurriedly snapped back to the present.

"It's okay to be sad, Luke," said Molly sincerely. "There's a lot of that going around these days."

"A lot of guys didn't come back from that war," said Walker. "I guess I don't have to say I'm sorry to hear about that. I had hoped he was still okay. I was never close to Jeff, but he was still my brother. I wish I could have known him better."

"And you, Buck," said Thompson, his pearly teeth shining prominently through the contrasting black of his hairy face. "Now tell us about yourself."

"Glad to. I've got Adrian connections that'll blow a microchip, Jacob. This can't be coincidence, all of us being here together, but I don't know how else to explain it. Simply phenomenal."

Morgan went on to describe to them his background and his recent mission while small groups of resident people gathered slowly around him as he talked. To his amazement, nobody had ever heard of his mission, apart from the small Adrian contingent.

"All of you, meet my wife Eva," said Walker as a young woman strolled up to the discussion. "And for starters she's not from Adrian, she's from Livingston, Montana. And no, we don't have any kids, at least not yet."

A light-hearted chuckle followed as they greeted the woman. Eva was a pretty blonde with long curls that made one think of the fairy-tale Goldilocks. Even her colorful sheepskin dress conjured up images straight from a happy children's story. Compared to the drab, worn appearance of the new arrivals, everyone in the compound seemed bright and prosperous.

"Livingston, Montana, you say? I once had a really good friend from there."

"Eva, this is Buck Morgan," said Walker. "He's been on a long space journey, and it seems everybody had kind of forgotten about him, I guess. Say, didn't you tell me you had a grandfather who was in the Astronaut Corps?"

"He was my father's grandfather, and his name was Jeremiah Smith. He was a really successful astronaut and writer. And you're Buck Morgan? Wow, I know all about you!" Eva exclaimed in amazement, looking up and down the handsome man in the flight suit. "I was always told you'd return someday, but somehow I never really believed it. This is phenomenal!"

"I'd echo that sentiment! Eva, we've got a lot to talk about! Say, you sure do look a lot like a girl I once knew—the one your great-grandfather married, in fact!"

"Plenty of time for catching up later. Let us show you around, folks," offered Thompson. "I want you to meet my wife, too. She's not from Adrian or Livingston, but she survived a lot getting here from California. Luke, why don't you climb to the lookout and make sure nobody's coming. Could be someone noticed our friends' fiery entrance."

"Sure thing, Jacob. You're right. I'll signal if we've got company."

"Company we don't want here. Unwelcome company, that is. God forbid. That's the last thing we need."

"Wow! A real farm," commented Barnes as they inspected fat animals and recently planted crops. "I haven't seen a large animal since the Concord seized our horses. The Lord is indeed providing for his people."

"He is. We took some animals off a Concord convoy we busted way back, and we've had some ever since. But we weren't sure it wasn't all over when you guys arrived. An intrusion like that from the bad guys would be the absolute end for us," Thompson observed. "We're expecting the Lord to put an end to this Concord insanity any minute now, but we're all hoping to be physically alive when it happens."

Questions formed and dissipated in Buck Morgan's mind at an astounding rate. He felt a strong stirring deep in his soul to understand more about all of this, but he didn't have much time, and he knew it was running out. Concord helicopters would almost certainly spot his shiny craft if they chanced to fly over, despite disguising cliffs, perhaps spelling doom for the entire population of this little niche of safety.

He hoped desperately that the authorities had been unable to track him here. Thankfully, just about all of the orbiting satellites appeared to be on the blink. He hoped the technology was defunct. Apparently for some time there had been no reason for the world government to have any orbital tracking capability, at least not until the *Ursa C* had appeared unexpectedly. Even if the satellites still worked, Morgan could be fairly sure Concord workers were unable to re-program them for such specialized duty. They should be secure for the moment, at least.

It was Molly, instead of Morgan, who enthusiastically related to Thompson the daring rescue of their captured family. She clarified again for Thompson the nature of Morgan's interstellar mission, a new notion to Thompson about which he knew nothing except bits from their earlier conversation. Morgan listened to her articulate account with great interest and was amazed at how well she understood the history of his interstellar mission. *At least someone on earth kept my memory fresh*, he thought quietly and thankfully.

Inside the main complex, Morgan marveled at orderly rows of dwelling places and mannerly, well-behaved children. There were over thirty families living in the compound. Most had fled here from surrounding cities and towns, but a few had survived perilous treks across half the continent after learning of the haven. *Wow*, he thought—*there's enough material here to write a whole library of books about their experiences*. Many of the families had come within an eyelash of death at the hands of the Concord.

"Buck, when I came here I didn't give a hoot about religion or anything else," said Thompson. "There were about four dozen of us to start with, but we were slowly killed off over a period of time until we were down to a handful. When Eva Smith and her mother showed up with old Abe, we made our last ambush to rescue them. I haven't killed anybody since. We did some tinkering with a radio we salvaged from the soldiers, and we were able to establish contact with a few more groups like ours around the world. After that more people showed up every few weeks, all with variations on the same tale. All of them told of making some important changes in their lives after friends or family vanished in the great disappearance. Most of them somewhere along the way had encountered a man like old Abe with a story to tell. What you see here now is our effort to live as normally as possible in what may be our last stand."

"Looks like a pretty prosperous last stand to me, Jacob. You never raid Concord outposts or convoys anymore?"

"Nope. It was unmitigated hate that motivated me to do that in the first place. I've given up that kind of vengeance. Anyway, we have too many women and kids whose lives are at stake now, like the ones you brought with you. We're completely peaceful. The only time we've used our weapons in a long time has been to ward off predators that come around with blood in their eyes. We know from our radio that a lot of areas lost many people to beasts, but we didn't lose a single person because we have these arms. We ate a lot of nutritious bear meat for a while, too. But Concord forces could easily wipe us out if they discovered us, so we don't want to challenge them in any way."

"When I left Earth a long time ago, nearly everybody had firearms, Jacob. How did the Concord police take them all away?"

"They didn't for a long time. Guns were illegal here long before the Concord took over, but enforcement was slack and a lot of people kept them anyway. When the Concord figured out how to re-program some old satellites to detect gunshots, it was all over for the average person. We knew that we immediately gave away our position whenever we used our arms, so we'd strike like a fox hitting a chicken coop and be gone before the helicopters could get to us. When the predator attacks started, we had no choice but to use them right here in our enclave. By then, though, they couldn't track us anymore. None of those tracking satellites work now, apparently."

"Are there still bears about?"

"Not many. This country is too dry for them to subsist here in big numbers. They like green grass and roots and berries and such, as well as meat. But there are still a good many cougars, and we all go armed whenever we leave the compound. They'll attack you just like you're a deer or something. No fear at all."

"Interesting. And scary. I'm sure you're right about the satellites being nonfunctional now, from what I've seen. How are your supplies holding up?"

"We're all managing well. We never run short of food. We haven't had any sickness. We pray a lot and study the Bible, and we teach it to our kids. Our great hope and our conviction is that the miserable events in the world herald the imminent climax of history. Molly tells me you may not be a Christian, Buck. I can tell you, Jesus died for us all, if we're willing to recognize the truth. Only through asking him to take control of my life and receiving his love and forgiveness have I been able to find true peace."

"No need to explain it, Jacob. I know all about it. I've read the Bible and I've lived a good life. And both my parents were Christians, so as far as I'm concerned I'm okay. Anyway, I'll be leaving shortly if I can get my lander refueled and loaded with water. I've got responsibility for a major starship, and I'm planning on seeking out an alternative star and heading there. If I find no inhabitable planet, I'll just keep going. One thing is indisputable, I can't stay here."

Molly listened to the two men silently, and after Thompson had gone she approached Morgan again on the subject. He was no more receptive than he had been with Thompson, but he promised to discuss it further with her later. Thompson left to go and prepare quarters for the Barnes family, leaving Morgan and Molly alone for the first time. They found themselves eye to eye, and the seasoned astronaut felt a little knot in his stomach.

"Buck, why can't you just stay here? I know the fuel on your lander is pretty much used up, so maybe you'll have no choice. Why the hurry to leave?"

"Little lady, I've already seen enough of this brave new world to make me sick. It's not the planet I left behind," Morgan replied. "Besides, there's the matter of my starship. I've got less than sixty days to get back up there and recharge it with water before the ecosystems onboard start suffering. There are almost a hundred different species of animals and nearly two hundred plant species on board. There's no future for them here. And I can't stand the thought of that ship falling into the hands of this evil empire."

"How far is it to another star?" Molly asked, the whole scenario stretching her imagination. A starship filled with animals. A Noah's ark with plants. It sounded marvelous to her.

"It depends. I'll get Calvin to do a little instant research. The star system I just explored—well—over four and a half years ago now—is forty-four light years away. Earth time, that is. You know what I mean."

"Sure is confusing to me. Is there nothing closer?"

"Oh, yes, there are closer stars. But none like our sun. It's pretty unique, you know. Everything has to be exactly right for a star to warm a living planet like Earth. I've probably pondered just how unsurpassed our sun is for supporting life more than any man in history. Even 47 Ursae Majoris doesn't match up perfectly with it."

"What's unique about the sun? I thought stars were stars, except for some being bigger, some smaller, some hotter, some cooler."

"When we started researching my interstellar mission, I did profiles on every star within a hundred light years of Earth. We even did a lot of complex deep space measurements on each one. Almost half are binary, or double stars that won't support inhabitable planets. Most of the rest emit so much destructive radiation that they would eliminate, rather than support, life."

"Do you have another star in mind as an alternative?"

"The nearest star with any possibility of an inhabitable planet is one called 51 Pegasai. I've eliminated the best hope in 47 Ursac Majoris, which has a very interesting planet nearby, but unfortunately you can't breathe its atmosphere. Fifty-one Pegasai is quite like 47 Ursae Majoris in that it's a singular star, it's approximately the size of our sun, and it emits a very tolerable radiation spectrum."

"Buck, what if none of them work out? You're finally lost in space?"

"I'll orbit the starship forever around a star somewhere. The renewables garden is self-perpetuating. Who knows, the way things are going here on Earth, it may contain the only life in the universe someday."

Molly sighed deeply and patted Morgan's hand. She knew her new friend had a horrendous task ahead of him. He did have the world's peak technology at his disposal, if he could only refuel and get back to the *Ursa C.*

"Buck, really, what's the use? In the end your whole quest will be futile. Can't you see that? Please stay here and...well...just get to know us. Be part of our family. Even become a person of faith in God rather than faith in science—I know you'll never submit to chipping. Stay and let's enjoy what we can of life in this wretched world."

"I just can't, Molly. What a wasted world we have here. I can't believe all that's happened. My world had its problems, but it had vibrant and optimistic aspects, too. This is not my world," he lamented, his voice almost cracking a bit as he spoke. He was surprised at his unaccustomed emotion and flushed slightly when he realized that it was apparent to Molly, as well.

"Besides, that huge lander out there is impossible to hide," he continued, regaining his composure. "Somebody with blood on his mind is certain to spot it. I've got to get it out of here, and the sooner the better. If those Concord guys burst in here and murder this band of brave people because I've exposed them—well, I just couldn't live with myself—even if I survived an attack like that, I mean."

"Can't we take it apart, Buck? Get it down and hidden? It just needs to be out of sight."

"First, I'm not willing to condemn my renewables garden to slow death, which is where it's heading minus 20,000 gallons of water. But that aside, they don't have anything here that would do what you're suggesting. The metal is an alloy that can't be cut and so are the few rivets used. It's practically indestructible. The only solution is to refuel it and fly it out of here. And I've got to do that fast."

"What kind of fuel does it use?"

"Liquid hydrogen and oxygen. The engines are actually from the horse-and-buggy era of space travel. But at least both components of the fuel are common elements. They aren't particularly easy to distill in pure form, though, unfortunately."

"Think Jacob might be able to help?"

"I hope so. All I really need is a line to water. The lander has its own fuel distillation kit. Let's go ask what he has available," Morgan suggested.

Thompson was helping Barnes and Sarah unload their belongings and transfer them to a picturesque bungalow on the edge of the settlement. Like all the other living quarters, it was nestled back against a stately cliff, out of sight from overhead.

"Buck, we're almost unloaded already. Everybody pitched in. I love these people!" Barnes greeted them. "I can't tell you how much I appreciate your bringing us here. Jacob thinks we'll be safe."

"Safe if we can get that lander out of sight," interjected Thompson. As the astronaut had already surmised, the sparkling vehicle was a dead giveaway of their position. As Morgan talked with Thompson, Molly pitched in, helping the Barnes family and the orphan girls get settled into their quarters. Baby Abraham toddled around trying to help, talking baby talk and generally getting in the way. Morgan picked him up, entertaining him with the colorful insignia on his uniform, to the child's delight.

"That's what I'm here to discuss with you, Jacob. I'm out of fuel and I need to take on more. I can't leave unless you can help me."

"What does that thing burn, sagebrush?" asked Thompson, a hint of humor in his voice. Morgan chuckled a little before he answered.

"I wish it did, Jacob. I need liquid hydrogen and oxygen, and lots of it," Morgan replied, going on to explain why disassembly was not an option, as well as the specifics of what he needed to do to generate and utilize the fuel he hoped to produce. He put the squirming child back on the ground, and he toddled away after his mother as Morgan continued, "In addition to making fuel, I need to load about 40,000 gallons of the purest water I can get."

"Buck, we have plenty of water, but the tap runs slowly. Before the war I worked in refrigeration, and if I'm not mistaken you've not only got to make hydrogen and oxygen in pure form, you'll have to pressurize it into a super-cold liquid. And from what you say about your equipment it may take a couple of weeks to generate and compress the stuff. But we'll help all we can."

Morgan winced a bit, but he knew that Thompson's estimate was probably accurate, far too long a period to be tenable. But there seemed no option.

"Jacob, what you're saying is right, I'm sure. But it means we're in big trouble. And I'm afraid it's my fault. It was my suggestion that we come here in the first place, and now I've jeopardized the lives of everybody in this enclave. Now I can't get the lander up and away for two weeks. What can we do?"

"We can pray, Buck. Don't worry about it. Just pray about it. We'll do what we can and leave the rest in the Lord's hands," Thompson replied confidently as Morgan shook his head, unconvinced.

Thompson set about immediately accomplishing the required arrangements. He directed several men to begin a camouflage project on the lander, using makeshift skin netting. Meanwhile, they retrieved the necessary hardware from the lander and moved it to the compound's lab, which was used primarily for producing and storing welding materials and for repairing farm implements. The facility was remarkably well supplied and quite adequate to do the needed refueling job, when Morgan added the necessary kit from the lander. Shortly the makeshift fuel facility was producing, albeit slowly, both needed elements.

"Buck, I really wish you'd simply stay with us. You seem determined to leave," Thompson commented as they toiled.

"I've got to, Jacob. I've just gone through this same discussion with Molly. I've got to leave—for your people and for me, it's simply best."

"Molly seems to be an uncommonly fine young lady, doesn't she?" Thompson observed. He watched Morgan adjust a critical valve and create a much-improved flow of pure hydrogen.

"Tell me more about Eva Smith—or Eva Walker, I guess it is. She and Luke are married, huh? And what about her mother?"

"Yep. Eva's a great lady, and a wonderful addition here. She knows a lot about cooking and folk medicine and she's taught us a lot. Unfortunately, Eva's mother died not long ago."

Morgan nodded. Yes, this is an interesting bunch of people, he thought as they toiled. He couldn't agree more. And down deep he couldn't wait to see pretty Molly Hancock again.

CHAPTER 43

May 2169

An unmistakable sound of helicopter rotors broke over the compound with astounding suddenness. Still air resonated from beating of the huge blades, sending out vibrations that shook the ground. People scurried out of sight instinctively and everyone held their breath as a flight of four Concord gunships seemed to hover over the sheltered valley. Had they spotted something suspicious in all that craggy terrain below?

It seemed an eternity before the flight disappeared over the rimrock. Jacob Thompson scrambled up the opposite canyon wall in an effort to ascertain their flight path. By the time he topped out for a better view, there was nothing in sight except bare sagebrush hills, distant peaks, and a ruddy blue sky.

Through his breathlessness, Thompson uttered a mighty sigh of relief. The flight had only seemed to hesitate, he guessed. Had the lander not been well camouflaged they almost certainly would have been discovered. Just a few more days and those huge fuel cells would be fully charged. While the bushy-faced leader had grown to love Buck Morgan, he would be deeply relieved to see the last of that lander and the awful security threat it represented.

Morgan and Molly had seen the flight, as well. During the two weeks since they had arrived here, they had seen four such ominous flights pass overhead. Molly had explained to Morgan why Concord helicopters observed a strict speed limit of twenty knots when flying below 5,000 feet above the ground so as to avoid killing "insect humans." It was evident that whirling helicopter rotors inevitably dashed countless insects into oblivion at low altitudes, but for apparent expediency this fact was simply ignored.

The two new friends had climbed a nearby hill to enjoy the sunset, a ritual they had begun only a few days after their arrival here. Morgan's time with the ruggedly attractive young woman was the space explorer's only respite from refueling work, and he looked forward to the hour each day. After a few such journeys, he had shyly taken her hand to help her up steep places. Gradually the two had begun to hold hands all the way up, though each pretended demurely that the reason for this was safety and convenience.

Morgan had retrieved his father's worn shotgun from the lander, and had loaded it with his makeshift buckshot. With predators about, he felt it wise to carry some kind of armament, and the old fowling piece was all he had. In nearly two-dozen trips up the scenic hill, however, they had seen no wildlife whatsoever except for an occasional soaring vulture silhouetted duskily against the sky.

As the flight of Concord warbirds faded into the distance and disappeared, they exchanged relieved glances. Molly looked in the direction they had gone and spoke first.

"Buck, you're working like a madman trying to escape. The helicopters aren't seeing us. Why don't you relax and stay a while?"

Morgan didn't reply for a long moment, but stared off toward where the noisy gunships had departed. He considered the words of this young woman he had come to admire and respect. He would have to measure his thoughts before voicing them and take great care not to cause any hurt. He turned back around to face her, the old shotgun draped casually over one shoulder in a manner like an old time quail hunter.

Molly had drifted a short distance away from Morgan as she mulled her own inner turmoil. There was a spurt of new growth in a sheltered corner of a dry wash below them, where a splendid tuft of avalanche lilies had emerged gloriously from a cleft below an overhanging rock. She was squatting, inspecting the delicate and rare white flowers, a vestige of beauty that seemed to defy contemporary ugliness by rising like a phoenix from seared earth.

Morgan caught sight of a flicker of movement on the rimrock, a mere dozen yards above the distracted girl. The twitch of black was the terminal tip of a tawny body that blended almost imperceptibly into the sandstone formation. Despite its natural camouflage, Morgan instantly recognized the creature. A cougar, coiled like a diamondback rattler ready to strike! Every muscle in the huge animal quivered, and its body swayed ever so slightly like a bird dog on point. The animal's yellow eyes were riveted hungrily on the woman. Before Morgan could utter a word, the cat launched itself silently and gracefully toward its unsuspecting prey.

Sometimes in situations of extreme danger, action moves in agonizing slow motion. Morgan was certain his body was responding rapidly, but his mind seemed to lapse into light-speed time dilation like he had experienced for so many years. The gigantic mountain lion hung in the air as if suspended between soil and sky, and its awful mouth was so wide open that Morgan could see every sharp tooth. Long, razor-like claws were unsheathed and extended to grasp the helpless victim, and it exhibited absolute singularity of purpose. Morgan's mind digressed instantaneously to his mother's unlikely and untimely death to just such a charge, and to the long-ago assault on the scientist Hansen. Horrifying dreams he had endured repeatedly in space seemed to be playing out before him now, stubbornly assuming reality in order to snatch away something precious from him once more. It was at the same time bewildering and terrifying, but was it immutable? Here was another one of the big cats about to ravish someone he—he—loved? The situation was happening so fast it appeared hopeless.

Pure instinct intervenes where rational and studied thought is impossible. Morgan never commanded his arms to move, never considered the antique device resting on his shoulder, never even thought about aiming it. As if driven by a computer on autopilot, the old Stevens Savage firearm was whipped forward while a practiced finger flicked off the etched slip safety, and the walnut stock was hoisted automatically to firing position. He didn't plan to lead the cat, but if he hadn't the sheer speed of its motion would have caused the load to miss its mark, or to do insignificant damage. His barrel swung to exactly eighteen inches in front of the cat's moving head, though he had no time to calculate distance to the animal nor to consider the velocity of its plunge. Old lessons and wholly involuntary mental calculation converged somewhere in Morgan's brain in a situation where absolutely no room for error was possible. The cat's head was a scant yard from the girl by the time he swung ahead of it and the shotgun exploded. Recoil force jarred hard into his shoulder.

The blast of nine big lead pellets slammed into the feline's head, literally blowing the animal in the opposite direction and almost decapitating it. The soft rear end of the 160-pound cougar cartwheeled solidly into Molly, sending her sprawling, but the beast was already very dead and quite harmless. Morgan trained the shotgun on the cat, but it was finished. He ran to Molly's side and helped her up. She was bruised and shaken, and there were speckles of cougar blood on her face and clothing, but she was otherwise unharmed.

"Got to reload," he said, fumbling in his pocket for another of his hand-loaded shells. "Could be another one."

He looked around while he broke open the breech and extracted the spent shell, and was amazed to discover that he had used the full choke left barrel. A shot from that barrel required that he pull the rear trigger so as to shoot a much tighter pattern of lead balls, a necessity time had not allowed him to consider. Instinct and practice from many years before had driven the entire sequence to a successful conclusion. To his great relief, there appeared to be no more of the cats for now.

"Oh, Buck, that's the second time you've saved me," exclaimed Molly as she dusted herself off while casting an eye toward the huge mountain lion sprawled beside her. Morgan wiped a few spots of splattered blood from her face as she looked back at him and said, "This is getting to be a habit."

Tears began pouring down her girlish cheeks as she pulled Morgan to her and wept in his arms. The astronaut felt an uneasy embarrassment, a most peculiar but highly pleasant sensation, as he returned a passionate hug.

"Old shotgun finally came in handy. Glad I made this buckshot. I melted down some bird shot," he explained as he comforted his friend.

Morgan checked the girl's bruised back, and found nothing really damaged. The curve of her shapely neck and her wide, sturdy shoulders had taken quite a blow, but those terrible claws had missed her entirely.

Morgan felt an odd, unfamiliar sentiment creeping over him as he inspected the traumatized areas and pronounced them fine.

They turned the great cat over and examined it. The animal was a well-fed tom cougar, and its hide was as smooth and supple as that of a mink. Morgan would certainly tell Jacob about this as soon as they got back to the compound. He had heard that cougar meat was quite edible, and unquestionably the pelt could be put to very good use.

They retired to a favorite vantage point as the sun sank lower, and cast long shadows that licked the ground for great distances and lengthened logarithmically as time passed. For a long time neither of them said anything, but Molly leaned back against Morgan comfortably, and both just enjoyed the respite.

"Thanks again, Buck," said Molly finally. "I still can't believe you've saved my life twice in the short time we've known each other."

"I think you're worth saving any number of times, little lady," said Morgan, looking his friend in the eye. "How old are you, anyway, Molly?"

"Twenty-one."

"A baby. I'm twice your age, in real time. And maybe a half dozen times your age in Earth time. Crazy."

"What do you mean? What's so crazy about it?"

"Oh, nothing. Just thinking, I guess. I'd sure like to have time to get to know the people here, including you."

"Well, as I was saying before that tomcat interrupted, you ought to consider just staying. You've saved my life, so why don't you remain with us and be a part of our lives, such as they are."

"Molly, what if we were sitting here like this, away from the rest, and that flight of helicopters zoomed into the compound, guns blazing? How many times does that have to happen to result in annihilation of the good people down there?"

Molly gulped aloud. She knew it could occur all too easily.

"Buck, it might happen whether you're here or not."

"I had Calvin run a set of probability calculations the other night, based on hard data I fed to the *Ursa C*. Chance of discovering this compound is less than one in a thousand, absent the lander. It's greater than fifty percent with it here. I've got to go, Molly. No matter how much it hurts."

"I see. You always have figured everything out scientifically, I'm sure. Those statistics are pretty devastating," she admitted. She lowered her gaze and noted again the beauty of the hidden valley below, so neat and clean and orderly. Could an objective mind like that of Buck Morgan really appreciate abstract aesthetics like that setting? Who was this strange man and how did he think?

"Will it really hurt to go, Buck?"

"Hurt? I've experienced real hurt only a couple of times in my life, when my dad was killed. And before that when my mom was killed, too. I was pretty young when Mom died, but I still get an awful agony deep down when I think about that time. Yes, this pain will be similar, I believe. I'm dreading it but, Molly, I don't know any alternative," he anguished, squeezing her hand gently, feeling once again the unaccustomed sensation of tears welling in his eyes.

"Don't forget, I've lost a few loved ones, too. And I didn't like it one bit, either."

To Morgan's absolute surprise, Molly leaned toward him and planted an emphatic kiss on his cheek. His senses began whirling like a spacecraft out of control, and he struggled to maintain his composure. Loss of poise was entirely new to him, and his mind reeled at this unexpected development.

"Molly," he strained through his emotions, his breath coming in short bursts. "Molly, are you feeling like I am?"

Morgan wondered at the propriety of his words, but he didn't know any other way to express it. There was no way to communicate such feelings in an exact and measured fashion. Before this wonderful woman had entered his life unexpectedly, he couldn't remember ever having experienced a truly romantic thought. Oh, there had been that long-ago prospect when he had been infatuated with JoEllen Thacker, but nothing ever really developed. He wasn't certain he even had romantic capability. Had the long years in space done something to him?

"Tell me how you feel, Buck. I'm new at this thing, you can bet, but I've sure had a head full of Buck Morgan since we met, if that's what you mean," Molly replied, adjusting her position next to him to accommodate his arm around her shoulder. He squeezed her tentatively, and she obliged and approved by drawing closer to him.

"I've got an indescribable burning in my heart, Molly. There's an excitement within me that I've never felt before. I don't know what to make of it. It doesn't compute."

"Let me tell you something, Buck Morgan. Ever since I was a little girl, you've always been a hero to me. My dear grandfather told me many times how selfless you were for giving your life and leaving behind a world of people who cared for you just to advance the cause of science. Like a knight in shining armor, that's how I've thought of you. I feel like a princess held captive in a castle somewhere and you're my long-awaited liberator. I must be pretty transparent, huh?"

"I was hoping my feelings were visible, too, Molly. I'm not very good at communicating something like this. But I can't stop thinking about you, day or night. I think I'm—I don't know how to say this, and I don't know how this will sound, Molly, but I think I'm falling in love with you."

Morgan studied Molly's eyes for a response, somehow knowing that it had to be positive. He longed to know her better, to share his deepest feelings with this marvelous creature—deep feelings, profound longings, and intimate desires which had never before been allowed to freely surface. Maybe potential for such emotions had been there all along— undoubtedly so, but their expression had been subjugated unmercifully to the god of science. These new sensations were so wonderful and captivating, so exciting and breathtaking, he now wondered if self-imposed lifelong deprivation had been worth the sacrifice. Perhaps so, even if only to get to this moment in time, when Molly Hancock was alive and mature and desirable.

"Buck, I'm feeling the same way. You know that without my saying it, don't you? How I wish times were more conducive to—uh—romance, I guess is the right word."

"Well, conducive or not, I feel like I feel. My mind tries to rationalize all these sensations and convince me that they're not real, that they're a product of years of isolation. But this is different from simple loneliness and need for companionship; it's like somehow my life was put on hold just to await nothing but you. Molly, I do love you. I'm certain of it. And for the first time in my remembrance I don't care how unscientific that sounds."

She knew how difficult such words had to be for Morgan, and she could sense veritable desperation in his search for appropriate language. The two had gradually drawn ever closer together as they talked and were gazing intently into one another's eyes. Neither of them needed to think about how right it was, or the difference in their ages, or how their feelings came to be so strong, as their lips came together in a gentle but passionate kiss. Buck Morgan, seasoned astronaut, high-speed hero of the twenty-first century, was treated to his very first kiss at age forty-one. As their lips melded into one, his head spun wildly out of control like a gyrating satellite, and intense pounding of his heart reminded him of the indescribable churning of nuclear pulse engines. There's no sensation like this to be found anywhere in speed and space and machines, his mind screamed as he groped for understanding of this awesome awakening of emotions.

Molly spoke after they parted, looking into those blue eyes that had seen more than anyone could imagine, and her own senses reveled inevitably in the same deep and powerful feelings.

"Buck, you know that I love you, too. I want to be with you always. Please don't leave," she pleaded, the imminence of losing him to the infinity of the universe bursting rudely into her mind once again.

The inescapable dilemma harshly intruded into the magic of the moment, imposing reality on the embracing couple once again. They clung to one another and kissed one more time before either spoke again.

"Molly, I can't even imagine how much pain it will be to leave you. If there were any possibility of a future for us on earth, I'd stay. I can assure you, I haven't decided to leave on a whim. You know that, don't you?"

"I believe you, but I really don't understand all of your reasoning," Molly pleaded, squeezing his hand lovingly again and again as they talked. "Why can't we just put enough fuel in the lander to fly it away from here a safe distance and leave it there."

"Molly, I've considered every possibility. Even if we could rid ourselves of the lander, I can't stand by and let my ship slowly die up there. Not only do I have onboard all of mankind's accumulated knowledge—plus more than any scientist ever dreamed about, incredible facts I learned on my journey—but I've got to think of my animals and the plants they depend upon. Molly, you wouldn't believe my renewables garden. This guy—the Father or whoever he is—wants them badly, and I've got to get it out of here lest they fall into his hands."

"But, Buck, how far can you go before you run out of fuel or die or just grieve yourself to death? You aren't supernatural, you know."

"Oh, fuel's no problem. For the planetary lander, yes, but not for the *Ursa C*. That's the beauty of antimatter conversion engines. Energy comes from the repeated conversion process. Inexhaustible is the appropriate word. Much more so than I am, I'm afraid. But the renewables section is also entirely self-sustaining. It's a complete ecosystem, designed to function forever, once I replace the water I robbed from it to fuel the lander."

"I see. So I guess you want to find a planet like Earth and colonize it with your renewables. Sounds like a good idea, but do you have time?"

"Who knows? I've been talking to Calvin regularly, and he recommends we set our sights on 51 Pegasai. It's over forty light years away, and it will take the *Ursa C* four years to get there. But I'm still young and there are several other options if I don't find what I need there. Calvin has the whole proposition detailed, if I can just get back onboard."

"Buck, what if you do find that planet you're seeking? What if you double or triple the scientific data in your computers? What if you even establish a successful colony on some planet? When your life ends, it's all futility anyway, isn't it?"

"Molly, I just don't think that way. No, it's worth it, given the situation on earth now, just to preserve the best of what this place once was. I've got to believe that. My mission has been altered by the unexpected catastrophe here, but I believe it's even more essential now."

Molly thought for a moment about the implications. Perhaps it was best, all things considered, for him to leave. The thought pained her heart profoundly and tears welled in her ebony eyes, moistening her long eyelashes and trickling down her cheeks.

"Buck," she sobbed gently, snuggling into his strong arms. "It's so incongruous, so tragic, like so much else in this wretched world. You'd establish a planet with no people—that seems to be the aim of the world government. And the Father's doing the exact opposite here—establishing a planet with no animals. What irony."

Morgan tried to comfort her but words of consolation were elusive. He finally returned to his original premise.

"Molly, I'm only certain about one thing: I can't stay here. These people here are at great risk because of me. The next overflight could be the end of them and us. These good people look like the hope of planet Earth to me," he said, staring pensively at the rocky ground and pushing over a stone with his leather boot. He turned to her and flashed an incongruous smile, a fleeting mirthful thought coursing his handsome face. "Who knows, maybe I'll return in a few hundred years to see how it all turned out."

"That's not funny, Buck, even if it is possible," Molly snapped with a brief grin. "Let me tell you my conviction. I believe with all my heart that Jacob is right—the culmination of history is at hand and I'm ready.

Every evidence I know anything about points to the fact that we're in the last days before the final return of Jesus Christ."

"You may be right. I have to admit, changes in the world square with what I've read about predicted future events. I had a lot of time onboard the ship to read at length, and I can tell you that I've been impressed by indications that it's all true. I plan to look harder at the evidence when I get a chance. Look, I've got to get back to the lab. Those fuel cells are getting close to full, and I've got to be there to shut off the process."

"Can we discuss this more, Buck?"

"Can we? Molly, we've got to," he answered with measured resignation. He then delivered another passionate kiss as he pulled her supple young body close to his.

The two descended the hill as usual, hand in hand. To anyone who observed, it would have appeared that there was nothing different.

But Buck Morgan and Molly Hancock had undergone a fundamental metamorphosis. They would never be the same again.

CHAPTER 44

May 2169

An aging synthetic pipe burst without warning, spewing a cloud of water vapor mixed with pure hydrogen and oxygen thousands of feet into the air. A billowing plume of the volatile material climbed high above the cliff that guarded their sheltered valley. Buck Morgan rushed in horror the rest of the way down the hill, leaving Molly behind in his haste. Something terrible had happened to his lander.

He arrived just as Jacob Thompson was closing a valve to the line, and as suddenly as it had begun, the hissing, spurting leakage ceased. Thank God there was no ruinous spark or any other source of ignition, Morgan thought. He entered the lab with his chest heaving for air in the high altitude's thin atmosphere. He propped his old shotgun hastily in one corner after he broke into the enclosure.

"Sprung a leak. I think you lost quite a bit of fuel," commented Thompson as Morgan approached. "Maybe—let's see—the reading shows about a third of it. Too bad, but we have plenty of water and we can start recharging as soon as we repair that line."

"Wow, guys, what happened?" asked Luke Walker, himself breathing hard from a mad dash across the compound. "Looks like a smoke signal you've lit. Calling all interested parties."

"Stop jawing and help us fix it, Luke. We need to splice that old pipe and seal it again with glue."

"Then let's get to it, Jacob. Say, I hope nobody spots that cloud. It's certainly a giant marker of our position," said Morgan.

"Maybe nobody will notice. It'd be pretty unhandy if somebody did. Visibility isn't very good because of all the atmospheric dust. And for your sake I hate that you can't leave as planned."

"For your sake and mine, Jacob. I sure am sorry."

"Don't worry about it. It wasn't anything we could have foreseen or prevented. And see, the cloud is dissipating already. We'll pray nobody saw it."

Molly raced into the lab belatedly, also gasping from exertion. All three men were already stooped over the ruptured line, so she surmised immediately what had happened. She ran over to them and stood for a moment catching her breath.

"Can I help?" she stammered through her deep inhaling and exhaling.

"Sure. Pray we can get this line fixed quickly and that we can make up for the missing third of my fuel," Morgan answered, a distinct despair in every word. He never looked up from the task at hand.

"A third of it escaped? Uh-oh. Another five or six days to replace it?"

"I'm afraid so. And we can only hope the bad guys didn't see that invitation we just sent them. You can pray about that, too."

"Oh, you're right, I didn't think of that! I hope not. Is there anything I need to do?"

"Not really. We won't be long repairing this, I hope. Check all those other valves to be sure they're firmly off."

Molly went along the row of valves, checked each one, and found each of them tightly shut. When she had finished she sat down in a chair that Morgan had at his makeshift desk and observed their frantic work. There being little else she could do, she looked idly about at the desk, which was filled with complicated notes on the fuel production process, obviously scribbled by Morgan as he planned the manufacturing. She could understand very little concerning the mathematical formulae, but in the scrawled notes she read a common thread of urgency. She felt a little guilty about reading the material without Morgan's permission, so she looked about for something else to occupy her mind.

Near the back of the desk was a faded green book. She strained a bit in the dark corner to read the title. *Heroes of the Cause* by Hilda Archer Prestone, it proclaimed in bold print.

"What cause?" she wondered out loud.

"What cause? Oh, you see that book on the table. Strangest thing, I had almost forgotten about picking that up," Morgan answered almost nonchalantly as he labored. "You might say it's a gift. That old woman I mentioned, the one at the Cape where I first landed, gave it to me. There's some information in there that I've got to share with you."

"Really? What kind of information?"

"That book is about heroes, all right. Heroes who helped bring about some awful changes in the world. It's very informative. I've been reading it the last few nights and I've discovered the answer to a mystery that has dogged me for many years. In fact, I had meant to tell you about it while we were on our walk, but we got sidetracked."

"Tell me now. If you don't mind that Jacob and Luke hear it, I mean."

"I don't mind at all. Molly, my father was killed a long time ago, in the year 2066, by an unlikely explosion that I always believed to be the result of foul play. A major fuel extraction facility on our farm had every modern safeguard that could be imagined, but it mysteriously blew sky high one day, destroying the building and killing my father. We never could put our finger on exactly what went wrong."

"How awful!" Molly gasped, holding her hand to her mouth in alarm. "Seems like I've heard something about that incident, now that you mention it. You say you suspected foul play? But you couldn't find the person responsible?"

"The main thing was that we had so little physical evidence with which to work. The state crime lab did all the tests they could, but everything was inconclusive. I left on my first deep space mission shortly thereafter and I was gone for six years. By the time I got back the case had been on hold for so long that nobody was interested in pursuing it anymore. And all possible leads in the case were too cold to follow."

"Tragic. What else can I say, Buck? But what does all that have to do with this book?"

"On page forty-five, where chapter four begins, is a section about a man named Sam Archer. He was a 'hero of the cause,' if you will. He was an agent for the species equality movement way back then. And he just happened to be the author's grandfather. The man carried out a covert campaign of sabotage and terror that few people suspected. Everybody knew he had some strange viewpoints, but nobody thought he was dangerous. He recorded a lot of gory details in a secret diary that somehow wound up in Hilda Archer Prestone's hands. His description of bombing Dad's facility is there in graphic fashion."

"No! He murdered your father?" She turned to the page number he had mentioned while Morgan continued speaking, and strained to read the print in the dim light.

"She doesn't mention that the explosion killed my father. The reader would never know anyone was hurt by the blast. But I know the truth. And Sam Archer was never held accountable."

"He won't get away with it ultimately, Buck," interjected Thompson, looking up from applying finishing touches to the ruptured line. "There is an all-powerful God who mediates such elusive concepts as justice and judgment. You can bank on it."

"Maybe you're right, Jacob. Matter of fact, somebody certainly intervened in this case. Here's the rest of the story. He didn't get away with it, you might say. The book details quite a few such 'innocent' crimes he committed, and almost deifies him for his exploits. But I remember that Sam Archer died a horrible death, disemboweled in a bar fight with a man he thought was his friend. And that man, a guy named Jesse Prestone, also died a gruesome death. His own son killed him a short time later. That son, an illegitimate kid whose nickname was Spot, was a classmate of mine in high school. Spot was a smart guy, but unfortunately he had the morals of a billy goat."

"Yuck! How horrible!" exclaimed Molly, once more covering her prim mouth. "But one has to agree, he got what was coming to him. How well did you know this so-called hero, Sam Archer?"

"Not very well, but ironically Dad did. They were friends of sorts, in fact. And get this—Sam Archer was the father of my best friend in high school."

"What? Why would he want to kill your father, then?"

"Because Sam despised us for our protein farming. I used to literally feel that hatred every time I was around him, but I didn't know what it was. My father apparently didn't tune in to it accurately. I remember Dad making numerous kind comments about Sam even when I would express my doubts."

"I'll never understand why anyone would kill a person just because they disagreed with their line of work or their hobbies, or whatever. But we've seen the same thing repeatedly," said Molly, remembering the death of her own father some years before at the hands of extremists.

"Sam Archer had another reason he felt so strongly. Despite Sam's objections, his son Monty, my friend, went to Alaska with Dad and me and came home with a different mindset because of the experience. Monty was an avid and outstanding outdoorsman all his life, at least up until I left. My memory of him is confirmed in a scathing indictment in Hilda Archer Prestone's own autobiography in the book. Hilda was my friend Monty's daughter, and she apparently hated him thoroughly. She wrote hero chapters about her grandfather, Sam Archer, and her great-grandfather, Clemon Archer, but she had nothing but contempt for her own father, and she makes it clear."

"Wow. Unbelievable. She hated her own father. What did he ever do to her?"

"Nothing is mentioned except that he held to a 'despicable philosophy of life,' to quote Hilda. The girl was apparently strongly under the influence of her mother, who was of like mind with Sam Archer. I lost track of Monty after my last trip back to Adrian, but I know he was divorced from Hilda's mother. Monty always did struggle in his relationships with women, I must admit. But I'd be astonished if he hadn't at least tried to care for a daughter. He became a man with a lot of personal integrity who was as trustworthy as he could be. He spent quite a bit of time with Dad during his last years, and they hunted quail together regularly."

"Is the rest of the book as seamy as this chapter?"

"Don't know," said Morgan, glancing at Molly briefly as he toiled. "I haven't had time to do anything but scan most of it. If we could travel back in time, though, I suspect it would be grounds for quite a few felony indictments. Unfortunately, it can't make any difference now. I will tell you something else interesting that comes out in the book, though. Hilda Archer was married for a time to a man named Alex Prestone, Jr. And my classmate Spot Prestone's real name was Alex, too, so that has to mean Hilda's husband was Spot's son. If that's so, Jesse Prestone, who killed Hilda's grandfather Sam, was her husband's grandfather. And then Spot killed his own father Jesse, as I said before. Pretty murderous family tree, wouldn't you say?"

"I'd sure say so. Is there more?" asked Molly.

"There is, but I haven't nailed down all the particulars. And maybe I can't. But Hilda's husband, Alex Prestone Jr., was some kind of war hero. Hilda dedicated the book to their son, whose name was Waymon Prestone. I wonder what ever happened to him. I'd suspect that he remained an obscure fellow."

"Waymon Prestone! Buck, he was the guru of species equality for my whole life," said Molly. "Everybody knew him. He had enormous influence."

"No kidding?" Morgan said thoughtfully. "Interesting."

Morgan didn't have time to dig for details. He and Walker left the control room and climbed up a ladder into the lander to inspect critical connections to fuel cells, a laborious and dangerous task that required a coordinated effort to accomplish safely.

Molly turned to Thompson as the two men left, knowing she needed some high powered counseling in view of her deep feelings for Buck. She was solidly committed to her faith now, and she knew Thompson to be likewise. There was something she remembered that bothered her immensely. She had to ask Thompson about it.

"Jacob, I've got a problem," she began, searching for words to express herself.

"Tell me about it. It's probably not uncommon to man. Or woman."

"I'm in love with Buck, I think. Or maybe I'm just completely infatuated. I've never met anyone like him. And I think he feels the same way about me. He refuses to consider staying here for anything, though. He hasn't exactly put it this way so far, but what if he asks me to go back into space with him? What should I say? That's my problem."

"I figured there was more to all that handholding than you two were telling us. You know, he's a lot older than you. Make any difference?"

"He's more than a hundred years older than me, Jacob. And no, that doesn't matter to me. I'm grown enough."

"Then what do you want to do? You want to stay here?"

"Yes. I mean no. No, what I really mean is I don't know what to do and you're the only one I know to ask. Buck is interested in what I believe, but he didn't crawl down that dark hallway with me that night when my life changed forever. He's not committed to anything in particular. He's seen the science god topple, and he'll never go for any other kind of false religion, so I have great hopes for him. And he despises the Concord, so he'll never submit to their authority. But he's made it clear he's too busy to consider any serious commitments right now. Would I be violating some kind of principle if he offered the opportunity, and I went with him?"

"It's the concept of unequal yoking you're talking about. Most Bible teachers say it applies to any relationship, marriage, business partnerships, and the like. When one chooses to associate officially for any reason, it must be considered. But most especially it applies to marriage. And if Buck's not serious about a commitment to faith, what makes you think he'd be serious about a commitment to you?"

"Good question. But unless I miss my guess, he's going to ask me to go with him. What happens if I do?"

"You mean if you get married? Or if you cohabit with him, but don't marry him? You will have to bear the consequences, either way, which will likely be worse than you'd encounter staying here. Molly, he's a fine, moral man, and I believe he would be a good husband. But one should never knowingly violate God's principles. I'd advise you to talk to him frankly about it. If he really wants you to go, he may have to make some changes in his own life. If it comes down to making choices, you choose God's way. It may be a price you both have to pay. To tell you the truth, we really don't have very much to offer you in the way of any alternative. Our life is brutally austere, to say the least. But I still think you'd be better off here than you would be married to an unbeliever, even one with a mansion in the sky."

Morgan and Walker shortly returned and reported the lander connections checked and secured. The problematic hose now repaired, they opened appropriate valves to begin anew the process of creating those precious elements. They watched carefully for any new leaks, and seeing no problem they eased the mixture back to maximum production. Flow began once more in earnest, the technical problem solved.

Morgan tilted his head slightly and cupped one hand over his right ear. He frowned and wrinkled his brow, seemingly straining to hear.

"Jacob, do you hear anything? It sounds like an engine in the distance."

"Now that you mention it, I do! Way off, but distinct. Trouble!" shouted Thompson as he hurried out the door. "Luke, spread the word, everybody in and hiding! Hurry!"

Morgan and Molly scurried off in opposite directions as their friends disappeared. The sound of an approaching vehicle grew nearer and ever more ominous by the second. They began yelling for everyone to take cover as they fanned out into the compound, everything else entirely irrelevant now. All that mattered now was to warn the encampment before the threat arrived. And maybe it was already too late.

CHAPTER 45

May 2169

"What in Gaia is that?" asked a uniformed patrolman as he gazed at a ballooning white nebula in the distant Rocky Mountain sky. The atmosphere was hazy and the sky had a red cast to, but nonetheless the towering cloud stood out starkly.

"How would I know?" replied the lieutenant who was leader of a four-man Concord patrol. "Let's go check it out."

The driver gunned the engine of their blue and white military vehicle toward the base of the revealing cloud. They knew there were some insurgents hereabouts somewhere and their orders were to seek them out and destroy them. Maybe this was the break they needed.

"Shall I call headquarters and advise them of our intentions, sir?" asked a corporal who was driving. "We're supposed to let them know any changes in plans."

"I know that," snapped the officer in an irritated tone. "No, they'll know soon enough if this is what we hope it is."

The lieutenant remembered all too vividly the tongue-lashing and outright ridicule he had endured recently. He had reported by radio that he had located rebels a few weeks earlier, and he had beamed with excitement as he bragged of his find over the air. It had turned out that his "rebel main base," as he had called it, was nothing more than a hot springs area with abundant mud flows and smoking steam vents. He was outraged and embarrassed by the unwelcome nickname of "Smoky" which had been affixed to him more or less permanently. There was still insulting snickering behind his back from lower ranking men, as well as caustic criticism to his face by fellow officers, always offered with a condescending smirk. He still contended that the formation had looked exactly like an active illegal encampment from his distant vantage point. The constant sarcastic jabs and vicious taunts had left an indelible mark, and he wouldn't make the same mistake twice. Besides, another such blunder and it might be more than laughs that came down on his head.

The vehicle sped toward the plume of smoke, sticking to relatively flat valley floor. They maneuvered westward toward the sinking sun and then toward the north around the base of an intervening high mountain. There was a maze of old roads everywhere, some of which required creative driving to negotiate. In a short time they had closed the distance and saw an opening up a narrow valley that seemed to lead straight toward the fading blotch of white.

The road became more narrow and bumpy as the canyon walls converged, and for a time the lieutenant was convinced that this would be another fruitless venture. He hoped he was wrong, because another laughable failure would be hard to explain to his superiors. Burning a load of rare fuel was inexcusable unless it yielded results. The vehicle bounced so violently from time to time that all four occupants were pounded against its ceiling repeatedly, and the lieutenant shouted obscenities at the driver to protest such rough treatment.

They crested a hill and saw what they were looking for. People were scurrying in all directions, perhaps several score of them. And what a perfect setup! There appeared to be nowhere they could easily escape.

"Shall I call headquarters now, sir?" asked the driver again.

The officer hesitated for a moment and his eyes narrowed as he considered his options. If he called headquarters he would receive some credit for the find, but the glory and promotions would go to the attacking force commander and the helicopters. If he proceeded on his own and wiped out these revolutionaries, the honor would be his alone and nobody could deprive him of higher rank. His forehead creased in thought, and he looked around at his small but heavily armed force, bristling with the world's best weapons. No rebel force had responded with armed resistance in a long time. They would prevail easily.

"No. We're men enough for this job. Ready your weapons."

"But sir, there are a lot of people down there!" protested the sergeant who was second in command.

"Shut up and don't worry. Prepare to attack. They're unarmed and we'll slaughter them. Move in!"

At his command the corporal accelerated again, covering the last half mile in a fraction of a minute, rolling in hard and fast. Terrified occupants of the compound were mostly hidden by the time they arrived, but a few men were still visible. As soon as they were in range the patrol started raking the dwellings with hissing, burping automatic weapons fire, though placement of the bursts was a bit erratic because of the vehicle's bouncing. A man caught out in a field was the first victim. He was dead in a tempest of slugs, as ripping lead particles tore him to pieces. He collapsed like a limp rag.

The simple strategy was to stop in front of each dwelling and riddle it with hot, high velocity bullets. Anyone who tried to escape a house could easily be cut down before they could reach safety. The vehicle was heavy with ammunition so there would be no shortage of firepower. As they figured, there was no apparent effort to resist and people in the first dwelling, that of Jody Barnes, never showed themselves. There were some anguished screams, but they ceased quickly, and the assassins moved on to the next house.

Stopping at the second home, they positioned four of their weapons and began to blaze away with murderous efficiency. Far down the way, they failed to notice the camouflaged landing vehicle, so intent were they on their sinister but satisfying duty. A woman fled the next house carrying a young child, but both of them died in a hail of inescapable particles.

"Buck, do you know how to use one of these?" asked Jacob Thompson grimly as he joined the astronaut back at the workshop. He was breathing hard from a mad dash around the compound. He produced two automatic weapons he had retrieved from his house. They could hear the horrifying noise of the raiders' buzzing guns, and they knew that each burst might cost the life of one or more of their charges.

"You bet, Jacob. This is an old auto! I trained with one like this when I attended the Point. Where did you get these antiques? Is this the kind of weapon you used to use?"

"No time to explain now, but you know Luke and I were in the Wyoming War," Thompson replied, heading out the door after handing

Morgan an ample supply of ammunition. "We had to use what we could get. Let's go, and let's be quick about it!"

The two men ran hurriedly across the lane that separated the houses from a steep cliff face. They dropped into a crack in the rocks that Morgan had never noticed before, and traveled quickly toward the incessant clamor of attacking weapons. They were able to run unnoticed to a position just a few score yards behind the murderous patrol, which was busy spraying yet another house with virulent fire.

"You take the two on the left, I'll take the two on the right," instructed Thompson clearly. "And for heavens sakes don't let them get turned toward us with one of those shredder guns. Any one of them can kill both of us easily if they do. And don't hit the vehicle, because we're going to need it."

Darkness was imminent as the two men positioned themselves a few yards apart and readied themselves. All four incredulous Concord patrolmen tried to spin around when they opened fire, but they were now the ones who didn't have a chance. Hot chunks of searing, old-fashioned lead ripped through them before they could retrain their weapons in the direction of their surprise assailants. It was over in an instant.

The two victorious men approached cautiously and rolled each one over to make certain he was dead. Their blue and white uniforms, so brilliant and menacing only a few seconds before, were now caked copiously with grisly, seeping blood mixed with sticky red-brown dirt that abounded in the area. Thompson lowered his weapon, relaxing for the first time, and Morgan did likewise. Nervous energy inflamed both of them, and the joy of success showed on their faces.

"Good show, Jacob. You were ready for them, weren't you?"

"Not ready enough. I wonder why these came alone. I had always figured we'd be so outmanned and outgunned we wouldn't have a chance if we were ever discovered, so I hardly considered contingency plans for defense. Looks like I should have. We might have saved the people in those four houses."

"First time I ever killed anybody. Weird feeling. So incredibly different from killing an animal."

People soon began emerging from undamaged houses, most of them choking with grief as they surveyed their dead, but nevertheless relieved that so many were still alive. Luke Walker's house had been next in line for destruction, and he ran up to Morgan and Thompson to express his gratitude. His hand firmly clasped that of his wife Eva, whose beautiful face was drained of all color by the sickening sight and smell of death.

"Couldn't get that old auto of mine to fire, Jacob. She's all locked up tight, so the only thing I could do was struggle and pray. Sorry I wasn't any help."

"Really? I wondered where you went. We'll have a look at it."

"Darn shame. I could've returned fire immediately. Pretty frustrating sitting there like a paper target holding a lap full of worthless metal."

"Surprise is all that got them, Luke. You know that. It's a blessing in disguise that you couldn't shoot, so don't feel bad. If you'd returned fire you and Eva would be dead. And so would the rest of us. Something tells me these guys wanted to take us without help from anybody. They'd have radioed home immediately if they had detected resistance."

All was absolutely dark and quiet in the four hardest hit dwellings. Only now did Morgan notice that the house of his cousin Jody Barnes was the most damaged of all, and literally was threatening to collapse from the awful pummeling it had received. Molly came running up and hugged him, but he was so intent on checking on the Barnes family that he hardly noticed her. He let the heated weapon in his hands slip slowly to the ground as he headed toward the home. When Molly became aware of the destroyed house and where he was going, she joined him in subdued silence.

Their door was completely shattered by gunfire. Morgan flashed his pocket perpetual handlight inside and discovered Jody Barnes' body wedged against the door, completely pierced with bullet tracks. He had died trying to use his body to protect Sarah and the two orphan girls, but high velocity ammunition had gone through all of them. Morgan and Molly looked with deep grief on the horrible sight of their crumpled corpses, so bloody and crushed that they were hardly recognizable. Both of them began to sob softly, clinging to each other for some measure of comfort.

Amid the heavy stillness of death and sorrow and darkness, there came a whimper that was totally unexpected. From a small corner pantry, a child started crying! How could this be? The little closet had likewise been virtually demolished by the terrible barrage. Could anything have survived such a holocaust? They looked at each other in surprise and simultaneously leaped toward the sound.

Opening the door, they heard loud cries but at first could see no little person. In the back of the dark space, the large metallic cooking pot stood with its sturdy lid jilted only slightly. Morgan shined his light into the recess and reached in to lift the lid. He then dragged the heavy pot out into the open. Impact craters on the ancient pot had barely scratched its impervious surface. Baby Abraham was alive and unhurt inside, nestled deeply into a bed of soybeans!

Molly picked him up tenderly and clutched the toddler in her arms as she said out loud a brief prayer of thanks. Morgan listened in agreement but with unbowed head, using the brief interval to check the squirming little body with his light. Sarah Barnes wasn't alive to see it, but her final desperate act had paid off.

They respectfully stepped around the pitiful sprawled bodies, and were met at the door by several members of the community. The somber expressions they bore turned to a mixture of joy and grief, an appropriate blend under the circumstances. Morgan moved away with Thompson for a consultation in the thick dusk.

"Buck, we've still got problems. They know exactly where this vehicle is located if its localizer device is working. And the chips in these dead Concord thugs do the same thing. As I suspected, these guys were hero hogs. They failed to report us, or surely the helicopters would have come in already."

"What do you suggest we do, Jacob? I'm listening."

"I'm moving everybody to another place I've discovered a few miles from here. I've already got them packing. I'm going to load these four fellows into their vehicle and drive them out away from here fifty miles or so. I'll try to stage it like they had a shootout among themselves over something. The Concord probably is unaware other people have guns anymore. Satellites can't detect gunshots now, I'm positive. The Concord has cleaned the guns out so well they think they don't need to worry about them."

"You know I'll have to stay here with my lander. I'd frankly feel a whole lot better if the rest of you could move to a safer place. If they don't attack me before I leave, it'll probably be safe to come back after I blast off. You planning to walk back fifty miles?"

"No choice. I'll take a backpack with supplies and water. It looks like it's going to rain tonight so that should obscure my tracks. If everything works out just right, we might come out of this thing with minimum losses and just maybe no suspicion about our being here."

"Oh, Jacob. One thing. Could you leave me one of those weapons?"

"No problem. Won't do you much good if the choppers come in on you, though."

"I'd just like to take some of the—the enemy—with me if I have to go. I can only get off a couple of rounds with my old shotgun."

"I understand where you're coming from. But I think it's the wrong attitude. It won't bring back the Barnes family."

"But I'd die happier."

"I told you already how to die happy. Why won't you listen to me, Buck? You've got a head as hard as a washpot. You remind me of myself, in fact. And I'm not the only one concerned about you. There's a lady who's pretty precious to you who's worried about you, too. Think about it."

The two men parted company as Thompson climbed into the vehicle and roared off with the dead patrolmen aboard. Morgan returned to the destroyed house and tenderly prepared the body of his cousin, as well as those of Sarah and the Hansen girls, for burial. The night was as black as fresh asphalt, so grave digging and interment would have to wait until dawn.

Back at the lab, Morgan checked to make sure the fuel production process was going well. Molly joined him, holding Baby Abraham tenderly in her arms.

"Is he still okay?"

"Fit as can be. Trying to talk. He's calling me 'Mum.' I can't tell he's any different than he was before the raid."

"He's the only relative I have left now, best I know. My fifth cousin."

"More than I've got left, Buck. We're going to have to take care of him, now that Sarah isn't with us anymore."

"Everything about child care is in the computers on the *Ursa C*. I'll call Calvin and get it."

"Probably not necessary. I've been around him a lot."

"True. I'll still check with Calvin to be certain. Baby Abraham's going with me, Molly."

"Really? Can you take care of a child?"

"If I have to, I'll figure it out. I was hoping I might have some help. I've been talking to Luke and Eva about going with me. And you know how I feel about you."

Molly sat down in one corner with the infant, her radiant complexion glowing in the dim light of lab machinery. She said nothing, but her earlier conversation with Thompson returned to her with absolute clarity. She honestly didn't know if she could ever stay here and let Morgan soar off into eternity with Baby Abraham, regardless of how the space explorer felt about her faith. And under any set of criteria she could conceive, he had every right as next of kin to determine whether the baby would go.

By midnight, the village was completely deserted except for the workshop where Morgan labored. His old shotgun sat ready in one corner, and the antique automatic rifle lay on a table. A soft rain was falling outside, and the night was quite cold and seemed as dark as a black hole. Quiet reigned in the poorly illuminated lab except for occasional whimpering from the orphaned child.

Molly sat feeding the baby fresh goat milk and wheat bread, and as she remembered her murdered friends she quietly shed a tear. Morgan noticed her crying and understood perfectly. He shared the same deep sense of loss and pain.

He walked over to her and lifted her chin toward him. In the midst of the gloom, deep blue eyes met dark brown ones once again.

He kissed her gently, and then turned back to his laborious task. There was a lot more riding on his success now. Deep in his heart he was sure of it. He didn't see how he would be able to stand it if he were wrong.

CHAPTER 46

June 2169

"Find him! And now!" menaced Father Hammer to his military commander, General Lawrence Foxx. The Father's angry eyes were so threatening, so terrifying, so filled with malice, and so devoid of mercy that they suggested the presence of Satan himself. The white-haired army officer had seen his share of troubled leaders in his day, but none of them were anywhere near as intimidating as this one. Never had he encountered anyone as agitated and demanding as his overbearing commander was at this very moment.

"Your Lordship, we are being hard pressed to stay up with rebels who are cropping up all over the world. We are executing thousands who refuse microchip implants but still their cause flourishes. Many of our resources are focused on locating and destroying vagrant preachers who seem to be spreading this rebellious attitude. They are most elusive, excellent Father, but we shall find and eliminate them."

"Forget the rebels. They are unarmed and easy to kill, no matter how many join them. They must wait. Find Morgan!"

"My Lord, we've alerted all units worldwide to be looking for him. Since he eluded our forces at the Cape and in Kansas, nobody has seen him at all. The clumsy patrols who failed you have been executed, most excellent Father. We will find him in a very short time, your Lordship."

"Get out of here, you silver-haired imbecile! I don't want any more of your lame excuses. I want Morgan and I want him now," growled the Father. His terrible eyes narrowed in frightful malevolence and his face contorted in a dreadful scowl. His words felt like super-cooled water falling on Foxx as he lowered his voice to a whisper. "You will meet with the same fate as those patrols if he isn't in custody by this time tomorrow."

Gripping fear seized the elderly officer, a panicky confusion that made him shake all over. He knew beyond doubt that this was no idle threat. He had earned some of the Father's benevolence, and had hoped that his loyalty would buy him a reprieve for any indiscretion perceived by his master. To be sure, the volatile strongman often flung abuse at him, but never had he threatened extreme measures so awfully and so directly. Nearly numb with terror, the veteran Concord general stumbled out of the palace in Rome determined to save his life if at all possible.

All Concord forces worldwide would be given a new focus: Forget Israel and stop searching for those pesky and elusive preachers for a time. Eliminating petty resistance movements would be put on hold while the army sought Morgan, and only Morgan. The rest could wait. The renegade nation wasn't going anywhere, nor were chip resisters, but the astronaut who had the keys to a present-day Noah's ark just might.

Foxx first called his staff together for an emergency meeting. The situation's gravity needed no explanation. Implacable determination showed on every face, and dour countenances were on all the assembled military experts.

They devised a comprehensive and detailed plan. All units would move immediately on a mission to search every possible location for the astronaut and his aircraft. The generals agreed that producing him alive would gain great favor for them with the Father, so they partially rescinded the shoot to kill order, effective immediately. If Morgan resisted in the least their forces were to destroy him, and somebody with historical and scientific leanings would be required to figure out how to use his lander to reach the orbiting starship and retrieve that priceless cargo. If he would cooperate, fine; if not, he was to be shot immediately.

All helicopters were to go on active alert and fly continuously for the next twenty-four hours looking for Morgan. The man or unit who found him was promised a special commendation and special privileges. Failure was not an option and success was commanded in no uncertain terms.

The first twelve hours turned up nothing of substance. Foxx was becoming more and more desperate, and he sent out an order for all units to send an hourly report of all activities related to the search. Any commander who had allocated insufficient resources or emphasis to the project was summarily executed and replaced by his second-ranking subordinate.

By this time the magnitude and importance of the chase had filtered down through the ranks to the lowest levels. An obscure private approached his unit commander with a theory that had been laughed at by his own immediate superiors. The essence of his argument was that four bullet-riddled soldiers found in the desert recently by the private's patrol had not been killed by regulation weapons. The private had mentioned this to his lieutenant and his sergeant but they had scoffed at his silly suggestion. The difference in size of the bullet holes had been so slight the men had been unwilling to consider whether they might be different from those created by regulation munitions. The patrol commander concluded that there had been an argument, and that the quarrel had erupted into murderous gunfire that had killed all four. Such a scenario was highly plausible and happened not infrequently in the tense and highly contentious Concord forces.

All personnel who had been involved in discovering the bodies were questioned at some length. Indeed, a hurried analysis of fragments of metal from the bodies showed that the lowly private was exactly right. An older weapon had been used to kill the men. It had to be insurgents! The sergeant and lieutenant were both led away to face a firing squad for their ineptitude, and the private received a much-deserved promotion.

But did the ambush of the patrol indicate that Buck Morgan was anywhere in the vicinity? Nobody really knew, but there was very little else to go on. The North American commander ordered all Concord helicopters in his theater of operations to the Rocky Mountain area that centered on the location where the doomed patrol had been found. Soon skies were being crisscrossed with the rhythmic beat of rotor blades.

This sudden increase in activity was not lost on Buck Morgan and Molly Hancock, nor on the deeply hidden band under leadership of Jacob Thompson. The larger group of people and their livestock simply melted into caves in the rocks, determined not to show their location. In the kind of terrain in which they were hiding, Concord choppers could land almost on top of their encampment and never know it was there.

Luke Walker and his wife Eva had rejoined Morgan and Molly after helping their friends finalize the move. The two couples had developed a growing friendship, and they were definitely closer since the unanticipated firefight with the Concord patrol. Walker had performed a poignant funeral service for all victims of the raid and had even asked for an attitude of forgiveness toward the four Concord patrolmen who did the damage. Morgan had been incredulous at such a charitable attitude in the man's prayer, and mysteriously he found himself a bit ashamed. He just couldn't help feeling glad that the attackers were dead. But he had learned to have a great deal of respect for Luke Walker's genuineness and compassion.

Walker took an increasing interest in the lander, and he had become familiar with its basic mechanics over the ensuing days. He was of immense help to Morgan in the ongoing refueling operation.

Thompson and his wife left their charges well hidden and elected to head back to the original settlement to see if they could offer any help in getting the lander ready to fly. The pair crouched under an overhanging boulder while another of the pesky flights of helicopters passed overhead. Thompson held no animosity or regret about Morgan's appearance having drawn a lot of attention their way. It was a dangerous world and nobody could predict such occurrences. But he would certainly feel a deep sense of relief when the lander was no longer protruding so prominently into the dusky atmosphere.

Buck Morgan, meanwhile, worked feverishly with Walker to finish refueling the camouflaged craft. His anxiety peaked as tanks neared the full mark, brimming with liquefied gases that should propel him skyward. He had already loaded the cargo hold with massive quantities of precious water to replenish the renewables garden of the *Ursa C*. He finished monitoring all gauges and turned to his newfound friend.

"Luke, I'm topped off. Would you shut off the valves?"

"I've got it, Buck. Consider it done," replied Walker, applying the needed closure. "Guess we're ready to ride now, huh?"

"Yes. I'll need all of the fuel to get back to the *Ursa C*. It's parked in a very high orbit. These Concord guys undoubtedly have spotted the ship, but apparently they can't do anything about it. Calvin has surveyed all the electronic activity down here, and he believes they can't even launch satellites anymore, much less rendezvous with an orbiting station of any kind. I saw the shuttle pads at the Cape and I can tell you they aren't going to launch anything from there."

"Calvin?" asked Luke. "You've mentioned Calvin before. You got another spaceman up there?"

"No, of course not. Calvin's the artificial intelligence complex on the *Ursa C*. I speak with him every day. He's got a lot more data on the Concord than they do on him, I can tell you that. We're in a critical water shortage up there, but all's been well on the ship otherwise. I've got to call him now and update our departure schedule."

Morgan picked up a portable radio unit from the lander and shortly had Calvin speaking on the device. He advised him of the completed refueling task and the tentative timetable for engine ignition. Walker appeared fascinated by the realistic voice from orbit.

Molly and Eva appeared in the door of Thompson's old home nearby, the youngster in Molly's arms.

"All done fueling? And you've got the cargo holds packed, too, huh?" asked Molly.

"With water plus some other raw materials we might need. Last chance for groceries, you might say," said Morgan.

"Buck, we've got to talk some more about this before you blast off."

"We'll talk in a few more minutes. It looks like everything is ready but I want to be sure. You can't be too careful about space flight."

Morgan crawled all over the lander, calling off items on a checklist held by Walker. He had to make absolutely certain all was ready. Attention to detail had kept him alive in space for his entire professional life, and he was determined this voyage would be no exception. But this trip had special significance and a truly critical need for absolute safety. It would be even more special, if only Molly would cooperate.

The feverish pace of recent days had left no time for walks, but now all was in readiness. They had to make time. There had been no helicopters overhead for several hours, and Morgan felt he had to return to the couple's special perch for a discussion of the most important topic he could imagine. Thompson had sent word via radio that he was coming, but he wouldn't be there for another hour or so.

Taking full advantage of the lull, and leaving Baby Abraham in the care of Luke and Eva, the two silently climbed to their hilltop overlook, staying out of sight. Morgan carried his ancient shotgun, reloaded with potent buckshot, as a usual precaution. They could see Walker and Eva roving about around the lander far below, while the child rambled about like children do. They sat staring at the pleasing valley, both of them blocking out the memory of recent tragedy there. They held hands without making eye contact. Appropriate words to express their deep emotions were hard to find. It was Morgan who finally broke the silence.

"Sweetheart, it's finally ready. You know I have to take off now. I plan to ignite the engines just after dawn tomorrow. Luke and Eva are going with me."

Molly sighed deeply but said nothing. Morgan knew without looking that her eyes were filled with tears. He gently put his fingers on her pretty chin and turned her face toward his.

"Molly, I can't stand leaving you. You know how much I love you. Come with me and we'll explore space together. Please?" he implored, his sincere eyes moist and his deeply masculine voice choking with emotion.

Molly buried her face in his embrace and sobbed gently. He squeezed her tenderly and waited for her to regain her composure. Finally she was able to speak, her sweet voice rich in feeling.

"Buck, darling, I love you, too. Now that Jody and Sarah are gone, you're truly the only friend I have in the entire world, besides these wonderful people we've met here. But there's something else more important that we have to talk about. I had an unscheduled counseling session with Jacob the night the pipe ruptured, and he advised me to discuss it with you openly. That's what I have to do, Buck."

"Come on, then. Out with it."

"You and I have entirely different belief systems, Buck. You've never given up on the god of science, even though it's a false deity. It has never, and can never, meet all your needs. There's only one way to true fulfillment and happiness, and that's the way of Jesus Christ. You say you've read the Bible, and that you know a lot about it. Do you understand anything about the Old Testament sacrificial system, and how it foreshadowed the coming of Christ as the perfect sacrifice for man's sins? Do you understand that there is no forgiveness of sins without the shedding of blood? Even pagans seem to understand that. But you somehow seem to think that by living a good life and doing the best you can, everything will be all right. That's deception, Buck. I can't live in a double world. I'd rather stay here and die without you."

"I see," said Morgan slowly. There was a long, uncomfortable pause before he continued. "Yes, I understand what you're saying. But if Luke and Eva can go, why can't you?"

Molly looked at him through her drying tears, discouraged somewhat by his question. If he didn't change, what were her options? She honestly did not want to stay behind, though she knew the undeniable facts. There was a chasm between the two of them that would not be bridged by blasting off. If Buck Morgan would not make the commitment she had placed before him, she had to make a decision. Would it be better to take her chances on planet Earth under the iron hand of the Concord, or be hurled into interstellar space with this man who did not share her beliefs. She had no real attachment to the world now, but this was still an unsolved and critical dichotomy.

"Luke and Eva know what they're getting into. And they have each other. But I can't get into an intimate relationship with you if you can't make a basic change in your life," Molly stated firmly but with deep feeling as tears welled once more in her dark eyes. "You're taking Baby Abraham, whether I go or not?"

"Of course. I'm his only relative, and I won't leave him here for murder by those Concord brutes. The ship was designed with renewables for just one person, but I have nine years of data calculations that show it will support up to five or six, perhaps even seven, with no problem. Will you, Molly? Make me deliriously happy and say yes. Please?"

"Buck, I can't do it as things now stand. I love you, but you're the one who has to make the real decision, not me."

"I've known those concepts you speak about since my boyhood, because my own parents went to their graves clinging to those beliefs," said Morgan, after which he drew a long breath and released a telling sigh. "Molly, I just can't magically change the way I feel. I've genuine doubts."

"All it takes is one step of faith, Buck. You don't have to become a Jacob Thompson or Abe Rosenthal overnight. Just ask God to make one small change in you, and trust him to do more."

There was a very long and uncomfortable pause as Buck gazed down the valley, his incisive mind dissecting the proposition. He even had thoughts of running it by Calvin before responding. He could feel Molly's watching and waiting, so he finally arrived at a decision.

"Okay, sweetheart, I'll take one step of faith. But I want you to know it's entirely on faith, what little I have. It's your turn to tell me what to do, Molly. And when I do this thing, we're going to get married, whether I'm a perfect Christian or not. What's next?"

"It's as simple as a few words, but as profound as all creation, Buck. Just follow after me."

There was something that happened to seasoned astronaut Buck Morgan that day, something he couldn't explain, something he couldn't reduce to a scientific formula. He followed Molly's words exactly, mouthing them like they were an ancient homily to be learned by rote. But as soon as she said "Amen," he felt a most satisfying and profound sense of peace. Thinking processes and nagging doubts were little changed, but a new creature, indeed, sat on the mountain above the encampment. Molly clung to him for the longest time after the prayer was over, and finally spoke.

"Buck, welcome to the family of God. I promise to love you forever. And so will God."

"And I promise to love you, little girl. Molly, I'm a little scared. I've never committed to do anything I wasn't sure I could handle. And this is certainly something I can't handle."

"You don't have to handle it, Buck. God will. Please trust him and take it one step at a time."

"One more thing. I already said you had to, but I need to rephrase it. Will you marry me?"

"Oh, yes, Buck—oh, yes! Jacob or Luke either one can perform the ceremony! Oh, God, thank you!"

"I guess now is as good a time as any to start this faith thing. God, help us get married and start a happy life together," said Morgan, looking into the reddish sky as he spoke. Molly smiled and hugged him again. The astronaut returned her look, and a twinkle developed in his sky blue eyes while an imperceptible shiver coursed his backbone. The idea of life with Molly aboard his incredible machine was a thrilling thought to be savored.

"And we still have to leave, Buck?"

"You've told me your feelings and I've responded. And you've heard mine, how I can't leave my ship to die. Now how are you going to respond?"

She silently considered the implications of departing the world again, closing her dark eyes so she could think more clearly. She had no living relatives, and she already felt closer to Morgan than to anyone else on earth. As a Christian, she believed firmly that it wouldn't matter, when her Christ appeared to claim his people, where she was in the universe. She believed it was all his anyway and that she would instantly be with her God at his call. And it wouldn't matter if she died elsewhere, either, because she believed that to be absent from the body was to be with the Messiah. Obviously Walker and Eva held the same belief, and her friends being along would make it much easier for her. She took a deep breath and made her decision.

"Okay, Buck. Let's get married, and then I'll go."

He hugged her warmly, and the two shared a fervent kiss.

"Thanks, love. You won't regret it," Morgan asserted softly, adding under his breath, "Thank you, too, God."

The pair descended the mountain, making necessary marriage plans as they descended. It would be indeed a simple wedding.

Thompson and his wife arrived a short while later to bid them farewell, and Thompson performed an impromptu wedding, using Luke's worn Bible as the basis for a simple ceremony. Buck kissed Molly after they exchanged vows, and there were hugs all around.

Thompson insisted that they all pray about the blastoff, and he and Walker did so with fervency. Morgan added a few halting words, the first public prayer of his life. The bearded man read a few passages from his Bible, each one rich with meaning and truth.

The older couple had just disappeared into a giant boulder field that marked the way to their hidden band when a remote radio unit lying on the table crackled to life.

"Commander Bucko, multiple hot metallic targets are converging on you from all sectors. Caution is advised," said Calvin's stoic voice.

There was no time to reply to the *Ursa C*. Deafening and ominous noise from innumerable rotor blades broke the accustomed silence. This time it didn't sound like a searching flight of helicopters, but seemed to reverberate from one end of the sky to the other. Two gunships wheeled over the crest of Morgan and Molly's mountain, bearing down on them directly. Another machine was also visible up a narrow gorge, a large troop carrier that swung in an arc over them and landed in an open field near the far end of the deserted compound. It immediately began spilling numerous armed men, who looked like ants emerging and fanning out, checking each house as they went. The tide of determined soldiers was unalterably heading their way. They could hear numerous helicopters in virtually all directions.

"Thank God everything is aboard! Molly, you and Eva take Baby Abraham and get in! Strap him into the seat next to you. Luke and I will be there as soon as we rip away the camouflage! And take this radio!"

"You get in and get ready to blast off, Buck. I'll get the netting off," said Walker, wielding a sharp knife in one hand.

Morgan looked at the oncoming horde of troops and the bedlam of approaching helicopters and knew there was very little time. He grimly tossed the automatic rifle to Walker and picked up his old shotgun. There would be little chance of success, but they would have to confront these first two helicopters before they would have any likelihood of cutting away the confining netting.

"Not a chance, Luke. Those gunships will kill you before you can do anything. Stay down out of sight," shouted Morgan.

They crouched amid the ubiquitous boulders as the deafening sound of the flying machines moved closer and closer, until finally they were virtually overshadowed by the apocalyptic craft. The pilots were plainly a little uncertain how to proceed, so they came to a hover just short of the lander. Morgan and Walker found themselves staring at the belly of the most efficient killing devices in the Concord arsenal, just scant yards above them.

The women and the baby were safely inside the lander, out of harm's way for the moment. The lowest helicopter was apparently going to land, and he was sitting almost on top of the two men and inching ever closer. Morgan could see the exact position of the pilot in the adjacent helicopter, and he judged from that information exactly where the one just overhead was located.

"Take that one, Luke," he shouted to his friend, and motioned to the more distant of the two choppers. Walker laid down a virulent barrage at the canopy of the gunship, instantly killing the pilot and causing the craft to lurch out of control and crash in flames.

In the confusion Morgan leaped onto the roof of the deserted lab and stuck the barrel of the old shotgun up as high as he could reach toward the belly of the helicopter, perhaps a couple of yards from the airframe. He estimated where the pilot would be located, and pointed the ancient barrels at that spot. He put his index finger on the front trigger and his middle finger on the back trigger, and when he thought it exactly right he discharged both barrels at once. There was a terrific jolt of recoil on his hand and arm as eighteen lead pellets of thirty-caliber size blew away a considerable hole in the metal, and a torrent of blood cascaded back out the opening. The craft suddenly spun right, then left, then nosed over into a nearby hill, creating another inferno. Neither downed craft had so much as fired a volley.

"Now go to it, Luke. Be careful! I'll have everything inside on go when you get up here," yelled Morgan as he ascended the ladder with his emptied shotgun slung over his back.

"Just get ready. I'll be okay," called the young man, slinging the old automatic weapon back around his neck as he shouted. He then set about cutting away tough leather camouflage netting, the strength of which could cause a disastrous launch failure if it weren't removed.

Concord foot soldiers couldn't miss the commotion and gunfire, and immediately they spotted the shiny, emerging craft. The silver bird now gleamed in the sunlight as netting dropped away, and the infantrymen at once ran toward it as a single massive unit. Another warbird popped over the hill, and the pilot could see billowing black smoke and raging fire from his conquered comrades. Nonetheless, little besides the prospect of glory from the Father filled his mind as he spied the lander. He turned the nose of his swift machine toward the lander, his gun sights zeroed on the shiny projectile. But what part should he shoot at? People were easy, but a big contraption like he was attacking was different. The lander looked unoccupied from the helicopter pilot's perspective, so the man spent some anxious seconds trying to decide how to capture the craft without setting down. He finally radioed that he had the lander under arrest, and then he backed off a short distance to await arrival of reinforcements, keeping the ship fully in his view.

As he hovered sideways inspecting his catch from another angle, the chopper pilot suddenly spotted Morgan in the cockpit of the silver bullet, feverishly working to begin the ignition sequence. A scowling face and eyes brimming with hate stared at Morgan through the double canopy, and determination showed clearly in the set of the Concord airman's unmoving lips. Turning to his gunsight, the aviator prepared to unleash all his firepower at the steaming lander.

The last view the chopper pilot ever saw was that of the ship through his scope, gleaming like a gilded chariot. Luke Walker, hidden in the rocks after pulling the camouflage free, placed another perfect volley of old time automatic weapon fire into the canopy, extinguishing the Concord pilot's life. The doomed machine nosed over into unforgiving ground as the pilot slumped forward and jammed the cyclic control. Walker was rocked by another mighty explosion as the helicopter's fuel tanks detonated and the machine disintegrated in flames, creating a titanic barrier that temporarily impeded the approach of onrushing Concord infantry. The young man then scrambled unharmed toward the readied lander as Morgan cheered him eagerly through the transparent canopy and gestured a hearty thumbs up.

As he clambered up the ladder, more than a dozen hissing helicopters approached from every point of the compass, looming like colossal dragonflies spewing fire and brimstone. Pellets of lead pattered against the advanced alloy frame and canopy of the lander, as harmless as raindrops to the vehicle, but deadly should one strike the vulnerable flesh of the struggling young warrior. He tumbled inside the ship as a barrage whistled and ricocheted all around him. One bullet creased his shirt and another nicked his arm. The hatch annunciator light immediately turned green as the port sealed. Morgan helped Walker strap in, and then quickly finished activating the familiar ignition sequence with no time to spare.

In desperation, one of the helicopters flew up to the very nose of the lander, almost touching the silver bird with its front gun turret, while whirling rotor blades loomed just microns from the apex of the craft. The Concord veteran driving the craft glowered intensely at Morgan, while a threatening frown creased his hateful face and bloodshot eyes shot malicious daggers. He seemed determined to use the front cowling of his machine to shove the lander over before it could launch.

Morgan was well into ignition countdown by this point, and he had no plans to be stopped now. He reached into his pocket and extracted the stun pistol, recharged to maximum and unused since he vacated the Barnes farm. He didn't know if it would work through so much intervening clear material, but it was worth a try. It was now or never, anyway. He put the pistol on highest setting and pointed it directly at the sulky-faced gunship pilot. When he activated the device, a look of horror displaced hate in the man's eyes as the craft rolled up and backward, almost doing a complete flip before crashing in flames. Debris from the blast rocketed skyward and briefly obscured the lander, while fire mixed with smoke once more engulfed disordered ground troops now teeming on all sides.

Mighty engines surged and flame stabbed downward with the force of a thousand jet engines, scorching the Rocky Mountain soil and shaking the very foundations of surrounding mountains. Gravity clasped at the ship with unyielding fingers as hydrogen and oxygen combined thunderously to deprive the earth of its prey, shooting the projectile and its human cargo skyward with multiple G forces. Takeoff was marred only by a harmless pattering of bullets against the lander's impervious hull. Several menacing helicopters capsized disastrously in a hurricane of departure turbulence, and all of them ended up as conflagrations of blazing scrap metal on the dry ground. Numerous Concord infantrymen were incinerated by the fiery departure.

Jacob Thompson emerged briefly, cautiously, from his hideaway to watch the streaking ship ascend magnificently. Yellow and orange fire trailed from behind the craft as it accelerated, and a white vapor trail formed in its wake. The noise was deafening even from more than a mile away. A crisp sonic boom caressed the land as if bidding it goodbye. Thompson lifted a hand in a gesture of farewell.

"Godspeed, friends," he murmured quietly before disappearing into his grotto once again.

And Earth released its grip on Buck Morgan.

CHAPTER 47

June 2169

"Calvin, adjust and lock trajectory to the *Ursa C*," commanded Morgan into his microphone as his craft thundered skyward. "Got us, old buddy?"

"Got you, Commander Bucko. You're locked and synchronized for rendezvous on the second orbit," came a punctual reply. A green-lighted flight profile appeared on the navigation console's big screen, with the starship poised symbolically at the apex of the envelope.

"Home free," breathed Morgan to his little crew. G forces began to relax while he throttled back at the familiar Max Q zone. After what seemed like only a few seconds he throttled up the lander to full power as atmospheric resistance subsided and all sound slipped behind the speeding craft.

"How's that arm, Luke?"

"Fine, Buck. Hardly scratched me. That's the third Concord bullet I've taken, and I hope it will be the last."

"We'll let Calvin have a look at it shortly. His medicine chest is awesome," said Morgan as he took a brief look at the slug's track.

Their hasty departure required some deft computer work by Calvin, since harmonization with the orbiting starship high above the earth was an absolute necessity. Walker was of substantial help in the copilot seat, despite his bleeding arm and a glaring lack of training and experience, and he followed Morgan's instructions exactly.

In less than two hours and an orbit and a half around Earth, the starship became visible to the naked eye through the canopy, initially as a tiny silver dot but growing larger minute by minute. Its sheer size and grandeur were overwhelming to the unlikely novices aboard as the massive craft began to dominate their entire view. The vaulted clear top of the lander allowed an excellent view of the magnificent machine, and repeated cries of astonishment were voiced as they approached ever closer to the *Ursa C*. Orbital synchrony was perfect by the time Calvin unlatched a huge docking bay, and it opened wide to receive the silver bullet onboard. Molly Hancock became a little nauseated from weightlessness and unaccustomed sensory disorientation while on the smaller ship, but the feeling vanished quickly as they were grasped by artificial gravity after the docking bay sealed behind them.

In anticipation of another planetary foray someday, Morgan connected the lander to the renewables outlet to slowly recharge during the planned upcoming flight. Fresh water they had brought would replenish the garden fully, with plenty of surplus to refuel the lander without any depletion of renewables. He coupled appropriate conduits to accomplish unloading, and watched carefully to make certain all was in order. He then proceeded to check his living charges for any adverse effect of his dehydrating absence. He could find no problem that renewed input of water would fail to solve in short order.

Morgan could see right away that he had a major new asset in Walker, who devoured details of the ship as he toured various components. The two women tagged along carrying young Abraham, and both of them marveled at the complicated and vast structure. The decision to go was unalterable for all of them, so they were eager to get to know their new home.

"Wow, Buck, this must be the most thrilling honeymoon in history," commented Molly as they toured the ship.

He leaned over near her ear and kissed her softly, and then whispered something in her ear that made her smile, then giggle. When Eva looked at her inquisitively, Molly just shook her head but wouldn't reveal what Morgan had said.

Their near-fatal encounter on the surface and the tragic premature demise of some of his new friends there had given Morgan cause to consider his options as far as influencing the outcome of the struggle on Earth. He checked the cockpit of the *Ursa C* to be sure everything was in working order, and hesitated thoughtfully as he examined the complicated console that controlled the frightening plasmafyer hyperlaser.

"Folks, before we finish the tour, I've got something important to discuss with all of you. Look at this unit," Morgan said as he patted the console and positioned them so they could see it well. "It can destroy Earth if we choose to use it. This is a laser that clears asteroids and other debris from in front of the ship. It could be an overwhelming weapon, though to my knowledge it's never been used that way. What do you think?"

None of them had ever seen anything so complicated. Numerous red and green eyes stared at them from the laser control panel, some winking and others a monotonous colored glow, the device giving every indication of being alive. Cooling fans whistled even while the monster slept, pumping refreshing air and water through its bowels so overheating would never be a problem, even with repeated use. As Morgan flipped the switch that placed the device in activated mode, a standby light disappeared and was replaced by a green asterisk. Walker grasped the implications immediately, but Molly blinked thoughtfully while Eva just stared, unsure what to make of Morgan's suggestion. He could see that he would have to explain further.

"What I'm saying is that this is the most deadly weapon in existence. The beam is normally scattered rather widely in front of the ship, but it automatically focuses tightly on discreet matter such as meteors and asteroid particles that are on a collision course with us. Look here, Luke, in manual mode I can focus it finely on anything I choose, so it could be a devastating piece of war-making equipment. We'd have to cook a whole shaft of atmosphere in order to burn a good sized hole in the ground, but it's up to the task."

Perhaps it was Morgan's recent battlefield encounters, perhaps it was the experience of killing an enemy for the first time, but for some reason his warrior training from many years ago was finally surfacing. Besides, this Hammer fellow deserved such a fate as he was suggesting. What about a little revenge for all the havoc and death that beast had caused? Didn't he deserve some kind of retribution?

"Buck, what are you suggesting? Destroying the world?"

"No, of course not. But I can't shake the thought that we could focus this thing on Rome and create a crater half the size of Kansas. That would rid the world of that evil emperor, or whatever he is. I don't know if that would be the best course or not."

"Man, I wish we'd had this thing in the Wyoming War. We'd still be riding free on the range if we had," lamented Walker. "But I don't know about using it now. If we're leaving anyway, it's seems like sheer revenge. I'd have to think about it, though I must say it's tempting."

"Buck, do you have any idea how many innocents might die if you did that?" Molly sighed. "And we couldn't even be absolutely certain that the Father would be in Rome. No, Buck, I know it's an attractive thought, but I don't think we should interfere. Besides, God will take care of him at the proper time. I've had enough trouble convincing myself I should even be vacating planet Earth, and I certainly don't think we should try to interject ourselves into the conflict any deeper than we already have."

"Okay. I just wanted your input. Whatever you think is what we'll do."

Satisfied with their reasoning, Morgan continued their tour of the amazing machine, a technological marvel that bristled with forgotten technology. In the control room, they all gawked at Calvin's handsome, wild-haired form, so lifelike that actual introductions were in order. Calvin waved at them and smiled, showing teeth that one would have sworn were made of real enamel instead of energized photons of light. His Jeremiah Smith locks waved untamed in all directions, so comical that it actually evoked chuckles.

"Eva, have you ever seen a picture of your great-grandfather? This is exactly what he looked like in real life," said Morgan.

"Handsome fellow, huh?" answered Eva.

"That he is—uh, was. In more ways than just his physical appearance, too. Greatest friend of my life, doubtless. Calvin here has kept him alive for me. Anything you want to know about your ancestor, Calvin knows, so just ask him. I don't think Smitty kept anything back.

Plot a course to 51 Pegasai, Calvin. We'll light up and get underway within an hour, if you're ready."

"Already done, Commander Bucko. Antimatter conversion engines primed and on standby," replied a pleasant voice from the holographic man, with appropriate inflection and a pride of workmanship showing in every word.

After the main control center, they visited the entertainment complex, where Morgan played a few bars for them on the superb piano. Despite lack of recent practice sessions, his rendition of *"Chariots of Fire"* was nonetheless stirring and superb. He concluded the masterful rendition to hearty applause from his companions.

"We've saved the music of Earth, in addition to some of the best creatures and plants. In here are all the songs ever composed up to the time I left," he said as he patted the computer terminal built into the keyboard of the instrument.

"Majestic," said Molly. "I can't wait to hear more. Do we have time?"

"Later. Once we're underway, that's a commodity that we'll have in plentiful quantity."

Continuing the tour, he demonstrated the main engine group, the complex navigation array, and many items of advanced hardware that made up the splendid ship. It was all more than impressive to the newcomers.

Molly was most fascinated, however, by the indescribable renewable resources garden, and especially the numerous animals she had previously known only from pictures. Her farewell to planet Earth was somewhat softened by tremendous newfound joy she was experiencing. After all, she reflected confidently, she was secure in her belief that they would all be reunited with their home planet someday, if her understanding of their faith were accurate. And she had every confidence that this man she loved, her new husband, would be there with her.

They were in a far corner petting some raccoons, playful animals that were utilized mainly as living garbage disposal units. They were startled when the plasmafyer hyperlaser activated automatically, emitting a perceptible drone and dimming the lights markedly as a sudden energy drain placed drastic stress the *Ursa C*'s powerful batteries. The device caused no noticeable effect on the ship's electrical systems when the antimatter conversion engine group was in operation, but when activated on fuel cell power it drew a crippling amount of current. Morgan rushed back to the forward control room, wondering if perhaps an approaching meteor had triggered such an event.

"Incoming radiation shower, Commander Bucko. Nuclear explosion at 680 nautical miles above Earth's mean sea level, orbital velocity, closing fast. The main mass will miss us by 1,500 meters, but some peripheral particles may brush the ship. Debris completely plasmafied, sir," reported Calvin. There was even a discernible hint of nervousness in the artificial man's voice.

Morgan gasped as he looked at the monitor, from which an eerie light emanated, blinding in intensity and ominous in meaning. Only one kind of force could cause such a light, so Calvin had to be right as usual. Nuclear arms had been banned since Terror War III, but this spectrum of radiation had to be a thermonuclear explosion! A blinding light coming through a porthole was adequate confirmation.

The debris from the blast was rocketing toward them at some 17,000 miles per hour, or almost five miles per second. It streaked past between them and the blue-green planet below, the cloud of radioactive material missing by only the narrowest of amounts. Close call, he breathed as the danger passed. Nervous sweat formed on Morgan's brow as he pondered how such a terrible close call could have occurred

. He glanced at his power output indicator, noticing that he had only enough standby power for one more shot with the laser. He deactivated automatic mode and placed it on manual. He didn't want to use his last gasp of power unless absolutely necessary. The monitor showed warning lights flashing insistently, so he began decoding signals the device was receiving, hoping against hope that no more nuclear warheads were headed in their direction. Where had such a primitive society found such deadly firepower?

"Calvin, if any more shots come our way, we can't afford to plasmafy unless they are going to be a direct hit on us. Plot trajectories and activate the laser only in an emergency."

"As you say, Commander Bucko. More incoming all sectors. Plotting as directed. Shall I initiate engine ignition sequence?"

"Affirm. Do it!"

The ship's scanning devices were now showing much more than antique communications satellites. There were streaking missiles everywhere, ascending menacingly in the general direction of their ship at modern orbital speeds. Totally surprised at this development, Morgan hurried threw the right switches to prepare his antimatter conversion engines for ignition. Calvin's attention was divided between supervising internal electronic components of the initiation sequence and monitoring incoming missiles, dual tasks he was well equipped to handle simultaneously.

"Luke, I'm a fool. I assumed they couldn't launch anything. They're throwing their whole ammo dump at us. Those weapons were supposedly destroyed more than a century ago. Obviously some of them survived. Now the Hammer is determined that we aren't going to leave."

"What can I do to help?"

"Pray. And get the women and baby to the center of renewables, where they'll be safest, and get them secured. Then get back here pronto. I've got some ideas."

The missiles were launched with little accuracy, fortunately, but there seemed to be no end to their number. It was as if the whole deadly arsenal of a superpower of old had been sequestered for just this moment of desperate revenge. Sophisticated guidance systems had been lost in the interim, but a hit from one of them would be no less devastating. From the distribution of streaking projectiles, it appeared that the weapons of mass destruction had somehow been spread out all over the globe. Several detonated with light-drenching explosions within a few hundred miles of the ship, but each was entirely ineffective, and ensuing clouds of debris passed by many miles from the spacecraft. It was just a matter of time, though, until one of the awful clouds of speeding radioactive dust and plasma plowed into the *Ursa C* with disastrous and deadly effect. Morgan and Calvin hurriedly set the engine ignition sequence in motion, hoping to get underway as well as power up in order to be able to use the plasmafyer hyperlaser with impunity. Adequate power would also allow him to deploy his faithful ion shield, which was virtually impregnable to radiation. For them to have a chance, he needed power and he needed it now.

Walker returned breathless just as the ignition sequence reached a critical stage, when energy input from the batteries was most essential for lightup of antimatter conversion. At this crucial juncture Morgan heard from Calvin what he had dreaded.

"Danger, danger, Commander Bucko!" boomed Calvin's pervasive voice. "Incoming missile on collision course for direct hit!"

A colossal ball of gas and high intensity radiation blossomed just in front of the ship. Morgan had no choice but to use critically low battery power to plasmafy the formidable cloud so it would hopefully pass by the ship harmlessly. Power standby cells depleted drastically as the laser flashed into the streaking nuclear holocaust, but its effect was dramatic. The material mostly disintegrated in an ensuing inferno as radioactive matter met pure energy in a clash of titanic proportions. Forked tongues of blue-white lightening streaked in all directions and screaming neutrinos and other subatomic particles poured like white-hot rivers of bullets from the cataclysm.

"Lock down tight, Luke!" shouted Morgan.

Both men hugged the floor and grasped any available handhold, but they had no more time to warn the women. Radioactive plasma slammed into the starship with an ear-shattering force, shaking the structure in a manner it had never before endured.

For the first time since the voyage of the *Ursa C* had begun, the hologram man completely disappeared in a flicker of neon-like light, though his image was intermittent for a brief interval. During some seconds the whole ship lost its artificial gravity field, and everything floated about in chaotic fashion. Fortunately, the weightlessness lasted only briefly before a backup system restored the field and everything and everybody came crashing to the deck once more.

Morgan could hear Baby Abraham crying far down the hall, and he was glad for the loud wailing. The little fellow had to be mostly unhurt, letting it roll like that. Walker was pretty much unscathed, though he had bumped his head and blood trickled down his forehead from a small cut.

"You okay, Molly?" Morgan shouted into the intercom as he manually monitored all the essential onboard systems for failure. He pushed previously unused reset buttons in rapid succession, and like a miracle Calvin reappeared with a powerful grin on his face, and with his hair even more disheveled than usual.

"Ouch, Commander Bucko. Dead centered my microprocessor element with gamma rays. No permanent damage," said Calvin. "Sorry I had to leave you so rudely."

"No problem, Calvin. But I'm glad you're back. Are you fully functional?"

"I'm scanning now. Nothing out of the green, I don't think. Just a couple of chips may need replacing."

"Good, because I need all the help we can get," asked Morgan from his workstation. "Can we light up the engines now?"

"Affirmative, Commander Bucko. But there is one bit of bad news. Engine linkage seems to be severed. I just found a red light in sigma sector."

Morgan groaned aloud. The engine linkage computer was irreplaceable. Without smooth linkage between the four engines, prag c was impossible.

"Continue ignition sequence on the prime engine. We've got to get one of them up and operative or we'll stay sitting here like a cat up a tree," said Morgan as he worked feverishly.

Power surged weakly into the ignition chamber, but there was no response whatever. It looked hopeless, and it appeared that they would stay floating in orbit like a clay pigeon for the Concord to shoot at until they were destroyed. Calvin reached to the panel in front of him and pulled a red breaker switch, whereupon he completely disappeared again and the ship's lights blinked out altogether. The prime engine immediately roared to life with a shudder that vibrated the entire fabric of the giant starship.

Now the craft would at least have ready energy for the laser, and they could maneuver as well. A moving target would make it much more difficult for the poorly guided missiles to hit them. Morgan reached for another obscure reset button near the back of the control console, and Calvin reappeared once more as if by magic.

"Good show, holo amigo. Welcome back. We're in business. I guess you draw enough power to make the critical difference today," said Morgan

"Insignificant voltage normally, but we were down below threshold for ignition. I had no choice, Commander Bucko," answered Calvin. "We're on the move, I see."

"Yep. Hold down the command room, Calvin. I've got work to do. Come with me, Luke, we've got to check on the ladies. And have a little conference, too."

Morgan and Walker dashed down a long hallway, relishing the lights and artificial gravity with new appreciation. Through one of the side portholes Morgan caught sight of another burst of nuclear energy flashing by, ominously close but still no threat to them so far. But he knew the missiles were continuing their assault unabated. They entered the renewables area and found their other passengers a bit shaken, and there was scattered soil and a quite a few displaced plants. Everything looked surprisingly okay otherwise. Eva was holding Baby Abraham, who had calmed considerably since the damaging impact, and Molly was sitting beside her.

"Buck, we're fine. Any damage?" asked Molly, arising as she spoke.

"Only minor. Molly, we've got to return fire or we're going to get killed," Morgan answered. "I have no alternative. Okay with you, Luke? Eva?"

"Oh, can't we just leave, Buck? I heard an engine or something start, didn't I?" said Molly.

"We're going to be in their range for a while if we don't do something. We've got power now, but we can't leave until we do some repair work, sweetheart."

"Let's do it, Buck. He's going to get us if he keeps up this barrage." said Walker grimly. "How much time are we talking about?"

"A couple of hours. I don't relish the thought of trying to be a repairman and fight a battle at the same time," declared Morgan. "Our engines won't link since that last barrage. We can hopefully ward off individual missiles, but if they score another direct hit like that it might be the end of us anyway. I need to maneuver for a shot at that guy's headquarters. That should give us a chance to reestablish the computer link between our engines. Can any of you think of anywhere else I could shoot besides Rome that might buy us some time?"

Molly plopped down in a corner, her face drained of expression. She had heard the question, and pondered it as she studied Morgan's face, strained more than ever by the feverish defense operation. She thought of innocent people on the ground, masses of oppressed people with no possibility of physical redemption under the grinding heel of authoritarian rule. She looked at the growing child in Eva's arms and looked back at Morgan, an undeniable question mark on her pretty face. Anyone living innocently in Rome would be better off dead, anyway. And if they had to blast any part of Earth into eternity to make their escape, there couldn't be a place that might do more good for mankind. Maybe it was God's will.

"You guys do what you have to. I'm not going to watch. Rome is where he usually stays."

"I agree, Buck," added Walker quietly. "Fire away."

Morgan had plenty of power now, even with only one engine operative, and with Calvin's flawless application of mathematics he blasted a pair of rising missiles before they had cleared the upper layers of Earth's atmosphere. They teamed perfectly and used the ship's complex tracking capabilities effectively. Soon the awesome laser was thrusting and parrying like the sword of a swashbuckling pirate of old. Morgan had no idea how many such missiles the Father had at his disposal, nor how long they would have to keep this up. At least the *Ursa C* was mobile now, and while the battle raged the ship was maneuvered until they held a geosynchronous orbit over Italy. Locking in coordinates of the Imperial City, Morgan prepared to deliver his deadly blow.

* * *

"My Lord, we are proceeding with all haste to destroy Morgan. He can't escape, Father."

"Don't tell me that rubbish, you bumbling idiot. Tell me when he's dead, and then you can live. But if he escapes, you'll be carrion like that stupid Foxx."

An awful stream of blasphemous expletives poured from the mouth of Father Hammer, so devastating that the targeted officer was briefly taken aback. He regained his composure with great difficulty and spoke weakly with stammering speech.

"Begging the Father's pardon, Great Master, I believe he may even now be very dead. Please proceed as planned for the Middle East. Our brave forces report that one of our missiles scored a direct hit on his ship."

"You'd better hope so. Ready my craft. I'll take a final report when I get to Israel," said the leader, his awful eyes burning a hole in the officer, his tone of voice sounding highly dubious of his underling's veracity. "And it had better be a good one."

The frightened officer who had replaced Foxx knew that the starship was not yet destroyed. Still, he desperately hoped to accomplish the task. The Concord's secret atomic weaponry was being thrown at the orbiting ship as fast as it could be readied and launched. If Morgan escaped, he

605

knew the whole officer corps of the Concord army could be executed, a massacre that his merciless master would not hesitate to carry out. He couldn't afford to intimate to Father Hammer that the starship was now mobile, so he purposefully did not divulge that latest observation to him. He'd do anything to keep the beast from another fit of murderous agitation.

"Father, my Lord, we must move you to your waiting ship. The Holy City awaits your conquering presence, and your army there is on full alert for immediate offensive action. We must leave if the invasion timetable is to be kept as planned."

"You can't deceive me, you fool. I know Morgan is still alive. Are you stupid enough to think that I don't know what's happening? Launch everything we have and you may yet save yourself. The ark and its animals must be destroyed if we cannot have them."

No one could say for certain why the dictator was so intent on preventing departure of the *Ursa C*. Much of it was simple pride, the unthinkable possibility of the omnipotent Father being outwitted by the ship's primitive and unenlightened captain. Perhaps he couldn't stand the thought of a single human being anywhere in the universe who was not under his control. Whatever the case, it was obvious that he would do everything in his power to kill Morgan and destroy his ship rather than let him escape.

*   *   *

Buck Morgan sensed desperation and determination in the staggering volley of missiles ascending toward them, and he knew he had to act quickly to save his ship. He couldn't avoid all of them forever. Morgan focused the plasmafyer beam for maximum penetration of the atmosphere, an adjustment that was necessary because the device had been constructed to function at maximum efficiency only in the vacuum of space. He entered the code for manual activation, and told Calvin to bring up an image of Europe into the laser console's monitor. By touching Rome's exact location on the screen with his finger, the computer automatically fixed the coordinates into the digital mechanism. He said a brief prayer out loud, then touched the maximum activation mode button, and the laser shuddered as energy built to devastating levels before discharging.

Hurtling downward as if from a celestial blowtorch, an ionized column of air sent out shock waves that created gargantuan winds of hurricane force. The energy struck the ancient city of Rome like an impossibly immense lightening bolt. Buildings collapsed like matchsticks, giant stones were hurled miles into the atmosphere, flesh and blood sizzled and exploded into lifeless particles of cookèd protoplasm. Like an infinite number of bullets, rocks and debris from the crater blasted outward in all directions, ripping through everything in their path. Nothing alive remained within five miles of the epicenter, and left was an enormous crater much larger than any nuclear detonation could have created. The tyrant fiend of Rome would doubtless be blown into micro particles by the death ray, Morgan thought with satisfaction as he surveyed the damage through his optical instruments. Sure enough, the missile attacks began to taper off immediately, and shortly they ceased altogether. It appeared to be over.

*   *   *

On the Appian Way just outside Rome, a still form lay beside an overturned blue and white vehicle. There were dead men all around the figure, all of them peppered and skewered by debris from the hyperlaser holocaust. The quiescent corpse was dressed in the black robes of a priest, and the entire back of his head was missing. The convoluted surface of the brain showed clearly through a gaping hole in his skull as he lay face down in the dirt. Over him crouched a big blonde man in similar attire, uttering some kind of strange incantation and placing his hands repeatedly over the massive wound.

A uniformed holographic cameraman beamed the devastating incident to Concord forces and to all operative three-vee receivers in every part of the world. A Concord radio broadcaster arrived within minutes and began relaying an audio description to a breathless planet. It appeared that the malignant Father was dead, even though he had moved far enough away from city center to miss the full force of Buck Morgan's desperate final strike.

*   *   *

Morgan set about the task of preparing the ship for interstellar flight. They would be sailing toward the winged horse of mythology, to the star 51 Pegasai, where hopefully a world like Earth awaited discovery. A new gladness pervaded Morgan's mind, a light happiness he had never experienced before. Even in his concentration, he couldn't stop thinking about his new best friend, Molly Hancock. He loved her ever more deeply, and now his heart burned with a passion to consummate their marriage. His head spun with questions about his newfound faith. After achieving prag c he wanted to spend considerable time...studying his Bible with Molly and...he couldn't believe it...*praying* with her.

Buck Morgan gazed out the window of the *Ursa C*, and lovely Molly stood beside him with her arm around his waist. They marveled at the breathtaking beauty of the blue-green planet below them. How Morgan longed to stay there, to revel in the beauty and bounty of his home. He yearned deeply to experience once again the mountains and the plains, to explore a hidden mountain basin for white rams, or pursue wandering caribou across endless, spongy tundra. Sadly, he knew that those wild creatures were gone forever, and he voiced his distress and disappointment again to his wife. An ancient proverb he had read popped into his mind, and he quietly spoke it aloud for Molly as they gazed, transfixed, contemplating the destruction of their planet's ecosystems.

"There is a way which seemeth right to a man, but its end is the way of death."

"How appropriate," said Molly. "There's been an awful lot of death on Earth because someone thought they knew a better way."

"I don't know if I'd want to stay on Earth without the creatures I knew as a boy. There's something irreplaceable that's gone forever."

"I suppose one would adjust, don't you? I mean if we could somehow eliminate the Concord factor."

"There was an American Indian chief named Seattle who said it best, Molly, about 300 years ago. He said, 'If all the animals were gone, man would die from a great loneliness of spirit, for whatever happens to the beasts also happens to man.' Man is in great danger of disappearing from the earth, apart from divine intervention. Well, my dearest Molly, let's go hunting."

"Hunting? For what? Oh, yes, we are going hunting, aren't we? For a planet, I mean."

"The ultimate hunt, I suppose. Is everybody ready?"

Walker and Eva, who had just finished settling into their quarters, joined them and they all took a final look down at the planet of their birth. There was a short pause as they said, each in their own way, a goodbye to their homeland.

All of them then walked to the flight deck, where efficient Calvin had already plotted a course to the selected star on the ship's complex navigation computers.

*   *   *

Far below, mobs of people had gathered around the dark figure Morgan had victimized on the outskirts of Rome. The Father stirred, first moved his hands, and then there was motion in his feet. The massive wound that had exposed his occipital cortex and his cerebellum was already pink with healing tissue. He sat up and rubbed his head, opened his eyes, and looked about with satisfaction. He glanced at Ersatzson and flashed a menacing and mirthless grin, a sentiment that was returned immediately by his spiritual brother. Christian Ersatzson stood up jubilantly, motioning with his hands over his head for the delirious crowd to shout in victory. A raucous cheer reverberated from the assembled throng of people.

Nothing could stop them now, they were certain. If power were available to achieve such a stupendous cure, they doubtless had sufficient power to complete the task before them. On to Israel they would go. Forget about the doomed spaceman and his worthless cargo, and let them wander the universe looking for an unlikely place to alight. The Father turned triumphantly toward the adoring multitude, and an awed silence fell immediately over the people. Without another word the hushed assembly bowed low and worshipped the man who had arisen from the dead before their eyes.

* * *

Buck Morgan set about preparing his finally peaceful ship for interstellar flight. Linking the complicated engines so they would function as a perfect unit took only a short while. Morgan was given an able hand by his fledgling copilot Walker, and they used only a few pieces of spare hardware to accomplish the repair. There was no other detectable damage from the close missile encounter. As he finished the job and took the pilot's seat, Morgan still contemplated the horrendous death and destruction that plagued his native Earth. Another thought crept into his mind as he worked.

"Uh, a certain angel has certainly been active down there lately," he commented as he completed the interstellar checklist with Walker.

"An angel? What do you mean?" asked Molly from over his shoulder.

"Apollyon and Abaddon. He's king of the abyss. A destroying angel. The name means destruction," Morgan replied. "It's from the Bible."

"Then he's been active, all right," Molly agreed. A telling smile crossed her petite face as she noted Morgan's observation. This husband of hers had tremendous potential.

Strapped securely in their seats, all of them felt the limitless energy of additional antimatter conversion engines firing up in sequence. Morgan fascinated Molly, performing one complicated task after another as he monitored familiar gauges and carefully applied power. Luke Walker was attentive to every step, with his sharp mind locked in learning mode as he noted every detail.

Energy level rising. Craft in motion. Sound speed. Escape velocity. Plasmafyer hyperlaser in the green arc. Mass inversion engaged. Speed building. All systems humming, climbing for prag c!

Stars in front of them became a dazzling blue color in their eyes as they approached prag c threshold. The *Ursa C* flashed briefly in the earth sky, and then the quintessential hunter was gone on his hunt for another world.

Printed in the United States
1431400001B/163